About the author

Meredith lives in Shropshire with his beloved wife. As well as being a dedicated sports fan, Meredith loves drumming, stand-up comedy, swifts and blackbirds. He began to lose his sight as a teenager but, despite the minor inconvenience of blindness, these days, he 'sees' life more clearly than ever.

RUNNING HARD

Meredith Vivian

RUNNING HARD

Vanguard Press

VANGUARD PAPERBACK

© Copyright 2019
Meredith Vivian

The right of Meredith Vivian to be identified as author of
this work has been asserted by him in accordance with the
Copyright, Designs and Patents Act 1988.

A CIP catalogue record for this title is
available from the British Library.

ISBN 978 1 784656 04 1
*Vanguard Press is an imprint of
Pegasus Elliot MacKenzie Publishers Ltd.*
www.pegasuspublishers.com

First Published in 2019

**Vanguard Press
Sheraton House Castle Park
Cambridge England**

Printed & Bound in Great Britain

Acknowledgements

To Roland Casson, Katherine Cox, Mandy and Anthony Dawson, Catherine and Bruce Diffey, Janet Finney, Moira Hudson, Kenton McCusker, Patricia Pollock, Ali Thurm, The Vivians, past and present (special thanks to Buzzard Sightings): with many thanks for your support, encouragement and enthusiasm — just what I needed at crucial times.

Dedication

For dearest Joanna — surely a miracle?

This book is in seven parts:

Part 1

The Runners

Frank

Frank Gordon was beginning to feel the calm settle inside him. He loved this moment — this was his time.

He looked down the track. The images were so familiar: the razor-sharp white lines of the lanes, the press of people 100 metres away, and now, right on cue, his father's red baseball cap held high.

Andrew Gordon looked up the track at his son. He could tell that the power was building. The other athletes were jumping, stretching, snarling and flexing. Frank was still. Andrew continued to hold his cap high, knowing from countless previous occasions that it was now the sole focus of Frank's attention.

Andrew's heart was hammering It always did in these last few seconds. He felt Janice's grip tighten on his arm: she was just as tense.

Robbie was chattering. He never got nervous. He had witnessed many of his big brother's races. Frank never lost, and it didn't occur to Robbie that he ever would.

Andrew and Janice had both been great runners. He had been a sprinter, Janice middle distance. They had won their races easily — until they broke into the higher echelons of athletics. They had continued to shine but had never quite managed to reach elite level. They both knew what it felt like when talent and potential ran out so close to the top. Frank was still shining. He had not yet been beaten — ever. Now, at fifteen, he was about to take on the best of the under 17s in the southern region. He had attracted a lot of attention. His times for the 100 metres were already making veterans shake their heads in wonder. He had been featured on radio and television, being labelled as one of GB's great hopes for the 1984 Olympics and, if he carried on developing at his current rate, even the Moscow Olympics in five years' time.

Robbie had been looking at the details of the other seven runners. He pointed at the list: 'Dave Johnson's time is the best this year but remember we saw Mark Robertson at Crystal Palace? He's definitely got the better technique.'

Andrew and Janice were silent. They couldn't bring themselves to speak. Robbie didn't seem to notice. He said, 'Frank's got his mask on: that's a good sign.'

It was true. Frank became so still seconds before a race that his face appeared waxen, as if he were in a trance.

This was Frank's biggest test so far. The opposition was older and had considerably more experience. Andrew knew that there were runners in the field who did not expect to lose. Normally Frank's competitors felt as if they were running for second place at best, but not this time.

Andrew thought back over the years of encouragement, early morning training, leaving with the dawn chorus to get to far-flung meetings, driving back late at night. He recalled the last year, the wintry mornings when he ran with Frank on their conditioning training sessions; the evenings in the gym building strength and endurance; the attention to detail on the start, the drive, transition, maintaining top speed, on finishing, on winning. He pictured Frank's face contorted in agony as he pushed himself to do another 150-metre sprint, having already done six against Robbie on his bike.

The press was here today. There had been speculation that Frank might become the first fifteen-year-old to run under 11 seconds. Frank cared about the time, very much. He had been measuring and recording his times, his height, his weight; the weights he could lift, the number of miles he could run, the amount and type of food he should consume. He had learned from his parents how to be knowledgeable in his sport; now, he was an expert.

Andrew looked around. He saw the cameras, the press gathering by the finishing line. Both he and Janice knew that they were reliving their athletic career through Frank. They had struggled to keep their excitement at bay. They knew that Frank might never achieve what they wanted for him. They also were acutely aware that by pushing him too much there was a risk of setting him up for ultimate failure. Frank had swept away their anxieties. He was utterly determined to be the best. Indeed, he was already far more ambitious than they had ever been; they were running to keep up with him.

'He's looking good,' said Robbie.

Janice put her arm around him and said, 'So are you.'

Robbie snorted. 'Hmmm, in the under 14s weediest boys' challenge?'

As usual, Robbie's ability to relieve tension galvanised them. They shouted at the tops of their voices: 'Come on, Frank!'

Frank heard the bellowed cheer amongst the hullabaloo but paid no attention. He never did. He had shut down to all external stimuli: it was just him now.

Janice looked across to where Frank's teammates and coaches were collected. Dave Willis, Frank's coach, looked back and grinned at her. He lifted his clenched fist and punched the air.

Frank breathed easily and deeply. He had trained until his lungs were about to burst, and his muscles burned. But Andrew and Dave had also taught him how to breathe — especially in the final few seconds before a race. He closed his eyes and counted slowly, holding each breath for three seconds. He let his shoulders relax.

Robbie pointed at Frank and said to his friend Ailsa, 'He's doing his crazy yogi breathing trick.'

'What's that?' she asked.

'Well he looks deep into a well of eternal spring water and reaches down and drinks deeply of it,' intoned Robbie in a low 'OM-like' voice.

'Really?' Ailsa asked, her eyes wide.

'No. It's how I describe his weird stuff. I think it's a load of shit, but he seems to believe in it.'

17

The loudspeaker crackled, and the disembodied voice announced, 'The next race will be the Under 17s boys' 100 metres.'

They heard the runners' names. When Frank was introduced there was a loud cheer from the Gordons and Frank's Briarfield Harrier teammates.

The starter called, 'On your marks.' There was some last-minute stretching and jumping and then they settled into their blocks.

Janice's fingers gripped Andrew's arm even tighter. They held their breath.

Robbie nudged Ailsa and said, 'Just watch this — you won't believe it.'

The crowd stilled and hushed.

As Frank put his fingertips behind the start line and his feet into his blocks, he felt power fizzing through him: he knew he was about to explode.

'Set!' barked the starter.

Andrew held his cap as high as he could. He knew Frank would see it: he had to have contact with his external world right now, to remove him from his trance and bring him out — this was the moment.

Frank saw the red cap held high.

The gun cracked.

The eight runners burst into frenetic motion. In the first few seconds, there was nothing to choose between them.

As the race continued it became apparent that there were two groups: potential winners and certain losers.

Andrew whispered, 'Come on, Frank, come on. You can do it!'

As they reached halfway, Frank felt himself unwind, and the exhilaration of more and more speed and power becoming available flowed through him like an unstoppable wave.

The crowd watched in awe as, in the space of a few metres, Frank's rivals seemed to go from breath-taking speed to ragged also-rans.

'Jeez,' whispered Ailsa.

'I told you!' cried Robbie watching his brother destroy the opposition.

Frank started to smile as he burst free from the procession that formed behind him. He felt everything relax as he cruised through to the finishing line.

The crowd was yelling, cheering and clapping. Cameras clicked as they captured Frank's image — grinning hugely, his long, dark hair flying.

As he slowed, Frank looked into the crowd. He saw his family cheering, their arms aloft. He raised his clenched fists to the sky in reply. He looked radiant.

The static of the PA system hissed again, and everyone listened to the result.

'Under 17 boys' 100 metres results — in first place: Francis Gordon in a time of 10.94 seconds.'

The other names and times were drowned out by the deafening cheers, whistles and applause from around the stadium. It had happened: the first time ever that a fifteen-year-old had broken the 11 second barrier.

Dave Willis ushered Frank towards the middle of the throwing area. They were followed by a gaggle of photographers and press men.

Andrew turned to Janice, 'I feel weak; I feel like I've just run the race.'

'I know,' she said, half crying, half laughing. 'You're going to have to carry me: I've lost control of my legs.'

'Come on, Al,' said Robbie, 'let's gate-crash the party.'

They dodged through the crowds and over the track to the infield. As they approached the melee, Frank saw Robbie and beckoned him over. He clutched his younger brother to him and lifted him high. They let out jubilant screams as they hugged each other.

'Is this your brother, Frank?' asked one of the reporters.

'No, he's my hero,' said Frank.

The reporter laughed and turned to Robbie… 'I guess Frank's your hero?' he asked.

Robbie paused and said, 'Well, he's pretty good but he still can't beat me.'

'Well done, Frank,' said Ailsa, overawed.

Frank smiled. 'Thanks for coming to watch. It means a lot to me.'

Ailsa blushed; she felt as though she'd been touched by something special.

There was a commotion as the television camera was wheeled towards Frank and the regional sports news reporter puffed into view. He threw away his half-smoked cigarette and said, 'Hello, Frank, I'm Giles Rumbelow from *South East Today*. Congratulations! What does it feel like to break the speed of light?'

Frank considered the question and said, 'I just like running; that's it really.'

'Of course, you know that you are becoming known as Flash Gordon — it's got a good ring don't you think?' Rumbelow said.

Frank said, 'I prefer Frank.'

'How fast do you think you can go, young feller?' wheezed Giles.

'Much faster. I think I can go much faster.'

Giles was being put into the shade by this boy's calm presence; he wasn't enjoying the feeling. He decided to put the kid back in his box. 'Of course, you still have a long way to go, young man.'

Frank studied Giles for a moment and said, 'I hope so,' and walked away leaving Giles searching for words, in vain.

'Here's Mum,' said Robbie walking beside Frank.

She ran up and hugged both boys.

'Brilliant, Frank, just brilliant. You're incredible.'

Andrew joined them. They were in a huddle: just them, the team, the unit, together.

'This way,' called a photographer.

The Gordons turned as one towards the camera, their exultant faces caught in the flash of light.

***

The school hall was full. Andrew and Janice were near the back, Andrew's parents sitting with them.

Next to Janice was her friend Sheila who turned to her now and said, 'Your boys are so different.'

Janice nodded. It was true. Frank was and always had been the athlete, right from his early days. With two top-level athletes as parents it wasn't surprising. She looked at her son now as he came into the hall. He was not yet sixteen but looked like a big man. He was well over six-foot-tall; his musculature was that of a twenty-year-old.

Students were allowed to wear what they wanted for Prize-Giving; Frank was wearing a black, polo-neck jumper with black, flared jeans. His hair was below his shoulders and, although he didn't care much about his appearance, he looked good. He didn't seem to notice that people's attention was drawn to him.

She looked for Robbie. There he was, shorter than the other boys his age, and much slighter. He moved quickly and with great determination. He had a charming, laughing face: utterly endearing, she thought, and not just to her.

Frank and Robbie were both popular — they had always had friends. She knew why: they were genuine, modest and friendly boys. She had over the years had so many compliments about them from friends, neighbours and teachers. Sheila was saying now, 'I can't believe how much Frank has grown, Janice. It seems only yesterday that he was a little boy. He used to help my mum with her shopping and he never ever accepted any payment; he wouldn't take anything. He's a real credit to you both. He's terribly good looking too: mm-mm, very tasty.'

Janice smiled at her friend. Sheila went on, 'I bet Robbie's going to be one with the ladies too: he's got that cheeky chappie thing that girls like.'

Janice reflected on their different lives. Frank was the sportsman; Robbie was the brains. Robbie had inherited her father's intelligence — it had skipped straight past her. Robbie was a brilliant writer. He had asked to be the editor of the school magazine as soon as he'd started at Newgate Grammar. The fact that there wasn't a school magazine hadn't been a barrier for him, nor for the school when they realised how serious he was about it. So, *Behind Bars* had been launched and over the last two years had carried a series of clever, funny and revealing investigative stories, as well as reviews, comic strips, skits and spoofs, and letters to the editor.

Mr Grant, the headmaster, welcomed everyone and one by one the awards were handed out. Then: 'It will come as no surprise to you to hear that this year's prize for outstanding sporting achievement goes to Francis Gordon. Come on Frank — up you come.'

There was a huge cheer from students, parents and teachers alike as Frank got slowly to his feet. Looking awkward, he walked to the foot of the stage and slowly mounted the three steps. He crossed the stage and approached the guest of honour.

'Well done, Francis. You have been a great ambassador for the school,' said the local captain of industry.

Mr Grant came over to shake Frank's hand and, gesturing to the microphone, whispered, 'Say a word or two, Frank, whatever you like.'

Frank looked out into the hall. He was suddenly overwhelmed by the sea of faces. Sheepishly, he examined the large silver shield he'd just been given. He looked up again and saw a red baseball cap and relaxed.

'Thank you. I'm glad I can run. I'm so lucky.'

Smiling broadly, he raised the shield and jumped off the stage and sat back down, his face beetroot red.

'And now for the final award tonight,' Mr Grant proclaimed. 'As you know we like to give a prize to an individual who has made a special contribution to the school and its reputation. This year we have seen Frank's incredible sporting feats, but he has a rival. This year one of our students won the *Guardian*'s 1975 national competition for best short story and for that achievement I am delighted to award this prize to another Gordon — this time it's Robert Gordon. Come on Robbie.'

Robbie rose slowly to his feet and staggered to the stage, limping, bent double. He struggled up the steps where he stood gasping for breath. He inched his way to the dignitary who handed him the silver cup. He stood limply at the microphone and said, 'It's great to win this award but knowing that I can run faster than my brother is what gives me the greatest pleasure.'

With that he scuttled off the stage and sat down, laughing delightedly with his performance.

'What a knob,' Frank said to the boy next to him. 'What a total knob.'

Later, as the Gordons walked away from the school, Andrew put his arm around Robbie's slight shoulders and said, 'Bloody well done, Rob.' They walked on ahead.

Janice and Frank walked more slowly behind. She said, 'You know Dad and I are so proud of you, Frank.'

Frank was silent for a minute then said, 'Robbie is going to be the really successful one; you know that, don't you?'

She punched his arm. 'You're both stars, and you'll both shine like stars.'

***

'If you ever change your mind, Frank, I'll be your personal trainer,' grunted Jim Brotherhood.

Frank was punching the bag as Jim leant against it. Part of Frank's training regime was with the Brighton Boxing Club and it had paid off in spades. The intense discipline of boxing training had been suggested to Frank by Dave Willis, and now he was one of the club's most committed members. He enjoyed the hard, driving work of the boxing sessions; and the competition from the other boys to be the fittest and strongest pushed him to the limit of his powers.

Now, he was punching hard with both fists. Not a raging torrent of blows: it was controlled physical force. The effort Jim was putting in to keep the bag from pushing him back was clear evidence of Frank's power.

'OK, time's up,' called Jim. He looked at Frank, who was breathing heavily but in control.

'You're good, Frank. Why don't you take up boxing properly?'

Frank smiled. 'Because I'm rubbish at it. I get hammered by my little brother.'

'That's because you let him,' said Jim. Although he had to admit that Robbie was good too. His determination never to take a step back demonstrated his unswerving belief in himself, even if his technique and fitness let him down. 'Well, if you change your mind,' Jim said, slapping Frank's shoulder as he went off for a shower.

On their way home, Frank and Robbie walked past the chip shop.

'Want some chips?' asked Robbie fishing in his pocket for change.

Frank shook his head, 'Wrong kind of food for me.'

'Rubbish, it'll put hairs on your chest,' Robbie countered and went inside.

When Robbie came out, Ailsa was with him, clutching a large bag.

'Oh, hello, Ailsa.'

'Hi, Frank,' she said colouring.

She was in the year below him, in Robbie's class, and knew that she didn't stand a chance with Frank. She couldn't even be in close proximity to him without feeling awkward. All of her friends liked him. He was so cool.

The door of the chip shop opened and some of Robbie's classmates came out.

'Wotcha, Frank, all right?' they chorused, keen to claim their closeness.

'Wotcha,' Frank said.

'Hey, you're out of your league, Ailsa,' one of them laughed.

She felt mortified and was about to go, when she saw Frank loom over the boy, 'What did you say?'

'Nothing, Frank,' said the boy. 'I mean, I didn't mean anything — sorry, Frank, I didn't mean anything.'

'Well don't say anything then,' said Frank.

He turned back to Ailsa and said, 'Where do you live?'

'Madison Road.'

'Come on then; we'll walk back with you,' he said.

'Yeah, good idea,' said Robbie and the three of them set off.

As they walked, Robbie chattered away, describing his forthcoming piece on Mr Hilton (the French teacher) who had spent time in a Japanese concentration camp during the war.

Ailsa was intensely conscious of her closeness to Frank who just sauntered along without talking except to ask enough of a question to keep Robbie prattling.

She wanted the walk to last and last: this was such an unexpected turn of good luck.

Frank liked Ailsa — a lot. She was quiet and studious; not quite shy, just reserved. She was a perfect foil to Robbie who loved to be in the centre of any group; Ailsa seemed to prefer to be out of the limelight. Frank knew that she was clever though. Robbie and she worked on *Behind Bars* together and some of its best articles had been her contributions.

'This is my house,' she said pausing at the gate.

'Ciao,' Robbie said. 'See you tomorrow for English.'

She nodded and turned to Frank who was looking at her in what she now knew to be his natural way — calm and level. She said, 'When is your next meeting?'

'A week tomorrow,' he answered. 'Do you want to come along?'

Her heart missed a beat, but she gathered herself and said, 'Don't you mind?'

'Mind? Of course not, I'd like you to come if you don't mind,' he said.

'Oh, then, yes, thank you.'

'Great, you've got a seat booked in our car,' Robbie said without hesitation.

'Bye for now then,' Frank said and began to walk off.

She looked after him. He was so big and yet so easy and gentle. She smiled at Robbie — he smiled back and nodded.

***

Ailsa spent the day with the Gordons. She revelled in their company. They were all so funny, kind and gentle. Well, Robbie wasn't so gentle. His sharp humour was hard to deal with sometimes, but she knew of old that he was really a total softie.

What became clear was the bond between the four of them. Although they were constantly chipping away at each other, there was something extra going on. At times, one of them would nod or comment as if in response to a remark when nothing had been said. She noticed how tactile they all were. They would pat each other's shoulders or backs, Frank and

Robbie were always punching each other, Andrew and Janice holding hands a lot. She felt so happy to be part of the team, but at the same time acutely conscious that she was an outsider too.

This time, she focused on Frank rather than the race itself. She saw his demeanour change: he warmed up like the others but then he went into what Robbie called his 'hypnoidal state'. She found it compelling; she guessed everyone else did too.

He won again, with the same breath-taking ease. This time she ran up to him and when he saw her, he hugged her too. She nearly cried with joy.

On the journey home, Janice said, '*The Brighton and Hove Gazette* are doing a feature on you, Frank. Ailsa, why don't you and Robbie write something and submit it to them?'

'Good idea,' said Robbie. 'We can describe all your weird fetishes and list your criminal convictions — well, not all of them, just the embarrassing ones.'

'What, including violent abuse of annoying brothers?'

'It'll be good fun — and experience,' Ailsa said, already picturing the time she would spend interviewing Frank.

'OK, let's meet after school next week,' Frank said. 'When and where?'

'After boxing on Thursday,' suggested Robbie, and it was agreed. Throughout the journey home, Ailsa wished that she could swap places with Robbie and just feel Frank's body pressed against hers.
Frank thought the same thing.

***

As Robbie and Frank walked towards the recreation fields where they had arranged to meet Ailsa, Robbie said, 'Do you fancy her then?'

Frank was quiet for a minute and said, 'Yes.'

'I thought so.'

'You don't mind, do you?' asked Frank.

'No, she's not my type. In any case, she doesn't fancy me.'

'Do you think she likes me?' asked Frank.

'Well, she's hard to read but I think she does, yeah. I'm not sure why though.'

As they approached the bench facing the lake, they saw Ailsa waiting for them.

'Hi,' she said, smiling.

Frank looked at her closely; she was different somehow.

'What's different?' he asked her.

'No glasses, Sherlock,' answered Robbie straight away.

'I'm wearing my new contacts,' she explained.

'Oh, well they make you look quite different,' Frank said.

'Better or worse?' she probed.

'Just as good,' he answered.

Frank stood by the lake and looked out across the water. Ailsa took in his body. She, like everyone else who saw Frank, couldn't get over his physical magnetism. The way he moved was in control but free and natural. Every step he took seemed to be effortless, as if he weren't quite connected to the ground. He picked up a pebble and lobbed it out into the water. She waited for it to splash. For a moment she thought he hadn't thrown it, then it plipped into the water near the far side.

'You're showing off, Frank; it doesn't become you,' Robbie said.

'Sorry, you're right,' Frank said and turned around to face them. 'OK, I'm ready for the interrogation.'

He looked at Ailsa as she turned the pages of her notebook. He looked at her bare legs: they were long and tanned. He could see the shape of her breasts through her T-shirt. He swallowed loudly. She was really sexy. He realised that he ought to sit down or his growing awareness of her body would cause him some obvious embarrassment. He sat down on the bench next to her.

'You ask the questions, Ailsa,' said Robbie, 'I know too much about him already.'

She sucked on her pencil and asked, 'Where did you learn that relaxation stuff?'

Frank looked at her quickly. She looked back into his eyes. God, she was so pretty.

'Well, Dad taught me. He used to say that he would have been a better runner if he could have channelled all of his energy into each race, not just his physical energy.'

'But how did you learn it? Not why do you do it?' she pressed.

He could feel the warmth of her body next to his. She was only an inch or two away from him. He wanted to press his bare arm against hers. He could feel his cock swelling. He was totally distracted.

'He's in one of his trances now,' Robbie observed. 'Come on, Frank, spit it out.'

'Well, er, I seem to have the ability to put myself into another place or setting or time. I don't know how, I just can,' Frank explained.

Ailsa moved her leg slightly and felt her calf touch Frank's. She felt a crackle of electricity rush through her.

'So, do you think you have special powers?' she asked.

'No, only a special family.'

Robbie shuddered. 'We can't put that in, not unless we want the readers to vomit.'

Frank pressed his calf against Ailsa's. The feeling was really good. He was beginning to overheat. He was suddenly extremely conscious of his mounting arousal. He drew away and reached into his bag and pulled out some water. He passed the bottle to Ailsa who took a sip from it. She handed it back without wiping it; he drank greedily.

'This is not exactly a free-flowing interview,' Robbie remarked. 'I tell you what: I'll write what I think will be a good story and then hand it to you, Ails.'

With that, he jumped up and said, 'I'll see you later.' And walked away.

They watched him go. Frank had put his bag on his lap — in an attempt to cover his hardness.

'What are you doing this summer?' Ailsa asked.

'We're off to Wales in two days' time,' Frank answered. 'We go every year. It's great: there are really long flat beaches and I just love running along them, free as a bird.'

Feeling a sudden sense of loss, she asked, 'When are you back?'

'The fifth of August,' he answered. 'Do you want to meet up then?'

'That would be lovely,' she said, still feeling the thrill of being so close to him.

'Good,' said Frank, 'I can't wait.'

For the first time in his life, he was looking forward to returning from holiday.

***

Robbie was preparing his article for the *Gazette*. He re-read what he'd written so far.

'Sibling rivalry is a familiar concept for many people. I compete with my brother all the time. The brilliant thing is that, even though we fight for "top dog" status, we each accept that the other one has the right to be so named.

'Frank is my hero. He will put his neck on the line for what he thinks is right. He'll even put his neck on the line for me, his annoying little brother, if he thinks I need it. He's like an old wise man even though he's only fifteen.

'He is of course a very fast runner. He always has been. But he's much more than that. He seems to understand everything, like he's seen it all before.

'I see him training early morning, during the day, in the evening. There is something single-minded about him. I'd even say he was slightly deranged. But he's not just a runner, oh no.

'He will carry shopping for old ladies. He picks up people's litter. He always washes his hands after he's had a dump. He has an excellent collection of porno mags.'

Robbie smiled. He was wondering whether he should share this version with Ailsa. He continued.

'Frank has got the hots for the co-editor of *Behind Bars*. She's my friend Ailsa. I think she's tasty too, but I know she doesn't see me — who would, when compared with Frank?

'I sometimes hate Frank. He's too perfect. Every now and then I'm tempted to trip him up or pour water over his head, just to let him know he doesn't get it right every time. The awful thing is that he'd probably laugh and say, "Nice one, Robbie, I'll get you back." He's great.'

Robbie looked out of the window and saw Frank walk up the path. He screwed up the paper and went downstairs.

'Did you give her one?' he asked as Frank came through the door.

Frank cuffed him around the head, quite hard, and said, 'She's too classy for that kind of language.'

'OK, did you engage in sexual congress?'

Frank smiled and said, 'Of course not. Anyway, I wouldn't tell you if we had.'

'I wrote an excellent piece about you: highly complimentary.'

'Yeah, like I really believe that,' Frank said.

'Want a game of table tennis? It's been ages since I last thrashed you,' Robbie asked.

'Thrashed me? You've never come close.'

'Today's the day.'

'OK, prepare yourself for total annihilation,' Frank said.

***

'I think this will be our last summer holiday all together,' Andrew said as he put the phone down.

'Why?' Janice asked as she came down the stairs with a case.

'That was Dave Willis. He says that Frank is being asked to join up with the national team in the autumn; that will mean that his time and what he does with it will be outside our control.'

'Brilliant news, oh, that is fantastic!' Janice exclaimed, clapping her hands. 'But I see what you mean: it's the end of our little era for now.'

'Where is Frank?' asked Andrew.

'Where do you think? At the track,' she answered.

'Well, we shall have to make this holiday the best yet,' Andrew said. 'We shall fill it with memorable events: fastest ever times along the beach, record-breaking performances at crazy golf, boozing for the boys, cooking for the girls, that kind of thing.'

'Robbie is going to find it hard without Frank around,' Janice reflected, ignoring his feeble humour.

'Never mind Robbie: what about me, and you?' Andrew replied.

'I know. We are going to have to toughen up a bit.'

Andrew looked out of the window in the hall and saw Frank looming up to the door. 'Here he is now.'

'Here he is, Mr British Athletics himself,' announced Janice as he came into the hall.

He looked enquiringly at her.

'Dave just rang you've been called up for autumn training with the national squad,' said Andrew excitedly, grabbing Frank's shoulders and shaking him.

Frank drew in a deep breath and held it. He exhaled and, as he did, he looked at them both and said quietly: 'Thank you. Thank you both so much.'

***

'Are we nearly there yet?' chorused Janice, Frank and Robbie.

'The next person to say that is going to suffer extreme sanctions,' warned Andrew.

They were now on their way to Wales. They had been driving for fifteen minutes and there were still at least four hours to go. Despite the long journey ahead, everyone was excited.

'Are we nearly there yet?' asked Janice with fake innocence.

'You're in big trouble, Mum,' Robbie warned her.

'Yes, you are, Mummy,' said Andrew, trying not to laugh himself.

'OK, what is my punishment then? Are you going to make me stand in the corner when we get there?' asked Janice.

'I know, Dad,' said Robbie, 'Why don't you limit her to only six gin and tonics a day for the holiday?'

'Hey, that's too harsh,' said Janice. 'I shall be a good girl now.'

But she couldn't help herself: she looked behind her, grinning and nodding to them: 'After three: one, two, three —'

'Are we nearly there yet?' they chorused again.

'No, we are nowhere near yet, and if you keep this up, I shall lose my rag and then you'll all be sorry!' yelled Andrew.

They all laughed, enjoying the moment: being together and on their way to their favourite place in the world.

'And for your next trick, Mum?' asked Frank.

'Why don't you play I-spy like every other family?' snapped Andrew.

'Yes, we need to change tack. Dad's already getting steamed up,' answered Janice.

'A spelling test I think,' said Robbie, knowing that he'd win.

'Good idea,' said Andrew. 'I'll go first. OK, how do you spell diarrhoea?'

'I knew you'd ask that,' Janice said. 'We can all spell it and have been able to since we first had it.'

'Go on then,' Andrew said. 'I don't believe you can spell it and I want the right accent in the right place.'

Janice paused for a minute then sighing said, 'Go on, Robbie, you do it.'

'D I A R R H O E A,' Robbie spelt out, 'and the accent depends on which country you're from.'

'Very good. And Frank, you can do haemorrhoid,' said Andrew.

'Well, that was a surprise,' groaned Janice.

'Oh, come on, Dad, that's too easy,' complained Robbie.

'OK then, you clever little tosser, you spell it,' challenged Frank.

'Frank, although we agree with your sentiment, please try and extend your vocabulary,' said Andrew.

Robbie reinforced the point, 'Yeah, come on, Frank, the presentation of your arguments and the rationale behind them indicates with absolute clarity and leaves us all with a veritable sense of certainty that you are in fact a knob head.'

They all started laughing. Andrew pushed back his red baseball cap and wiped his eyes with the back of his hand. At that moment the lorry they had been overtaking moved into their lane. Janice screamed, '*Andrew!*'

***

The only one to escape fully was Frank. Andrew and Robbie were killed instantly. Janice's injuries were horrendous. She broke both her legs and a number of ribs, and flying glass etched itself into her face. Months of skilled plastic surgery brought her face back to a semblance of its previous appearance, but still it wasn't her face.

Frank could not stop reliving the moment. He saw a therapist twice a week but could never come to terms with even saying how he felt, never mind making sense of what had happened.

Every day, he went to the hospital to be with his mother. He sat beside her with his head down, her fingers in his, gripping hard. They didn't speak. They didn't know what to say. They had nothing to say.

Frank's appearance changed. He moved differently; he now shambled where before he had bounded. His tanned face was white, his long hair lank. His eyes were dark and had retreated into deep sockets.

When Ailsa went to the hospital to see him and Janice, she stood and stared at him. Her eyes filled with tears.

'I'm so sorry,' she whispered. 'I'm sorry, I'm sorry, I'm sorry.' She shook her head to stop herself saying it, but she couldn't help herself.

Frank didn't move or say anything. He wanted to put her out of her misery, but he didn't know how.

Ailsa and Robbie had been firm friends for three years. He knew how close they had been. He also knew that he, Frank, had grown to like her too and now he felt so guilty that she was crying with him and not with Robbie.

Frank could not get the overwhelming feelings of guilt out of his head. He knew that what had happened was not his fault, but he cursed himself a hundred times a day for being there and not doing anything to prevent the loss of his dad, little brother, and of everything that mattered in his life, in their lives.

He wished he could pick up his mother and run away with her. He wanted to be with her on his own, where no one could see them and feel pity for them.

'I'll come again,' Ailsa had said. She left a card with him. He read it.

'Dear Frank,

I don't know what to say. I wish I did. All I can think of is that I miss Robbie so much — he was my best friend by miles.

I wish I could help you in some way. Please tell me if I can.

With all my love

Ailsa x'

Frank closed his eyes. He gripped the card in his hand. He made himself fold it and put it securely in his pocket. He didn't call Ailsa. He couldn't bring himself to.

***

After the orthopaedic surgeons had done all they could for the time being and Janice's convalescence was under way, the two remaining Gordons moved. Janice's parents lived in north London and it was decided that she and Frank should live near them. Late that year, with Frank now sixteen, they moved to their new home.

Janice knew she should work at the exercises the physio had recommended for her, but she didn't have sufficient concern for herself to summon the energy. She now used a wheelchair most of the time.

She would only go out if Frank went with her. This, she knew, was partly fear for herself but mostly it was the dread of being separated from him. She was scared for him; she couldn't stand the thought of his being alone and what might happen to him.

Their new home was a council flat in north London. She had resisted going there, but her parents had insisted. They wanted to be able to look after her and Frank.

Frank had become overwhelmingly protective of Janice. If she was awake when he went to bed, which was always late, he would sit with her in silence, holding her hand as if she were a tiny child. He would do anything and everything for her, but nothing for himself. He had given up.

'You are going to have to go to school,' Janice said one day.

'What's the point? Really, what is the point of it?'

'Well, I know it will be hard, but we've got to move on if we can — and that means doing the best you can at school.'

'I can't face it. Please don't make me.'

Janice left it. She didn't want him to go to school either, but she knew that he must. She had had a letter from the local education authority telling her that Frank must go to school, never mind his unfortunate circumstances.

So, one morning, Frank reluctantly and with overwhelming trepidation went to the nearby comprehensive. It was not like his old school. It was rough. The kids were tough. There was a wilder and harsher feel to the school; it made Frank feel uneasy.

As he walked up the drive, past the lounging teenagers smoking at the gates, he heard a voice yell, 'Bloody hell, who's this zombie?'

The boy's friends laughed and jeered at Frank as he passed them.

'Give us your cap, zomboid!' shouted another one.

Frank was wearing one of Andrew's red caps. He never left the house without it. It was faded now. It no longer smelled of Andrew, but for Frank it was a lifeline.

He attended the lessons, went to the canteen where he had a glass of water, more lessons, then home. He didn't talk to anyone.

On his way out he heard more comments, 'I think he's the one that pushes the ugly spastic around the park.'

Frank paused momentarily then carried on.

'How did it go, love?' Janice asked as he came in through the door.
'Fine.'

She knew it must have been tough. She wanted him to tell her how it really was so that she could be strong for him, not the other way around. She had given up life for herself, but she so desperately wanted him to be able to rebuild his own, to become the old Frank once more.

The next day Frank went in again. He went with the same detached feeling of hopelessness. As he approached the gates, the collection of smokers were there.

'Hey, zombie boy, what's your name?' one called out.

Frank ignored him.

A couple of them detached themselves from the group and walked up to Frank, blocking his path.

'You were just asked a question,' the taller one said. 'What's your fucking name?'

Frank looked down and waited for them to part. They didn't. He didn't feel fear, or anger, in fact he didn't feel anything.

'OK, well, if you won't talk to me, I'll take your nice little cap and you can beg me for it.'

He reached over and took Frank's cap from his head and put it on his. The gathered teenagers cheered and whistled.

Frank looked at the boy. He saw the cap and felt venom rush through him, but he kept his cool and just took the cap back and put it on his head.

His persecutor wasn't done. He took the cap again and started to run and skip around singing, 'I've got the cap, I've got the cap.'

His friends started clapping and cheering in rhythm.

Frank felt his muscles relax, for the first time for months. He burst across the driveway, grabbed the boy and, without effort, picked him up and flung him like a rag doll over the three-foot wooden fence into the car park. He walked around to the sprawling youth, picked up his cap and went into school.

Thirty yards behind him he heard one boy say, 'I think he wants to keep his cap.'

When he got home that afternoon, he sat down next to Janice.

'I lost it today, Mum,' he confessed.

He told her what had happened.

'I don't blame you,' she said. 'I'd have gone demented if it had been me.'

He felt her take his hand and say, 'Do your best, Frank, I trust you always to do the right thing.'

But Frank was sure what lay ahead. He knew he had inadvertently set himself up for more of the same.

The next morning, they were waiting for him. He looked at the ground as he approached them. This time they were silent but as he walked past them, he heard a throat being cleared and one of them gobbed on him. He kept going. He could cope easily with that.

The day went by as usual. He didn't talk to anyone. He didn't hear anything. He was lost inside himself. He felt other pupils looking at him. He was aware of the lessons but didn't absorb anything. The bell rang for home time. He got to his feet slowly. He felt so tired, empty.

This time there was no one at the gates. He was relieved: at least he wouldn't have to face his mother's disappointment in him.

He walked down the street and cut along the footpath behind the garages. As he turned the corner, he saw a group of teenage boys.

'Ah, here he is — our favourite zombie.'

Frank stopped. He knew what was coming and decided to let it. He put his bag down and waited.

They moved up to him. The boy he'd thrown over the fence stood in front of him and pushed his face into Frank's.

'You're going to be sorry you fucked with me, you creep.'

The other boys were pressing in around him too.

'I've seen you with your ugly bitch of a mother; you're going to have to share her wheelchair for a while.'

Something snapped inside Frank. He suddenly felt elation, good again. Power rushed through him. He let it fizz and crackle like a drug — he guzzled on it.

He drove his right fist hard into the boy's stomach and felt breath whoosh into his face. He stepped away and brought his other fist up into the other's lowered jaw and saw his head snap back. He collapsed. Frank turned to the boy beside the first and punched him hard in the side of the head. He went down. Frank wheeled around to another of them. He was backing away, but Frank took two fast steps, caught him by his long hair, spun him around and smashed his fist into his temple. The boy went down. Frank looked around and saw the other three backing away. He moved towards them, his hands by his sides. His heart was racing; he felt his strength coming back in waves. He suddenly ran at the middle of the three, catching him by the neck, and ran him straight into a lamp post. The metal clanged as the boy's head crashed into it. Frank looked at the other two and moved towards them.

'Get away from me, you're a fucking nutter,' one of them was crying.

The second was running, desperate to escape.

Frank looked at the one who was left. He looked scared and pathetic. His mates were crying, apart from one, who was clearly unconscious. Then Frank felt limp. He knew he'd lost everything. Picking up his bag he walked home.

'Hello, Frank,' Janice called.

He put his bag down. He went to Janice, knelt beside her and put his head in her lap and started to cry — gut-wrenching, wracking sobs. She heard his muffled agonised voice, 'I'm sorry, Mum, I've let you down, I'm so sorry. I've let you down. I've let you down. I'm so sorry.'

She stroked his head, 'It's fine, Frank. You can never let me down.'

They stayed like that until the police car drew up outside.

***

Frank's worst fear, that he would be arrested for GBH, or even murder, didn't materialise. Although the police were called to the scene of the fight, and an ambulance, the whole event had been witnessed by two separate passers-by. They had impressed on the police that it was Frank who had been waylaid and looked as if he'd be the victim before he fought back. However, the police, social services and the school had made it clear that he should leave immediately and start at a new school, one — for Frank's welfare — not in the same catchment area.

So, Janice and Frank packed up again and this time moved ten miles north, to a small London overspill town.

'I can't see the point of going to school,' said Frank. 'I want to stay around and make sure you're OK.'

She was resolute, 'No, Frank, you're going to school, and I don't want to discuss it further.'

This time though she understood that she must prepare the ground more carefully for Frank. She just hadn't had the energy or the foresight to think what school life might be like for him. She knew that if he was to go to school, even for the next few months, she would have to give him every chance of getting through it unscathed — and preferably benefiting from the effort he would have to make. To help him, she knew she would have to toughen up herself.

She made an appointment with the headmistress and went along to the school with the Education Officer recently allocated to Frank's case

She pushed her way into the head's office and extended her hand.

'It's very good to meet you, Mrs Gordon,' said Miss Court looking carefully at the woman in the wheelchair.

She knew something about the tragedy the other woman had survived, in terms both of the loss of her husband and son and the appalling nature of her injuries. She saw the scarring and the deep lines of trauma etched in her face. She saw the grey hair and the sharp cheekbones. But most striking was the fierce determination that emanated from her. She felt the hard grip of Mrs Gordon's bony fingers and understood the strength in this woman.

'Please call me Janice,' she said.

'Thanks, I will; and please call me Victoria.'

Janice similarly weighed up the other woman. She was bright, breezy and strong. Yes, she thought, strong was the right word. She was of average height, fit and healthy looking, a bustling no-nonsense sort. In fact, in manner rather as she imagined a headmistress should be. Not in appearance, though. She was younger than Janice had expected — maybe early forties — and very attractive. She looked nice: sensitive as well as capable.

The headmistress said, 'I know a little about your terrible loss, Janice. I am so sorry — for everything that has happened to you and your family.'

Janice inclined her head and said, 'Thank you. I'm here, though, to talk about Frank. I am desperate for him to have a fresh start, one which can help him build his life again.'

Victoria looked down at her notes and said, 'I see he is a wonderful athlete.'

Janice smiled sadly. 'Well, he is or, maybe I should say, was. He is an exceptional runner. He is exceptional in so many ways. But he is badly damaged by everything that has happened to him. He is very vulnerable, and I just cannot bear to think of him coming to any further harm.'

Victoria looked into Janice's face. She saw the anguish, the pain and the absolute love there. She nodded and said, 'I shall make it my personal business to give Frank a positive experience at this school and I shall endeavour to help him have the chance to grow again.' As she said it, she knew that she was taking a risk. She had a strong grip over the school, the staff and the students. But she also knew that there were many variables that she could not control. She went on, 'Janice, I must tell you that this school has its fair share of problems: not every student is a perfect pupil. Not every teacher is the most sensitive. We have some difficult issues to deal with on a daily basis. But I promise you that I shall do my best for Frank.'

Janice looked at Victoria's strong, open face. 'Thank you,' she said.

The Education Officer cleared his throat, 'Frank has anger problems — you need to be aware of that.'

Janice shot him a look and snapped, 'No, he is the calmest, gentlest boy you will ever meet. What happened before was the result of him being victimised, and he defended himself.'

The Officer nodded but pressed the point, 'I know, Janice. That is true. I also believe that he has a huge reservoir of rage that will come out at some stage. That is what worries me.'

Janice said nothing. She knew that it was probably true. She looked at Victoria, 'Please do your best for my boy. Please.'
Victoria said, 'I will,' and meant it.

***

Victoria looked around the staff room as she spoke, 'Right, I want this to go well. This is an incredibly fragile boy. He has been let down once by the school system and I don't want the same thing happening again. He is talented, but his confidence, self-esteem and resilience have been blasted from under him.'

'Talented is an understatement,' said Phil Wilson, head of PE. 'He is THE Frank Gordon, fastest ever fifteen-year-old. Seriously, he's destined for great things, definitely Olympics.'

Victoria Court nodded. 'He's capable of great things but I fear he can do terrible things too.'

She described the recent beating Frank had handed out. Some of her teaching staff flinched when they heard how Frank had stoved in one boy's head.

'So, this is the point. We are going to have to be on the alert for any taunting or teasing, any scenario which might appear to be the precursor to a trigger point,' Victoria stressed.

She looked at Phil Wilson. 'I want you to take him under your wing, Phil; you'll be taking him for English as well as PE.'

Phil nodded. He was really intrigued to meet Frank. He already knew of his reputation of course, and he was excited at the prospect of being able to rehabilitate Frank into the great athlete he clearly had the potential to be.

Victoria read his mind. 'I don't want you to imagine that a couple of encouraging words are going to turn him back to the old Frank. I spent half an hour with him last week and he's very badly damaged, Phil. It's going to be a long haul and I doubt we'll see him get through it. No, I just want you to look out for him — just to ease his way a bit.'

'OK — I'll give it a go. But if I see any sign of enthusiasm for getting it back, I really want to make the most of it. He is something special you know.'

Victoria nodded and thanked him. She looked at her notes and said, 'We've got Katy Walker coming back today. She's had a rough time and her parents say that she's really troubled at the moment. Phil, you've got her in English, haven't you?'

'Yeah, looks like I've picked a hell of a week to give up smoking,' he joked.

'There's another one. I've had Anthony Alexander's mother complaining that her son is being bullied,' she went on.

Phil groaned, 'I've got him too this morning — I've picked a hell of a week to give up drinking.'

Victoria Court smiled but, looking around at all the staff said, 'We're all going to have to be on the lookout for these people: they've got some serious issues and I want us to be part of their solutions, not their problems.'

***

'Right, shut up, you horrible lot, I want your attention!' bellowed Phil Wilson.

He was popular amongst his pupils. He was young, had the right clothes and attitude to gain the respect of teenagers: he too was a rebel. He liked to demonstrate his difference from the other more established teachers and the kids warmed to him for it.

'There is a new boy starting today. He is with the head right now but he's coming along when she's done with him. He's had a very serious family tragedy and we need to look after him a bit. He's a cool kid and I'd like us to treat him with some kindness and respect. Do you hear me?'

He looked around the room and saw a few heads nod.

'No, I want more than that. There are thirty of you and I want to see thirty heads nodding.'

There was general assent.

'Right, it's our old friend today: *Of Mice and Men*.'

There was some rustling as bags were picked up, books produced. There was a knock on the door. Miss Court walked in, followed by Frank.

Anthony

Anthony sat in church, depressed. He did not believe in God or Jesus, or that the time spent in church would make him believe what for him *was* make-believe. Anthony was sure that there was no God. If there were then, surely, He wouldn't allow him to feel such loneliness.

Anthony suspected that it was his fault that he was always on his own. He stood out from the boys who lived around him. He spoke well, he was mannerly and respectful and wore sensible old-fashioned clothes. He was utterly different in every way to the foul-mouthed yobs he saw on the streets with their flares, huge collars and surly expressions. The biggest difference though was that every one of his contemporaries had friends. He saw other boys playing football or cricket, or going off to play tennis, or standing around smoking and talking. He so wanted to be like them. Anthony also knew that other boys had all sorts of games that he only vaguely knew about. His family didn't even have a television. His father was adamant that 'television was an excellent instrument for bringing the poison of society into their home', and as he didn't want his family to be subjected to the 'loathsome behaviour of common people' he could not see why any rational man would tolerate a television in the house.

Anthony's father was old — fifty — ten years older than his wife but, although she was so much younger, in some respects she was even more old-fashioned. It was she that insisted on Anthony living up to his father's standards and moral code. So, Anthony had grown up with ways of thinking and behaving that were natural to him but which he knew were not normal for other boys his age.

There were some aspects of behaviour that had been drummed into him and which he really did believe in: the importance of honesty, taking responsibility, acting like a gentleman. On the other hand, he was also a rebel. He felt more and more strongly that he was going to free himself of the straitjacket that his parents insisted he wear.

Mr and Mrs Alexander and their son Anthony lived in Hampstead. They were comfortably off, as they might say. In fact, Anthony knew they were rich. You didn't get to live in a house like theirs in a leafy avenue in Hampstead without loads of money. But what did they do with their money? Nothing worthwhile that he could see. Their holidays were with his grandparents in Scotland — in a dark, cold and unfriendly house. They never had any luxuries that he knew other boys' families had. They didn't even have a car he could be proud of or boast about. His parents drove an old Wolseley, which boys at school laughed at as it chugged in and out of the school car park. He couldn't show off about his father's job: he wasn't even sure what his father did for a living. He knew it was something in the City, possibly a bank, but that was all.

Anthony's conversations with his parents were formal. They had always been Father and Mother to him. Boys at his school talked about their parents as Mum and Dad, and some were even on first name terms. He had never once played football with his father. He had never played cards with his mother. He had never played anything with either of them.

The only person that he had ever formed a relationship with was his eccentric grandmother. She was his mother's mother. She was, of course, old but she was funny. She loved to do rebellious things like disappearing in the evenings to smoke cigarettes or reading books her husband had disapproved of; and she had glossy magazines with lurid titles and front covers. Anthony's education into a wider world had come about through his two weeks of contact with her every year. He loved to read the paperback books she lent him, and he particularly enjoyed her magazines with their stories of what his father would have called 'floozies and harlots'. In the last two years she had introduced him to smoking: he loved it. It wasn't the smoking itself; it was the act of daring that was required, of being 'bad'.

Granny talked to him as if he were an equal. She would ask him about school, what he liked, what he hoped to do when he left school. She told him about her early life, she loved to regale him with the story of her expulsion for being caught cavorting with a young man. He had grown up trusting her absolutely. He told her how unhappy he was and how strict his father was and that he never had any fun with other boys. She sympathised and reassured him that life would get better one day, he'd just have to have patience. She always told him that he could talk to his mother, that she loved him so much. Anthony could never see any evidence of this. His mother only ever seemed to love his father.

Granny was the only person he told about the bullying he suffered at school. She listened to him and shook her head sadly. She seemed to understand how he felt. She hugged him and told him that, 'One day you'll get your own back. Be patient, dear Anthony.' He kept her words in his head, but he had become increasingly certain that she was wrong.

Now, eating his dinner in silence, he thought about what he had just done. The thrill of it was making him jittery. He fumbled with his knife and it fell to the floor.

'You are a clumsy oaf, Anthony,' snapped his father.

'Sorry,' Anthony mumbled, and bent down to pick it up.

'Don't use it again, Anthony,' said his mother. 'Go and get a clean one.'

Anthony got up and went into the kitchen. As he went, he heard his father say, 'How did we manage to spawn such a cretin?'

'Shhh, he will hear you,' cautioned his wife.

'I don't care if he does: it might make him buck his ideas up.'

Anthony, hearing the exchange, felt his face redden. He was used to these comments and jibes but as he got older, he was becoming more and more sensitive to them.

He walked back into the dining room and sat down again.

'What happened to you after church?' asked his father.

'Nothing.'

There was a loud clatter as his father banged his cutlery down.

'Don't say nothing, you idiot,' he barked. 'You disappeared for five minutes, so clearly you were doing something.'

Anthony thought quickly; he would have to say something credible.

'Well, yes, I was doing something but nothing interesting is what I meant.' He went on, 'I was picking up the kneelers that hadn't been put back.'

'Why?' asked his father. 'You don't normally, why today?'

'Mrs Armitage asked me to help.' He was close to getting into dangerous waters. He'd picked Mrs Armitage as his alibi as she was vague in the extreme and he had seen her picking up kneelers, she might not remember if she had asked him to help or not.

'Well done, Anthony. Perhaps you can help every week you're at church,' said his mother.

'Hardly a major effort,' said his father. 'He could be doing all sorts of things to help in church and why he has to be asked I don't know; you should just do them without being prompted.'

Silence fell over the room again except for the sound of cutlery on china.

Anthony felt hot. The prospect of being caught for what he'd done was unimaginable. It was bad enough just saying that he'd done 'nothing', never mind taking twenty-five pounds from the collection plate. He had loved the feeling though: the adrenalin rush had thrilled him. And there had been something else. He thought about it: it was the sense of doing something that would impress all the boys who hated him. He would be considered heroic if only they knew.

He had seen the plate just inside the vestry curtain as he'd queued to leave the church. He sat down to tie up his laces as the parishioners filed out. Anthony waited for his father to leave; he was always the last one, determined to tell the vicar how the sermon could have been greatly improved. As soon as he was out of the door, Anthony took the few paces to the vestry and slipped inside. There was a lot of money on the collection plate, pound notes and a load of change. He looked through the gap in the curtain and, seeing no one, he quickly gathered in the notes and stuffed them into his pocket. Again, he peered out through the curtain and, seeing an empty church, he walked to the main door. It was only then that he saw Mrs Armitage on her knees picking up kneelers.

She looked up and saw him. He smiled and said, 'Hello, Mrs Armitage.'

She nodded hello and he sped off.

Now, as before, the feeling of euphoria was wearing off. He had been charged with excitement last term when he'd opened the door of the car in the school car park. He'd quickly looked around and, seeing no one about, opened the glove compartment and pocketed some mints, a pair of sunglasses and a pen. He had quietly shut the door and felt the intense thrill of being bad. The moment was exquisite but not what happened next. He was gripped by his ear and spun around to face a large, indignant man in a suit.

'You're in big trouble, my lad!' The man held out his hand for Anthony's swag. 'Come on, let's see Mr Cunningham,' the man said, and marched him to the headmaster's office.

The next few minutes had been horrendous. Cunningham was ingratiating to the man and thanked him for bringing the miscreant to justice. He turned to Anthony and smiled. He just stood there smiling. Finally, he said, 'So, Alexander, I wonder what your dear father is going to say about your behaviour?'

Anthony knew, his father would be demented with rage. He shuddered at the thought.

'I should expel you, boy, but that option is not available to me. However, I do have an appropriate penalty to hand.'

He leafed through a book and then picked up the telephone and made a call.

'May I speak to Richard Alexander, please?' The headmaster's voice was calm and pleasant. 'It's Douglas Cunningham.'

After a few seconds he said, 'Ah, Alexander, it's Cunningham at St Luke's. Yes, all is fine, but I do need to seek your permission to cane your boy. I'm afraid he has been caught stealing. Yes, I agree, stealing is beyond the pale and as you say does need to be nipped in the bud. Yes, thank you, Alexander, I shall. Yes, I think that would be a very wise course of action.'

He put the phone down and smiled at Anthony. 'Your father is in complete agreement that you should receive the cane. He told me not to spare the horses, and I shan't.'

He walked to the bookcase and pulled the long, whippy cane from behind it.

Anthony remembered the swish of the cane, the crack it made as it struck him, and the grunting urgency of Cunningham, and subsequently the shouting and yelling of his father and the week's imprisonment in his bedroom when term ended. He could hear his father's high-pitched lectures, day after day, on the disgusting nature of stealing: that it was in direct contravention of God's word, that it showed utter disrespect to those who loved and cared for him.

However, Anthony also remembered the adrenalin rush of opening the car door and rifling through the glove compartment. It had been thrilling and he knew he would steal again.

Now, after the event — as then — he was beginning to feel sick. Sick at the thought of what he had done, stealing money from a church, money given by people he knew. Sick at the thought of what his parents would say to him if they ever found out.

He decided to get rid of the money. It held no value for him beyond the extraordinary excitement that had swept through him as his fingers closed around the notes. He thought that he might just put it in the large plastic guide dog outside Boots the next opportunity he got. This struck him as a good idea, as the value of the money might be greater to a poor charity than a rich church. But he also pictured Mrs Armitage: she lived alone and seemed to him to have very little wealth to spare. He knew that she would have put money into the collection this morning and he felt now as if he'd stolen directly from her, not the rich old men like his father.

He made up his mind. He would go to Evensong this evening and leave the money near the vestry and hope that someone would see it and assume that it had been dropped earlier.

'I'd like to go to Evensong today,' he told his mother.

She was reading in the drawing room. 'Oh?' she looked up, her eyes questioning.

'Yes, to be honest, I think I should be putting a bit more effort into my relationship with God,' Anthony said, hoping that he didn't sound implausible.

'Well, I'm sure your father would agree with that,' she answered. 'Be back straight after. Supper is at eight p.m.'

Anthony walked to the church at six p.m. He had the cash in his pocket; it felt like a lead weight. He had no clear plan but hazily pictured the money being restored with no one the wiser.

The doors were open. He walked in uncertainly, looking towards the vestry to see if anyone was around. He gripped the wad of notes and saw that just inside the vestry curtain was a low chest with a gap between it and the wall. He looked around the church quickly. There were three people already there, but they had their backs to him. He couldn't see the vicar and guessed that he was either in the vestry or yet to arrive. He stood motionless; his ears pricked for sounds coming from behind the curtain. There was no sound or movement. He bent down and, pushing his hand inside the curtain, he inserted the money behind the chest. He stood up and moved quickly to a pew near the back, his heart thumping.

The service came and went. At the end he went to the door where the vicar was waiting to shake hands.

'Good evening, Anthony,' said the vicar, 'it's very good to see you tonight.'

'And you,' mumbled Anthony and made to go.

'Thank you so much for your generosity. I was really touched by it,' said the vicar.

Startled, Anthony looked into his eyes and saw something that made him want to cry —absolute kindness.

***

Anthony walked along the long, main school corridor on his way out. As usual he was on his own. He had been at St Luke's for eight years now, arriving at prep school when he was seven. In that time, he hadn't made any friends. Instead he had been beaten up, taunted, ridiculed — a butt of derision for pupils and teachers alike.

He knew his appearance didn't help him. He was slight; he had fluffy fair hair, and a pale milky complexion, the whole package making him look like a weakling. Furthermore, although he had a soft voice, he had adopted the supercilious speaking style of his father which seemed to aggravate everyone.

In the rough and tumble world of a boys' public school he was entirely ill-equipped. He was terrible at ball games, and at best was only average at running and swimming or climbing ropes or wall bars. When it came to PE or participation in team games, he was a laughingstock. No team wanted Anthony foisted onto it. He was always the last pick, and audible groans were heard when he found himself allocated to a team.

Over the years he had been tripped up, pushed down stairs, punched viciously in the stomach, locked in the caretaker's shed all night, had had maggots put into his rice pudding; his shoes had been thrown on to the roof of the main school building; he'd been buried in the compost heap, and sworn and laughed at so much he had lost count years ago.

He had never spoken about his ordeal to his parents. He didn't expect them to take him seriously and in fact he suspected that his father would think that a bit of harmless banter was good for him.

Anthony knew he made matters worse for himself. He might look pathetic, but he was by no means weak. He could not win a fight, but he was smart, and he could outwit his school mates. He would answer back with biting wit and sarcasm — this just made things worse for him.

Although the school masters knew of the bullying, they didn't seem inclined to do anything about it. They even seemed to find some of the pranks played on him amusing. Last year, when Anthony had had one half of his head shaved, Mr Mitchell had said, 'Anthony, remind me never to go to your barber.'

In amongst the sniggers and titters of his fellow pupils Anthony said, 'I wouldn't waste my time recommending anything to you, sir.'

That had earned him a detention during which he had had to write 'I shall never make clever dick comments to Mr Mitchell again' five hundred times. Instead, every tenth line he wrote 'I shall make clever comments about Mr Mitchell being a dick again and again'.

He had been rather pleased with his adaptation of the punishment, but this backfired on him. Mr Mitchell checked the lines and, discovering the alternative versions, had escorted him to the headmaster's office.

'Alexander, this is filth and I shall not tolerate filth in this school. I am sending these lines to your parents and recommending a strict penalty for you when you get home,' said the headmaster.

Sure enough, when he got home for the next half term holiday, he received a frosty reception from his parents and was restricted to his room for the whole week. Although the confinement had been an inconvenience, it had in some ways been a blessing. It had meant that he had not had to interact with his father, and it had allowed him to spend all week doing what he loved — reading.

Now, the summer term of 1975, Anthony was once again plunged back into loneliness and the usual spate of physical and verbal abuse. He watched his mother drive away from the school car park. She didn't wave or even look in his direction. Had he known she was crying he would have been very surprised.

'Welcome back, shit face,' said Davies, with whom Anthony shared a dorm, along with eight other boys.

'Hello, Davies,' Anthony said, 'did you have a good break?'

'None of your God-damn business,' Davis growled and walked off.

Anthony sighed and made his way to his dorm. Once there he sat on his bed and put his head in his hands. He felt like crying. He wanted to cry out loud and for someone to hear and tell him he wasn't a 'spoilt baby', 'queer', 'pathetic little worm' or any of the usual abuse. He wanted to cry and be heard by someone who would tell him he was brave, clever and, most of all, that they liked him.

After lunch in the refectory, on his own as usual, he walked back along the long corridor towards the door out to the quad. As he passed by the school secretary's door, he saw that there was a key ring with at least half a dozen keys on it hanging from the lock. He felt his heart start to thud as the now familiar excitement washed over him. He quickly looked up and down the corridor and with no one in sight moved to the door and slipped the keys from the lock and into his pocket. He walked quickly down the corridor and out into the quad.

He went straight out towards a bench on the far side of the grounds and sat down. He took the keys out of his pocket and studied them. There were six keys, three Yale and three mortices, one of which was larger and sturdier. It was clearly designed to unlock an old door. He took it off the key ring — no easy feat as it was thick and unwieldy. Finally, it was off, and he put it in his inside pocket and stood up. He walked quickly back to the main corridor and down it to Mrs Irving's door. As he approached, he could hear her voice, presumably on the telephone. He walked straight past and along to the far end of the corridor. He slipped into a small alcove, the doorway into the steps up to the next floor. He peered back along the length of the corridor and waited. He only had a few minutes before the start of his next lesson: he must get the key ring back before it was missed.

He saw Mr Cunningham walk into Mrs Irving's room and then both of them leave together to go down the short corridor leading to his office. Anthony sped back, looking towards Cunningham's office as he passed. Then, seeing the coast was clear, he took out the bunch of keys and put it in the lock of Mrs Irving's door. He was a few steps back down the corridor when he heard her voice behind him, 'Hello, Anthony, you seem to be in a hurry?'

Anthony turned to face her. He smiled. 'Yes, I've got to rush for English.'

'Yes, you mustn't be late for Mr Negus,' she said. She was a nice woman, thought Anthony and, because he had become a keen student on such matters, cast a quick glance at her breasts. As he had hoped, they were large and heavy looking.

'Go on then, scram,' she said.

He looked away from her breasts and into her face. She seemed to realise what he'd been looking at; how embarrassing. On the other hand, better that than suspect him of taking the key.

'Yes, goodbye then,' he said and walked quickly away.

***

After supper Anthony walked out of the school, across the grounds to his favourite bench. It faced towards the lake and the countryside beyond. He took out the big old key and looked at it carefully. It was heavy, ornate and he deduced from its sheen that it was well used. He realised that it would be missed, and probably already was.

He jumped up and started walking quickly around the school, taking in as many doors as he could. There were plenty of doors to look at, but he knew he could ignore any new or newish buildings. He went up to the chapel and saw that its heavy oak door had a keyhole that would have a key like his. He tried it, nothing turned. He now knew, though, that he was looking for a door in the original part of the school — built at the same time as the chapel.

This meant that it was probably in the east wing and one of the office doors. His stomach and heart lurched — maybe he would be able to get into one of the offices and actually find something worth having?

He was running out of time to do any more work on the project now. He slowed his walk and sauntered towards his dorm. Taking off just his shoes, Anthony got into bed. He settled down for a long wait.

Bit by bit his dorm mates filed in. They were laughing and joking as usual. Some of them threw a comment at him, and all sniggered at their brilliance.

'Hey, Alexander, you're in bed early; having a wank?' said one.

'We've been planning your next punishment with Mr Mitchell; it's going to be such fun.'

'Yeah, it'll involve razor blades and vinegar.'

Anthony ignored it all. He knew that if he answered back, he'd be pulled out of bed and trussed up in his sheets, or some such penalty. Above all, he needed to stay under his bed clothes tonight.

Gradually everything quietened down. At ten p.m., Mr Roberts, the house master, called 'lights out' and shut the door.

How long would he have to wait? He had to be sure that everyone was asleep before he could risk moving. He decided to wait until midnight. To keep himself awake he thought of Mrs Irving's breasts. He imagined her undressing in her room. He pictured her undoing her blouse and standing in front of the mirror admiring herself. He wondered whether she would be pleased to see him watching her as she undid her bra. He decided that she would be. In fact, he saw her in his mind's eye turning around to see him standing there and, cupping her breasts, saying invitingly, 'Anthony, I want you to suck my nipples.'

He moved forward and hesitantly touched her heavy breasts. He looked up at her and saw her nod to him.

He bent down and took her nipple in his mouth. He sucked on it — it tasted so sweet. He found the image of Mrs Irving, his mouth on her nipples and the thrill of his imminent criminal activity incredibly arousing. He felt his hard penis with his hand and almost moaned out loud at how good it felt. He started to rub it; it felt wonderful.

He heard a door shut outside the dorm; he jumped. His erection subsided immediately; he did himself up. He scolded himself. He needed to be focused and alert.

The chapel clock had struck eleven ages ago. He thought it must be approaching midnight by now. He was ready.

At last, he heard the deep slow chimes. Listening hard, he could hear nothing other than the sound of sleeping boys. There was almost no light coming into the dorm. He strained to see but could only just make out the shape of the room. Confident that he would not be seen, he pushed back his blankets and got up. He carefully lifted the bed clothes and pushed his pillow under. It didn't look like a sleeping body, but in the dim light neither did it look like an empty bed.

He put his shoes on and then a pair of socks over them. He looked around once more then moved quickly to the door, turned the old, round knob and slipped through, closing the door silently after him. He stood still, hearing only the pounding of his heart. He loved this feeling, the adrenalin rush.

There was more light now. After the darkness of the dorm it seemed brilliant. But it came only from wall lights at the top and bottom of the stairs. They lit the way for him but still left the corridor and hall below in deep gloom.

He sped to the top of the old staircase, making no noise. He gripped the heavy, oak bannister and considered his next move. The staircase was in two halves. The first was twelve steps, the second, at right-angles to it, was fourteen. He knew that almost every step creaked and groaned. He made up his mind, straddled the bannister and slid down to the small landing. He did the same for the second flight. He would have to risk the noise on his return trip but then he'd be almost home and dry and, in any event, he was only thinking about the present. That was becoming the fascination of his sorties into stealing — the wonderful feel of 'now', only now.

He suddenly remembered the key. His heart leapt: did he have it? His panicking fingers went inside his trouser pocket — there it was. He grasped it firmly, drawing power from it. He was cross with himself: how could he have been so reckless not to have double-checked?

He walked quickly across the hall, through the heavy door into the short corridor with the offices and went straight to Cunningham's door. He looked down at the keyhole. It certainly appeared as if his key would fit it. There was only one way of finding out: he inserted the key and turned it to the left, to unlock it. It wouldn't turn. He felt his excitement and thrill leave him like air from a pricked balloon. He had so wanted his key to fit the headmaster's office: of all the offices, this was the one.

He withdrew the key, then pushed it in again as far as it would go. He turned. Nothing. He withdrew it minutely, just in case the fit wasn't snug. Again, nothing turned.

There were three other doors in the corridor. He ran to each one, but the key would not open any of them.

He stood still. Disappointment was beginning to crash through him. He remembered the key to the garden shed in the large rear garden of his home. That lock had been put in upside down, or the wrong way around, and you had to turn it anti-clockwise to unlock it. He tried the key in the head's office lock. It turned smoothly. With elation he quietly turned the handle of the door, it was still locked. He could not understand it. There must be another lock. He looked up and down the door: nothing. Maybe it was bolted from the inside. He nodded to himself, that must be it. Then, in a flash he realised his stupidity. He turned the key to the right, turned the handle and the door opened. It had been unlocked all the time.

He slipped in, shut the door silently and stood stock still, breathing hard.

There was light coming in through the windows. It was from a lamp post in the car park. It illuminated the room well enough for him to see shadowy outlines. He knew the office, but not well. He could make out the square shape of it. He could see Cunningham's large, dark desk and the looming shape of the bookcase and the two armchairs in front of the desk. He moved around the desk and sat down in the heavy leather chair. He scanned the desktop, took in the neat row of pens and pencils, a large glass ash tray, a blotting pad.

The desk had two sets of drawers, with one longer one across the top. He started with that one. He rummaged around. Nothing caught the attention of his fingers. He wasn't sure what he was looking for, but it wasn't papers or stationery. He tried the drawers on the right. Again, nothing interesting. He moved to the left set. He opened the top drawer, thrust in his hand — a book. He pulled it out: it was the book Cunningham had leafed through when he'd rung up his father. He put it back. There were other papers in the drawer, and the next.

Now the third drawer. He reached inside and grasped a wooden box. He pulled it out and put it on the desktop. Lifting the lid, he gaped at what lay inside — although it was a new sight to him, he recognised it of course. He replaced the lid and hurriedly put the box back. It had repulsed him.

He tried the next drawer. This had a packet of cigarettes, a lighter, and a silvery box which, when he opened the lid, revealed a large number of thick cigars. He thought of his granny and smiled. He'd love to take this box and its contents and give them to her. He took one cigar: he felt he deserved it.

Putting the cigar box back he moved down to the final drawer. This one contained a leather case. He lifted it out, unclipped it and discovered a video camera. He put it back. He wanted to find something that he could take, as a memento of his nocturnal visit. But he did not want to take anything that would be missed.

He looked around: there was nothing else in the room apart from the two armchairs and low coffee table.

He got up from the desk and, leaning against the wall to make sure he didn't trip on the wires of the telephone, he noticed for the first time that there was a door there. Its handle was white, the same colour as the walls; in the dim light it hadn't shown up at all. He turned the handle. The door opened to reveal a small room. He couldn't really see what was in it. He moved into the room, groping his way. As soon as he let go of the door it closed behind him. He froze, his heart thumping; could he open it from the inside? Yes, there was a handle.

He shut the door again and explored the small room. It was square, had an armchair and some bookshelves. There was no window in the room and the door he'd come into was the only one.

He was intrigued by the room. He wanted to see more of it. He decided that he could risk a light if only for a second or two.

He flicked the switch by the door and was dazzled by the overhead light. He could see at once that his blind exploration had been accurate except for one thing: there was a television set attached to the far wall. Beneath it was the same equipment used to play the videos he and his classmates had made during Art, last term. He wondered what old Cunningham would be watching in his little cubby hole. There was a pile of video boxes on a small table next to the chair. He looked at the labels, *Exam Nerves*, *Spelling Test*, *First Day*, *Taking Temperature*, *Punishment*.

Intrigued, Anthony loaded *Punishment* into the player, turned on the set and pressed the 'play' button; the screen flickered. He turned off the overhead light and sat down in the chair.

He heard Cunningham's voice say, 'Right, it's all set up; ready when you are.'

The screen lit up to reveal Cunningham's desk. Then, into the picture came Mrs Irving. She sat down behind the desk and started talking.

'You've been such a bad boy. You have let the school down, your family down and most of all you have let yourself down. You will be punished, and you will take it like a man.'

Anthony gaped at the screen. Then he heard Cunningham say in a quavering pitiful voice, 'But it wasn't my fault; all the other boys made me do it.'

'Shut up, you nasty little piece of shit!' Mrs Irving shot back at him. Her voice was harsh, full of malice and loathing. It was not her usual voice — indeed she had seemed to grow into a totally different person. 'Come towards the desk, you little worm!' she commanded.

Anthony was spellbound.

Cunningham's figure appeared — his back to the camera.

'I'm sorry,' he whimpered.

'Too late, boy!' she snapped.

Anthony's attention was rapt. He could not believe what he was seeing. Then it became even more bizarre.

Mrs Irving stood up and slowly and deliberately took off her clothes. Anthony felt his face redden; his breath shorten as her body was revealed. Every now and then she looked towards the camera and moved slightly to make sure she was in full shot.

She looked at Cunningham and said, 'What's that lump in your trousers, boy?'

She leant across the desk, her breasts dangling. Anthony felt his penis harden at the sight of them.

'It's my willy,' whispered Cunningham.

'So, you are here to be punished and all you can do is get an erection?' Mrs Irving said, scornful. 'Pass me the cane, boy.'

Cunningham reached behind the bookcase and handed it to her.

She took it and walked around the desk to the camera. She stood in front of it and stroked the tip of the cane against her nipples, then opened her legs and rubbed the cane against her large, dark bush of pubic hair.

Anthony had never seen a naked woman. He was shocked by the sight of Mrs Irving's body; he was captivated by what he saw, but he was also feeling increasingly repulsed.

'Mmmmm, I'm going to enjoy this,' she murmured. Then, in a menacing voice, 'Drop your trousers and pants, boy.'

She stepped to one side to reveal the headmaster pulling down his trousers and pants, exposing his hairy, saggy bottom.

'Bend over,' she commanded.

He leaned forward, proffering his buttocks to her.

She took up position to the side of him — her target fully exposed to the camera, her lumbering, naked body just in view.

There was a swish and a loud crack and a cry of pain. Anthony saw the old man's buttocks go red. The cane cracked again, and again, and again.

After six strokes Mrs Irving ceased her assault.

'I hope that will be a lesson,' she hissed.

'Yes, Miss,' Cunningham whined.

Then, he turned around. His penis was semi-erect, a long dangling thing that looked utterly ridiculous.

'You'll have to do better than that, boy,' snapped Mrs Irving.

The images flickered and went black.

Anthony was shocked by what he had seen. The sight of Mrs Irving's naked body had been titillating at first, but as the film had progressed, he felt more and more sorry for her and ashamed of himself. The sight of the headmaster's penis had turned the whole thing into something utterly grotesque. Claustrophobia overwhelmed him. He just wanted to get out of that cell-like room, away from the office and back into bed — now.

He got up from the chair, ejected the tape from the machine, replaced it in its case and put it back amongst the pile. Panic was beginning to get hold of him. He took in a deep breath and stood still for a few seconds: he knew he must stay calm.

Anthony edged out of the room, shutting the door silently. He tip-toed back through Cunningham's office to the door. He opened it, slipped out and sprinted back to the foot of the stairs, paused, then ran back to the office. He opened the door and dropped the heavy key under the big bookcase; he had no further need of it.

He raced up the stairs — two steps at a time. He thought he must be making a racket, but he couldn't help it, so just kept on going. Pausing outside his dorm door, he caught his breath, opened the door, and went straight to his bed. Nothing had changed. No one was awake, everything was normal.

***

The next morning started the same as every other one.

'Get up, Alexander, time for your normal bout of victimisation!' shouted thick, ugly, stinking Bagnall.

Anthony opened his eyes to see the boorish, leering face grinning inches from his.

'Bagnall, you're an ugly bastard,' said Anthony. He couldn't help himself.

Bagnall pulled the blankets off Anthony's bed, grabbed his ankles and hauled him on to the floor. Encouraged by the whooping and yelling of the others, he dragged Anthony towards the foot of the bed.

The door opened, and Mr Roberts looked in. 'Leave him, Bagnall,' he said in a resigned voice.

'Oh, sir, he was very rude to me and it would be totally unfair if he got away with it,' protested Bagnall. The other boys yelled their agreement.

Mr Roberts shook his head and left. Anthony got to his feet. He ignored the laughter and cruel grinning faces around him.

He thought about the events of the night before. If only these ignorant thugs knew of his daring escapade, perhaps they might respect him. Probably not. Maybe he was destined to be despised no matter what he did.

He reviewed what had happened. It was completely unbelievable. He was even wondering whether it had been a dream. It felt like a dream. It had all the usual characteristics. He reached under his bed and touched the cellophane wrapping of the cigar. That was at least proof that he'd been to Cunningham's office, but the film?

The rest of the day's lessons went by in a blur. He saw Cunningham walk ahead of him at one point. Anthony pictured the naked posterior, and the dangling penis. It was impossible to believe it all.

Then, his worst nightmare began to come true. During maths, Mr Roberts appeared in the door and asked Mr Cameron if he could spare Alexander.

'Of course, he's all yours,' Cameron said.

As they walked along the corridor the house master said, 'I'm sorry about this, Alexander, I don't know what the issue is, only that Mr Cunningham needed to have a word with you straight away.'

Anthony knew. His mind went back a few hours. He pictured his night's activities and only now wondered at his stupidity. How could he have hoped to have got away with his ridiculous venture. He tried to think what he'd done to incriminate himself. The only thing he could think of was that Mrs Irving must have realised that when the key to the headmaster's office went missing, she'd seen him skulking around only moments before.

They paused outside the office door. Mr Roberts knocked; they heard a voice ordering them, 'Come in!'

Anthony went in, Mr Roberts behind him. Cunningham looked up. Normally he had a cold, dispassionate facial expression; today there was something alive about him. He looked at Anthony and said, 'Come in, Alexander.'

'Do you want me to stay?' asked Mr Roberts.

'Yes.'

'I have never liked you, Alexander,' started the head. 'You aren't the right kind of pupil for this school. But the person I despise more than you is your father. He makes me feel physically sick. He is an arrogant and conceited man, a bully and a fraud.'

Anthony looked into Cunningham's face. He seemed deranged: there was spittle at the corner of his mouth.

'I hated him when we were at school together, and I've hated him ever since. When I heard you were coming here too, I tried to block it, but the governors insisted because of your dear papa's clout in the city.' At this he started to laugh.

'Well, I can now get rid of you — without any fear of comeback or criticism. I can get rid of the shit, and the shit's shit of a son.'

Anthony was staring at him. What was wrong with the man?

'You're probably wondering what this is all about?' went on Cunningham.

Anthony said nothing. He knew what it was all about perfectly well.

Grinning now, Cunningham explained, 'He's been arrested. He has been charged with fraud. He is currently in the kind and loving care of those charming boys in blue, the Metropolitan Police.'

Anthony's mouth was open.

61

'Well? Aren't you going to say something?' sneered Cunningham.

Anthony didn't know what to think, never mind say. His first emotion had been one of relief: he hadn't been caught. Then, his head spun. His father arrested. For fraud?

'I don't know what to say, sir.'

'You can say goodbye, Mr Cunningham, goodbye St Luke's and goodbye to your nice big fancy house in Hampstead,' crowed Cunningham. 'You'll leave in the morning; your mother is collecting you. Make sure you have everything ready and packed after breakfast. Now get out.'

In a daze Anthony turned and left the office. Mr Roberts came with him. He said, 'Sorry, old man, but maybe it's better for you somewhere else.'

Anthony thought about this. Yes, he agreed wholeheartedly.

***

In bed he tried to process everything that had happened. If the events of the night before hadn't been bewildering enough, todays had rendered him senseless. He had had a brief conversation with his hysterical mother. She had simply said that Father had gone away for a few days.

He tried to sleep but his mind kept racing. The boys in the dorm had asked him what he was doing as he packed up his belongings. He stayed silent. Davies and Bagnall wrestled him to the floor and shouted in his face to tell them what was going on — he shut his eyes and went limp. Finally, they delivered a punch into his solar plexus and left him gasping on the floor.

The night seemed to last forever. He went over and over in his mind all the insults, the punching and the kicking, the humiliation. The awful memories made his heart pound. He wanted to get his own back on these morons. He wanted so much to make his tormentors feel what he had felt all these years.

Suddenly he got up. Throwing caution to the wind he dressed, went out of the room, down the stairs and straight to Cunningham's office. He didn't look around cautiously this time; he turned the handle and the door opened. He marvelled for the first time how lax Cunningham was about security when there was so much in his office that he ought to keep well and truly locked up.

He went into the little back room and took the video from the pile. He checked it was the same one — yes, there it was: *Punishment*. Then he went to the third drawer down in Cunningham's desk. He opened the box and lifted out the gun. It was much heavier than he'd imagined. He gingerly hefted it. It shocked him. It felt brutish and violent. It made him feel as if he'd picked up a cosh rather than a gun. He held it out in front of him in his right hand. The weight of the gun made it waver he couldn't hold it steady. He had an overwhelming desire to know what it felt like to shoot someone, anyone. He found his index finger curling around the trigger. Swallowing he lowered the gun; he knew he must stay calm.

On impulse, he took the cane from behind the bookcase. He put the video and the gun case on the desk and tested the strength of the cane in his hands. It was bendy. He put it over his knee and snapped it in half. The sound of it echoed around the room like the crack of a pistol. He snapped the two halves. Then again and again until he had a collection of splintered bits of cane by his feet. He gathered them up and put them neatly on Cunningham's blotting pad.

He took the gun out of the box and put it into his pocket; it was incredibly heavy and cumbersome. He placed the video case into the gun's box. He left the office, feeling good, in control — maybe for the first time in his life.

***

Instead of going up the stairs to the dorm, he walked quickly to the gymnasium. He ran through it to the fire door at the back. He opened it and slipped out. He took off one of his shoes and put it between the door edge and jamb: it must not close whilst he was outside. He didn't know what time it was, but he could see a faint glimmer of light and knew he only had minutes left.

With just one shoe, carrying the box, and with the heavy gun in his pocket, he ran awkwardly across the rugby pitch to the hedge separating the road from the school grounds. He wriggled under the hedge and pushed the box as far as he could. He crawled back out, looked carefully along the boundary to the car park, weighing everything up. All was quiet still.

He sprinted back to the open fire door, slipped in and closed it. He put his shoe back on, ran to the stairs, flew up them and back into the dorm. He got into bed and waited for his moment.

***

Anthony lowered his face until it was inches from Bagnall's, 'Wakey-wakey.'

The boy opened his eyes and looked at Anthony. His first reaction was to shout abuse, or punch him, but the gun three inches from his head silenced him.

Bagnall's face went white; Anthony smiled.

'Get out of bed, little man; it's time for your punishment.'

Bagnall started shaking. The other boys were waking now.

'Get the fuck up, you wanker,' Anthony ordered, jabbing the gun into Bagnall's face.

Bagnall was gibbering, 'No, no, please no.'

'Leave him, Alexander; it was just a bit of fun,' Davies said.

Anthony turned to him. 'This is just a bit of fun too, Davies, my old friend.'

He clubbed the gun against Bagnall's face and snapped, 'Get up, you bastard!'

Bagnall scrambled out of bed. He retreated until his back was against the wall. Anthony faced him and, holding the gun in both hands, he aimed it at Bagnall's chest. With his thumb he pulled back the hammer and said, 'Put your hands in the air — and Davies, you come and pull down his pyjamas.'

Bagnall raised his hands pleadingly. Davies didn't move.

'Do it, Davies; do it right now.' Anthony's voice was calm and steady.

Davies went across to Bagnall, who was snivelling. Davies pulled the other boy's pyjama bottoms down to his ankles and retreated quickly to the corner with the other boys, all of whom were cowering in silence.

'You are going to get a bullet each,' said Anthony, looking quickly in their direction, 'so watch Bagnall get his so you can see how it's going to work.'

He looked down at Bagnall's shrunken penis and started laughing.

'Not so hard now are you, Bagnall?'

Bagnall wet himself.

Anthony couldn't help himself laughing even more.

He aimed at the boy's dribbling member and pulled the trigger. The click was deafening.

***

Anthony knocked on Cunningham's door. He heard the normal, peremptory: 'Come in!'

He walked in and went straight to the edge of the desk and said, 'Oh dear, what on earth has happened to your tickling stick?'

Cunningham got to his feet. He looked down at Anthony and was about to start to roar when Anthony held up his hand.

'Tidy up your splinters, calm down and be sensible. I shall leave as soon as my mother gets here. You won't ever hear from me again and I shan't ever hear from you. If I do ever hear from you, I shall make available to as many people as I can this year's cinema epic starring Mr Cunningham and Mrs Irving — it's called "Punishment". Rather apt don't you think?'

Cunningham had gone white. He looked at Anthony and said, 'You will never get away with this; I shall find it and then I shall find you.'

Anthony smiled. 'Let's just let sleeping dogs lie. It's better that way.'

Mr Roberts came into the office without knocking. He took in the scene.

'We need to call the police: Alexander has just threatened Bagnall and the other boys in the dorm with a gun.'

Anthony looked questioningly at Cunningham, who had bent to the drawer in his desk where the gun was kept. He stood up and looked at Anthony.

'We'll sort it out internally, I think,' said Cunningham. 'There's no need to involve the police.' He looked down at his splintered cane then said, 'I want Bagnall, Davies — and any other boy involved in the incident — here in five minutes. They're not to talk to anyone about what has happened. Do you understand, Mr Roberts?'

'Very wise,' said Anthony and turned to leave. 'I shall keep my end of the bargain: forever — as long as you do.'

Cunningham was silent.

***

Anthony got into the car beside his mother. They drove away.

As they accelerated up the road, Anthony said, 'Stop, Mother, just for a second.'

She stepped on the brakes and turned to him. 'Why?'

He got out of the car and ran to the roadside. He moved quickly along, crouching down as he inspected the roots of the hedge. He bent down, grasped the box and pulled it free from the foliage. He ran back to the car and they drove away.

***

Five months later, Anthony started at his new school. He and his mother had moved in with his beloved, eccentric grandmother in her large, ground-floor flat to the north of London.

Mr Alexander had been convicted of fraud and sentenced to five years' custody. He was now incarcerated in Lewes Prison. Anthony and his mother had never spoken of what his father had done. In fact, they never spoke of their past life in Hampstead. They did talk now, though. Meals were chatty and cheerful affairs. Her husband's downfall seemed to have breathed life into Margaret Alexander. She was quite different. It

66

was as if mother and son had both broken free of the abusive and oppressive prison, he had imposed upon them.

They had gone together to meet the headmistress of the new school. Anthony had liked her: she was the polar opposite of that bastard Cunningham. Miss Court was warm and reassuring. His mother had explained that Anthony was a bright boy and was keen to do well at school. She had begun by being vague about what had happened to them but then had held up her hands and came out with the fact of it. 'My husband, Anthony's father, has been sent to gaol.' She explained that things had been difficult for Anthony and they had had a negative effect on his schooling.

Miss Court had said to Anthony, 'Well, I shall do my best to ensure that this is a positive experience for you, Anthony. We are always pleased to have high performing pupils here.'

He said that he was looking forward to it. He liked the look of her. In fact, he thought she was nice looking — quite pretty in an old woman kind of way.

'Good luck!' his mother said as he got out of the car three days later.

'Thank you, Mother. It can't be any worse than St Luke's,' he said, smiling.

Dressed in his usual outdated clothes and sensible shoes, he walked up the drive to the large 1960s concrete building ahead of him. He heard a coarse voice say, 'Hey, shithead, what's your name.'

He turned to see a tall boy with a sneering face pointing a finger at him.

'Anthony Alexander,' he answered.

The tall boy looked at Anthony. He saw a slight boy, pale, weedy. He heard a recently broken, stuck-up voice that immediately got on his nerves. He hissed, 'Keep out of my way, shitface.'

Anthony felt his blood run cold: not again — please, not again.

Gary

For as long as he could remember, Gary wanted to be like his brothers. They were his heroes. He was the youngest of three boys. Derek and Kevin were five and two years older, respectively. They had always been able to do everything he wanted to do — run faster, fight better and, more recently, swear, smoke, get served in pubs, pull birds.

But, up on a pedestal, was his dad: a heavy drinking, foul-mouthed man; people were scared of him. Even Gary's brothers were in awe of their dad. Gary's mother was too.

Brian Abbott worked in a factory, according to him: 'welding lumps of metal on to bigger lumps of metal'. He hated his job, his bosses, the low pay. He loved being with his mates, discussing tits, pints, horses, snooker and how awful their wives were.

Gary couldn't remember a time when he hadn't wanted to grow up like his dad. He had always tried to impress him. Bit by bit, Gary could tell he was becoming more and more like his brothers and his dad, and he was glad.

Gary enjoyed being the school bully throughout primary school, and he had fought hard to attain 'top dog' status at secondary school too. He had made it. He had had to face some challenges from boys with big reputations, but he'd coped with them easily. He would have fights at school or, often, after, and come home excited at the prospect of telling his brothers about what had happened. They usually jeered at him, but he knew that they were impressed. However, it was his father's good opinion that he coveted the most.

Over the years, Gary had never thought that his father's abrasive and sometimes violent manner was anything other than heroic, apart from one thing. Every now and then his old man would get pissed up and come home looking for trouble. On these occasions, Derek, Kevin and Gary kept out of the way. It didn't do anyone any good to cross the old man when he was drunk. Gary's mother took the brunt of it; the boys disappeared.

Gary liked to instil fear in people too. He seemed to be able to do it effortlessly. He just copied his dad. Gary would swagger around at school or in and about town, staring into people's eyes, chewing gum nonchalantly, or smoking; he would dare people to face up to him — they didn't. If anyone ever stared back, Gary would put his face into theirs and sneer at them, 'What's your problem?' or, 'Think you're hard enough?' or, 'Don't make me laugh!'

He used to enjoy football, but he found that, although he was good at it, he had, in the last year or two, lost his touch. He didn't mind he preferred to smoke, spit, swear, belch, and be hard. He had a little group of fellow hard-boys — Steve, Paul and Phil. They wandered around together, looking tough and causing trouble. It was great fun.

Gary's brothers had girlfriends. They were sexy and smart-talking. When they visited the house, Gary liked to hang around with them. He often thought they quite fancied him. They offered him cigarettes, sat with their legs crossed so he could see their thighs, or leant forward showing their tits. They talked about sex — it turned him on. Often when they left, he wanked himself off thinking about them. He imagined roughing them up a bit, making them look both scared of and grateful to him. But, after he'd come, he would feel depressed and deflated — dirty and angry with himself. He didn't know why; it was always like that.

He liked to leer at the girls at school, especially the more developed ones. He wanted to have sex with them but, although he had the big guy status at school, none of the girls showed any interest in him. None of his gang had a girlfriend. They acted as if they did, and often talked about what they had done with girls. They all knew that their boasting was just that, but it was good fun anyway. They talked about the girls in their classes and said what they would do if given the chance which, to date, had not come their way.

Gary's favourite time of all was Sunday. Recently he had started going to the pub down the road with his dad and brothers for a few pints, then back home for dinner and then *The Big Match*. It was brilliant, getting drunk with his dad; being in with all the blokes in the pub, listening to their jokes and remembering them for when he was back at school; then the swearing, the belching and farting as they watched the match. He really enjoyed the dinner too. His mum would make a lovely roast, and then apple crumble and custard or something like that. They would all then sit in front of the telly whilst his mum would clear everything up. Later, they would crack open some cans and watch comedies or sometimes play darts. He loved it.

The best part of it all was that he was now bigger than his brothers and, although slimmer than his dad, he was taller. He felt as if he was fast becoming the top dog in his family too. Life couldn't get much better.

***

For Gary, school was a waste of time. He didn't want any qualifications — why would he? His dad hadn't needed any, and neither of his brothers had even managed to finish school.

Gary and his retinue mostly turned up for lessons but that was only because that bitch the headmistress made it difficult for him if they didn't. They would delight in disrupting lessons, laughing and jeering with each other and scoffing at the kids who did want to learn.

There was one subject that he did enjoy: English. He liked Mr Wilson, who was cooler than the other teachers. Mr Wilson didn't mind challenging Gary and his friends, and even stood up to them when they were getting lippy. Gary had attempted to intimidate Wilson in the early days, but he had had to back down when Wilson had called his bluff. Since then Gary had been quiet in English and, without realising, had started to enjoy it.

In the last couple of weeks, they had been studying *Of Mice and Men*. Gary liked its gritty nature, imagining himself in the West, working with tough blokes and enjoying the camaraderie. However, what had surprised him was the soft and touching relationship between George and Lennie; and when George had shot Lennie to save him from the inevitable lynching, Gary had found himself crying.

For the first time in years, he had made an effort with his homework. Mr Wilson had asked them to respond to the question: 'Was George right to kill Lennie? Explain your answer'. When handing out their exercise books, Gary had seen 'See me' and had got into a rage. He had often seen those words for his homework, but this time had expected better — he'd worked hard on this and he wanted some recognition. He was in for a surprise. Mr Wilson had called out, 'Gary, come up here please.'

Gary had pushed back his chair and slouched up to the front. He looked sulkily at Mr Wilson who said, 'Ladies and gentlemen, I present to you Mr Gary Abbott, a literary genius.'

The class had laughed, keen to see how Gary would take the sarcasm.

'I'm not joking; here you are — ten out of ten. Well done. It's an excellent essay and I'm going to read it out, as I think everyone can benefit from hearing it.'

Gary reddened. He was still seriously wound up; he didn't know how to respond. He sat down again as Mr Wilson read out extracts.

'Where the fuck did that come from?' Steve whispered to him.

'Fuck knows! I just wrote down what was in my head,' Gary answered.

At the end of the lesson, Steve, Phil and Paul started singing the theme tune to *University Challenge*. Gary looked around him and said to everyone in earshot, 'Piss off. It was nothing.'

As he left the room Mr Wilson said, 'Have you got a minute, Gary?'

Gary paused, not looking at Wilson, who said, 'I've got a feeling there is more to come from you; you're not the stupid oaf I thought you were.'

Gary did his best to look like the stupid oaf he wanted people to see but couldn't help being pleased. He snorted loudly and scuffed his way out of the room.

Walking down the corridor he looked for his friends. He was feeling mixed up. He had tried his best with the essay. He had been pleased to have been praised for it. Mr Wilson's comments had made him feel good. But he was desperate to be hard, to be mad, bad and dangerous. He was struggling to reconcile his feelings and right now he didn't want to face his friends and their taunting. What he got was worse than that.

'Well done, Gary,' said Anthony Alexander. 'I got ten out of ten too.'

Gary turned and looked at Anthony. He hated this little, poncey, shit of a wanker with his posh voice, his frail, feeble body and his fucking arrogance. Here he was, talking to him like he was his friend or something.

Gary moved quickly towards Anthony and grabbed him by his hair. 'Keep away from me, you little shit,' he growled, 'and don't you ever speak to me again.'

Anthony went still; his eyes glazed over.

Gary looked down at Anthony as if he had trodden in shit, then pushed him violently into the wall.

'Hey, Gary, mixing with the clever kids now: too brainy to hang around with us!' laughed Steve as he, Phil and Paul walked back towards him.

'I want to get out of this dump,' snarled Gary striding off down the corridor.

***

'You like her?' asked an incredulous Phil of Steve.

'Yeah, what about it?' Steve said.

'Well, nothing if you want to fuck the back end of a bus,' Phil answered. Paul agreed.

'Yeah, but look at the knockers on it,' Steve said.

Gary chipped in, 'Well, my dad always says, you don't look at the oven when you're putting the meat in.'

'Exactly,' Steve said, grateful for the support.

They were sitting in the canteen, wondering what to do with themselves. The object of Steve's longing looked across from the nearby table and flicked two fingers at them.

'I think she fancies you, Stevie boy,' Paul said, smirking. 'You can see the desire in her eyes.'

'You'll see. I always get my girl,' Steve said.

The girl and her friends all got up and as they walked by one of them said, 'Jeez you're a bunch of Neanderthals.'

When they were out of earshot Phil whispered, 'Is that good or bad?'

'Who cares? They're just a bunch of scrubbers anyway,' said Paul.

Gary was feeling dissatisfied with life. The chit-chat of the others was getting on his nerves. He wanted to read *Of Mice and Men* again but knew his friends would jeer at him. He also wanted to cause some trouble somewhere. He was feeling mixed up, restless.

He'd felt ashamed when the girl had called them all Neanderthals. He didn't like the insult and wanted to make someone pay for it. He got up, saying, 'I'll see you later,' and walked off.

He heard Steve say, 'He's probably off to the library to write a play or something.' The others sniggered their agreement.

As Gary left the canteen, he walked past the queue of younger kids waiting to go inside. As he went past, he elbowed a few of them in the guts and looking back saw a couple of them bent over gasping for air. He felt marginally better. He decided to go home. He was sick of school.

When he got home, he found his mother in the kitchen ironing.

'What's up, love?' she asked.

'Nothing,' he grunted.

He went upstairs and stretched out on his bed. He was totally wound up; he wanted something in his life to happen, something, anything.

He reached under Kevin's bed and pulled out a mag. He flicked through it enjoying the feeling of arousal that the naked girls always gave him. He wondered what the girl in the canteen would look like naked. Phil and Paul had been right: she was ugly, but her tits seemed huge to him and he thought that maybe it would be nice to fuck her. He got his hard knob out and within seconds had come. He wiped up the mess and lay back on his bed.

As usual, the relief of ejaculation had got rid of some of his energy and restlessness, but he now felt the normal depression. He threw the glossy mag on the floor and said out loud, 'You're a fucking loser, Gary; you're a total loser.'

Gary went downstairs. He took *Of Mice and Men* with him. He joined his mum. He liked being in the kitchen when she was ironing: the warmth, the smell, the rhythmic sounds made him feel safe.

'Cup of tea?' she asked.

'Nah.'

He sat down at the table and opened his book.

'What's that?' she asked.

'It's the book we're reading in English. It's called Of Mice and Men.'

'Any good?'

'Well, yeah. It's about these blokes in America and a load of trouble they get into.'

'That doesn't sound a laugh a minute. What's good about it?'

'Well, I thought it was a load of rubbish to start with but, it's funny, I got to feel sorry for the main characters and then one of them has to shoot the other one and it was sort of sad.'

'Sounds awful,' she said.

Gary was quiet. He closed the book. He turned to his mother and asked, 'What did you like best at school?'

She too was quiet for a while. 'I liked reading I suppose; I don't really remember much about it.'

Gary looked properly at his mother. She was a small huddled woman, a little mouse really, but she had the kindest face of anyone he knew.

'How old are you, Mum?' he asked.

'Very old — at least, I feel it,' she answered.

'Seriously. How old?'

'Forty-five.'

'What did you want to be when you were my age?' he asked.

'I think I wanted to be a hairdresser, then an air hostess, then a hotel receptionist, then I wanted to get married — and then I did.'

'But don't you look back at your life and wish you'd done those things?'

'I've been all right; don't you worry about me.'

'No, seriously, I mean a career or something,' he pressed.

'Sometimes. Why do you ask?'

'I don't want to stay on at school or anything, but sometimes I think I should try and be good at something.'

'Like what?'

'That's the trouble: I don't know.'

She made herself a cup of tea and sat down opposite him. She let out a tiny gasp of pain as she lowered herself into her chair. 'I used to like to read, and I especially liked writing stories when I was a girl.'

Gary noticed that she sounded quite young now, not the old lady he was so used to. He asked, 'What were the stories about?'

'Well, I liked to imagine myself in different places, maybe in a film, or on a desert island; or sometimes I would imagine I was Princess Elizabeth,' she said, smiling.

'Did you show anyone your stories?'

'No, I was too embarrassed.'

'Have you got them now?' Gary asked genuinely interested.

'No, of course not,' she laughed. 'They were terrible.'

'Maybe they were good, and you didn't realise,' he said.

'Who do you think would be interested in them?'

'I am,' he said, and he meant it.

They both went quiet. Gary was suddenly aware that he didn't know his mother at all. She was always in the background in his house. She made their meals, washed up, did all the stuff that mums do and that was about it.

She saw him looking at her. 'What? What's up?'

'Nothing,' he said, feeling awkward.

She said, 'Do me a favour?'

He looked at her.

'Read me something from your book.'

He opened the book and read. She listened. He read very well, she thought. He even gave the characters different voices.

He stopped after a couple of pages. He felt a bit silly, reading out loud.

'I'd better get on,' he said.

'Gary?'

'What?'

'Do your best at school if you can; I wish I had.'

He was quiet. Then he said, 'I got ten out of ten for my English homework.'

'That's brilliant,' she said, delighted.

'Do me a favour though: don't tell Dad.'

She nodded, understanding.

***

That evening Gary met up with the others. They liked to walk through the town at night, feeling hard and part of the action, although apart from them there was no action.

They lived in a commuter town with one main shopping street with a few pubs along it. They would buy some chips, smoke fags, leer at girls, throw insults at any kids they saw. They went to The Wellington some nights: it was the only pub where they could definitely get served.

Now they sat on a low wall, waiting for the bus.

'What did you do this afternoon, Gaz?' asked Steve.

'Sat around at home, getting bored,' said Gary.

'You would have enjoyed Maths this afternoon,' said Paul.

'I doubt it,' Gary replied.

'Yeah, it was funny,' Phil said.

'I doubt that,' Gary said again.

'That little shit Anthony Alexander only told old Lamb that he was wrong,' Steve laughed.

'About what?'

'Lamb was explaining something about triangles and the little shit-face said, "Excuse me, Mr Lamb, but I think you'll find that that's not strictly correct".' Steve was mimicking Anthony's posh voice.

'Lamb totally went for him and told him to go and see Court,' Paul said.

'I hope he got some serious shit, I hate that bastard,' Gary grunted.

He went over to the cigarette machine outside the newsagent and started hitting it. He had dislodged some money out of it before but, this time, no joy.

The bus came along. They went upstairs and sat at the back. They all lit up cigarettes and looked around the top deck. A few seats ahead of them was a young couple kissing.

They started wolf-whistling. Steve said, 'Go on, my son, give her one for me.'

The couple drew apart. The boy looked at them. Gary stared back. The boy tried to outstare Gary but then looked away. He said to the girl, 'Come on, let's go.' They got up and went downstairs.

The boys yelled and cheered and advised the couple to fuck off out of it.

'Fucking wimp,' said Gary who, for a split second, had been excited at the prospect of a fight.

Phil reached across and pulled the emergency handle; a loud alarm filled the bus.

'You wanker, what did you do that for?' Paul said.

'I dunno; I thought it'd be a laugh,' Phil said, wondering why he'd done it too.

The bus stopped; the driver came heavily up the stairs.

'Get off, you lot,' he said.

They didn't move.

'Get off. You're out to cause trouble and I don't want any of it,' he insisted.

Gary said, 'You going to make us?'

The driver, a middle-aged man, looked at Gary and saw the aggression in his face.

'No, I'm going to go and call the police if you don't get off,' he said.

'For fuck's sake come on you lot,' Gary said and moved to the stairs. As he approached the driver, he leaned in close and said, 'I won't forget your face.'

When they got off the bus, they shouted and gestured to the driver.

'What now?' asked Steve.

Gary looked in the bin by the bus stop, reached in and pulled out a bottle. He spun around saying, 'This,' and threw the bottle hard at the closing doors of the bus. It smashed — glass flew everywhere. They sauntered off, laughing.

***

As they reached the roundabout at the centre of town, a car hooted. The driver's window was wound down and they heard, 'Oy, you nasty little fucks, why aren't you in bed?'

Steve said, 'It's your dad, Gaz.'

Gary looked at the car and recognised his dad's beaten up Cortina. It pulled into the kerb and the passenger door was thrown open.

'Get in, lads — let's burn some rubber!' shouted Mr Abbott.

'Brilliant, come on,' Phil said jumping in, with Paul and Steve getting in the back.

Gary felt excited. He loved being with his dad. He was proud of him and he knew Steve, Paul and Phil thought he was brilliant. He got into the back seat and pulled the door shut.

'Right, my lords, where would your majesties like to go?' roared Mr Abbott.

'How fast can your car go, Brian?' asked Paul.

'Hmmm, depends on how drunk I am,' he replied.

'How drunk are you then?' shouted Phil, excited at the joyride in store.

Brian Abbott rolled up his shirtsleeves, drew in a deep breath and roared, 'I'm pissed out of my fucking mind!'

With that, the car roared into life. It whipped around the corner and went careering up the road, wheels spinning, the smell of hot rubber filling their heads. As they went faster and faster the boys went mad —

this was going to be one hell of a roller-coaster. They were yelling Mr Abbott on to go faster still. The car was all over the place, swerving around cars in front and narrowly missing vehicles coming towards them.

Up ahead they saw that there were roadworks: the road was reduced to one lane. The temporary traffic lights were red on their side, with a car in front of them. Mr Abbott pulled up behind and started to hoot. The car in front stayed still. Abbott continued to sound his horn. 'What's that fucking poof waiting for?' he cursed. 'The road is clear — why doesn't he just go?'

He put his hand on the horn and held it there. 'Come on, you wanker!' he growled.

The door of the car in front opened and a middle-aged man got out and walked back towards them. The Cortina's headlights illuminated his smart suit and silver tie. He motioned to Gary's dad to wind down the window. He did.

'What's eating you?' the man asked.

'We're trying to get on and you're in our way,' slurred Abbott.

'Yes, but the light is red. May I suggest you just calm down and observe the Highway Code?'

There was a silence, a long silence.

Brian Abbott was sheepish, 'Sorry.'

The man nodded and started to walk back to his car. Abbott got out and, walking quickly after him, grabbed the man's collar, whirled him round and head-butted him savagely in the face. The man collapsed in a heap at his feet.

Abbott looked down at the prone figure, 'You pompous shit, don't you ever talk to me like that again.'

The passenger door of the car in front opened and a woman ran back. She started screaming at Abbott, 'You bastard, you've killed him — you're a lunatic!'

Gary's dad started laughing, 'Sorry, me lady, I'm afraid your little chap tripped and fell into my head.'

He got back behind the wheel and started the engine. He turned to the boys and said, 'Home, gents?' pulled out round the other car, mounting the pavement opposite, and sped off.

That night Gary heard his mother's cries, again.

***

The four of them were smoking their cigarettes outside the school gate the next morning.

'Your dad is amazing,' Phil said. 'It was like being in *The Sweeney*.'

'Yeah, that posh bastard went down like a sack of potatoes,' Steve said.

'Your dad's so cool, Gaz,' said Phil.

Gary was silent. He lit a cigarette and inhaled; it made him feel sick.

'Is he like that all the time?' asked Paul.

'Come on. It's time to go in,' Gary said.

Gary loved his dad, he really did. He wanted to be like him; he wanted to live like him. He hated him too: he hated him so much he wanted to kill him.

As they walked towards the door into school Phil said, 'Gary's in one of his moods.'

Suddenly white-hot with anger, Gary stopped and looked at Phil. 'What?'

Phil moved a pace back. Realising his mistake, he put up his hands defensively. 'Nothing, Gaz, nothing; all's fine.'

Gary controlled himself. He paused, let his breathing come back, and he smiled, 'Sure, come on. Let's waste another day.'

***

'OK, we're going to play the balloon game today,' Mr Wilson said.

He explained, 'You're all in a balloon and it's going down fast. The only way you can be saved is if you vote one person out. You all have to present an argument that will persuade your fellow balloonists that you should be saved. You've got ten minutes to get your arguments together and then I'll call you up in alphabetical order.'

Gary sighed. He did not want to play. He wanted to brood and feel alone.

He put his hand up questioningly.

'Yes, Gary?' Wilson said.

'Sir, I've already fallen out; you can forget about me.'

'Don't worry. I saved you and helped you back in.'

'Bad luck, Gaz,' Steve said.

'Right, we're in the air and we are beginning to drop out of the sky. We need to lose someone. Who's first… ah, Gary Abbott. Right, up here, Gary let's hear why we should save you.'

Gary sighed. He rolled his eyes. He stood up and walked up to the front. He turned around and faced the class. He was silent for ten seconds. He looked at his classmates and said, 'Whatever you think of me, you're wrong. Whatever you think I shall do, you'll be wrong. Whatever you thought I might say, you'd be wrong.'

The room was silent. Gary went on.

'I will make it my business to ensure that this balloon gets the success it deserves. I won't rest until we can look each other in the eyes and say, 'we did our bloody best'. Nothing will get in my way to secure victory for this balloon — you can rest easy on that score. When we look back on this day, we will remember how strong we were, how brave we were, and how lucky we were to have each other.' Gary felt strong and certain. 'I'll make sure we're OK.'

He looked around the room. People were gaping at him. He suddenly felt like a complete prick. He had gone too far. He mumbled, 'That's all.'

He went back to his desk and sat down.

The room was still silent. Mr Wilson said, 'Thank you, Gary. Now Mr Anthony Alexander, up you come.'

'This'll be a load of shit,' Steve said.

'Before I start,' said Anthony and that was as far as he got. Steve started, then Paul, then Phil, then the rousing chant which was impossible to resist, 'Out! Out! Out! Out! Out! Out!'

Anthony looked at Mr Wilson, who shrugged. Anthony walked back to his desk and sat down.

One by one they all outlined the benefits they could bring to the balloon trip. Gary didn't engage with the game any further. He felt like such a jerk. Why had he said what he'd said?

He'd been really impressed when he'd heard Brian Clough talking at the weekend and he'd read it again in the paper. He hadn't meant to say it out loud: it had just appeared without him even thinking.

Mr Wilson said, 'Katy Walker, you're our last balloonist, what have you to offer?'

Gary watched Katy walk to the front. He liked her. No, he really fancied her. Everything she did was a bit over the top. It wasn't just that she was pretty, it was that she was different. She had a sexy body too, nice tits.

'Ladies and gentlemen, I present to you an overwhelming argument, one which will make you realise that to eject me from the balloon will mean that it will crash to the ground and our journey will end in disaster.'

Katy had the attention of the room.

'However, if you choose to eject me then I shan't mind, oh no, not I.' She paused. 'And why is that? Simple: because I can fly, I can fly, I can fly,' she yelled.

With that, she slipped off her platforms, jumped onto the desk in front of her and, with arms outstretched, leapt from desk to desk to desk around the room, over people's heads to the front, then down the sides and back again. She bowed.

There was a tumultuous round of applause, with everyone cheering and whistling.

Gary looked at Katy and, as she beamed around the room, he said, 'Brilliant, fucking brilliant.'

She heard and smiled at him.

***

Gary, Steve and Phil were playing cards on the edge of the pitch. They were vaguely watching Paul who was playing for the school against their local rivals. The card-players were notionally reserves, but none of them had any intention of playing. They were really only there to get out of maths. There was a shouted exchange at the far end of the pitch and the three looked over.

'That's typical — Paul is on the ground: he spends more time lying down than playing. I think he might be a fucking homo.'

'Yeah, but look who's causing all the trouble,' Steve observed.

'Who is it?' asked Gary shielding his eyes to see what was going on.

'That prick we saw groping his girlfriend on the bus last night,' Steve said.

'Which one?' asked Gary.

'That one,' Steve and Phil said, pointing.

Gary looked at the players. He could see a body on the ground which he assumed to be Paul but couldn't see the faces of any of the other players. He didn't say anything. This was not the first time he'd noticed that his eyesight wasn't as good as the others'.

When he got home later that day he went through to the kitchen and found his mother sitting, just staring into space. She said, 'Hello, how's life?'

Gary sat down and pulled the newspaper over. He flicked through it idly. He looked at his mother to ask her a question but saw that she had an ugly, dark bruise around her eye.

'What's that?' he asked.

She rubbed her eye and laughed, 'Oh, nothing; I banged it on the corner of a door last night.'

Gary was quiet. He knew he'd always known.

'When did you start wearing glasses?' he asked.

'Hmm, I think I was about thirteen; I'm not sure — a couple of years younger than you. Why? Do you think you might need glasses?'

'Nah. Anyway I wouldn't wear them even if I needed to,' he said.

'Well, if you need them it's better to get used to them now, otherwise your eyes might get worse.'

'I'm fine; don't go on about it. Anyway, maybe you need stronger glasses if you keep walking into doors.'

'I don't keep doing it,' she said.

'Well, I've seen other bruises on you before today.'

She went quiet, then got up and started getting vegetables out of the larder. Gary watched her; her movements were stiff and careful.

'I think Kevin's bringing Tina home for dinner tonight,' his mum said.

Gary grunted. He liked Tina. She was the same age as him but went to a different school. She was really sexy. He liked to imagine her coming around one day and finding just him at home. He pictured her moving close to him and saying, 'Gary, you're much nicer than Kevin, can I be your girlfriend now?' The scene always made Gary feel horny and he was sure that Tina must be able to see his erection.

'Have you got a girlfriend?' his mum asked.

He got up suddenly and said, 'Got to go. I'll see you later.'

He went upstairs and lay down on his bed. He picked up *Of Mice and Men* and started reading it again. He felt sorry for Lennie and George and hated Curly. His favourite scene was when Lennie crushed Curly's hand. But he really wanted to be like Slim, the foreman of the workers. Slim was calm, had dignity and natural authority. That was how Gary wanted to be. But he suspected that people thought he was like Curly, just a bully.

He thought back to the balloon game earlier that day. His ridiculous speech had been the result of his desperation to be respected by the other kids. He had been bruised by the 'Neanderthal' remark from the girl yesterday. He didn't want to be seen as an ignorant bully; he wanted people to look up to him, to admire him.

In need of some strenuous exercise, he pulled his weights out from under the bed and started lifting. He always enjoyed the sensation of his muscles tensing and relaxing; it made him feel powerful and in control again. He did as many press-ups as he could, followed by sit-ups. That was better: he felt much more like himself.

He heard the front door open and Kevin come in.

'Mum, we're hungry. Is dinner ready?' he shouted.

Gary went downstairs. The hall smelled of Tina's perfume — he breathed it in.

He went into the front room where Kevin and Tina were watching the telly.

'Hi, Gary,' Tina said. 'How are you?'

'All right,' Gary grunted, trying to be cool.

'Mmm, I'm sure you're bigger than Kevin these days,' she said.

'No, he ain't,' protested Kevin.

'Yes, he is,' Tina insisted. 'Look at his muscles.'

Gary was loving this — getting Tina's approval above Kevin. He looked at Tina, she was so sexy. She had loads of make-up on; her T-shirt was low cut and he could see her tits easily from where he was standing. She looked up at him and winked.

Kevin looked at Gary looking at Tina's tits and said in a low voice, 'Wouldn't you like to go and play in the sandpit, Gary?'

Gary heard the threat in his brother's voice and went through to the kitchen.

'Oh good. Reach up and hand me that saucepan, Gary,' his mum said.

'You can reach that,' he said. 'It's just above your head.'

'Yes, but I'm busy with the onions,' she said.

Gary handed it to her. As she took it, she let out a little gasp of discomfort. She coughed to cover the moment and said, 'Put the knives and forks out, will you.' He did, in silence.

Derek came in then. He said, 'I've just seen Dad going into the Red Lion with some blokes from work.'

Gary looked at his mum; she made no comment.

Derek lit a cigarette. Gary wanted one too. He said to Derek, 'Give us one of them, will you.'

Derek passed the pack to Gary who took one and lit it from the flame of the gas stove.

They leant against the walls as their mother fried onions and sausages.

'Did you say hello to Tina?' asked Mrs Abbott.

'I didn't bother; she had her tongue down Kev's throat,' Derek answered.

Gary felt a flash of envy.

'I was talking to my foreman today, Gaz. He says that there'll be a job for you at our place when you leave school.'

'Doing what?' Gary asked.

'I don't know, Thickhead; something on the line, drilling or soldering something that will be as unskilled and dull as you,' Derek answered.

'Great, I can't wait,' Gary said.

'Yeah, well it's good enough for me, so I don't see why you should be so fucking lippy.'

'Shhh. What will Tina think of us?' Mrs Abbott said.

'She'll think we're a bunch of losers, and she'd be right,' Gary said.

'Speak for yourself, you little shit. I've got a hundred quid in my pocket — what have you got?' Derek said.

'He's got his schoolwork,' said Gary's mum.

Derek laughed, 'Oh, you get CSEs for beating up other kids these days, do you?'

'No, Gary is doing very well in English, actually.'

Gary said quickly, 'Leave it. I'm hungry: come on, Mum, serve up will you.'

After dinner, Kevin and Tina went out; Derek and Gary watched the telly.

'Dad'll have had a skin-full by the time he gets home,' Derek said. Gary nodded. He was already thinking that.

***

Brian Abbott came home at nine o'clock. Kev and Derek were in the front room watching the telly; Gary was there reading his book. Mrs Abbott was in the kitchen. They all heard the door crash open and the harsh voice of Abbott as he stumbled into the hall.

'Have you had a nice evening?' his wife called to him as he lumbered into the front room.

He looked blearily in her direction and grunted.

'Did you win?' asked Derek.

'Win what?'

'I thought you were in the darts match tonight.'

'Fucking waste of time that was; I didn't even get to play in the team.'

'Why did you stay then?' asked his wife.

'Because I'm in the fucking team, of course. I had to support the boys, didn't I?'

He sat down heavily in his armchair and lit up.

'What's for dinner?' he asked.

'Bangers and mash,' she answered.

'Well, let's have it then.'

She went back into the kitchen.

'Go and get me a beer, Derek.'

Derek got up and fetched a can. He handed it over.

'Ta.'

He cracked the can and took a long frothy swig, some of it spilling down his chin.

'Ah,' he said, smacking his lips.

His wife came back in with a tray. She handed it to him.

He looked at the plate. 'What's this?'

'Sausages, mash, onions and cabbage,' she answered in a quiet voice.

'Yeah, but what's this?' he pointed at the congealed gravy.

'Well, I've been keeping it warm for you,' she answered.

He looked at her through half closed eyes. 'Don't insult me; don't feed shit to me. One of you go and get me some fish and chips,' he ordered. 'You can take this shit away,' he said to his wife, handing the tray carelessly to her.

Derek got up and went out.

'He better be getting my dinner and not going off to screw that tart he's been seeing,' Abbott grumbled.

He swigged at his can again.

Gary had his book in front of him, but he wasn't reading it.

'What's on the telly?' asked Abbott.

Gary answered, 'It's going to be *Sports night* soon.'

'What's on, a match?'

'No, it's boxing and something else.'

'Great, I feel like a fight myself,' Mr Abbott said, chuckling.

The door banged, and Derek came in with a bag. He handed it over.

Mr Abbott unwrapped the fish and chips and said, 'No pickled onion; where's my pickled onion?'

'Sorry, Dad, I forgot it,' Derek said.

'For fucks sake, am I living with a bunch of imbeciles?'

He started shovelling chips into his mouth. He said, 'No, we're not all thick here: I see Mr William Shakespeare is with us reading his little book.'

Gary didn't look up. This was danger time.

'What are you reading?'

'It's just a book,' said Gary.

Abbott and Derek laughed.

'I might be a cretin, Lord Fucking Muck, but I think I can recognise a book. What is the name of your fucking book, please?'

'It's called *Of Mice and Men* and it's a book we're reading at school,' Gary answered.

'Mice and Men? Which are you Gary, a mouse or a man?'

Gary shut the book and said nothing; he didn't know how to answer, not without enraging his dad.

'Let's have a look at it,' ordered Abbott.

Gary reluctantly passed it over.

'It's only a little book: is that all the school thinks you can manage?'

Derek sniggered.

Mr Abbott took a long drink from his can and started choking as the beer went down the wrong way. He spluttered onto the book.

'Ooops, it's got a bit wet — but then you're a bit wet, aren't you, Gary?'

Gary was getting wound up now. He didn't like confrontations with his dad when he was like this, none of them did.

'Oooo, you are getting wound up, Mr Shakespeare?' taunted Abbott seeing his son's face darken.

'Can I have the book back please, Dad?' Despite his growing anger Gary's voice was calm.

'Certainly, my good man.' He took the book and tore it into three parts. 'There you are: you can manage it a bit more easily now.'

Gary took the book back. He left the room. He hated his dad so much right now he thought he might kill him.

***

Gary went out. He couldn't bear to stay in the house. He called for Steve. They called on Phil and Paul.

They walked around the estate and ended up in the old bus shelter at the bottom of the hill. They had cigarettes stolen from Steve's dad and a bottle of Dubonnet from Phil's mum.

Gary was in a bad mood. The other boys were wary of him. As soon as he had turned up at his front door, Steve had sensed the aggression in him. Now, as they talked, they were agreeing with anything that Gary said, just to pacify him.

'Here comes the bus,' said Phil, looking up.

'We'd better start swimming,' joked Paul.

'You're a fucking jerk,' Gary said.

They went quiet.

The bus pulled up and some girls got off.

'Hello, hello: I recognise these lovely ladies,' Steve said.

'Hello, girls,' said Phil. 'Looking for some action?'

Heather, Janet and Paula looked towards the boys, recognising their classmates.

'Oh God, look who it isn't,' said Heather, 'the four ugliest boys in the world.'

'What've you been doing then?' asked Paul.

'We went to the pictures and then had a few drinks,' answered Janet.

'Which pub?' asked Phil.

'The Red Lion.'

'How come you get into the Red Lion? We don't get served there.' Steve complained.

Heather was scornful, 'Why do you think that is? Look at yourselves. You look like four stupid kids.'

The girls did look older than them. They were heavily made up, tight tops and jeans accentuating their figures.

'How much did you drink?' asked Paul.

'A few,' the girls giggled.

'Well, we've got some booze — want some?' he said.

'All right,' said Paula, and reached for the bottle.

'You're quiet,' said Janet, looking at Gary.

'Yeah, what's wrong with you?' asked Heather.

'Nothing.'

Gary was sitting in the furthest corner of the shelter, not engaging with the banter. Heather sat down next to him and said, 'Why do you hang around with these losers? You're much nicer than they are.' As she spoke, she took a long pull from the bottle.

Gary grabbed the bottle from her and took an equally long swallow.

'Leave us some,' Steve said, taking the bottle.

The little group proceeded to empty the bottle and throw insults. They were now pushing and shoving at each other to stay on the bench.

Heather was pressed up close to Gary. She put her hand on his crotch and whispered into his ear, 'Does that feel nice?'

It did feel good. Gary turned his face to her, and they kissed clumsily.

Heather started stroking his cock; he felt hard immediately. He reached to her breasts and grappled with them. He moved his hand between her legs, but she pushed it away.

'What's wrong?' he asked, indignant.

'I don't want that.'

'Yeah, but it's what I want,' and he put his hand between her legs again.

She levered herself away from him and stood up.

'Come on,' she said to the other girls, 'I'm off.'

'Fucking bitch,' Gary spat.

'Didn't manage to get your end away then, Gary?' Phil asked, his voice was jeering.

Gary sprang to his feet and pinned Phil against the bus shelter wall.

'OK, OK, it's cool, nothing meant by it,' Phil said.

'Leave it out mate. He was just being a tosser: he can't help it,' Steve said, pulling at Gary's arm.

Gary shrugged him off and started walking away. He wanted to get away — from everything.

***

Gary got home just before midnight. He went upstairs to the bathroom. He sat on the toilet and put his head in his hands. The shitty drink was making him dizzy and the fags made him feel really sick suddenly.

The day had been horrible. Everything was a mess. He was mixed up and wanted to get out of it. Nothing seemed to go his way anymore. He'd thought that Heather wanted to get off with him. She'd been giving him all the signals. Then the stupid cow had got all straight and serious just when he thought something might happen, for once.

He thought back to the scene with his dad earlier. That had really upset him. It was only a stupid book, but it had felt much more than just that. Why did his dad become such a total prick when he got drunk?

Gary leaned his head against the bathroom wall, nearly asleep. Then he heard his father's angry cursing next door.

'Yes, you will; yes, you fuckin' will!'

Gary heard his mother's whimpers, 'Not again; please, no, not again.'

There was a heavy crash against the wall and his father's voice, 'Shut the fuck up; just do it, for fuck's sake.'

Gary heard the sound of his mother crying, and then bedsprings creaking.

'Please — no, not again.'

Then her voice was shut off by a loud blow. Then came the sound of his parents' bed rocking; his mother was quiet, his father grunting like a pig.

Gary stood up and lifted the lid of the toilet; he got onto his knees and vomited. He knelt there for several minutes, his stomach heaving every few seconds. He rested his head on the toilet seat, desperate for its cool relief. After an age, he stood up. He brushed his teeth and washed his face. It was quiet next door. He shuddered.

***

Gary went down for breakfast as usual. His dad and brothers had already gone to work. His mother put some toast in front of him with a cup of tea. He didn't dare look at her. He was too embarrassed. He was scared too.

'Where did you go last night?' she asked.

'Just out with Steve, Phil and Paul.'

'Just out?'

'Well, we kicked around the estate for a bit.'

'I'm sorry about the book,' she said.

'Doesn't matter.'

'Well, I've done my best to stick it together again,' she said, and pushed it across the table.

The book was back in one piece with a lot of Sellotape down the spine.

'Thanks, Mum,' he said, and looked up at her.

'Another door?' he asked, as he saw the vivid red mark on her cheek.

'Come on then, time to get going,' she said.

***

During register the headmistress came in. She whispered to Miss Arnold, the form tutor, then turned to the class and said, 'I want to see Gary Abbott, Steve Hunter, Phil Armstrong and Paul Nuttall in my office in five minutes, please.'

Everyone looked round at the four, who were looking at each other.

As soon as the register was taken Miss Arnold said, 'OK, you four had better go.'

They scuffed their way slowly to the headmistress's office. Steve said, 'What's this all about?'

Gary said, 'I bet it's that fucking bitch Heather. I bet she's complained about me.'

They knocked on Miss Court's door. She opened it and ushered them inside. Standing by her desk was a policeman.

'Here they are, officer, they're all yours,' said Miss Court.

The policeman looked at the four of them. He said, 'We've had a report of some criminal damage two nights ago. You have all been identified, with one of you being seen to throw a bottle at a bus. What do you have to say for yourselves?'

Miss Court said, 'Don't bother lying just say what happened.'

No one spoke. The boys looked at the floor. There was a long silence.

Gary spoke. 'It was me. I threw it.'

'Which one are you?' asked the policeman.

'Gary Abbott.'

'Why did you throw the bottle?'

'I dunno,' Gary answered, 'I suppose I just did.'

'Well, suppose I just ring up your parents and talk to them about it. Will your mother or father be at home now?' asked the policeman.

'No, don't ring my mother, please don't,' Gary blurted.

There was a long silence.

Miss Court said, 'I realise this is an extremely serious offence, constable, but is it possible that it is a matter that the school can address?'

'Well, not really; I have to take action. The offence occurred outside of school time and off the school premises.'

'I wonder whether, if these lads promise not to cause any more trouble and you allow me to impose sanctions, we can leave the matter here?' Miss Court continued. 'I think that would be best all round, don't you?'

The policeman looked at her. She was tough, he could tell. He looked at the boys again.

'What do you have to say?' he asked.

They shifted uneasily. Finally, Gary said, 'I'm sorry, it was stupid, and I wish I hadn't done it.'

The other boys nodded their agreement.

'Right, all right. I'm warning you boys: I am going to write up a report about this and I do not want to see your names again. Any further problems and it'll be much, much worse next time.'

He got up and went to the door. He said, 'I recommend a harsh punishment, Miss Court,' and turned and left.

The headmistress sat down behind her desk.

'OK, I know you won't be able to tell me what was behind it all; I don't want to know. The question is what is the right kind of punishment for you? Any ideas?'

The boys looked down in silence.

'I personally don't believe in the cane, but Mr Earnshaw does.'

This they knew was true. Earnshaw was the deputy head and he was famous for his caning.

Victoria Court was quiet as she stared at each of them in turn. Finally, she said, 'This is what I want. In the next five days, you will all do a piece of work on which a teacher must compliment you. I won't tell any of your teachers about the challenge: it's up to you to earn the praise. If you don't achieve it, I shall be forced to talk to your parents and explain what has happened. Does that sound fair?'

The boys nodded.

'OK, now get out, and pull your socks up. Gary, you can stay.'

Steve, Phil and Paul scuffed their way out.

'Mr Wilson told me about your excellent essay, Gary. So, you already know how to achieve a good mark.' She went on, 'What's wrong with you, Gary? There's something going on: do you want to tell me?'

'Nothing, Miss,' Gary mumbled.

'You've got some potential; you're not an idiot. Why do you behave like one, and a thuggish one at that?'

Gary was silent.

'Do your best to keep your temper under control: it will be the end of you if you're not careful,' she warned. 'Off you go, then — I don't want to see you again for a while.'

Gary turned and left. He breathed a sigh of relief. The thought of the filth talking to his mum right now filled him with — what? He wasn't sure. He didn't want the police to see his mother and ask her questions about her face. Nor did he want his mother to know that he'd been in trouble with the police. He loved his mum; he wanted to protect her from any more pain.

As he walked back to his form, he vowed to himself that, no matter what the provocation, he would stay out of trouble.

Katy

John and Anna Walker had wanted a child for the entirety of their fifteen-year marriage. They had finally begun to accept the probability of never conceiving. In fact, their sex life had long ago waned to a once a month basis in any event. So, when the doctor told Anna that she was pregnant neither she nor John could quite believe it. Anna gave up her job as an assistant librarian the moment the amazing news was confirmed. John had wholly supported her decision — nothing was going to complicate or jeopardise Anna's pregnancy or the health of their baby. His job, in the housing department of the local council, was secure and, although only modestly paid, it did bring in enough money for them to manage and plan for the future — a future with their child at the centre.

The moment they had dreamed of arrived — in the middle of the night and a month earlier than expected. They waited for the ambulance in an ever-increasing state of agitation. Anna's contractions were rapid and, although she was doing her best to stay calm, she felt that everything was slipping out of control. With no sign of the ambulance they decided to drive to the hospital. John, even more frightened than his wife, drove erratically, his mind racing and his heart thumping. Anna cried for him to drive faster as her contractions continued to come hard and fast.

As the car rounded a corner, minutes from the hospital, it bumped over a kerb and crumpled into a bollard. The engine cut out. Cursing savagely, John tried over and over to get the car going — the engine was dead. He ran into the road to wave down the first car he could see. John frantically explained the situation and the 'good Samaritan' agreed to take them to the hospital. When John opened Anna's door to help her out her unconscious body sagged against him.

John sat in the waiting room, his head in his hands. He was drowning from the weight of his fear, rage with himself but, most of all, sickening feelings of guilt. Finally, the midwife came in and sat next to him. She heard John say through his sobs, 'Tell me everything is OK, please.'

She said calmly and slowly, 'Anna is fine, and so is your daughter.'

John let out a deep groan of utter relief, 'Oh God, thank you God.'

The midwife was silent for a full minute then said, 'I'm so sorry, John, your other daughter didn't make it.'

***

Anna and John wept uncontrollably at their daughter's funeral. Afterwards, when it was just them and their little girl Susan, they talked about their loss properly for the first time.

'It's all my fault: will you ever be able to forgive me?' Implored John, holding his wife's hands.

'There's no fault; don't punish yourself. I worry about Susan: I think she'll grow up feeling that something is missing.'

Anna asked her consultant what the chances were of her being able to conceive again. He said that, in view of her age and the complications surrounding her recent delivery, another pregnancy would carry significant risk. 'I'm sorry, Mrs Walker.'

The news was a bitter blow to them, but they didn't give up. Their next step was to look into adoption. John discussed the situation with the adoption team at the council. He explained that they were looking for a baby to grow up with their own bereaved daughter: was it possible that a baby could be found? They attended the introductory classes, passed through the various hoops of proving their parental suitability, and succeeded in gaining the approval of the final panel.

One year after the birth of Susan and the death of her twin, John and Anna were introduced to their new daughter — and Susan's sister — Katy.

* * *

As it turned out, their dream for an adopted daughter of the same age as Susan was almost fulfilled. Katy was just four weeks older than her new sister. They decided to make Katy's birthday the same as Susan's and, from the moment of Katy's arrival, treated the girls as twins.

The adoption team didn't give explicit advice about talking to Katy about her adoptive status but encouraged Anna and John to answer any direct questions that Katy might ask in the future. Being keen to do the right thing, Anna and John took the advice seriously. They agreed that they would tell Katy that she was adopted and why they had been so determined to find a twin for Susan, but only when they felt that she was of an age to understand.

* * *

Even as a very young child, Katy was challenging. She seemed highly sensitive to change and reacted badly when she didn't get what she wanted. However, as time went by, she grew into a lively and generous girl, whose abiding love was her sister — a love absolutely reciprocated.

Susan and Katy looked similar: both had dark brown hair and dark eyes. They were of similar height and build, with Katy being slightly taller and certainly more athletic. In personality, however, they were quite different. Susan was calm, steady and a 'good girl'. She was very much cut from the mould of her parents. Katy was the opposite. She was full of life, always ready to take on a challenge or a dare, keen to seek out adventures. At school they were both bright, although Katy rarely put any effort into her work; unlike Susan who was a model student. They were most similar in one particular aspect — they loved each other completely. They were inseparable. From the earliest days of their sisterhood they formed the strongest of bonds. They shared a bed, their toys and their treats. If one was upset, the other was too. When one was happy the other was glad.

In the early years, John and Anna often discussed how and when they should tell Katy the truth. As time passed, the need for doing so occurred to them less and less and, without their even noticing, they left the subject alone altogether. Every now and then there would be an instance when it seemed they would have to address it but, somehow, each time, the matter was avoided.

One day, before the girls had started school, Anna took them swimming. Katy saw a heavily pregnant woman in the pool. She exclaimed, 'Look, Mummy, she's the fattest lady in the world!'

Anna shushed her and explained that the lady had a baby inside her. This was very intriguing to the girls who wanted to know if that was where all babies came from, including themselves.

'Yes, you were once in my tummy and then you popped out to say hello,' Anna said. She reddened slightly as she said it but didn't see it as a lie, rather it was just a simple explanation.

Years later, they had their astrological charts drawn. They needed to know what time of day they were born. Anna had pondered the question carefully then said, 'Well, I'm not sure exactly; you see I was unconscious, and the birth happened when I was away with the fairies.'

'But was it day or night-time?' pressed Katy.

'I am sure it was very early in the morning, still dark anyway.'

Then Katy asked the question she had been dreading: 'Who was born first, me or Susan?'

'You were first, and then Susan came along very soon after,' Anna said, hoping that the subject would change soon.

'Which one of us was more painful?' Katy asked. She knew that this was an important part of giving birth.

'Run along! I don't know I wasn't conscious,' Anna ended the subject, not wanting to get into any further half-truths.

Both girls were popular but had different friends. Susan's group was made up of sensible, polite little girls. Katy's friends were more often than not little boys, and the naughtier they were the more she liked them.

Susan scolded Katy that her friends were silly show-offs and not like her own friends. Katy didn't mind she liked to shock Susan and reported to her the dares she had been set and how she had managed to achieve them. Susan was always upset and shocked, much to Katy's delight. By the time Katy was eight she had smoked cigarettes, dropped her knickers for curious boys, had climbed and fallen out of trees, been caught shoplifting sweets, and had sworn at a teacher. Susan remained a model pupil. But, despite their many differences, they each loved the other more than anyone else in the world.

As they grew up, they noted and spoke of their uncanny power — the ability to 'sense' what the other one was feeling. They would stick up for and rally around each other no matter what. This had been the case at their ninth birthday party. They always had a joint party, with their separate friends invited. Anna, in particular, found these events stressful. Managing to create an environment that suited both groups of friends was increasingly difficult. On this occasion Katy was upstairs in the room she shared with Susan, wrestling with two boys from school. She was pinned down by one of them whilst the other tied her up with the cord of her dressing gown. Susan didn't know why she thought to look upstairs for her sister, but she did. On opening the bedroom door, she saw the two boys laughing as Katy became more and more enraged by her predicament. Susan yelled at them to let her sister go, they didn't. Susan rushed into the bathroom, picked up a pair of nail scissors and ran back to Katy to free her. Rounding on the boys, her scissors pointing dangerously, Susan screamed at them to 'get out of our house'. They saw her fury and ran. As soon as they fled, Susan collapsed in a flood of tears and only calmed down when Katy comforted her.

In their last year at primary school they were both chosen to appear in the end of term production of *The Wizard of Oz*. Katy, of course, was Dorothy, whilst Susan had a minor part. Katy was totally energised and excited by it all, Susan terrified. They rehearsed together in their bedroom, Susan reading the parts of all the characters with whom Katy's role had contact. The majority of their home rehearsal time was spent practising Susan's three lines over and over again. On the day of the performance, Katy stood behind Susan, just out of view, ready to prompt her sister. As Susan dashed off the stage, elated yet shivering with nerves, Katy hugged her, grinning like a lunatic, telling her how proud she was. Although Katy stole the show, it was Susan's successful performance that gave her the most joy.

John and Anna watched them grow up with enormous pride. They were warm and loving parents and loved both girls equally. They knew how lucky they were to have such wonderful daughters. However, they both realised that although Katy's coming into their lives had been a miracle, she was going to stretch their resolve to the limit.

***

Things started getting really difficult when Katy became a teenager. On their thirteenth birthday, they had their usual joint party. Susan wore no make-up, was wearing a T-shirt and jeans and trainers. Katy wore lipstick, mascara, eye liner; her hair was piled high on her head. She wore a tight, white top and short red skirt, with high platform shoes. When Anna saw her, she said, 'Katy, what do you look like?'

Katy was excited, 'I know! Melissa helped me get ready. Don't I look amazing?'

Melissa was Katy's older friend. Anna didn't think she was a very good influence. Katy met her at the youth club she attended every Friday night. She came home breathless, talking about all the older teenagers she'd met, what they said, what they wore and how she wanted to be like them.

'Katy, you look like... well, you don't look very well brought up, if I'm honest,' said Anna, doing her best not to prick her daughter's balloon.

'But it's what young women look like these days, Mum,' Katy explained.

Anna didn't have the heart to say that she thought that Katy looked like a tart, so she left it.

When John came home from work with the party still going, he said to Anna, 'What did you let Katy dress up like that for?'

'Ha, you try telling her then,' Anna retorted.

John knew his daughter well enough not to broach the subject now.

As they got ready for bed, Katy and Susan, still sharing a room, were reviewing the party.

'You know Adam was staring at you the whole time,' Susan said.

'Really? Brilliant! I think he's gorgeous.'

'He's a total idiot, Katy — a show off; and he's completely thick.'

'Yeah, but he's really tasty: you have to admit that.'

'No, he's stupid. Honestly, there's nothing to like.'

'I bet he's got something hidden away,' giggled Katy, 'and I think I shall track it down.'

'Oh, Katy.' Susan tried to be shocked, but she knew her sister: this was how she was these days.

'Who do you like then?' Katy asked.

'No one really; although Jenny's brother is quite nice,' Susan admitted.

'He's so boring, Sooz. Plus, he wears the worst glasses I've ever seen, and they're held together with Sellotape.'

Susan had to admit that Ian, Jenny's older brother, did look a bit square, but she liked his studious appearance. She didn't want excitement and adventure: she dreamed of a boyfriend with whom she could talk about books and music and go for walks in the country.

'Well, I don't want to have a boyfriend if you don't have one,' Katy said.

'Don't worry about me: you go off and have fun with your trendy little boys,' Susan said with bored superiority.

'OK, I will,' Katy said.

Two days later she and Adam were snogging in the back row of the cinema.

Every Friday night, the girls went to the church youth club. They were both popular but for different reasons. The organisers liked Susan because she came up with ideas for events, games, trips away, and helped organise them. Katy was popular with the boys, because she was sexy and provocative. She didn't really want a boyfriend: the excitement of flirting and the possibility of what might happen were what she craved.

As their bodies began to mature, Susan continued to wear modest clothes, not keen on displaying her changing shape. Katy loved the fact that she was becoming curvy and couldn't see why she shouldn't show herself off. Her parents kept telling her to be more like Susan but to no avail.

Despite her increasingly daring ways, Katy remained kind and loving to Susan. She wanted her sister to have everything good. Katy encouraged her to dress up more and take chances with boys, as she did. Susan was happy with her lot.

One night, Susan found Katy sitting on a toilet seat in the youth club, crying.

'What's wrong, Katy?' she asked, kneeling down to comfort her.

'I told Stewart that I didn't fancy him and to fuck off, but he kept on at me and pushed me into a corner and started groping me,' Katy answered through her sobs.

Susan held her close then told her to get her coat. She went out into the main hall and, seeing Stewart, went up to him. He was complaining to his friends, 'She's such a prick-tease; she makes out that she's desperate for it but then acts all innocent.'

Susan strode up and without preamble kicked him hard between the legs. She turned on her heel and went off to collect Katy. The room had gone quiet, except for the comments of a few admiring onlookers.

Katy was too proud to go home. She went back into the hall to search for Stewart. She saw him kneeling on the floor, curled up in pain.

Looking down at him she said, contempt in her voice, 'What's happened to you?'

'He's had an attack of Walker revenge,' said one of his friends laughing.

***

During her starring role in *The Wizard of Oz,* Katy had discovered her love of performance. She joined Mayfair Studios stage school, to which John took her every Saturday. She was full of the excitement of it. She was learning to dance and act, but singing was her greatest love.

John spoke to the tutors every now and then to find out how Katy was doing. He heard: 'Amazing voice...', 'She's a natural...', 'She could go all the way...'

Katy was increasingly excited at the real possibility of a life in show business. She told Susan everything that she was doing at the school and how much she enjoyed the world of performance.

One day she came home from Mayfair and said 'Suzy, Mr Kelly, the singing teacher, said I should think about finding an agent. He thinks I could get onto *Opportunity Knocks*! Can you believe it?'

Susan could see that Katy shone brightest when she was performing and stressed to her sister how important it was that she carry on and make the most of her talent.

When they chose their options, Katy selected Drama and Music. Anna was anxious about Katy's direction but, to Anna's surprise, John backed their daughter up, 'I think we should encourage her; she really is talented: maybe she could make it? We ought to support her.'

The next school year was a great one for the girls. Susan was getting high marks in her subjects, all of them. Katy was doing very well in her preferred subjects and had played Lady Bracknell in the school production of *The Importance of Being Earnest,* to great acclaim. They both had various forays into romance: Susan's were with studious boys who were too timid to press their advances, whilst Katy's boyfriends — invariably short-lived — to her great satisfaction, could not keep their hands off her.

That Christmas, they sneaked a bottle of sherry upstairs and were working their way through it. Susan had two glasses and said that she'd had enough. Katy carried on swigging from the bottle as they talked.

'Do you want to go all the way one day with a boy?' she asked.

'Well, one day I do but not with any old boy; it's got to be with someone special,' Susan answered. 'How about you?'

'Well, I've got pretty close a few times, but something always stops me going too far. Also, the boys I've been out with have just been boys; I usually have to show them what I want and it kind of spoils the whole thing. All they want to do is juggle with my tits and get me to wank their cocks.'

'Katy, that's terrible,' Susan said shocked, but laughing too.

'Well, it's true. I want a bit of stroking and kissing and grown up stuff,' Katy said.

'Me too. Plus, I'd like to go out for a nice meal first, and then see a play or something,' Susan agreed.

'Never mind a play, just give me a fast car,' Katy said glugging more sherry.

'How are we going to explain the missing bottle to Mum and Dad?' asked Susan.

'They won't notice, they've had this bottle for years. Listen,' she went on, 'I've got something to tell you.'

Susan looked at Katy, wary.

'There's this guy at stage school. He's a bit older but I quite like him and I'm sure he's got the hots for me.'

'What's his name?'

'Gavin.'

'How long has he been going?'

'Well, he doesn't go he's one of the teachers.'

'How old is he?'

'Hmmm, maybe thirty, maybe a bit more. Does it matter?'

'Thirty!' Susan said, almost shrieking.

'Yeah, but he's really young and modern; he's not like a teacher,' Katy said.

'But, you're only fifteen, Katy,' Susan protested.

'I know that, dummy.'

'Has he done anything or said anything?' pressed Susan, worried now.

'He looks at me in this sort of, you know, that way. He's always praising me and saying I should stay a bit later to practise, that kind of stuff,' Katy said.

'But that might mean anything; it might be because he thinks you're talented and will go a long way?' Susan suggested.

'Yeah, that's true, but I caught him looking at my tits the other day and I could see he had a hard on,' giggled Katy.

'Oh, Katy!'

'He's terribly good looking, Suzy. I really fancy him.'

'Be sensible — nothing can come of it, except a load of trouble.'

Katy knew that it was silly, but she began to dream of being with Gavin, and couldn't wait to see him again.

'I shall be getting a lift home, Dad,' Katy said, as he dropped her off outside the rehearsal studio.

'Oh, who from?'

'One of the teachers lives near us,' she answered.

'Who?'

'Oh, Davina, she teaches dance.'

In fact, she had no idea whether she could get a lift home, with Gavin or anyone else. She didn't care, all she knew was that she wanted Gavin.

Gavin's class that day was early afternoon. She loved watching him. He was so sexy. He had long, golden hair, parted in the middle. His clothes were chic: he always wore hugely flared, velvet loon pants, a waistcoat and skinny ties. He smoked long black cheroots and made his own coffee. He knew, and had worked with, television and theatre stars, and often regaled his students with anecdotes from the West End and Hollywood.

Katy stared, transfixed, her heart thudded at the thought of being with him, being touched by him, giving herself to him.

Gavin was preparing them for a production of *A Midsummer Night's Dream*. Katy landed the part of Titania and was enjoying the license to play a part with sexual undertones — which she played as overtones. At the end of the session she asked Gavin, 'Is there anything you can think of that will make my performance any better?'

'No, Katy, you are perfect in every way. But if we could spend more time together, I could give you ideas about how best to use your body to real effect.'

His words thrilled her. She had spent hours imagining them together: in his car, in his bed, in long grass in the country — all her images were of him taking off her clothes and revelling in her body.

'Gavin, you don't live near me, do you? I need a lift home tonight and I'm just wondering who will be able to take me.'

'I'll happily take you in my car,' he said, staring into her eyes.

At five thirty she walked with him to his car. She had put on some lipstick, a dab of scent and had spent a few minutes making sure that she looked perfect for him.

'This is my car,' said Gavin as they reached a battered Ford Anglia.

He saw her expression and added, 'It's the car I drive around town, I leave my better car at home.'

'Is that the Jag you told us about?' Katy asked.

'Yes, I bought it with my earnings from my part in the last *Bond* film.'

As they drove, she felt her heart fluttering at his proximity. She was aware of his hand moving to the gear lever, inches away from her knee. She slowly moved her leg closer and closer.

Gavin asked her questions as they drove. He wanted to know about her friends, her school, what she did in the evenings. Finally, he asked her, 'I expect you have lots of boyfriends?'

'No, none. I find boys my age far too immature.'

'Really?'

There was a long silence. Gavin turned to her and said, 'You are a lovely young woman, Katy; you deserve someone special; you know.'

'I would like someone in my life, but I don't know where I'll find the right man,' she said, willing his hand to touch her knee.

The car stopped at traffic lights. She saw his hand resting on the gear lever. She edged her knee against his fingers; the touch was electric.

'Katy, I think you are a beautiful young woman; I find you very attractive.'

'Do you, Gavin? Do you really?'

He put his hand on her knee and said, 'Oh yes, I do, really I do.'

She closed her eyes: it felt so good, so right. She wanted to take his hand and move it up her thigh. She looked at him. He looked back, smiling. Katy saw his face properly, for the first time. She saw a pock-marked old man with oily, lank hair. She breathed in sharply, her mouth and nostrils filled with his stinking, coffee- and cigarette-fuelled breath.

Lifting his hand carefully off her knee, she said, 'Oh, Gavin, I live just down the road on the left. You can let me out now.'

'Really? I thought we might go for a longer trip, out into the country,' he said, with a whine in his voice.

'No, I must get home now: my parents are expecting me.'

With the mention of her parents she suddenly felt ashamed, upset and a little frightened.

'Are you sure, Katy? You know I shall make certain everything is fine for you: you needn't worry about anything.'

She knew what that meant. She had to stop this right now.

'I'll get out here,' she said reaching for the door handle.

Pulling up sharply to the kerb he said, and edge in his voice, 'Well, all right, if that's what you want.'

She opened the door and got out. 'Thanks, Gavin, I'll see you next week,' and slammed the door shut.

She watched the old car pull away. She closed her eyes and took in a deep breath. What had she been thinking of? He was horrible!

Now what was she going to do? Still five miles from home, far too far to walk, and no money in her pocket. She groaned. She walked to the nearest telephone box and, reversing the charges, rang home. Her mother answered.

'Hi, Mum, is Sooz there?'

'Yes, where are you?'

'Oh, we're just working a bit later; I wanted to check something with her.'

'Hold on, she's upstairs.'

'What's up?' Susan asked a few seconds later.

'Listen,' whispered Katy, 'I need to get a taxi home, but I haven't got enough money. Have you got any?'

'Yeah, I've got a few quid — will that be enough?'

'I dunno. Probably. I'm going to get the taxi to drop me off at the end of the road. Will you meet me there in fifteen minutes with the dosh?' Katy asked.

Susan said yes and rang off.

When she got out of the cab, Katy put her arms around her sister and started crying.

'I'm such an idiot,' she said shaking all over.

Back in their bedroom, Susan said, 'He sounds repulsive, what got into you?'

'I don't know; I just love it when men fancy me. It makes me feel special,' Katy answered, now feeling ashamed and dirty.

'Well, you're safe now,' Susan said, cuddling her sniffling twin sister.

**

Summer holiday that year saw the Walkers in the Dorset seaside town of Swanage. They were staying at a caravan park just outside the town. They had had fun, now the holiday was nearly over.

The sisters had been on the beach every day. Katy liked to show as much of herself to the public as she could, whilst Susan was predictably more modest. Susan read books voraciously; Katy flicked through *Melody Maker*, *Nineteen* and, when she could afford it, *Cosmopolitan*.

Lounging on their towels, they became aware of a boy watching them. He was about their age and although he was reading a book his gaze kept moving in their direction.

'Which one of us is he looking at do you think?' Katy whispered.

'You, of course.'

'How can you tell?'

'Because you're the sex bomb, not me.'

'He's nice, don't you think?' Katy said.

'Yes, very nice.'

Katy couldn't help herself, she sat up and started rubbing sun cream into her arms. As she did it, she made sure that her breasts were facing the boy, and for good measure she rubbed cream into her thighs too.

'You are terrible, Katy; you might as well ask him if he wants to jump on you.'

'But I do want him to.'

They passed away the next hour looking at the boy and enjoying being looked at. Anna and John came along midway through the afternoon and joined them.

'There's going to be a concert on at the bandstand tonight,' John said. 'An evening of Glen Miller.'

'Wow, that'll send us all crazy,' Katy said.

'Oh, come on, Katy, it'll be fun,' said Anna.

'What's fun for a couple of geriatrics isn't quite the same for cool cats like us,' Katy said.

'I'll come, Mum; I'll enjoy it,' said Susan.

'Oh, all right — I'll come if you force me.' Katy gave in. She said loudly, 'What time is it and where?'

Anna said, seven thirty p.m. at the bandstand.

Katy looked in the direction of the boy; she saw him nod. She smiled.

Later that day, they were standing in amongst several hundred holidaymakers in front of the Victorian bandstand. The band started to play, and the old-fashioned tunes gave the evening a romantic atmosphere — even the girls felt it.

'He's here,' said Susan spotting the boy from the beach a little way back.

Katy looked round and saw him. She smiled and waved at him. He smiled back.

'He's on his own. That's a shame,' Katy said.

'Why?' asked Susan.

'Well, I had hoped he might have a friend you could get off with, thickhead,' Katy said.

'Don't worry about me, I'm fine.'

As the evening progressed, the boy edged closer until he was standing slightly behind them but to the side. Katy couldn't help herself looking round at him every now and then. He was nice looking, maybe a bit older than her, dressed fashionably. He looked cool.

Just then the band leader announced that they would be having a break but that the talent competition was going to follow.

'What talent competition?' Katy asked, suddenly interested.

John looked at his programme and read, 'If anyone has a talent and wants to be in show business why not enter our Star of the Future talent competition.'

Katy squealed, 'I'm going to have a go! What shall I do?'

'Why don't you do that lovely Mary Hopkins song, "Those were the days"?' said Anna.

Katy tutted. 'Boring.'

'How about a Beatles song?' John suggested.

'Dad, you're so out of touch.'

'You do that Lulu song really well,' said Susan.

'Yeah, "Shout": that's perfect,' Katy said.

She looked to see where to put her name down and rushed off.

'She'll win I'm telling you now,' John said smiling.

Thirty minutes later, the band leader announced, 'Ladies and gentlemen, we are very lucky tonight: we have eight classy acts to enjoy, and we'll be starting with one of the country's leading impressionists, Dazzling David Dodd.'

There then followed an embarrassing three minutes of Frank Spencer, Harold Wilson and Bruce Forsyth, and some desultory applause. Several more acts came and went and then the Walkers heard:

'Now, is it Lulu? — No: it's the one and only Katy Walker!'

John, Anna and Susan applauded wildly.

Katy came on to the stage. Unlike the previous contestants, she strolled on slowly and with confidence. She went up to the band leader and held out her hand for him to kiss. She turned to the audience and smiled broadly. Then, she undid her hair and let it fall down over her shoulders. She took the microphone from its stand and walked to the front of the stage.

She turned to the band leader and said, 'I'm ready, are you?'

'We can't wait,' he said.

She looked at her family and after a slight pause she opened her mouth and sang the raw, throaty cry of, 'Weeeeellll,' and then let go.

Katy was electric. Her movements, voice, energy — her sheer presence rendered the audience spellbound. As the song continued so the electricity increased. Halfway through the song the crowd started clapping and stamping their feet and by the end they were shouting for more. Katy bowed; her face wreathed in smiles. She put the microphone back on its stand, gave the band leader a huge hug and kissed him on both cheeks.

As she came back to her family, people parted for her as if she were royalty. Susan hugged her and said, 'Not bad for a novice.'

'Well done that was amazing!' people were saying around her.

'Yeah, it was OK — I lost it a bit towards the end, but I thought it was OK,' Katy said, her eyes alive with excitement.

She had loved every single minute of the performance. She had been in control — in charge of everything around her. It had felt like the rush of some drug: she wanted more and more of it. The attractive boy was forgotten completely: she just wanted to get back on stage.

***

Two weeks before the girls' sixteenth birthday, Anna said to John: 'You know we are going to have to face the music soon.'

'I know. I've been dreading it. What never occurred to me was the effect it would have on Susan, as well as Katy.'

'I can't believe we've been so stupid as to leave it this long,' Anna groaned.

'Do we have to tell them?'

'Not tell them. Surely we have to?'

John thought for a long while. 'Well, maybe not. No one will ever find out. We don't know anything about Katy's parents. It's not likely that there'd be any contact from them all these years later.'

'We did make a commitment though: you remember, don't you?'

'Only to ourselves.'

Anna was silent. Finally, she said, 'John, I'm prepared to risk it. I can't bear the thought of anything changing our life, their lives.'

'OK, mum's the word,' John agreed.

***

The two birthday events came and went, both girls loving their special days.

Susan invited her four best friends and Katy to join her for afternoon tea, and then on to London to see a play at the recently opened National Theatre. John and Anna covered the costs but stayed at home, allowing the girls the excitement of visiting London on their own. It had been an amazing night out — both girls loved the experience.

Katy's trip had been to see a musical in the West End. She had asked Susan to go but her twin had said that she preferred to see a play. In fact, she'd known that Katy wanted to take her stage academy friends and the evening would be far too frenzied for her taste.

Katy came home after the show starry-eyed. She was full of who she'd seen and talked to at the stage door. The excitement of London nightlife and the thrill of a live show enthralled her. She clapped and cheered with everyone else but, really, she was envious: she wanted that acclaim.

The next day the four of them had their Sunday lunch together as usual, Katy reliving the excitement of the night before. John and Anna were quiet, noticeably so.

'Sorry, I'm going on too much,' Katy said.

'No, honestly, it's lovely to hear everything about it,' reassured Anna, 'it's just that Dad and I have something to say.'

She looked at John, who cleared his throat.

'OK, we want you both to, um, the thing is, well, here's the thing,' he stopped and looked at Anna.

'Oh no, this is going to be horrible news, isn't it?' said Katy.

'Not horrible,' said Anna, 'but it will come as a... a very great surprise; and we probably should have explained sooner, but...' She drew in a long breath and said in a steady voice, 'Sixteen years ago I gave birth to two little girls. One was Susan. Our other baby died during her birth. Dad and I were devastated. We had lost our baby and, Susan, you lost your twin sister. We couldn't bear it. We decided that we must do something, for all of us. I wasn't able to have another baby, so we adopted a little girl the same age as Susan. That girl, Katy, is you.'

The silence in the room crashed around them.

Katy spoke first, 'But that can't be true. How can it be right? We are twins. Susan and I are twins. We've always been twins. I know we are — we are, aren't we?'

She turned to Susan for reassurance, for the evidence she needed. She went on, 'Why are you saying such a terrible thing, what has got into you, Mum?'

Susan was white. She was shaking her head.

Anna looked steadily at her girls. She said, 'I know it's a shock. A sudden thing to hear out of the blue. It doesn't change anything — you are still our wonderful twin girls whom we love equally and absolutely.'

John said, 'It's true, Katy; Susan, it is true — everything that Mum has said is true, especially how much we love you both.'

Katy was shaking her head. Tears filled her eyes. 'But who am I? Where am I from? Who *are* my parents? What am I supposed to do now? I'm what?'

Anna started to explain but Katy put her hands up as if to defend herself against an attack. 'Stop, I don't want to hear it, I can't hear it. Stop it, Mum, stop this now.'

'We understand how upsetting this is,' John started.

Katy looked up; her expression shocked them. 'No, you have no idea: you have destroyed me, you have destroyed us.'

She violently pushed back her chair and got up. She looked down at her parents, who loved her so much but had suddenly become strangers. She raged at them, 'I can't believe you lied to us for so long. You lied all along. Why? Why did you lie?'

John said, trying to stay calm, 'Nothing's changed, Katy. We're still your parents, Susan is still your sister, you are loved by us all.'

'Everything's changed,' Katy screamed at them. 'Everything's fucking changed for ever.'

'Not for us,' Anna said.

'But what about me?' Katy whispered. 'What about how I feel?'

Susan spoke up. She sounded scared, 'And what about me? You have just taken away my twin sister.'

'You see, you see, do you see what you've done?' Katy screamed at them. 'Perhaps now that your real daughter is upset you might realise what you've done.'

'No, stop that right now!' John said, standing up. 'You are both our real daughters; nothing has changed for us: we love you both equally.'

'But everything has changed for me,' Katy said, crying. 'Everything.'

John sat down, unable to answer.

Katy picked up her glass and threw it at the wall above her parents' heads. It smashed, sending a shower of glassy splinters around them. There was silence and then she ran off, slamming the door after her.

Susan looked at them. 'I don't know what to do. I don't know anything anymore. Help me understand?'

Anna was crying now, 'It's my fault. I couldn't handle the death of your sister. I felt I'd lost everything, and most of all I felt as though I'd lost you your sister.'

'I can understand that, I think, Mum, but why did you let us grow up believing we were twins?' Susan asked.

'Looking back, we should have made it clear from the start,' said John. 'But day by day it just became truer and truer: that you were twins and that we had twins after all.'

'So why tell us now?' asked Susan. 'Why ruin everything?'

There was a long silence and then Anna said. 'Because Katy's mother has got in touch.'

They heard Katy's feet on the stairs and the front door open and slam shut.

***

Katy ran blindly out into the street. Her mother's voice was still ringing in her ears 'That girl, Katy, is you'.

She shook her head as she stumbled along the pavement, trying to erase the memory. She could not get rid of it. She couldn't even avoid it: it was hammering in her head like a pneumatic drill.

She careered past people, oblivious to traffic and unaware of where she was going. She kept running, desperate to get away from the moment, the place and that memory.

She instinctively turned down the footpath to the fields in which she and Susan had played so many times, building camps, dreaming of their futures. She was in urgent need of a sanctuary now, somewhere safe, reassuring, home.

She vaulted over the barbed wire fence and ran hard across the field to the scrub and bushes to their favourite childhood place: she pushed her way through the branches and brambles until she found the den. She sat with her knees pulled up under her chin, her arms tight around them. Her breathing began to slow and, as it did, she felt the racking sobs start to sweep over her. They were uncontrollable, heaving, gasping sobs of utter loss.

Slowly she came to. She heard her pleading voice saying, 'No, it's not true, it can't be true.'

She opened her bag and pulled out some tissues and blew her nose. She took out her packet of Bensons. She lit one and inhaled deeply.

Her parents' revelation seemed like a lifetime ago. She still couldn't get her head around what it meant. She understood the facts, but she could not comprehend what they meant for her, for her world, for the foundations of her life.

She thought of Susan. How was she feeling? She had had her twin taken away from her too, but at least Susan knew who her parents were. In fact, Susan had come out of this very nicely. She, Katy, was the loser. How was she going to manage on her own? Who could she turn to, now that she had lost her twin sister?

As she thought of her lying parents, her fury ignited all over again. They would be in the front room, all complacent and understanding. If they understood anything at all, they would have realised how devastating what they were going to say would be. They expected her to take this appalling realisation and simply get on with her life, as if nothing had happened. Why? She could not stop her mind shouting 'Why?'. Why had they even said anything? What had got into them? They had had a million opportunities to tell her and Susan the truth: every day had presented a chance to open up the subject and allow it to just come out. She remembered so many times she and Susan talked about being twin sisters, with her mum and dad part of the conversation.

She looked around the grassy walls of the den. It felt good to be in here, in her own world where nothing could get in and surprise or harm her, not like at home.

She lit another cigarette. This one was good too. She felt the nicotine rush through her. The dizziness that was threatening to make her feel sick felt comforting: she wanted to feel like shit.

Beyond the den, she could hear birds whistling and chirruping and leaves blowing in the breeze. She wondered at the ordinariness of it all. Couldn't the birds tell that the world had turned upside down? She put her cigarette out and lay down, her face in the flattened grass. The earthy smell of the foliage and soil was reassuring. Her eyes closed, she slept.

***

Waking with a start, Katy was totally disorientated. She could not think straight. Where was she? Everything was pitch black, nothing was familiar. Gradually her mind cleared, and it all came back to her, with a sickening rush.

She suddenly felt scared: not because she was alone in the dark, in a now damp little hollow in the bushes, but because she felt so alone. What was going to happen to her? She wanted to be in the world she had left behind only hours before. But that world had gone — she couldn't return to it now.

She shivered violently. She was cold, damp and bursting for a pee. She pushed her way out of the den and squatted down to relieve herself. As she did, she suddenly felt vulnerable. Although it was very dark, she felt conspicuous, as if everyone could see her and knew the truth — that she was a fraud.

She picked up her bag and started to move back through the undergrowth and out into the field. She walked quickly across it. She knew it very well and, although she couldn't see much of anything, her steps were assured, unlike her reeling mind.

Through her sluggish mind came the sound of voices. She opened her eyes and listened. Yes, some boys were approaching. As the footsteps neared, she forced herself to sit up and get ready to react to whoever it was. The boys came into the entrance to the shelter and sat down opposite her. There were three of them. They suddenly became aware of her in the deep shadow; they started.

'Jesus, you shocked me,' one of them said.

'Hello, darling, on your own?' another said.

'Fuck off, Phil, you prick,' she said thickly.

'Katy Walker, is that you?' Steve said.

'No, it's fucking Cilla Black,' she answered lifting the bottle to her lips. 'Want some of this?'

'Yeah, what is it?' Gary asked.

'It's my piss,' she answered.

Gary reached out and took the bottle and sniffed at it. He raised it to his mouth and took two long swallows.

'Don't go mad,' Katy said, reaching for it.

Gary passed it back, puffing out his cheeks as he felt it hit.

'I'll have some; what is it?' Phil said.

'It's too strong for a kid like you,' Katy slurred, taking another long swig.

'Fuck off,' he said, stepping across and taking the bottle.

He took a gulp and started coughing and spluttering.

Steve laughed and said, 'Here, give it to the grown-ups.' He snatched the bottle and glugged.

'The rest is mine,' Katy said, reaching for her cigarettes.

'What are you doing here?' Steve asked.

'What's it lucking fook like?' she answered. She was feeling very drunk now and was only dimly aware of where she was.

The boys laughed at her drunkenness. Steve moved over to sit next to her. He asked, 'Where are all your nice little friends?'

'Haven't got any.'

'Well, we're your friends now,' he said taking the bottle and drinking again.

'I'll have one of your ciggies,' said Phil, helping himself.

'Yeah, thanks, Katy,' said Steve taking one too.

Katy's eyes had been shut but she opened them now and looked vacantly at them.

'What are you doing here?' she asked, her mind dull.

'Looking after you,' Steve said.

Katy closed her eyes and fell against him.

'She's totally pissed,' said Phil. 'No one in her right mind gets that close to you, Steve.'

Gary picked up the bottle and drained it. He hurled the bottle across the road where they heard it smash.

Katy woke up. 'Is that my bottle?'

'Well, it was, and it's gone,' Gary said.

She got to her feet and staggered towards him; her fists clenched.

'Sit down,' he said pushing her back onto Steve's lap.

Steve caught her and let his hands cup her breasts. Massaging them he said, 'You've lovely tits, Katy.'

'How would you know, Steve? You've never felt a pair of tits in your life,' said Phil.

'They're lovely,' Steve said continuing his assault.

'Get off me,' Katy mumbled.

Steve carried on with his groping. Gary and Phil were watching, fascinated.

'Oh, you're so pretty,' Steve said.

Katy giggled now and started moving her bum on Steve's lap. 'What is that I'm sitting on, a cocktail stick?'

Gary and Phil laughed. Phil moved towards her and tried to kiss her. She rubbed her hand against his crotch and said, 'Get your prick out, little man.'

Phil lost his nerve, he stepped away. She jeered at him.

Katy felt so soiled now, she couldn't resist a compulsion to degrade herself completely. She staggered to her feet, pulling her tee-shirt up and over her head. She went up to Gary and said 'Want some? I don't care who fucks about with me now, even you, Gary Abbott.'

Gary didn't move. His eyes were riveted on her breasts. She pushed him in the chest. Off balance, he fell back onto the bench. She knelt down in front of him and clumsily fumbled with his flies. She finally undid them and reaching inside she pulled out his penis. She bent her head, took it in her mouth and started sucking.

'Jesus, Gary, you, lucky bastard,' shrieked Steve.

Katy's world was spinning out of control. Her stomach began to heave, and then she was gagging. She puked up all the venom inside her — vodka, cigarettes, the anguish of her loss, everything.

'Fucking hell!' screamed Gary as he felt the hot vomit hit him. 'Jesus! Fucking hell! Get off me, you bitch!'

Steve and Phil were screaming with laughter now.

Katy sat back on her heels, then rolled over onto her side, her face against the dirty floor of the shelter.

Gary was on his feet slapping vomit off his trousers, pants and genitals. He kicked Katy hard in the arse. She groaned but didn't move.

'I'm getting out of here,' he snarled.

As he moved away from the shelter, a car drew up. The passenger door opened, and Susan jumped out.

'Gary, have you seen Katy?' she cried at him.

He ignored her and strode off.

Susan looked into the shelter and gasped. She knelt down beside Katy, joined by John.

'Katy, what's happened to you?' Susan was crying.

Steve and Phil were sidling out.

'What has happened here?' John said to them.

'Nothing, she just can't handle her drink,' Steve said, and he and Phil bolted.

Susan was cradling Katy's head and whispering to her, 'Katy, oh Katy, everything's going to be all right; please, Katy, open your eyes, please.'

John bent down and putting his hands underneath his comatose daughter heaved her up and carried her to the car. Susan opened the back door and he hefted Katy inside. Susan went around the other side, got in and awkwardly covered her with a blanket. She put her arm around Katy and kissed her face, crying. 'Don't go, Katy: stay with me. Please stay with me.'

***

Katy stayed in hospital overnight. John, Anna and Susan came to collect her the next morning. When they saw her waiting just inside the main doors, they were shocked. She was a pale, frail and listless figure. She followed them slowly back to the car. Susan looked back and seeing her sister looking so fragile took her gently by the arm. She said, 'We're going to be fine, Katy. Don't worry. Everything's going to be all right.'

Katy looked down at the floor and said quietly, 'How can that be true? I'm lost.'

Susan gripped her arm tight and said, 'No, I've got you. I'll never let you go.'

Later, John said to her, 'Katy, I am going to talk, even though you don't want to hear it.'

She stared out of the window and ignored him.

'The reason why we had to tell you the truth is because we have been contacted by your birth mother. She has expressed a desire to meet you. We cannot deny you that if you want to. Do you want to?'

Katy was silent.

After five minutes wait, John said, 'Think about it, Katy. We want to do the right thing for you.'

She looked at him, then at her mother and said, her voice flat, 'But what is the right thing?'

Victoria

Victoria wanted to be a teacher from the moment she started school. She hero-worshipped her first teacher, Miss Nightingale. Victoria loved her because she knew so many things, was kind and gentle, but was also very strong and wise. Victoria often came home from school eulogising Miss Nightingale — that she knew how to do joined-up writing, could spell every word in the world, could run faster than everyone in the school and could make cuts and bruises better just by using magic.

Victoria was a good girl, but she did get into trouble. She didn't mean to — it was just that sometimes she found herself in situations that didn't quite turn out as she'd planned. She had been found locked in the boiler room of the old school, only because she thought there might be buried treasure down there. She'd got stuck up an oak tree in the garden next to the playground while attempting to retrieve her friend's satchel, thrown there by the boys. She had held up the traffic in the high street outside the school to help a frog cross the road. She was brave and kind, never afraid to do what she felt was the right thing.

Victoria loved her father. He was very tall, strong and handsome. When Major Court came home, he lifted her high into the air and told her that she was the greatest girl in the world. She yelled and laughed and asked for more and more. They ran races, played cricket and swung from a rope in the garden. What she loved the most though was sitting at the top of the tall tree in their garden and planning their future adventures.

But her father was only an occasional visitor. She got used to him coming and going. She knew he was important and that he had to be away a lot. Then, he went away all the time: 'fighting the Germans,' she explained to her friends.

Victoria loved her mother, but she was always too busy to play with her daughter. She didn't understand games like her father did. At the start of the war, her mother joined the ambulance service as a driver and was often out of the house at night. But Victoria was a resourceful little girl. She knew that she had to get on and be helpful. She did jobs around the house, peeling and chopping vegetables from the garden, sweeping the kitchen floor, helping Mrs Christmas next door, with whom she would stay when her mother was out driving ambulances.

Victoria was rather scared of Mrs Christmas. Although she was kind, she was also very strict. She had a no-nonsense manner which made Victoria do exactly what she said without question. If Mrs Christmas said to do something, then everyone seemed to jump to it. Even Victoria's father took orders from her. Before he went away, he whispered to Victoria, 'Make sure you always do what the sergeant major says.'

The only person who wasn't scared of Mrs Christmas was her husband. Although Dr John Christmas was easily the biggest man Victoria had ever met, he was also the kindest and most gentle. Victoria loved Dr Christmas, or as she called him, Uncle John. He listened to her, encouraged her, was impressed by her adventures, was utterly sympathetic no matter what she did or said.

What Uncle John was best at, was reading stories. She often went next door for the evening, first reading to Dr Christmas and then listening to him read: his deep, kind voice bringing to life all her favourite characters and their adventures. She loved cuddling up close to him, breathing in his warmth and smell, feeling completely safe and secure.

Victoria, her mother and neighbours became horribly familiar with the sound of air-raids — the harsh immediacy of fighters taking off from nearby Northolt, or the ominous drone of German bombers making their inexorable way up the Thames, towards them.

When the sirens went off, Victoria sought out John Christmas. She had no doubt that he was big and strong enough to hold up the whole house if a bomb ever came really close to them.

'Are you the strongest man in the world?' she asked once, looking up at him with wide eyes.

'Nowhere near the strongest. Are you the brightest star in the universe?' he asked.

'I'm just a girl, silly.'

'No, you are the brightest star I know by a million, million, million times the brightest.'

'Brighter than the moon?'

'Let's have a look.'

They went out into the garden and looked up into the night sky. Looking at the shining, silver disc she heard her friend's deep voice say, 'It's very bright, but it's tiny and dull compared to you, Victoria.'

'But it's a long way away; if we were closer it would be brighter than me wouldn't it?'

'Ah, but if you were closer to it, then it would think you were even brighter.'

Victoria wasn't sure, but he sounded so certain that she guessed that he was probably right.

'I'll prove it to you,' he said and bending down he picked her up and sat her on his shoulders.

'You see, you're much closer to it now but it hasn't got any brighter.'

'I'm going to stand up; then I'll be even closer.'

She carefully got to her feet, his hands under her arms, holding her steady.

'You won't let go, will you?'

'Don't you worry I'll keep you safe.'

They heard the sirens in the distance.

In the early days of the war they heard bombs only in the distance; then closer. Then they saw the horrendous explosions as bombs landed. They saw at close quarters the damage they were wreaking they were surrounded by people whose lives were destroyed and ended. One morning, after a near miss, Victoria looked out of her bedroom window

125

She walked back down the footpath and out onto the street. The lights suddenly seemed dazzling. As she neared the parade of shops, she saw the 'Open' sign on the door of the off-licence. She paused; she would love a drink now. She combed her fingers through her hair, brushed off her clothes and entered the shop.

'Hi, how are you doing?' she said to the woman behind the counter.

'Good evening, sweetheart, what can I get for you?' she said, looking at Katy and seeing a tall, confident girl in her late teens.

Katy had put her birthday money into her bag before she'd left the house; she was glad: she wanted a big drink.

'A bottle of Smirnoff please, and twenty Bensons.'

'Sure, that'll be £3.80 please.'

Katy handed over a fiver and put the bottle and cigarettes into her bag.

'Aren't you cold, love?' asked the woman.

Katy was only wearing jeans and a T-shirt — she was bloody freezing.

'Yeah, but I only live down the road,' she said and left.

As soon as she had gone three paces, she opened the bottle, lifted it to her lips and took a gulp. It burned its way down her throat, her chest and settled into her stomach. It made her feel immediately better and warmer. She kept walking. She had another swig. It felt good, even better. She was beginning to feel light-headed already: exactly what she wanted.

As she walked away from the town she kept on drinking. Slowly her mind became fuzzy; she was beginning to forget the reality of the day and, as she walked and drank, the pain was drifting away too.

After a while, she saw the old wooden bus shelter. She approached it cautiously: tramps sometimes used it for overnight stops. It was empty. She sat down in the corner, hidden from view. She lit a cigarette. Again, she inhaled deeply. This was better. She was feeling more like herself.

She lifted the bottle to her lips. It was half empty already. She took a mouthful, some of it dribbled down her chin. She laughed and said aloud, 'You're turning into a wino yourself, my girl.'

She closed her eyes. This wasn't a bad place to spend the night.

and cried out: 'Mother, come quickly! Mrs Shenton's bath is in the street and it's full of glass and clothes and everything!'

***

In the summer of 1941, Sylvia Court decided that it was time for Victoria to be evacuated out of London. She had resisted the temptation to send her away till then: she couldn't bear the thought of her daughter disappearing from her life as well as her husband. But when Mrs Shenton was killed, she realised that she had no choice but to send her little girl away.

Victoria explained to Dr Christmas that she had to go: 'Mummy says it's for the best because it isn't safe here anymore. You mustn't be sad though. I'll write to you and I'll think about you all the time.'

He smiled, 'You are a kind girl, Victoria. Mrs Christmas and I will miss you but you're doing the right thing to go somewhere safe. We are going away too. I am joining the army and might even be with your father somewhere. So, we'll all still be together and then one day we can all meet up again, probably very soon.'

'Promise?' she asked, looking into his face.

'I promise you — one day: I'm sure of it,' he said, trying not to let her see his tears. He turned away for a second, took something from his desk and gave it to her. She looked at the tiny wooden object.

'It's a dog,' she said beaming, 'a little dog.'

'Yes, I found him in my garden. I've got his friend, see?'

He held out his hand: another wooden dog, just like hers.

'What are you going to call yours?' he asked.

She looked at the carved figure carefully, then up at her huge friend, standing in front of her wiping tears from his eyes.

'Can I call him after you? 'Christmas' is a good name for a dog, don't you think? What will you call your one?'

'Victoria, of course.'

'But, he's a boy.'

'Oh, well, how about Victor?'

Victoria laughed, 'Perfect.'

***

Sylvia Court put her seven-year-old daughter on a train at Waterloo, with her case of clean clothes, her copy of *Swallows and Amazons*, her four *William* stories, and her little wooden dog. She arrived in Dorchester where she was picked up by the Reverend Roger Wright, a middle-aged vicar, and his wife and daughter.

'Welcome, welcome, you are very welcome,' he said ushering her to his battered, old car.

He and his wife were kind and loved to have fun. They played all sorts of games with Victoria, outside and in, and were always laughing. But it was their daughter that Victoria loved the best. Eleanor was thirteen and nearly grown up. She was Victoria's new heroine. Eleanor taught Victoria how to play tennis, to swim (in the river at the end of the vicarage garden), to whistle, light a bonfire, and paint and, it seemed to Victoria, a thousand other things. Although Victoria went to the village school, she had extra lessons with Eleanor. Eleanor had set up one of the many empty vicarage rooms as a classroom and she even had a blackboard on the wall so that she could write sums, spellings and riddles.

Victoria and Eleanor were inseparable. They went for long walks together, talking about their hopes and dreams. Eleanor wanted to be a famous writer. She tested her stories out on Victoria who became lost in the imaginary world Eleanor conjured up for her. Victoria told Eleanor that she wanted to be a teacher, just like her.

Victoria said to her friend one day, 'I think I'd like to stay living here with you, Eleanor; it's much nicer than London and after Uncle John you are my best ever friend. Can I stay, do you think?'

Eleanor sighed, 'Oh, Victoria, if only you could! You will be going home to live with your parents soon, when the war is over.'

But the war didn't end, and Victoria's dream seemed to be coming true.

Victoria was a bright girl. When she was nine, Mrs Wright asked her if she would help her with the little children at Sunday school. Victoria had agreed with alacrity. She loved being a teacher and modelled herself on both Miss Nightingale and Eleanor — a mixture of stern and loving but, most of all, fun.

In the early days she kept in touch with her parents and the Christmases. She began to write less and less as she became ever more settled in Dorset. She used to get lovely long letters from Uncle John, but they stopped coming; she didn't know why. When her mother came to visit, she asked, 'Do you think Uncle John has found another girl to be friends with, Mummy?'

Mrs Court had gone quiet then said, 'No, I think he is very busy with the war; but, Victoria, I've got some wonderful news.'

Victoria went cold.

'I've heard from your father: he's coming home soon.'

Victoria felt terrible. She wanted to see her father, of course, but she didn't want to leave; she couldn't imagine life back in boring old London, and definitely not without Eleanor.

Her mother went on, 'It's not safe for you to come home yet, Victoria. Would you mind staying here a little longer? The Wrights say they are happy for you to live with them, if you don't mind?'

Doing everything in her power to control her sheer joy, Victoria said, 'I shall do my best to manage, Mummy.'

In the Spring of 1944, Eleanor told Victoria about her liking a boy at the tennis club. She pointed to him when they were there one day.

'That's him. What do you think?'

Victoria saw a tall, fair boy hitting the ball very hard.

'He's quite nice. What's his name?' she asked.

'Nigel. Don't you think he's handsome?'

Victoria could see that he was, but not wanting to share Eleanor with him she said, 'He's all right, but I don't think he's the right type for you.'

'Why not?'

'Well, I bet he can't whistle, or put up a tent, or go fishing, or any of the things you can do,' Victoria explained, thinking of all the most amazing abilities Eleanor had.

'Silly! Of course, he can do those things; anyway, I'm more interested to know if he's a good kisser.'

Victoria was shocked. 'You don't want to kiss him, do you?'

'If I get the chance.'

Victoria hadn't realised that her friend thought about boys like that. This was all news to her.

Some of Eleanor's friends arrived as they sat waiting for a court. They were all chatting about boys and who they liked and who was horrible. Victoria suddenly felt left out and lonely. Eleanor noticed and said, 'Don't worry, Vic, you'll get bitten by the bug soon, I know you will. In the meantime, you're still my favourite person.'

She meant it. She loved her little sister Victoria: she was so plucky, full of fun and energy. But Eleanor did spend more and more time at the tennis club, especially with Nigel. Victoria had to admit that he was nice, always friendly and, after a while she began to accept that maybe she could share Eleanor with him. She was invited around to join Eleanor for tea at Nigel's house one afternoon; she had gone and had had a wonderful time. Nigel's mother was friendly too. She asked Victoria what she wanted to be when she grew up. Victoria said straight away, 'I'm going to be a teacher and when I'm really old I shall be a headmistress.'

Nigel had an older brother, James. He told Victoria that he was joining the army soon and was making the most of his freedom. 'I want to do as many things as possible before it's too late,' he explained.

He said to Eleanor, 'I hear you are good at tennis, Eleanor.'

'Not really, just average,' she said.

'May I give you a game one day?'

'Sure, any time.'

Nigel laughed and said, 'You've no chance, James: she often beats me.'

'Hmm, we'll see about that,' James said.

'Did you enjoy the tea?' Eleanor asked Victoria on their way home.

'Very much. Nigel's family is nice, especially James. Do you think he is too old to be my boyfriend?'

'Oh, dear Victoria, he's about eighteen: you're only ten. Don't worry, though: I'm sure someone will come along for you soon.'

Later that week, James and Eleanor went off to play. Victoria wanted to go along to watch, and be ball-girl and umpire, and ensure that James won all the disputed calls. But she had been asked to help Mrs Wright and her friends with the preparations for the village Whitsun fete. As soon as she could get away, she dashed off down to the tennis courts to cheer on James.

When she arrived, no one was there. She walked to the far end and recognised Eleanor's bag under the bench. Guessing that they were looking for a lost ball, she crawled through one of the gaps in the fence. There was no sign of them. Mystified, she pushed her way into the shade of the trees and bushes. She paused: yes, that was Eleanor's voice. She moved quietly closer and could now definitely hear her; she was crying and saying, 'Stop! Stop! — No!'

Then she heard James say, 'You want it, Eleanor, you know you do.' Victoria heard Eleanor cry in pain and then a muffled scream.

Wriggling past a holly bush, she saw them Her blood went cold. Eleanor was on her back; she was crying. Her dress was pushed up, her blouse ripped. Between her bare legs was James. His trousers and pants were down around his ankles; he was shoving something in and out of Eleanor. Victoria realised what it was. She had seen little boys' willies, this was horrible, more like a spike.

James was pinning Eleanor's arms above her head with one hand, his other hand was clamped over her mouth. Eleanor was trying to fight him off, but he was just too strong for her.

Victoria was transfixed by what she saw. She knew vaguely what was going on, but she couldn't believe it. What she was sure about was that Eleanor did not want it to happen and she had to save her. Without thinking she ran up to the writhing couple and shouted, 'James! Stop it! Stop it now!'

Whether it was her total conviction that he would stop or just that she shocked sanity back into him was impossible to say. He looked up at the small figure standing over him and froze.

'Get up, James,' she ordered again.

James looked down at Eleanor and released her arms. He scrambled off her pulling up his pants and trousers. He looked at Victoria again and then ran away.

Crying hysterically, Eleanor feverishly covered herself. Victoria was crying too.

'Did he hurt you?' she hesitantly asked her friend.

Eleanor put her head in her hands and shivered violently. After a minute she got up, Victoria took her hand and they pushed their way through the bushes back to the court. Eleanor picked up her bag and pulled out a cardigan and put it on.

'Thank you, Victoria. I don't know what to say. What James was doing was horrible. I didn't want it. I promise you; I didn't want it. You believe me, don't you?'

'Yes, of course.'

'And another thing: you must never tell anyone about what happened. It was dirty and horrid, and it must be our secret,' Eleanor said, looking hard into Victoria's eyes.

Victoria nodded. She understood.

***

Ten days later, the Normandy landings heralded the end of the war. It was also the end of Victoria's Dorset life.

Her mother came to take Victoria home. When it was time to go, she and Eleanor hugged each other with all their strength. They were too upset to say anything and as her train gathered speed, Victoria couldn't bring herself to lean out of the window and wave.

More upset was in store.

On their train journey home, her mother said, 'Victoria, your father isn't how you remember him. He was a great hero and did some wonderful things, but he has been injured. When you meet him again you mustn't expect him to be the same.'

Victoria said she understood. Her main concern though was whether Uncle John would remember her. She asked, 'Is Dr Christmas all right?'

'I don't know. They moved away when he joined the army; I don't know what has happened to them.'

Victoria felt a great wave of sadness sweep over her. She had promised Eleanor that she wouldn't tell anyone about James but had thought that it would be safe to tell him her Uncle John. He would have definitely made everything all right again; he always did. She dug the little wooden dog out of her pocket. Even now, after all this time, it still had the power to comfort her.

'What's that?' her mother asked.

'Just a memory,' Victoria sadly closed her hand around it.

After a long and tiring journey, they finally arrived back home. When they entered the house, Victoria noticed the change straightaway: it was dirty, dark, but most of all it smelled funny.

'Come and say hello to Father, Victoria.'

Victoria went into the living room and saw an old man sitting with a blanket over his lap. Swallowing, she made herself sound cheerful and said, 'Hello, Daddy.'

She heard a stranger's frail voice, 'My dear girl, thank you for coming home to me.'

He held out his arms. She felt his body convulsing as he cried into her hair. She couldn't help herself crying too. She had lost Eleanor, then Dr Christmas, and now her father. Then with horror she realised something else: he had no legs. Feeling sick, she moved away from him and said, 'Would you like a cup of tea, Daddy?' and so her life was set.

***

Victoria's life narrowed to home and school. She did more and more around the house as her mother became increasingly busy with her job at the Town Hall and her evening work at the cinema box office. She took her father for walks in the park, pushing his rickety wheelchair with all her might, and helping him manage everyday life.

She came home from school, telling her father all about what she had learned, who she had played with, what had gone well and what was worrying her. He listened, was sympathetic, encouraging and very proud.

Despite everything that he had lost, he had retained his love for his little girl.

***

Victoria took her responsibilities at home seriously but nonetheless grew up to be a vivacious and attractive girl, always laughing and ready for fun.

As Eleanor had predicted, Victoria was attracting the interest of boys. She was invited out for walks, to the pictures, to dances. She was happy to accept invitations. She enjoyed the company of boys. But not physical contact. If she was ever with a boy who showed any inclination to hold her hand, or even to ask her for a kiss, she would simply move away or say, 'I'm sorry, I just want us to be friends.'

Although Victoria told her father most of what was going on in her life, it was only Eleanor with whom she truly confided. They had stayed close and corresponded regularly. Eleanor had broken off all ties with Nigel. When Victoria wrote to her, she said, 'I am struggling, Elly. I like boys, but I don't want them to touch me. What shall I do?'

Eleanor had written back, 'Don't worry. I'm sure everything will be all right: you'll find someone right for you. I have.' It was true: Eleanor had found Michael, a charming and kind man. They were going to get married.

But things did not get better for Victoria. No matter what she tried to think about, when she was close to a boy, she felt sick, panicky and scared.

Nevertheless, Victoria didn't let it get in the way of her studies. She was determined to do her best and be a success. She worked hard and gained a distinction in her School Certificate at sixteen. She stayed on into the 6th form and in 1952 gained three A levels.

To celebrate their exam successes, Victoria and several friends organised a dance at the nearby social club. Her father had said, 'I want you to be the Belle of the Ball, dear. Go and buy yourself a special dress,' and he had pressed some money into her hand.

Victoria spent hours getting ready for the party. Finally, she came downstairs to show her father. He looked towards the door as his daughter entered the room. He felt his heart tighten and his eyes became moist. She was lovely: tall and shapely, with long auburn hair. Her green eyes sparkled with excitement at the thought of the night to come. What was most striking though was her strong, intelligent face. She looked impressive: someone to be reckoned with, someone special.

Although she had gone with her usual trepidation, the evening had been perfect. She had danced, laughed, drunk wine and felt as happy as she ever had. The band had played slower numbers and she was being asked to dance by many of the young men in the hall. She happily accepted and enjoyed their attention.

'Will I see you again?' asked Richard, as they danced together.

'Of course. I'm going to University College, London; I shall carry on living here,' she said.

'Good, I'm glad. The thing is, I really like you, Victoria: can I be your special friend?'

She hugged him and said, 'You are special, Richard.'

He looked into her eyes and said, 'No, I mean really special.'

She felt his hand on her waist slip down to her bottom; for a moment she enjoyed it, but then felt the old sensation welling up in her. She said, 'Oh, Richard, can we just be friends for now?'

'Of course,' he said, but she could tell that he was disappointed. She was too: she liked him a lot and wanted him to kiss her; she just couldn't face the prospect of it.

When the evening came to an end, she kissed Richard on the cheek, and they agreed to meet again soon.

'How did it go?' her father asked the next morning.

'It was wonderful, Daddy, it really was.'

'I bet you had dozens of admirers'

'Well, a few,' she admitted.

'Anyone special?'

'Not really; I prefer to keep my options open.'

'Well, that's wise,' he said.

Alfred Court was secretly pleased. He wanted Victoria to have a happy life away from home but when she wasn't in the house his life was bleak and grey. He had been imprisoned during the war and without Victoria he was a prisoner still. He knew that his wife was having an affair; it might have been going on from before he came home. He understood she was an attractive, middle-aged woman, he a broken old man. He also knew, though, that his wife's lack of warmth and care for him made his dependence on Victoria that much greater.

Soon after Victoria's party, he asked Sylvia to sit down. He cleared his throat and said with as much strength as he could muster, 'It is time for you to go, Sylvia. I cannot bear to hold you back any longer. You have your own life and I want you to enjoy it.'

He looked for her reaction. He saw it: it was relief. She closed her eyes and said, 'I cannot leave, Alfred. I must stay with you, for Victoria's sake. We can't hold her life back, you know that.'

He nodded and said, 'When it is time for her to go, I shall make her go too. Now, it's your turn.'

She went. He knew that it was what she wanted. In letting her fly, he felt strong: he'd been able to give her the gift of a second chance.

When she came home that day and heard the news, Victoria was not sad. She realised what it meant — her tie to her father had just become ten times stronger. But Victoria was tough: she was never going to let her father down.

***

University went in a blur. She continued to split her time between care for her father and her studies. She bore her father no resentment. She often recalled the energetic, adventurous man of her early life and although, physically, he had left her a long time ago, his mind was still clear and very much alive. They would often read books, plays and poems together, analysing them as they went, working as a team on her essays. When she was at lectures or attending to university life in general, neighbours would come around and prepare meals for him and accompany him on walks around Ealing common. He welcomed the company and he was grateful for the help, but he lived only to see his daughter. For her part, Victoria was happy to come home each day. She had made many friends but felt no strong urge to be with them rather than at home with her father.

She occasionally heard from her mother, who had moved to north London with her gentleman friend. One Saturday, she took two trains to go and visit her. She was happy to see her mother looking so well and, as they parted, Victoria knew she was saying goodbye forever. She wasn't sad: they had drifted apart, probably when she went to Dorset, if not before.

In 1955, Victoria gained a First in English Literature. A year later, with the teaching certificate under her belt, she began applying for posts. With her academic record and evident enthusiasm for education, she soon found a school that was keen to take her on. She taught English at a tough secondary school, where the pupils really only wanted to get out and earn some money. In the early days, she was disillusioned but gradually found ways of talking to her students which earned their respect and interest. She brooked no nonsense from them: right from the outset she had a reputation for being strict, but funny too.

One day the head of English said to her, 'You're a natural, Victoria; you're really doing very well.'

She liked him, Paul Cousins. He had been at the school for eight years after serving in the Navy during the war. He was in his mid-thirties. He was calm, quiet and thoughtful. Victoria told Polly Braithwaite, the art teacher, that she thought Paul was nice. Polly said, 'Watch out Victoria; he is nice, but I think he's desperate for a new wife.'

'Why, what's happened to his old one?'

'Direct hit, I think.'

'Oh, the poor man,' Victoria felt herself drawn to him even more.

When he asked her if she'd like to go out for a drink, she said yes. Paul was more mature than men her own age. She warmed to him; she felt instinctively safe with him.

They had a lovely evening. They went out again, this time to the pictures. They had a meal the week after. Slowly, she and Paul began to get close.

During one trip to the pictures, Paul had taken her hand. It gave her that familiar feeling of panic, but she fought against it and squeezed his in return. Outside her front door, he kissed her cheek and thanked her for a lovely evening. She had enjoyed it too. She had to admit that she was hoping that, at long last, the past might be behind her.

On their next trip, they drove out to Richmond and walked along the Thames tow path. Standing in the evening sun, close together, Paul said, 'You're beautiful, Victoria.'

She smiled back at him. 'Thank you, kind sir, you're not so shabby yourself.'

When he parked the car outside her house, neither of them moved. She was breathless. Would he kiss her? She wanted him to, but she was scared. He leaned towards her and, putting his hand under her chin, tilted her head and kissed her. The touch of his lips on hers made her heart thump: surely, he must hear it? She felt his hands stroking her hair. She sat still, telling herself to stay calm and enjoy the moment.

He drew away and said, 'Can we do this again soon?'

Still feeling jittery, she smiled and nodded. She was grateful to him for his gentleness; she really liked him.

Later that evening, she lay in bed and tried to work through her feelings. She knew that she wanted physical contact with a man. When she touched herself sexually, she felt a flare of arousal, but the same old sickening feelings returned, a recurring nightmare.

She liked and respected Paul and was sure that he was kind and sensitive. She imagined what it might be like to lie in bed with him next to her. She made up her mind.

During lunch the next day he thanked her again for a wonderful evening and said, 'Would you like to go cycling one day?'

'Yes, I'd love it.'

So, that Saturday morning they set off on their bikes. She hadn't cycled since Dorset and was a bit wobbly to start with but soon regained her confidence.

'Whose bicycle is this?' she asked when they stopped for a rest.

He was quiet for a minute then said, 'It's Margaret's, my wife's; it's great that you are getting some use from it.'

'Will you tell me about her?'

Paul was silent again, then he said, 'She was very lively, much more outgoing than me. You remind me of her in many ways.'

Victoria wasn't sure how to take this. She didn't want to be like his dead wife, but on the other hand she liked him a lot and any similarity to her must be a compliment.

'Well, I feel very honoured,' she said.

They cycled along the Thames to Hampton Court where they enjoyed exploring the building and grounds. They walked hand in hand beside the river: it felt good.

After an evening meal in a pub, they arrived back at his house. He invited her in. She took her courage in her hands and went inside.

They sat on his sofa and talked for a while. He put on an Ella Fitzgerald record; they just listened, close together.

At last he said, 'May I kiss you?'

Too nervous to speak she nodded.

He kissed her. As before his gentleness made her feel brave. She kissed him back, the rush of arousal fizzing through her. She felt his hands stroke her hair, her neck, her shoulders. This time she wanted more.

He pulled away and looked into her eyes.

'You're very beautiful,' he said.

She smiled and snuggled into him.

He stroked her back; she pressed herself hard against his chest. They kissed again. He moved away and ran his fingers down her throat to the buttons of her blouse. 'May I?' he asked her, his fingers pausing.

'Yes please,' she croaked.

She thought she could hear her heart pounding as he slowly and tenderly undid her buttons. As her dress fell open, she moaned softly as his hands grazed her breasts. She closed her eyes and tried to relax.

'Would you like to take off your bra?' he whispered.

She reached behind and undid it. Self-consciously, she took it off and sat still, looking down, feeling vulnerable but — thank God, she thought — very aroused.

She looked at him, waiting for his next move, only to see that his head was in his hands. Suddenly he cried out, 'Oh, no! Margaret…Margaret!' and turned away from Victoria.

Instinctively she wanted to console him, but then felt horribly exposed and ridiculous. She put her bra back on, and quickly did herself up.

Paul was sobbing.

She sat still, not knowing what to do. She was beginning to feel resentful. She wanted to escape this was awful.

He suddenly seemed to remember that she was there. 'I'm sorry, Victoria, please forgive me.'

She nodded and said, 'I understand, Paul. In any case I think it is time for me to go now. Thank you for a lovely day.'

She rose and went to the door.

'Victoria don't go. Please stay. I'm sorry, Victoria, I'm sorry.'

'It's all right, Paul; it's time for me to go, really.'

***

After that evening Victoria and Paul did not continue their relationship. She had taken a step that had left her feeling vulnerable and degraded. She could no longer think of Paul in a sexual way: to do so made her shudder.

Over the next five years, her life continued on its familiar course — on the one hand caring for and sharing with her father and on the other deriving great satisfaction from putting her considerable energy and creativity into her pupils. Paul had left to go to another school and at the age of twenty-six she was now head of English.

'You are my wonderful girl,' her father had said when she came in and told him of her promotion.

She confided most things to him — everything, in fact, except how she felt about men and relationships. This subject she shared only with Eleanor. She had told her of her brief and upsetting experience with Paul and that she had begun to accept that a relationship just wasn't going to be part of her life. Eleanor had shushed her and said, 'Victoria, you are a lovely girl; you are bright and energetic, a real sport: you'll find someone — I know you will.'

'Do you ever think about what happened?' Victoria asked.

'I do. I can't help it; it just rushes back into my mind at odd times. I just try and block it out. I screw up my eyes and think of something else — anything will do,' Eleanor admitted.

'I get it, too, and it didn't even happen to me,' Victoria said. 'The picture haunts me at least once a day.'

'I told Michael what happened before we even got married,' Eleanor said. 'That was incredibly helpful. He was so sweet and kind. He just made me feel clean and whole again — well, mostly, anyway.'

Victoria was happy for her beloved friend. Part of her own dread-filled thoughts had been about what effect the event had had on Eleanor. That she had been able to begin to deal with it was a great relief to her.

'I've not really got close enough to anyone to get intimate, apart from with Paul,' she said.

'You will, Victoria, I'm sure of it.'

But Victoria was not sure. She was now in her late twenties. Her father, although frail, was not ill and would live for many years yet. Indeed, she hoped he would. She knew that, even if she were able to find a man with whom she could get close, her father's need for her would certainly make a relationship complicated, and maybe impossible.

She often grew angry with herself for even agitating over such matters. She had a very good career, a loving, albeit burdensome, relationship with her father and she generally felt that her life was not at all bad. Friends sometimes spoke to her of being 'broody', but Victoria didn't recognise that feeling — 'Just as well,' she sometimes thought grimly — though she enjoyed being with children and was very close to her goddaughter: Eleanor and Michael's little girl, Barbara.

When she reached thirty, she applied to be head of English at Ealing Grammar School for Girls. She knew it was a long-shot — her age and gender were definitely against her — but she got it. This was a significant step up for her. At last she had pupils who genuinely wanted to do well, and in Miss Court, they found a teacher who could inspire them to achieve great things.

She decided she must learn to drive. She took lessons and passed her test first time. Her father helped her buy a car: a Morris Traveller, roomy enough to put the wheelchair in the back. She was thrilled with it. She felt liberated and that she had given her father freedom too. Every weekend they drove to the coast, or into the country. They felt like pioneers. On one occasion, they were on the promenade at Worthing looking out to sea. Alfred Court said, 'I promised your mother that I would let you go, Victoria — the time has come.'

Victoria didn't reply for a minute. She was trying to work out her reaction to his statement. Her overriding feeling was to reject the notion out of hand. She had nowhere that she wanted to go or anyone with whom she wanted to be. However, she also knew that her life was passing her by there was more to the world than her career and her life at home with her father. In the end she said, 'But Mother had someone. I don't.'

'Yes, but if you stay looking after me, you'll never find anyone,' he answered.

'But, Daddy, it's not like that. We look after each other,' she protested. It was true: even now she needed to have him nearby for encouragement, security, his love.

But they agreed that she would consider it, and her future. She did think about what would happen in the long term, often. However, she could never find the right time or reason for change, and so her life continued to pass by. It wasn't that she was totally content: in fact, she often felt dissatisfied and unfulfilled. The prospect of being alone for the rest of her life was a dread which came to haunt her with growing frequency. She chastised herself for her weakness. Her mind told her that she had to break free, but she knew, in her heart, she was trapped. Her frustration was at its worst at night. She would often toss restlessly, trying to rid herself of the suffocation of regret, resentment and impotence. She found herself seeking sexual relief from the negative emotions building up in her. She masturbated urgently, desperate to find a calmer place. When she climaxed, it was never enjoyable; she always felt dirty and depressed and although her body would relax afterwards, her churning mind could not.

In the mornings, life seemed better again. She found herself putting her own hopes and dreams into the heads of her pupils. She particularly enjoyed the time she had with her sixth formers. They looked to her for guidance and inspiration; she did not disappoint them. At the wheel of the school minibus, she took her charges on trips to West-End theatres, to international football matches at Wembley and — her greatest challenge — on a long weekend to Paris.

She made many casual friends through her work and her interaction with neighbours. But she remained very definitely a single woman caring for an elderly parent.

The deputy headship became vacant. Victoria could see that the school needed modernising: the attitudes and behaviours of teachers, the curriculum and the facilities. She wanted to lead the changes. She applied and at the age of 36 she was given the authority to shake the place up.

As the late '60s moved into the '70s, her father became increasingly frail. He preferred to stay in one room and listen to the radio, or just sleep. For her fortieth birthday, they had planned to eat at their favourite Italian in Hammersmith, but when she had come home from school that day, she saw that he was not going to be able to go out.

'I'm sorry, do you mind if we just eat in tonight?' he said, looking distressed.

She smiled; she didn't mind. She had a sense that this was going to be her last birthday with her father, and so it proved. Only a few weeks later, she came home and found him dead in his chair. She knelt down in front of him, took his cold hand in hers and held it against her heart. She felt scalding tears running down her face. Leaning into his bony frame, she wrapped her arms around him and squeezed him tight to her. She heard herself saying, 'Thank you, Daddy, thank you for everything.'

***

When she met her mother at the funeral, Victoria was shocked. She too had aged — of course she had — but the once vivacious and energetic woman was now a frail old lady. Mrs Court saw her daughter for the first time in twenty years and marvelled at how her little girl had turned into such a beautiful woman. They had been unsure how to greet each other. In the end, Victoria had taken her mother's hands in hers and held them.

'Hello, Mummy, it's lovely to see you.'

They had sat together during the funeral service and then stood hand in hand as the coffin was lowered into the ground.

'How are you getting home?' Victoria asked once the few friends and neighbours had gone.

'On the bus.'

'I'll drive you home; you can show me your house.'

Victoria was in for another shock. Her mother's home was not a house: it was a tiny one bedroom flat in total chaos.

Victoria asked, 'Where is Stephen?' She could see no evidence of her mother's partner.

'Oh, we went our separate ways years ago.'

'Why didn't you tell me?' Victoria asked in exasperation.

'Well, I suppose I thought you wouldn't want to know.'

'Oh, Mummy, of course I'd have wanted to know.'

Victoria felt a wave of guilt. She had deleted her mother from her world: she had no right to be annoyed at being excluded from her life. She soon realised that her mother was not just physically frail. Her conversation had been as messy and muddled as her home and, worse than that, she had repeated the same news several times. Victoria hadn't had much experience of senile dementia, but she had a good sense that her mother was very much on the road to having it.

She spent the next two hours straightening and clearing up around the flat. It was a futile exercise, she knew, but she had to do something. She filled the bin with detritus and washed up pots, pans and crockery and knew in her heart of hearts that her life of caring wasn't yet over. The realisation of it filled her not with despair, or resentment, but with relief. After her father had died, she had started to feel anxious. She knew that she would have to take responsibility for her own life at last, something that she felt ill-equipped to do.

'Well, Mother, we're going to have to sort a few things out,' she announced.

***

It soon became apparent that her mother was not able to cope with life in a safe or healthy way. There was no question of her continuing to live alone: it was simply a question of with whom she should live and where.

Victoria weighed up her options. She had been at her present school for ten years and felt ready for a new challenge. She wanted to get away from west London and the house she had lived in all her life. She also felt that, for the sake of her father's memory, she should not bring her mother to live in the house that was so redolent of him.

She looked for senior teaching posts in her mother's home area. After just two weeks of trawling the Times Educational Supplement, a vacancy for a head teacher came up in a school a ten-mile drive from her mother's home. Victoria knew of only one headmistress in north London — and that only because of a recent feature in the TES — but this did not deter her.

As she walked up the drive to the front doors of the school, she took in its square, concrete form. This was a big school. It had evidently seen better days. The main block was looking faded but there were modern offshoots that suggested the school hadn't been forgotten altogether.

She made a good impression during her interview. Her energetic and determined manner and her belief that she could and would make the school fulfil its potential convinced the panel. When she was offered the job, she took it.

The school had a tough reputation. The town, on the outskirts of London, had been an overflow for bombed-out Londoners, and a sense of community had taken some time to emerge. Also, the established grammar school siphoned off higher-achieving pupils. She was under no illusion that this headship was going to be an easy one. But Victoria was thrilled to get the job.

She rang her mother immediately on hearing the news. 'Start looking for a house, Mummy. We're on the move.'

The next few months were a tremendous strain for Victoria — selling her home, moving into a new one, moving her mother into it, and starting the biggest job of her life.

On her first day at school, she asked for all pupils and teachers to be present for an assembly. She stood on the stage and looked at the hall as it filled up. Her heart thumped as more and more people took their places; the seating area in the gallery over the rear of the hall was now also full. She thought of her first day at primary school and remembered the awe she felt, how much she had looked up to Miss Nightingale. She imagined her father's pride: his daughter, headmistress of a school this size. She thought of John Christmas; would he be proud of her too? She smiled as she remembered standing on his shoulders, looking at the moon.

As the hubbub quietened, she stepped towards the edge of the stage and said, 'Good morning, everyone, my name is Victoria Court. I am absolutely delighted to be with you today. Some of you will want to do well at school, some don't care, some actively want to be somewhere else. What I promise you all is that I shall do my very best to make your experience of this school as good as possible. I shall try my hardest for you; all I ask is that you try too.

'I am sure that sometimes we shall laugh together; we shall learn together; we shall have successes and disappointments. We shall have disagreements — of course now and then we shall differ — but we will have many, many, times when things go very well: I'm looking forward to it all.

'I shall do everything I can to make this a healthy place and between us we are going to make it a place in which we all share a real sense of pride.

'I want to know how you feel about the school. I want to know when things are going well and how we can improve them. If you have ideas or solutions let me know. If you have a complaint tell me how you think it can be put right — I really like creative people.

'I'm determined that this school will be a vibrant place: a place to look back on in years to come and talk about with pride. Believe me, I am a very determined person.'

She paused, the hall was still and silent.

'I look forward to working with you all.'

She stood still for a few more seconds, her gaze steady.

***

Victoria came home to the rented house she and her mother shared. She felt exhausted but elated. The day had gone well. She had met the majority of her teaching team, had had some contact with pupils and had walked around and explored. She had a positive feeling about the school and her place within it. Life at home, though, was not so clear cut.

Settling down with her mother was not easy; every day was a challenge. Sylvia Court's mental state meant that she forgot or muddled up much of what Victoria told her. Victoria had an ongoing fear of fire, flood and burglary. So far, nothing seriously untoward had taken place but she was sure that it was just a matter of time. She arranged for a lunch to be delivered each day, then for a carer to come mid-morning and afternoon to check that everything was safe.

As her mother's health declined, Victoria's impact at school increased. She had established a strong teaching team and had developed a reputation for being tough, fair and a good laugh. She played on the teachers' netball team against pupils, took part in the performance of *A Christmas Carol*. She was familiar to all her pupils, and she had got to know many of them in person.

Two years after their move, Victoria decided she must look into the local care homes for her mother. She had hoped they could have managed much longer than this, but Sylvia Court's short-term memory had diminished to almost nothing. She had started getting lost if she left the house, having to be helped home by neighbours, strangers and, on one occasion, the police. After comparing and contrasting the various options Victoria explained to her mother that she would soon be moving.

***

Victoria went through to the lounge of The Beeches and looked around. There she was: her mother was half asleep in front of the large television from which came the sounds of a cowboy film.

'Hello, Mummy, how are you?'

146

Mrs Court opened her eyes and, seeing that it was her daughter, closed them again.

She had been there for several weeks now but was still to come out of her shell. She had not forgiven Victoria for forcing her into this prison. In fact, The Beeches was warm, comfortable, and the staff seemed to be treating the residents with respect and dignity. Victoria had been very careful about her mother's new home and she was confident that she had made a good choice. However, she also felt a horrible sense of guilt — she had effectively incarcerated her mother for the rest of her life.

Sylvia said, 'I don't know why you come here: I know you hate me.'

'Of course, I don't hate you! I come to spend time with you.'

'The only nice one around here is Jo.'

'Who's Jo?'

'The only person who bothers to talk to me like I'm a human being,' she answered.

'Well, I look forward to meeting this wonderful person.'

'Jo's my friend, not yours.'

'I know. She's your friend, absolutely nothing to do with me.'

Her mother smiled to herself, enjoying her own special relationship.

'Jo isn't just your friend,' said a tiny lady two chairs along.

'Well, who's asking you?' Sylvia shot back.

'Come on, ladies — I'm sure Jo is friends with both of you.'

The two old ladies shook their heads emphatically.

'Shall I do your hair for you, Mummy?'

'No, I want Jo to do it.'

'OK, how about a crossword — or does Jo do those too?'

Her mother was silent.

'I'll be back tomorrow, earlier than usual. Is that OK?'

'Don't bother. I expect Jo will be here, so I shall be busy.'

As Victoria left, she asked at reception, 'Is Jo going to be here tomorrow?'

'I hope so. It will cheer everyone up.'

The next day Victoria arrived at three p.m. She walked to the lounge and saw that there was a meeting in progress. She sat on a chair out of the way and watched. A man was sitting with his back to her listening to an elderly man talking about his work in the nearby film studios.

When he finished his story the stranger said, 'Fascinating, Don. You must have met lots of film stars?'

Don nodded and burst into a long list of actors.

'How about you, Muriel? Ever met anyone famous?' the stranger asked.

Shyly Muriel said that she'd once met Jane Austen.

'Really, how exciting, what was she like?'

'A quiet little thing, rather timid as I remember,' she answered.

'How about you, Sylvia?' he asked.

Victoria watched her mother get animated and launch into a long tale of when she had had lunch with Errol Flynn.

The man nodded encouragingly and whistled in amazement. Sylvia looked very pleased with herself.

Victoria looked around. The collection of disparate individuals was now a single group. This never happened. When she came, everyone was only concerned with themselves and paid no attention to anyone else. She looked at the man. There was something about him that made everyone focus on him. He had them captivated.

When Sylvia stopped to breathe, he turned to the woman on his left to ask her about her memories and noticed Victoria. He looked at her steadily.

Victoria face reddened. She suddenly felt like a little girl, not sure how to react. She glanced away for a second but thought better of it and looked back at him.

'Hello, are you a new resident?' he asked.

'No, I'm visiting my mother,' she answered quickly, not realising that he was teasing her.

'Ah, well it's nice to meet you. My name's Joe.'

Victoria didn't know what to say.

'And you are?' he asked.

'Oh, sorry, my name is Victoria Court. Sylvia's my mother,' she answered, self-conscious.

He stared at her, then smiled and said, 'Great! Would you like to join our discussion?'

'Er, no, I'm happy here — thank you.'

The residents were getting restless.

Joe turned back and said, 'Right, let's have a song now,' and he launched into 'Daisy, Daisy'.

After several more songs, it was time for tea. Victoria went over to her mother and sat down beside her. Sylvia was glowing.

'Did you enjoy that, Mummy?'

'Oh yes. Joe comes to visit me all the time you know.'

Victoria looked across the room to where Joe was handing out cups of tea. She was intrigued by him. He wasn't exceptional in any physical way: average height, strong looking but not huge, maybe middle forties? There was something about him though. She saw how the residents' demeanour lightened up around him. They all wanted him to stay talking to them as he went about the room.

He must have felt her gaze on him; he looked across at her and smiled. She coloured again — damn. She carried on watching him. He moved confidently, in control. She was beginning to see what he had that was affecting her — he had authority. He had the authority that she normally had and, somehow, he had stripped her of hers.

'You like him too, don't you?' her mother said, smiling knowingly at her daughter.

Victoria looked at her mother and said, 'Well, he seems like a friendly chap. I expect he's very popular.'

'Oh, he is. Even the gaolers like him.'

Victoria looked at his face. It was kind, open and intelligent. There was something else: he looked as if he knew everything; as if he knew what was going on in other people's minds, maybe her mind.

He came over to their side of the room and asked, 'Tea isn't it, Sylvia? Milk and two sugars?'

'Yes please, Joe,' she answered, sounding like a teenager.

'How about you, Victoria?' he asked, looking at her full on.

'Tea, milk, no sugar, please,' she said in a rush.

He handed it to her. She felt him come close; she leaned back to stop herself being overpowered.

'Thank you,' she said.

'Do you come here often?' he asked.

'Yes, I'm here later though, normally,' she said.

'Ah, that makes sense. Perhaps we'll meet again one day?'

'Hmm, perhaps,' she said.

'Bye then,' he said and moved along.

She looked around the room. He had everyone's attention. What was going on? Who was he? What was he?

***

She saw him in the first row of students for assembly. He left early pushing a tea trolley, cups and saucers rattling. Then she found him typing at a desk in the secretaries' office; he was wearing Eve Chalkley's funny, old pink cardigan. He smiled at her and said, 'Ah, would you like a cup of tea?'

She looked at his hand as he held out a cup; she liked that hand. She took the cup and put it down. She examined his fingers, his palm, 'You're not really a typist, are you?' There was no reply. 'I'm not really Jane Austen, by the way. Don't you mind me not wearing any clothes?'

'Not at all; anyway, I hadn't noticed,' said Joe.

'Well, that's a relief. Go on, it's your turn.'

She looked at his hands as they stroked hers. She said, 'Are you sure you don't mind me being naked?'

'Are you sure I'm not a secretary?'

'No, I like you like that.'

He started stroking her wrists and arms and suddenly she felt incredible arousal. She took his hands, pressing them against her breasts, then moaned at the electric shock of pleasure.

He said, 'Maybe you're someone else?'

'Don't worry, Joe, you're doing fine.'

'Shall I keep on guessing? Till I score top marks?'

'Fine, don't mind me.'

He ran his hands down her belly, up and down her thighs, her inner thighs.

'Oh, lovely.' She opened her legs. She urged him, 'I don't care who you are, just touch me, please, touch me,' and shuddered as she felt his fingers. Knowing something wasn't quite right she said, 'Are you sure? I am naked — I'm not normally naked. You won't tell the governors, will you?'

'I don't normally wear this cardigan, so we're both all right, aren't we?'

Victoria felt his fingers stroking her; she knew it was wrong, but she didn't care. She arched her back, willing him to be inside her. Then he was on top of her, his weight pinning her down. Her hips rocked as he entered her. The image of James flashed into her head. She tried to dash it away, but it stayed. She screwed up her eyes to rid herself of him and heard herself cry out, 'James! Stop it! Now!' But he wouldn't. She couldn't stop him. Awake now, she rolled into a ball, hugging herself tight. Huge waves of bitterness swept over her. She let the gut-wrenching sobs rack her body. She felt sick and dirty and utterly alone.

Part 2

The Start

Frank was only dimly aware of the packed classroom as he walked in behind the headmistress. He heard her introducing him to the class. He stood still waiting to be told what to do. The teacher came over to him and said something. Frank felt his hand being shaken.

Victoria looked around the room for a spare place. The chair next to Anthony Alexander at the front was unoccupied. She paused for a moment: was it a good idea to put these two together? She cast the thought aside; to start rearranging students now would create a fuss that she knew Frank wouldn't want.

'Here you are, Frank,' she said, pointing to the chair. 'Have a seat.'

Frank did as he was told.

'Thanks, Phil,' she said, looking meaningfully at her colleague. 'I'll see you later.'

Feeling self-conscious, Frank sat down. He hated standing out and he could feel that all eyes were on him. He put his bag down, pulled out a pen and a blank exercise book, closed his eyes and waited for time to pass.

Anthony felt dwarfed by Frank. To start with, no one ever sat next to him, so he had become used to the extra space. But not only was the double desk now shared, someone who seemed to be twice his size was looming over him.

When Frank had appeared behind Miss Court, he had looked like a giant. It wasn't just that he was tall, he was big too. Anthony had started taking note of the physique of other boys. Since he had left St Luke's and moved to this awful run-down, suburban town and its apology for a school, he had decided to toughen up a bit. The campaign had been recommended by his granny when he and his mother had moved in with her. He told her of the full extent of the bullying he'd faced for all those years and she'd been quite matter of fact, 'You're going to have to fight back, Anthony. Don't stand for it anymore.'

His successful exit from his last school, with all its derring-do, had confirmed to him what he had always believed: that he wasn't the downtrodden whipping boy that everyone had thought. Following his granny's advice, he started working on his fitness. He lifted weights — well, bags of sugar — and did press-ups and sit-ups. He now looked at himself every night in his bedroom mirror to measure the difference all the work was making. Although he was getting taller, he wasn't as big or strong as he would have liked; but he could definitely feel himself growing in confidence, if not physical stature.

Since he'd started at the school, he'd had plenty of the usual swearing, teasing and scornful comments. Most of them came from the ignorant fool Gary and his sniggering friends. He started off by ignoring them, but now he was beginning to feel the drive for revenge building inside him. The last time he'd felt it, he'd acted, and he was prepared to do so again.

'Hello, Frank,' he said.

Frank turned towards Anthony and stared. Anthony shifted uneasily in his seat. He stared back. What was this shambling oaf staring at him for? Was this stranger already lining him up for some kind of attack?

Frank's heart had missed a beat. He stared at the skinny kid and heard himself say, 'Hi, Robbie.'

'It's Anthony,' Anthony corrected him.

Frank looked at him again, and mumbled with embarrassment, 'Oh, I'm sorry.'

Frank felt stupid. He hadn't really believed that Anthony was Robbie — how could he be? Just for a split second, though, there had been something about Anthony that had brought his brother back to him in a horrible rush of hope. He blinked back tears now, trying to get the image of Robbie's broken body out of his head.

'Leave him alone, you wanker. Didn't you hear what Wilson said?' Gary hissed.

Gary was in a seriously bad mood. He hadn't been able to sleep the night before. Once again, his father had come home drunk and there had been the usual swearing and threats to him and, of course, to his mother. When his parents had gone to bed Gary rushed downstairs and out into the garden where he'd sat on the ground crying. He tried to wipe the hideous scenes out of his head by rubbing furiously at his eyes — it hadn't worked. Now, he felt like shit.

To make matters worse, Katy Walker was back at school. The last time he'd seen her she'd been lying on the floor of the bus shelter semiconscious. He had attempted to block that evening out too. Seeing her walk into the classroom this morning had brought the disgusting images racing back. He remembered everything, mostly the absolute rage he'd felt towards her for what she'd done to him but, this morning, he'd been shocked by her appearance. Katy was normally bright and bubbly; today she was pale, withdrawn and looked about ten years older. She saw him looking at her when she came into the room; she just looked away, as if he were a piece of shit on the floor.

'Up yours,' Anthony said to Gary over his shoulder.

'You what?' Gary said, rising to his feet.

'Right, settle down everyone,' shouted Mr Wilson.

'It's that ape causing all the trouble, like normal,' Katy said, pointing at Gary.

She'd come to school against her will that morning. Her mother — well, the woman pretending all these years to be her mother — had been going on and on about going back and, in the end, she'd just wanted to get away from the house: anywhere was better than there. Susan had cajoled her into it too. They hadn't had any real conversation for over a week now and, despite herself, Katy missed her sister.

The night of the bus shelter was a blur to Katy, but she remembered enough of what had happened to feel like throwing up again at the very sight of Gary Abbott. Now, as usual, he was winding everyone up.

'Watch out, Gary mate, remember the last time you and "deep throat" got together,' jeered Steve.

Gary turned to him, fury in his face. Steve stopped smirking.

Katy stuck her finger up at Gary.

Gary put his head in his hands; it was already turning into the worst kind of day. He liked this lesson, normally — it was the only one he did. He wanted to talk about the book and, if possible, he wanted Wilson to say well done to him again. Now, as usual, everything was slipping away from him and descending into the normal shit. He felt sick, sick of everything.

'Right, we're going to dramatize *Of Mice and Men*,' said Mr Wilson. 'I'll be the narrator and I'm going to pick some of you to play the parts.'

Everyone got out their copy of the book. Gary pulled his out of his bag; despite his mum's efforts it fell apart again.

'What's happened to your book, Gary?' asked Wilson.

Gary went red, 'Nothing,' he said, the shame reaching boiling point.

'He couldn't read the whole book, so he decided to break it into smaller parts,' laughed Anthony.

'You can fuck off, you little shit,' Gary snarled.

Frank's heart sank. He'd only been in the classroom five minutes and he was being thrown right back into violence. He took a deep breath and sought the calm he used to find so easily. He couldn't find it.

Katy laughed at Anthony's jibe.

Mr Wilson walked over and looked at them closely. Even without them saying anything, the enmity was palpable. He allocated players for the parts, deliberately choosing sensible heads.

Gary hissed again, 'I'm going to get you, you little wanker.'

Frank turned around to look at Gary. Gary looked into the big kid's eyes. They were dead. He stared at Frank, waiting for him to back down, Frank did not look away.

Frank took in Gary's size, sullen expression, and the evident challenge in his face. He felt energy begin to grow in him. He wanted to look away, to get away, but he could feel that oh-so-familiar power building — it was calling him.

'Everything OK, Frank?' asked Mr Wilson.

Frank turned back and looked down.

Steve whispered to Gary, 'He's a fucking freak.' Gary nodded.

As the lesson progressed, Gary calmed down. He now regretted his threat. He wasn't concerned about Anthony; he had had enough violence for a while. The sound of his father's brutish voice and the picture of his mother's puffy eyes were searing through his head.

Anthony was regretting winding Gary up: why had he done it? He'd got into his mind that he could take on the bullies, but this time he didn't have a gun, he didn't have the back-up of incriminating evidence and, although he lifted bags of sugar every night, he was pretty sure he couldn't beat Gary Abbott in a fight. He sank lower into his seat as the minutes ticked by.

Frank thought back to his mother's words as he'd left home that morning, 'Just ignore everyone and come back home to me safe.'

He had kissed her cheek and said that was all he wanted to do, and it was true. Now, here he was, getting into a state again, and spiralling towards another incident.

Katy was feeling wobbly too. She had wanted to get away from the house, but she certainly had not wanted these awful feelings, all of which were being brought back by Gary Abbott. Seeing him had been sickening; and hearing the stupid joshing jokes of him and his friends had brought that awful day and night back to her with horrible clarity. She suddenly felt overwhelmed by feelings of revenge. She wanted them to feel as humiliated as she had, as she still did.

At last the lesson ended. Chairs were pushed back, and chatter and laughter filled the room.

Anthony packed his books away quietly. He said to Frank, 'Do you know anyone in the school?' Frank shook his head.

'Well, I'm your first friend then,' and held out his hand.

Frank took it for a second; it felt good to touch someone kind, just the briefest of contacts.

'Anthony's found himself a bum chum,' sneered Steve.

Rather than joining in with the hilarity, Gary ignored the comment and got up to go.

'Where are you going to do him, Gaz?' asked Phil.

'Leave it,' growled Gary.

'Come on, he's got it coming to him, remember what he said to you,' chivvied Steve.

'He hasn't got the balls,' said Katy as she walked past them.

'You can fuck off,' said Gary, seeing red.

Frank was beginning to fear the build-up of energy that was now running through him. He got up and walked out.

'Lost your new boyfriend, shithead. Now what are you going to do?' sneered Paul.

'I'm not scared of you imbeciles,' said Anthony, and got up to go too.

'Come on, Gary, sort him out once and for all,' Steve said.

Anthony sped out of the classroom. The little gang followed him.

'Keep away from him, you moron,' shouted Katy, following them.

Everything speeded up. Anthony had to get away from the chasing pack. He slipped out through a side door and into the car park. He ran along the front of the school towards the lavatories. He was breathing hard. He knew he was going to get beaten up badly if he couldn't evade them. He cursed his stupidity: why did he always have to provoke them?

Gary, Steve, Phil and Paul — followed by Katy, screeching, 'Wankers! Wankers! Wankers!' — emerged into the car park. They looked up to see Anthony disappearing into the bogs. They sprinted after him.

Victoria Court's attention was caught by some activity outside her office window. She'd been discussing her ideas for a new science block with three of the school's governors. She saw Anthony Alexander running hard past her window. A few seconds later she saw Gary, Steve, Paul and Phil running after him. Then, seconds later, Katy Walker, screaming like a fishwife.

'Excuse me, gentlemen, I'll be right back.'

Anthony dashed into the lavatory, panting: where could he hide? Nowhere. He could go into a cubicle, but someone was in there and the other one had had its door pulled off.

He heard the running steps approaching the door and he turned to see the triumphant faces of Steve, Phil and Paul, and the glare of Gary. They came in and stood in front of him.

Katy Walker burst in shrieking, 'You are a total waste of space, Abbott, you are a fucking waster!'

Gary stood still, deflated; he did not want this. He felt like crying. He could hear his mother's pleading voice and the sounds of his father's violence. He closed his eyes.

'He's all yours, Gary,' crowed Steve.

Anthony knew he was facing a beating. He'd been hit before. This time, though, he was going to fight back.

'Come on then, if you think you can beat me,' he said and adopted a ludicrous nineteenth-century boxing posture.

The boys started howling.

'Jesus, Gary, looks like you've got a fight on your hands,' Phil screeched, almost crying with laughter.

At that point the cubicle door opened, and Frank came out.

'This can't get any better,' Steve screamed, 'the Boy Wonder's brought his queer friend with him.'

'Come on, Abbott, are you scared?' Anthony sneered.

Suddenly Gary's pent up rage overwhelmed him. He put his bag down and as he moved towards Anthony, he heard Steve's voice yelling, 'Get him, Gary, get him!'

There was a wet, thudding splat.

After a long, shocked silence Steve said, 'Fuck.'

Everyone gaped at Gary. He was down on his knees and elbows, head in his hands. Blood was pooling around him. Breathless sobs were coming from his muffled face.

Frank was standing in front of Anthony and above Gary. He stepped back and looked into everyone's eyes one by one. His voice was slow, calm, it had an absolute ring of finality, 'He walked into the door, that's all.'

The lavatory door flew open and Victoria Court rushed in, followed by Phil Wilson. She took in the scene. She looked closely at everyone, her gaze coming to rest on the whimpering boy on the floor.

She whirled around to confront Phil Wilson, 'This is not what I wanted — not at all.'

She turned back and said gently, 'Let me see your hands, Frank.'

Frank, passive now, held them out. His right hand was red, already swollen and angry. She looked into his face. He couldn't hold her gaze.

She suddenly realised that Katy was in the toilet. She barked at her, 'What the hell are you doing here?'

'I wanted to stop that gorilla,' Katy said pointing at the figure on the floor.

Victoria bent down to Gary. She lifted his head slightly. Blood was streaming from his nose.

Steve, Paul and Phil edged towards the door and slipped out.

Victoria said, 'Get an ambulance, Phil.'

He ran off.

She bent down to Gary, 'Can you hear me, Gary?'

He didn't answer. She put her hand on his head, smoothing his hair, soothing him. 'Come on, old chap, let's get you into the medical room.' She looked at Katy and Anthony, 'Help me get him up.'

Between them they helped Gary to his feet. He was groggy, unable to support himself. They lowered him onto the toilet seat. She held him against her, supporting his weight.

'Katy, get me some towels, please. Wet them, then ball them up.'

She did as she was told. Victoria pressed the makeshift compress gently to Gary's face. The soggy paper became red in seconds. She held him tight against her and murmured, 'Don't worry, Gary, everything's OK.'

She looked at Frank, Anthony and Katy. 'This is the end. I'm telling you now: it's over. I'm taking over from now on.'

Part 3

Drive Phase

Victoria made her way slowly back to her office. She had made commitments to Frank's mother: she'd failed to honour them. She knew how troubled both Anthony and Katy were: she'd let them down. She'd taken responsibility for ensuring that Gary would be dealt with appropriately after his run in with the police, and now he was in hospital. All in all, it was her worst day ever in teaching.

She popped her head around Mrs Chalkley's door and said, 'I'm hoping that the Three Musketeers have gone?'

The school secretary nodded her head. 'Yes, they've left but...'

'Thank goodness. I don't want to be disturbed for the next thirty minutes. I just need time on my own. Can you keep me out of trouble?'

'Well, the thing is, there is someone here to see you. He's waiting in your office.'

Victoria sighed. She was desperate to put her head in her hands: to find a few minutes peace before gathering the strength to write up what had happened, inform the parents, liaise with the hospital and on and on and on; not to mention think through what she was going to do with the perpetrators or — as she felt certain they were — victims.

'Who is it?' she asked.

'His name is Marshall. He's here to discuss some work placement opportunities.'

'I'll give him a couple of minutes then can you come in and remind me of an urgent meeting?'

'Right, what's the name of the meeting?'

'Hmmm...say it's with the governors; he won't know the difference.'

She turned to leave.

'Er, you are a bit...mmm...stained? Are you all right?'

Victoria looked at her blouse: it was covered in Gary's blood.

'Ah, I'll clean up in a minute. Let's get rid of this chap first.'

She walked to her office door, opened it and went inside. She stopped and stared at the man standing there.

He said, 'Oh, hello. Here you are'

She was momentarily dumbfounded but then collected herself.

'Joe! What a surprise.'

'Sorry. Your secretary said to wait in here,' he said.

'Yes, yes, of course. Sit down. Let me organise some coffee.'

'No, don't go to any trouble. You've obviously got other matters to deal with — and that's just what I can see, never mind what's under the surface,' he said.

She blushed. Although it had been a week since the dream, its effect had not diminished. She pulled herself together.

'There's been a bit of an incident and I got rather caught up in it,' she explained, looking down at her blood-stained blouse.

She moved around her desk and sat down. She felt a bit more confident behind the heavy, wooden barricade.

She looked at Joe. She tried to work out what was unusual about him; there surely was something. It wasn't his physique or his face. He was strongly built but not exceptional. He was good looking but not especially handsome. It was his stillness: that was it. He was calm; he seemed to be at peace. He also had unsettling eyes: they were dark brown, deep set, and incredibly steady. When he looked at her, she felt he could see inside her, as if he were reading her mind.

'Don't look so worried; I'm here to help you,' he said.

She stared at him. Was he reading her mind right now?

Attempting to get back some control she said, 'What can I do for you?'

At that moment the door opened, and Mrs Chalkley looked in, 'Your meeting with…'

'It's OK, I'll go along later,' Victoria said.

'Oh, OK, I'll let them know,' Mrs Chalkley said.

Victoria said, 'So, how can you help me?'

He was silent for a long time, just looking at her, appraising her. Finally, he said, 'Do you want to talk about what's just happened?'

Victoria swallowed. She did want to tell him. Suddenly she felt compelled to reveal everything to him.

She closed her eyes and drew in a deep breath and said, 'It was just one of those everyday school incidents that the head gets involved in. It will blow over like they always do.'

He nodded. Had he understood her: that she couldn't say, but had been sorely tempted to tell him? And, tell him what?

'OK, so let me tell you how I can help you,' he said. 'But before I do, would you like a few minutes just to unwind and feel more like yourself?'

She looked at him. Was he playing with her? He was in her office, her school, he was a casual visitor, but he was making her feel like the guest being put at ease. She did want to compose herself though, get cleaned up a bit.

'Yes, I'll be back in five minutes.'

She went to the staff lavatories and stood in front of the mirror. She looked at herself. She was a bit of a mess. There was blood over her cream blouse, on her face, and hands. Her auburn hair was all over the place and her eyes were staring back at her like a stranger's. She filled a basin and splashed water on her face and hands. She took some paper towels and held them to her face, her eyes tightly closed. She took several deep breaths and willed herself to just calm down. After a few moments she felt her pounding heart begin to slow. She studied herself again. Apart from the blouse, she looked relatively normal — well, apart from the hair. She brushed it back into shape with her fingers.

She walked back to Mrs Chalkley's office and knocked on the door.

'Please can I borrow your cardigan?'

'Yes, of course. It's not the most stylish garment in the world,' she said pulling her pink cardigan off the back of the chair and handing it to Victoria.

'It's a lot classier than blood stains,' she said, shrugging it on. 'Thanks, Eve. I'll wash it and bring it in tomorrow.'

She went back to her office.

'You look much more like yourself,' he said. 'I particularly like your top-of-the-range school secretary cardigan.'

'Stop doing that,' she said.

'What, guessing correctly?'

'Yes, it makes me feel as though you are playing tricks on me.'

'Sorry, it's a bad habit, I know.'

'So, come on then, what's your pitch?' she said. She was feeling better now; she was ready to show him who was in charge around here.

'Right, I'm looking for some of your best students to help me with an event I am arranging at The Beeches.'

'Oh, what kind of event?'

'One of the residents is going to be a hundred soon and we are putting on a little party for her. We're inviting her friends and family, plus the press and the mayor and of course making a big fuss of her. I was told that you sometimes organise placements for your fifth form as preparation for work and I wondered if you had any that might want to help us?'

'Sounds lovely; how many do you want?'

'Maybe three or four, I'm not sure yet.'

'What will they be doing?'

'They'll work with me to plan it, send invitations out, contact the great and the good and help the residents get involved in it all too.'

Victoria studied Joe. She heard herself say, 'I've got an idea, but I don't know if it's a good one. May I share it with you?'

She had surprised herself. She hadn't wanted to show him that she had any uncertainties. But he made her want to confide in him.

'Fire ahead. I'll keep an open mind and tell you what I genuinely think,' he replied.

'Well, there are four students in this school that need help. They really do. I have the feeling that although they are struggling right now, they all have great potential and I want to help them. The problem is that they are on the edge of life: for one reason or another they are all on the brink. I'm determined to help them, but I'm not sure I can do it alone.'

Joe was silent, then said, 'Do you want me to meet them, and get a sense of them myself?'

'Yes, yes, that's a good idea. Plus, it would be good interview practice for them.'

'OK, but may I make a couple of things clear?' he said.

'Sure.'

'First, and foremost, I shall have the welfare of the residents of The Beeches as my guiding principle. If I think that there is any risk involved, I shall say no straight away.'

She nodded. That reassured her: that must be right.

'Second, I want to meet them individually and on my own.'

She paused before answering. What did she know about him, really? She mustn't hand over responsibility for them; she must stay in control as long as they were her students. On the other hand, they would be job-hunting soon, and the interview practice would be useful.

'OK, but I want you to meet them here in the school, so that they realise the school is ultimately responsible.'

'OK, do you have a room I can use — not a formal room?'

'Yes, there is a small room attached to the library.'

'All right, what's the next step?' he asked.

'I shall speak to their parents and get their go-ahead, then get back to you.'

He looked into her eyes. She held his gaze.

'I get the sense that this is really important for you. Am I right?'

She nodded and said, 'Yes, you are right. I have a personal interest in this, and I want you to recognise it, and to help me with it.'

'I understand, I think. I am very flattered that you trust me. I shall do my best for them.'

When he'd gone, Victoria thought back over the last few minutes. What had happened? Why had she been so willing to put Frank, Anthony, Katy and Gary into the care of a stranger? Or, just as importantly, why was she even contemplating their being able to help with an old lady's birthday party. It had been Joe. He had some kind of weird power over her. She didn't like it. The more she thought about it, the more her reservations deepened.

She picked up the phone and rang The Beeches. The phone was answered, and Victoria said, 'May I speak with Veronica Harper please?'

'Who's calling?' answered the receptionist.

'Victoria Court, Sylvia Court's mother.'

'Hold on.' Then, 'Putting you through now.'

'Hello, Victoria,' said the business-like voice of the manager, 'what can I do for you?'

Victoria liked Veronica: she was like her, professional and straightforward.

'Well, it's a funny question. I wonder if you could tell me anything about Joe Marshall. It's just that he and I are arranging work placement opportunities for four of my students and I don't really know anything about him or his role at The Beeches.'

'Oh, I know. He is somewhat mysterious, isn't he?' Veronica Harper answered with a smile in her voice.

'Good, so it's not just me then,' Victoria said. 'Go on, spill the beans.'

Veronica laughed, 'No, he's totally reliable, I promise. He works in the garden, he chats with the residents, he helps with serving meals, and generally does odd jobs. Plus, he's organising Grace Simpson's 100th birthday party.'

'Why?' asked Victoria.

'Why what?'

'Why does he do all those things? Hasn't he got something better to do?' Victoria asked. 'I mean, what is his real job?'

'That is his job,' Veronica answered.

'Well, how do you know he is so trustworthy?' Victoria asked, conscious that she was beginning to sound suspicious which, if she were honest, was exactly what she was feeling.

'Well, he came with references from some very reputable people and plus, he is just a thoroughly decent and kind man,' the manager answered, now sounding a bit defensive.

'Thanks, I didn't mean to doubt you or him; it's just that I've got my students to think about.'

'Yes, I understand that. But I have my residents to think about too and I wouldn't let anyone who represented any kind of risk to them come into contact with them on such a close basis,' Veronica said sounding serious.

'Yes, of course. That's true,' Victoria said, realising that she had pushed the other woman a little too far. 'Thanks Veronica, forgive my nosiness, won't you?'

'Of course. He's all right. I'd say we were very lucky to have him with us,' Veronica said.

Victoria said goodbye and put the phone down. She felt better about Joe. She wanted him to be trustworthy — for Frank, Anthony, Katy and Gary. And for herself.

***

'Mrs Gordon?' Victoria asked as the phone was answered.

'Yes?'

'Hello, Janice, it's Victoria Court from the school. I just want to tell you a couple of things that have happened today.'

'Oh no — please tell me everything is all right?' Janice's voice was urgent.

'Well, Frank was involved in an incident today. He punched a student. However, I believe that there was a great deal of provocation and he certainly did not go looking for trouble. Rather it followed him.'

Apart from Gary, Victoria had spoken to all those involved in this morning's fracas. She'd managed to piece together the various elements of the story.

Janice Gordon said, 'This is terrible. Is he OK?'

'Yes, a bruised hand only. Although I think he is very upset by it,' Victoria replied, already thinking about what she was going to tell Gary's parents.

'No, I mean is the other boy OK? Frank is terribly strong you know.'

Victoria looked at the blood on her blouse and remembered Gary's almost unconscious state. She said with as much confidence as she could muster, 'I think he'll be all right.'

'Is Frank going to be in trouble?' Janice's voice was breaking.

'I've talked to Frank. I have reassured him that I understand what happened and why. But I have stressed to him that I don't want violence at this school.'

'Thank you, I'm very grateful to you. I'm sure Frank will be too,' Janice said, breathing out with relief.

Victoria went on, 'Also, I want to ask you if you are happy for me to put him forward for some work experience at a nearby old people's home.'

'I don't think he'll want to. He's very sensitive about new and different things right now,' Janice answered.

'But are you happy for me to ask him?'

'Yes, but be prepared for him to say no.'

Next, she rang Mrs Alexander. She was not surprised to hear that her son had been involved in an incident. 'Was he being bullied?' she asked straightaway.

'Well, it appears to me as if he has been a target for bullying. I hate bullying and I am putting a stop to it,' Victoria said.

'It's not the first time. He has told me that it has happened but that he's going to deal with it,' Mrs Alexander said.

'Well, it has been dealt with today and I believe that this will be the last time we have to have this kind of conversation. Also, I want to ask you if I can put him forward for some work experience in an old people's home?'

'Yes, please do; he needs a focus. He is a very clever boy and he gets easily bored. Please do find him something that he can get his teeth into.'

Victoria put the phone down and wondered how Gary was doing. She knew that he was going to be the most difficult one of the four but perhaps the neediest.

She spoke to Anna Walker. 'Mrs Walker, you told me something of Katy's circumstances. She was involved in an incident today which I feel sure was because of her difficult recent experiences. I am not going to take any action, but I am worried about her mental state. An opportunity has come up that I think might give her something of a distraction, something else to focus on.'

Anna said, 'I'm terribly worried about Katy. We don't seem to be able to talk to her about anything right now. If you can help her, please do.'

'Well, I would like to put her forward for some work experience, how do you feel about it?'

'What kind of thing?'

'Helping to arrange a 100th birthday party for a lady at The Beeches. I think it might be a lot of fun.'

Anna said, 'It's worth a try… see what happens. She used to love parties.'

Victoria rang the hospital to check on Gary. He was being treated in the casualty department. He had a broken nose and was being kept under observation.

She rang his home again. She'd tried several times since the incident but there had been no reply. This time the telephone was answered, and she heard a timid voice, 'Hello?'

'Mrs Abbott?'

'Who is this?'

'Mrs Abbott, this is Victoria Court, Gary's headmistress at Hillside School. I'm ringing about Gary.'

'He's not in trouble, is he?' the small voice said, sounding scared.

'Well, he was involved in a scuffle and he's in the casualty department at the hospital. He has a broken nose and they're keeping him in just to make sure there's nothing else amiss,' Victoria said, trying to sound reassuring.

There was silence. Victoria was quiet too. Then, through the hiss of the connection, she heard Mrs Abbott crying. 'It's my fault, it's because of me.'

'Why do you say that?'

'It's my fault,' she repeated. 'I'm a terrible mother.'

Victoria kept quiet, listening hard.

'I'll go down there and look after him,' Gary's mother whispered finally.

'That's a good idea,' Victoria said wanting to reach out and hold her. 'Before you go, may I ask if you are happy for me to put Gary forward for some work experience at The Beeches?'

'I'll have to ask my husband about that. He'll know best.'

Victoria paused but then said, 'Lovely, thank you. Let me know, won't you?'

'I will,' said Mrs Abbott and put the phone down.

***

'You should have heard the sound, it was awful; it makes me feel sick just to think of it,' Katy said to Susan as they walked towards the canteen.

'But what were you doing there anyway?' Susan asked.

'I was chasing after that idiot, trying to get him to leave that poor boy alone.'

'Who, Anthony?' Susan asked.

'Yes, it's always him they pick on. I know he's a bit weird but he's harmless and, really, he's never going to be a threat to them, is he? Well anyway, when Frank hit Gary it was like he'd punched a rotten melon or something. It was sort of terrible and fantastic at the same time.'

'Then what happened?'

'Well, it was so funny. It was like time had stopped. No one said or did anything. There was just nothing. Then Frank looked at us all and in this spooky way he told us that Gary had walked into a door. We all just nodded, like we were under a spell or something. Then Miss Court rushed in and things went back to normal.'

'What did she say?'.

'She was flipping furious; then she went quiet — then for a minute it was funny.'

'Funny?'

'Well, Gary was sitting on the loo lid, Miss Court was sort of cradling him, and then she said that she was taking over. I don't know what she meant, but she was quiet and sort of final. That's it really.'

'What's wrong with Frank, do you think?'

'I don't know but I tell you what, there's something going on: he's not like the rest of us.'

'When he came into the classroom I thought, well, he looked sort of half asleep. Do you know what I mean? It was like he was sleep-walking,' Susan said.

'Hmmm, something awful has happened to him, poor boy.'

'Well, we can sympathise with that,' Susan said.

They were quiet for a while. They could see the long queue to get into the canteen, so they sat down on a wall and waited.

'How are you feeling?' Susan asked.

'I don't know. I am still mad at Mum and Dad. I feel really sad about it all. I don't know how to feel, if I'm honest. The thing is — who am I? You can't answer that. They can't. I can't. I'm a mystery person. I know you're my sister, but you're not really. What am I supposed to feel? I don't know.'

Her voice was cracking. She pulled a hankie out of her pocket and blew into it.

'I know. I feel terrible too. Nothing's changed really, but at the same time everything has.'

They were silent again.

'Then that stupid letter — that's what caused all the damage,' Katy said. 'Who the fuck is this mystery woman who happily gets rid of me and then thinks she can just turn up and I'm hers again, as if none of us matter.'

Susan agreed. She was furious with Katy's real mother. If she hadn't sent the letter, nothing would have changed, and their lives would have carried on in the easy, loving way they always had.

'What are you going to do?' she asked.

'I'm going to ignore it. Don't worry, I'm not going to let her selfishness wreck our family even more than it has already,' Katy said.

As she said it, she didn't feel as sure as she sounded. She had taken the letter and screwed it up and thrown it into the bin. Five minutes later she had fished it out and it was now in her bottom drawer where she kept her most important things.

***

'So, what happened today?' Mrs Alexander asked Anthony as he came in after school.

'It was amazing. There's this new boy at school. His name is Frank. He's had something terrible happen to him and we were all warned to be nice to him. Well, he sat next to me and I said hello, and we shook hands, and he called me Robbie. I don't know why. Then that awful boy Gary — you know the one that is always swearing at me and threatening me

— started to taunt me. It was just like normal but this time there was a different feeling about the whole thing. I was ready this time and I started answering him back. You know Granny told me that I had to face up to bullies, so I have been getting ready to tackle him and today I got the chance.

Then at the end of the class Gary and his stupid friends started chasing me and, anyway, we all ended up in the boys lavs and then I started telling Gary that he was a coward, just like Granny said, and then Gary came up to me and then this new boy Frank, who was there, punched Gary so hard he dropped like a stone and just lay on the floor crying. It was amazing. I was going to punch him, but I didn't get the chance. Anyway, Miss Court rushed in and then it was all over. Gary just stayed on the floor — there was blood everywhere. It was a shame that Frank punched him because I was going to, and he got in just before I did. Never mind, he gave him a tremendous shot. Frank is a lot bigger than me so maybe he is better at punching than me anyway, I'm not sure though, I've been training. Then, an ambulance came, and Gary was taken off.

Miss Court was really angry with everyone. I could tell she was furious. Mr Wilson, the English teacher, looked really nervous when he was talking to her; he was like a naughty boy. He looked quite funny standing in front of her. Then we all just drifted away. You know that girl Katy, the one who does singing and dancing? She was in there too. I'm not sure why, she was screaming at Gary but then she went quiet. The whole thing was like a dream now I think about it. I walked out into the playground and saw Frank sitting on a wall on his own. I went up to him and told him he was pretty good at punching. He didn't say anything. I got the feeling he didn't want to talk to me. I told him that I was going to punch Gary, but I didn't get the chance. Frank said he was sorry. I think he was sorry that he had got there first, I wasn't sure. He said it in a funny sort of way. He's really quiet you know. I think he might want to be my friend. I told him that if he wanted a friend that would be fine by me. He just nodded. I told him that I'd look after him if he was worried about anything. I think he's shy; he just needs a bit of time to get to know me. What do you think, Mother?'

'I think you're being a kind boy,' she answered.

'Well, when it was lunchtime, I went with him to the canteen and we sat next to each other. It was interesting. Gary's henchmen — you know, those ignorant, ugly brutes I've told you about — they all came in and looked at us. For the first time ever, they ignored me. They just walked by and didn't say anything at all. I think they've got the message now — that I mean business and they can't bully me like they thought they could. Katy and her sister sat at the table next to us. They're nice girls, you know, not like some of the girls there. Katy said to us that she was pleased that we'd sorted out Gary. That was nice of her. Frank didn't say anything. I think he might be shy of girls. Then this afternoon I showed Frank where everything was around the school and he seemed to be pleased about that. I can't really tell much about him. He doesn't say anything. I think he's a nice chap though. Do you think I should ask him around one day? We could play chess. Or, he might like to look at my books, to see if there is anything that he'd like? I think he's a bit lonely.'

Anthony's grandmother had come into the kitchen and was listening. Anthony turned to her, his eyes shining with the excitement of the day's events.

'Did you hear all that, Granny?' he said.

'Two things, Anthony,' she said. 'Please pay attention. First, don't say anything to Gary when you next see him; I think he might want to get his own back.'

'But Granny...'

'No, this is important: you and Frank have established your position. Now let it go.'

'Oh, all right,' Anthony said.

'Second, I think that you should give Frank a bit of time to get used to you. He might just need to find his feet.'

'Sure, yes. Well, I could ask him around tomorrow after school. What do you think? I don't know if he plays chess and, even if he does, he's unlikely to be my kind of standard, but perhaps he'd like a lesson. One thing I should tell you though: he's a bit grubby; well, not really grubby, more unkempt. He's got really long hair, and his clothes are all crumpled. He is clean though; he doesn't smell or anything. In maths this

177

afternoon I sat next to him again. I think he fell asleep. Mr McManus saw him, but he didn't say anything. I think all the teachers have been told to leave him alone. After the lesson I asked him if he wanted any help with maths. He just shook his head. It's a pity. I'd like to help him. He's really big. I think we could do some weights together. Yes, that's an idea: I'll ask him back to lift weights, not play chess. He might prefer that. Anyway, at home time I walked with him down the road. I asked him if he had any brothers and sisters. He didn't answer. He lives near us, at the end of Drayton Road. I shook hands with him when we said goodbye. He shook my hand and said "Thanks, Anthony". He seems like a nice chap, don't you think?'

Mrs Alexander put down her book and said, 'Very nice, but I think you were nice too.'

'Really? Oh, good,' said Anthony, pleased.

'Miss Court rang today. She told me there had been an incident. She also said that there was a work placement opportunity at The Beeches, the old people's home near here. She wants to know if you'd like to be involved.'

'Yes, that sounds like it might be good fun. Maybe they're all like Granny,' Anthony said.

'I don't think so — she's not the norm you know,' Mrs Alexander said, picturing her mother smoking cigars and reading scurrilous magazines.

'I doubt it, Anthony,' confirmed his grandmother.

'Well, it might be good fun anyway,' Anthony persisted. 'I wonder if Frank will be asked as well.'

***

Janice Gordon looked at her son as he came in through the door. She knew he must be feeling terrible about what had happened. Her heart went out to him. She wished she could take his pain from him and see him grow back into her old Frank.

'I know what happened, Frank: it's all right, don't fret,' she said.

He hung his head.

'Let me see your hands.'

She saw that his right hand was horribly swollen.

'Let's wrap that up straight away,' she said and wheeled her way to the fridge. She got a bag of peas from the ice box and wrapped it around his hand.

'Victoria Court rang me and explained that someone had been causing trouble and you just got mixed up in it,' she said, keen for him to be reassured but also wanting to hear more from him about what had happened.

Frank sighed and said, 'I can't keep away from trouble, Mum, no matter what I do. This time I even got out of the way but it all just followed me. I'm a jinx: there's something about me that attracts damage and pain.'

'That is total rubbish. Stop that childish talk!' she snapped. 'Don't you let me hear that talk again — I will lose my rag, I promise you.'

He couldn't help smiling. 'OK, I won't say it, but until it stops happening, I'll keep on thinking it.'

Janice was quiet. She knew she wouldn't be able to just tell Frank not to feel something, especially when it was such a powerful emotion. Instead she said, 'Well, you may be right; let's see, shall we?'

They were quiet for some time then she said, 'Victoria asked if you would like to have a go at a work placement, helping put on a special birthday party for a very old lady at a nearby home. I said I'd ask you. What do you think?'

Frank laughed, but it was not a happy sound. He said, 'Yeah, and I'm going to be the life and soul of a happy birthday party, aren't I?'

Janice laughed too. He was right. There was nothing jolly about her Frank right now.

'Well, I don't think they want you to do the entertainment, just help organise it.'

'No thanks. Not right now, Mum.'

She thought for a moment. She'd been thinking that it might be a good idea for him to focus his attention on something other than himself and his grief. It had been seven months since the crash, and he was getting more and more withdrawn.

'I want you to do it. Do it for me please, Frank,' she said.

He closed his eyes in pain. She knew she was going to put him through an ordeal, but she felt in her bones that he needed to begin to move on, get going again.

'Why?' he asked.

'You're a kind, gentle boy and there's a very good chance you'll meet someone who needs your friendship, care and concern,' she said. 'I want you to give yourself to someone who needs you, someone who will feel the Frank magic.'

Frank laughed again, a mocking sound.

'Seriously, Frank. I've been to places like The Beeches. There are people with no one to talk to, no one who cares about them. There will be someone there who will love to have you talk to them. Do it for me and for him or her?'

'I talk to you, I care about you,' he said.

'But I'm the one that wants you to do this, Frank, and I am going to insist.'

Frank was silent for a long time. Finally, he said, 'OK, for you I'll do it. But if I feel that it's not right, I'll leave immediately. I can't get caught up in any more aggro.'

She nodded. 'Well done, my brave boy, you are the strongest person I've ever met,' she said, tousling his hair.

'No, I'm the weakest,' he said, 'far and away the weakest.'

**

Gary got out of the taxi outside his house. His mother followed him. They went indoors.

He was feeling terrible. He had a thumping headache, his face was so sensitive it felt as if it had been badly burned, and he still felt unsteady when he walked.

It was now after six and he knew his father and brothers would be at home. He'd been dreading this bit. He knew what their reaction would be when they saw him.

It had been bad enough with his mother crying next to him in the hospital and on the drive home. He'd been embarrassed by her; now he knew he was going to be shamed by the others.

He walked into the front room on his way to the kitchen.

'Fucking hell look at the state of you!' his father said, gaping at Gary.

Kevin and Derek looked up and stared at him, then all three of them started laughing.

'Tell me you were fighting at least five other blokes,' Kevin said.

Gary ignored him. He kept going into the kitchen. He heard them joking about him as his mother closed the door and they were alone.

'Sit down, love,' she said.

He hung his head, then, feeling the pressure of his broken nose, sat up straight.

'I'll make you something to eat and then you're to go to bed,' she said.

He stayed silent. He didn't know what to say. He wanted to cry but he knew he couldn't. His face hurt badly. His head was full of a boiling mass of vicious, dirty thoughts. He could think of nothing except his total humiliation and the pounding reminder of it caused by the damage to his face.

As he listened to the kettle boil and his mother scraping potatoes, he dared for one minute to think back to what had happened. He wasn't quite sure even now. He remembered Anthony Alexander standing in front of him, his fists up in a mockery of a boxer's pose. He felt the drive to punch that smug little face rush through him again. Then, something had hit him, and he was down. From that moment on everything was a blur. He knew that the headmistress had been there, and he could remember leaning against her. Nothing else though. What had happened? Had he walked into something? He could not believe, would not believe that Anthony had hit him so hard.

His mother's voice started him back to the present, 'Tomorrow we'll go to the opticians.'

Gary said nothing. He had known that his sight wasn't great; he'd known for a couple of years. The idea of turning up at school wearing glasses was something that he just couldn't contemplate. In fact, turning up at school with his face looking like a punch bag was more than he could accept right now.

He felt his mother's hand on his shoulder. She started to stroke his head. Her touch was hesitant but when he didn't move it became stronger. He liked it.

'Don't worry, Gary, it'll make you look like a boxer,' he heard her say.

Her touch was making him cry. He started to shake. She moved around to his side and put her arms around him.

'Sssshhhh, it's all right now, love,' she crooned softly to him.

The kitchen door opened, and Mr Abbott's harsh voice interrupted them.

'What happened then?' he asked.

Gary was silent.

'Don't bother him, dear,' Mrs Abbott said, getting back to the potatoes.

'I think I've got the right to know what has happened to injure my own son,' he shot back at her.

'I'm not sure, Dad,' Gary said.

'Well, I'm going to find out,' Abbott snapped. 'I'll ring up that fancy pants headmistress and ask her.'

Just then the phone rang. Gary's dad went into the hall and answered it.

'It's your mate Steve,' he shouted to Gary. He picked up a can of beer, opened it, slurped deeply, belched loudly and walked back into the front room.

Gary didn't want to talk to anyone; he looked at his mother imploringly.

She picked up the phone and said, 'Hello, Steve, this is Gary's mum.'

She listened and then said, 'He's back home but he's a bit shaken up. The doctors said he'll be all right though.'

After a pause she said, 'What do you mean?'

Then, 'Who was it?' and then, 'Oh.'

Finally, she said, 'I'll tell him you called,' and she put the phone down.

She came back. 'Apparently you walked into the edge of a door,' she said.

Gary thought back. He didn't know how, but at least it explained things. 'Was he sure?' he asked.

'Yes, he was quite definite. He said that there was a new boy there who told them that was what had happened,' she said.

Gary remembered the new boy. He had been there, that was right. He started to feel a bit better. Maybe he hadn't come out of it so badly after all. He had been scared that somehow, unbelievably, Anthony Alexander had punched him. No, that was impossible: it must have been a door he just hadn't seen.

'I do think maybe glasses might be a good idea,' his mother said.

Maybe she was right. He closed his eyes. Something else now was making him feel like shit. He suddenly said, 'I know about Dad and what he does to you.'

There was a sharp intake of breath from her and then silence.

'Why do you just take it?' he asked, turning to look at her.

'It's nothing, really, it's nothing,' she said trying to smile at him.

'It doesn't look or sound like nothing,' he pressed.

'Well, it's just him with a pint or two inside him; it's nothing. Anyway, he doesn't mean anything by it.'

The door opened, and Mr Abbott came back in, twisting his empty can in his hands.

'Gary walked into a door, Dad,' Mrs Abbott said.

Gary's father scoffed and said, 'Well, that's stupid but at least no one gave you a beating; I couldn't have that.'

Mrs Abbott remembered her conversation with the headmistress earlier in the day.

'The school wants Gary to do some work practice at The Beeches: what do you think?'

'Wiping arses? Great, that'll suit him nicely,' Abbott said with contempt.

'Well, I think it would be nice to do something like that, better than something menial, anyway,' she said.

'Go on, say more, you mean you don't want him to do a menial job like I do,' he said, and pulled out another can from the fridge.

'No, I didn't mean that, dear. Miss Court wants him to do it.'

'Ah, Miss Court. I'd wipe her arse for her if she asked me; in fact, I'd do a lot more than that if I had the chance,' Gary's dad said, leering.

'Shush! What a thing to say,' his wife said, embarrassed.

Mr Abbott went off chuckling.

'Will you do it, Gary?' his mother asked.

Gary hadn't told his mother about the recent incident with the police; he was ashamed to. He hated his mother finding out he'd been in trouble. All she ever did was try to do the best she could for him, and he gave her nothing back.

'Do you really want me to?' he asked.

She looked at him closely, surprised by his answer. She wanted the best for her Gary: he was her last hope.

'Yes, I'd like it very much.'

'All right, I'll do it,' he said trying to sound keen.

She smiled. He saw her face light up. He saw a little, happy girl, just for the briefest of moments.

**

Victoria went through reception and looked around the lounge for her mother. There she was, asleep in her chair, her customary state these days.

Victoria sat down and looked at her mother. She could not quite come to terms with the sight of this old lady, once so attractive and vibrant, now so doddery and with almost no grasp of reality.

Victoria sighed and closed her eyes, grateful to have a few minutes of peace. It had been a tough week. She was under a lot of pressure right now: expectations from governors, parents, students and staff — and absolutely no money with which to meet them. She was short of one Physics and one French teacher and the caretakers were on strike. There was some extensive damage to be sorted out following an arson attack. Then there had been the fight on Monday morning. That had been the lowest point of all. She had at least persuaded the perpetrators to have a go at working here with Joe: that had pleased her. She guessed that there had been some hard, parental work undertaken to persuade and cajole them to do something like this and she was grateful. She smiled to herself. She knew that a big part of the gratitude she felt towards them was stimulated by the pleasure she was going to derive from telling Joe that she had found him some volunteers. She knew they weren't exactly willing, but at least they had come forward to have a go; that was in itself a success.

She was excited at the prospect of seeing him again. Although she'd only met him twice, and for a few minutes only each time, he seemed to have moved permanently into her head.

She held her mother's hand. It wasn't like her mummy's hand, it belonged to an old lady. Still, there was something comforting about it, reassuring. Victoria let out a long breath, closed her eyes and slept.

She woke up. Opening her eyes, she saw him looking at her. She stared back at him, confused and awkward.

He smiled and said, 'You looked so nice like that, a little girl with her mummy.'

She sat up and rearranged herself and said, 'Not so little, I'm afraid.'

'No, that's true, not little; nice though. May I?' he asked as he sat down next to her.

'Be my guest.'

'How's your week been?' he asked.

'The usual: up and down.'

'You must tell me what it's like to be a headmistress.'

'It's fantastic. I'm very lucky.'

'That's great — what a brilliant thing to say. How come it's so good?'

'It's what I always wanted to be, and now I am.'

'You are lucky. Not many people know what they want, and even fewer achieve it.'

'What about you?' she asked, aware that she knew nothing about him.

'Well, I like what I do here.'

'What do you do here, apart from charming the old ladies and arranging parties?'

'That's about it really, as well as looking after the gardens.'

'Is that all you do?'

'All? That keeps me out of trouble, thanks very much.'

Victoria looked at him again. There was much more to find out. Joe had a quiet authority, a way about him that was compelling. She didn't think he was the typical odd job man at a care home. Her mother stirred next to her.

'Hello, Sylvia, how are you today?' he asked.

'Well, now that you ask, I feel like a prisoner, the same way I always do.'

'Hello, Mummy,' Victoria said.

'What are you doing here? I've told you before I don't want to see you.'

Victoria sighed heavily. She wanted the best for her mother, but she couldn't ever get her to understand that this was the best place for her.

'It's tough, isn't it?' Joe said quietly to her. 'Believe me, I'm sure you've done the best thing possible for her.'

She looked at him, gratitude in her eyes.

'I've got you some applicants for the party project,' she said.

'Oh, well done! When can I meet them?'

'Any day next week; just let me know when you want to come in and talk to them.'

'Monday?'

'Sure, what time?'

'How about three p.m. onwards?'

'OK, I'll make sure everything is set up.'

'Don't tell me anything about them, just their names. Is that OK?'

She thought for a second: what should she tell him? 'Well...'

Before she could go on, he said, 'Really, I don't want to know anything.'

'All right, I agree,' she said, trusting his judgement but not sure why.

She went on, 'I must tell you something, though, something that you won't necessarily pick up and that is important to understand.'

He looked at her, attentive.

'There are some difficult dynamics for all of them, and between them. They won't be natural teammates, that's for sure. In fact, now I think about it, I am flipping between its being a good idea and a complete disaster in the making.'

'Shall we have a go, though?' he asked. 'I want to try, if you are up for it.'

She looked at him. She wanted to tell him everything: about the unlikely party organisers, about her own fears and cravings. She shook her head, to herself.

'Yes, let's try, but we must be careful and trust our judgement,' she said.

'OK, that's great. Will you excuse me?' he said.

She felt disappointment, 'Of course, don't let me hold you up.'

He got up and went to the trolley and started rattling plates and cups. He looked over to her and said, 'It's good working with you, Victoria; it's going to be fun.'

She smiled. 'Yes, I think so too. Thank you.'

'He's my friend, don't you try and steal him from me,' Sylvia said.

Victoria ignored her and watched Joe serving tea.

***

'Hello, Katy,' Joe said, 'do come in.'

He held the door open for her as she walked into the small room.

'Take a seat,' he said, pointing to the easy chair.

He had rearranged the room, piling up books and magazines on a side table.

'Thank you for coming along,' he said.

Katy thought back to the conversation she had had with her mother. Anna had said, 'I know you're going through a hard time, Katy, and I wish every minute of every day that we'd told you the truth years ago. It's done now; we must all try and move on even though it's painful.'

Katy had sighed and said nothing.

'You've been a recluse for days. How about having a go for this work placement Miss Court has suggested,' Anna encouraged.

'Because I don't want to?' Katy had answered.

'It'll be good for you,' Anna pressed.

'Please don't make out you know what is good for me, not after what you and Dad have done.'

'That's not fair, Katy. We've always done our best for you, and we are still trying.'

Katy sighed again. She was gradually beginning to lose her fury at her parents' long-term deceit. She loved them dearly and her natural warmth was getting in the way of her righteous indignation.

'Well, what do you know about this placement anyway?' Katy asked.

'Only that it's to help put on a hundredth birthday party for an old lady at The Beeches.'

'What do I have to do?'

'I'm not sure; I think the first step is to have an interview with someone from The Beeches.'

Now, here she was, sitting in front of this stranger. She had come down to the library with Miss Court, who said that it would be wonderful if Katy could get this job, she was sure that it would suit her very well.

'My name is Joe Marshall,' said the man.

She eyed him up. He looked all right, quite nice in fact. He was broad and fit looking; he had a kind face, but he looked a bit tough too.

They sat in silence.

Finally, he said, 'So, you need to tell me about you; I need to tell you about the little project I am arranging. Do you want to go first or second?'

'First,' she said.

'Brilliant, fire ahead.' he said.

'Well, there's not much to say about me. I am sixteen. I enjoy singing and dancing and acting. I have a twin...' she stopped momentarily and started again, 'I have a sister called Susan who is the same age as me.'

'So, you are a performer?'

'I love it; that's what I enjoy more than anything else,' she answered.

He said, 'What do you like about it?'

She suddenly became wary, 'Well, I just like it, I suppose.'

'Is Susan a performer too?' he asked.

'No, she's much more academic.'

'Are you very close?' he asked.

She looked away then said, 'We're like twins really.'

He let silence fill the little room.

Katy looked at Joe for a moment then said, 'I'm adopted; I've only just found out.'

'Thank you for telling me,' he said, 'I appreciate you being so candid with me.'

She said, 'I know it's not really what you're supposed to talk about in an interview, but I can't help thinking about it — all the time in fact.'

'It must have been a terrible shock?' he suggested.

She nodded, her eyes filling with tears.

'Tell me more if you want to.'

She drew in a deep breath then in a rush she described the last two weeks of her life.

She went on. 'When I'm with my parents now, it feels as if I am with a couple of impostors. It's not that I don't love them still, it's more like I don't quite know them anymore.'

He said, 'A total upheaval.'

She nodded.

They were silent.

'And Susan? How are you two getting on?'

She wiped away a tear and said, 'Fine really, we're getting back together slowly, but I feel like there is a gap between us now, like we've been separated somehow.'

'I guess she feels it too?'

'Yeah, she does,' Katy answered.

More silence.

'I wonder how Susan is managing to deal with the knowledge that her twin died all those years ago?' he asked.

Katy opened her eyes wide. She looked at him and then put her hand over her mouth.

'Fuck! — Oh, sorry. Do you know, I never even thought about that,' she admitted, looking forlorn. 'I've been so busy thinking of myself, that it never even occurred to me.'

'I'm not surprised: you've had a big shock; a traumatic one I'd say.'

'Yes, but Susan has too,' she said looking woeful.

'I think you're a very generous person, Katy.'

'Well, I thought I was, but actually I've been a bit of a bitch recently.'

'I'm sure I would have been too in your position,' Joe said.

They were quiet for a moment.

'May I tell you about my plan?' he asked.

'Sure, that's what I'm here for,' she said, focusing her gaze on him.

'There is a wonderful woman living at The Beeches; she's going to be a hundred in a month's time. We want to make sure that she has a great day, but also that her family and fellow residents do too. We want to put on a party that will be something special.'

'Great! I love parties,' Katy said.

'I want some help to make it all go with a swing. Would you like to be part of it all?'

'Have you arranged any entertainment for it?' she asked.

'I've got some ideas, but I need someone to bring it all together,' he said.

'I'm your girl!' she beamed.

***

As Victoria Court and Anthony walked along the corridor, she listened to his chatter.

'I'm really looking forward to getting involved, Miss Court, being part of something different and being able to help do something worthwhile.'

'Good, I'm sure you'll be a great asset to the project, Anthony. Good luck with the interview.'

'What's he like? Is he friendly, serious, old, young, how should I be with him?' he asked.

Victoria thought for a moment and then said genuinely, 'He's all of those things as far as I can see. You must just be yourself and you'll do well, I am sure.'

She knocked at the door. Joe opened it.

'Hello, Anthony, do come in.'

Joe looked at Victoria; he winked and closed the door.

'Thank you very much for coming along, Anthony,' Joe said as they shook hands.

Anthony had a small hand but a vice-like grip.

'Where did you learn that handshake?' Joe asked.

'My father always said that a firm handshake is the best way to make an early impression.'

'Well, he's probably right. Do you take after him?'

'Well, not really,' Anthony answered.

'May I ask how old you are?' Joe asked.

'I'm sixteen. I know I look younger but I'm growing fast.'

'Is size important?' Joe asked.

'Well, it is if you want to compete around here.'

'Compete in what way?'

'You know, compete with the bigger, tougher boys,' Anthony said.

'At sport you mean?'

'Yes, but more generally,' Anthony answered; then said, 'and just on an everyday kind of basis. You see, there are plenty of ignorant louts about and I'm not great at fighting back yet.'

'You know the pen is mightier than the sword?' Joe asked.

'Indeed, I do, thanks to Edward Bulwer-Lytton. But unfortunately, that doesn't stop ignorant thugs taking their petty frustrations out on me,' Anthony said.

Anthony had surprised himself. He hadn't intended to blurt his feelings out loud.

'Do you always speak your mind?' Joe asked.

'Yes, I always have done.'

'Let me guess, your father's influence again?'

Anthony just nodded this time. He was warming to this man, but he did not want to talk about his father, not with anyone.

Joe outlined the plans for the party.

'That sounds great. What do you want me to do?'

'What are you good at?'

'I'm good at working out things, planning things, thinking through problems; I suppose I'm quite resourceful. I like talking to people too, if I get the chance.'

'You sound ideal to me: consider yourself hired,' Joe said, holding out his hand to shake on the deal.

Anthony did his usual vice impersonation — Joe did the same.

They smiled at each other.

***

Victoria opened her office door and saw Gary sitting outside.

'Hello, Gary, all set?' she asked.

He looked up at her. Her heart went out to him: he had a classic shiner.

'Let's go,' she said, leading the way.

They walked in silence. As they approached the door to the interview room, she paused and, turning to him, said, 'This is a good opportunity for you, Gary, I really admire you for giving it a go.'

He didn't answer; he just looked at the door. She knocked, and it opened.

'Hello, Gary,' Joe said leading Gary into the room.

He said, 'My name is Joe Marshall,' holding out his hand.

Gary felt his hand being squeezed hard. He looked at the man's face: there was something unusual about him. He couldn't decide what, though.

Joe turned away from Gary and looked out of the window for a long time. Finally, he turned back and said, 'What I want, is to make someone very happy, and all the people who love her to be happy too. Can you help me do that?'

'I don't know. I doubt it.'

192

He didn't want to be here; he was only here because his mother had played her guilt-trip game on him.

Joe was quiet again. After another long pause he asked, 'If we were successful in creating a happy time for that person, how would that make you feel?'

Gary shifted uneasily. He didn't know what the right answer was. He knew what his father would say — something like, 'Is this a fucking interview or a session with a shrink?'.

'I suppose I'd be pleased,' he answered.

'Oh, that's good, because that is what is going to happen,' Joe said with total conviction.

He explained what he had in mind.

'What are you best at, Gary?' he asked.

'In what way?'

'What gives you satisfaction? A sense of achievement?'

Gary didn't know how to answer this one either. He thought for a while then said, 'I dunno…It was nothing special, but I enjoyed writing an essay about *Of Mice and Men*, and it got good marks.'

He felt a bit embarrassed. It was hardly something to crow about.

'I love that book,' said Joe. 'Who is your favourite character?'

Before he knew better Gary answered with equal enthusiasm, 'Slim: he's the strongest one.'

Joe nodded and said, 'Yes, he's a leader; he has natural authority. Are you like Slim?'

Gary wanted to say that he was, but he felt awkward, instead he said, 'Dunno, you'll have to ask other people that.'

Joe said, 'I like Slim, but I also warmed to the weaker ones like Candy, Crooks and Curly's wife.'

'Yeah, but they weren't really weaker; they were victims of society,' Gary said.

Joe nodded and said, 'You're right, that's true.' Then, 'Could I read your essay one day, Gary?'

'If you want,' Gary said, clamming up again.

'Yes, I would like that very much — especially as we are going to be working together over the next few weeks.' Joe stood up and put out his hand.

'Oh, is that it?' Gary asked, surprised and a bit disappointed that it was suddenly over.

'Yes, that's it. I'd really like you on the team,' Joe said.

'Why?' Gary couldn't help himself asking.

Joe looked at Gary and said, 'Because every group needs a Slim.'

***

'I know this will feel like an ordeal you can do without, Frank, so I'm really impressed by your agreement to take it on,' Victoria said to Frank as they walked.

Frank was quiet. She was right, he could do without it. He definitely wanted out and right now. He'd promised his mother though, and he would have to grit his teeth and get on with it.

Victoria knocked on the door.

'Hello, Frank, I'm Joe Marshall, do come in.'

Joe looked at Frank, Frank looked at the floor.

'No one has told me anything about you, Frank, nothing. I want you to tell me anything you like, everything or nothing. All I want to do is put on a lovely party for a lovely old lady; will you help me?'

Frank crossed and re-crossed his arms. He felt his bruised knuckles and wrapped his left hand over them.

'Are you a team player or an individual?' Joe asked.

Frank looked up and said, 'Individual I suppose.'

'Why is that?'

'Well, you don't have to rely on anyone, and no one can let you down.'

Joe nodded and said, 'Yes, I get that. Have you been let down then?'

'If getting killed counts, then yes.'

'Who was that?'

'My dad and brother.'

After a long silence Joe put his left hand out to Frank and said, 'Give me your strength Frank; let me have some of it will you?'

Frank looked at Joe's hand. He took it, and felt his hand being squeezed. He squeezed back, unsure why, but wanting to.

Joe smiled at Frank and said, 'Thank you, Frank.'

***

Joe heard a quiet knock on the door. He got up.

'May I come in?' asked Victoria.

'Of course, this is your gaff after all.'

They both sat down. She looked at him.

'Give me five minutes,' he said.

He closed his eyes. His jacket was off, and his sleeves were rolled up. He had muscular forearms. He was tanned and looked as if he must spend a lot of time outside. His face was relaxed, and he seemed at peace. She felt rather voyeuristic watching him like this, as if she were spying through a keyhole. She got up quietly and stood with her back to him, looking out of the window.

Joe sat very still. After a few minutes he said, 'Thank you, I needed that.'

'How did it go?' she asked, turning around to face him.

'Well, pretty well, I think. But I have to be honest with you, it's been some time since I had to confront so much raw pain and anguish in such a concentrated time and place.'

'I know. That's what I feel too,' she said. 'I feel a bit guilty now that I've loaded such a major set of issues on to you.'

He smiled and said, 'No, there's no need to feel guilty. I take it as a great compliment that you think I can work with them. What's more, I would really like to. So, it's thanks from me to you that is needed. Now that I've met them, can I make a couple of comments?'

'Sure, go ahead.'

'I get it that Gary has been bullying Anthony, and I assume Frank punched Gary, but how does Katy fit into the group?'

'I'm not sure how or why but Katy has developed a vendetta against Gary; something has happened, but I don't know what. I think though that somehow her recent family issue is caught up with her problem with Gary.'

Joe said, 'OK, here's my next one: what are their parents like?'

Victoria thought for a moment and said, 'Well, I don't know them well of course but... Katy's are decent — together and conservative. Frank's mother is made of steel and is very loving; they're close. Anthony's mother seems rather distant; his father isn't around. Gary's father is difficult, rather a bully I think, and his mother is a timid woman. I'm sure there's much more to tell but that's it in a nutshell.'

'I think the success of our venture is going to depend very much on Gary. He's seen as the public enemy by the other three. How strong is Gary, do you think?'

Victoria thought back over her experience of Gary and said, 'Hmmm, I'm not sure. He's bright; he is a sensitive young man, but the problem might be his home life rather than him.'

'I've told them all that I would like them to be in the team, but I didn't say anything about who else was involved. I need to do that next — do you agree?'

'Well, yes; unless you plan to have them, all working at different times, then it's got to be done.'

'Can you and I do that together?'

'Yes, that's a good idea; I'd like that. Also, can I continue to be involved in some way? I feel very responsible for them. This whole thing might be their chance of a new beginning.'

He looked at his watch and said, 'It's late — past your home time, isn't it?'

'Ha, ha, if only. I've got loads to do before I can go.'

'That's a shame: I was going to buy you a pie and a pint. Well, that is, if you'd like to join me. But I guess you're very busy with other things and other people?'

Victoria felt a flutter in her stomach — excitement and fear. 'Yes, I would like to, but perhaps another time,' she said

'Do you mean that or are you just saying it?' he asked.

'Yes, I mean it,' she said, wondering whether she did.

'OK, well how about I nip over to The Beeches, chat to Grace, and then come back in an hour or two?'

She felt flustered now. This was going a bit too fast. She admonished herself: she was not a schoolgirl; he wasn't asking her to marry him, for goodness' sake. She breathed evenly and looked at him. He looked back — he was weighing her up.

He said, 'I've got an idea: ring The Beeches and let me know what you want to do when you've had a chance to sort your stuff out here.'

She felt grateful to him for giving her the space to decide what to do. Once again, she had a sense that he was reading her mind.

She tried to think her way into his head. She was normally good at working out people's motivations and what was going on 'between the lines' but she could not see into this man's head at all.

'To be honest, Victoria, I'd really appreciate a chance to unwind a bit and I can't think of someone I'd rather do that with right now. But, you're a very busy person and will have many other commitments, so I'd understand totally if it's not a runner.'

'Oh, it's not that I've got lots of commitments, it's just that I hardly know you. For all I know you could be a mad axeman, or worse,' she said.

He smiled and said, 'Good point! I'm not an axeman. Actually, I'm harmless, and a frail, sensitive sort of soul.'

'Sensitive but not frail, I think,' she said. 'I'd love to have a drink with you, I'll meet you at The Beeches at seven thirty — will that be all right?'

'That's great, I'll be ready.'

***

Margaret Alexander looked at the clock and saw that she had fifteen minutes before Anthony came home. She poured herself another shot of vodka and lifted it to her lips. She felt the glass clack against her teeth in her haste to get the mouthful down her throat.

Since her husband had been locked up and she and Anthony had moved to live with her mother, she had almost joyfully found relief and oblivion in alcohol. She had never been a drinker when she and Richard had lived in Hampstead. He had disapproved of strong liquor and because she was so intent on performing the role of the perfect wife, she had done what he had wanted. Now, with his malevolent influence far away, she had actively chosen alcohol as her way of coping. It was all part of her break from the imprisonment that had been her previous life.

She refused to drink in front of Anthony. Another part of her determination to leave the past behind was to be a better mother to him. She felt intense guilt at having deserted him for so long. In ways she now understood to have been cruel, she had left him to cope with life whilst she strove in vain to satisfy her husband. Now, Anthony was her focus and she did not want to let him down anymore.

Every day, her feelings of guilt and then revulsion at herself increased. She knew that her lack of demonstrative love towards Anthony had damaged him. She also knew that she had been complicit in his life of anguish at the hands of bullies — her husband being the primary culprit. She cursed herself.

She wanted so much to make amends to her son, but just did not know how. Despite everything that he had been through, Anthony remained cheerful, optimistic and, if she were honest with herself, he was more caring to her than she'd ever been to him.

She thought about him now. He was finally beginning to grow. His voice had broken and although still spindly, he was not the frail little boy he had been. She knew from her mother how badly Anthony had been bullied. She screwed her eyes shut at the thought of her little boy being miserable for so long: why had she been so blind to it for all those years? She wanted him to be popular, but Anthony was like his father — he spoke his mind regardless of the effect on those to whom he spoke. She drained her glass and got up to put away the evidence.

The front door opened and closed. She vowed she would say something today. She had to act and not just continue to adopt her current victim mentality.

'I met the chap from The Beeches today,' said Anthony as he came into the kitchen.

'How did it go?' she asked.

'It was good; he's really nice. I think he might be a bit strict, but he seemed like he would be a good boss.'

'So, are you going to work there?'

'Yes, it was decided almost straight away.'

'What are you going to do?'

'I don't really know. I told him all the things that I'm good at and he seemed to think they would be useful skills. I expect I'll be in charge of something important.'

Margaret suddenly said, 'Stop. Stop right there.'

Anthony looked at her astonished. 'What? Stop what?' he asked.

With the vodka rushing through her veins, she took in a deep breath and said, 'I've been thinking a lot about you and me recently, Anthony. I know that in the past I've been a pretty useless mother. I know it's true — don't argue. The thing is, and I hate to have to say it, I always behaved as your father decreed. He wanted you to be brought up his way, and I was too weak to do anything else. I'm sorry, Anthony, I have let you down for far too long.'

Anthony was totally amazed by his mother's outpouring. He said, 'But, what do you mean? You're you, I'm me, what else is there?'

She shook her head. 'That's just it, I am not how I've been with you all these years. I've been downtrodden for so long you don't even know what I'm really like. I'm not even sure what I'm like myself anymore. What's more, I don't know what you're really like either. I just see your father in you, and I don't believe that is your real personality.'

They were both silent.

'The thing is, Anthony,' she explained slowly, 'I've allowed you to become more and more like your father and that has been a terrible mistake. I've decided to change that now, I am going to try and make amends. Will you let me?'

Nodding, he said, 'Yes, but what do you mean?'

'I'm going to try to be myself, my real self. I want to learn how to be a mother all over again. I'm going to try and help you find yourself too. Will you help me?'

'Of course, what are we going to do?'

'We're going to be honest with each other — about everything. To start with, I am going to tell you something about me that I am going to change. Then, I want to tell you something about you that I want you to change. Is it a deal?'

Anthony nodded. He was confused and slightly uneasy. This was not like his mother at all.

'I drink vodka, Anthony, a lot of it,' she said simply.

Anthony looked at her and said, 'I know, Mother.'

'You know?' she said, feeling rather stupid suddenly.

'It's all right though; I know you've been under a massive strain recently.'

She smiled and said, 'So, my first great disclosure is something of a damp squib.'

'Well, what's your second one?' he asked.

'OK, how about this. Your father, and of course my husband, is an arrogant, boastful man who thinks the world is inferior to him. Do you agree?'

'Totally, absolutely,' he answered.

'Where has that got him?' she asked.

'In prison.'

'Exactly, not a great success. So, do you agree that behaving like him is probably a bad idea?'

'Yes, I hate the way that he is; he is a bully himself really,' Anthony said.

'Yes, he is,' she said softly. 'But here's the crux: you have to make a special point of avoiding his characteristics if you can. So, when I asked you about what you might do at The Beeches what might be a good answer: one unlike something your father might say?'

Anthony thought for a minute. His face cleared, and he said, 'Well, how about: "I'm not sure; whatever they would find useful"?'

His mother smiled. 'Perfect. Do you think I'm terrible for saying such awful things about your father, and about you too?'

Anthony looked at his mother. He suddenly felt as though he were seeing her for the first time.

'No. On the contrary, I'm very grateful to you,' he said.

'The thing is, people react badly to certain behaviours. Sometimes it is hard to go against the grain, but maybe it's worth a try: what do you think?'

'Like you've just done?' he said.

'Exactly.'

'Well, I'll give it a go and see what happens. May I ask you for something?' he asked.

'Yes, I would like that,' she answered.

Anthony paused and then said, 'Will you teach me about drinking booze?'

She smiled and said, 'Why, what a thing to ask one's parent.'

'Well, I want to be like everyone else. The boys in my class are always talking about how many pints of lager they've drunk, and I haven't even had one in the whole of my life.'

She got up, a little unsteadily, turned to him and said, 'Come on, then — let's have our first lesson. Go and get Granny; she'll want to be involved too.'

***

When Gary's chat with Joe was over, he found Steve, Phil and Paul waiting for him outside the school gates.

'Well, was it a total waste of time?' Steve asked.

'I dunno. It was a bit weird,' Gary said.

'So, what's it all about?' Phil asked.

'There's some old bag at the care home down the road who's going to be a hundred and they're putting on a party for her,' Gary explained.

'What are you going to do other than cause trouble, get into fights, and get kicked out?' Phil asked, laughing.

Gary looked at him and scowled.

'I'll see. I'm not sure if I'll bother,' he said.

'What was the bloke like?' Steve wanted to know.

Gary considered his answer. 'Well, he was a bit funny. He made me feel sort of nervous. He was all right, just a bit funny, like he was setting traps for me or something. I guess he was OK. I wouldn't want to tangle with him though.'

'I think that about your dad: he's not someone to mess with,' said Paul.

'No, this bloke wasn't like Dad. He was intelligent, sort of wise or something, I dunno,' Gary said.

'Ha, I'd love to see you tell your dad that he wasn't intelligent,' Paul sniggered.

'Yeah, well your dad ain't Mastermind,' Gary said.

'He's all right; he's not totally thick,' said Paul.

'Bit like you then, except you're totally cretinous,' Steve chipped in.

'I'm going home; I'll see you tomorrow,' Gary said.

'Hang on, aren't we all going down the town for a bit?' Phil asked.

'You can. I'm off home,' Gary said starting to walk.

'We can see if we can get into the back of the newsagent again,' Paul suggested.

'What for? Just to nick a few bottles?' Gary asked. 'You lot really are pathetic.'

'Oooo, Mr Perfect has spoken,' Steve said.

Gary didn't want to hang around with them; he wanted to go home and tell his mum how he'd got on. He started walking quicker towards his house.

'Too good for us then, are you?' Phil called after him.

Gary ignored him.

'Oh, leave him alone. I think his brain got scrambled when Frank hit him,' Paul said.

Gary stopped. He turned around. He walked back to them.

'What did you say?'

'Nothing. It was nothing,' Paul said.

Gary looked at each of them in turn. Finally, he spoke to Steve, 'You told me I walked into a door.'

Steve shrugged and said, 'Yeah, well, you broke your nose, doesn't matter how, does it?'

Gary felt his heart start pounding. He didn't know how to deal with this. He could not let this go by without taking some action. He looked down at the ground. He was suddenly full of bitter rage. They saw his fists clenching.

'Why did you lie to me?' Gary's voice was quiet.

'Well, we all just thought it was better to leave it alone, you know; what was the point of saying what really happened?' Steve said, not really sure himself.

'We wanted you to come out of it all right,' Phil put in.

Gary was trying hard to work it out. Was the fiction better than the fact? If everyone knew he had been knocked down by that weirdo, then his reputation would be in tatters. But he would have to do something about Frank, there was no doubt about that.

He heaved a deep breath and said, 'Yeah, well, let's leave it as it is. I'm still off home,' and he walked off.

'How did it go, love?' asked his mum as he came into the kitchen, 'I've been wondering about it all afternoon.'

'Fine.'

'Will you work there then?' she said looking pleased.

'Yeah, if I want to.'

'How lovely, well done,' she said sounding so proud it made him feel terrible.

'Yeah, but I haven't decided if I will yet,' he said.

'Oh, go on, it'll be great.'

'How do you know, you don't know anything about it,' he said.

She looked hard into his eyes and said, 'It's better than anything your dad or brothers have ever done; just helping other people is a good thing.'

Gary sat down and put his elbows on the table. She looked at his downcast face and asked, 'What's wrong?'

'Steve and that lot just told me something — it really pissed me off.'

'What?'

'Don't tell Dad, will you?'.

'All right. If you don't want me to.'

'Well, there's this new kid at school. He's had something bad happen to him and we've all been told to leave him alone.'

'Yeah?'

'Well, Steve told me that I didn't walk into a door: this kid hit me.'

'Oh, well that's terrible,' she said. 'We should tell the school.'

Gary shook his head.

'Why not? That's an assault,' she said.

'Yeah, but the thing is, I was going to hit someone else when he did it,' Gary admitted.

'Who?' she asked, looking distressed now.

'This little shit who gets on my tits the whole time,' Gary said.

'Oh, Gary, what do you want to get involved in hitting people for?'

'Because that is exactly what we do in this fucking family,' he shot back at her.

She gasped at his venom.

'I'm sorry,' he cried out, putting his head in his hands.

She turned away from him.

'I won't tell your dad about this. But you must promise me, Gary, keep out of trouble. You'll get into big trouble soon if you're not careful. You'll be involved with the police and I couldn't bear that.'

She turned around to him, held his hand and pleaded, 'Promise me, Gary, keep out of trouble?'

He felt her frail hand in his. He looked up at her face. She looked small and fragile, really desperate.

'I promise,' he said.

***

The Walkers were eating their dinner. They sat around the table in silence. It was their custom to eat together and until the recent upset it had always been a happy sociable tradition for them.

Katy felt her heart beating quickly. As she'd walked home after her interview with Joe, she had rehearsed in her head how she wanted the conversation to go tonight. Now the time had come, and she wasn't sure if she could do it.

Finally, she cleared her throat and said, 'I've got something to say and it's important.'

The other three stopped eating and looked at her.

John Walker prepared himself. He had found the last two weeks to be total agony. He felt guilty, but also unfairly done to by Katy and by her birth mother. He was ready to stand his ground now and argue that he wasn't the villain he had been painted.

Anna's heart sank. She knew they had lost Katy. She was resigned to hearing her announcement that she was going to leave them. Anna knew that she and John had made a terrible mistake and she was ready to pay the price.

Susan looked quickly at Katy. Her sister did not look angry or ready for more battles. Instead she looked small and vulnerable. With her heart in her mouth she said, 'What is it, Katy?'

Katy drew in a deep breath and said, 'I've been a bitch. I have. I've been incredibly selfish. All I've thought about is me. I've been obsessed by me. It has been hard for me, but I'm not the only one suffering. I don't know what to feel about me, and what it all means for me. But when I think about what it means to you, I suddenly feel even worse.'

'Don't, Katy…' her mother said.

'Please, let me finish,' Katy insisted.

She looked at Susan and said, 'I suddenly thought today that you are just as affected as me.'

'Not really; it's not the same,' Susan said.

'It's not the same, but it's still terrible,' Katy said.

She looked at her mother and said, 'You lost your baby, Mum, I'm so sorry.'

Anna closed her eyes and bowed her head.

Katy looked at her father and said, 'You've been carrying all our hopes and this family secret all this time — it must have been weighing you down.'

John said nothing. He just looked at her.

Katy went on, 'Well, the point is, we're all a bit fucked up, aren't we? It's not just me is it?'

'That just about sums it up, but please don't swear like that,' John said.

'Oh Dad, this isn't the time for niceties. We're not a fucked-up family. We are a close, strong and loving family. I want that family back,' Katy said. She looked at them all, then sat back, empty.

There was a long silence.

Katy stood up suddenly and rushed out of the room saying, 'Now, let's leave it there — I'm going to explode if I don't get out now.'

They heard her rush up the stairs, crying.

'Please God, let her be back with us,' Anna said.

***

Janice Gordon looked at Frank. He was sitting in his chair staring out of the window. She wondered where his mind was. In one way, she hoped that he was just mindless, with no agonising thoughts about his father and brother, of their former life. She doubted it though. She could see the pain on his face. She wanted so much to be able to help him but didn't know how.

She looked towards the mantelpiece. She looked there hundreds of times every day. In the middle of it was a large photograph of the four of them. They were all smiling hugely, such elation in their expressions. It had been taken at one of Frank's meetings. There he was, looking tanned and strong and all-conquering. Next to him was Robbie, small and fair and utterly unathletic, but with a funny knowing smile. Flanking them were Andrew and herself, looking proud and as happy as it was possible to be. She looked at Andrew, he was wearing his red baseball cap, but it was slightly askew, Norman Wisdom-like. She smiled at her husband, but with such pain and loneliness it looked like a grimace.

'Frank, would you bring me over the picture on the mantelpiece please?' she asked.

Frank got up and brought it over. She looked at Andrew closely. Frank stood beside her as she looked at the photograph. She held it so that it was between them and they could share it.

Frank knelt down next to her. They stared at the picture as if it was alive; it captivated them.

'Do you know what I see?' she asked.

'No.'

'I see them. I see them, and I think they are trying to tell us something.'

'What?'

'I don't know,' she whispered. 'What are they saying to you?'

After a long silence Frank said, 'Calm down, let the power build in you, let it out when you're ready.'

'You're right. I get that too.'

'But I've lost my power: I'm weak, I feel so weak,' Frank said.

She took a gamble and said, 'Look at Dad's cap — he looks ridiculous.'

Frank looked. She sensed him concentrating on the cap. She said with absolute authority 'You're still strong, Frank. You are believe me and believe Dad, and Robbie too. We all know you too well to be wrong.'

***

It was seven thirty. Victoria was nervous about going out with Joe, but excited too. Although she had made a throwaway joke about his potential penchant for axes, she was still uncertain about him. Who was he? All she knew was that he worked at The Beeches.

When she walked into the lounge, she saw Joe sitting next to one of the residents. She was leaning against him, fast asleep. Joe seemed to be daydreaming, gazing into space. Victoria surreptitiously watched him. He was holding the old woman's hand in his; perhaps she was his mother?

There was very little activity in the lounge. The television was on, with one or two residents paying attention to it but the others were all dozing. She wondered, as she often had since her mother had moved here, at the shrinking horizon of a person's life once they hit 'old age'.

She walked slowly towards Joe. As his attention turned to her, she saw genuine pleasure in his face.

'How wonderful,' he said, 'I've been looking forward to seeing you.'

She smiled too. 'Well, your offer of a pie and a pint was utterly irresistible.'

He gently let go of his companion's hand and said quietly to her, 'Grace, will you excuse me?' She carried on snoring.

He stood up stretching. 'Where would you like to go? Your wish is my command.'

'Can we get out of the town do you think?' she answered.

'Sure. Your car or mine?'

'I'll drive,' she said without hesitation.

As they drove, they said little. She glanced at him now and then; he looked straight ahead.

'If you don't mind me saying, you're a very good driver,' he said, looking at her now.

She was pleased to get the compliment, but also felt a little patronised.

'Oh, and what makes you qualified to make such a judgement?' she asked.

He studied her face, perhaps checking to see how much she'd meant her challenge.

'Sorry. Thank you,' he said.

'For what?' she said, surprised.

'For putting me in my place: you must always do that.'

She felt a flash of guilt and said, 'Oh, I didn't mean to — I was just interested.'

'No, you must stick to your guns now. You were making a point, a good one: don't back down,' he said.

'You're right. I was making a point, but I didn't want you to feel you had to say sorry as a result of it.'

'We're going to do well, I think. What do you think?' he asked.

'Hmmm, by "well" what do you mean?'

'I mean that we shall get on well.'

'And your conclusion is based on what exactly?'

'On the basis of three things: one, you are extremely intelligent and insightful; two, you speak your mind, which I also like and, three, you are extremely attractive. All these things are excellent, plus they are all true of me too,' he said, with a straight face.

She laughed.

'Why are you laughing?' he asked.

'Well, you are so…' she paused, looking for the right word.

'Don't say, let me find the word for you,' he looked out of the window then said, 'Right?'

She laughed again and said, 'I'm not sure if you're arrogant or overly confident, or yes, maybe it's just that you are right.'

'You see, we are going to do well,' he said, looking pleased.

'Now, Mr Marshall, I must warn you that I am going to grill you and get answers to my questions,' she sounded serious.

'Oh good, me in the spotlight, my favourite subject,' he said.

They pulled into the gravel car park of a pub.

'Stay there,' he said and got out of the car and walked around to her door. He opened it for her; she got out.

'That's very chivalrous but completely ridiculous,' she said.

'Good, I didn't want to have to do it every time.'

They walked into the pub and sat down.

'So, should I get the drinks as I am the man, or would that be totally ridiculous?' he asked.

'Good question. I'm a woman; I'm in a pub which, although it is open to men and women equally, is still a bastion of male oppression of women and I would appear to be behaving inappropriately if I got the drinks. Plus, everyone would think you were a very poor male specimen if you allowed me to.'

'Ah, but should we maintain the status quo, or should we challenge it?' he asked.

'How about we go up to the bar together, I ask for my drink, you ask for yours, we both reach into our respective purses and wallets — I pull out a pound note, you pull out a pound note and I say, "I'll get it on expenses." We'll look as if we are business colleagues.'

'Hmmm, OK. Then I shall buy the next one and some food on my expenses?' he said.

'Yes — good one.'

They did just that. They sat down at a table and smiled at each other.

'I feel as if we've been in a scene from a television programme,' he said, 'maybe Coronation Street?'

'You should have asked for a pint of bitter not a glass of wine,' she pointed out.

'I don't like beer,' he answered. 'Anyway, how come you're drinking whisky? Surely as a headmistress you should be drinking a sweet sherry?'

'OK, so shall we just accept that we don't have to conform to any assumptions, either our own or society's?'

'Nice one. That suits me very well,' he answered. 'Never mind that — when are you going to start your interrogation?'

'Now. Why are you so keen to be interviewed: is it a double bluff?' she asked.

'Ah, you nearly trapped me. No, it's a rare triple.'

She ignored him and said, 'What do I need to know about you that would make me in any way anxious for my students?' she asked.

Joe was silent.

She looked at his face. His eyes drew her in; she couldn't resist their pull.

'Nothing. There is nothing about me that represents any risk to them, and I promise you that I am no risk to you either,' he said.

'Oh, I'm not worried about me,' she said.

He looked at her again. She felt herself floundering. She wanted to curse out loud — how did he make her feel so transparent?

'Next question: how come you work at The Beeches?' she asked.

'That's easy. I enjoy doing the things that I do there — gardening, talking, laughing,' he said.

'Well, maybe what I really meant is...' she started to say before he cut in,

'Listen, with me, always say what you really mean; you don't need to come at it obliquely.'

She nodded and said, 'Right, OK, I suppose I thought you might have a different job, judging by how you are, you know, what you're like. I don't know being a handyman at an old people's home isn't quite what I would have guessed; that's all.'

'Well, if you mean "why don't I have a better paid job?" That's easy: I have enough money not to worry about wages; I can just please myself.'

'I feel like I'm pulling teeth,' she said. 'How did you make your fortune?'

'My Godmother left me a mint.'

'Lucky you,' she said. 'Was she a fairy godmother or a real one?'

'Both, really, I suppose.'

'Do you have a wife, any children?'

'No wife, no children, no one locked in my attic either,' he said.

'It's weird. Every time I ask you what I think is a good question, one which will reveal something important I seem to get some knitted fog. What do you say to that?'

'You are looking at me as if I am a naughty boy sent before the beak,' he said.

'There you go again, wriggling.'

'OK, I admit it. I am a private person; I like to keep myself to myself.'

'Forever?' she asked.

'I don't know. I like the idea of getting to know someone so well that I can share everything, but I haven't had that experience so far, that's for sure. How about you? Have you ever had such a degree of trust in someone else that you feel able to share everything?'

She was silent for a long time then said, 'No.'

'Would you like to be able to?' he asked.

'Yes.'

'Thank you; thank you for being honest with me — more than I am with you,' he said.

'We mustn't get bogged down with too much navel gazing,' she said. 'Time for another drink, I think.'

'I'll get them. Expenses again?' he said.

When they drove home after more drinks and steak and chips Victoria felt as though she'd had more personal interaction with a man than she'd had for ages, possibly ever. Joe was unlike anyone else she'd ever met. He was funny, questioning, challenging, searching — without limit almost. He seemed to be able to talk about anything without awkwardness or guile, except about himself. She enjoyed talking to him immensely. Their two hours together had flown by and when she saw that it was nearly ten o'clock, she felt disappointed, not ready to end the evening at all.

In contrast to her failure to discover more about him, Joe had drawn from her all sorts of information about herself. She had told him about her life, from her early days before the war, her absent father and her love of John Christmas, her time in Dorset with Eleanor, her undergraduate years, and her life as a teacher. She had felt her face warm as she'd skipped over the last few days of her time as an evacuee and hoped that Joe hadn't noticed. As she'd mentioned Eleanor's name, though, she had felt a strange compulsion to tell Joe about what had happened. She'd resisted the temptation: she had promised Eleanor that she would never talk about it. Keen to avoid the memory, she said,

'You're very good at staying private.'

'Thank you, that's a nice compliment,' he answered.

'It's not one; it's an accusation.'

'Oh, you mustn't worry about me. Honestly, I've nothing to talk about; you're much more interesting.'

'Well, as my students would say, that's a load of shit.'

'No, look at you: you had an ambition and you've made it become a reality. Look at me — nothing to write home about.'

'Don't forget you're going to change the lives of four damaged people for the better,' she said, serious.

'Is that my homework, Miss?'

'Yes, it is. I believe you can do it. You won't let me down, will you?'

Joe was quiet for a long time. Finally, he held out his hand and she took it. As she felt his fingers tighten around hers, he said, 'It's a deal, but will you do something for me?'

She nodded, 'If I can.'

'I have something important to share with you. I want to tell you but now's not the right time. Can I hang on to it for a bit longer please?'

She looked at his face. For the first time, he didn't look as confident, and she felt stronger than she had done with him yet.

'Yes, but don't leave me dangling for too long, I might start to get suspicious,' she said.

'So, it's a deal?'

'It's a deal. I shall keep my end of the bargain: you needn't worry about that.'

Part 4

Transition

'Thank you very much for coming along. It's really good to see you again.'

Joe looked around the small office. There couldn't have been a less comfortable gathering of potential teammates. Gary was staring out of the window, savagely chewing gum. He had been the last to arrive and when he saw who else was there, his sullen expression had turned instantly to one of accusation. He looked at Joe and then Victoria with silent fury. As Gary had entered the room, Katy's expression had turned from uncertainty to disgust. Now she was looking sulky. Anthony had been dismayed at the arrival of Gary: he looked tense, very much on edge. Frank sat slumped in his chair; his eyes closed. Victoria's demeanour was the epitome of determination and authority.

Joe said to her, 'Before I start, would you like to kick us off?'

'Thank you, Joe. I am very pleased that you have all been chosen to participate in this wonderful opportunity. I'm sure you'll all make a great contribution.'

'Thank you,' said Joe. 'So, this is what it's all about. There is a lady living here who will be a hundred years old next month. Everyone wants her to have a great day — that includes the staff, the other residents, friends and family. Also, we think it's a good opportunity to tell the town about The Beeches: what it's like and what a great job it does for elderly people. So, to achieve what we want there's plenty of work to do. Do you have any thoughts about what needs doing?'

The four sat still. No one wanted to be the first to speak. Finally, Anthony said carefully, 'I suppose we need to tell people about it?'

'Great, yes, we need to do some publicity,' Joe said.

'The place will need to look at its best on the day,' Anthony said again.

Gary sighed loudly.

Joe ignored Gary and said, 'Yes, inside and out.'

Anthony was about to suggest something else when Joe said, 'Hang on, Anthony, let's see if anyone else has some ideas.'

'Well, we shall need to decide what we are going to do on the day,' Katy said.

'Yes, very good.'

He looked at Frank and Gary — nothing doing. He looked directly at Gary until he caught his eye. Joe raised his eyebrows.

Gary puffed out his cheeks, looked out of the window and said finally, 'Maybe we should ask the old lady what she wants.'

'At last! I wondered who was going to say that,' Victoria beamed. 'Well done, Gary.'

Gary tutted and looked out of the window again.

'All right. So, we have some good ideas already. I think we ought to speak to the boss about everything. I'll see if she's available,' Joe said and got up to leave.

'It's time for me to go too. Good luck with everything,' Victoria said.

They walked to the reception together.

'Thanks for coming,' Joe said, 'it was really important that you were there at the outset. I hope you'll keep being involved?'

'Of course. I hope I can come to the event too?' Victoria answered.

'Definitely. Consider yourself a guest of honour. When can I see you next?' he asked, as she pushed open the main door.

Victoria really wanted to go out with Joe again, but she didn't want to seem too keen and, in any event, she was still feeling apprehensive about any kind of intimacy. She paused, then said, 'I'm very busy right now — er, soon?'

Joe searched her face and said, 'Tonight?'

Victoria coloured.

'No, sorry, Victoria, I'm too pushy; tell me what you want,' he said.

'Tonight, yes, lovely,' she heard herself say.

Back in the office, the four teenagers sat in silence. It was Anthony who spoke first. He'd been trying to think of what to say to Gary. He knew that Frank and Katy were all right, better than that in fact. He liked Frank a lot; he wanted to help him if he could. Katy was amazing; he would do anything to get her to like him. It was Gary that was the problem for him. He knew he had to get on with him if this whole exercise was going to be a positive one.

'Listen, Gary, can we put our enmity behind us and start again?' he asked.

Gary snorted. 'Only if you use words that make fucking sense.'

'Anthony, you have to remember that Gary is half ape, half cave man,' Katy explained.

'Look, I didn't want to come, and I really don't want to be with you tossers,' Gary snapped back.

'No, listen. That was my fault,' Anthony said. 'Seriously, I know I'm annoying; let's start again.'

Frank shifted his position and rested his chin on his clenched fists.

Gary saw and suddenly felt anger building up in him. He was being pestered by Anthony, and next to him were the two people who had most recently totally humiliated him. He stood up suddenly and was about to walk to the door when it opened. Joe stood there. Next to him was a tiny old lady. She was about four feet tall, totally shrunken, her face a mass of deep wrinkles.

'Ah, Gary, great: would you hold the door for us, please,' Joe said.

Gary really wanted to get away but if he pushed past them, he would flatten the old lady. He did as he was asked.

'Here you go, Grace, you take this chair,' Joe said.

Very slowly she lowered herself into the chair. Joe sat beside her. He looked at Gary and said, 'Thanks, Gary, would you shut the door?'

Gary looked out towards freedom. He glanced back at the tiny woman. He could feel a flush of guilt and shame sweep over him as he thought back to his mother's voice urging him to come along. He shut the door and sat down. He saw Joe was looking at him; was he pleased?

The four young people looked at Grace. She looked back at them.

She said, 'Don't imagine that I am a frail little old lady. I am a very tough old woman, very tough indeed.' Her voice was faint and quavering, but she had no trouble commanding their attention.

Gary, Frank, Katy and Anthony shifted uncomfortably. Each of them had been feeling pity and wondering how they should or even could relate to someone so old. Now they realised their mistake.

'Thank you for helping me plan my party — I want it to be the best party ever,' she said.

'We're all really pleased to be part of it,' Joe said. 'We'll do our very best to make it go with a swing, won't we?'

Anthony said, 'Definitely.'

Grace looked at Gary and asked, 'Are you Gary?'

'Yeah.'

She looked at him for a long time and said, 'I've heard great things about you.'

'Me?'

'Oh yes, I'm looking forward to getting to know you.'

Gary looked to Joe for clarification.

'Grace knows about all of you,' he explained. 'She is our leader and we all have to account to her for who we are and what we do. Grace has allocated areas of responsibility for all of us.'

He took a piece of paper from his pocket and handed it to Grace. She looked at it closely and read, 'Gary, you are going to be responsible for press and publicity.'

'Me?'

'Yes, you,' she said.

He sat back and crossed his arms, feeling cornered.

'Hello, Katy, how are you?' Grace asked.

'I'm fine, thank you. How are you?' Katy answered.

'Very well. You're very pretty I must say,' Grace said.

'Oh, thank you,' Katy said, disarmed.

'I'd like you to be in charge of all entertainment,' Grace said.

'Great. Thank you. I'll do something special.'

Grace looked closely at Katy and nodded.

'Hello, Anthony, how are you?' Grace said.

'Very well, thank you.'

'I'd like you to be in charge of catering,' she said.

'Catering?' he repeated, a bit surprised and disappointed.

'Yes, I hope that's all right for you?' she said, looking at him.

'Well, I'm not very good at cooking,' he said.

'Don't worry, you'll be fine,' she said with certainty.

'OK, I'll try.'

'And you must be Frank?'

With great reluctance Frank opened his eyes and said, 'Hello, it's very nice to meet you.'

Grace said, 'I want you to be my right-hand man. Will you be that for me?'

'If that's really what you want?'

'It is, thank you, Frank.'

'I'm responsible for the gardens and odd jobs,' Joe said.

'Thank you all, you are very kind to me,' Grace said. 'Now, Frank, will you help me back to my room? It's time for me to have a snooze, I think.'

Frank got up and moved to her side. She grabbed his arm and pulled herself up; he dwarfed her.

They walked slowly to the door, Frank concentrating hard on helping her get there without her toppling over.

'Bye!' she called to them all and slowly left the room.

'I'm in room 21,' she said to Frank as they inched their way along the corridor.

They finally reached her door and they went in. She lowered herself into a rocking chair.

After a couple of minutes getting her breath back, she said, 'You'd never guess I used to be fit and lively.'

Frank didn't know what to say, so he stayed quiet.

'Sit down for a minute,' she said.

Frank sat on the edge of her bed.

'Joe told me about your loss, Frank. I'm very sorry.'

'Thanks.'

She gathered herself and said slowly, 'You may think I am an old dear and haven't much to offer you, Frank, and you'd be mostly right. I live in this place and have no real contact with your life. But, may I tell you something about me that I'd like to say, and it's about your situation?'

Frank looked at the very old woman. He had had many people tell him how he should be feeling, what he should do, what his father and brother would want, what they would say. He was sick of the advice and other people's desperation to make him feel better, to help them feel better. But this old lady was trying to help him, and he didn't want to offend her.

He said, 'Sure.'

She took in a deep breath and said in a whisper, 'I know it's not the same, but I lost my husband and little brother in 1899 in the Boer War. I miss them so much. I was only twenty-tree, my husband Jack was twenty-six and my brother Julian was twenty-two.'

She paused, caught her breath, and continued, 'It's not the same for you, I know. Your loss was unexpected; I was at least prepared for it a little. I felt angry, guilty, punished, scared, helpless, lonely, but mostly an overwhelming sense of sadness. I still do and it's three quarters of a century ago. Can you believe that? Can you, Frank?'

'Yes, I can,' Frank said.

'What can you do to help me with my loss, Frank?' she asked.

'I don't know; nothing probably,' he said.

'There is. Will you share it with me?' she asked.

'What?' he asked.

'Will you listen to me talk about them? I realise that it might be a bit dull, but you'd be helping me, you know; you'd help me bring them back a bit,' she said.

'Well, if you want to tell me about them, then I'd listen,' Frank said.

'Thank you. Can we do that next time you're here?' she asked.

'Yes, of course.'

He waited for further instructions from her. But after her effort she now seemed exhausted.

'Bye then,' he said and got up to go.

At the door he heard her thin voice, 'Thank you, Frank, I shall look for some photos of them for you. Will you bring some of your dear father and brother for me?'

'I will,' he said and went out.

Joe said, 'Welcome back, Frank. We've been thinking through our various jobs. I think that now I shall just take you all on a tour of the place so that you can meet people and get familiar with the venue.'

***

After their tour and introductions to staff and residents it was time to go home.

Joe thanked them again for coming and said, 'So, three thirty again tomorrow — is that OK?'

They agreed, with varying levels of enthusiasm.

As soon as he was outside, Gary moved away from the others and lit up a cigarette. Joe followed him.

'Have you got five minutes, Gary?' he asked.

Gary inhaled deeply from his Number 6 and said, 'Suppose so.'

'Let's go and sit in the garden,' Joe suggested.

They sat on either end of a bench and looked at the tree-lined lawns.

Gary felt uncomfortable. He was struggling to understand this bloke. He was so different to anyone else he'd ever met. What unsettled him most was the way he didn't say anything. Gary had grown up with men who just said what came into their heads; they didn't sit and stare like Joe did. He glanced at Joe now — he seemed to be just staring into space. Gary looked away again. The silence was getting to him. He didn't know what was expected — he was sure something was though. He took one last drag of his cigarette and threw the butt into the bushes.

'What?' Gary said.

Joe said, 'Thanks for making the effort to come along today. I'm sure it took a lot of strength to even contemplate it, never mind turn up.'

Gary turned to look at him. Joe's eyes were on him, knowing. Gary looked quickly away.

'The others are going to need you, Gary; especially Anthony I think.'

Gary said in a rush, 'I don't know what I'm doing here. I can't do anything; I can't do publicity, and I certainly am not going to help Anthony Alexander, no way.'

'Why not?'

'Why not what?'

'Why not any of it,' Joe said.

'Coz, well, I'm rubbish at school, and I don't know, and coz that little shit gets on my nerves, that's it.'

'What's wrong with Anthony?'

'He talks like a posh prat and he makes me feel stupid,' Gary said without thinking.

'But you're not stupid, are you?'

'No. Well, I dunno; maybe I am.'

Joe was silent again. Gary wanted to go now. There was something about Joe that made him blurt stuff out.

'Anthony is clever, but I think he looks up to you; in fact, he probably wants to be like you,' Joe said.

'Me?'

'Yes,'

'Why?'

'Maybe because you've got what he'd like?'

Gary snorted, 'Like what?'

'Hmmm, well, probably because you're big, hard, drink beer, smoke fags, wear modern clothes, and you're intelligent too.'

Gary didn't know what to say.

Joe went on, 'All I'm saying is that if you stay involved in this party thing you can make a very big difference to how it all goes; everyone will benefit from what you bring — much more than you realise. As I say, I think Anthony will particularly like working with you. I know that I will.'

No one had spoken to Gary like this before. Although he was embarrassed, Joe's words had given him great pleasure. He looked at Joe again: he looked strong and confident, but he also seemed incredibly kind. Gary swallowed.

'I'd better go,' he said.

'Me too. Thanks for talking, Gary, I appreciate it.'

'I'll start my article for the paper,' Gary said and got up.

'I look forward to reading it — and don't forget your essay: I want to read that too.'

Gary shambled back to his house. He used to like going home, being with his dad and brothers. He liked the feeling of being an adult with the adults he'd grown up respecting and admiring. Nowadays it felt different. He found himself much more often in the kitchen than the living room, talking to his mother — about what? He wasn't sure he could quite say what they talked about. He knew it wasn't football or birds, or booze; whatever they talked about, he liked it.

When he got home that day, everyone was in, including Tina. She and Kev were sitting at the bottom of the stairs with their arms wrapped around each other, snogging. Tina broke away to look at him. Her lips were swollen; she looked sexy.

She said, 'Hello, Gary, you're looking nice.'

'No, he isn't. He looks like the same useless turd he always does,' Kev said, and pulled her face back into his.

Gary walked past them and into the kitchen. He really wanted to do to Tina what Kev was doing.

'Hello, dear, how was your first day at work?' his mum asked.

'OK, I suppose. We didn't do much,' he answered.

'Wipe any arses?' his father asked him.

'Of course not,' Gary said, irritated.

'Why's that then? Do you need extensive training for that? I'd have thought you'd be a natural at it.'

'Don't listen to him, Gary. Tell us what you did do,' his mum encouraged.

'It doesn't matter,' Gary said and turned around back into the hall.

He pushed past the necking couple. Kev had his hand up Tina's T-shirt. 'Get off, Kev, not in front of Gary,' she said, slapping his hand away.

He went up to his room and lay on his bed. He was fizzing with unused energy. He felt like a fight more than anything. Right now, he wanted to beat the shit out of his brother, and his father too. He wondered how he could go from admiring them to hating them so quickly. He wanted to fuck Tina too. Jesus, he wanted that. Usually he would call up Steve and go out with him and the others. Thinking about them made him feel like beating them up too. He felt his fury rising, he had to get out of this dump.

He jumped down the stairs, over Kev and Tina, and left the house, slamming the front door. He started running, down the street to the old industrial estate. He hadn't run properly for years. He never made any effort in PE anymore. Now, the strain of running hard was beginning to tell on his heart and lungs. He kept going though. He ran along the long straight road that went through the middle of a variety of factories, one of which was where his father worked. He'd got his second wind now and he was enjoying the feel of effort and speed. He'd forgotten he could run fast: it felt good.

He reached the far end of the service road and was about to turn back when he saw a bus coming. He carried on running to the nearby stop and stuck out his hand.

Gasping he said, 'Edgware Station,' and handed over some change. He got off at the station and went through the barrier without a ticket and got on the first tube out. He was feeling a million times better than before — strong and confident. He'd managed to escape.

***

Katy, Frank and Anthony walked out of the grounds of The Beeches together. They were silent, uneasy with each other.

Anthony broke the silence and said, 'I don't know about you, but I definitely drew the short straw. I haven't got a clue about catering; I don't know why I got that job. I suppose Joe knows what he's doing but I'm sure I won't be much use.'

'I think he's really cool,' said Katy. 'There's something unusual about him, don't you think?'

'Definitely,' said Anthony. 'What do you think, Frank?'

Frank had been hoping to stay out of the conversation, but he knew now that, when Anthony was around, he'd be brought in whether he liked it or not.

He said, 'Yeah, he's all right.'

'Listen, I know you said that Gary hit his head on the door the other day, but I just wanted to say that I thought it was brilliant what you did to him,' Katy said, looking directly at Frank for the first time.

Frank shrank. He said nothing.

'Yes, it was amazing — just what I wanted to do but you beat me to it,' Anthony said.

'Anthony, you're such a prat,' Katy said. 'As if you could have done that.'

Anthony looked disappointed but said, 'Well, maybe I couldn't have done it, but I definitely wanted to.'

'Me too,' Katy said.

Frank surprised them, 'It was awful. It was the last thing I wanted: I hate violence.'

'Why?' Katy asked.

Frank's voice was suddenly harsh, 'Because people get hurt; they get hurt badly and it always ends badly.'

Katy took in Frank. He didn't look like someone who got into fights; she wondered what made him feel so strongly. But she had seen at first-hand what damage he could do and guessed that maybe he'd had some trouble in the past.

'Have you got into trouble before, then?' Anthony asked, thinking along similar lines.

'Leave it,' Frank said, wishing he'd stayed quiet.

Anthony said, 'I've had some trouble in the past, but I've always been on the wrong end of it.'

'I'm not surprised,' Katy said.

'Why?' he asked.

'I don't know if you mean to, but you do wind people up a bit,' she answered.

'I definitely don't mean to, and I'm trying to change how I come across. It's just that I tend to speak my mind and that seems to upset people,' he said.

'Well, plus you've got that stupid posh accent,' she said.

'I can't help that.'

'Yeah, but if you can tone it down a bit that would definitely help.'

'All right, I'll try. Maybe I should swear a bit, smoke cigarettes and act stupid?' he suggested.

'Give it a go. You never know.'

'I'm going to try and get on with Gary, even though he's so awful,' he said.

'Why? He's been so horrible to you!'

'Well, mainly because I want to do my best for Joe and Grace, and because I feel a bit sorry for him.'

'Sorry? For that useless thug?' Katy said.

'Well yes; there's something a bit pathetic about him, don't you think?' Anthony said.

'Definitely: he's such a loser.'

'I think there's something wrong with him; it's as if he's got to be fighting something all the time,' Anthony said.

'All I know is that he's a total shit and he gets on my nerves,' she said.

'I agree with Anthony,' Frank said out of the blue.

The other two looked at him.

'For Grace's sake we should get on with him,' he said.

'What was she like, Frank?' Anthony asked.

'Fine. She's fine,' Frank answered.

'She's definitely got her faculties,' Anthony observed.

'The trouble with Gary is that he's always surrounded by that bunch of cretins,' Katy said. 'They really are pathetic, thick as shit and twice as ugly.'

She and Anthony laughed, and even Frank smiled.

They carried on walking. They were an odd trio: Frank by far the tallest but the quietest, and hunched, trying to be invisible; Katy exuberant and twirling around every now and then, looking like a grown-up toddler at a children's party; Anthony, energetic, bright, chatty.

'I'm really sorry about whatever has happened to you, Frank,' Anthony said. He'd wanted to say something for a while but wasn't sure whether to broach the subject.

'Yeah, I'm really sorry, Frank,' Katy said.

'Thanks,' Frank mumbled.

'Anything we can do to help?' Anthony asked. He really wanted to help Frank; he felt he owed him so much already.

'No. Thanks, though.'

'You'll let us know, though, won't you?' Anthony said.

Frank nodded. He could feel tears beginning to form; he didn't want them to see him cry.

'Have you got any brothers or sisters?' Katy asked.

Frank was silent. Katy and Anthony looked at him. He'd stopped walking and was leaning into a privet hedge, his face in his hands.

Dismayed, Katy cried, 'I'm so sorry, Frank. I didn't mean to upset you — please forgive me.'

She walked back to him and took his hand. As she did, she saw his face was wet with tears.

Katy was crying now, 'Oh Frank, I'm so sorry. I'm such a thoughtless cow.'

Anthony edged up to Frank's other side and, not knowing what to do, patted his shoulder.

Frank squeezed his eyes tight shut and drew in a huge shuddering breath. He pressed his back into the hedge and slid down to sit on the foot-high brick wall at its base. He sank his head into his hands again. The other two sat either side of him, close.

They heard his muffled voice say through his sobs, 'My dad and little brother were killed in a car crash a few months ago.'

'You poor thing,' said Katy, 'I'm so sorry.'

'That's terrible,' said Anthony.

They sat like that for several minutes, none of them knowing what to do or say. Finally, Frank drew himself up and wiping his face with his hands he said, 'Sorry about that, sometimes I can't help losing it.'

'I could do with a drink,' Anthony said, hoping that he sounded grown up.

'Me too, what shall we do?' Katy asked.

'You can come to my home: my mother has been teaching me to drink,' Anthony said.

'Wow, what a great mum,' Katy said. 'I have to drink in secret.'

'We've got lager, port and vodka in the house,' Anthony said. 'Come on, let's go.'

'Great — although I have a bad relationship with vodka,' Katy said.

They got to their feet, shepherding Frank as they walked purposefully to Anthony's house.

As Anthony went through the front door he called to his mother, 'I've brought a couple of friends around for a drink.'

Margaret Alexander rose from her chair, suddenly feeling very drunk. It didn't matter that Anthony saw her like this, but strangers were another matter. She looked in the mirror in the living room and saw her blurry face. She touched her hair into some kind of shape and turned to face the door as it opened. She saw her son smiling at her; he looked so happy to have his friends with him. Then came a very pretty girl with long, chestnut hair, followed by a huge unkempt boy who looked worse than she felt.

'Do come in,' she said, 'sit down and make yourselves comfortable.'

'This is Katy, and this is Frank, my colleagues at The Beeches,' Anthony said.

'It's very nice to meet you,' his mother said.

Anthony said, 'Any chance of a drink, Mater? I thought a can of lager or a glass of port or something might be nice.'

His mother didn't really want visitors right now. She said, 'Oh, well, I'm not sure.'

'Don't worry, just a snifter,' Anthony encouraged.

'We shan't stay long, Mrs Alexander; we thought it would be nice just to toast the success of the project,' Katy explained.

'Exactly,' said Anthony.

'All right, that's a good idea. I shall join you if you don't mind,' Margaret said. 'Is there someone missing?'

'Yes, can you believe it: my nemesis, Gary Abbott,' Anthony answered.

'Not that awful bully?' she said.

'That's him,' Katy said.

'He's involved in the party for the old lady?' Margaret asked incredulous.

'I know it's unbelievable,' Anthony said, 'but we've decided to give him a second chance.'

Anthony had given a can of lager each to Katy and Frank and was opening one himself. Margaret helped herself to a very small vodka: she didn't want them to get the wrong idea.

'Where's Granny?' Anthony asked.

'She's playing bridge tonight; she'll be back later.'

'Cheers!' said Katy and they clinked their cans and glass together.

Anthony chatted cheerfully as they drank their drinks. Katy and Margaret Alexander joined in; Frank was quiet. They had another can each. Anthony said, 'Shall we get some fish and chips?'

'Good idea,' said his mother.

'I'd like to go home soon; my mums on her own,' Frank said.

'Do you have to?' Anthony asked.

Katy shot him a look, and he coloured and said, 'Of course, Frank, but you can ring her if you like and see if you can stay a bit longer.'

'I don't like to leave her for too long,' Frank said.

'Well, ring her anyway,' Anthony pressed.

Frank did. Janice was delighted to hear that he was with some new friends and told him to stay. 'As long as you want to, of course,' she said.

'How about you, Katy, can you stay?' Anthony asked, hoping very much that she could and would.

'I can stay out any time,' she said, sounding defiant.

'I'd like you to ring your parents though, Katy.' Margaret said.

Katy rang home. Susan answered.

'Where are you?' Susan asked.

'At Anthony's flat,' she whispered. The telephone was in the hall, but she didn't want anyone to overhear.

'Anthony who?' Susan asked.

'Anthony Alexander, of course.'

'What?'

'He's very friendly and we're having a good laugh,' Katy said.

'Who's we?'

'Frank too.'

'Frank?'

'He's such a poor, sad boy,' Katy whispered.

'Well, how long are you going to be?' Susan asked.

'We're about to have fish and chips. Maybe another drink?'

'I'm worried about you, Katy; I don't like it when you go out and get drunk.'

'Anthony's mum's here — although she's already blotto,' giggled Katy.

'Right, I'm coming over to make sure you're all right. What's the address?'

Ten minutes later Susan arrived. She took in the scene quickly. Katy, Anthony and Frank were already a bit drunk; so was Mrs Alexander. They all seemed to be having a great time.

'It's very nice of you to come, Susan,' Anthony said, showing her to a seat and passing her a can of lager.

Katy explained the odd combination of personnel involved in their Beeches project and ended with, 'Who do you think is the fourth member of this crack squad of operatives?'

Susan shook her head.

'Gary Fucking Knobhead Abbott!' Katy screeched. She suddenly remembered herself and, turning to Mrs Alexander, said, 'I am so sorry; my language is terrible.'

'Don't worry, Katy,' Anthony said laughing. 'We're always swearing, aren't we, Mother?'

This was news to his mother, but she stayed quiet. She was having a wonderful time. She felt like swearing herself. She hadn't had such fun since before she was married. She was so happy for Anthony too.

'Gary? No — you're joking!' Susan said.

'I know, talk about square pegs,' Katy said.

They carried on in raucous fashion, their tiddly laughter sounding up and down the street as they went for their fish and chips.

Anthony was having the best time of his life. He'd always wanted to have some friends around to have fun with, and here he had three people, all of whom wanted to be here with him.

Frank too was feeling better than he had for months. His loss of control earlier on had been terrible but now he felt much better, aided by beer and the kindness of his new friends.

Katy hadn't thought about her parents, her new unexpected parent, or any family matter at all. Susan being here was cool too. She loved having her sister around: she gave her strength and confidence.

'Have you got any records, Anthony?' Katy asked.

'Of course, we have tons of them. What do you want to hear, Mozart, Beethoven, Strauss?' he answered getting up.

'Strauss?' Katy scoffed 'Can't you do better than that?'

'Oh, like what?' he answered, deflated.

'They're wonderful, of course, Anthony,' said Susan kindly, 'but I think Katy meant anything a little more modern?'

'Not really, have we, Mother?' he asked.

Margaret Alexander shook her head sadly and said, 'No, I'm sorry. We need to do something about that.'

'Don't worry. Have you got a radio?' Katy asked.

'Yes, it's in the kitchen; I'll get it,' said Anthony.

Katy fiddled with the tuning knob and soon they heard Brotherhood of Man singing 'Save all your kisses for me'.

Katy stood up and started singing and dancing along to the music. The others whistled and clapped.

After her performance, Katy sat down and knocked back her can of lager.

'You're amazing, Katy,' Anthony said.

'You are, Katy — what a talent,' Margaret agreed.

'It's nothing. We're all good at something,' Katy said.

'What are you good at, Frank?' Anthony said.

They all looked at him. He had been more animated than usual, and he'd drunk more than anyone else. Now, he felt uncomfortable in the glare of attention and said, 'Nothing, I'm just ordinary.'

'You're brilliant at punching,' Katy said.

Frank shook his head. He didn't like this conversation. Susan, less drunk than the others, noticed and said, 'How about you, Anthony, what's your special talent?'

Anthony thought; he wasn't sure what to say. He was good at stealing, holding guns to people's heads, gaining revenge, and he was clever too. He didn't want to say any of that so instead said sadly, 'I'm good at getting bullied.'

'Not any more you're not, not now you've got your own gang,' Katy said, rather more drunkenly than she'd meant.

Anthony's face flushed with happiness. He smiled broadly. He couldn't believe how much his life had turned around, in just a few days.

Here he was with his own group of friends, and with his mother, all getting drunk and having fun.

'Time for more booze,' he said.

'What is the time?' his mother asked.

'Nearly nine thirty,' said Susan, conscious of it getting late and her sister getting drunk.

'Let's nip down to the off-license and get some more cans,' said Katy.

'They won't serve me,' said Anthony. 'I've tried, and they just laugh out loud.'

'They'll serve me, and they'll definitely serve Frank,' said Katy. 'Come on.'

They pooled their change.

'Don't forget me,' said Margaret putting in a pound note.

'Great, let's go,' Katy said, and they all followed, leaving Mrs Alexander smiling in her chair.

Anthony popped his head back into the room and said, 'Thank you, Mother, we're having a lovely evening.'

She smiled at him and said, 'Hang on to them, Anthony. I think they'll look out for you.'

***

Gary sat on the top deck of the bus and reflected on his evening. He'd been to London a couple of times before, with Steve and the others. Then, he'd been primarily concerned with making a lot of noise, attempting to chat up girls, and getting drunk. This time, on his own, it had been different.

After the hour's journey into central London he had just wandered around, not really sure where he was or where he was going. He walked up and down Oxford Street and Regent Street, looking in at the shop windows, excited by the bright lights and the crowds all around him. He felt liberated, away from his drab, stupid and ugly home and town: able to go anywhere, be anyone.

He loved the novelty of everything — it was all so different. He had seen more pretty girls in one evening than in the whole of his life. He admired the look of the professional men in suits; they seemed clever, in control. He stared at dossers in doorways, feeling their cold and hopeless acceptance. Music had been everywhere, drifting out of shops, blaring from pubs, a penny whistle on a street corner, a busking guitar. He had stopped outside a Chinese restaurant and wondered if he dared go in: what would he order? How would he eat it? Would they understand English? He shook his head and walked on, choosing the safety of a Wimpy Bar instead. It was the first time he'd ever gone into a restaurant on his own. He felt cool and adult. He listened in to the voices around him. Although he was on his own and everyone else was in a group, he felt at ease. He was totally absorbed by everything and everyone around him: he loved it. He also felt free for the first time in his life. He was not expected to be anyone or do anything. He could do what he liked and right now all he wanted was to be himself, his new self.

When he left the Wimpy Bar, the big shops were closed but the streets were still exciting. Buses and taxis sped past, carrying their passengers... where? He wondered at the exciting lives of all these people, their everyday existence so full of adventure, excitement and variety.

He jumped on a bus and went upstairs. Pressing his face against the window he imagined what it must be like to live here, where you never saw the same person twice, where it was possible to be who you wanted to be. He saw young people everywhere, but not like the ones he knew these were beautiful, fashionably dressed, cool; they looked like pop stars to him. He felt a powerful craving to be like them, part of their lives.

As the bus drew away from a stop, he heard feet pounding up to the top deck. He looked over to the steps and saw a group of black kids. They were loud, confident; they had a breezy nonchalance that made Gary feel uneasy. They sat around him at the back. He felt suddenly out of place and intensely conscious of his whiteness. He didn't like being the odd one out, the minority; he felt conspicuous and vulnerable.

In his school there were just two black kids, Jacob and Joshua. They were regularly taunted and abused. Gary was like everyone else he knew at school: he treated the black kids like shit. It occurred to Gary suddenly that Jacob and Joshua laughed at the treatment they got because they had no choice. Gary felt a hot flush of shame as he remembered how he treated them, what he called them.

The black kids sitting around him now were not like Jacob and Joshua. These weren't malleable smiling boys: they had an edge to them; they were threatening. Gary wanted to be away from here — and quickly — before he drew attention to himself.

He was about to get up and go downstairs but suddenly felt nervous. If he got up, they would start on him; maybe they'd call him names or worse. He watched them out of the corner of his eye, waiting for the right moment to go. He saw one of them rolling a cigarette, he realised from its size that it must be a joint. He hadn't seen one before, although he knew that some of the lads who had left school last year smoked blow. He watched surreptitiously as the large cigarette was manufactured and lighted. He smelled the herby scent of the weed and saw the joint being handed around. He was fascinated.

The group were suddenly aware of Gary's interest. He saw them all look hard in his direction, challenging him.

'You want some?' said one of them, sounding menacing.

Misunderstanding, Gary said quickly, 'Er, no, sorry,' and looked away.

'No, I mean do you want to try some?'

Gary felt a rush of relief. He'd thought he was going to get a kicking.

'Sure… yeah, why not?' Gary answered. He did want to try some; he was definitely up for new experiences tonight.

The enormous joint was passed over to him. He felt a bit nervous — of the situation and of his first experience of drugs — but he smiled and took it and did as they had done: dragged the smoke deep into his lungs. He handed it on.

'Good?' his new friend asked.

'Great,' Gary said.

There was an animated chorus of approval and he felt a heavy hand slap him on his back. He smiled back at the group.

Two hours later, as the bus back from the tube station took him home, he thought back to the brilliant few minutes he had had in the impromptu party. He had found himself grinning inanely with the gang, laughing at absolutely nothing and feeling incredibly close to his new friends. He marvelled at how quickly he had moved from wanting to get away from imminent danger to being sad at leaving them. He'd felt slaps on his back as he left the bus; they'd opened the window and shouted cheerful goodbyes to him.

Now, staring out of the window, he saw the familiar rows of drab council houses and empty streets: the most boring town in the world. Gary's heart sank.

As the bus turned into the High Street, Gary walked down the steps and got ready to jump off. The bus drew up on the corner by the Red Lion. As he got off, he thought he might look into the pub to see if his father or brothers were in there; then he checked himself and thought better of it. The last thing he wanted now, he realised with a jolt, was to spend any time with them. He felt disgust at their brutish manners and coarse ignorant ways. Instead he walked slowly towards his house, hands buried in his pockets, his feet dragging.

He came to the parade of shops that comprised the chip shop, the Golden Bengali, the off-licence and the Kwikfix Exhaust Centre. As he approached the Indian restaurant, a young man came out of the side entrance with a bag of rubbish. He hoisted it into the large metal bin on the side of the pavement. As he did so, three blokes came out of the chip shop.

One said, 'That's the right place for the shit you serve, Abdul.'

One of the others, a bloke in a black leather jacket, laughed and said, 'Here, have some proper English food not that Paki crap you eat.'

With that, he threw a handful of chips at the young Asian man. His friend followed suit.

The young man looked away and was about to turn back when the first youth said, 'Aren't you forgetting your manners? You come over here and make money from serving up shit and you can't even say thank you for our generosity.'

Gary watched the expression on the young man's face turn from fear to anger, then it slipped back to one of humble indifference. The louts were intent on making their point. They walked up to him and stood in front of him. Black leather jacket took more chips and thrust them into his face and said, 'Thank you, sir, is all you need to say.'

Gary was sure how this was going to end. He knew because he had seen his father behave like this all his life. He knew because it was how he himself behaved. The three drunk guys would have to end up either making the young man run away or they would have to give him a beating. They had forced themselves into it.

Before he knew what, he was doing, he said, 'Come on, lads, leave it out.'

All four turned to him.

'What the fuck's it got to do with you?' asked one.

'It's not worth it, mate, just let him get back to his work,' Gary said in a matter of fact voice.

The three blokes looked at Gary. He was like them, and they even vaguely recognised him.

'Aren't you Kev Abbott's brother?' one asked.

'Yeah, what about it?'

'Well, Kev can't stand these stinking fucking wogs either.'

'What's that got to do with anything?' Gary asked.

'You're not going to let that fucking Paki treat me like shit, are you?'

'That's not what I saw,' Gary said.

They stared at him. He had suddenly become their target, the Asian man forgotten.

Black jacket picked up a chip from his soggy bag of grease, threw it at Gary's face and said, 'You can show our little coloured friend what good manners are like, you say "thank you, sir".'

Gary swallowed and clenched his fists. He tried one more time, 'Let's just go home,' he said.

'Good idea, once you've said thank you for our kindness.'

'Well that's not going to happen,' Gary said and prepared himself.

***

238

As they came out of the off-licence, Katy, Susan, Anthony and Frank saw a little knot of youths gathered outside the chip shop. They took in the scene — Gary was there facing three angry-looking young men. Slightly behind Gary was a young Asian man.

They heard one of the youths say, 'Why do you want to get a kicking for a piece of Paki shit?'

Gary said nothing. This was not going to work out well. He was outnumbered but, more importantly, these blokes were pissed up and would have no inhibition, nor would they be able to stop punching or kicking once they'd started. He'd been in a similar position before, but then he'd been doing the kicking.

Frank put down the bag of lagers. He felt the familiar conflicting emotions — the exhilaration of letting go his energy, the shame he knew he'd feel afterwards.

Katy was in a state of conflict too, she hated Gary so much she was looking forward to seeing him get a beating. But there was something horrific about the bloody sound of fists on flesh. Plus, unbelievably, Gary seemed to be defending the young man.

Susan was scared. She had had enough of fury and hurt. She gripped Katy's arm to pull her away.

Anthony wasn't feeling any of this. His mind had gone into overdrive. Something in the situation had reminded him of himself, the victim of people's intimidation. He weighed up everything in a flash and walked straight up to the young Asian man and said,

'Hello, Sadiq, how are you?'

Everyone gaped, Sadiq in particular.

Katy took Anthony's lead and walked into the middle of the group and said, 'Hi Gary, we wondered where you'd got to.'

Suddenly the fray was just a group of people, the moment had gone, and the violence had evaporated as quickly as it had started.

The three thugs ambled away, laughing. One of them looked over his shoulder at Gary and nodded — what was it, a warning?

'How do you know him, Anthony?' Katy asked.

'Who, Sadiq? I've never met him in my life before.' Anthony laughed.

'My name is not Sadiq, but I think it might be from now on,' the young man said.

'You, brilliant bull-shitter, Anthony,' Katy said. 'You had me fooled.'

Anthony couldn't stop grinning.

'Thank you for your help,' the young man said to him, but then turned to Gary and said, 'especially you.'

'What happened anyway?' Katy asked.

'He stopped those men from attacking me,' "Sadiq" said. 'He was very brave.'

They all looked at Gary. He avoided their eyes. He had been ready to fight but now the adrenalin had washed away he was feeling shaky and embarrassed too.

'It wasn't anything,' he mumbled.

'Come on, let's go home and drink our drinks,' Anthony said. 'Do you want to come, Gary?'

Gary looked at them. They looked at him. He wanted to be with people right now, decent people.

He said, 'All right,' and they moved off together, sticking close.

***

'How on earth are we going to get them to cooperate with each other, or better still create a happy environment for Grace?' Victoria asked Joe.

They were driving back from a meal out in a country pub several miles out of town. Joe was driving this time.

'I honestly think that simply being out of their normal and familiar settings and being thrown together will help them all to just get on with it,' he said.

She said, 'I'd like to think you're right, but they are all so different, and they all bring with them such a load of baggage.'

'I suspect that the more we keep out of the way the better it will be,' he said. 'Attempting to guide a load of frogs back into a bucket never works.'

Victoria nodded. He was right. She so wanted everything to work out well. She felt compelled to make it work, no matter what.

'You're a very good driver,' she said.

'Thank you. Now, here's a funny thing. I take the compliment without feeling patronised; why is that?'

'Because you're a man and you expect to be complimented?'

'Well if that is true then I could just as easily say that you felt patronised because you are a woman and you expect to be patronised, even when the comment is genuine,' he pointed out.

She pondered on this then said, 'Ah, but when you've been patronised enough times by men, you can't help but be sensitive about it.'

'Of course, that's true, but if you're a man and you get a compliment a few times then you get used to that too,' he said.

'So, what's your point?' she asked.

'Well, I think my point is that if I think a woman is a good driver, or good at anything, then I think I should be able to say so without fearing that I am offending that woman,' he said. 'After all, I don't think I should be held accountable for the behaviour of all men towards all women, should I?'

'No, but I think that perhaps you should be aware of the fact that all women have been oppressed by all men for a very long time and therefore have a right to be sensitive on such matters.'

'Aware of, yes, but am I culpable? Anyway, should I really say... I think you are an excellent driver, oh, by the way, women have been oppressed by men for centuries but despite that I am different, and I like your right hand turns in particular?'

She laughed and said, 'You poor, poor, man, how miserable we cruel women make your life.'

'Thank you, I rest my case.'

'Just as well. It was sounding a little tired.'

They were silent.

He said, 'Conscious of course that by saying that you are a smart, witty, attractive woman I am guilty of continuing to perpetuate crimes against womanhood, I wilfully do so and accept whatever sentence you judge is appropriate.'

'You shall have a suspended sentence, pending a sufficient amount of good behaviour for an unspecified time.'

'Oh no, I hate good behaviour,' he protested.

Victoria had had a lovely evening. When she'd rung the Beeches a few hours after leaving Joe, he had suggested they go out for a meal. She had changed after work and she had tried to look her best. As she brushed her hair, she had thought that she still looked like an attractive woman, not as pretty as in years gone by, but not bad.

Part of her felt anxious still. She was enjoying being with a man, a man who made her think, who challenged her and who commanded her respect. She felt worried, though, that maybe she was getting into another situation where she might lose her dignity or, worse still, be flattened by disappointment. But she couldn't help herself: she wanted more from Joe. She really did. She was attracted to him and was being increasingly drawn to him. She watched his hands on the steering wheel. She speculated what they would feel like on her body, gentle or rough, urgent or hesitant. She wondered what his body would feel like pressed against hers.

'What are you thinking?' he asked.

She blushed. 'Oh, nothing really; just thinking back over past times.'

'Do you want to share them?'

'I would like to, but some things are very hard to say out loud,' she said.

'I know. I've got some of those.'

'Yes, that's a point: you said you wanted to talk about something. Something with which you needed my help?'

'OK, how about we do a deal. If I show you mine, will you show me yours?'

'All right, but how can we measure the nature of our revelations? You might tell me about a deep and meaningful experience, but I'll just tell you my favourite colour is purple,' she said.

'Hmmm, good point. Any suggestions?'

Victoria felt her heartbeat quicken. Could she risk it all again? Plucking up her courage she took a deep breath and said, 'We have to promise that we each tell something that we've never shared with anyone else, except the people involved.'

'Can it be something really important. Something that has had a profound effect on who we are and how we are?' he asked.

'Yes, it must be that,' she answered.

'I trust you, Victoria, but are you sure you trust me?' he asked.

'I don't know — I want to though.'

'OK, well, how about this: I'll tell you my issue first, then when you've heard it you can decide if you still want to tell me yours,' he offered.

'That's very gallant, but that's not fair on you,' she said.

'Yes, but I'm a gentleman,' he reminded her.

'But I think we've done that old chestnut, haven't we? I can't have it both ways: we are equals.'

'So, are you saying that we have to both be prepared to exchange no matter what?' he asked.

Swallowing, suddenly apprehensive but resolute she said, 'Yes, I want to.'

'Right, hang on a minute: I've got an idea,' Joe said.

He pulled into the side of the lane and stopped. He turned on the light and leaned towards her.

Victoria's breath caught in her throat for an instant: what was he going to do? Was he going to kiss her? But instead he reached into the glove compartment and pulled out a notepad. He scrabbled around for a pen and found one.

'OK, what about this. We each take a piece of paper and write down the very thing we are anxious about but which we want to get off our chests. We read what the other person has written and then decide as to whether we want to learn more. Is that OK?'

Victoria nodded. This was it. She wanted to be free of the cage James had put her in all those years ago. She wanted it more than anything. She took the pen and paper he held and wrote.

Joe took the pen back and scribbled something on his paper.

'All right, let's swap, and we must read at the same time,' he said. She nodded.

He read 'My best friend was raped'. She read 'I killed a man'.

***

Anthony led the way back to his house, adrenalin still rushing through him. It was the same feeling he had had following his various stealing adventures but this time there was no subsequent wash of shame.

'Mother, this is Gary,' he introduced the tall boy. 'He's the other member of our group.'

She stood up. She wanted to let this boy have a piece of her mind. However, she was surprised that the others all stood around him, as if they were shielding him.

She held out her hand and said, 'Welcome, Gary, I've heard a lot about you, but it's not been good.'

There was an awkward silence. Gary looked down. The moment was broken by Anthony's excited voice telling his mother what had happened, highlighting Gary's heroics.

Anthony's Granny came into the room during the account of the fracas. She looked at Gary and, with her usual straight talking, said, 'You're still a shit for bullying Anthony though, aren't you?'

Gary reddened and scuffed his feet. Anthony leapt to his defence, 'Oh, that's all in the past. Are you going to have a drink, Gary?'

Gary took the can Anthony offered him. He was beginning to get his equilibrium back. He looked around the room. He couldn't quite reconcile recent events with his present situation, sitting here in Anthony Alexander's flat — Anthony Alexander's! — next to Frank, opposite Katy Walker of all people. He put his hand to his eyes to wipe away the past. The others were looking at him.

'What?' he asked.

It was Susan who spoke. 'I just want to say well done, Gary: that was a very brave thing to do.'

'Yes, it was,' Katy added.

Before he could even think he said, 'But it was Anthony that got us out of the shit.'

'Where did you get the name from?' Katy asked Anthony.

'Well, there's a cricketer called Sadiq Mohammed and it was the first name that came into my head. I don't even know whether they're the same nationality; they're probably not, now I think about it.'

'Very ingenious, Anthony,' said his Granny. 'So, how do you all feel about your jobs at The Beeches?'

'Yes, tell us all about it,' Susan encouraged.

Over the next hour, they talked through the events of the day. Even Frank opened up when he spoke about Grace and what she'd told him about her husband and brother.

'What a strong lady she must be, losing her husband like that,' Anthony's grandmother said.

'She is,' Frank said.

'But Frank, you're going to get through, I know you will,' Katy said.

Susan, Margaret, Anthony's granny, and Gary looked at her and then at Frank.

He looked stricken again but summoned up the strength to say, 'I lost my dad and brother last year, in a car crash.'

'Oh, how awful, Frank, I'm so sorry,' Margaret said.

Gary said suddenly and with horrible bitterness, 'I wish I could lose my dad.'

The room went quiet. Gary turned to Frank and said, 'I'm sorry, I didn't mean anything about you. It's just that my dad is, well — I can't stand him.'

'It's late. Time to go, I think,' Margaret said.

They all got up and started getting ready to leave. Susan cleared up cans, glasses and fish and chip wrappers.

'Thank you, Mrs Alexander, and you too, Anthony's Granny, and you too, Anthony: it's been a brilliant evening,' Katy said.

'Thanks for letting me come too,' said Susan.

'It's been great. Thanks for coming,' said Anthony, sorry that the evening was over but still on a high at how events had panned out.

'Bye,' Frank said.

'Cheers,' Gary grunted.

Once the door had closed, Anthony sat down and looked at his mother and Granny.

'That's the best day of my life,' he said.

'Do you know what? It's about the best day of my life for a very long time too,' Margaret said.

'Do you know what? I would have brained that Gary, but actually he wasn't bad at all. Funny isn't it?' Anthony's granny said.

'That's because Anthony has won him over,' Margaret said smiling.

'You're right. I told you, Anthony: I told you that life would pick up,' the old woman said and went over to him and hugged him hard. 'Now, where are my cigars?'

Outside the four young people walked home.

'Where do you live, Gary?' asked Katy.

'Drayton Road.'

'Fine, we're going that way. How about you Frank?' Katy asked.

'Near the station.'

They walked in silence together. They paused outside Gary's house. He was ashamed: there was an old car on bricks in the front garden, pieces of wood and metal, an old mattress and a bike wheel was propped up against the overflowing dustbin. However, his greatest concern was that they might hear his father's drunken cursing, or worse.

'Bye then, see you tomorrow,' he said and went quickly to the front door.

They chorused a good night and carried on to the girls' house.

'Thanks for telling us about what happened, Frank; it must be very difficult for you,' Katy said.

'It is. I still can't believe it's happened,' he said.

'Well, you can talk to us any time you like,' Katy said.

'Thanks.'

He left them and walked slowly on. He felt lighter and stronger than he had done for some time. Upon impulse he started to jog along the quiet residential street. It felt good just to run. He didn't go mad; he just gradually picked up speed and, in a few minutes, he was outside his house. He unlocked the front door and walked inside. His mother was sitting alone, a book in her lap.

'Welcome home, stranger,' she said.

She looked at her son. He was puffing a bit. His face looked different, more alive perhaps.

'Have you been running?' she asked.

'Just a jog along the street.'

'How did it feel?'

'Not too bad, not bad at all.'

She smiled at him. 'Well done, you. Have you had a good time?'

'I have. It's been pretty good actually,' he answered, surprising himself.

'That's great.'

'I met the old lady that we're doing the party for. She told me that her husband and brother had died when she was young.'

'What a coincidence,' Janice said.

'I don't think so; I think this bloke Joe knew all the time,' Frank said.

'You smell of beer, Frank. I hope you're not going to turn into a boozer and undo all your training?' she teased him.

'Don't worry, Mum. I'm fine,' he said, and he did feel good: he felt as if he was beginning to push back up.

***

Victoria felt like cringing away from Joe. She forced herself to sit centrally in her seat. She looked steadily out of the windscreen into the darkness. The silence was horrible. She wanted to fill it with something, anything.

Finally, Joe said, 'I'm happy to go first, but if you want to, then just say. Or we can just drive home and forget it all.'

She tried to speak but nothing came out. The car was suddenly too small; he seemed very large, oppressively so.

She said quickly, 'You first.'

Joe nodded, took a deep breath and said, 'Thank you, Victoria. I can guess what you're thinking. OK, this is my secret. Nearly six years ago I

247

was convicted of murder and was sentenced to fifteen years in prison. The reason I am here now is because my conviction was revisited, and it was reduced to five years. However, the fact remains that I am an ex-convict: I have spent five years of my life in a high security prison and my nearest and dearest friends for that time were very tough, angry and, in society's eyes, bad people to be around. I have to say too that although I didn't mean to kill this man, I had fantasised about doing it and even today can still feel great satisfaction from doing away with him.'

He paused. She was silent.

'May I go on?'

'Yes.'

In a rush, Joe said, 'My father died before it all happened. My mother wasn't coping with life. She had relied on him heavily for everything really. She lived in a nice big house but couldn't keep it going on her own.

'I moved in with her on a temporary basis, just to help her through the early days of losing Dad. After a few months, I said I would have to move back to my own home and pick up my life again. Because she was anxious about living alone, she decided to take in a lodger, the brother of a friend who had also recently died. She wanted the companionship; he needed a roof over his head. No one could have anticipated what was going to happen.

'Victoria, this man was a bad man. He obviously had his eye on the house and her savings. The first time I met him I smelled a rat: he was so ingratiating to her, and to me. He couldn't do enough for her; he made himself indispensable. He took her out for meals, which she paid for; he drove her around in his flashy car; he treated her like royalty.

'She started dropping her friends and wanted only to be with him. He didn't have a job — he'd been made redundant, apparently. I asked her what she really knew about him: she just said that he was a lovely man and he needed her help. The next thing I heard, she told me that they'd become a couple. I was appalled.

'Every time I met him; I was more convinced that he was up to no good. I couldn't persuade my mother to look at the facts: he had nothing; she had plenty — he was exploiting her. She then told me that she'd lent him some money to start a business: £500.00. Although she didn't have to worry about money, she certainly wasn't so wealthy that she could just throw around that kind of cash.

'I decided to have a quiet word with him, just to make it clear that I was onto him. He smiled at me and said, "Please don't fret, Joe. Your mother and I love each other deeply. You don't need to worry about us, young man". What he said next shocked and scared me: "Joe, you're a kind and thoughtful son — I know that — and because you care about your mother's welfare, I am advising you to keep well away from us. If I find that you've done anything to jeopardise our relationship, I shall kill her, and then you". I stared at him; I couldn't believe it. He smiled at me, nodded and said, "That's right, old chap, you heard."

'I told him that he couldn't get away with it, that I'd never let him. He just smiled. I started shouting at him, but he put up his hands and said, "Joe, time for you to run along and leave us alone. We're going to live our life together, happily ever after."

The next day my mother rang me up to say that he had asked her to marry him and she'd said yes. I went to the Police, thinking surely, they could help. Can you believe it? He'd already got there and had told them that I was violent and abusive towards my mother and that he thought I posed a significant threat to her safety. I was powerless to do anything about what was happening.

My mother kept ringing me up to tell me all the wonderful things that were happening: their holidays together, their new car, that she'd put the house in both their names, the amazing success of his new business. I tentatively suggested that maybe he wasn't quite what he seemed. She said, "Joe, I know you don't like Giles, but you have to understand that I love him and that there is nothing you can say that will make me change my mind. He said you were against him, and that I must let him know if you say anything bad about him."

Victoria, what was I supposed to do? I started to think through more and more violent ways of getting shot of him. I contacted a couple of people I knew who might be able to help me persuade him to just disappear. Then, I thought — no — bringing in a couple of 'heavies' was like something from a B picture! But as the weeks ticked by, I started to think that I'd have to do it.

I got a phone call from my mother's next-door neighbour saying that she hadn't seen her for a few days and was beginning to wonder if she was all right. I have to say, Victoria, that I was getting really scared. The whole thing was sending me a bit round the bend. I was imagining all sorts of awful things and, each day, developing greater hatred for my mother's precious Giles.

So, in a state of complete desperation, I rang my two friends and gave them the go-ahead to deal with him. The plan was for them to rough him up, to make it clear to him that it was time for him to leave and that, if he went, no further action would be taken. It was all set up to take place the following night, but it never happened.' Joe paused again. He waited for her to respond.

Finally, she said, 'What happened?'

'After I had spoken with them, I went out and got drunk. I remember thinking: don't get other people to sort out the mess, do it yourself. I left the pub, really drunk, and went to my mother's house determined to have it out with him. I parked my car and walked down an alley between the neighbouring houses. I saw someone walking towards me: it was him.

'I told him that if he didn't leave the house by the next day, I would make him. He laughed at me and asked: why wait till the next day? Why not make him leave now? I was drunk, Victoria; I didn't know what I was doing. I suddenly saw red. I picked up the nearest object. It was a brick. I don't think he saw what it was because he just laughed at me. That laugh sent me over the edge. I stepped towards him and threw the brick at him with all my might. He didn't move. The brick hit him full in the face. I can still hear the sounds of that moment now. They are etched into my mind: his mocking laughter and then the wet slap of the brick hitting his head. He went down like a sack of potatoes. I just stood there. I hadn't planned to hit him — although if I think about it, I hadn't given anything any thought at all. My head was messed up; I was crazy. After a few seconds, I weighed up the situation. I could see his still body on the ground. I knelt down and touched him. He was lifeless. I assumed he was just unconscious. I got up unsteadily and tried to think what to do. It was obvious: I had to call an ambulance.

'For a second, though, I just stood there. The thought had occurred to me that he might be dead, in which case maybe I should just leave him there and get the hell out of the place. I wanted to — I was really tempted to. I couldn't. You may well be thinking that I am a bad man, and I guess that I am in some ways. But my conscience suddenly kicked in and I ran to the nearest phone box to call an ambulance and the police. I waited with him till they came. By the time they arrived I knew he was dead. I'd put my coat over him to keep him warm but there was no movement, no breath. He was taken away by the ambulance and I was taken away by the police.

'I told them exactly what had happened, from the day he moved into my mother's house, through to the moment I killed him. It was an open and shut case. I was guilty and that was that. I pleaded guilty but with mitigating circumstances in the hope of a manslaughter conviction. As it turned out, my nemesis still had power over me. It transpired that he had telephoned the police earlier that day to tell them that I had been threatening him with a gun. The police searched my house and — surprise, surprise — they found a gun in the shed. The prosecution persuaded judge and jury that I had planned the whole thing and had only confessed to what had happened in an attempt to gain a lesser sentence. So, instead of a few years in prison, I ended up with a life sentence of fifteen years with no hope of parole for good behaviour.'

Joe had been talking slowly and steadily. He had been staring ahead, as was Victoria, as if they were both watching the same film.

He turned to her at last and said, 'Any questions so far?'

She shook her head. She was finding the whole thing too difficult to grasp. The blackness of the outside world contrasted starkly with the interior of the car which was half lit by the inside light. Every now and then a car swooshed by, startling her. She hugged herself.

'So, there I was, a prisoner, a murderer — wondering every day what I must have done in an earlier life to have suffered such a fate. I appealed but, without any new evidence, it was a lost cause.

But, Victoria, although I did not mean to kill him, I had wanted to hurt him; I had wanted to kill him if I'm honest. I started to imagine that maybe I had actually meant to go out and murder him in a demented state. Could it be possible that I could have become so irrational that I had got hold of a gun? Did I really plan to kill him? Had I hidden the gun and wiped it out of my mind? I began to doubt myself and my sanity. I began to believe that I was guilty. Also, people in prison for murder all claim they are innocent: was I any different?'

Joe paused, for a long time, then went on.

'Day by day I got used to my lot. It was tough in prison. I had to cope with the toughest ordeal of my life: the clanging of those doors, the locks being turned; the shouting — screaming sometimes; the overwhelming stench. When I found I was able to cope, it gave me strength. Being able to help other people cope gave me more strength. My mind began to clear. Around that time, two people became incredibly important: the first, someone who taught me everything that I now hold dear; the second, a benefactor. I would like to tell you about both of them one day. May I?'

Victoria looked at Joe for the first time since he had started his account. She saw his calm face, his kind eyes. She wanted to hear more; she found him utterly magnetic, despite what he was saying.

'Go on,' she said.

'I met someone, someone influential. He listened to me, he believed me, and he started to make investigations into what the police had failed to explore properly. I suggested that the murdered man must have had some history. If my mother had been a victim of his modus operandi then surely others had too. So, my friend arranged for a private investigator to look into his past and see if any paths led anywhere useful. Gradually it became apparent, as I had suspected, that my mother was not the only one to have been targeted by him. He had left a trail of victims and some of them had very bitter memories of how they'd been treated. All that was interesting but mostly it was reassuring — he really was a shit: it wasn't just me imagining it. But the key discovery was that a gun matching the one found in the shed had been bought by this man only days before I killed him. At last there was a real breakthrough. My friend was able to put together enough evidence to secure an appeal — the result of which was that the charge of murder was dropped and replaced with a conviction and sentence for manslaughter.'

Joe puffed out his cheeks and looked across at Victoria.

'There's a bit more. My benefactor? Why do I work at The Beeches? Who is my fairy godmother? I'd want to protect my saviour's privacy, really but: he is a journalist, he lives locally, and he is an amazing man. Without him I would still be incarcerated and for the next ten years. My work at The Beeches? Well, our wonderful ninety-nine-year-old lady, Grace, is his mother.'

Victoria didn't know what to say. She wanted to tell this man that she was sorry for him, that she cared about him, that she wanted to hold him and make the past go away, that she was now a bit scared of him, that she was struggling to be in the same confined space as him, that she loved him, and hated him. She thought that maybe this was all a dream. She surreptitiously pinched her hand, just to check. It hurt. This was real.

At last she said, 'What about your mother?'

Joe said, his voice flat, 'She never spoke to me again.'

Victoria's pity overtook her shock, 'I don't know what to say.'

'I know; it's too big to grab hold of, to absorb,' he said.

'It is. Thank you for telling me though. I guess it took a lot. In fact, now I think about it, it must have taken enormous courage. I feel privileged that you trust me enough to tell me.'

'I wanted you to know, Victoria. You need to know about me, before we go any further.'

'Further?' she asked.

'Yes, I want us to go further but there had to be a point at which you must find out the truth, and where you must have the right to say that you don't want any more to do with me.'

Victoria was torn. She didn't know what she wanted. She closed her eyes and tried to work it all out. She had gained a sense of the nightmare he had been going through, but was that reason enough to kill a man, even if the act had been provoked? Did she want to end everything now, just when she had started to get close to a man, a man she was drawn to so powerfully? She waited in the hope that he would say something that would help her work it out.

'I know this is difficult, Victoria; it's hard to know what to think, how to weigh it up, what to do,' he said, as usual guessing what was in her head. 'Yes, I am not a murderer, but I have killed a man. I have a lot of mud sticking to me. I arranged for him to be hurt. I have been a close associate with some of the country's least acceptable people. All these things, when combined, make up an unpleasant and unsettling whole. I would understand if you found it all too murky to handle.'

She nodded. These were her feelings; it was no use pretending.

Joe said, 'I think we should go home. Let's leave it for now. It's not fair on you to have to deal with all this — it's too big to just hear it and accept it as if nothing has changed.'

She suddenly felt guilty, 'But, we had a deal. We knew the other one had a difficult and upsetting story to tell. I can't just let you take the hit without me taking my turn.'

As she said it, she knew she was right, but she also knew that she was not in the right frame of mind to reveal either what was in her heart or her past.

'That's very generous of you, Victoria. I appreciate your courage and your respect for me. I have a suggestion. Will you do me the honour of telling me yours when it feels right? Now is not the right time, I'm sure of it.'

She looked at him full on. He had again read her mind; he was prepared to let her off the hook, forever if she wanted it.

***

Their parents were in bed when Katy and Susan got home. The girls tried to keep quiet, but Katy was drunk and couldn't stop herself knocking into doors and furniture.

'Is that you two?' their mother called down the stairs.

'Yes, we're fine,' called back Susan.

Anna Walker came downstairs and looked carefully at them both. She said, 'I've asked you not to go out late during the week, look at the state of you.'

'We're fine. Don't lecture us,' Katy said.

Anna didn't rise to Katy but instead pointed to the coffee table near the door and said, 'You have a letter, Katy. I think it might be important.'

Katy saw the letter. She picked it up, folded it in half and went upstairs.

Anna really wanted to know what was in the letter, but she knew her daughter very well: now wasn't the time to press her for information, or anything else come to that.

'Stick with her, Susan, won't you?' she said.

Susan nodded and said, 'I will, like glue.'

Although they had their own bedrooms, Katy and Susan had always shared. Since the Walkers' recent upheaval, Katy had moved into what had, over many years, changed from hers to the guest room. She had felt compelled to impose a physical barrier between herself and the 'real' Walker family. She was missing them now, though. She wanted to share her thoughts, feelings and the events of the day with Susan in particular. Susan too felt lonely without her sister near. She imagined her plucking up the courage to open the letter. She resisted the urge to knock on the door and pop her head in; she knew Katy would come to her if she wanted to. Katy did. Susan's door opened quietly, and she slipped into bed with her sister.

Susan said, 'Have you opened it?'

'No, I haven't dared to yet.'

'Do you want to?'

'I'm not sure. I want to know but at the same time I hate what she did, and what she has done to us.'

'Me too,' said Susan. 'She has a lot to answer for.'

They were quiet. They lay on their backs, side by side.

Katy said, 'What would you do?'

'I'd ask you,' Susan answered.

'That's not much help.'

'No.'

'The trouble is, I don't want to discover that my real mother is a prostitute, or a lunatic or, worse still, that I'm the daughter of a rapist,' Katy said.

'None of that makes any difference to who you are or how I or we feel about you,' Susan said.

'But it does, don't you see?' Katy exclaimed angrily.

'Why?'

'Because who they are is who I am,' Katy said, through tears.

'Only if you let it be,' Susan said gently.

'But how can I stop it being true?'

'I don't know. Maybe the only way is to find out and then deal with what is real rather than imagined.'

Katy fell silent. Susan was right, but it was easy to say, much more difficult to do.

'I know you don't need me to say it but nothing that you learn from opening that letter will make any difference to me, or to Mum and Dad. It won't change you in our eyes,' Susan said.

'You believe that is true, but you don't know because it hasn't happened yet. You don't know — you can't know. Believing is different to knowing. That's the problem I'm having but from the other way around. I believe it may ruin everything for us, but I don't know, and I am scared to take the risk. It has already had a massive impact.'

'That's true,' Susan acknowledged, then said, 'but we've already had the big trauma; anything more will be easier to come to terms with, don't you think?'

'Maybe, but that's just what you hope isn't it? You don't know,' Katy said.

'I suppose so, but isn't it better to deal with what is rather than what might be?' Susan encouraged.

'Yes, it is,' Katy said. She reached across and turned on the bedside lamp. She took the envelope and tore it open. She paused for a moment. She felt Susan's hand on her arm. She took a deep breath and read the single sheet of paper.

'PO Box 1673
London W1

'Dear Katherine

I have spent a long time wondering what I would say to you if and when I wrote. Every day I changed my mind, first about whether to write, and second what is the right or best thing to say to you.

I have tried my hardest to imagine what it must feel like to discover that you are adopted, and to hear from your birth mother.

Your parents wrote to me to explain that you did not know that you were adopted. I can't guess with accuracy of course but I imagine that you had and are having very strong feelings of shock, confusion, anger, grief, loss, uncertainty, fear, and many more.

So, my first words were always going to be and still are: I'm so sorry. Sorry for many things. I'm sorry that I let you go but, looking back I am sure it was the right thing to do for you. I would not have been a good mother and I wanted you to have a wonderful mother, and father, with brothers or sisters. I hope so much that you have them now. I always dreamed of having the protective blanket of a family around me — I hope to God that you are safe and secure with the people you love, and who love you.

I am sorry that after all these years I have come along to upset your applecart. In the previous paragraph I talk about the safety and security of a family and then I deliberately throw in a hand grenade and maybe I have ruined everything for you. I waited until you reached sixteen so that you had had the chance to have strong foundations under you, so that you would be able to cope with my sudden appearance and the effects that knowing about me must have. I am very sorry that I have imposed myself onto your family. They may well hate me for my approach to them and you. Perhaps you hate me too. I have often hated myself.

Finally, I am sorry that I am so weak. I haven't stopped thinking about you for the last sixteen years. I have never had a day when you have not popped into my mind, maybe for a second, sometimes for hours. I have tried to resist temptation and stay out of your life but finally I caved in and here I am.

If I were you, I would want to know about me. Here are some basic facts:

I was twenty when you were born. I am now thirty-six.

I was a singer then.

I had a very brief relationship with someone much older than me, a married man.

Your father is a decent man and I bear him no grudge, and I hope you won't either.

I have had some very tough times — my life has been turbulent — I am now beginning to get myself into shape: hence my overwhelming desire to find you and finally know you.

I know I have given up the right to be your mother — that role is now with someone else. I pray though that we might be able to have a relationship, one which can grow into something important for both of us.

My dear Katherine, you may well despise me. I can see how that could be the case. I ask you though, give me a chance. Give me one chance to know you, and for you to know me.

Write to me at the above address if you want to but, if you don't want to, will you write and say so?

With my love and sincere best wishes to you

Jane'

Katy passed the letter to Susan and waited for her to read it.

'How do you feel?' Susan asked after she'd scanned it.

'Well, it's not as bad as it might have been, but it doesn't really say much does it,' Katy answered as she re-read it.

'She seems quite nice, sort of understanding, don't you think?' Susan said.

'Yeah, I suppose so. But who is this older man? Why has her life been so turbulent? Why couldn't she keep me? There is just loads of holes in the story,' Katy said.

'At least we know where your performing genes come from now,' Susan said.

'Yeah, I suppose so. But even that's just a comment: what kind of singer is she? Is she any good? Is she a professional?'

'She might be famous,' Susan said excitedly.

'She might be a total drunk or drug addict too,' Katy said.

'What do you want from her anyway?' Susan asked.

'Nothing. I just want my nice peaceful family back,' Katy said.

'No, that's not you, Katy. You love the drama: admit it.'

Katy was silent. Susan was right: she was intrigued and rather excited by this new development. She had spent the last couple of weeks in a state of agitation — she still felt mixed up — but gradually she was coming to terms with the reality of it all. But what was real? The letter did nothing to help her get a sense of certainty or identity.

'Do you think you will write to her?' Susan asked.

'Dunno,' Katy said. But she knew already that she would: she had to find out more.

'You can't kid me, you liar! I can read you like a book,' Susan said laughing, and jabbed Katy in the ribs.

'Will you help me, Suzy?' Katy asked.

'Of course, we'll all help you,' Susan said and, turning to her sister, hugged her fiercely.

***

Victoria wrestled with her dilemma. Joe had given her a way out. She could go home now, think about what he had said, weigh it up, get used to it and regroup. She could go home now and never see him again: that possibility was tempting. She wasn't quite sure why she was feeling the need to get away — after all he wasn't a cold-blooded murderer, he was a victim of circumstance.

'What do you want to do, Victoria? Shall we go home?'

Victoria shook her head. She said, 'No, I am going to fulfil my part of the deal.'

'Only if you want to; I'm happy to wait,' Joe said.

'I wanted to tell you before you told me. What you have told me has upset me; it has shocked me, and I'm now feeling as if I don't know you at all. But I also think that you've earned the right to hear my story, and I have a debt to pay.'

'There's no debt, Victoria, but I do want you to tell me, I have to admit,' he said.

Victoria's heart was thudding, and she was finding it difficult to breathe as she formulated what she should say. She was scared to call to mind and describe James' violation of Eleanor: his grunting, Eleanor's desperate horror and fear.

Victoria said in a rush, 'I saw my dearest and most loved friend being raped and it has left me with a wound — a scar that won't heal. She was sixteen. I was ten.'

Joe said, 'That is awful. I'm so sorry.'

In her head, Victoria was back in the woods behind the tennis courts again. She was oblivious to where she was and with whom she was sharing the tiny space. She carried on, 'He was like an animal — he was treating her like an animal, my beautiful friend, my lovely, gentle, kind friend.'

She put her head in her hands and started crying, huge shuddering sobs.

After several minutes, Victoria began to compose herself. He handed her his handkerchief and she took it, blew her nose noisily and gave it back.

'Keep it, you might need it again,' he said.

Victoria was feeling awkward now. She hadn't told anyone about what had happened. She had wanted to, many times, but she had promised Eleanor that she never would. She had always imagined that if she did reveal herself and the dreaded feelings, she would regret it immediately. Now, she felt uncomfortable and self-conscious but not regretful.

She heard his calm voice, 'Do you want to tell me more?'

She told him again about her childhood in Dorset during the war and her relationship with Eleanor and the events leading up to and during the attack by James. She heard her own voice intone the nightmare; every detail described.

'The poor girl — and you too,' he said. 'It sounds grotesque — and shocking — utterly appalling.'

'She's managed to deal with it better than me, I think,' Victoria said.

'You saved her, Victoria: you overpowered James,' Joe said.

'I would have done anything to save her. I would have killed him if I'd had to.'

They were silent for a while.

'May I ask you a difficult question, Victoria?' he asked at last.

'Yes,' she said, steeling herself.

'I am feeling an overwhelming need to comfort you — to hold your hand, for you to hold my hand... to give you a hug — anything really. But I am also scared to, in case it brings back those awful feelings all over again.'

Victoria listened to him and, just as she had many times before, wondered if he really could read her mind. She craved physical comfort; she wanted to be held right now. She was scared though that, in seeking it out, she would feel everything that he had predicted so accurately.

They both stared straight ahead.

'You're right, Joe,' she whispered finally.

He nodded.

'The thing is, I'm stuck in the past. I've got caught in that terrible few minutes all those years ago. I have never been able to break out of its grip. I think I would do anything to break free, anything,' she said, her voice pleading.

'Would you let me help you?' Joe asked.

'Yes, if only you could.'

'I believe I can.' Joe started the car and drove off.

They sped along a quiet lane which gradually started to go up hill, round a couple of zig zags then they crested the hill and turned into a gravel car park. Joe turned off the engine. He climbed out, walked around to her side and opened the door. She got out.

'What are we doing?' she asked, anxious.

'You're going to take control,' he said and walked across the gravel to the edge of the hill. She followed.

'You're brave, Victoria, I know you are. You are going to be truly courageous now. You will confront James and cut him out of your life forever: you are about to shake off that terrible burden; it will be gone and will never return. But listen, Victoria, if you want to stop what we are about to do, you can. Trust me, Victoria.'

She could just make out the shine of his eyes: they were looking into hers. She braced herself and said, 'OK. I don't know what you mean, but I'm ready.' Victoria wondered what she was getting herself into. She didn't seem to be able to resist Joe and had to admit that she didn't want to.

They stood next to each other and looked down from the top of the hill. They were a long way up, overlooking the lights of the town.

There was no sound other than the buffeting noise of the wind.

'Fill your lungs, Victoria,' Joe said. 'Look out to the end of the world. You are free now. Nothing that happened all those years ago can hurt you. You said that you would do anything to save Eleanor. You did save her, and you have protected her ever since. Your role is over. You have done your job brilliantly. Now it's time to say to yourself, "Well done: a job well done".'

Victoria thought about this. She knew he was right but that didn't change how she felt.

'But there is something awful I haven't told you,' she said.

'Do you want to?'

'When I said I would have killed him if I'd had to, what I really meant is that I wish I had killed him. I wish I'd killed him when I had the chance.'

'Stay there,' Joe said.

He walked off quickly, and after a few seconds he came back.

'Shut your eyes, Victoria.'

She paused, then closed them. All she could hear was the wind blowing and then Joe's voice, very close, almost in her head.

'Just listen to what I say. Just hear what I say and absorb it. This is important, please do it: you are looking for Eleanor right now. You are walking across the tennis court; you see her things at the back. You are confused but you guess she and James are looking for a ball behind the fence. You go under the fence and start to look behind the bushes. You hear something: it's Eleanor. You move closer and see them. They are on the ground. You move closer still; you see Eleanor's face. She is petrified. You want to help her. You see that James is on top of her. You see that he is between her legs. You see him attacking her. You know that you must do something to save Eleanor. James is brutalising her. She is scared, she is being hurt, she is being horribly abused. You see James taking away Eleanor, destroying your beautiful friend. You cannot let that happen. You will not let it happen. You see what James is doing and you must stop it. You will stop it. You see Eleanor looking at you — she is pleading with you to save her. You see James and what he is doing, and you know it is terribly wrong. You know it is wrong because Eleanor does not want it. She doesn't want it and you must stop it. You decide that the only thing to do is kill James. You look around and you see a heavy stone. You pick the stone up,' Joe pressed the rock into her hands. 'You move closer to James and you lift up the rock. You look at Eleanor's face to make sure that it is what she wants you to do. Eleanor looks at the rock and she shakes her head. It is not what she wants Victoria. It is not what she wants because it is the violence and the horror that is making her scared. She does not want violence. She wants peace, safety, security, love. Eleanor wants you to stop what is happening. She does not want any more violence. You look at James. He is out of his mind. He does not know what he is doing. He is mad. He is a child. He is a weak child. He is hurting Eleanor, but he does not know what he is doing. You must stop him; you must save him too. You must save both these people, Victoria. You must save them both. What can you do? Put the rock down — what else can you do? What can you do, Victoria? What can you do to save your beautiful friend? What can you do to save this boy who does not know what he is doing? You must save them both. What can you do? You know what you must do now. Now. Now!'

Victoria screamed, 'James, stop it! Stop it now!'

For a fraction of a second her anguished, guttural cry crashed about her, then the wind whipped it away.

Joe spoke with absolute conviction, 'He's gone; he's gone now. You've done it, Victoria; he's gone. Eleanor is safe. You have saved them both and you have saved yourself too. You have been carrying around this terrible weight for more than thirty years. You can let it go now. You can cast away that terrible burden: you are free now. Throw away that awful weight now, Victoria, just throw it away.'

Without knowing what she was doing she lifted the rock up high and launched it off the top of the hill. As she did, she screamed again; this time it was a scream of release.

Joe touched Victoria's shoulder; she turned to him. He wrapped his arms around her and held her tight. Her body heaved as she tried to control the horribly raw emotions sweeping through her.

***

Gary sat at the kitchen table. He was jotting down his ideas for an article to send to the local paper. He'd been mulling it over ever since he'd left The Beeches all those hours ago. It seemed like a lifetime since then. He remembered his conversation with Joe. He had listened to what he had said, and his initial reaction was to dismiss it. But as he'd travelled up to London, he had heard Joe's arguments over and over. He had been right; he was right. Gary knew that he could contribute, and he could also destroy. Up until now he had been intent on destruction, cynicism, wanton vandalism, but he knew in his heart that these were not going to get him anywhere — except into more and deeper trouble.

He had enjoyed his trip to London. Every part of it had been great. He had felt as if he had left something of himself behind when he'd been there; he knew what it was — he had left behind his horrible, stupid, thuggish identity. Then, when he had got off the bus back home, he'd been faced with a trial was he going to return to his old ways or stand up and be someone he could respect. He had thought it was going to end badly but, unbelievably, he had been saved by the least likely person he could ever have imagined.

When he'd got home, no one had been in. His mother was still at bingo. His father and brothers were out; he knew where they'd be. He had been relieved — he had no interest in being with them.

He'd come into the kitchen and read the note from his mother, 'Your dinner just needs heating up. Your new specs are by the bread bin. See you later.'

He picked up the glasses case. He didn't dare open it — there was no way he was going to wear glasses! Curiosity got the better of him, though: he opened the case and lifted out the black-framed, plastic glasses. He resisted the sudden urge to smash them on the cracked old worktop and instead put them on. He looked at his mother's note again. He was shocked. Her writing jumped out at him: it was bigger, blacker, clearer. He looked around the kitchen. Everything leapt at him. He couldn't believe the difference they made.

He walked into the hall and stood in front of the mirror. He noticed two things. The first was that everything looked much clearer — he saw himself properly for the first time in ages. But he also saw himself with glasses on a total prick, like the kind of kid he'd have laughed out loud at.

Now, as he sat writing, he was watching the point of his pen moving as words appeared on the page. He was fascinated by the clarity of the little images emerging in front of him, as if by magic.

The front door opened and closed quietly. He knew it was his mum: the others barged in noisily.

The kitchen door opened, and she said, 'Hello, love, how are you?'

'OK.'

She looked at him and smiled. 'You look great in those; what do you think of them?'

'They make me look like a total prat.'

'Don't say that. They really suit you. They make you look very clever,' she said.

'Well, I'm not really clever, and I don't want to look like a prat,' he grumbled.

She put the kettle on and sat across from him.

'Didn't you want your dinner?'

'I had fish and chips with some friends.'

'Who, Steve and that crowd?'

'No, some other friends, new ones.'

'Nice?'

'Yeah, all right.'

'What are you writing?'

'Just an article for the old lady's party.'

'Did you meet her?'

'Yep, today.'

'What's she like?'

'Old, really old. But she was sharp though. She was like a young person in an old lady's body,' he said, remembering Grace and her knowing eyes.

'Can I see?' his mum said, gesturing towards the page.

He pushed it across. She read:

'Grace the Centurion

'What was the world like 100 years ago? No cars, no electricity, no television, countryside everywhere and not a strike in sight. But was the world any better than today? We can find out, simply by asking Grace. She was there and she's still here today.

'The Beeches' oldest resident is about to turn one hundred. She remembers the good and bad old days, not just the second world war, nor the first world war but the Boer War too. She can remember Queen Victoria's golden jubilee, what it felt like to celebrate New Year's Eve on the 31st December 1899 and much, much, more.

'Her first journey in a car was seventy years ago, it went 20 miles per hour and Grace remembers feeling thrilled and scared at travelling so fast.'

'That's all I've done so far. What do you think?'

'It's like a proper newspaper article. You're really good.'

'Well, I made it all up. I haven't spoken to her yet, but I'm expecting that kind of stuff,' Gary admitted.

The kettle started whistling and Mrs Abbott got up to make tea. The front door opened, and loud rough voices reached them. Gary quickly took his glasses off and folded up his paper.

The kitchen door opened, and Mr Abbott walked in.

He said, 'Great. Make us a cuppa, Jen.'

He looked at Gary and said, 'I'm only going to tell you once: never stick up for a Paki again. If I hear you have, I shall give you such a beating you won't be able to walk for weeks.'

Gary looked at his dad. He didn't need to know how the events of the evening had reached him, the fact was that they had, and he now had to face the music.

'Honestly, Dad, he wasn't doing anything wrong; he was just putting out a bin.'

Mr Abbott sat down opposite his son. He leaned across the table, his face inches from Gary's.

He growled, 'This is England. English people are white, they eat English food, they speak with an English accent, they go to English places for holidays. England is in Great Britain. Great Britain, son — not shit Britain, not Brown Britain: Great Britain. Those stinking wogs can get the fuck out of this town and this country. People like you standing up for them are no better than them. Believe me, you made a big mistake tonight and you better not do it again. Do you hear me?'

Gary heard Kev come into the room behind him.

'Here he is. Jesus, you're an embarrassment, Gary; your name is shit down the pub,' Kev said.

'He's all right; he understands now, don't you, Gary?' his father said.

Gary swallowed and sat still and quiet.

'Answer me, son, don't you fucking ignore me,' his father growled again.

'Let it go, Dad,' said his wife.

Abbott whirled around and shouted, 'Keep out of this; this is between a father and his son, nothing to do with you.'

'It's late; let's leave it alone,' she said again.

Gary watched his father's red, boozy face go purple. He said quickly, 'I get it, Dad, I hear you.'

Mr Abbott didn't seem to hear him. He got up and reached across to his wife's arm and wrenched her around to face him.

'How many times do I have to tell you? Never, never, never cross me. Don't you ever cross me again,' he yelled into her face, spraying her with spittle.

Jenny Abbott looked tiny and frightened; she reminded Gary of a dog he'd once seen being beaten by its furious owner.

'Now where's my fucking tea?' Abbott said, letting his wife's arm go. 'Come on, my love, make your hubby happy,' he said, stroking her hair. She shrank away but caught herself and turned to make the tea.

'I'm off to bed,' Gary said.

'Good boy — remember what I said,' his father's voice was now soft and gentle.

Gary went to his room. He got into bed and closed his eyes. He closed his eyes to everything dirty, ugly and rough. He thought back to the joint he'd shared with the black kids on the bus, the young Asian man, of the hour he'd spent with the others at Anthony's house. He wondered if Joe would have been proud of what he'd done today. He hoped he would be. He imagined talking to Joe about himself, about his family. Maybe Joe could help him? Whatever happened, something had to change he couldn't bear it any longer.

***

Victoria felt herself calming down. The images that had flooded through her mind as Joe had retold the awful event had shocked her, had overwhelmed her. It was as if she had been there again in real life, except that, this time, she had been in control. She was still clinging to Joe now. She was not sure she felt strong enough to let go of him. Holding him now, being held, was so reassuring, comforting.

As her breath came back, she became increasingly aware of his body against hers. She felt a rush of desire. She pressed herself against Joe's chest; she wanted to get closer and closer to him, to climb in. She had also felt his hardness for just a second — dare she feel it again? She tentatively moved her hips forward: arousal flooded through her as his erection touched her. They stood still; their bodies pressed together. His hands moved up and down her back. She shivered and pressed herself harder against him.

She heard him say, 'Are you OK?'

'Yes,' she said, and to her surprise she meant it.

She lifted her face, her lips parted. He kissed her. They were locked together, their arms tightly around each other, kissing passionately.

He drew away, 'Come on, let's get back into the car,' and led her back.

He opened her door for her, but she closed it again and opened the back door and got in. She slid across the back seat and took his hand, he got in beside her. He closed the door after him and turned to her. They kissed again. Joe stroked her hair, gentle, soothing. She felt his hand on her neck, her shoulder. As his hand ran down her arm, she felt his fingers graze her breast; she groaned with pleasure. She took his hand and pressed it to her chest. He cupped and fondled her breasts through the fabric of her blouse and bra. She broke away and started to undo the buttons of his shirt. Her fingers were fumbling and hectic; he gently pushed her hands away and slowly undid his shirt. As soon as the last button was undone, she pulled open his shirt and ran her hands up and down his body, exploring, stroking, touching every inch of his chest and stomach. Her fingers found his nipples and stroked then squeezed their hard points. She took her hands away and started to undo her blouse. She was rushing; her fingers wouldn't obey her.

'Will you do it?' she asked.

'Are you sure?' he asked.

'Do it,' she commanded, 'undo my blouse.'

He kissed her again. She felt his fingers gently undo her buttons. As his hands moved, she felt them against her breasts, every tiny touch making her gasp. He undid the last button and gently parted her blouse. She leaned forward and struggled out of it, and seconds later reached behind her and unclipped her bra.

'Ow!'

'What's wrong?' he asked.

'I hit my elbow. It's a bit cramped in here.'

'Sorry, I'll bring my caravan next time.'

'Next time?'

'Sorry, I mean if there's a next time.'

In response she took his hands and held them against her breasts.

'Oh, Victoria,' he breathed into her ear as he stroked her. He put the flat of his hand against her nipple; she moaned and arched her back against his touch. She pulled his face towards hers and kissed him hard.

'Ouch! My turn.

'What?'

'I'm at a funny angle; I can't wait to get my caravan.'

She laughed, 'This is fun. Are you having fun?'

'Yes, Victoria, I'm having a ball, thank you.'

He kissed her, her lips, her eyes, her chin, her throat, then down her neck. She put her hand behind his head. His lips and tongue moved down her cleavage and then she felt his mouth on her nipples. She cried out with pleasure.

'Are you OK?' Joe's voice was worried.

Victoria laughed again, 'Yes, sorry, it was pleasure not pain.'

'Phew, I was worried there.'

'I'm OK, Joe, honestly.'

To prove it to herself she inched her fingertips up his thigh towards his crotch. He leaned back and undid his flies; wriggling awkwardly he pulled down his trousers and pants, freeing himself.

She felt his hand take hers and draw it to him. For a moment she was uncertain; she held her breath. She ran her fingertips up and down him, hesitant at first, then more confident.

She heard herself say, 'Will you touch me?'

His voice was gentle, calm, 'Sure. Where?'

She took his hand and put it on her thigh. He stroked her slowly, softly. She lifted the hem of her skirt and he moved his hand up, probing between her thighs. She parted her legs, his caressing fingers moving higher. She gasped as she felt his touch. He gently stroked her through the silky material of her underwear. She lifted herself up for a second and, as she did, she pulled her pants down slightly. She felt his stroking fingers.

'Mmmmm, don't stop, Joe.'

He moved his fingers again; she caught her breath. She searched for him as he gently stroked her. More confident now she moved her hand up and down on him; his breath became ragged.

Awkward in the limited space, she put her arms around him and kissed him deeply. Looking into his eyes, she said, 'I want this so badly; you won't despise me for it, will you?'

'Oh, Victoria, I promise you; I respect you more than anyone I know.'

'Really?'

'Absolutely.'

'Promise me, Joe: you're not just saying that, are you?'

'He kissed her, 'I promise you, Victoria.'

'Good.'

Manoeuvring herself in the confined space, she wriggled out of her pants. When they were off, she straddled his lap. He lifted her skirt and held her buttocks. She put her hands on his shoulders and gently lowered herself until she felt him.

'I'm scared,' she whispered in his ear.

She heard his voice, 'It's fine, Victoria. We'll look after each other.'

She said through sobs, 'Joe, this is my first time. I really am scared.'

'Oh, Victoria. Then I'm a very privileged man; I'm just sorry we're not somewhere more fitting for the occasion.'

Despite herself she laughed, 'At least it's not behind the bike sheds.'

In answer he moved his hand between her legs. As she felt him touch her wetness, she shuddered and let her weight sink down. There was a slight resistance and then he was inside. She let out a deep low groan of relief.

Victoria was still. He murmured soothing sounds, stroking her hair, kissing her face tenderly.

'Are you OK?'

'I'm fine, Joe, more than fine.'

Victoria felt stronger now.

'And you, are you OK?'

'What, canoodling with my favourite headmistress? I can't think of anything better in the world right now.'

'Good, me too,' she said; it was true.

She pressed her breasts against his face.

'Victoria, you are utterly beautiful,' he said.

'Do you really think so?'

'Yes, utterly beautiful.'

She started to move, rising and falling — slowly at first, then quickening, faster, harder. He moved in rhythm with her. As she rode him, she was aware of him deep inside her; it made her feel strong, in control.

Joe was thrusting his hips in rhythm with Victoria's increasing urgency. She heard his voice, 'Victoria, you are wonderful; let yourself go — let go.'

She was only dimly aware of her cries, of her frantic movements; all she could think of was her desperate need to come.

She felt his hand move between their bodies. As she rose up, he slipped his fingers between her legs and touched her. She gasped, held her breath for a lifetime — then it was as if something had burst inside.

Victoria let the waves of ecstasy sweep over her. She heard Joe's gasps, and then she felt the hot flood spurt into her. As he came, she felt herself tighten around him again and again.

He pulled her to him. She heard his whisper close to, 'My lovely girl, you are safe, you are safe now.'

Slumping against him, she was sobbing again. This time, though, her cries were of relief, of release.

They stayed like that for a long time.

***

Anthony's inexperienced drinking bladder was playing havoc with him. He got up to go to the lavatory. On his way back, he saw that there was a light on in the sitting room. He peered in and saw his mother asleep in her chair. He walked over to rouse her and noticed that there was a letter on the coffee table next to her. He recognised his father's writing immediately. He paused for a moment before picking it up. He read quickly:

'Margaret

'Life continues to be diabolical. Everything here is unimaginably horrific. The food is disgusting. The staff treat me with utter contempt. The inmates are without exception the lowest dregs of society. I am, in short, in hell.

'I think a lot about all the everyday aspects of life that I have had taken away: freedom, the respect of others, decent food and drink, the right to make a living, to sleep in a clean bed, in a warm house, not to mention the quite reasonable expectation of being able to choose with whom I associate. All those things, that you now take for granted, have been taken from me.

'You took them away, Margaret. You have done this to me. You decided to make my life a living hell. Why did you do it? I gave you a beautiful house, with everything in it that you wanted. I gave you everything and, in return, you have destroyed me.

'Your behaviour is loathsome; your actions mean that I must now live like an animal.

'I wonder if you have told Anthony what you did? I wonder how he would feel if he knew you had sent your husband to prison and his father to his death?

'Maybe you would do me the honour of writing to me to explain why you have banished me to this bloody hell-hole? I guess that you won't; you will not have the courage to tell me what I have a right to expect — an explanation.

'I shall continue to write to you despite your protests. I shall continue to do my best to make your life as wretched as mine, be assured of it.

'Richard.'

Anthony re-read the letter. He tried to get his drink-fuddled brain around what he was reading. He looked at his mother; she was watching him.

'What does it mean?' he asked.

She leaned forward and took the letter from him. She read it again and then screwed the paper up.

'Your father is quite mad, Anthony. Let's talk about it in the morning.'

Anthony shook his head, 'Tell me what it's all about — just the facts.'

She yawned.

'I'm exhausted. You and your friends completely finished me off.'

'What did you do to him, Mother?' he persisted.

She was matter of fact, 'I assisted the police with their enquiries, and it was me that furnished them with much of the paper evidence that was decisive in his conviction.'

Anthony sat down and considered what she'd just said. He hated his father. Life without him was so much better. He and his mother were enjoying getting to know what it felt like to have a close, loving relationship.

He said, 'I'm glad; I think you did the right thing.'

'Thank you, Anthony. That means a huge amount to me.'

'Has he been writing to you a lot?'

'Yes, I get letters all the time. Some are abusive, some are pitiful, all are about me having wronged him — making me out to be at fault. Listen, Anthony, it's so horrible I don't want to talk about it anymore.'

He asked, 'Do you want me to write to him, to tell him to stop?'

She shook her head and said, 'No, you must keep away from him. Don't have any contact: it's not something you should get mixed up in.'

'But I am involved — you are my parents after all,' he argued.

'I'm your mother. You mustn't think of him as your father anymore. He is someone to avoid at all costs. He is poison.'

'OK, if that's what you want,' he said.

As Anthony got back into bed he thought about his father and how he had treated his mother and him. He had been the worst bully of them all. His harsh, critical voice came back to him, even now making Anthony feel foolish, helpless and utterly scorned. Anthony had never had a positive comment from his father, just words of contempt and criticism. He thought back to how his parents had interacted. He realised now, for the first time, that his mother too had been the focus of his father's opprobrium. Just as Anthony had done, she'd acted; she had taken control. He must help her, back her up, play his part.

He brought his father into his mind's eye, looking directly into his haughty, hard face. He felt anger sweep through him: even at long-distance Anthony could feel him trying to control their lives and exact revenge.

***

Frank dreaded sleep. Every night he dreamed — tearing metal, screams, sirens, desperate but futile attempts to save his father, Robbie. Whatever the nightmare's image, he was always absolutely powerless.

This dream, still vivid in his head, was different but just as disturbing. He was with Grace in her bedroom when she'd said, 'So, you're a good runner, Frank?'

Frank said that he enjoyed running but was out of practice. Grace told him that she loved to run and challenged him to a race. Although Frank protested, he now stood on the long, straight path behind The Beeches with Grace. She looked tiny and frail, almost unable to stoop to adjust her blocks. Before he had had a chance to get ready, Joe had fired the starting pistol and the race had begun. Grace set off, her small feet shuffling, stick clutched in her hand like a relay baton, face set and determined. Frank gathered himself and was about to run when he saw his father and Robbie waving at him. He couldn't believe his eyes. He focused on them. Yes, it was them. They were both wearing red baseball caps. He saw that Grace had moved several yards down the path and was making slow but steady progress.

He heard his father's voice shout, 'Come on, Frank. You can do it!'

Frank's heart was thudding in his chest. It was them. He must get to them whilst he still could. He started running. Instead of the burst of speed he had been expecting, he found his legs were so heavy he could hardly move them. He gritted his teeth, heaved his feet one after the other — they felt as if they were glued to the path. He was at least moving now but as he looked down the track, he could see that, unbelievably, Grace was beginning to get away.

He heard Robbie's voice cry out, 'Come on, Frank. Please, Frank. You can do it — come on!'

Frank was panicking. He was getting desperate. No matter how hard he tried he could not speed up. His fists were clenched, eyes bulging, his lungs were on fire. He remembered to relax; he tried to let his hands go loose, to breathe more easily. Nothing happened. Up ahead he saw Grace reaching the end of the path and his father and Robbie cheering her as she crossed the finishing line. They looked down the path to him, shook their heads sadly and, one on either side of Grace, walked with her back into The Beeches.

Frank heard his cry of agony echo around the concrete walls, 'Come back! I'll run harder, just come back and I'll win again. I promise you I will win again. I will. I will.'

They didn't come back. Frank was left stranded, his lungs heaving, muscles burning, his sadness an enveloping, concrete coat.

Frank got up and had a pee. He was soaked in sweat, still breathing hard from the exertion of the nightmarish race. He went back to his bedroom and took out the scrapbook that his father had kept. It charted all his races from primary school days right through to the successes of the summer, only last year. He read the articles and flicked through the photographs. He saw his quotes and those of his parents, coach and of his rivals. He was now unsure if the boy he saw and read about was really him.

One of the last articles was a cutting from the Brighton and Hove Gazette.

Frank read:

'Frank Gordon's not Flash'

'When I first met Frank Gordon, I expected a highly confident, maybe even arrogant personality. After all, being the fastest fifteen-year-old in the country must make you feel like Superman. Well, let me tell you, Frank is the most modest, understated and decent boy I've ever met.

'When I saw him run for the first time at an athletics meeting, I couldn't believe my eyes. There is something awesome about him. The gun cracked, his competitors were running like the wind and then they all seemed to start running backwards as he swept past them. When he broke the tape, he was exultant for an instant, then he became modest Frank again. That was the day he broke the eleven second barrier. It was an amazing moment.

'Frank's younger brother, Robbie, proudly explained to me Frank's extraordinary ability. I thought the special gift he had was running fast, which it is. But Robbie described to me the process that Frank uses to find peace and calm prior to a race, a state that enables him to gather all his strength and deliver it with the entirety of his mental and physical power. Seeing Frank in action, both the calm before and then the storm, was truly incredible.

'Since then I have got to know Frank. He is someone that people admire. His contemporaries look up to him. Younger boys want to be him. He seems to have effortless authority, and something else — although it's a funny word to use for a fifteen-year-old boy — Frank has grace too.

'Commentators are talking about Frank as a future Olympian. Who knows what will happen between now and Moscow — or beyond? I have a very strong feeling, though, that Frank Gordon is going to achieve great things.'

Underneath the article he read 'By Ailsa Carmichael, Guest Contributor'.

Frank's eyes filled with tears. His life had been perfect then. He remembered sitting next to Ailsa by the lake. He thought back to how she had made him feel. He remembered her coming to see him and his mother at the hospital. He had never contacted her; he didn't know how to. He knew her address but what could he say? He felt guilty that he'd never called or written. Now it was too late. He looked at her name at the foot of the article. Frank felt searing guilt. He had let Robbie down. Robbie would have wanted him to get in touch with Ailsa, to check how she was feeling — she had lost her friend after all. He felt his fists clench; he looked around for something, or someone, to punch. He saw himself in the mirror: he looked like a wild man — long ragged hair, crazed staring eyes, teeth bared. He looked down at the picture of himself next to Ailsa's article. He saw a tanned and powerful young man, with a calm smiling face. The contrast was shocking. He closed his eyes and breathed deeply and slowly. Gradually, he felt everything calm. He carefully put the scrapbook down, turned off the light and got into bed. He put his hand on his heart and felt its beat slow and soften. He heard his father's voice telling him 'slower, calmer, deeper'. He let himself fall.

***

The tremors of her orgasm were still shivering through her. Victoria did not know what to say, do, or even think. She had just had sex with a man in the back of a car, for God's sake! She wanted to giggle and cry at the same time.

Although she felt incredibly self-conscious, she didn't want to move. It was wonderful just being here with this man, so close, so intimate. She wanted to feel him inside her still, but his penis was shrinking away. She almost blurted out 'don't go' but instead pressed her face against his.

'Are you OK?' he asked.

'I'm fine,' she said in a tiny voice.

'Me too,' he said.

'I don't know what to say,' she said.

'How about 'the suspension moved for you'?'

She laughed.

He said, 'I'm taking you home and putting you safely into bed.'

He lifted her, she scrambled onto the seat next to him.

'It's all a bit messy,' she said, conscious of her own stickiness and his.

'Have you got my hanky still?' he asked.

'I've absolutely no idea. I couldn't tell you where my own clothes are, never mind yours,' she said, laughing again.

They rummaged around for underwear and did their best to tidy themselves up. When they were fully clothed and done up Joe leaned across and put his hand behind Victoria's head and brought her face to his. He kissed her tenderly.

'You're wonderful,' he said.

She smiled and kissed him hard back.

They drove back in silence. When he pulled up outside her house Joe said, 'Can I come in, you know, just to make sure you're all right?'

'Joe?'

'Yes?'

'Did you hypnotise me or something: you know, before we...?'

Joe looked into her face, then said, 'You asked me for my help. I've learnt how to use it to help people. I wanted to help you. Did I do the wrong thing?'

'Not this time, no. But, Joe, you won't do it again, will you? Not without my say-so?'

'No, I promise.'

She took his hand and led him to her front door. They went inside.

**

Gary woke up to the sound of cursing and smashing crockery.

'Leave it,' Kev said from his bed on the other side of the room.

'What the fuck is going on?' Gary said groggily sitting up.

'I said leave it,' his brother said again, insistent.

Gary got up. He walked to the door and listened.

'Get back, or I'll throw you back,' Kev snarled.

Gary laughed scornfully and said, 'Yeah, like you could — I don't think.'

Kev sat up. Gary turned around to face him. He looked down in his brother's direction, making out his shape in the gloom.

Kev capitulated, 'All right, fuck you. Don't say I didn't warn you.'

Gary put his jeans on and walked out on to the landing. His mother was coming up the stairs.

'What's going on?' he asked.

'Nothing. Dad's fallen over in the kitchen; he's all right.'

Gary switched the light on and stared at her. She had an angry red mark across her face.

'Turn that off, Gary, please,' she implored.

Gary turned the light off. He was happy to. His mother's face looked awful — not the effect of his father's hand, but her look: fear? Shame?

'I'll go and help him,' he said.

He went into the kitchen and found his Dad snoring on the floor. He was surrounded by debris. He had obviously slid along the kitchen worktop and brought everything down with him.

Gary stood looking at him. He could not quite associate this drunken wreck with the powerful, heroic figure he had grown up admiring so much. What he saw now was a pathetic man, pitiful almost.

Gary started picking up broken crockery and the variety of kitchen items scattered around him. When the floor was mostly clear he bent down to hoist up his dad. As he regained consciousness, Mr Abbott started grumbling and then, properly coming to, he began to fight Gary off.

'Get the fuck off me, you bitch,' he growled.

Gary stood back. His father looked up at him through half-closed eyes.

'Gary, what are you doing here?' Abbott said in confusion.

'Mum asked me to come down and help you,' Gary lied.

Abbott looked around him. He was evidently unsure of where he was or how he'd got there.

'Help me up, you wanker,' he growled.

Gary reached down and with a mighty pull managed to get his father unsteadily to his feet. He steered him into the front room where he collapsed on the couch and started snoring almost immediately.

Gary went back into the kitchen and carried on clearing up the mess. He didn't notice his mother standing by the door.

'Thank you, Gary. Don't worry about Dad; he can't help it,' she said.

Gary looked over at her and said, 'Even if that's true, you can stop it can't you?'

'He's my husband, Gary,' she said.

She went into the front room. He followed her to the door and looked in. She was wrapping a blanket around the unconscious form of her husband. She sat on the arm of the couch and bowed her head. Gary left them to it. The scene was too awful to witness any further.

***

'I'm feeling a bit wobbly,' Victoria said as they stood together in the kitchen.

'It's been a long day, I'm not surprised,' Joe said. 'May I suggest something?'

'Of course.'

'Why don't I run you a nice hot bath; you get in, warm up, then I'll put you to bed?'

'That sounds lovely.'

She was feeling exhausted. Her sense of self was completely out of kilter. She could not quite process what had happened to her over the last few hours. It had all started relatively normally, but with Joe's revelation, her telling him her own awful memories and reliving them and then what had happened in his car: it was all too much to take on board.

She sat in her armchair and looked at her hands. She heard him in the bathroom, then the kitchen. He seemed to be busying himself and she was glad. She didn't want to talk to him; she didn't know what to say. In fact, she was feeling so tired and knocked about, all she wanted to do was go to bed.

He came in and pressed a mug into her hands. She sipped it. She felt the sweet tea warm her.

'I know it's a cliché, but hot sweet tea does have miraculous powers,' he said, then disappeared again.

She drank her tea. It was bringing her around and back to some semblance of reality.

He came back into the room and took her mug and said, 'Your bath is ready, me lady.'

She allowed herself to be led towards the bathroom. He left her at the door.

She undressed quickly. Her body didn't feel like hers. She glimpsed herself in the bathroom cabinet mirror. Her face didn't look like her face.

She got into the bath and let the hot water seep comfort into her. She stretched out. The warmth of the silky, soapy water was wonderful. She tentatively touched herself. She felt different, unfamiliar; she liked it.

After a few minutes she got out and dried herself. She put on her dressing gown and shyly went downstairs. Joe was sitting with his eyes closed. He looked like a complete stranger in her living room. What was

281

this man doing here? The funny thing was, though, he also looked like someone that she had known for a long, long, time.

'How are you feeling?' he asked, looking up at her.

'Very tired,' she admitted.

He nodded. He stood up and said, 'Time for bed then,' and led her to the stairs. She didn't protest. Normally she didn't like being told what to do but right now she wanted someone to take care of her.

They went into her bedroom. He pulled back the bed clothes and she took off her dressing gown and quickly got in. He smoothed the blankets and pulled them up to her chin. He sat down on the edge of the bed. He stroked her hair and said, 'What a day, eh?'

'Mmmmm,' she murmured. Her eyes were closed, and she was almost asleep already.

He bent down and kissed her on the forehead.

'Good night, Victoria.'

'Good night,' she whispered.

The light was switched off. She vaguely heard him open and close the door. She could feel sleep begin to overwhelm her. She suddenly felt scared. What if she never saw him again? What if she woke up and it had all been a dream? Maybe it would be better if it had been, then at least her life wouldn't be complicated by it all. She opened her eyes and felt her mind racing. Her heart was beating quickly now: she'd gone from comfort, and relief at being in her own safe bed, to panic. She thought of how incredible it had been to be held by a man, someone to keep her safe, someone she could keep safe. She wanted that back; she could not let it slip away. She sat up. Had he left the house? She listened with all her might: there was no sound downstairs. She got out of bed, feeling like crying again. Surely, she hadn't lost him.

She opened her bedroom door and cried out, 'Are you there?'

She heard the plaintive sound in her voice. No answer came. She went back into her bedroom and looked out of the window. There he was, opening his car door. She forced the sash window open and called in her loudest whisper:

'Joe?'

She couldn't see his face; he was just a dark smudge in the night. He was still. Then, he leaned into the car to retrieve something, straightened and closed the door.

He called up, 'What light through yonder window breaks?'

She laughed. She ran downstairs to open the door. As he came in, she threw herself at him.

'I'm sorry, I know I'm being a baby — I don't want you to go,' she said.

He said, 'I was hoping against hope you'd call me, but I didn't dare say anything in case it all broke around us.'

'I know. I felt the same thing. I don't want it to break I want you to stay.'

She pushed the front door closed, took his hand and led him upstairs.

'Come on, your turn for a hot bath, my laddie.'

She went into the bathroom and turned on the taps. Joe followed her in and started to undress.

'Can I stay with you?' she asked.

'Sure, that would be nice,' he said.

She sat on the loo and watched him take off his clothes. He lowered himself into the bath. She stared at his body. He looked across at her and asked, 'What are you gawping at?'

'You.'

'And?'

'How did you get to be so muscly?' she asked.

'Gardening now, but don't forget I had five years in prison with very little to do except stretch my mind and body.'

She knelt beside him and kissed him.

'I'm feeling very daring all of a sudden,' she said.

'Really? What do you plan to do? I'm in a very vulnerable position you know.'

'This.' She opened her dressing gown and leaned over the edge of the bath to kiss him.

'Any good?' she asked.

'Nice, very nice indeed.'

He brushed her breasts with the back of his fingers, grazing her hardening nipples.

Victoria closed her eyes with pleasure. When she opened them, she saw that he was hard.

'I'm getting into bed, I expect you to be outside my door in five minutes, all present and correct,' she instructed him.

'Yes, Miss.'

He slipped into bed beside her. She rolled onto her side and faced him. 'Hello, fancy meeting you here,' she said.

'I did what I was told.'

'Not against your will I hope?'

She felt his hardness pressing against her belly. 'Ah, apparently not.'

They kissed slowly and deeply. She wrapped her thigh around his waist.

'This is so weird. I can't believe I'm having sex with a headmistress.'

'I can't believe I'm having sex with a gaolbird,' she answered.

He pushed her gently on to her back. She lay there, eyes closed, ready for him. She felt his hands run up and down her stomach, then between her legs.

'Yes please,' she whispered.

He knelt between her legs and stroked her. As his fingers quickened, she heard a strange voice cry, 'Fuck me, Joe.'

He moved up her body, kissing her nipples, throat, lips. She felt the touch of him between her legs and then he was inside her. She groaned and pulled him in deep.

'That's it' she said. 'That's where I want you.'

They moved slowly and gently at first. Then their movements became urgent. She heard his panting breath in her ear and then he seemed to lose control. Again, she felt the hot rush inside her. She held him tight. She would not let this man go.

Part 5

Maximum Velocity

Her alarm clock went off at six thirty as normal. For a few seconds Victoria couldn't conjure consciousness. She didn't recognise the clattering bell: it didn't fit in with her dream at all. Groggily she turned off the clock. She put her head back on the pillow and tried to remember what day it was, what had happened last night — surely something had, something big, she knew it in her heart. Then, her mind cleared, and she sat up suddenly. She gasped.

Lying beside her was Joe. He was watching her.

'I'm sorry, you shocked me,' she said, conscious of her nakedness.

She fell back and pulled the covers up to her chin.

'You don't have to behave like a vestal virgin, you know,' he said smiling.

'Well, I'm not used to waking up with strange men in my bed,' she protested.

'Strange?'

'Very,' she said, nodding to emphasise the point.

He reached across and took her hand in his. It felt strong and reassuring to her.

'I'm not strange. It's the others — they're strange,' he said.

She turned to him, 'Did it all really happen?'

'I hope so. It was amazing.'

'I'm so pleased. I was scared I might have dreamed the whole thing.'

'No, it happened — all of it; although it feels like an amazing dream to me too.'

'May I?' She snuggled up against him. He felt warm and comforting. 'I'm going to have to go to school in a few minutes. I have a job to do, you know,' she said.

'I know, and I must get on too. Shall we meet again in similar circumstances?'

'And what might those be?'

'In a state of undress, and in a warm bed and with nothing to worry about?'

She felt desire rush through her at the thought of it.

With a huge effort of self-restraint, she got up. 'Your ideas do have some worth, and I shall give them due consideration. However, it's time for me to get going. Come on — sling your hook.'

***

'Jane

    This is Katy.

You did a pretty good job of guessing my feelings and the impact you have had on me and my family. Well done you.

I want to tell you that you are THE MOST selfish person in the world. You have damaged my family and me horribly and all because you want to get to know me, someone you decided to give up in the first place. I think the expression having your cake and eating it is appropriate, don't you? It's very easy to talk about 'tough' and 'turbulent' times. Did you say that just to excuse your behaviour?

Tell me more about why you gave me up. How can a mother hand her baby over to someone else? How do you think that makes me feel about you now?

Just so you know I have a mother, father, and sister who love me, and I love them. We would rather die than let one of them be handed over to someone else.

    Katy.'

Susan watched Katy writing the letter. She was stony-faced, hunched up; her knuckles were white as she gripped her pen.

'May I read it?' Susan asked.

'I don't know if it's what I should say, it's just what came into my mind,' Katy said, handing the letter over.

'Blimey, you haven't held back, have you?'

'Well, what does she expect me to say? Does she have a pretty picture of me running into her arms like some kind of fairy tale?' Katy said.

'I guess the best thing is just to be as honest as possible, say how you feel.'

288

'And this is how I feel right now. I'll probably change my mind, and then I'll change it back again. I don't know what I'm feeling half the time. I'm totally mixed up and it's horrible,' Katy said, wiping her eyes.

They heard their mother calling them for breakfast. Katy folded up her letter and put it in an envelope and addressed it.

'How are you?' Anna asked Katy as she came downstairs.

'All right.'

Anna was desperate to know what yesterday's letter to Katy had said and what her reaction would be to it. She knew better than to ask though.

Katy sat in silence as she ate her cereal. She knew she was being horrible to her mother, but she couldn't bring herself to talk to her, and certainly not about the letter and what it had contained.

'Are you going to The Beeches again?' Susan asked.

'Yep.'

'What time?'

'Three thirty.'

'I wonder what it will be like. It was so weird the way last evening went. I still can't quite believe that Anthony and Gary were there, and poor Frank too.'

Katy reflected on the day before. She had enjoyed the afternoon meeting Grace, and she really liked Joe. Then they had all ended up getting pissed — and that was after the near punch-up outside the chip shop too! Susan was right, it was surreal.

'How do you think you'll all get on this time?' Susan asked.

'I think Gary will be back to normal. He won't be able to resist the pressure of his stupid, thick friends; he'll be the same as usual, I bet you any money.'

'I hope not. I thought he was quite nice behind all that tough guy act,' Susan said.

'The funny thing is that I think Anthony's the tough one really. I know he looks a bit weedy, but I get the feeling there's more to him than we realise.'

'He's funny, like he's trying to be grown up the whole time. If you all have another drink together, you'll let me know, won't you?' Susan asked.

'Of course. I think we'll all be a lot more sensible this time though. We've got a job to do after all.'

'Are you talking about the Beeches?' Anna asked, coming to join them.

'Yeah,' Katy said.

'Did it go well?'

Katy nodded again and got up to get ready for school.

When she was upstairs Anna asked Susan, 'Is she all right?'

'She's just mixed up, Mum. She's a bit all over the place,' Susan whispered.

'Stick close, won't you?' Anna said.

Susan nodded.

'And, how are you?' Anna asked.

Susan looked down. After a minute she said, I'm just trying to get on with life, and not worry about it. It's hard though — I'm mixed up too.'

Anna sat beside her and gave her a cuddle.

'You're doing brilliantly, my love; you are keeping us all sane in amongst all this madness.'

'I promise you, Mum, Katy still loves us. She is just struggling to work everything out, that's all.'

Anna hugged her daughter and got up.

'That's all I needed to know.'

Susan was hesitant, then, 'When things have died down a bit can we talk about my real twin?'

Anna came back and stood behind her daughter. She put her hands on her shoulders and said, 'You have two real twins, one who died and one who lives with you now.'

'I know. You don't need to worry I understand. I just wonder about the other one, that's all,' Susan said.

'So, do I,' Anna sighed. 'Let's talk later, when Katy is at The Beeches.'

Katy's heavy platforms came thudding down the stairs.

'Are you coming, or shall I go without you?' she asked Susan.

'Give me five minutes.'

'Too long, I'm off,' Katy called, slamming the door behind her.

***

'May I have a word, Anthony?' his mother called to him as he was leaving the house.

Anthony looked into the sitting room.

'Granny and I were talking about the events of last night. It occurred to us that yesterday evening might mean different things for different people,' she said.

'What do you mean?'

'Well, I know we had a nice time with them but today they will be with their normal friends: they might not want to go back to how they were last night; they might be a bit shy?' she suggested.

'I thought that too. Especially Gary. I think he'll be all tough again and will pretend nothing happened,' Anthony said.

'Yes, that was what I was thinking too.'

'How should I be then? What do you suggest?'

'It's hard to know. Maybe just a smile at each of them, just to let them know you share something, but not much more than that. Unless — they might be full of it; I just don't know,' she said.

Anthony walked to school thinking about it. He hoped with all his heart that it was not back to normal. He'd had such a good time. He'd really liked everyone, even Gary. He hoped they liked him too.

He turned into the school gates and walked past the normal knot of smokers.

'Here he comes, tosser of the century,' Steve shouted out as he saw Anthony.

Anthony looked over at him and saw Paul and Phil there too. They grinned at him and in perfect coordination gave him the wanker sign. Gary wasn't there though. Anthony walked past them without pausing.

His first lesson was maths; it was his best subject. He was in the top class and only Susan Walker of last night's 'party' was in his class. He sat at the front in his usual place. Seconds later Susan came into the classroom with two of her friends. He looked at her and when he caught her eye he just nodded hesitantly.

She smiled and said, 'Got a hangover by any chance?'

Anthony went red. He didn't know how to answer. He was thrilled that she had spoken to him, but this was more than he'd expected.

'I'll live,' he mumbled, embarrassed.

'Katy is in a right old mess,' Susan said smiling.

'Really? Poor her,' he said.

Susan moved away, her friends following, gaping at her and then Anthony.

He opened his textbook and pretended to read. He had gone from nobody to a big drinker who got pissed with Katy Walker, of all people. He felt at least a foot taller and, for once, not a total freak.

***

Janice saw Frank putting his scrap book into a large carrier bag.

'Oh, who are you showing that to?' she asked.

'The old lady, Grace. She's going to show some old photos to me. I don't suppose she'll be interested in my stuff, but I did promise her.'

'She sounds like an amazing person.'

'I think she is, although she seemed hardly alive when I left her yesterday.'

'When's her big day?'

'It's not till next month but I think Joe wants everything cut and dried well in advance.'

'What's he like?'

Frank paused. He hadn't really given Joe much thought. He didn't give anything or anyone much thought these days. He spent his time in a fog, not really knowing what was going on around him.

Finally, he said, 'Well, he's a sort of a grown-up grown up.'

'What does that mean?'

'Yeah, I know it sounds weird. He's the sort of bloke that people look up to I suppose; he's calm, confident, like a leader,' Frank said.

'He sounds interesting. Can I meet him?'

'I expect so. I'll let you know.'

'Will you show him your scrapbook?'

Frank suddenly felt shy. He wanted to, but he was embarrassed. He dreaded coming over like a little boy desperate to impress.

'We'll see,' he said.

Janice left it. She knew what was going through Frank's head. She wanted to tell everyone about her amazing son — not just his running but about him as a person too. She also knew that Frank wasn't up for being in the limelight and maybe never would be again.

'Hope the day goes well,' she said and punched him in the stomach, hard. Frank gasped and doubled over, just in the way he used to when Robbie punched him. He straightened up and stooped to kiss her cheek.

'Thanks, Mum, I'll see you later.'

When he got to school, he joined the queue waiting to go into Mrs Burn's history class. He ignored the laughing, jostling group and thought about Ailsa. He couldn't think of her without the associations of last summer, of Robbie, of a time that seemed so long ago it was more like a film now than reality.

He saw Gary walking towards him. He was shambling along looking sullen. When he drew level with Frank, he looked at him and nodded. Frank nodded back.

'Hey, Gaz, where've you been?' shouted Phil.

'Nowhere,' Gary said and stood with him, Steve and Paul.

'Done the essay?' Steve asked.

'What do you think?' Gary muttered.

'Same here,' said Paul.

'I've dunnit. It was a piece of piss,' Steve said. 'I've still got to get some good marks to show that cow Court,' he explained.

'I did that days ago,' Phil said proudly. 'All I had to do was make a poxy screwdriver and that was it.'

'What you done, Gaz?' Steve asked.

'Court made me get involved in a group organising a party for an old dear down the road, that was it,' Gary answered.

'Blimey, poor old dear!' Paul said.

'You don't know shit about it. It's not so bad.'

'What are you doing then?' Paul asked, unconvinced.

'Well, I'm writing an article for the newspaper,' Gary said, feeling defensive.

'You? Write an article?' Paul said, even more amazed.

'What about it? It's not that big a deal,' Gary said, pissed off by Paul's scornful reaction.

'Who else is involved?' Steve asked.

Gary said, 'Just some others.'

'Yeah, who?'

Gary was embarrassed. He didn't want to say. He knew what their reaction would be. 'Does it matter?' he said at last.

'Anyone we know?' Phil pressed.

Gary was hyper-aware of Frank in front of him, hearing the whole conversation.

He thought back to the evening before. He'd enjoyed himself with them. They'd been good fun, even Anthony.

He said quickly, 'Anthony, Katy and Frank.'

There was a brief moment of silence then they started laughing in unison.

'You're lying! That is a joke! Come on, who is it?' Steve crowed.

Gary reddened and said, 'No, really.'

'Jeez,' Steve said.

'How are you going to stop yourself giving Alexander a kicking?' Phil asked.

Gary glanced at Frank. He hadn't moved. Was he listening?

'They're all right,' he mumbled.

'What a bunch of freaks though,' Paul said, unaware that Frank was behind him.

Frank said, 'Want to say more?'

Paul started at Frank's voice, 'Uh? Oh — no, nothing; nothing, that's all I wanted to say.'

There was quiet around them now. The hubbub had become silence.

Frank suddenly felt self-conscious. He hadn't wanted to get involved; it had just been a flash of anger. It was gone now. He turned around again.

The sound of chatter and giggles started up.

'You fuckin' arsehole, you're a total knobhead,' Steve whispered to Paul who was now trying to look cool.

Gary felt shitty. He should have stood up for his new gang. Instead it had been Frank.

'I'm off,' he said, and started walking away.

'Where?' Steve asked.

'Nowhere,' Gary said slouching down the corridor.

'Jeez, there's something wrong with him,' Steve said.

Gary heard the comment. Steve was right. There was something wrong with him.

Mrs Burn was coming towards him.

'Where are you going, Gary?' she asked.

'Bogs,' he said and kept going.

She looked after him. Then, as she turned back to the group of students another figure walked past her. It was the new boy, Frank. She was about to say something but let the moment pass. She was aware of Frank's situation: she knew better than to query where he was going.

The group began to file into the classroom. Steve, Phil and Paul watched Frank walking quickly after Gary.

'What the fuck's that all about?' Steve said under his breath.

Frank caught Gary up quickly. As Gary went out through the door into the car park, he turned to see Frank right beside him. He stood his ground and waited.

'I wanted to apologise for what happened in there,' Frank said, pointing to the toilet door.

Gary looked at Frank. He didn't seem threatening now. He looked genuinely regretful.

'Doesn't matter. I think I look cool with a broken nose anyway.'

Frank smiled and nodded. 'Where are you going?' he asked.

'Fuck knows,' Gary answered. 'I just had to get away.'

'Me too.'

'Are you going to The Beeches later?' Gary asked.

Frank nodded.

'Me too. On the way there I was going to go into the newspaper office; we could do that now.'

'All right,' Frank said.

They walked down the street in silence, self-conscious in each other's company. Gary got out a packet of Number 6. He proffered them. Frank was about to say no but changed his mind. He took one and, standing closely together, they lit their cigarettes from the match Gary held.

'What's in there?' Gary asked Frank, gesturing to his large carrier bag.

'Something that Grace asked me to bring.'

Gary wanted to ask 'What?' but he didn't. He was beginning to get Frank's measure. If he didn't want to say something, then he wouldn't.

Gary cleared his throat noisily and spat into the gutter. He chucked his cigarette butt into the road.

'You don't smoke, do you?' he said to Frank.

'No,' Frank admitted and ground his unsmoked fag under his foot.

They reached the high street. After a short walk they stopped outside the newspaper offices.

'What shall I say?' Gary asked.

'Not sure. Just tell them what you're doing and see what they say, I guess.'

Inside the office was a reception counter with two women sitting behind it. One, the younger, was on the phone, the other looked up as Gary and Frank entered.

Behind the counter was a glass wall and through it they could see several desks with people sitting at them. There was a buzz of noise and activity. Phones were ringing, calls were being made, handsets were being banged down followed by laughs and curses. The room was thick with cigarette smoke.

'Can I help you?' asked the older woman.

Gary said, 'Er, I'm writing an article and just wanted to see how I could get it in the paper.'

'What's it about?' she asked. She weighed Gary up. He looked like a thug to her, scruffy. He didn't smell very good either. She glanced at the other boy; he looked even worse.

'It's about an old lady at The Beeches who is going to be a hundred next month. We, well, I, well we, want to say something about her in the paper.'

'Oh, that's a nice human-interest story,' she said reappraising Gary.

'So, what do I have to do?' he asked again.

Behind her a phone was crashed down loudly and a young man said exultantly, 'I got him! He's available — now — on the set! Can you believe it?'

He got up, flung his leather jacket around his shoulders and, picking up pen, notebook and briefcase, marched out.

Gary watched him go. He couldn't help asking, 'What's that all about?'

'Oh, he's been chasing a story all week, something about one of the people appearing in the film they're making up the road at MGM,' she said.

'Really?' Gary said, impressed.

'So, how about you write up something about the old lady and bring it back when you're ready and we can go through it then?' she said.

'OK, how many words?' Gary asked.

'Hmmmm. Give me five hundred and we can see what it's like,' she said.

'All right, any ideas about it?'

'Our editor always tells new recruits to use Kipling's 'Six Honest Serving-men'. Do you know it?'

Gary looked confused for a moment and then nodded. 'Thanks,' he said.

He looked at the younger woman. She was tasty. He stared back at her when she glanced his way.

'Are you all right?' the first woman said to Frank.

Frank shook his head and walked outside.

'What's wrong with him?' the woman asked Gary.

'I dunno. Anyway, thanks, I'll be back in a couple of days.'

When he got outside, he turned to Frank and asked, 'What's wrong?'

'Oh, it's just the usual stuff. My little brother used to be in and out of newspaper offices. He even managed to get a job as a volunteer in one once.'

'The one who died?'

Frank nodded.

'I'm sorry.'

'Thanks,' Frank said in return.

They walked back up the road to school. Gary was elated, for the first time for ages. He had been excited by the newspaper office. It had been a surprise. He had expected it to be like a library. It was the opposite — loud, lively, young.

He said, 'OK, I'm sure this is a stupid question, but apart from making cakes who the fuck is Kipling?'

'I know Kipling was a writer. Maybe it's one of his stories?'

'Oh, right, thanks,' Gary said. He was feeling stupid again. He decided to go to the library when he got back to school.

***

Victoria stretched and stood up. Her day had started like no other day and, despite the fact that she was attending to plenty of usual and everyday matters, it still felt strange. She was sure that everyone could tell what had happened to her the night before. When she had arrived in her office she couldn't concentrate on work; her mind was racing. All she could think about was seeing Joe again. She finally understood why teenagers wandered around school with their minds elsewhere: hers was on some other planet.

Now, she turned around and looked out towards the front gate. She was aching to leave and was imagining what the evening would have in store for her. The sight of two boys broke her spell. She watched the unlikely duo shamble up the school drive.

Gary looked energised. She'd never seen him like this before. Poor Frank looked like a ghost. They were definitely walking together though: that was quite remarkable.

She walked out of her office to the main door and went down the three steps to greet them.

'Bonjour, messieurs?'

They both looked in her direction but didn't answer.

'Been somewhere interesting during lessons?' she asked.

Gary had turned into sullen, cretin mode and Frank remained in hangdog silence.

'You might not want to answer me but I'm going to insist,' she said, this time more serious.

'We've been to the newspaper office,' Gary said.

'Oh?'

'I'm going to submit an article,' Gary continued. Then he couldn't stop his enthusiasm bubbling over. 'It's about the old lady we're helping at The Beeches. I'm going to have an article published. I'm using er... erm... Mr Kipling's friends.'

Victoria wanted to laugh at Gary's evident unfamiliarity with Kipling's poem but mostly she was just happy that Gary was suddenly alive with enthusiasm for anything.

'Nice one, Cyril,' she said. 'That sounds fantastic.'

She looked at Frank.

'And you, Frank?'

'He came with me,' Gary said.

'You are doing well with this project. Don't let it get in the way of your actual lessons though, will you? Do you hear me?' she said Gary shrugged; Frank was unresponsive. And then she couldn't help herself: 'How are you getting on with Joe?'

'He's all right,' Gary said, surly again.

'And you, Frank?' she asked.

'Fine.'

She left it. She said, 'I'm sure I can find the poem, Gary; give me five minutes and I'll get a copy for you.'

She disappeared into her office.

'What do you think of Joe?' Gary asked Frank as they waited outside.

'He seems OK.'

'Do you trust him?'

'In what way?' Frank asked, puzzled.

'Oh, I don't know. I was thinking I might ask him something.'

'I don't know him. He seems OK, that's all,' Frank said.

They were silent as they leaned against the concrete pillars of the main entrance.

The school bell started ringing for lunch time. Kids started spilling out of doors. Miss Court came back out with an envelope. She handed it to Gary.

'I love this poem. I had a friend who read stories and poems to me when I was little; he said this one reminded him of me.'

'Who was that?' asked Gary.

'I called him Uncle John. He was a very kind man.'

'Why did it remind him of you?'

'Because I used to ask questions all the time — just like you. I hope you find it helpful.'

'Ta,' Gary said.

'Good luck then,' she said to both of them and went back inside.

Gary opened the envelope and pulled out the single sheet. He read it thoughtfully. Frank watched. He saw that Gary was holding the paper incredibly close to his face. He didn't say anything but couldn't help thinking that maybe he'd caused Gary's obvious sight problem.

'Any good?' he asked when Gary began to fold up the page.

'I dunno, it's a load of shit if you ask me,' Gary said, but he put it back very carefully in the envelope.

Frank watched Steve, Phil and Paul shamble past them forty yards away. They were looking at him and Gary with open interest. Frank looked away.

'Hey, Gaz, we're off for some chips — you coming?' Steve called over.

Gary looked up.

'Naa, not today.'

'All right stick with your new friends then,' Steve answered, and they wandered off.

'See you later,' Gary said to Frank, and walked off towards the library. After a second, he turned back and said, 'Wanna come?'
Frank pushed himself off the pillar and joined him.

***

'Fuck,' said Katy under her breath. Then, feeling the wave of regret sweep over her she said it again, loudly.

She was standing next to the post box, which now contained her letter to Jane. She had been certain that it was what she wanted to say when she'd left home but as she got closer and closer to posting it, she had become more and more doubtful. Finally, she decided just to post it and be damned. As she let it slip from her fingers and into the box, she instantly regretted it.

She thought briefly about various ways of retrieving it, all of them fanciful, then she walked quickly into school.

As the bell rang for break, she bolted out of art and waited outside Susan's maths class. As usual she was shilly-shallying, talking to Mr Mitchell, plus other students, discussing something indecipherable with brackets and letters. She saw that Anthony had joined in the discussion. They seemed very animated. Katy could not begin to see what was so fascinating. She waved at Susan who finally noticed her. She came over.

'What's up?' she asked.

'I've sent the letter,' Katy said.

'And?'

'I wish I hadn't. It wasn't what I wanted to say.'

'Oh,' said Susan. 'Hmmm.' She thought for a minute then said, 'Why don't you send another one explaining that the first one wasn't quite right and that this one is the right one?'

'Have you got a stamp, and an envelope?' Katy asked.

'Do I look like a post office?'

'Honestly, Suzy, you're not much help, are you?'

Susan dug around in her bag and fished out a crumpled stamp.

'Here you are. Add it to the enormous list of favours you owe me.'

'No envelope?' Katy asked.

'No, you'll have to make one or — shock, horror — buy one.'

Katy ignored her sarcasm and said, 'Right, give me the stamp; I'll cadge an envelope from the office.'

She sat down and started to write quickly onto a page of an exercise book,

'Dear Jane,

This is the version I want you to read. Forget the first one. Well, maybe read this one as well as the first one.

The thing is, I am mightily pissed off with you. But I do want to know more, and I guess it might be interesting to meet up. I don't know, I'm sort of confused, and a bit emotional.

I do love my family, and I do not want anything to upset us anymore. You understand, don't you?

So, tell me about you, I am interested.

I hope you'll write again soon.

Katy.'

She showed it to Susan. 'What do you think?'

'It's fine. I think you can relax a bit: she's probably confused too,' Susan said.

'Hallo, Katy,' Anthony said as he walked towards the door.

'Wotcha,' she said. 'See you later?'

'Yes. Want to walk down together?' he asked.

'OK. I'll see you at the gate at quarter past three.'

'Great,' he said and wandered off.

She walked quickly to Mrs Chalkley's office and knocked on the door. She opened it and went in.

'Hello, Katy,' Miss Court said.

'Oh, hello. Sorry to bother you.'

'That's all right. I'm just doing some photocopying. Do you know Kipling's 'Six Honest Serving-men?' she asked.

'Mr Kipling?' Katy asked uncertainly.

'No, Rudyard.'

'Er, no.'

'It's very useful to know it. Ask Gary when you see him next.'

'Gary?' Katy said, surprised.

'Yes, it's for him.'

'All right. Well anyway, do you have an envelope I can borrow?'

'Borrow or have?'

'Well, have, I suppose.'

'I'm sure we can manage that.'

She went over to the stationery cupboard and picked up a foolscap envelope and handed it to Katy.

'Thank you.'

'How are you getting on with Joe?' Victoria again couldn't resist.

'Oh, well, he's all right so far. Early days though.'

Victoria nodded.

'We're meeting again today. One thing's weird: we're all getting on OK,' Katy said.

'Everyone?' Victoria asked.

'Yeah, I know. Doesn't sound possible does it?' Katy laughed.

'Long may it last.'

She put a sheet of paper into an envelope and they both walked to the door.

'Do you like Joe?' Katy asked.

Victoria blushed. She turned back into the room to hide her sudden display of embarrassment. She said, 'He seems all right, so far. As you say, early days.'

Katy said thanks and walked off towards the car park to the nearest post box. As she reached the usual group of smokers she heard, 'Hey, Katy, you going to get your tits out again?'

She looked towards the voice and saw Steve, Phil and Paul grinning at her. There were a few other kids with them, all looking on with interest.

'In your dreams, you knobheads,' she said and walked past.

'Oooo, can't take a joke?' Steve said.

Katy stuck her finger up at them and kept going. Even now the letter she had quickly scribbled was making her feel unsure. What did she want? She had to admit to herself that the thought of her birth mother being a famous singer was exciting. She also thought of Anna and of how much she loved her mum and immediately felt disloyal. Reaching the red post box, she shoved the letter inside. She put her back to it and closed her eyes. Was she playing with fire? She screwed her eyes tight shut and counted to ten and then walked back to school, slowly this time.

***

'Hello?' Victoria said.

'Hello to you, too,' Joe said.

'How's your day going?'

'Well, it started very nicely and, so far, it's fine. I have to tell you that I have been thinking about you a lot, with plenty of very exciting images coming into my head.'

'Like what?' she asked.

'Cars, baths, potting sheds, headmistress's offices, and all of them involving temptresses — well, one temptress in particular.'

Victoria smiled.

'Can I see you later?' he asked.

'Yes.'

There was a pause. Then she said, 'I must get back to work. I thought you might want to know that your little working party has started to bond.'

'Oh, how so?'

'Not sure. Katy said they were getting on well. I can't quite believe it, if I'm honest,' she said.

'Nor me. I'll keep a pinch of salt handy if you don't mind.'

'Want to come for dinner?' she asked.

'Yes please. I'll bring a bottle.'

'Bye, then,' she said.

'Bye-bye, Victoria,' he said and put the phone down.

Smiling, Victoria replaced the receiver.

***

'Hi, lads,' said Phil Wilson as he neared Gary and Frank outside the library.

They nodded at him.

'Got a minute, Frank?' he asked.

Frank stopped and waited.

'I just wondered, have you thought about doing some sport, a bit of training maybe?' Phil Wilson asked.

Frank looked at him for a second and then shrugged, 'No, I've not thought anything.'

'Oh, that's a shame. Let me know if you want to talk about it, won't you?' Wilson said.

Frank nodded, and he turned to walk away.

'I could do some private sessions if you wanted,' Wilson pressed. 'You know, after school?'

Frank felt a flash of anger rush through him. He turned back and took a step towards the teacher.

'I said no, didn't I?' he said looking into Wilson's eyes.

Phil Wilson was a powerfully built man; he was not one to be intimidated. Now, though, with Frank's physical presence suddenly in his face he was stopped in his tracks; he felt like a naughty boy in front of the teacher.

'Sure, totally, I've got it,' he said, putting his hands up.

Frank immediately calmed down. 'Sorry, I don't want to do anything right now.'

This time he did walk away.

Gary gave Mr Wilson a questioning look, then he turned to walk off with Frank.

'What's that all about?' he asked Frank.

'I don't know. I think he got me confused with someone or something,' Frank answered.

Gary said, 'Tell me if you want to, don't if you don't.'

Frank considered the offer. He was beginning to like Gary. He had thought that he was just an ignorant bully, but he was showing himself to be more than that, quite a lot more.

'Thanks, Gary, let's leave it.'

'Sure, that's fine.' Then, 'Is it true that you get a telegram from the Queen when you get to be a hundred?'

'I think so; that's what people say anyway.'

'It's not exactly something worth having, is it?' Gary said.

'I think it might mean a lot to really old people.'

'I want to interview Grace later, I'll ask her,' Gary said.

They went into the library and sat down at a table. Gary took out his article and read it again. Frank put his carrier bag on the floor beside him and closed his eyes.

They were silent for a while.

Behind their table was a group of younger students. They were cracking jokes and laughing loudly at their funny one-liners. Frank got up and walked off to a quieter area. The occupants of the noisy table gathered their possessions and got ready to leave. One of them leaned down to pick up his bag and at the same time opened up Frank's bag and peered inside. He looked around quickly and pulled the large scrapbook half out of the bag. The sound of rushing feet filled the air and then he felt someone's hands pinned around his neck. He saw the wild fury of the face inches from his. He let the scrapbook fall back into the bag. Tears came into his eyes as Frank's hands squeezed like vices.

The clatter of activity stilled as everyone watched in horror.

Gary got up and touched Frank's shoulder and said, 'Frank, it's all right now.'

Frank came to. He let go of the boy's neck.

'I'm sorry,' he said to him.

Mrs Evans came out of her office.

'Get out. I'm not having violence in my library,' she shrilled at Frank.

'I'm sorry,' Frank said. He picked up his bag and walked out.

Gary put his papers back into his own bag and followed him. He turned to the frightened boy and hissed, 'That'll teach you to piss around with my friends.'

***

306

Anthony and Katy walked away from the school. There were a few jeers from the usual suspects as the odd couple turned down the road towards the high street.

'You are quiet today,' Katy observed.

'Sorry, I'm trying to sort out a problem my mother and I have got at the moment,' he said.

'Oh, anything you can tell me about?' Katy asked.

'No. Thanks though. It's awful and in any case it's not really something that anyone can help with, more's the pity,' he answered.

'I don't want to piss on your parade, but I've got myself into a right mess too,' Katy said.

'I'm sorry to hear that — want to tell me?' Anthony said.

Katy stopped and looked at him.

'I'm a bit embarrassed about it. It's such a difficult subject, and it affects my family, and much more than that. I honestly don't know what to say. The actual thing is simple but it's sort of much more complicated.'

Anthony nodded and said, 'Funny, mine's a bit like that too. I had thought of talking to Joe about it, I don't know who else to tell.'

'What do you think he'll say?' she asked.

'I don't know. It's just that he's not connected in any way and he seems to be sensible and, um, well, he might have some ideas.'

'Yeah, he's a bit like that,' Katy agreed.

'Would you tell him, do you think?' Anthony asked her. 'It's just that if you were going to, then I would tell him about my situation too. It might be better if we both did; do you see what I mean?'

'Hmmm, maybe, I'll see.'

They were quiet for a while, then Anthony said, 'Listen, I know I'm a bit different to the rest of you but it's just because I have been brought up differently. I want to be like you and everyone else.'

Katy laughed. 'Like who? I'm a mess. Look at Gary, you can't tell me you want to be like him. Then there's poor Frank: I hate to think what his life is like.'

'Well, actually, I would quite like to be like Gary. He's not going to be picked on and bullied, is he?' Anthony said.

'Hmm, I'm not sure. He's probably just as miserable as the rest of us.'

'Well, I suppose it's true that people aren't what they seem once you've got under the surface a bit,' Anthony said.

They came out on to the High Street and walked past the scene of the previous night's fracas outside the Indian.

'I just want to pop in. You can come in if you want,' Anthony said.

They went inside. It was quiet.

'Hello,' Anthony called uncertainly.

A door opened, and an Asian man walked towards them saying, 'Can I help you?'

Anthony said, 'Thank you, yes, I wonder if I could ask you a question. We have a friend at The Beeches — you know, the old people's home — who is going to be one hundred years old soon. We want to organise some refreshments for her party, and I thought it would be a good idea to have some Indian food, you know, to remind them all of the Raj. I thought that we could say that The Golden Bengal was providing the food and then we could promote it in the local newspaper. We are putting an article in there to let people know. What do you think?'

'Was it you that helped my son last night?' the man asked.

'Well, we didn't really help much. It was our friend Gary who did,' Anthony said.

'Hold on, wait a minute.'

He disappeared through the swing doors and came back with the young man of last night's events.

'Hello, Sadiq,' Anthony said, smiling.

The young man laughed and said, 'It's still not Sadiq, it's Haroon, but it doesn't matter hello again.'

He was looking pleased to see Anthony but even happier to see Katy.

Katy said, 'What's happened over there?' pointing at the roughly fitting wood across the window by the door.

'What do you think? We had a brick through it last night,' Haroon said.

'That's terrible,' Katy said, 'I hope no one was hurt.'

'It's normal. We get our windows smashed many times,' Haroon said.

Anthony and Katy were silent.

'Yes, we would be happy to provide the food for your party. My son will help you with it,' the older man said. 'I don't think it will be traditional food from the Raj though, we're not from India.'

'Don't worry about that. It's just the idea of it really; it doesn't have to be authentic. We're going to see the old lady now — we can let her know,' Anthony said.

'When is her birthday?'

'A few weeks away, I think,' Katy said.

'OK, come back when you want to discuss it further; we shall be very happy to see you,' Haroon said, looking directly at Katy.

Anthony and Katy left. They walked along the high street.

'You see, you're not the only one to be bullied,' Katy said.

Anthony nodded.

'How old do you think Haroon is?' Katy asked.

'I'm not sure, maybe eighteen, twenty?'

'Hmmm,' Katy said.

Anthony looked at her. He'd noticed Haroon had been staring at Katy. He felt a bit jealous now. But he knew she was out of his league. He didn't really know what his league was. He'd never spent any meaningful time in the company of a girl, ever. He found girls incredibly attractive; nearly every girl he saw, he imagined what it would be like to be with them, kissing, having sex, just talking.

He said, 'Did you like him then?'

'I dunno. He's kind of nice I suppose,' she said.

'He definitely liked you.'

'Hmm, well I probably won't see him ever again.'

'You will if he comes along to Grace's party,' Anthony pointed out.

'Oh, well, that's true I suppose; I hadn't thought of that,' Katy said.

They turned into the car park of The Beeches. They entered the building and signed into the visitors' book.

'Same room do you think?' Anthony asked.

They went down the corridor and knocked on the door of the office they had been in before. The door opened, and Joe was there. He smiled and gestured them in. Frank and Gary were sitting next to each other in silence.

'Come in, join the party,' Joe said.

Anthony and Katy sat down in the two other chairs and waited.

'Thanks for coming along again,' Joe said. 'I am very pleased to see you all.'

He looked at them all in turn. They were watching him warily, as if they were waiting for something important to happen. No one wanted to go first.

Joe said, 'Will you excuse me, I am just going to see how Grace is today.'

He left the room.

The four of them looked down: at their feet, their hands. Frank shut his eyes.

A minute passed by, and another one.

They breathed a big sigh of relief when Joe came back into the room.

'OK, Grace isn't feeling great. I think we might have to do our best without her today. I want today to be productive though: has anyone anything to suggest? Any ideas? Have you had any brainwaves?'

They were silent.

He said gently to Frank, 'What's in your bag, Frank?'

Frank had been hugging the large carrier bag against his chest. He now looked awkward and put it on his lap. 'It's just something Grace asked me to bring along. She was going to show me her photos and asked if I had any; nothing very interesting.'

Joe said, 'I'd like to see them. Would you show them to me, and to the rest of us?'

Frank sat like a statue. Suddenly he got up. He took the scrapbook out of the bag and gave it to Joe and left the room.

'What do you think we should do?' he asked the others.

'I think he wants us to look at it,' said Gary. 'That's what he is saying.'

Joe looked at Anthony and Katy. They nodded their agreement.

Joe put the large book down on the desk and lifted the front cover. For the next ten minutes they stood over it as Joe slowly flicked through it. Every page had newspaper headlines, articles, train tickets to destinations around the UK, programmes, plane ticket stubs, and photographs: photographs of Frank as a much younger boy, then older and bigger, with his family, with team mates, training, receiving awards, of moments of celebration as he crossed the finishing line — always first.

The Frank in the pictures looked very different to how he was now. He was big, strong, confident; he filled every picture. He was supreme.

They stared at the picture on the last page. They saw Frank, in the middle of a family group. They all looked so happy.

The little group clustered around the scrap book was silent.

Joe closed it again and they sat down.

Katy put her head in her hands and started crying. The others shut their eyes to blot out their sadness for Frank.

Joe looked out of the window. Frank was sitting on a bench in the garden, hunched and alone.

'Stay here, I'm going to ask him to join us.'

As Joe walked along the path towards him Frank heard him say, 'Jeez, you are a very strong guy, Frank.'

Frank laughed mockingly and said, 'No, I'm a complete weakling; I lost it again today.'

'No, you're made of solid steel, Frank. Come on, come back and join us. We want you to be with us, we need you.'

Frank levered himself to his feet and followed Joe back.

As he came into the room the others looked up. Frank could see that they were shocked.

He said for them, 'I know, it's hard to believe that it's me.'

They just stared at him.

Joe said finally, 'I don't know what to say, Frank.'

'Nor do I. I think that's part of my problem: I just don't have anything to say. There is nothing to say. I never lost a race. Now I've lost everything. I never learned how to lose.'

Another long silence.

'Except my rag, I keep losing my rag,' Frank said at last.

Gary thought back to Frank's reaction with Mr Wilson earlier and the scene in the library; he remembered the look of savage fury in Frank's face. Anthony and Katy thought of the moment Gary had had his nose splattered by Frank's fist.

'Thank you for showing us your memories, Frank. I think you're very brave,' Katy said.

'But I'm a coward. I keep running away,' he said.

'You didn't have to show us the scrapbook; you didn't run away from that,' Anthony said.

'I was going to show it to Grace, so I'd already got used to the idea of showing it,' Frank explained.

'Katy and Anthony are right though: you could still have decided not to,' Joe pointed out.

'I'm just so tired of having to deal with it all on my own, that's all,' Frank said.

Gary, Anthony and Katy were quiet. Frank's words had hit home for each of them.

'In my experience, limited though it is, everyone is dealing with something on their own. Sharing something difficult does take courage, but it usually helps in the end,' Joe said to no one in particular.

Gary felt his heart thudding. He wanted to say something, but he didn't know how or where to start. He looked at Joe, did he dare? Joe looked at him and raised his eyebrows.

Gary blurted out, 'Fuck it. OK, it's my turn. My dad is a drunk. He's violent. He is beating up my mum every night. He is forcing her to do things,' he paused for breath. 'He's a fucking animal and I'm scared for my mum. I'm really scared. I keep thinking he's going to kill her.'

Gary's voice ended in a strained whisper.

There was a shocked silence in the room.

'I don't know what to do. I don't want to ring the police; they wouldn't do anything anyway. I can't stop what's happening. My mum doesn't do anything — I don't think she can. She's got no choice but to just stand there and be smacked about the place,' Gary said, tears running down his face.

He went on, 'She's so small, and gentle. All she does is make his meals, clear up after his mess, make excuses for him. He's a total animal and she just takes it.'

There was a long silence. Finally, Joe said, 'It sounds like a living nightmare, Gary.'

Gary nodded. 'I used to look up to him. I thought he was so brave and tough. He's not. He's a drunken bully. He should be locked up.'

Anthony jumped in, 'I'm sorry, Gary. My father's a bully too. There's one big difference — he is locked up.'

Everyone's head turned to Anthony.

Anthony said, 'I'm sorry, I didn't mean to steal your thunder, although I realise it might sound like that. I just couldn't stop myself. Just for the record my father is currently in prison: he was convicted earlier this year for serious fraud. Now, I'll shut up again.'

'This is turning into some kind of weird dream,' Katy said.

Joe got up and looked out of the window, then said. 'Katy?'

'Oh, sorry, well, I've got some weird stuff going on too but honestly I don't want to tread on anyone's toes.'

'You might as well say, otherwise we'll feel like circus freaks,' Gary said.

'I think we are freaks,' Anthony said. 'I know I feel like one.'

Joe cut in, 'OK, this is what I think. No one here is a freak. We're all dealing with difficult stuff. Katy, if you want to say something that's fine, but only if you want to. Then, we'll all have the chance to say more if we want to. Agreed?'

They nodded.

Katy took in a deep breath. She made up her mind.

'Right, it's simple really, but complicated too. Three weeks ago, I discovered that the people I thought were my parents aren't. The girl I thought was my twin sister isn't. I now discover that I have a real mother who had me adopted when I was a baby. She has now written to me to say she wants to meet me. I've written to her to tell her that I think she's a selfish bitch. I've written again to say that I didn't mean it. I hate my parents — the ones that adopted me — but I love them too. I don't know who I am, what I'm doing, where I'm going. I am a total mess.'

Silence filled the room again.

Joe said at last, 'Thank you, Katy, for sharing your situation with us. In fact, you all amaze me. You are so brave and trusting to share such awful situations.'

Frank, Anthony, Gary and Katy all looked at him. They were expectant. They wanted him to do something to help them.

He said, 'We have some choices, but we also have an obligation. Let me start with the most important thing. We now have in our possession information that is private, sensitive and precious. We are going to treat each other's trust as if it is pure gold. We are never going to tell anyone anything about what we now know, not anyone. The only time we can share anything that we have learned is if the person to whom it belongs says so. Is that clear?'

They nodded.

'You now have choices to make. Do you want to talk more about what you're going through? Do you want help with it — do you want us all to get involved in helping? Do you want to step back out of all of this?'

He looked around the group and said, 'Katy, what do you want?'

'I want help; I'm lost.'

'Anthony?'

'Well, I haven't told you everything, so I'd like to say more and maybe get some help?'

'Gary?'

'I haven't got anything else to say, but I've got to do something, anything.'

'Frank?'

'I've got nothing left to say, but I think I need help, and I would like to help.'

'Sorry, I should have said that: I'd like to help too,' Anthony said.

'Me too,' Katy said.

'And me,' Gary said.

'And I want to help too,' said Joe. 'Between the five of us I think we're a powerful outfit, I really do.'

***

Joe looked at each of them in turn. They were looking back at him. He held each of their gazes for a second or two. As ever, Frank had shrunk back into himself. Gary looked very edgy, as if he was about to make a bolt for the door. Katy was hugging herself. Anthony looked eager, ready.

Joe said, 'I suggest we talk about each other's situation, see what we can do in each case and then agree a plan. What do you think?'

They all nodded, wary but willing.

'OK, alphabetically speaking, you're first Anthony. Do you want to go for it?'

Anthony looked at the others. They visibly relaxed.

'What I am going to tell you is hard to say, hard to believe and makes me feel totally humiliated. But I've got to do something about it, as I think you will see,' Anthony said, looking down.

'Only share what you want to; we've all got something to share so we're all in a similar position,' Joe said.

Anthony closed his eyes and, after a deep breath, said in a long burst, 'Well, my father was arrested a year ago. He went to court and was convicted of fraud and sent to prison for eight years. Basically, he was convicted of stealing millions of pounds by illegal trading on the Stock Exchange. He had been doing it for a long time. I had no knowledge of it, but I think my mother did. When the police came to investigate him, she gave them some papers which were critical in his conviction. I only found out last night. Yesterday I also found out that he has been writing to her, blaming her for everything, telling her that what he is going through is her fault.'

Anthony stopped. He was breathing hard. He looked at Joe. Joe looked kind, calm, interested. He reminded Anthony of the vicar when he'd returned the money, all those months ago.

'That's one half of the story but the other half is worse in a way. My father is a nasty and abusive man. He has bullied me all my life. He has bullied my mother all their married life. I never realised that he was a monster until he was gone. He treated me like a worthless animal. He never hit me or even threatened to, he just talked to me as if he hated me.

He talked to my mother in the same way. He was contemptuous of us both. I never had any friends. I never saw a television. I have spent my life feeling lonely or afraid... and so despised.'

Anthony stopped again. His breathing was ragged now. His face was red and there was such distress in his appearance that he looked as if he were going to burst into tears. But he went on.

'Over the years, as he became more and more malicious and abusive, I became increasingly resilient. I don't know how. I knew that one day I would be free of him. I know that there is something about me that makes people hate me. I can't help being the way I am. I always thought that one day people would realise that I'm not too bad, that they might suddenly see the real me, not someone to be laughed or sneered at, put down or beaten up, but someone who has ideas, is stronger than he looks: more interesting, more friendly, just a nice person.'

He paused again and looked around.

'The last two days have been the best two days of my life. I can't believe that I am actually sitting here with you all, especially you, Gary. I am thinking at last; I have arrived. But just when life is beginning to pick up, the monster has reached out to get me again. He has written to my mother and says he wants to see me. I know what he wants to do: he wants to divide me from my mother and get me on to his side against her. He's evil, I'm sure of it. There is something very bad about him and he makes me feel sick just thinking about him.'

Anthony sat back, he looked exhausted. Again, he spoke, quietly this time.

'Well, that's it. A sorry tale, don't you think?'

There was a long silence. Joe broke it, 'Thank you, Anthony, well done for getting it out and letting us hear it. Anyone want to say anything?'

The others were silent. They were trying to absorb it all.

Anthony spoke again. 'So, the posh voice, the manner that everyone despises, everything that people see — that's not the real me. But I don't even know what I'm like in real life; I've never had the chance to find out.'

'What do you want to do?' Katy asked at last.

'Good question,' Joe said.

'Find a way of killing him?' Gary suggested.

'If only I could. No, what I want is for him to be out of my life forever. I want to erase him completely,' Anthony said.

'That's so weird: that's what I have started to think about my dad too,' Gary said.

'Hold that thought, Gary. Let's work out Anthony's plan first,' Joe said.

'Sorry,' Gary said.

'No, it's a good point: you and Anthony do have something in common but they're also very different situations.'

'Maybe you should write to him to tell him to leave you and your mum alone,' Katy suggested. 'After all, he can't do much to you from prison.'

'I thought that. But the letter I saw this morning was so horrible, it made me feel sick,' Anthony said.

'Can't you just burn the letters?' Gary asked.

'Yes, but he's still going to keep writing them and trying to control us.'

'Can you tell the police?' Katy asked.

'Maybe, but I'm not sure what they can do to stop someone writing to his wife,' Anthony said.

They all stopped to consider the predicament.

Then Frank said, 'Do you want revenge, Anthony?'

Anthony looked at Frank closely. He weighed up his answer then said with horrible determination, 'Yes, I do. I want him to pay for what he's done to us.'

The other four were slowly beginning to realise that Anthony was not the boy they had thought him to be. He was well spoken, mannerly, had nothing of the coarse or surly appearance of the other teenage boys they knew, but they saw that there was a hard edge to him, an inner strength that unnerved them.

'What kind of payment do you have in mind?' Joe asked.

'I want him to feel like a worthless dog, like a beaten cur; I want him to be beaten like a cur and I want to do it.'

The others swallowed uncomfortably. The venom with which Anthony had just spoken chilled them.

Anthony looked around him. He seemed to waken from a dream.

He smiled and said, 'Phew, I don't know where that came from — scrap all that. I just want him gone, out of our lives.'

'Er, um, I'm feeling like a complete shit,' Gary said suddenly. 'I am a complete shit; I have been a total shit to you, Anthony.'

Anthony looked at Gary. He smiled and said, 'Don't worry about it. I had you beaten senseless a hundred times in my dreams.'

The humour lifted the room. There was suddenly energy and life and relief flooding through them all.

'This is mental. I think my head is going to blow,' Katy said.

'Shall we have a break?' Joe asked.

'No, let's keep going, now that we've started,' Katy said.

'So, Anthony, any ideas?' Joe asked.

'I know it sounds weird, but I think I ought to go and see him and tell him what I think — that he has wrecked our lives and he's not going to do it anymore.'

'Are you allowed into prisons?' Katy asked.

'Yes,' Joe said, then went on: 'How do you know what you'll say when you get there, Anthony?'

'I thought I'd write it down, practice a bit, then just say it.'

'OK, that's a good idea but I think it might be really hard. Have you thought about what he'll say, how you'll feel?' asked Joe.

'Not really. I only thought about it this morning.'

'What does everyone else think?' Joe asked.

'I think it might be really hard: he'll make you feel like a shit, like he used to,' Gary suggested.

'I agree,' said Frank.

'Then I'll have to practise,' Anthony said.

Joe said, 'Have you discussed it with your mother?'

'No, and I don't want too. She's had to deal with him for too long; I don't want her being bothered by anything about him ever again.'

'Frank, what do you think?' Joe asked.

Frank shifted uneasily in his chair then said, 'Use everything you have in your favour, eliminate all potential obstacles and train till you vomit.'

'There you go — that's what it takes,' Joe said.

'How can he train though?' Gary asked.

'We can act it out, can't we?' Katy said.

'Yes, we can try and work out the variables and put Anthony through it as many times as possible,' Joe said. 'What do you think, Anthony?'

'I think that's right: put me to the test.'

'When?' Katy asked.

'Whenever you want to do it,' Joe said to Anthony.

'Now?'

***

Anthony came into the room. He was accompanied by a prison warder. He looked ahead and saw his father sitting on the far side of a table. He looked around. There were other people in the room, but he couldn't take in anything except the grim, haughty, and contemptuous face of his father. Anthony sat down opposite him.

'I knew you'd come and see me. I knew I only had to click my fingers and you'd come running,' Richard Alexander said. 'So now you're here, what have you got to say for yourself?'

Anthony swallowed hard and said, 'I'm here to tell you to leave us alone. We don't want anything more to do with you. You've ruined our lives once: that's it — no more.'

Anthony's father looked back at his son. He saw the effort the boy was making.

'Get out. You disgust me. You have nothing over me. You are, and always have been, a pathetic little mummy's boy. You can rot in hell along with your bitch of a mother. I shall make you both pay; I shall always beat you, boy.'

Anthony wasn't beaten.

'How are you going to win? You're stuck here in prison. We're free.'

319

'Free? You'll never be free of me you little wretch. I shall infect your mind whilst I'm in this place; then when I get out, I shall poison your life — forever.'

Anthony tried again. 'Threats don't bother me, Father. I'm not scared of you.'

Richard Alexander laughed out loud. 'You are, Anthony. Your dreams are full of me. You see me smiling every time life kicks you, and life kicks you all the time. It kicks you because you are pathetic, weak, a loser. You'll never beat me. You will never be strong enough.'

Anthony was white now. He had started to shake. He thought for a minute then put his hands up and said, 'OK, let's stop for a minute.'

They all relaxed. Joe got up and walked around to Anthony. He put his hand on his shoulder and gripped it hard.

He said, 'Bloody good, Anthony. I had to work really hard that time.'

'Tell me he's not really like that, Anthony,' Katy said.

Anthony looked up and said, 'I know it's hard to believe but, yes, that's exactly what he's like.'

'Maybe we need to do it differently,' said Gary, his role as warder over.

'Any ideas?' Joe said.

'How about we take away his power? At the moment we're feeding him,' Frank said.

'Yes, good point,' Joe nodded.

'How do we do that?' Katy asked.

'Anthony, what do you think? Joe asked.

'Well, he's very clever. He can win an argument with anyone. There's something hard and cold about him; he doesn't seem to care what people think of him. It's like he doesn't need anyone,' Anthony said.

'The fact that he's writing horrible letters means that he is trying to achieve something though,' Katy said.

'Yeah, but what?' Gary asked.

'Maybe he just wants revenge for what your mum did?' Frank suggested.

'Yes, but I think there is more than that,' Anthony said.

'Well, it might not be this, but do you think he needs to feel that he is in control? In a place where he has no control maybe he needs to feel that he can just snap his fingers and make people jump to his beck and call?' Joe asked.

Anthony nodded as he thought about this.

'Maybe I should just ignore him then, just let it go?' he said slowly.

'How would you feel then?' Joe asked.

'I'd feel as if I'd let him win,' Anthony said. 'I can't stand the thought of that.'

'So, somehow, we have to find a way of ensuring that you have power over him?' said Katy.

'That's great, but how?' Anthony said.

'Well, what do you want, Anthony?' Joe asked.

'I want him out of our lives, I want him to realise that we have absolutely no interest or concern or anything for him, and that we are doing very well without him.'

'So, how about you go and see him but totally ignore him the whole time?' Katy suggested.

'That's a good idea. I bet that will wind him up — that would make my dad's blood boil,' Gary said.

'How about it, Anthony?' Joe asked.

'Maybe. I don't know if I can hold my nerve though,' Anthony said uncertainly.

'I think it's about how you prepare,' Frank said. 'If you prepare properly, with a very clear vision of yourself — what you'll do, how you'll react, how you will arrive and leave — then you'll feel in control.'

'Is that what you do, Frank?' Joe asked.

Frank nodded and said, 'I learned that, no matter how much physical training you do, you have to prepare the same amount mentally too. In particular you have to be calm, almost not there.'

There was a knock on the door. Startled, all five of them turned. The door opened, and the manager stood there.

She said, 'I'm really sorry to interrupt. May I have a quick word, Joe?'

'Sure, excuse me for a minute, I'll be back in a jiff,' he said to the other four.

When the door closed behind him, they stretched and yawned.

'This is such a weird day,' Katy said.

'I know, I was thinking that. I thought we'd be talking about a party and instead we're planning a trip to prison!' Gary said.

'Are you really going to see your dad?' Katy asked.

'Yes, I think it's the right thing to do,' Anthony said.

'Do you want us to come with you?' Frank asked.

Anthony looked at him, then at Gary and Katy.

'Would you?'

'Of course — try and keep us away!' Katy said without pausing to ask Frank and Gary.

They nodded their support.

Joe came back in and sat down.

'I'm going to have to nip off shortly. Before I do, are we clear what to do next?' he said looking at Anthony.

'Yes, I'm going to arrange a visit to see my father, as soon as possible.'

'We're going too,' Katy said.

'Will you come as well?' Anthony asked Joe.

'Yes, if I may. I'll drive us all down there. Meanwhile, Anthony, you have to prepare well, get everything done that you need to do. Remember what Frank said.'

***

They all left together. Joe came with them. He shook hands with each one outside their houses.

At Frank's he turned to him and said, 'Your situation is very different to the others', Frank. We shall all want to do something helpful for you. You know that, don't you?'

'I don't really want anything, at least nothing that can be given to me,' Frank said.

'I know, but will you give some thought to what you might want to do, to achieve, to try? We all want to do something, but I know that that in itself might seem like an extra pressure. So, if what you want from us is nothing but our time, then say so. If you want more, then say that too. I don't think we shall be satisfied with nothing though.'

Frank was silent for a second then said, 'I'm more concerned about my mother really.'

'OK, give that some thought too.'

'I will.'

'See you tomorrow, Frank,' Joe said, slapping Frank on the shoulder and walking off.

Frank watched him go. Joe was confident, unhurried but purposeful. He drew level with a group of boys kicking a football around the street. He slowed to let the ball roll past him but intercepted it, dribbled past three startled players and shot hard into the makeshift goal. He leapt up and whooped his joy. Then, as if it hadn't happened, he continued his measured walk up the street.

Frank couldn't help smiling. He felt good around Joe. He went inside and up to his room. Lying on his bed he went through his pre-race drill of counting down, of slowing his breathing, of running through every element of the race in his mind's eye. He was beginning to feel the familiar surge ignite in him. Then, it all disappeared in a flash as the jangling, screaming violence of the crash punched him again and again. His heart was pounding it was deafening him. He lay still. He calmed. It was a bit better this time. He actually managed to get back some of the control he'd been looking for, and which had eluded him for so long.

He sat up. He took a pen and a piece of paper and started to write.

***

'How did it go?' asked Susan as Katy came into her room.

'It's been another strange day. Totally mixed up. I don't even know where to start and, in any case, I can't tell you much,' Katy said, collapsing on Susan's bed.

'Tell me what you can then.'

'Well, I posted the letter to Jane, I mean my mother — well, you know that bit. I posted the second one; you know that bit too. Honestly, I'm losing track of everything. Then I went with Anthony to The Beeches, but we stopped off at the Golden Bengali. We saw that Haroon, the one we saw last night. I tell you, Suzy, he's gorgeous; I think I might see a bit more of him. Then Anthony and I went on to The Beeches where we've been ever since.'

'How was Anthony?' Susan asked.

'He's all right. He's a nice boy. He really is, despite how he talks and what he looks like.'

'I know. It's funny — he's nothing like people imagine I'm sure.'

'Well, then we all talked about ourselves. I told them about everything that's happening to me.'

'Really? Wow, I bet that took some doing, didn't it?'

'Well, put it this way, it wasn't that amazing compared with what everyone else told me. I can't tell you though: we're sworn to secrecy.'

'So, Frank, Anthony and Gary all have something happening to them?'

'Yeah, and that's it; no more.'

'OK, how was the old lady?'

'We didn't even see her. She wasn't very well, so all the time we were just talking with Joe.'

'I wish I was part of the team; it sounds like you're having a ball.'

'Hmmm, well it's not exactly a laugh a minute you know.'

'No, I know that — it's just that you're all getting into something different, unusual.'

'Yeah, you're right. It is actually quite exciting in a way.'

'So, how do you feel about Jane?'

'I don't know, I just don't know. I hate her, and I want to meet her too. I keep wondering what she's like. Am I like her or my real dad? Maybe I'm not like either of them. I could have loads of brothers and sisters: people I meet in the street might be my relatives.'

'Well, maybe we'll find out one day. If you ever meet her, can I come with you?'

'I hope you will — although I think I might want to be on my own at the actual moment. But if you could be there to mop me up after, that would be brilliant.'

'What did the others say when you told them?'

'Well, I thought my situation was bad! You wouldn't believe what they're going through. Don't ask though: I won't tell you.'

'I know something about Frank, don't I?' Susan reminded her.

'Yeah, but that's only half of it.'

'Oh no. No other sad things for him, that poor boy?'

'Stop it. You'll wring it all out of me and I promised not to tell.'

'No, you're right: don't tell me more.'

'I can't tell you more, but we're all going to visit a prison,' Katy said. 'Please though, Sooz, please don't say anything.'

Susan laughed and said, 'If I just stay quiet for thirty seconds, you'll tell me everything anyway.'

'No, that's it. But maybe Anthony won't mind you knowing, shit, jeez, I can't help it,' Katy groaned.

'Leave it, Katy; that's it, no more.'

***

Anthony was at home. He was reliving the role play they had gone through earlier. He was feeling fired up by the time he had had with the others, wound up by the interaction he'd had with his pseudo-father, and now he was trying to piece together a new normality. He went into the kitchen.

'What do I need to do to visit Father?'

'Don't tell me you want to?'

'I do; I'm not sure why. It's been nagging me for ages now: I do want to visit him. It's not that I want to see him, or be with him, it's more that I want to see him in prison, where he deserves to be.'

'I strongly urge you not to, Anthony. You know what he's like.'

'Yes, he scares me; he makes me feel small and pathetic; he will probably ignore me. But it's something that I want to do, I've got to do.'

'I can't go there with you. I just cannot face him. You understand, don't you?' She looked at him for reassurance.

'Yes, it's OK, Mother, I understand. Anyway, I would like to go on my own.'

'Really?'

'Well, actually I am going to go with Joe and the others. We were talking about it.'

'You told them about him being in prison?' Margaret Alexander was shocked.

Anthony nodded. He realised his mistake.

'I can't believe it! It's so shaming,' she said, her hands over her face.

'It's OK, honestly. They didn't think anything. Anyway, they all had problems that are just as bad, worse really,' Anthony said, trying to calm his mother.

'How can it be worse than us? Your father is in prison. He hates us; he is trying to abuse us from afar: what can be worse than that?'

Anthony thought about Frank's awful tragedy and his spectacular running, Gary's mother being beaten up, Katy not even knowing who her mother was, or her father.

He said, 'Believe me, we're not alone in the trauma business.'

His mother turned to him and said, 'Is this Joe looking out for you all? Is he a decent person do you think?'

'I think he's amazing. He's definitely looking out for us all, more than I've ever known anyone do before,' Anthony said with certainty.

'What do you know about him, though?'

Anthony thought about this. It hadn't occurred to him to ask about Joe. He made a mental note to fill in some gaps.

'I don't know anything about him. I'll find out,' he said.

***

Jenny Abbott was in the kitchen when she heard the doorbell ring. She wiped her hands on her apron and went to the front door. Waiting there was a middle-aged man in a dark blue suit. He wore a broad-brimmed hat and horn-rimmed glasses.

'Yes?' she asked.

He smiled at her, put out his hand and said, 'Good evening, my name is Peter Gregory. I'm from the Prudential. I would be delighted if you would spare a few minutes for me to tell you about some amazing new insurance policies the Pru is bringing out. Yes, before you tell me that you've got insurance, that you're busy, that your husband isn't in, that you've got dinner on the way, let me tell you that I've been sent out from head office to hand out personally some extra special deals. You're on my list — not everyone in the street, just this house. Now, it will only take a few minutes to talk you through it all; I've got all the bumf here and, I promise you, you'll not regret a single second of our time together. As I say, I'm Peter Gregory, the Man from the Pru. Your name is?'

'Mrs Abbott,' she said.

'Oh, come on now: tell me your first name. Let's be pals,' he said smiling.

'Well, it's Jen,' she said.

'Jen. Are you a Jenny or a Jennifer?' he asked, still smiling.

'Jenny.'

'Good, I love the name Jenny; may I call you that?'

'Umm, well, er.'

'Jenny,' he lowered his voice, 'let me tell you about these deals inside. I don't want your neighbours getting wind of them. How about we have a cup of tea and then I'll be out of the way.'

She felt herself being drawn to this man. There was something compelling about him. She looked at her watch. The black strap showed up against her frail white wrist.

'Well, five minutes only,' she said.

'Fantastic! Lead the way.'

She showed him in and led the way into the kitchen.

'Do you mind sitting in here?' she asked.

'This is perfect: the heart and soul of any house,' he said beaming.

He sat down at the table and put his books and folders out in front of him.

'What time does your husband come home from work, Jenny?' he asked.

'In a few minutes, although sometimes he has a drink or two at the Red Lion on his way home.'

'Well, I hope to meet him too, if possible. I want him to be in the know too. Got any children?' he asked.

'Yes, three sons, all grown up now,' she said, rinsing out the teapot.

'Tell me about them. I'm sure you are keen to give them the best future you can possibly provide for them?'

'Yes, of course. Well, Derek and Kevin work at the same place as my husband, and Gary is in his last year at school.'

'Ah, I remember those days so well. When everything seems easy and the future is forever,' he said, leafing through his books. 'Why don't you sit down, take the weight off your feet for a few minutes?'

She did, grimacing slightly as she lowered herself into the chair facing him. She saw that he'd noticed.

'The possibility of a bright, safe and happy future is so important, don't you think?' he said.

She nodded. She looked into his face. He was watching her closely. He suddenly seemed a bit too big for the small kitchen. She got up again.

'How do you like your tea?' she asked.

'Good, strong and hot, no sugar please.'

'I really can't waste too much time: I do have dinner to make; they'll all be back soon,' she said.

'I understand. I'm just grateful to have your company for a few minutes.'

She looked at him out of the corner of her eye. He didn't look so big now.

She put a mug of tea in front of him and sat down. Now, he seemed to have shrunk a few inches. He was sitting low in his chair and had his face in his folders. She relaxed again.

'So, one or two questions, just to get us started, is that all right?'

'Yes.'

'Tell me what you would like to be able to do in the future, you and your husband, once the young gentlemen have flown the nest.'

'I don't think 'gentlemen' is quite the right word for them,' she said smiling.

'Ha, lusty lads, are they?' he asked, smiling in return.

'Yes, they're quite a handful; lovely though.'

'Sure, I know what you mean. But about you and your husband, tell me what you see in the future for you two.'

She glanced at his face. He was flicking through a brochure.

'I don't know,' she said.

'Well, the thing is that the Pru has a policy aimed at you. If you pay into it for a few years, you can draw it out to pay for a wonderful holiday, some home improvements, a new car — that kind of thing,' he read.

'To be honest, I just think about today. I don't look into the future,' she said.

Peter Gregory sipped his tea. He'd gone quiet. A minute before, he'd been hale and hearty; now he was silent.

After a while he knocked back his tea and said, 'Do you ever feel like making a fresh start? Putting it all behind you?'

She looked at him. What was he talking about? 'No, I'm very happy as I am: my boys and Brian, we have everything we want.'

'What do you want though, Jenny? What would you like in particular?'

She was feeling uncomfortable now. This conversation felt really strange.

'I think I'd better get on: they'll be back soon,' she said and got slowly to her feet.

'Good, I'm really looking forward to meeting your husband,' he said.

They heard a door slam overhead and then heavy feet on the stairs. The kitchen door opened, and Gary came in, he stopped and stared.

'Which one of your boys is this, Jenny?' Peter asked.

'This is Gary, the clever one,' she said.

'Very good to meet you, Gary. I'm Peter Gregory, the Man from the Pru.'

Gary was rooted to the spot. Peter stepped towards him and shook his hand.

'Want a cuppa, Gary?' his mother asked.

'Er, no, ta.'

'I was just talking to your mother about the future, what she dreams about, that sort of thing,' Peter Gregory explained.

'Oh, well I'm just out. Dad will be home soon you know,' Gary said looking at Joe.

'Good, I want to talk to him about what the Pru can offer.'

'Do you want me to stay?' Gary asked his mother.

Joe shook his head.

'No, you're fine to go out; I'll leave your dinner in the oven,' she answered.

Gary walked to the hall door, his eyebrows raised as he looked at Joe, who winked at him.

They heard the front door close. 'What a nice young man,' Peter said.

'He's very clever. I think he might be a writer one day,' Jenny said.

'I always say to people that they must have dreams. If you have a dream, you're much more likely to achieve it than if you don't have one. In fact, I like to talk about dreams. Will you sit down for a minute and let me talk to you about your dreams,' he said, pointing to the chair.

Not sure why, she sat down.

'I know this is a bit weird, Jenny. I'm going to talk to you about dreams. Is that all right? It will just take a couple of minutes. You don't have to do anything except listen to me. Honestly, if you can bear to listen to my voice for a couple of minutes, then that is all that I need.'

She heard his voice: it sounded calm and soothing. She was tired. She really did want nothing to do for a couple of minutes. She nodded her agreement.

'I've learned from the people I see that life catches up with us sometimes and it's really hard to stop and wonder if we are doing the right thing, making the best decisions, exploring all the choices we have available to us. We tend to think that what we've got now is what we'll always have. It feels as if we are trapped. Actually, we all have choices, and the people who are healthy and well are the ones that make good choices. Jenny, you have choices, like everyone else.'

She listened to his voice. Her eye lids felt incredibly heavy, in fact, all she could think of was how tired she was, how heavy, how sleepy. She felt her eyes close. She actually felt as though she were about to fall asleep with a complete stranger talking to her. Suddenly she didn't care, she relaxed and gave up.

'I have an idea that sometime soon you are going to be presented with choices that will need you to be strong and determined. I think the true Jenny Abbott is going to emerge: the true one, the one who is capable of making strong decisions, of being brave, courageous, strong. You used to be unsure as to what was the right thing to do, but now it is all becoming clear to you. When the time comes you know that you are sure, certain, positive. You are feeling so relieved about your certainty that your spirits are lifting you feel lighter, more confident, more alive. At last, it's going to happen. The moment you've been waiting for is finally coming and you're ready for it. You are, Jenny, you really are ready.'

For some strange reason Jenny felt light-headed. She could feel her heart thumping with adrenalin; she was bigger, stronger and more powerful — she felt elated.

'The time is coming, Jenny, very soon. You are ready for it and it is making you feel in control, at last.'

She was smiling.

'Now, how about another cup of tea?' Peter Gregory said. 'I'm parched.'

Jenny opened her eyes; she shook her head to clear her mind.

'Yes, coming right up,' she said.

She poured another cup, her mind still scrambled; but she felt good, she really did.

'So, I shall probably have to go soon. It's a shame I'll be missing your husband.'

She looked at him again. She smiled at him.

'I'll tell him you came if you like?'

'Ah, I wonder if this is him now?'

The front door slammed shut and seconds later Mr Abbott came in. He looked at Peter Gregory and then his wife.

'This is Mr Gregory from the Pru; he has some offers on insurance policies.'

Peter got to his feet and said, 'What a pleasure to meet you, Mr Abbott it really is.'

'You don't know me. How do you know it's a pleasure?' Abbott asked. He looked at the stranger. He was a bit too smart and a bit too clean-cut for his liking.

'I'm only going on what your wife has told me, but you're right: it's good to meet you in the flesh.'

'We're not interested in insurance; whatever happens to us is going to happen insurance is a total waste of time and money,' Abbott was dismissive.

'Well, maybe saving up for a holiday, a car, something nice in the future: how about that?'

Brian Abbott took a can from the fridge, opened it and took a long swig. He belched loudly; his wife turned to the sink in embarrassment.

'Sorry, Jen, can't help it. She doesn't like me burping in front of people, I don't know why.'

'Ah, the first drink of the day — it's always the best one,' Peter said.

'Well, that's true, but this is my fourth.'

Gregory laughed and shook his head then said, 'You're a proper good, old-fashioned bloke, I can tell. None of this waiting for the sun to go over the yardarm for you.'

'You what?'

'I remember the days when I could get drunk at work and no one cared one jot,' Gregory said.

'Not at the Prudential, I hope?' Jenny said.

'No, long ago, when men were men and suits were suits.'

'Wanna drink now?' Abbott asked.

'I shouldn't but, yes, thank you.'

'Come on. Come into the front room. You can tell me about your crooked scams with the Pru,' Abbott said.

They went into the living room. As he left the room, Gregory caught Jennifer's eye; he smiled and tapped his nose. She smiled back.

***

332

When he'd seen Joe in the kitchen, Gary had been shocked. He'd come very close to blurting out something, but Joe's eyes had told him to keep quiet. What was he up to? Gary's brain was working overtime now. One thing he'd been sure about though, his mother seemed very relaxed about him being there. Normally she was timid with strangers, but not Joe. She had been talking to him as if he were a long-lost friend.

Gary was now walking aimlessly. Only a few days ago he would have rung up Steve and they would have gone out to slouch on a street corner, smoking, threatening, sniggering. The idea filled him with embarrassment. He used to enjoy being a thug: now he was ashamed of himself. What had happened to him? He wasn't sure.

His mind wandered back to the incident in the bus shelter when Katy Walker had been so pissed up. He screwed his eyes up to rid himself of the images. God, he'd been horrible. He wished with all his might he could go back to the scene and make it a different one.

He found himself walking towards Anthony's house. Something beyond his control was drawing him there. He rang the bell and waited. The door opened, and Anthony stood there.

'Hello, Gary,' he said, smiling broadly. 'Come in! Please come in.'

Gary followed Anthony inside. Mrs Alexander was there.

'Hello, Gary,' she said. 'This is a surprise.'

It was a surprise to him too. He wanted to be somewhere safe and secure; for some weird reason, being here felt like home.

'I'm sorry to just turn up but I wanted to talk to Anthony about something,' he said.

'No, you're very welcome. You can always come here if you want,' Anthony said.

There was a pause and then Anthony said, 'Let's go into my room.'

Anthony was reeling. Never in his life had anyone other than he or his family ever been in his bedroom. He was feeling self-conscious and embarrassed. What would Gary think? Would he find him and his possessions completely boring? How amazing was it? Gary Abbott coming into his room!

Anthony sat on his bed and pointed at his chair for Gary to sit.

Gary looked around. It was bigger than his bedroom, had one less bed in it, and was incredibly tidy. He saw hundreds of books: on shelves, on the windowsill, piled up neatly beside Anthony's bed.

'Have you read all those?' he asked, impressed.

'Of course, some of them a few times.'

'No wonder you're so clever.'

'Well, when you don't have any friends and there isn't a television you have to fill in the time somehow,' Anthony said.

Gary nodded and fell silent. He felt like a shit again.

'Anyway, never mind my sob stories: what's happened?' asked Anthony.

'Er, right. The thing is, something weird has just happened and I wanted to tell someone, and I knew where you lived, and I thought that maybe we could talk about it?' Gary explained.

'Sure, yes, good idea,' Anthony said, keen to know more.

'I was in my bedroom and went downstairs. I was going to talk to my mum but who do you think was talking to her?'

Anthony thought for a minute then said, 'The police?'

Gary shook his head. 'No. Although that's not a bad guess. No, it was Joe.'

Anthony blinked at him.

'Yeah, I didn't say anything, obviously. I ignored him, although I must have looked surprised. I just went out and left them to it.'

'That's really strange,' said Anthony.

Gary nodded.

'How does he know where you live?' Anthony asked.

'He must have made a note of the door number when he walked back with us earlier.'

'Well, I suppose he wanted to meet your mother; maybe he was talking to her about you?' Anthony suggested.

'I thought that, but that can't be it because he pretended not to know me, and she didn't say anything like — I don't know — 'here is Gary now', that kinda thing. Anyway, he was pretending to be someone else: he told her that he was working for the Prudential, selling insurance. He had a load of brochures and stuff.'

334

They were both silent as they thought about it.

'I'm scared that he was going to talk to her about what I said earlier, you know,' Gary said.

'He wouldn't do anything that would put her or you at risk though, would he? He's too clever for that,' Anthony reassured him.

'Yeah, but he doesn't know my dad, and he usually comes home around now. I wouldn't give Joe much chance with my dad,' Gary said.

'Is he as bad as that?' Anthony asked.

Gary thought for a minute and then said, 'He's a fucking nightmare.'

They heard the phone ring next door and Mrs Alexander answer it.

'Anthony, it's for you,' she called.

'Me?' Anthony said in surprise. He'd never had a call, never.

He went into the hall, picked up the phone and said, 'Hello?'

'Hi, Anthony, it's Katy.'

'Katy?'

'I wondered, well, we wondered if we could pop round,' Katy said. 'Me and Susan.'

'Um, well yes, of course, of course, please do,' Anthony said delighted.

Then he remembered his guest, 'Gary's here, is that OK?'

'Gary?' he heard Katy say.

'Yes, he just popped in for a chat.'

'Erm — yeah, sure, that's cool,' she said.

'It's a pity Frank isn't here too,' Anthony said.

'Well, why don't you ring him up and ask him?'

'I don't know his number.'

'You prat! Get it from Directory Enquiries; that's what I did to get your number,' Katy said.

'Oh, yes, good thinking.'

He put the phone down.

'More guests coming, Ma,' he said laughing. 'Just call me Mr Popular.'

'Oh, well, that's good, isn't it?' she said a bit unsure.

'Yes, it's just another one of our meetings,' Anthony said. 'I'll just see if I can ring Frank.'

***

Frank had finished his letter to Ailsa when he heard the telephone ring. He got up and answered it.

'Frank, this is Anthony Alexander, from school.'

Frank smiled at Anthony's overly formal greeting.

'Hello, Anthony.'

'I, well, we, were wondering if you'd like to come around. Gary, Katy and Susan are here, and it didn't seem right without you. You'll come around, won't you?'

Frank paused. Did he want to? He suddenly felt lonely.

'Thank you, Anthony, yes please.'

He heard Anthony's smiling voice say, 'Splendid, come as soon as you can.'

Frank went into the living room and said to his mother, 'That was the boy I was telling you about, Anthony. He's asked me around to his place.'

'Do you want to go?' Janice asked.

'Yes, but I'll stay here if you want me to.'

'Silly. Be off with you. I'm fine. Have some fun, Frank: that's what I want.'

'Sure?'

'Very.'

***

Frank followed Anthony into his bedroom where Gary, Katy and Susan were sitting, Gary on the chair and the sisters on the bed.

They cheered when they saw him. Frank's face flushed.

'Right. First of all, thank you very much for coming along everyone. I feel very honoured to have such noble guests in my humble abode,' Anthony said.

'Anthony, you knob, you sound like you've just stepped off the set of Upstairs Downstairs,' Katy said laughing.

'Sorry,' Anthony said.

'Don't listen to her, Anthony. I like how you speak,' said Susan.

'Well, anyway, now we're all here, Gary had something to tell us — but the problem is Susan,' Anthony said.

'Oh, sorry, I shouldn't be here,' Susan said, suddenly aware of her outsider status.

'Well, the thing is, I wondered if we could ask her to be part of the group?' Katy said.

They looked at each other.

'I don't mind,' said Gary.

'Nor do I,' Anthony said.

They looked at Frank. He was sprawled on the floor. He took up a lot of space.

'Susan, I used to be a good runner. Now I'm a loser. You know the rest.'

'Frank, you're being a knob now. He was the fastest runner in the country. He's not a loser, he's still a total winner,' Katy said, very proud.

'My dad's a fucking bastard and he hits my mum,' Gary said.

'My father's in prison for committing fraud, and he's a bastard, too,' Anthony said.

'And you know my story,' Katy said. 'It's your story too.'

'Thanks everyone, thank you for letting me join in,' Susan said.

'Tell them what happened, Gary,' Anthony said. He marvelled that he was able to tell his nemesis what to do. Gary didn't seem to mind. He told them about Joe.

'He's up to something; I don't know what, but he does things for reasons,' Katy said.

'Susan, we spent this afternoon planning a trip to visit my father — what I would say and how to deal with him,' Anthony said. Then, to all of them, 'How about we think about what Gary should do about his father.'

They looked at Gary.

He said, 'What? What can we do?'

'I saw an episode of *The Sweeney* where a woman was being beaten up by her husband; it was awful,' Katy said.

Gary closed his eyes and swallowed. 'It is terrible, fucking awful. I can't bear it. I can hear him swearing and shouting; then she starts crying, not loudly but sort of whimpering. Then I can hear him hitting her, and then there's this awful sound of crashing as she falls against things.'

Katy said, 'In *The Sweeney*, Dennis Waterman had a fight with the husband, and he took the woman away. I know that isn't going to happen here, but perhaps we should call the police?'

'Yeah, but what will happen then? My old man will get his own back on her.'

'I think there's something like a home for battered women,' Susan suggested.

'Yeah, but if my mum goes there, then he'll just track her down and drag her out again,' Gary said.

'But they must have security, otherwise it's not very safe, is it?' Katy said.

'Well, we could find out, couldn't we? Maybe in the library?' Anthony suggested.

'But how would we get her there, or anywhere?' Gary said.

'Maybe that's what Joe is thinking; maybe he's one step ahead of us?' Frank said.

They looked at him. They all nodded.

Anthony said, 'Right, we need to talk to him tomorrow. Meanwhile, I'll go and get the telephone directory.'

He came back with it.

He read out loud, '*Refuge for women at risk of domestic violence — see Social Services.* Hang on, here's the number: 953 3972. There's no address. Shall we ring it up?'

'Should we? I'm not sure. What if they want to know details — my name, my mum's name, worst still my dad's name?' Gary said.

'I'll ring it. I'll just pretend I'm the daughter, but I'll keep my identity secret,' Katy said.

They looked at Gary. He looked back, unsure.

'It's worth a try, Gary,' Frank said.

Frank's calm voice galvanised Gary. 'OK, go on then,' he said.

They trooped into the hall. Katy dialled the number.

***

'Wanna fag?' asked Brian Abbott as he and Peter Gregory sat down in the front room.

'They're against my religion, thanks though.'

'Suit yourself. What's in it for you?' Abbott asked.

'What in particular?'

'Flogging insurance to poor people like us — what do you get out of it?'

'Good question. Well, it's a job. I get paid for it plus, to be honest, I want the people who buy a policy to get some benefit from it.'

'I'd rather spend my money on beer and fags and fuck the future.'

'Fair enough, it's your money.'

'I sometimes think that maybe I should put some money into a bank but then it'll just go towards the salary of someone who does fuck all for a living when I'm working my bollocks off.'

Peter Gregory smiled.

Abbott took a long slurping pull from his can and belched again.

'Have you met my boys?'

'I met Gary. He seemed like a bright lad.'

'Bright! He needs to watch out: he's getting a bit too big for his boots. I'm going to have to put him straight on a few things before long.'

'Hmmm?' Peter Gregory answered.

'Yeah, talking to Pakis, thinking he's cleverer than the rest of us; I'm not having that.'

Gregory stayed quiet.

'Want another one?' Abbott asked, pointing to the can by Peter Gregory's elbow.

'No, I'm fine — thanks though.'

Abbott levered himself to his feet and scuffed his way to the kitchen, 'Something nice for dinner, gorgeous?'

Jenny said, 'Stop it, Brian, we have a guest.'

'Nothing wrong with showing my wife my appreciation is there?'

'Stop it, it's not right.'

'Fucking hell, it's like living in a monastery around here.'

Abbott came back into the room with two cans.

'Are you married?' he asked.

'Not anymore. I got divorced a while ago.'

'You can play the field then: you're lucky.'

'My work takes up all my spare time I'm afraid.'

'Work? Selling insurance ain't exactly work is it?'

'Long hours though.'

Abbott lit another cigarette.

'May I ask you a question?' Gregory asked.

'Ah, here we go, the hard sell.'

'No, I'm interested: why are you talking to me?'

Brian Abbott looked at him, gulped from his can, dragged on his cigarette and said, 'It's not often I get any intelligent company around here. My boys are always out, pulling birds, or can't be arsed to talk to me. Jen's always in the kitchen and seems to have forgotten how to talk. To be honest, it sounds bloody stupid: I get a bit lonely, in my own house; fucking ridiculous I know.'

'Oh, well thanks for asking me to join you. May I call you Brian?'

'Sure, you can call me what you like: Sir, Your Lordship, Your Excellency, anything like that,' Abbott chuckled.

'Have you always lived around here?'

'Thirty years. My folks moved here after the war.'

'Are they alive?'

'Dead as door nails.'

'Oh, I'm sorry to hear that.'

'Don't be. My mum was ill most of the time and my father just got drunk and beat my mum and me up, just for a laugh.'

'I bet that was tough.'

'Not really; put hairs on my chest.'

'I think it's important to have respect for your father.'

'Damn right.'

'I'm going to have to get off in a minute — time waits for no man.'

340

'You sure? I'll ask Jen to do you a dinner if you want.'

'Thank you, but no, I'd better go.'

'Aren't you going to sell me some insurance?'

'I don't think so. I think you've got things just how you want them.'

'Yeah, I have, most of the time.'

'Good luck, Brian. Thanks for the drink.'

Hands clasped they looked at each other.

'Bye then, Brian. Good luck,' Gregory said again, and went to the front door. He looked back at Abbott walking towards the kitchen, calling to his wife, 'Fucking smart-arse. Not bad though. Dinner ready yet?'

***

'Social Services,' said the female voice.

'Hello, I'm ringing for some information,' Katy said, the others listening.

'Yes?'

'Well, it's my dad. He keeps coming home drunk, and then he hits my mum and I'm scared. I don't know what to do. Can you help?'

Katy listened attentively, then said, 'Not really, I don't have any relatives nearby, and I don't want to tell anyone what's going on.'

Another pause.

'She doesn't want to tell anyone. She just takes it, every night. Can she come and stay somewhere or something?' Then, 'No, no, er, no, I don't want to say my name, do you mind?'

Katy gestured for a pen and paper, Anthony handed her his pen and pushed the telephone directory towards her.

'How do I do that?' Katy asked.

Katy scribbled something down then said, 'But is it safe? What's to stop my dad finding my mum?'

More silence.

'Thank you, that's very helpful.'

She put the phone down and they went back to Anthony's room.

'So, this is the situation. We have to get your mum to contact social services herself or go to the police and then they'll arrange for her to go

341

to a refuge if they think that that is the best thing to do. They don't give the address out. I suppose it makes sense doesn't it?'

They all looked at Gary.

'Naah, she wouldn't do that. She'd think she was a failure, or that she was letting my dad down, or letting us down.'

'But, staying at home, Gary, that's not right either,' Katy said.

'I know,' Gary said, hanging his head.

'Could you talk to her? See if she would think about it?' Susan asked.

'Maybe. She might listen, but I don't think she'd do anything.'

'We should talk to Joe about it,' Frank said. 'He's met her now and maybe he'll have an idea.'

They murmured their agreement to this.

'What a fucking mess,' Gary said. 'The thing is that I've only just realised what's been going on. I know it's hard to believe but until the last couple of weeks I didn't even realise. I thought my dad was just a laugh, a bit of a drunk, but that was all. I mean, he used to get angry and we'd all be scared. But I didn't realise he was attacking my mum like he does.'

'Well you know now, and you're trying to do something about it,' Katy said.

'Can I change the subject? Will you tell us more about your situation, Katy?' Anthony asked.

***

Victoria's phone rang.

'Hello?'

She heard Joe's voice, 'What are you doing right now?'

She smiled. She'd spent the day waiting for the moment for him to ring.

'I'm washing my hair, tending to my dairy farm, completing my translation of Plato's long-lost parchments and of course my schoolwork but I might be able to spare a minute or two.'

'Good, may I come around? I'm desperate to get away from something, and I can't wait to see you again.'

'Sure: jump on your steed and gallop over,' she said, trying to stay cool.

'Hi-Ho, Silver!' he cried and put the phone down.

Her mind had been in a whirl all day. She'd had to pinch herself several times. She still wasn't absolutely sure that what had happened last night might not turn out to be a dream. But it had been his voice on the phone, and he was on his way over now.

Twenty minutes later his car was there, and it was him walking up to her door. She opened it and stood there, uncertain.

'I wonder if I can interest you in an exciting insurance policy?' he said.

She laughed and said, 'I had been wondering what you might say to me, or what I'd say in return. I didn't get close.'

'Good. I am a man of mystery, after all.'

He put his arms around her and hugged her hard. She felt his body tight against hers. It felt absolutely wonderful.

She led him into the kitchen, 'What was the 'something' you had to get away from?'

Joe sat down and sighed deeply. Victoria was quiet too. He looked all done in. She stood behind him and touched his shoulder.

'Want a massage?' she asked.

'Oh God, I can think of nothing better right now.'

She put her hands on his shoulders. She hadn't massaged a man before, other than her father whose frame had withered to just skin and bone. She felt Joe's physical power under her fingers; it thrilled her to touch him so intimately.

'That's amazing,' he said.

'Tell me what you want to, but don't feel obliged,' she said.

'Well, our little team has emerged — individually and collectively, with unbelievable results. I have just spent a little time with the most obnoxious man I've ever met; and believe me I've met a few. Plus, Grace wasn't well enough to see us today and I'm beginning to worry that her time is fast running out.'

'Oh no! What a shame.'

'I know. I'd begun to think that she might be invincible. She was struggling yesterday evening, and she was bad again today.'

'Did you tell them she is so frail?'

'No. Believe me, there was far too much other stuff to broach it. I was very conscious of protecting Frank from anything like that — Frank in particular, but all of them would be upset to think she wasn't going to make it.'

'I know. I spoke to Gary today; he seems really excited about what you've asked him to do.'

'That's great.'

Victoria rested her hands on his shoulders. She wanted to hug him and let him know that he was safe now. She felt shy though. She still hardly knew him.

'May I hug you?' she asked.

'I'd love that.'

She moved around, and he shifted his chair to face her. He rested his head against her chest, and she put her arms around him and felt his around her. They stayed still for several minutes.

Finally, she drew away and went to put the kettle on.

'Who was Mr Obnoxious?' she asked.

'Do you mind if I don't say? It's all tied up with stuff that we're trying to sort out and I need to keep things confidential.'

Victoria felt a flash of resentment. She wanted to know about him, who he mixed with, what was important to him. She felt ashamed immediately.

'Of course, I understand. You've obviously all bonded.'

'I know. Something has happened for them; I'm not exactly sure what. There's some kind of energy and group dynamic that's been happening that I haven't seen take place: they have become a really strong little unit. It's amazing really. I think that they are going to stick together and try and sort some things out.'

'Gary and Anthony included?'

'Yep. I know it sounds impossible.'

'What did you do, or say?'

'Nothing. It all happened without me.'

'Not quite, Joe. You created the opportunity; you gave them the chance and the environment.'

'Yes, you and I did that. But they've picked up the ball and it's them that are running with it.'

'What is the ball, or can't you say?' she asked.

'I can't say but I can tell you that each of them is struggling to deal with something major and I'm going to try and help them — although if I'm honest I think they'll manage on their own.'

Victoria faced him again.

'You'll keep them safe, won't you?' she asked.

'I'll protect them, the best that I can.'

She moved close to him again and bent down and kissed his lips. She felt his hands move up and down her back; she shivered with pleasure. They kissed harder and with more urgency.

'Would you think me a loose woman if I suggested we went to bed?'

'No, I'd think you were a mind reader.'

'Come on then, you can protect me too.'

'Ah, so that's what it's called these days,' he answered as he got to his feet.

For a moment they stood together face to face. He pulled her into his arms and held her close. She felt him harden against her.

'Now,' she said and turned and ran up the stairs, 'if you think you can catch me.'

***

'So, that night in the bus shelter, that was the day you found out?' Gary asked Katy, feeling like a complete shit all over again.

Katy nodded. She had kept her eyes shut the whole time she'd told her story. It had poured out of her. All five of them were quiet; no one knew what to say.

Anthony turned to Susan and said, 'It must have been terrible for you too?'

Susan looked at him and nodded. She said, 'It's much worse for Katy though: all of a sudden finding out that you're not the person you thought.'

'So, what next?' Anthony asked Katy.

'I'm waiting for her to reply to my letter — well, both letters.'

'What do you want to happen?' Frank asked.

'I don't know. One minute I feel like I want none of it to have happened. Then, the next minute I think it would be amazing if my real mum turned out to be a famous film star or something. Then I get scared and wonder if she's a drug addict or something awful.'

'You don't have to do anything you don't want to, do you?' Anthony said.

'No, but I'm scared that once I've contacted her, I shall be in too deep. I've already opened the door a bit and God knows what will happen next.'

They were all quiet again, thinking through the implications.

'How are you getting on with your parents — well, you know — your old parents?' Anthony asked.

'Terrible. I hate to be with them; I feel like I can't trust them.'

'You *can* trust them: you know that, don't you?' Susan said turning to her sister.

'I know. I just keep thinking about them lying about it all this time.'

'They're the same people though, aren't they?' asked Anthony.

'Yes, they're the same. But I'm different now. I've got a load of stuff in me that I didn't even know I had.'

'We think you're the same person, Katy, whatever happens,' Susan said.

'I know that, but I am different, don't you see?'

'It's like me, like all of us,' Frank said. 'We're the same person despite all the shit that's happening, but it is the shit that makes us different.'

As usual Frank's words seemed to sum up what they were all struggling to say.

'I suppose we have to deal with it, whatever it is. I know that's what I'm going to do,' Anthony said.

346

'What are you going to do?' Susan asked.

'I'm going to see my father in prison. I'm hoping to go there this weekend, if Joe can take me.'

'We're all going,' Katy said and looked around the room.

They all nodded.

'Can I come too?' Susan asked.

'Of course: you are part of the gang now,' Anthony said.

'I hope he's got a big car,' Susan said.

'I'm sure we can all cram in. Anyway, we can go by train if not.'

'Where is the prison?' Susan asked.

'Lewes; it's in Sussex, I think.'

Frank looked up sharply and said, 'Really?'

'Yes. Near Brighton, I think.'

'No, I meant is it really Lewes Prison?' Frank asked.

'Yes. Why?'

'Well, that's near where I used to live.'

'Ah, well you don't have to come, Frank, if it's awkward, but I hope you will,' Anthony said. He really wanted Frank to come along, he felt much safer and stronger with Frank nearby.

Frank was quiet.

'I'm going home,' Gary said suddenly. 'I don't like to think about my mum being at home with my dad.'

They all got up; the bubble they'd been in suddenly burst.

'So, see you all tomorrow then?' Anthony asked, feeling a wave of loneliness. He had already got used to having friends around him.

'Of course. We're not going to disappear, you idiot,' Katy said, jabbing him with her elbow.

Anthony felt like a million dollars.

As they left the house, Margaret Alexander came to the door.

'You're not going already, are you?' she said, disappointed for Anthony.

'Sorry, Mrs Alexander, we'll see you another time,' Susan said politely.

'Bye then,' Anthony said, watching Susan put on her coat.

He liked Susan. She was quieter than Katy but just as pretty. She looked at him and smiled and said, 'See you in physics then?'

He nodded stupidly; she smiled again.

Outside, Gary, Frank, Katy and Susan walked together.

'Another crazy day,' Katy said.

'Totally fucking mad,' Gary said.

'You put things so sensitively, Gary,' Katy said to him, trying not to laugh.

'Well, it has been fucking mental — everything,' Gary said.

*****

'Dear Ailsa,

I don't know if you remember me, it's Frank Gordon, Robbie's older brother.

Anyway, I am just writing to thank you for your card, eight months late I know, and to see how you are.

My mum and I are doing OK. We live in a town north of London, where the film studios are. We've had a tough time since the accident and some awful things have happened. Anyway, I'm writing to say hello, and to make sure you're doing all right.

I guess you must be missing Robbie. I know I am.

I keep on thinking that one day I'm going to wake up and discover that I've been in a dream the whole time. I know that won't happen now, but I wish it would.

I don't run any more. My mum says I should, but I don't think I can even if I wanted to.

What are you doing? Still writing? If you wanted to write to me, I promise I'll write back straight away next time. If you don't want to then I'll understand.

Bye then.

Frank.'

Frank had read and re-read the letter. He felt horribly guilty that he'd not written to her before now, but he hoped that she would understand. Would she want to be friends with him? Maybe not now that Robbie wasn't around. As he thought of his little brother, he felt hot tears stinging his eyes, for the millionth time. He buried his head in his hands once again. Would he ever be able to think of the past without breaking up? He wondered how his mother must be coping. How did she cope? She put on a brave front, but she'd lost her husband, her son, and her legs.

He went into the living room where she was sitting.

'Howdy, Pardner,' she said.

He sat beside her.

'Hello.'

'How are you getting on with the old lady's birthday?'

'No progress today, she wasn't very well. But, it's funny, the others and me are getting on really well with each other. I thought it was going to be a nightmare but actually we seem to be getting on all right.'

'I'm so glad, it's time for you to start to get going again,' she said, taking his hand.

'What about you though, Mum?' he said, looking at her.

'I'm all right, I'm getting through it.'

Frank knew this wasn't true, but he didn't know what to do to help her.

'The thing is: all I want, Frank, is for you to begin to get your life back. I know it's hard for you, but that's what I want. That's what your dad would want, and Robbie too. Can you imagine how they'd feel if they thought that you didn't fulfil your potential? Or, put it the other way: wouldn't you want Robbie to do everything in his power to be the best he could be, for you as well as for him?'

Frank was silent for a long time then said, 'But I'm scared. I'm scared I can't. I think I've lost my nerve. In fact, I'm sure of it. I keep imagining I am going to lose all the time. Every dream I have I come last in whatever I do. It's not just running; I can't help thinking about everything going wrong. I'm carrying so much misery around with me. I like the others I'm working with for Grace's party, but they've all got a load of horrible stuff going on and I can't help feeling it's because I've turned up. I know it's not my fault, but I just can't help but feel I'm a jinx to everyone. Why didn't I die in the crash, Mum? Why didn't I die? I wish it had been me — why couldn't it be me?'

Janice held her son's hand as he cried. She knew how he felt. She felt the same. Every day since the crash she wished she'd been killed too, especially if it meant that Andrew or Robbie could have been saved.

'All I know is that I've now got a responsibility, Frank. I have to make sure that the things that they wanted to achieve are made possible by what I think and do. If I can do anything towards their dreams, then I must do it.'

'What were their dreams?'

'For Andrew, it was for you and Robbie to be successful at running and writing. For Robbie, it was the same. You can achieve half of their dreams Frank. I know it's hard, but you can try, can't you?'

Frank shuddered. 'Not without them I can't.'

'It won't be without them. You are part of them: you're who you are because of who they were and what they did and cared about. Anyway, I don't believe they've gone. I think that somehow they are with us, somewhere.'

'It's not the same. I can't feel them at all — I can't talk to them; I can't hear them. I can only miss them.'

'I know, Frank. It's the same for me. What shall we do?'

Frank had been thinking about what to do for a long time and had slowly begun to find certainty. He had resisted it. He felt that to take the easy option was not what he'd been brought up to do but the words his mother had used had struck a chord with him. She had said that they were there, somewhere. Perhaps he could join them too? He'd be with them then. He looked at his mother and caught himself. He saw her strength and her vulnerability. He shuddered again. How could he think of leaving her? It would break her once and for all.

'What are you thinking?' she asked.

'I'm so scared, Mum. I'm scared of everything and everyone,' he said, gripping her hand hard.

'Me too, Frank, me too.'

'What are we going to do then?' he asked, sounding to his ears more and more like a little boy.

Janice gripped Frank's hand even harder and said fiercely, 'We've got to be fucking tough, that's what.'

350

Frank had never heard his mother swear. Her words shocked him. He looked at her and saw in her face such determination it made him flinch. She stared at him, into his eyes; he stared back at her. She didn't look away: she was challenging him, and he knew it. He felt his father's and brother's power sweep through him. It jolted him. He shivered.

'Yes,' he said quietly. 'Yes, Mum, you're right.'

He got up, his body twitching and restless. He started pacing around the room.

'Go for a run, Frank. Get out there and run,' she said. It was a command.

'I will.'

'Now. Just go now.'

He stopped moving.

'Now!' she ordered again.

He bent down to her and hugged her and then went out.

Seconds later the phone rang.

***

'You fancy Anthony, don't you?' Katy said to Susan as they walked along the street.

Susan coloured and said, 'Well, I wouldn't say fancy, but he's sort of quite nice.'

'Sort of quite nice: what does that mean?'

'I don't know. He's kind of all right.'

'I used to feel sorry for him, but I've realised that he's not the drip I thought he was,' Katy said.

'I know he's got loads of ideas, and behind his posh manner he's just like us really,' Susan said.

'He's not cool, or good looking or anything though,' Katy pointed out.

'I know; but he's kind and funny, and incredibly intelligent.'

'What makes me laugh about him is his attempt to be cool. Listening to him swearing is ridiculous — and the way he and Gary talk to each other nearly makes me laugh out loud. Honestly, one posh boy meets the badger's arse,' Katy said, laughing now.

'I think it's sweet, the way they've become friends.'

'Well, I have to admit Gary isn't what I thought he was. He's actually got a brain in his head, and he's quite soft really.'

'You never told me what happened in the bus shelter that night.'

Katy shuddered.

'I don't want to think about it to be honest, and anyway I can't really remember. I was so pissed I probably did all sorts of stuff. I remember being sick and blacking out.'

'Gary didn't do anything horrible, did he?' Susan asked, remembering how he'd walked away from the scene just before she'd found Katy on the floor, exposed and senseless.

'I don't think so, but I honestly can't remember.'

'It seems like so long ago, but it's only a few weeks.'

'Yeah, thinking about that day makes me feel sick all over again.'

'You've done really well. I was so worried about you.'

'I don't know what I'd have done without you: I was in such a mess. The funny thing is that, although we're not even related, I feel closer to you now than even before,' Katy said, turning to her.

Susan stopped, turned and wrapped her arms around her sister; they hugged each other.

'Life's strange isn't it? Not only are we going through something totally unexpected, we've now got caught up in other people's lives and all of their problems. People I couldn't have possibly predicted we'd even speak to, never mind get close to,' Katy said.

'I know, and what crazy stuff too. Can you imagine what it must be like to have a dad in prison? Or, have a dad who should be put in prison?' Susan asked.

'Maybe my real mum was in prison, that's why she gave me up,' Katy said. 'Maybe she killed my dad and was put away in a loony bin. Or, maybe she had an affair with a film star: who would it be? Maybe Roger Moore or Tony Curtis — or Paul Newman?'

Susan laughed and said, 'Your imagination is getting carried away: it'll be something much more ordinary than that.'

'But how come I love performing so much and — come on — you've got to agree I'm bloody good.'

'Though you say it yourself? Well you'll probably find out soon. You should make sure you're prepared for whatever happens you don't want to feel totally deflated.'

'I know. I've gone through all the possibilities,' Katy said in a quiet voice. She had dreamed of super-stardom with her new mother, but she knew that the chances were that her mother was someone quite ordinary who'd just had some bad luck sixteen years ago.

They had reached their house and were going in as the telephone rang.

'Katy is that you?' she heard Anthony's voice.

'Yeah, what is it?' she asked. He was sounding agitated.

'Gary's just rung me. He says his dad is going mad; he wants us to go around. He thinks it's time to get his mum out of the house.'

'Shit! OK, we'll go around now. Are you going too?'

'Yes, but I want to get hold of Frank and he's not home.'

'OK, well, let's go to Gary's anyway,' Katy said.

Dropping her bag on the floor, she explained what was happening to Susan.

'I'm telling Mum we're off,' Susan said.

'Don't bother, she won't care.'

'Of course, she will, you idiot.'

Moments later they were running down the street.

***

Gary's voice had sounded desperate. Anthony had heard fear in every word.

'I tried to have a joke with him, but he told me to fuck off,' Gary had said, 'so I did.'

Anthony had asked hesitantly, 'He's not hurting your mother, is he?'

'Any minute. He's just winding up to it. The awful thing is that my mum's acting really weird and it's making things worse.'

'What's she doing?'

'Ignoring him. She's acting as if he isn't there and that's winding him up something chronic.'

'Do you want me to come around?' Anthony had asked.

'I don't know what to do, but maybe if you and the others were here it might help,' Gary answered.

Anthony tried Frank first. It was funny in a way, Frank himself seemed like he was lost but his presence calmed everyone down. Frank was out though.

He'd rung Katy and Susan and they had agreed to meet him at Gary's house.

He got himself ready, put on his big coat and left the house.

***

Gary got back from the telephone box to find his father in the kitchen opening another can. He looked around for his mother.

'Where's Mum?' he asked.

Mr Abbott looked at his son without comprehension.

'Having a shit probably; that's all I get in this fucking house, shit.'

Gary ran upstairs and heard his mother in the bathroom.

'Mum, you all right?' he asked.

The tap stopped running and he heard her blowing her nose.

'Mum, talk to me.'

The door opened, and she came out. The left side of her face was red.

'Mum, say something.'

She stopped and, seeing him properly at last, said, 'It's nothing, love. I'm fine. It's over now.'

'I'm getting you out of here, now — right now.'

'No, I'm fine.'

'But, Mum, he's dangerous: he's going to really hurt you.'

She looked at Gary and nodded her understanding and said, 'It's all right, Gary, I'm ready. I really am.'

'For what?' he asked.

'I'm ready. I've decided.'

She went downstairs. He followed, hoping that the others would be here soon.

***

Frank just jogged at first, but the further he went the more he speeded up. He felt his stride lengthening and the dimly remembered feeling of power started to seep back into him. He found himself in Meadow Park. Once his feet touched the short grass, he pressed the accelerator and waited for the surge. It wasn't there. He didn't know what to expect. He had anticipated a sluggish response: he'd been out of training for months and he felt generally out of condition. But he couldn't help being disappointed. He craved the familiar wave of euphoria that made him feel like a warrior.

Reaching the far side of the park he stopped and turned around. He was breathing hard but was not out of breath. He closed his eyes and stilled his mind. Slowly the sounds of the town slipped away, the picture in his head brightened. He looked down the track and there was his father with Robbie. They were waving at him. They were smiling. He smiled in reply. He saw his father look at the stopwatch and show it to Robbie. Robbie had his notebook at the ready. Frank's heartbeat slowed. He felt calm again, in control. His father held out his hands, palms down, the signal to slow down still further. Robbie was gurning behind his father's back, then gave him the wanker sign. Frank laughed out loud and shook his head. Seeing his son laughing, Andrew Gordon whirled round and caught Robbie in mid-gesture and clouted him around the shoulder. Robbie collapsed to the ground shrieking, 'Where are social services when you need them?' The two of them became serious again. Robbie looked up the track to Frank, his thumbs up. Frank nodded. The energy began to bubble and swirl inside him, deep, somewhere he couldn't describe. He looked towards the finishing line, nearly ready. His father's red cap was brilliant, shimmering and dancing, beckoning. Frank felt the adrenalin suddenly release inside him. He was ready to go. He stared down the track and saw his father's face, Robbie's face: they were shining and bright — they looked absolutely alive. He saw his father take

355

his cap off and hold it high. Frank felt a massive jolt strike him — he ran he flew; he smiled, exultant.

***

'Keep out of it, Gary,' Kevin said, as they met in the hall.

Gary heard his father's guttural voice through the closed kitchen door.

'Yeah, and let Mum get beaten up again,' Gary said to his brother.

'You can't do anything with him when he's in this kind of mood; you'll make him worse. The best thing to do is get him so drunk he ends up senseless.'

'Meantime Mum gets a few more punches to her head, is that what you want?'

Kevin went up the stairs, ignoring his younger brother.

Gary listened at the door.

'You've always hated me, Jen, don't argue you fucking hate your own husband,' Abbott growled.

'Don't be silly, Brian, of course I don't,' Jenny said.

'Now you're fucking laughing at me. You think I'm just a fucking drunk, don't you?'

Jenny was silent.

'Don't you? Answer me. Be honest for once in your pathetic little life,' Abbott roared.

Gary heard a tentative knock on the front door beside him. He opened it. Katy and Susan were standing there, looking scared.

Gary didn't know what to say to them. He just stood there.

'Shall we come in?' whispered Katy.

They all heard Gary's dad screaming, 'If you don't answer me, I shall kick in your fucking head.'

The three looked at each other helplessly. Gary looked over their heads and saw Frank running on the far side of the road. He waved at him. Frank saw the group and ran over.

They looked at their new friend. Something had happened to him. He had grown. He was like a giant.

'Frank, thank God,' Susan said.

'What's up?' Frank asked. Then he heard a chair scrape back and Gary's father's voice rasp, 'Right, that fucking does it.'

Frank's arrival galvanised Gary and he turned and rushed into the kitchen followed by the others.

They saw Mr Abbott with his hands around his wife's throat.

'Stop it, Dad!' Gary commanded.

Brian Abbott looked round at his son. His face was beetroot red. There was a deadly coldness in his eyes.

Jenny Abbott looked at her son. Despite the situation and her husband's hands tightening around her neck, she did not look frightened. She seemed to be calm and composed.

'Here comes the cavalry, led by my own fucking son.'

'Let go of her, Dad — be sensible, please, Dad,' Gary said trying to pacify him.

Abbott let go of his wife and lurched towards Gary, his fists bunched.

Gary stood still. He felt Frank edge beside him.

'I'm going to teach you the lesson of a lifetime, you little fucking shit. You think you're better than me, you're not. You'll end up drinking, beating your wife and then you'll end up fighting with your son. That's how it goes, Sonny Jim.'

'No, Dad, we're not going to fight; no one is going to fight,'

'Oh yes they are, you little fuck,' Abbott said, and took a shambling unsteady step towards his son.

'No, they're not,' Anthony said, pushing past Katy, Susan and Frank and standing next to Gary. He was holding a large revolver and aiming it straight at Brian Abbott.

They all gaped.

'What the fuck?' Abbott said, blinking.

'No one's fighting, no more violence,' Anthony said, his voice steady.

'Who the fuck are you?' Abbott said.

'My name is Anthony Alexander, and I'm not going to leave until everything is calm.'

'Oooo, Anthony Alexander is it? And who's your brother — Little Lord Fauntleroy?' Abbott said, beginning to chuckle.

'Please be sensible, Mr Abbott. I have a loaded gun and I am not afraid to use it.'

Gary's father was now beginning to laugh uncontrollably. He put his hands up.

'Please, sir, please don't shoot me.'

Anthony's thumb cocked the revolver.

'Sit down, Brian. Sit down and grow up,' Jennifer Abbott said. Her voice cut through the tension. Everyone looked at her, shocked. She stood up straight. Her face looked hard and her voice was cold.

'You what?' Abbott said, even more startled.

'I'm telling you, Brian, to sit down and grow up,' she repeated.

She moved to him and took his arm. She was dwarfed by her bulky husband but suddenly seemed in control. She guided him to a chair and firmly pushed him into it. She looked at her son, at Anthony's grim face, at Frank, Katy and Susan. 'I'm fine now, thank you all. Everything is fine now,' she said and turned to her husband.

She held his head against her and said, 'It's over, Brian, it's over now.'

They saw tears spill from his closed eyes as she cradled his head.

***

Victoria lay on her back staring at the ceiling. Next to her was Joe. They had been still and silent for several minutes. Victoria was in total conflict. She had craved close physical contact and emotional intimacy for all of her adult life. She had wondered time and time again if she would ever find it and as the years had gone by her belief in its possibility had begun to weaken. Now, out of the blue, had come this man. This man who seemed to be able to read her mind, who was kind and generous, who could make her laugh but made it possible for her to cry too. She turned her head to look at his shadowy form beside her.

'What are you thinking?' he asked.

'You're the mind reader.'

'No, I am just a lucky guesser.'

'Guess then.'

'OK, you're thinking it's high time I made this wonderful man a piping hot dinner served with wine and soft music?'

'Nowhere near. In fact, not only wrong but, also, it's never going to happen.'

'Oh, what a shame. Maybe I'll have to make you something. Do you like Marmite or marmalade?'

'Don't side-track me. I know your tricks now. Have another stab.'

'Hmmm, it's probably along the lines of "how did all of this happen?"' he said.

'You're right, of course,' she sighed. 'But what's the answer to the riddle, clever clogs?'

'Something in the stars? Or its fate, or destiny? Or, each of us was bound to meet someone or other and we just happened to be each other's someone or other?'

'I don't think it's the last one. We're not very typical, so our chances of finding someone that was going to feel — let alone be — right are slim I'd say.'

'Are we that different? I think that we're pretty normal. Our circumstances might seem unusual, but only because we don't know anyone who has had the same set of things happening to them. Perhaps what we think are singular to us are just variants of other people's lives?'

'No, I don't think that that's right. Maybe other people have events or experiences that are generalizable to what has happened to us but only if they are similar in personality would those people be something like us as a result.'

'Hmm, well — I don't know I just potter along and do what I'm told.'

'I'm telling you that you are unlike anyone that I've ever met, and I've met a lot of people. What's more, I have to tell you that part of what draws me in is that I don't know anything about you. I'm liking the man of mystery bit.'

Joe was silent.

'OK, you can still talk you know; even secret agents can chew the fat now and then.'

'I don't know much about you, Victoria. Will you tell me your life story?'

'You already know it. Anyway, why do you want to know about me? If it's important to know about someone, why don't you share yourself with me?'

Joe said, 'OK, I understand. The thing is this: what if I do tell you all about me, my life from cradle to the present day, and you find that I'm not who you thought I was or could be? Then our relationship would be dented, tarnished or even ruined. Isn't it better just to be what we are now — and from now on — rather than worry about what was?'

'But, Joe, how will we know what we have in common, our ideas and beliefs, our shared experiences, our different perspectives? They all come from before we met: can't we share them?'

'I know what you mean; I understand. You may well wonder why I'm so reticent. It's just that I like to live in the moment — to forget the past and let the future take care of itself.'

'Ah, "forget"? A breakthrough at last. What do you want to forget?'

'You've unlocked me. I'm putty in your hands. It's all over.'

'You idiot, you're just wriggling now,' she said jabbing him in the ribs.

'I say forget because I don't like my past; I want to forget it. It isn't who or what I am now.'

'Isn't who or what you are now informed by who or what you were? I can't see how the two can be separated.'

'That's what worries me, Victoria. That is exactly it. You cannot fail to be affected by who or what someone was irrespective of who or what they are now. Your judgement will be informed by your own prejudices and preferences — do you see?'

Victoria thought about it then said, 'Maybe you should just tell me and see what happens. After all, this is not just about you. I'm half of the equation and if I'm unable to accept who or what you are then that tells you something important about me.'

'Good point. You're good at this, Victoria.'

'Never mind the flattery: what's your next move?'

'No move, I'm not ready for it. I'm sorry.'

'I'm struggling with this, Joe. We are thrown together; we are physically and emotionally close. I have invested a lot of myself already in you and us. I'm suddenly feeling that everything is built on sand and I don't like it.'

'I do understand, Victoria, but you are going to have to trust me; that's all I can say.'

'That's not good enough for me, I'm sorry.'

They were silent. Victoria was very close to tears, but she was not going to give way to any sign of weakness.

Joe sat up and rubbed his eyes.

'I'm struggling too, Victoria. I want you to trust me but I'm behaving in an untrustworthy way. I need to go away and think about it all. Will you let me do that?'

'How long are your deliberations going to take you?' she asked, with an edge to her voice.

'Long enough to be sure I am making the right decision.'

Victoria lost her patience. 'Go on then. Off you go and consult your conscience or whatever higher power you refer to in such matters.'

Joe got out of her bed and started putting on his clothes. He glanced at Victoria. She was looking away from him.

He said, 'That's long enough. I've decided.'

Victoria looked up, 'And?'

***

The five of them backed out into the hall. They could hear Gary's mum whispering to her husband, 'It's all fine now. It's all over, Brian.'

'I've got to get out,' Gary said. He opened the front door and strode off down the street. The others followed him in silence. They hurried towards the High Street.

'Gary — hang on — let's go in here,' Katy called as they went past the café on the corner.

Gary stopped and looked back. He seemed surprised to find them there. They waited for him to walk back towards them before going inside.

They crowded around one of the little tables, hunched together, close and conspiratorial.

Gary pulled out a packet of Number 6. He opened it. There were three cigarettes in it. He pushed the packet into the middle of the table. Katy took one, and Anthony. Gary took the last and struck a match.

'Whadda you want,' asked the Italian owner. He looked suspiciously at them: they looked like trouble.

'May we have five coffees, please?' asked Anthony.

'You gonna pay?'

'Of course, what do you take us for?' Anthony asked.

Muttering, the owner walked off. They heard the tumultuous sound of a coffee machine.

Katy looked across the table at Anthony and said, 'What shall we call you from now on? Dirty Harry?'

There was a moment's pause then they started to laugh. They became hysterical, choking on nervous energy.

Finally, wiping his eyes, Anthony asked, 'Who's dirty Harry?'

They fell apart again.

'No trouble! This is a nice place, respectable,' the owner shouted over to them.

A couple sitting near them got up and left, tutting as they went.

'Sorry, we're good citizens, apart from Billy the Kid over there,' Katy said.

They collapsed again.

Slowly they calmed down.

'That's not a real gun, is it?' Susan whispered to Anthony.

'Oh, yes, it is,' Anthony said, pleased with himself.

'Where did you get it?' Katy asked.

'Ah, well, it's a long story; I'll tell you one day,'

'But it's not loaded, is it?' Susan said.

'Yes, it is.'

'For God's sake keep it hidden, you'll get us all arrested,' Katy said.

'Don't worry, it's hidden away inside my coat,' Anthony reassured them.

'Get rid of it, Anthony. It'll get you into trouble; it's not worth it,' Frank said. He sounded different to normal. They all turned to him.

'Frank, what has happened to you?' Susan asked.

'What do you mean?' Frank answered, self-conscious.

'Yeah, what has happened to you? You're totally different somehow?' Katy asked.

'Nothing, nothing's happened, honestly,' he answered, still not sure what they were getting at.

'You seem to have grown twice the size,' Anthony said.

'Yeah, that's it, exactly,' Susan said.

Frank felt bigger, he couldn't deny it.

'Well, it's nothing really. It was just that I had a quick run and for some reason something clicked, and I felt OK, better than I have for a long time, well, since the... a long time.'

'Flip, it's done the trick all right,' Katy said.

Their coffees arrived.

'How are you feeling, Gary?' Susan asked him.

Gary stared at his coffee. He shrugged and said, 'Like: shit, that was the worst thing ever.'

They nodded, wanting to show their support but unable to find the right words.

'I would have fired the gun if he'd done anything, Gary,' Anthony said.

'Don't you ever do any such thing,' Susan said.

'It's funny: I felt really powerful, in control, like the other time,' Anthony said.

'What other time?' Katy asked, wide-eyed.

'Oh, nothing really, just to get my own back on some bullies at my last school,' he said.

Gary looked up sharply. He looked down again, his lowered head hiding his feelings.

'What do you think will happen now with your mum and dad?' Frank asked Gary.

'I don't know. I can't get my head around it. You've seen what he's like. But when we left, well, that wasn't normal, totally not what he's normally like.'

'Your mum seemed really strong, Gary, I had no idea. I thought she was well, a bit, um, you know, a bit…' Katy trailed off.

'Weak?' Gary offered.

'Well, I suppose so.'

'She is normally. Normally she just takes whatever he throws at her, literally.'

'Good for her,' Susan said. 'Taking control is a brilliant thing if you can do it.'

'I'm scared to go home now, in case it all kicks off again,' Gary said.

'Do you think it will?' Frank asked.

'Normally it would; this time it was different. Not because of us — in fact I think we all made it worse. No, it was mum, she was so, well, she was like another person altogether.'

'Do you want to stay at my house tonight?' Anthony asked Gary.

Gary looked at him. He was beginning to like Anthony a lot.

'Um, what would your mum say?'

'I think she'd be fine about it. She knows you're all right from last night,' Anthony said.

'Well, I think I will then. Home is the last place I want to be right now.'

'I'm sorry, I'm going to have to say something. You two are doing my head in,' Katy said. 'A few days ago, and you would have happily killed each other, now you are blood brothers.'

Neither Gary nor Anthony replied. They were a bit embarrassed by her remark, but not unhappy.

'Have you had any more thoughts about going to see your father?' Frank asked Anthony.

'Yes. I rang up the prison and apparently I can go along any time during visiting hours and if he's prepared to see me then I can see him.'

'You're not going on your own: we're all coming along, remember?' Susan said.

Anthony looked shy suddenly, 'But, do you really want to come? Won't it be boring?'

'Boring? A trip to a prison? When are we next going to do that?' Katy said excited.

'I don't think you'll be able to go in though,' Anthony said.

'It doesn't matter; we'll be your supporters,' Susan said.

Anthony smiled at her.

'We're all in it now,' Gary said. 'You've seen my little shithole of a life. We've got to be part of the shit you're in too.'

'Well, if you put it like that,' Anthony said smiling.

'Lewes is close to where I used to live,' Frank repeated.

'Do you want to go back?' Katy asked.

'I'm not sure. My life is so different now, I think it might be a mistake.'

'Perhaps you should talk to Joe about it, see what he thinks?' Anthony suggested.

Frank nodded. After his sprint across Meadow Park he had felt elated, just like the old days. He had carried on running hard down the residential streets, slowly decelerating as he went. He had seen a letter box across one of the side streets and had veered in its direction. He had taken his letter to Ailsa out of his pocket, paused a moment and then popped it inside. Thinking of it, of her, of meeting her again, he felt excited and very, very, scared. He would talk to Joe, see what he thought.

'Come on, let's pay and get out; I don't think we're very popular in here,' Katy said, standing up.

They left and walked down the street in a tight-knit group. They went past Gary's house — it was quiet.

They reached the Walkers' house and stopped. Katy turned to Anthony and hugged him. He looked embarrassed but hugged her back. He turned to Susan. She hugged him too.

'Please get rid of that gun, you idiot,' she whispered.

'I will.'

The girls hugged Gary and Frank.

'See you tomorrow,' they all called.

Shortly after, the boys came to Frank's house. This time it was a less effusive parting but still each of them felt the need for physical contact: a punch from Gary, slaps on the back from Frank, Anthony shaking hands with Frank.

'The last few days have been so peculiar, Gary,' Anthony said as they walked towards his house.

'I know. It's been weird as fuck; I can't keep up with what's going on,' Gary agreed.

'I don't want to worry you, Gary, but I think we've got some company,' Anthony said, looking back.

Gary turned and saw three figures fifty yards or so behind them. He couldn't see their faces, but he guessed who they were. They must have been following for a while, waiting for numbers to decrease.

'They're the lot from last night,' Anthony confirmed Gary's hunch. 'What shall we do?'

'Deal with them. I could do with a bit of aggro right now,' Gary said, and turning around stood to face the oncoming group.

They walked up to Gary and stood inches from him.

'You've got this coming, Abbott, you cunt,' black jacket spat into Gary's face.

'I can't wait,' said Gary, pushing his face into the other's.

The three swarmed around Gary, punching and kicking him. Gary fought back. They struggled for a few seconds, the sound of punches landing, grunts and swearing filling the air. Then, a monstrous explosion deafened them. The four grappling bodies froze. They looked at Anthony. He was standing still, the gun in his hands.

'Move away, you lot,' he said pointing the gun at the three assailants. 'Step back and remove yourself from the area.'

The four were stupefied, rooted to the spot.

'I said remove yourselves. Right now.'

He levelled the gun at the one in the middle.

'I shall shoot you if you don't go now; and if I see you again, I shall shoot you then,' Anthony said, icy.

Gary stood beside Anthony and looked at the other three.

'I'd do what the gentleman says if I was you,' he said.

'Fuck you, you are dead meat, Abbott,' said black jacket.

Anthony squeezed the trigger and again the gun boomed.

This time the three turned and ran. Anthony fired again behind them.

'Come on. Let's get out of here — now!' Gary said, pulling at Anthony's arm.

They ran hard, turning down an alley between two ends of terraces and careered towards some scrubland. Gary knew this area well. There was nothing but bushes, brambles, a bog, old cars, and general wasteland.

'Get rid of it, Anthony,' Gary whispered hoarsely.

In the gloom he could just make out the shape of Anthony bending down and hurling the gun with all his might into the darkness. They heard it splash into a bog in the distance. They continued running along the alley as it made its way back out into more residential streets.

They slowed to a walk.

'We'll never find it now. What a shame,' Anthony said.

'If you got caught with it, Anthony, you'd be sent to prison for possessing a weapon, for threatening people with it, for causing a riot, fuck knows what else,' Gary said.

'Yes, but it's been very useful tonight,' Anthony said. He'd enjoyed having the power again.

'Whatever happens, you must never, ever admit to having a gun. Do you understand me?' Gary said, looking straight into Anthony's face.

Anthony nodded. He knew Gary was right.

They reached Anthony's home. They went inside.

'You're late, Anthony, and Gary too, that's nice,' Margaret Alexander said.

'We've been working on Grace's party,' Anthony lied easily. 'We lost track of time.'

Margaret Alexander looked at Gary, 'What's happened to you?'

Gary's face was bloody, and his eye was swelling.

'Oh, I walked into a lamp post. I wasn't wearing my glasses,' Gary said, only now aware of the throbbing pain in his face.

'You need to put something on that bruise. Witch-hazel should do it.'

She disappeared into the bathroom, coming back with a bottle. She wet some cotton wool and dabbed Gary's face. Anthony looked on.

'It's OK for Gary to stay here tonight, isn't it? His mother isn't very well, and they need more space in their house at the moment.'

'Of course, if it's all right with your parents?' Mrs Alexander asked Gary.

'It's fine, honestly,' he answered.

'You can put some cushions on the floor in your bedroom, Anthony. Gary can have your bed.'

'Sure, that's fine with me.'

Anthony marvelled at the extraordinary set of circumstances that had turned Gary and him from bitter enemies into close friends. Gary Abbott, someone he had loathed, and who had despised him, was about to get into his bed. He laughed out loud.

'What's so funny?' Gary said.

'Oh, it's nothing.'

The phone rang.

***

'Before you start, I want to get dressed. I'll see you downstairs,' Victoria said.

He nodded and left the room. She got out of bed and put on her clothes. She felt scared. As she came down, she took in a deep breath and prepared for the worst.

'Right, are you ready?' Joe asked. He was standing, staring out of the window, his back to her.

'Yes,' she said sitting down at the table.

'What I'm going to say is easy on the one hand but complicated on the other. You may well say: "that's it, I've heard enough, please leave". You may think a million other things. I want to tell you everything, Victoria, because I care about you deeply; I really like you, and I want to spend much, much, more time with you. But I need to know that you respect me, that you trust me, that you are feeling those things based on the facts and not on what you hope is true.'

'Yes, I understand what you're saying. Now please get on and say it.'

'I told you that I killed a man, and that it was just an instinctive reaction, an act of blind rage. That wasn't true. I planned to do it. I waited in ambush for him and went armed with an iron bar. I killed him with a single blow. I wasn't let out of prison early. I served my full time. There was no gun found. That was all fantasy. I'm sorry, Victoria, I am a cold-blooded killer.'

'No, I don't believe it,' Victoria burst out.

'I'm sorry I didn't tell you the truth before. I've been regretting it ever since. I didn't want to lie. I just couldn't bear the thought of you hating me, losing respect for me, being scared of me. I knew immediately that it was a mistake, but I couldn't take it back. I should have done. I'm sorry.'

Victoria's head was spinning. Her eyes were wide and staring. Sitting opposite her was a murderer. Only minutes before she had been in bed with this man, a brutal man, a killer. She shook her head.

'I wish I hadn't lied to you,' he said.

'Me too,' she whispered.

'I killed him, and I meant to. I was rightly convicted of murder and I was sentenced to twenty-two years life imprisonment. I was not pardoned. There was no framing, I am a killer and, although I was driven mad by the behaviour of the man I killed, I wish with all my might that I had not done it.'

Victoria felt cold. There was a long silence.

'Is that it?' she asked at last.

'That's it in relation to the awful part of me. There're the parts before and after prison — not that dramatic — and then there's the part during prison. How much do you want to know?'

'Everything.'

'Well, I can honestly say that my time in prison was the best thing that could have happened to me. It wasn't a happy or pleasant time. Of course not. It was a challenging, brutal and often lonely time and place. It was also where I grew up, where I discovered myself, what I could do and what I could achieve. If it hadn't been for prison, I would be something and someone quite different.'

'Joe, I can't bear this. This is a nightmare. You've become a stranger, and a horrible one, in a matter of minutes. Minutes ago, I thought I… well, that was then.'

Joe was silent.

'My God, to think I trusted you to look after the interests of four damaged young people. I can't believe I've been so gullible. What was I thinking of? I've been so irresponsible.'

'I realise that you will find this hard to believe, but I would do anything to protect those kids, Victoria. I shall do my best for them no matter what. I really…'

Just then they heard gun shots somewhere nearby.

***

'Have you told Mum and Dad that you've written to Jane?' Susan asked Katy after they'd said goodbye to the others.

'No, and I'm not going to either.'

'It might be nice if you did, you know. You don't have to give details, just say enough to keep them from worrying.'

'I don't want to. It's too complicated. I am really struggling to know what to do, what to say, what to say to who, everything. If I tell them anything they'll want to know more and more, and I'll just get snappy and wound up.'

'I know. It must be weird and difficult and all that. Couldn't you just say that you've written a letter to say hello and you're not sure what is going to happen next?'

'Hmmm, maybe. I'll see.'

They went inside.

'You're late. Where've you been?' John Walker said.

'Don't start, Dad,' Katy said.

'We've been with a couple of friends, the ones we're doing the party with, you know, for the old lady,' Susan said.

'Ah, how's it going?'

'Fine, although it's not quite working out as any of us had imagined,' Susan said thinking about recent events.

'How are you, Katy?' he asked looking at her.

'Fine.'

Anna came into the room.

'I've left your dinners in the oven; do eat them, won't you?' she said.

Katy went upstairs without answering. Anna and John looked at Susan who shrugged helplessly.

'I'm sorry. I can't persuade her to let up,' she said.

'Don't worry. We'll wait for her to come home to us,' John said.

'What if she doesn't?'

'We will do everything we can, and we know you will too. She knows we love her and in the end that is what counts,' Anna said. She sounded certain, but Susan wondered what was really going on in her mother's mind.

'She has written to her, but she doesn't know I'm telling you,' Susan said.

'What did she say?' Anna asked.

'Just asked her more about herself I think, nothing much.'

'Thanks, Susan, you're playing a great hand, looking after all of us,' John said and came over and hugged her.

'It's horrible. I feel so disloyal.'

'Not for long — keep going. We all know what you're doing and how hard it is,' he said.

Katy's heavy shoes clumped downstairs again.

'Talk later,' Susan said to her parents and followed her sister into the kitchen.

They all heard the gun shots.

'I can't believe it! Please tell me it's not Anthony with that stupid gun,' Susan whispered to Katy.

'It wouldn't surprise me: he was a bit weird with it. It was like he thought it was a game or something. What a prat.'

'Don't you like him?' Susan asked.

'Of course, I do. He's funny — a bit odd — but, yeah, I like him.'

'I'm worried about him, what's he gone and done.'

'Ring him up,' Katy urged.

'I will in a few minutes. If it's anything to do with him then he'll have to get home first.'

***

Victoria's rational mind saw Joe as someone who had committed the ultimate crime. He had meant to kill a man and had done it. What could have provoked him to such an act?

But she knew she wasn't rational right now. She had fallen for him, completely. She loved what he had done for her and how he made her feel. She knew that Katy, Gary, Anthony and Frank looked up to him, respected him. She had seen her own mother and her fellow residents swarm around him. What was he all about? Was he a con man? Could it be that everyone was as gullible as her? He did have tricks, there was no doubt about that: the way he seemed to be able to read her mind was amazing. But she realised that there was nothing mystical about it, just that she let out subtle messages and he was, she knew, extremely empathic and observant. So, he made her feel special — in fact, he seemed to make everyone feel special.

'I'm finding this very difficult, Joe. You've killed someone, and you lied to me about it. What am I supposed to do now? I don't think I can handle this.'

Joe closed his eyes in resignation. After a pause he said, 'Of course, there's much more to tell. Here is a snapshot of my life before and after prison. I did two years National Service, in Germany. When I came out, I got a job in an insurance company and did very well. I made plenty of money, was seeing a beautiful girl, should have been set for a normal, successful life. Then my father died, my mother met Giles and the rest you know. I wasn't a bad man: I was driven mad by badness. I wish that I hadn't killed that man, but I suspect that if I were faced by him again, I would kill him again.'

Victoria remembered how she had felt when she thought back to James and what he had done to Eleanor. Was it the same thing? She had wanted to kill James, but she hadn't. Would she have killed him if he hadn't stopped his attack? She was having doubts now; she had lost her moral compass.

***

'Was that you?' Susan asked in a whisper.

'What?' Anthony whispered back.

'The shots.'

'Did you hear them?'

'Of course, we did, you idiot! Everyone must have heard them.'

'Really?' he sounded pleased.

'Oh, Anthony, you'll be arrested,' Susan said.

'Only Gary was hurt.'

'You didn't shoot Gary, please tell me you didn't.'

'Of course not, no! He was fighting those horrible brutes we saw last night, and I scared them off with my gun.'

'But you didn't shoot them, did you?'

'No, although I was tempted.'

'How's Gary?'

'A few cuts and bruises; I think he's all right.'

'Where's the gun now?' whispered Susan.

'I threw it away. It's lost forever now, I think,' Anthony sounded regretful.

'Thank God. Honestly, Anthony, you're your own worst enemy, you really are.'

'But you still like me, don't you?'

'I'd like you much more if you grew up a bit. What do you think you are, some kind of vigilante?'

'I'm sorry, Susan, I was just caught up with the excitement of it all. I'll behave from now on, I promise.'

'OK, I don't want you to change too much — just don't do anything so idiotic again.'

'Susan?' Anthony asked hesitantly.

'Yes?'

'Well, you know we're going to visit my father in prison,' Anthony was whispering now.

'Yes.'

'You will come too, won't you?'

'If you're sure you really want me to.'

'I do.'

'Why?'

'Well, you're one of the team, aren't you? And anyway, well, I think you're really nice and I'd feel a lot better if you came as well.'

'Oh, well, that's nice of you. Then, yes, I'll come along for the ride.'

'Really?'

'I said yes, didn't I?'

'Oh, yes. Great… Good. Lovely.'

'Anthony?'

'Yes?'

'You will be sensible, won't you?'

'Yes, I will be, from now on.'

'Good night then.'

'Goodnight, Susan, thank you.'

'You put the phone down,' she said.

'No, you go first.'

'No, you go first.'

'Ladies first.'

'Oh, all right then.'

'Well, go on then.'

'I'm going to.'

'Susan?'

'What?'

'I was just checking if you were still there.'

'I am.'

'Yes.'

'Right, I'm off — good night, Anthony.'

'Good night. Thank you, Susan.'

'After three?' Susan suggested.

'One, two, three.'

They put the phone down together.

***

'Then something else happened to me,' Joe said.

Victoria looked at him. She was willing him to say something to make everything all right.

'Let's hear it.'

'Someone came into my life. He helped me turn things around.'

'The journalist?'

'You remember.'

'Of course, I remember. I remember everything you told me, because I trusted you. Now I don't believe anything you tell me. How can I trust you? All I have to go on is what you tell me, and you're not exactly a reliable witness are you?'

'No, I'm not,' Joe conceded.

'The thing is, Joe, you are a manipulator. I get the feeling that everything you say and do is designed to make people think or act in the way that you want. You've wrapped me around your little finger. I've seen you do it and I've let you. You're crafty. I don't know what you're all about.'

'Would it help if there was someone else you could talk to, someone who can vouch for me?' Joe asked at last.

'Like a third-party testimonial?'

'Yes.'

'But whoever you choose will be part of your web of intrigue. Is there anyone who knows you that I can trust?' Victoria asked.

***

Anthony turned off his light and got into his makeshift bed. The last time he'd shared a bedroom was at St Luke's. Here he was with another school bully, but this time it was his friend.

'Sorry you had to see that stuff with my dad,' Gary said.

'No, I'm sorry that I wasn't much help,' Anthony answered.

375

'Not much help? You and your gun — that was unbelievable. Don't forget you scared off those fuckers too.'

'I'm glad I did something helpful.'

'It's been a fucking crazy few days, hasn't it?' Gary said, not for the first time.

'Fucking mental,' Anthony said, liking the sound of the words.

'Anthony?'

'Yes?'

'Don't swear, it's not very nice.'

'Fuck off,' Anthony said grinning.

'Anthony?'

'Yes?'

'I'm sorry.'

'Me too.'

'Why are you sorry?'

'For being such a wanker.'

Gary laughed.

Anthony said, 'I've got a question for you.'

'Yeah?'

'What happened between you and Katy?'

Gary groaned and said, 'It was awful. I can't tell you, but it was terrible. I didn't know what I was doing. I wish it hadn't happened.'

'She's amazing, don't you think?'

'Yeah, she is. I was so fucking stupid — a total cretin in fact.'

'Susan's nice too, don't you think?'

'Yeah, she is; they're both nice.'

'What do you think is going to happen to your parents?'

'I don't know. I can't work out my mum. She was so different to normal today.'

'Do you think it's got anything to do with Joe being round at your house?'

'I dunno. I tell you, though, that was weird seeing him there. She was talking with him like they were old friends. There's something funny about him — do you know what I mean?'

'I certainly do. Do you remember today, when we were role-playing the trip to see my father in prison? Well, Joe played the part of my father as if he knew him! It was uncanny. I could almost believe he was my father.'

'I really like him though, don't you?' Gary asked.

'Yes, I do too.'

They were silent as they thought about the events of the day.

Gary spoke first, 'So what's going to happen tomorrow?'

'I don't know about tomorrow, apart from school, but the day after is the trip to see my father. At least I hope so.'

'What does your mum say about that?'

'She doesn't want me to go.'

'Why not?'

'She thinks he'll get into my head, like he always has done.'

Gary was quiet, then said, 'Do you hate him?'

'Absolutely, I despise him. Do you hate your father?'

'I know this might seem weird, but this evening I felt sorry for him: for the first time in my life I felt sorry for my dad.'

'Why?'

'Because he looked so pathetic, such a loser.'

'My father isn't a loser, he's evil,' Anthony said.

'Do you reckon?'

'Yes, he's evil; he must be to be able to behave like he does.'

'Fuck, maybe you should keep away from him then?'

'I thought that, but I've got to try and free my mother from him.'

'Yeah, that's true; but if he's that bad what can you do?'

'I don't know, but I've got to try something.'

'I 'spect you'll think of something,' Gary said, respect in his voice.

***

'May I have a drink?' Joe asked.

Victoria got up and opened a cupboard and took down a bottle of whisky. She opened it. She'd been saving it for medicinal purposes: it was needed now. She poured two glasses, but not large ones. She wanted to keep her wits about her.

Joe said, 'OK, there is someone.'

Victoria steeled herself.

Joe knocked back his whisky. 'I had been in prison for — maybe ten years? We heard that the BBC wanted to come in and do a documentary about life in gaol and had chosen our beloved residence. There was a great deal of excitement at the prospect of the television coming into the place. I think that many of us thought that it might be a chance to show to the world how innocent we were, and that natural justice would kick in and we'd be freed. I remember the morning vividly. We'd been warned to be on our best behaviour and do exactly what we always did. The first thing we saw was the governor walking around the wings with a little group of men, cameras, microphones, recording equipment — what you'd expect, I guess. We all stared at them, feeling like animals in a zoo. They stayed with us for a week, interviewing us, filming us in the library, garden, the yard, everyday places for prisoners. The chap in charge interviewed some of us in our cells. Mostly, though, they just began to blur into the fabric of the place. I never saw the programme. I think it was broadcast in the early 1960s. I remember it was all filmed around Christmas time. In fact, now I think about it, I have a feeling that it was an attempt to capture what it might be like to have Christmas in prison. Did you ever see it?'

'I didn't, but I do remember it. It was a Stewart Simpson documentary, I think.'

'That's right. Stewart is Grace's son.'

Victoria gaped at Joe.

'What are you thinking? How did a convicted murderer become friends with a famous documentary maker and journalist, to such an extent that we are now still friends and I am organising his mother's birthday party?'

'Yes, that and other things too.'

'Like, how are you ever going to know whether you can trust anything I ever say?'

'Yes, mostly that.'

'I know. That's what's troubling me too. I know that what I'm telling you is true but how can you know that it's true.'

Victoria sipped her whisky.

'I've got a partial solution,' he said.

'Yes?'

'How about we ring Stewart up and you talk to him?'

'Stewart Simpson? Ring him up, just like that?'

'Yes. Maybe speaking to him might be helpful?'

'But won't he mind?'

'I don't know; but I want you to begin to trust me again and if it helps you get at the truth then it's worth a try.'

Victoria felt unsure, out of her depth. She knew Stewart Simpson by reputation. He'd been a journalist and had started making television documentaries in the 1950s. He'd been the presenter and producer of *Real Life* and was regularly on television and radio as a social commentator. She looked at Joe. He looked back at her. His gaze was steady and open.

'All right give him a ring,' she said finally, not convinced that Joe was telling the truth even now.

Joe went over to the telephone and dialled a number. He waited.

'Stewart, it's Joe…' 'No, everything is fine. Grace was very tired today; I think the excitement of meeting the kids yesterday was a bit too much for her in one go… Well, it's an odd request. Are you free for a few minutes…? OK, it's like this. I've met someone called Victoria. She's special. We are getting on very well. I want her to be able to trust me and for obvious reasons it's not easy. I have described my unfortunate past. I was wondering if you'd tell her what you know about me, just as an additional bit of insight, just — well I don't know really — an alternative viewpoint?' Joe nodded as he listened. 'Yes, I understand that. All you can do is say what you know, nothing else… Great, thanks, Stewart. I'm going to leave the house so that it will be just you and Victoria.'

Joe put the telephone down on Victoria's desk. He beckoned her over. She sat down. He picked up a pen and wrote, 'Ring me if you want to see me again.'

He squeezed her shoulder and left. She felt the pressure of his hand last after he'd gone. She wanted to feel it there again. She cleared her throat and picked up the telephone and said firmly, 'This is Victoria Court. To whom am I speaking?'

***

Frank lay in his bed. He smiled at the memory of Robbie gesturing behind his dad. He had felt his body fill with life and joy as he'd seen them both cheering him as he'd crossed the finishing line in Meadow Park. He had flown past them and slowed to a stop. He didn't turn around. He knew they were still there: he could hear them chattering and laughing. Instead, he had jogged back home, posting his letter to Ailsa in the post box at the end of Gary's street. He had carried on down Drayton Road and had seen Gary, Katy and Susan at the door. What had happened after that had been shocking, in Gary's house, and then exhilarating in the café. He shook his head in wonder — life was crazily out of kilter right now.

He stretched out fully. He filled his bed completely tonight. He knew why. He had come back to life. His mother had made him do it. When he had put his faith in her total belief in him, his dad and Robbie were there for him too. Were they ghosts? He wasn't sure. He knew they were there and that was all that mattered.

***

'So, if she gets the letter tomorrow maybe I'll get a reply the day after?' Katy said to Susan as they lay in bed together.

'Who knows? Yes, maybe.'

'What will she say? I bet she's wondering right now if she'll get a letter from me in the morning. She's probably nervous too.'

'Maybe. Maybe, though, she's got six kids and they're taking up all her thoughts and energy,' Susan suggested.

'Yeah, or maybe she's rehearsing for a part in the West End, starring in a new show. Maybe she's going to be in the *Eurovision Song Contest* next year, or — how about this? — she's the first woman to read the news on television.'

'That's Angela Rippon, you idiot,' Susan said.

'Well, maybe Angela's my mum.'

'Have you seen her?'

'No, does she look like me?'

'I don't know. Anyway, I thought you wanted to be a singer, or an actress, or a dancer, not a newsreader.'

'Well, how do you know Angela Rippon can't sing, or act, or dance?'

'Shut up! Your mum is probably a typist, or a cleaner or something ordinary.'

'Well, in which case it's my dad who's world famous.'

'What does it matter what they are? You're the one who's going to be famous.'

'Yes, well that's true, I suppose.'

'Now please shut your brain down. It's like being with a whirling dervish.'

'What's that?'

'I don't know, but it's something like you.'

'All right, how about a pillow fight then?'

Susan groaned but smiled at the same time. Her sister was beginning to come back.

***

She heard the familiar voice say, 'My name is Stewart Simpson. It's very good to talk to you, Victoria.'

'I feel that this is rather presumptuous, just ringing you up like this; it's late and you don't know me from Adam,' she said.

'I know. Joe has a way about him that makes out of the ordinary behaviour seem every day.'

Victoria was already feeling relieved. That Stuart should say such a thing about Joe straight off made her realise that he really did know him.

'Are you sure you don't mind talking, just briefly?'

'No, it's fine. The thing is, I owe a great deal to Joe and I'm happy to help him out when I can.'

'From what I understand, he owes you too, doesn't he?'

'Well, in which case we're even.'

Victoria paused. She felt she owed this stranger an explanation. But before she could frame a question or set the scene he said, 'What I'm going to do is tell you what I think might be helpful and then you can ask me questions, is that OK?'

'Yes, perfect, thank you.'

'Has he told you about the documentary?'

'Yes.'

'Right, I shall go from there. We were in the place for a week. On my first day there, we were filming mealtimes, filming the prisoners as they moved around the place. I was just sitting and observing really. My attention was caught by this man. He seemed different to the others. He was calm, self-contained, composed, I suppose. He talked to the other blokes, he laughed with them, he listened to them. But he seemed slightly separated from them too. In fact, this is the best way to describe him: he seemed to be their boss, or their officer. I've seen a lot of people in military settings, as a serving soldier and a journalist: Joe came across as if he were the leader in amongst the ranks. What struck me about him was the way he seemed to be looking after the others around him. I saw him reading something to one man. Another time I saw him put his arm around the shoulders of someone. He joked with others. He edged one chap away from a near bust-up. It was as if he was looking out for them all. At the same time, I saw them being drawn to him. The funny thing is, Victoria: I found myself being drawn to him too. Before I knew what was happening, I was setting up the cameras in and around where he was. It was fast becoming a piece about Joe Marshall, not prison at all.'

'Did you talk to him?' Victoria asked.

'Yes, but not in the way you might expect.'

'What happened?'

'He talked to me — that was the funny thing. I was in my usual place, off to one side of the canteen and, as usual, watching him. He was writing something for a young man — a letter I suppose. He finished writing, read it back to the young chap and then handed it to him. He looked up at me and stared straight at me, like he was measuring me, weighing me up. I felt like a little kid caught out. Me, a middle-aged man, quite famous, someone used to dealing with authority, challenging authority. This man suddenly made me feel like a little boy. What was going on?'

'What happened?'

'Nothing. I just looked back, then away. The thing is that, for a split second, I had the impression that he could read my mind, could see what I had thought was secret, private, hidden away.'

'I know. He does that to me, too,' Victoria admitted. 'What next?'

'Well, later that day I was talking to my main cameraman and I turned around and I saw that Joe was walking off. I followed him. He went into the library and sat down at a table. I plucked up my courage — yes, isn't it weird to even say that — and I sat down next to him. He looked up and said, "You're wondering whether to tell me something, but I can't tell what it is." I nodded. It was true.'

'What was it?' Victoria asked.

There was a pause then the familiar voice said, 'I was struggling with something, something difficult, something that I hadn't shared with anyone ever. The thing is, I was being faced with a horrible decision and everything was beginning to implode around me. That Joe had picked it up without even talking to me made me suddenly want to tell him everything. I looked at him: he just seemed so calm and understanding. I had known him only a few days, and not at all to talk to, but here I was about to tell him aspects of my personal life that I'd never shared with anyone. And do you know what? I was happy to.'

'I'm glad it's not just me,' Victoria said.

'So, I told him. You don't need to know the details, suffice it to say that I was in a very difficult situation and I couldn't see my way out of it. Before I could stop to think, I had told Joe everything. Think about it: I was in a prison library, there were people all around us, and yet the only person I was aware of was this man. It felt like he had hypnotised me — yes, that's what it was: I was in a sort of trance.'

'What did he say to you?'

'He was very clever, he said... "sounds interesting. Is it for television or a film?" I looked at him blankly, what did he mean?'

'What did he mean?'

'I suddenly realised that as I'd been talking, others had been listening — warders, prisoners — goodness knows who had heard what. I realised that what Joe had done was to make it appear as if it were fiction, as if it were a plot line. I came to. I nodded and said, "Not sure yet, what do you think?".'

'What did he say?'

'He said, "Sounds like a fly on the wall documentary to me".'

'Then what?'

'Then he said, "Thank you for telling me about it; I really appreciate you sharing it with me. Tell me more when you're ready".'

'Did you?'

'Yes, but not then. We finished filming. We put the programme together and that was it. But, from that day on, Joe and I began to write to each other. Bit by bit I told him more about my predicament, which, by the way, involved my wife and a family matter. I found myself becoming more and more drawn to him. I sought his counsel, his support, his encouragement.'

Victoria could still feel the pressure of Joe's hand on her shoulder, she shivered. 'Didn't that worry you? I mean, that you were becoming too reliant on him?'

'No, that's the funny thing. As I opened up to him, the more he told me about himself. There was never a time when there was an imbalance. I'd never met anyone quite like him for ease of communication. I bet you're finding that too, aren't you?'

'Well, sort of. He was really reticent about his past but then I pressed him into telling me everything and although it was the right thing to do, I'm still regretting it.'

'Yes, I understand that. Joe's no saint. I think it's because he's done bad as well as good things that he understands people so well. It's as if he's thought it, done it, or stopped himself doing it, and therefore, whatever anyone tells him, he can relate to it. Remember too that he was the listening ear to a load of serious offenders. What they would have told him would shock and appal most people, Victoria. I can't advise you about him. I can only tell you that as far as I am concerned, he is completely trustworthy. For example, I bet he hasn't told you anything about me or what I was struggling with back then, has he?'

'No, nothing.'

'I wish you well, Victoria. Joe is a complex man. Don't compare him with other men.'

'Thank you. Thank you very much indeed. I am still unsure of him, and of myself, but what you've told me has been helpful.'

Victoria put the phone down. Although she was reassured to some extent, she was far from easy in her mind. Joe was a sensitive, intelligent and empathic man. He had also done some bad things. Which was the real Joe? She realised that no one person could be known fully by another: that was a fundamental part of being human. She knew that everyone had secrets, every single person had done things that they regretted — or nearly done regrettable things which only chance had prevented. She picked up the telephone and dialled the familiar number.

'Hallo, 453 5620?'

'Hello, Michael, it's Vic.'

'Hallo, stranger. How's life?'

'Hmmm, topsy-turvy. How about my favourite family?'

'We're mostly fine. Elly's got a new job. I'll let her tell you; hang on, here she is.'

'Great timing, Vic. I've got exciting news.'

Eleanor's voice brought immediate relief to Victoria: it always had. Of her friends, she'd found over the years it was only with Eleanor that she could really confide. 'How wonderful! What is it?'

'Senior editor for Riverside Press. I can't believe it! It's my dream job.'

'Brilliant! You deserve it, Ellie. I'm so pleased for you. I hope you're cracking open a bottle?'

Eleanor's voice was smiling, 'Yes, we're already halfway through a bottle of Cinzano. I wish you were here, Vic.'

'Me too.'

'Anyway — any news from your end?'

Victoria wondered if this was the right time as this was a special moment for Eleanor. Should she spoil it for her? She found herself blurting out, 'Oh, Ellie! I've met this man. His name is Joe. He's funny, intelligent, kind. We've been out a few times, nice meals, drinks, conversations. We, er, well, erm — oh sod it — we've become lovers. Ellie, I'm all jumbled up. I really like him; I like him a lot. The things we talk about are really important: you know, the meaning of life and all that. We also just laugh a lot about silly things. I mean, yesterday we spent half an hour deciding which was best with an aperitif — peanuts or crisps? Half an hour ago we got into a huge argument about nature and nurture and whether killing a man could ever be forgiven or justified.'

'Blimey! Why?'

'Oh, Ellie, because he's killed someone.'

'Bloody hell!'

'What am I going to do?'

'Dare I ask if he meant to kill whoever he killed?'

'Yes — yes, he did.'

'Oh, bloody hell!'

'But, Ellie, don't get the wrong idea. He's so lovely and funny, and I love being with him. He's not like a traditional murderer. Oh, I know that is ridiculous. There's no such thing, I know. I mean, he's not like one of the Krays: he's not a villain is what I mean.'

Eleanor was silent.

'I think he's a good man, Ellie. I want him to be one, anyway. The problem I'm having is that he's not telling me stuff and then it kind of gets revealed and I'm not sure I can trust him. Tell me what to do. You're wise: what should I do?'

Victoria heard her dear friend's breathing.

'Ellie?'

'I don't know. I can't tell. I'm a bit drunk; my mind's fuzzy, Victoria. You've thrown me a hand grenade: I can't take it all in. I trust you to do the right thing, though — you of all people know what the right thing is. Erm, forgive me for asking: is everything good in the, er, bedroom department? I only ask, well, because; I mean it's not the be-all and end-all, but what with the dim and distant past — you know?'

'It's absolutely lovely.'

'Is he kind to you, Vic? I think kindness is the most important thing.'

'He is — so far anyway: apart from recent revelations, that is.'

'Well, why not just see what happens? No commitments, no long-term plans, just see what happens and then decide?'

'Thanks, Ellie. I wanted you to say that; that's exactly what I wanted to hear. Erm, you see, I think I'm in...er — You're right. I'll wait and see.'

'Oh, good. I'm terribly excited, Vic. Tell me more, when you want to. But, Vic, you will be careful, won't you? Promise?'

'Yes, of course I will. I promise. Wish me luck, won't you?'

***

'Hello?' said Joe.

'It's me.'

'How are you doing?' he asked.

'All right.'

'How did you get on with Stewart?'

'He was very kind and helpful.'

'What do you want me to do, Victoria? I shall keep away. I shall also tell the kids that I've had to change plans for Grace. I shall do the right thing by them and you. What do you think is the right thing?'

Victoria closed her eyes and counted to ten. She drew in a breath and said, 'You're the mind reader, you tell me.'

'Not this time, Victoria. You must tell me what you want.'

'You've got one more chance, Joe. Don't mess it up.'

She heard his long, drawn out, 'Phew.'

Victoria smiled, but she was still uneasy.

'Victoria?'

'Yes?'

'I'm really sorry. I know I'm pushing my luck, but there's one more thing I have to tell you. It's...'

Victoria cut in, 'Oh for heaven's sake, Joe! Can we do it tomorrow, please? I need to clear my head.'

'Of course. Let me know when you're ready.'

***

Victoria walked into the canteen. She queued up for her turn at the counter and chose cheese pie with chips and beans, her favourite. She turned to look around for a seat. It was her custom to eat with pupils when she could: she enjoyed it. Today there were a few spare chairs and indeed more became available as she scanned the canteen.

The table that caught her attention was in the far corner. She made her way over. Gary, Anthony, Frank, Katy and Susan were huddled together in deep conversation. As she approached, Gary saw her and nudged Anthony next to him. They leaned back in their seats and looked up at her.

'May I join you?' she asked.

Susan pulled out the chair next to her. They were silent.

'How's it going?' Victoria asked.

'How's what going?' Katy asked.

'Things?'

'Very well, thank you. Things are just fine and dandy,' Anthony answered.

'Great. How about plans for the big event?'

'Oh, pretty good; everything's coming along,' Katy said.

'Great. Anything you can tell me about?'

The group was silent. Victoria looked around them. Something was up. That this strange collection of people was sitting together was peculiar in itself, that they were clearly hiding something made her think of the evening before and all her suspicions of Joe came rushing back.

She couldn't help herself asking, 'How are you getting on with Joe?'

Their expressions changed; they all relaxed.

'Fine… great… very well,' echoed around the table.

'When are you seeing him next?'

'This afternoon, at The Beeches,' Susan said.

'I heard that Grace wasn't very well yesterday; I hope she's going to be all right.'

'Who told you?' Gary asked.

Victoria blushed, then stammered, 'Oh, I had a quick chat with Joe yesterday.'

Her fluster was noticed by them all. She went on, 'He told me that you're getting on famously.'

They looked pleased.

'Miss Court?'

'Yes, Anthony?'

'What is Joe?'

'What do you mean?'

'I just wondered what his job was. Do you know?'

'Ah, um, well as far as I know he's a gardener and helps out at the Beeches. Why do you ask?'

'Well, I just wondered, that's all. He knows lots about all kinds of things and I wondered if, well, what his background was?'

'I think he might be a spy,' Katy said.

'I thought he was an insurance salesman,' Gary said.

'Or perhaps he's a magician,' Susan mused.

Victoria smiled at them. 'He could be all of those things; he's rather unusual, that's all I know. What do you think, Frank?'

Frank looked up. She studied him for a moment. He looked different: something had happened to him. He thought for a minute and then said, 'I think he could be whatever he wanted to be.'

They all seemed to like that answer, and so did Victoria.

Victoria ate her lunch quickly. They started to chatter inanely, clearly not wanting her to know what they'd been talking about before her arrival. She wanted to stay and chat with them, but she didn't have the time, and, in any event, they seemed to be so close-knit that she felt like an intruder.

'Bye for now. Good luck with it,' she said as she stood up.

'Bye, Miss,' Katy said, rather too quickly.

Victoria smiled and walked away. They huddled together again.

'Phew, that was close,' Anthony said.

'What's the big deal? You're totally entitled to visit your dad,' Katy asked.

'Yes, but I don't want my mother to know and also I don't want Miss Court to know that Joe is taking me, I mean, us.'

'Why not?'

'I don't know. I suppose she might think he's a bad influence or something, and if she thinks we're doing things in secret she might call everything off,' Anthony explained.

'I think she fancies Joe,' Katy said, giggling. 'Did you see her blush when we were talking about him?'

'I don't think people their age fancy each other anymore: it's more dinner parties and classical music, that kind of thing,' Susan answered.

'Of course, they do — they're not that old,' Katy insisted.

They started getting up to leave. Susan began collecting plates; Anthony took them from her. They filed out towards the door, edging past tables. Anthony's vision was obscured by the pile of crockery and he failed to see a foot move out from under a table. He felt himself pitch forward and crash to the floor. As he fell, he heard yells of excited laughter.

'Perfect timing, Steve,' Phil screeched.

Steve was laughing hysterically as he, Paul and Phil looked down at Anthony sprawled on the floor amidst broken plates and strewn chips.

Hearing the commotion, Victoria turned at the door and looked back. She could guess what had happened from the exultant laughter of the perpetrators. She was about to walk towards them but stopped in her tracks.

Anthony was brushing bits of food off himself as he got up. Then he bent down to pick up the wreckage.

'I suppose you have servants to clear up your mess back at Alexander Palace,' Paul sniggered.

Anthony ignored him. Katy was helping him to clear up. Frank and Gary were looking on, ignoring the sneers and jibes of Gary's former friends.

'Come on, Gaz, aren't you going to help your little friend?' Steve asked Gary, a challenge in his voice.

Victoria started to smile as she saw what was about to happen.

Phil looked up as he saw Susan, struggling under the weight of the large bucket of scraped-away food, walk up behind Steve and Paul. She hefted it high and emptied the contents over the heads of first Paul, then Steve and, before he could avoid the torrent of chips, gravy, beans and custard, over him too.

There was a massive cheer from around the canteen as the three were engulfed.

'I suppose you have servants to help you clean up your mess,' Susan said.

She looked up to see the advancing dinner ladies and, beyond them, Miss Court smiling broadly. Susan smiled back at her. Victoria turned and left the canteen, shoulders shaking, tears in her eyes.

***

Joe walked into the little office he had commandeered at The Beeches. He saw Katy, Gary, Anthony and Frank waiting for him. There was someone else with them, an attractive girl with chestnut hair and a serious expression.

'Hello, Joe,' Anthony said, cheerful as ever.

'Afternoon, all. How goes it?'

There was a general chorus of greeting. The energy and high spirits in the room were palpable.

The new girl stood up and said, 'Hello, I'm Katy's sister Susan. Would it be all right if I joined in?'

'Fine by me; it's up to everyone else.'

'She's ever so helpful and sensible,' Katy vouched for her sister.

'I think she should join us; she's brilliant at dealing with shits and wankers,' Anthony said.

They all laughed at Anthony's language.

'I don't think that that kind of ability is quite what we need, but I'm sure Susan will fit in very well,' Joe said.

'What are we doing today?' Gary asked.

Joe looked at Gary. He thought about his trip to the Abbott house and what he had encountered. He saw that Gary had been in a fight.

391

'I think it would be good to talk through what ideas you've come up with and I know Grace wants to see you, Frank. Plus, are we still up for a jaunt tomorrow, Anthony?'

'Definitely, if it's all right with you.'

'Who else is coming?'

'We all are,' Katy answered straight away with an uncompromising look.

'Great. It'll be a tight squeeze but I'm up for it if you are.'

He looked at Anthony. 'Have you checked what you need in terms of giving notice, identification, that kind of thing?'

'Yes, everything's in order.'

'I think you might need parental agreement, Anthony; is that all OK?'

'Ah, well that might be tricky.'

Joe looked questioningly at Anthony.

'I wasn't going to tell her you see.'

'What does everyone think about that?' Joe asked them all.

They were quiet. Then Frank said, 'Better to tell her, Anthony; you'll feel better if it's out in the open.'

'I agree,' Susan backed him up.

Anthony swallowed and looked uncomfortable.

'Did you want to keep it to yourself?' Joe asked.

'Well, the thing is, my mother doesn't want me to see him, or to have anything to do with him.'

'What do you think you should do then?' Joe asked.

'I know I should talk to her. I just wanted to avoid it.'

'We can all talk to her,' Katy said. 'I'm sure she'd understand.'

Anthony smiled but shook his head.

'Thank you, Katy, but I'll do it on my own. I think that would be best.'

Joe said, 'I shall need her OK before we go, Anthony. Will you ask her to ring me, or write me a letter?'

'Yes, I will. What's your telephone number?'

'It's 4306.'

They all pulled out pens and papers. Susan had a hardback notebook, Katy wrote it on her hand, Gary wrote it on an old bus ticket, Frank on the corner of his scrap book which he was still clutching, and Anthony produced a propelling pencil and entered the number in a leather-bound address book.

***

'Sit down, Frank,' croaked Grace as he stood hesitantly in the doorway.

He looked at the old lady. She was sitting in her armchair, huddled up in a big fluffy blanket.

'I see you've brought your life history with you,' she said, looking at the large scrapbook under his arm.

'Yes, but we don't have to look at it if you don't want to.'

She looked at him.

'I do want to see it. I want to show you my pictures too.'

Frank pulled up a hardback chair and sat down next to Grace. He totally dwarfed her. He stood up again and pushed the chair away and pulled over a small coffee table and perched on that; they were now at the same level. He opened the book and slowly turned the pages for her. She stopped his hand now and then to read a headline or to study a picture. After several minutes they reached the last of the articles.

'Who's Ailsa?'

'A friend of my brother.'

'She obviously likes you.'

'Yes.'

'Do you like her?'

'Yes, but we've lost touch.'

'Why?'

'Because I'm an idiot.'

'I doubt that, Frank.'

'Well, I wrote to her yesterday, probably too late.'

'Did you see what she wrote?'

'Yes, I've read it a few times.'

'Did you notice that I'm in it?'

Frank frowned, he read it again… 'Frank has grace too.'

Grace said, 'That's funny, don't you think? You've got me, and I've got you.'

He nodded and said, 'Can I see your photographs?'

She pointed to an album on the top shelf of the bookcase opposite them. He lifted it down and brought it to her.

'You can look through if you want,' she said.

He turned the old pages. He saw black and white images of Grace as a young woman posed with a variety of similarly old-fashioned people, some young and some old.

'There's none of my husband or brother of course: they died before photographs came along for ordinary people.'

'Who's this man?'

Grace looked at the picture of her with a tall man in uniform.

'That's me with my second husband. He's rather grand don't you think?'

He was very grand, Frank agreed.

'Is that your son?' he said, pointing at a little boy on Grace's husband's shoulders.

'Yes, that's Stewart. Do you know who he is?'

Frank shook his head.

'He's Stewart Simpson, the television presenter,' she said.

'Really?'

'Yes, really. He's done ever so well.'

Frank wasn't really sure who he was but knew his name. He carried on turning pages then as the pictures became more modern, he started seeing a very familiar face. He studied the photographs closely.

'This is him, isn't it?' he said.

'Yes, he looks terribly young there,' she said. 'That's his wife in the next one.'

Frank saw Grace with young children.

'They're my grandchildren; aren't they beautiful?'

Frank thought that they looked like normal kids, but he didn't say so.

He reached the end and closed the album.

'Thank you for showing me your treasures, too, Frank; they must be very precious indeed.'

'Yes, but it's all ancient history now.'

Grace nodded then said, 'I know I'm nothing important to you and what I say has no real value, but may I give you some more advice?'

Frank shrugged.

'No, I want you to tell me if I may, or not; either way I want you to tell me.'

Frank looked closely at the old lady. She looked steadily back at him. She was about two feet smaller than him and maybe half his weight. Despite her age and infirmity, he felt as if he was shrinking, she seemed to be growing in front of his eyes.

He said quietly, 'I would love some advice, please.'

Grace reached over to her bedside table and picked up a small purse. She opened it and took out two brass discs. She held them tight in her tiny hand. Frank watched her closely.

'These are medals. One was given to my husband and the other to my brother. I have taken them everywhere I have ever gone. They are with me all the time. I take my husband and my brother with me everywhere. I know that, no matter what happens, they are with me. They look after me. But this is the important thing: they come with me — they never hold me back. They are light. They are strong. They are indestructible. They will last forever and, they will always be with me. They never hold me back, never: they don't want to. They want me to be at my best, in everything that I do. You understand me, Frank, don't you?'

Frank looked at the old lady in front of him. He heard her words ringing in his head; he saw the conviction in her eyes. He sensed her own inner strength as if it were a physical force. He nodded.

***

The others stared at Frank as he came into the room. He paused slightly at the door. He looked at them questioningly.

'What's up? What's happened?' he said.

'Nothing. It's just, well, every time I see you, you look as if you've grown six inches,' Katy said.

'Are you taking some kind of drug?' laughed Anthony.

Frank looked embarrassed and sat down.

'Grace wants to talk to all of us — you're next Katy,' Frank said.

Katy jumped up.

'Which room is she?'

'Twenty-one.'

'Is she all right?'

'Yeah, she's amazing,' he said.

Katy left the room.

'How tall are you, Frank?' Anthony asked.

'About six foot three.'

'How tall are you, Gary?' Anthony asked.

'Six foot, I think.'

'Oh, you make me feel like a midget,' Anthony said.

'It doesn't matter how tall someone is, you idiot, it's what they're like as a person,' Susan said.

'I agree,' said Joe.

'You're not that small anyway. How tall are you?' Susan asked.

Anthony sat up straight and puffed out his chest, 'Five seven.'

'OK, so you're a bit shorter but who's the most intelligent one here?' Susan asked.

'Depends on what you think of as intelligent. I don't know anything about anything interesting, but I can do algebra,' Anthony said.

'Good answer,' Joe said.

'If you want to change anything you should wear different clothes,' Gary said.

'I don't know, I think Anthony is bringing back the pre-war look,' Susan said, trying not to smile.

'I suppose I am a bit old-fashioned,' Anthony said.

'A bit?' Gary snorted.

They studied Anthony's clothes: he was wearing straight trousers; his shirt had small collars; his tie was tied neatly; his shoes were well polished black brogues. Anthony looked at what the others were wearing:

Gary had on a pair of faded corduroy baggies; his shirt had wide collars; he was wearing the school tie, but it was tied so tightly as to be merely a knotted string; his shoes were huge, two-tone wedges. Frank was wearing a denim jacket and flared jeans — and very old trainers.

'Hmmm, I see what you mean,' Anthony said.

'And your hair, Anthony: do something with your hair for Christ's sake; you look like something out of the last century,' Gary said.

'All right, I take your point, although I do think it's good to maintain standards.'

'Yeah, if you want to look like a prick,' Gary said, laughing.

Anthony looked dejected. Feeling guilty for putting him down, Gary said, 'You know more about guns than the rest of us.'

Joe looked up at him sharply, then turned to Anthony.

'Meaning?'

'Oh, we were near a gun going off last night and Anthony thought that it might be a Webley,' Susan said quickly.

Joe looked questioningly at Anthony.

'I don't know anything about guns; it's just that my grandfather had one and it's the only type of gun I know.'

'How close to the gunshots were you?' Joe asked Susan.

Susan coloured as she paused, 'It's hard to say, maybe a few streets away; sound travels in a funny way doesn't it?'

'Frank?' Joe asked.

'Susan's right: we weren't close, it just sounded close.'

'That's right,' Gary said.

'How did you get the cut eye, Gary?' Joe asked.

'Oh, just a scrap,' Gary answered.

'With anyone in particular?'

'Nah, just a couple of kids. It wasn't anything.'

Joe looked around the room, 'You'll let me know if I need to know anything, won't you?' he said.

'Don't worry, Joe, we won't let you down,' Anthony said.

'What did Grace think of your scrapbook?' Joe asked Frank.

'I think she thought it was pretty good; she seemed interested.'

'I'm not surprised — it's amazing. You're amazing.'

'You are, Frank. We all think you are,' Susan said.

Frank looked embarrassed again.

'Are you going to start running again?' Anthony asked.

'I'm thinking about it. I'm not sure.'

'What's stopping you?' Gary asked.

'I'm a bit scared: I think I've lost my nerve.'

'What are you scared of?' Anthony asked.

'Everything.'

'We'll look after you,' Anthony said.

'I know it's not a real fear. It's irrational.'

'Not really, Frank. I'd say it's totally rational,' Joe said.

'Me too. You've had a terrible time, Frank: it would be funny if you weren't a bit scared,' said Susan.

'Do you think?' Frank asked, he sounded surprised.

'Of course. It's obvious — well at least to anyone looking on,' Anthony said.

'OK, so what do I do to get over it?'

'Any ideas?' Joe asked looking at each of them in turn.

'I'd rather not talk about it, sorry everyone,' Frank said.

'If anyone can sort it out, it's you,' Gary said.

They all looked at him.

'I agree, Gary,' Joe said.

'Me too, and I know Katy thinks you're wonderful,' said Susan.

'You are amazing, Frank,' reinforced Anthony. 'That's exactly what you are.'

Frank couldn't hide his tears.

***

'You're very lively, aren't you?' Grace said to Katy.

'I'm sorry, I'm not great at sitting down,' Katy said. She'd been floating around the room, looking at ornaments and pictures, and gazing into the mirror over the basin.

'So, what do you plan for our entertainment on my birthday?'

'Well, I thought I could do a few songs, maybe a dance routine, and how about a monologue? I could do some Shakespeare, or something a little more modern. What do you think?'

'So, what you're saying is that it's going to be a one-woman show, and we shall get what you want to perform?'

Katy was quiet for a minute, not sure if Grace's question was a mild rebuke or a tease.

'I suppose I could ask the other residents what they'd like. Or, I could arrange for some other people to come along and do something. It just seems a shame to waste my extraordinary talent that's all.'

Grace chuckled, 'You're very funny; you really are.'

Katy beamed.

'You remind me of my granddaughter, Chloe,' Grace said.

'Is she stunning too?'

'That's enough, Katy, it's wearing thin now. Will you sing me a song?' Grace asked.

'Sure, what would you like?'

'Something from long ago.'

'Like The Beatles, do you mean?'

'Are you teasing me, you naughty girl?'

'OK, give me a few titles and I'll see if I know any of them.'

'How about "Stardust"?'

Katy smiled, 'I do know that, it's one of my grandma's favourites. I can play it a bit on the piano too, although it's a bit tricky.'

Katy cleared her throat and sang. When she'd finished, she turned around to look at Grace. Her eyes were closed; she looked as if she might be dead.

Katy knelt and took one of her hands and squeezed it.

'Was it terrible?' she asked.

Grace opened her eyes and smiled, 'No, it was lovely: just as I remembered it.'

Katy breathed a sigh of relief.

'I imagine your parents are very proud of you.'

'They are, but they're not my real parents. I'm adopted.'

'It's who brought you up that counts, not the person who gave birth to you. You know that, don't you?'

'Yes, I know. It's just that I suddenly discovered that I had another mother, another family — the real ones.'

'Real isn't really the right word is it?'

'Well, natural then.'

'Some people aren't naturally good at being parents, just good at conceiving.'

'I know. It's still hard to come to terms with though, when you're not expecting it.'

'Do you have any brothers and sisters?'

'Yes, I have — who I thought was my twin sister and that's another thing: she isn't really my twin and I'm terribly upset that she isn't.'

'How does she feel?'

'She feels the same but she's much wiser and more mature than me.'

'What's she like?'

'She's just down the corridor. Would you like to meet her?' Katy said.

'Yes, please.'

Seconds later Katy ushered Susan into the room.

Grace looked at Susan. She looked like a studious version of Katy.

'You look like twins to me, although my eyesight isn't very good these days.'

Both girls smiled, pleased with the verdict.

'We are twins really; nothing has changed,' said Susan.

'You are wise, just like Katy said.'

'Did you?' Susan said, turning to Katy.

'Well, I said loads of things; that was just one of them. I listed all your faults too.'

'Are you going to find your real parents?' Grace asked.

'Yes, I think so. Although, it's just my mother who got in touch.'

'Don't expect too much, dear. Life isn't usually a fairy tale.'

'That's what I keep telling her. She's probably a dinner lady or something like that,' Susan said.

'Yes, but maybe she's something exciting too: maybe she's a pop star; maybe she's on the television all the time,' Katy said.

'Will you let me know?' Grace asked.

'Of course, I will. Thank you for even being interested. My parents aren't bothered.'

'That's not true or fair! They're worried and scared,' Susan said with sudden force.

'Hmm, well let's see,' Katy said.

Susan was about to retort when Katy nudged her and pointed towards Grace. The old lady's eyes had closed, and she was snoring slightly. Katy straightened the rug over her lap, and they got up to go.

'Come again,' they heard Grace whisper.

'We will,' they both said.

***

'So, OK to meet here for nine a.m.?' Joe said.

They all nodded.

'I reckon we should allow three hours to get there — you'll check visiting times and all the necessary identity requirements, Anthony?'

'Don't worry, I'll have it all sorted out,' Anthony said.

'You will bring that letter from your mother, won't you?'

Anthony nodded.

They called goodbye to him as they left. He closed the door and picked up the phone on the desk.

'What shall we do now?' Katy asked, as they walked down the drive.

'I've got to do a bit of shopping,' Anthony said.

'What are you after?' Katy asked.

'Well, I'm going to buy a pair of baggies,' he answered.

'You, wearing baggies!' squawked Katy.

'Why not? That's what all the other boys wear,' Anthony answered aggrieved.

'Yes, but you're not exactly like the other boys, are you?' Katy said laughing.

'Gary wears baggies,' Anthony pointed out.

'To be fair, Anthony, you're not really like Gary, are you?' Susan said.

'Yes, but maybe I want to be like him,' he answered. 'You'll come with me down to Fosters, won't you, Gary?'

Gary said, 'It's on the way anyway.'

'How about you, Frank?' Gary asked.

'Um, well, I need to check something with Joe, so I'll see you tomorrow.'

They all looked at him; he looked away.

'We'd better go home, Katy. We need to spend some time with Mum and Dad.'

'Do we have to?'

'Yes, come on. Let's go.'

They went off in their separate directions.

'Are you going home today?' Anthony asked Gary.

'I better had. Not sure what will be waiting for me when I get there, though.'

They both reflected on the scene of the evening before.

'Do you think he'll be drunk still?' Anthony asked.

'To be honest, I don't know. I've never seen my mum behave like that, and I've never known him give in to her before.'

They turned on to the High Street.

***

'Hello, Victoria.'

'Hello, what are you up to?' she answered.

'I'm at a loose end. I wondered if you wanted to come out to play?'

'What have you got in mind?'

'A little trip.'

'Sounds intriguing. Tell me more.'

'Later, if that's OK?'

'Yes. But remember; I don't want any more secrets or nasty surprises.'

402

'Understood. By the way, we're going to visit Anthony's father in prison tomorrow.'

Victoria fell silent.

'It was decided by them; they all want to go. I offered to take them.'

'I assume Mrs Alexander knows all about it?'

'She will shortly. He's just off to go and tell her, and get her agreement, of course.'

'How will you know if he has or not?'

'He's bringing a letter from her.'

'I'm a bit uncomfortable about it, Joe.'

'If his mother is OK with it then it's nothing to do with us really, is it?'

'What, apart from the fact that you're driving him there you mean?'

'He wants to go, the others want to go with him, I have the time and — assuming his mother agrees — her consent too. Honestly, Victoria, I feel OK about it.'

Victoria considered her anxiety. What people did in their own time was up to them; Joe was right about that. But she had explained to their parents that their children were going to help with the arranging of a party for an elderly woman, not go on a prison trip with a convicted murderer. She said, 'I don't want to be a wet blanket, Joe, but I feel responsible for this and I want to be sure everything's out in the open. You understand, don't you?'

'Yes, I get it. What do you want to do?'

She thought it through. What was the actual issue? It was a day trip, that was all. The only real fly in the ointment was Joe's involvement. She was prepared to risk herself with him — if there were any risk — but could she, in all conscience, put Frank, Anthony, Gary and Katy in a risky situation? She made up her mind, 'I'm going to come along: be the responsible adult. I need to supervise this outing. If any of them don't like me being there, then I'm sorry, he or she will have to drop out.'

'Great! That's fantastic. I'm really happy with that. The only issue is going to be space in my car. Frank will have to go in the front, and you can all fight for places in the back.'

'You silly man, I can take some in my car.'

Joe said with great cheer, 'Deal! Thank you, Victoria; that's just smashing. Actually, you may be able to help us with something — something I've been worrying about.'

'Oh?'

'I think Anthony is going to find his visit to see his father pretty difficult. He's told me a bit about him; he sounds like quite a handful. I'd like to help Anthony prepare before going in and I have an idea. Will you help?'

'As long as it's in Anthony's best interests, I'd like to help. What do I need to do?'

'I'm not sure yet. I need to work it out. Thanks, Victoria; we're going to be a great team.'

'So, what time are you picking me up, then?' she asked.

'Seven p.m. — is that all right?'

'Sure. See you later then. I'm looking forward to it.'

Joe put the phone down. There was a quiet knock. He stood up and opened the door.

'Hello, Frank, want to come in?'

Frank came into the room and stood there uncertainly.

'Want to sit down?' Joe asked.

Frank sat down. He looked uncomfortable. There was a long silence then Joe said, 'How are you getting on with Grace?'

'Fine, she's a great lady.'

Joe nodded. 'How about you and the others?'

'Fine. We've sort of found a way of getting on, very well in fact.'

Frank sat slumped in his chair; his fingers knotted.

'Something's worrying you?'

Frank nodded.

'Is it about the trip tomorrow?'

'Yes,' Frank said almost in a whisper.

'Well, I've got an anxiety about it. If it's OK with you may I share my uneasy feeling?' Joe asked.

'Sure,' said Frank, sounding relieved.

'Well, I'm having a slight reservation about the wisdom of it. I know Anthony is keen, but his father isn't exactly lovey-dovey and maybe by going we're making things worse between them. What do you think?'

Frank considered the question. He looked at Joe and said, 'Honestly, I don't know. We all want to look after him, and maybe by going it will help them come to terms with each other. I know that if someone could take me to see my father, no matter what the circumstances, I'd be very happy about it.'

Joe nodded, then asked, 'Does it make any difference that his father is in prison do you think?'

'Maybe. But they're father and son; the place doesn't change that fact. Plus, if his mother is fine about it then all we're doing is making it happen. We're not deciding anything or taking any action that isn't wanted.'

'You're right. Thank you, Frank. I appreciate the advice.'

They were quiet again. Finally, Frank said, 'I'm scared.'

Joe waited, then said, 'Is it the drive? The car?'

'Yep.'

'Will it be your first time since?'

'Well, I've been in a couple of cars but not for several months and, in that time, I think I've developed some kind of phobia about going in a car. It's stupid, I know, but just thinking about it makes me feel sick and trembly.'

'I don't think it's stupid, Frank; you'd be abnormal if you didn't feel something. I'd have thought being at least anxious was natural.'

'The thing is that I want to go, and I don't want to let Anthony down, but I don't think I can manage it.'

'I'm sure Anthony would be disappointed, but you could tell him that you're uneasy about driving. He's a sensitive chap; he'd understand why.'

'I know, but I want to be there, part of it all. Plus, there's another reason.'

'Go on.'

'Well, I was sort of wondering if we could make a slight detour to see an old friend of mine, well, a friend of my brother's. She lives in Brighton, only a few miles from Lewes.'

'I see.'

'But now I'm feeling so scared of getting into the car I don't know if I can do either.'

Joe looked at Frank, 'Tell me about the ring, Frank.'

Frank looked at his right hand.

'It was my brother's. I think it came from a Christmas cracker one year. I found it in his stuff after the accident. I just like to wear it.'

Joe nodded and said, 'You're a very strong person, incredibly determined: you can beat the odds. I believe that you can get on top of this fear — I'm sure of it, in fact. Do you believe you can?'

'I used to believe I could do anything, but that was before... you know.'

'Yes, I know that your view of life has changed, but you are still Frank Gordon; you are still special.'

Frank didn't say anything.

'If I could do something to help you with this, would you want me to?'

'Yes, can you help?'

'I believe I can, but before we do, I want to ask you a question: is that all right?'

'Yes.'

'OK, so here you go. Answer this: which is faster, a horse or a bucket?'

Frank looked at Joe, confused.

'Which one, Frank?' Joe pressed him.

'A horse I suppose.'

Joe asked, 'OK, but is it right to write about right or left?'

Frank opened his mouth to answer but Joe went on, 'Would the mean of an average be mean to another, do you see what I mean?'

Frank was shaking his head. Joe carried on, 'I want you to count down from fifty in threes, starting at sixty-four. Start now, Frank; do it out loud.'

Frank was looking dazed now. He was staring at Joe who was looking serious, insistent.

'Come on, Frank, it's quite simple; if it makes it any easier why don't you do it in Greek, or Latin, or Morse code, whichever one you want. Now off you go, in thirds from Thursday onwards.' Joe went on, 'And what about this, wouldn't it be just wonderful to fall asleep now and let all the worries and pressures and uncertainties drift away, just drift away, simply drift away, and now as your eyes close, Frank, feel that sensation of total relief sweep over you; let your eyelids be as heavy as they want, just for a second; let them close, for a long, long, time if they want to.'

Frank's eyes were closed. His head had lolled forward; his breathing was deep and slow.

Distantly he heard Joe's voice, 'Well done, Frank, you're safe now. You are completely safe and secure. You can relax now. At last you can let go. I really admire the way you have decided to do what is right for you, to take on your next challenge. That's typical of you, Frank. So, here's the fact of the matter: you have the power to do amazing things; you know that. You are a determined person and you feel at your best when you have achieved your goals. You know that feeling of crossing the line first: you remember that feeling don't you, Frank?'

Frank nodded.

Joe went on, 'You worked really hard to win your races; you fought hard and you were at your best. You've had some tough times and you have wobbled a bit, quite understandably, but it's just a wobble. Now you're getting ready to get going again, to take on new challenges. The thought of getting back to your best is exciting: it's making you feel that adrenalin pulse through you again. The feelings of achievement, of victory, of relief at reaching your destination after all the effort, the ups and downs: you want those feelings back again. They are yours to have, Frank. You can have them, and you know they are on their way. Now, in a minute I want you to touch your silver ring with your left hand. When I say, "touch the ring", I want you to put your fingers on it. When you do, you will feel a jolt; you will get a rush of energy, of certainty and belief — it will feel like a wave of power. When you touch the ring there will be that rush and then it will be followed by something extraordinary: you will feel relief. Yes, that's right — relief that everything is safe, secure, at peace; relief so powerful you can relax into it. You can let it cover you like a wonderful fog of tranquillity; a cloak that is so warm and comfortable it will make you feel as easy and content as you have ever been before: ten times happier, and relaxed. OK, so, Frank, touch the silver ring with your fingers and let that feeling sweep over you.'

Frank put the fingers of his left hand on the silver ring. The moment he did so, he let out a long, audible sigh. His face was smooth and at peace.

'Well done, Frank. It's amazing isn't it? So, from now on, every time you touch that silver ring, you feel these feelings: belief in yourself, that wonderful sense of achievement, relief — absolute and complete relief. Whenever you touch the ring you feel relief wash over you like a blanket, a cloak, you can relax totally into that feeling. Just as you feel safe, secure, relaxed and at peace now, just as you feel relief moving through your body now, you feel relief every time you touch that ring, Frank, every time. No matter what, where, when, who you're with, no matter how you're feeling that ring brings you relief — every time.'

Frank sat still.

'In a minute, Frank, we'll get ready to go, but just for a moment you can just enjoy the feeling — the feeling that you can have whenever you want it. All you need to do is touch that ring and you feel relief; relief, Frank, every time.'

They sat together in silence.

'It's time we went, I think. Are you ready, Frank?'

Frank stirred, yawned and stretched.

Joe said, 'I'll see you in the morning, Frank, nine a.m. — is that OK?'

'Yes, I'll be there.'

'Will you tell me where you want to get to tomorrow?'

'Yes, it's near Brighton.'

'Bye then, Frank. See you in the morning. I think it's going to be a good day, don't you?'

Frank's left hand went to his silver ring. 'Yes, I do.'

***

Gary slouched into Fosters Menswear. Anthony followed.

'What do you want?' Gary asked.

'The same as you, black corduroy, the baggier the better.'

'They're over here,' Gary led Anthony to the rack of huge, baggy trousers.

Anthony looked at them. He put his hand out and felt the material. He breathed in their smell.

'I've never bought a pair of trousers before; can you believe that?' he said.

'There's a surprise,' Gary said.

'Well, it's easy for you: you come from a normal family, not like me,' Anthony said.

Gary snorted, 'Normal? Don't tell me that what you saw last night is normal.'

'No, I mean normal as in just being the same as the people around you. You and Steve — you know — your friends: you're all the same in terms of how you've been brought up, with the same kind of standards and expectations.'

'You talk a load of shit, Anthony.'

'I'm right though, aren't I?'

'I suppose so — although I don't know what normal is any more.'

'Do you think you're going to be friends with them again?'

Gary made a dismissive sound and said, 'I don't know, they're pricks, childish jerks; maybe when they grow up a bit.'

'Well, I'm not exactly mature, am I?' Anthony said.

'Yeah, well you come from a different background, plus at least you're intelligent, not like those toss-pots.'

Anthony couldn't help himself smiling. Hearing himself being compared favourably with boys who only days before had had so much power over him made him feel a foot taller.

Gary saw him smile and said, 'Don't worry you're a toss-pot too. What do you want baggies for anyway?'

409

'You're wearing them: why did you buy them?'

'Coz, well, coz that's what's in fashion I suppose.'

'Well, there you are then. It's the same for me.'

'Yeah, but you're different; you don't have to be like the rest of us.'

'But I want to be that's the point. I've been treated like an alien for the whole of my life and I want to be the same.'

Gary considered this but said, 'I think maybe you're better off being different, being yourself. I think being different from everyone else is cool; you stand out that way.'

'Maybe if you stand out in a way that other people think is cool or attractive then, yes, I agree. Standing out because you're a posh prick isn't so good.'

Gary laughed.

An assistant came over and Anthony pointed at the trousers.

'What size are you?' the assistant asked.

'Twenty-eight-inch waist, not sure how long,' Anthony answered.

The assistant handed him two pairs. 'Want to try them on?' he asked, gesturing to the changing room.

'Hmm, maybe I should,' Anthony said and disappeared behind the curtain.

Two minutes later he re-emerged wearing the trousers. Gary looked up from the leather jackets he'd been studying and burst out laughing.

'What's wrong?' Anthony said, crestfallen.

'They're fucking huge, Anthony; you could fit into one leg.'

'Well, that's because they're baggies, thickhead,' Anthony said.

'Yeah, but you look like, well, like a …. They're absolutely flipping' stupid.'

'I don't care; this is what I want.'

He walked to the till and took out a five-pound note from the inside pocket of his blazer.

As they left the shop Gary said, 'I'm not walking with you: you'll make me look as wacky as you.'

'I thought I already had.'

'Jesus, you look like a total prat,' Gary said, but nevertheless they walked back along the High Street together.

***

Katy and Susan walked home together. They took their usual detour — past the film studios. MGM and EMI took up most of the northern end of the main road through the town and, although activity had dwindled in recent years, there was still evidence that this town was where films were made. Katy liked to hang around outside the MGM main entrance, just in case someone from the 'business' spotted her and engaged her in conversation.

'Roger Moore was here at the weekend,' she said as they sat on a wall, Susan reading a book, Katy looking up and down the slip road to the studios.

'Big deal,' Susan said.

'I wonder if he's my father,' Katy mused.

'Who? Him?' Susan asked looking at an overweight man lifting boxes off a forklift truck.

Katy punched her lightly.

'Don't be stupid; I've obviously got talent in my genes.'

'Maybe that man has too. Not everyone with talent gets to be a film star you know.'

'I know. Let me dream, though, won't you?'

They got up to go.

'Nice legs, darling,' Katy's 'father' called across to her.

'Up yours, you old lech,' she shouted back sticking up two fingers.

'That's no way to talk to your beloved parent,' Susan chided.

They talked as they weaved along the busy pavement.

'Poor Anthony. Fancy having a father in prison!' Susan said.

'I know — what a disgrace for his mum, and she's so nice too.'

'I wouldn't be surprised if Gary's dad ends up in prison too; he's an awful man.'

'That was terrible last night. I didn't know what was going to happen — anything could have happened.'

'Gary's mum seemed so nice and gentle.'

'Oh no, please no! Please tell me that's not who I think it is,' Katy said pointing across the road.

Susan looked and said, 'It is. Oh dear.'

They saw Gary and Anthony walking in the same direction as them, the latter with enormous billowing legs trying to keep up with Gary's longer stride.

'What does he look like?' Katy said giggling.

'Don't say anything: he's probably really proud of them.'

They slowed down and watched the comic pair disappear down a side street.

'They're the weirdest couple of all time,' Katy said.

'They're rather sweet, I think. It's like they've found each other in the wilderness.'

'Eh? What book did you get that from?' Katy scoffed.

'I didn't. It just occurred to me.'

They turned into their road. Katy grabbed her sister's arm and pointed, 'Look, maybe it's her.'

Parked fifty yards from their house was a Rolls Royce, its occupant, if there was one, obscured by tinted glass.

'No, it can't be. Don't be silly, Katy,' Susan cautioned.

'It might be. How often do Rollers park in our street?'.

'Well, if it is anything to do with you, you're better off just acting normally.'

They walked slowly past the car. Katy couldn't help casting a sideways look into the driver's window as she went.

'Calm down, Katy. It can't be anything to do with us. Waiting in a Rolls Royce isn't exactly good camouflage is it?'

'I suppose not. Still, I wouldn't mind a car like that one day.'

'I thought you liked to cruise around in Ford Anglias,' Susan said.

'Shut up, that was a mistake. He was a sleazy creep: I've learned my lesson.'

They reached their house.

'Another evening with the drabs,' Katy sighed.

'Don't be horrible. They love you much more than anyone else does; you do know that, don't you?'

Katy grunted.

'Let's get on with it then. We've got an adventure tomorrow anyway.'

'Yes, I wonder what it's going to be like.'

***

'See you tomorrow, then,' Anthony called, as Gary walked quickly away from him.

'Yeah.'

Anthony knew Gary was anxious about going home. He was anxious too. He didn't know what his mother would say about the planned trip and, although he had been confident in his reassurance to Joe, he was far from sure she'd agree.

'Hello, Mummy dearest,' he called as he went through the front door. As usual at this time of the evening, Mrs Alexander was watching the television, glass in hand.

'Hello, dear,' she said.

Anthony didn't waste any time.

'I'd like to go and see Father tomorrow. Joe is going to drive me and the others. He will only take us if you write him a note to say you agree to it. I know that you'll be thinking that it's a bad idea — that we should keep away from him, that if I go then I'll be encouraging him to stay in touch, and I know that that is the last thing you want — but, and please believe me: I am going to tell him that he should stop writing to you, that neither of us ever want to hear from him again and that, as far as we are concerned, he is persona non grata. You're probably worried that he'll twist and turn and, before I know it, he'll be getting into my head — well, that concerns me too. But I've given it a lot of thought. I've spoken to Joe and the others: I'm ready for him, Mother, I really am. I need to see him. I need to get him out of my head, and to get him out of our lives.'

Anthony sat back and looked at his mother's face. There was no reaction from her.

'Mother?' he said.

She looked at him.

'He is a terrible man, Anthony. He is clever, very clever. He will try and manipulate you. Don't you think I thought I could manage him all these years?'

'I know, but he's in a weak position. We're in control now. Plus, I've got you, and my friends. You've got us looking after you. He can't hurt us anymore, I'm sure of it.'

Margaret Alexander got up slowly and went into her bedroom. She came back holding something small. She went to the desk in the corner of the room and carefully wrote a note. She folded it up and popped it into an envelope.

'Shall I mark it for Joe, then?' she asked.

'Yes please, Mother. Thank you.'

She handed the envelope to him and the small object she'd been holding. Anthony took both. He pocketed the envelope and examined the ring in his palm. It was her wedding ring. He looked at her.

'When you see him, tell him that I never want to see it or him ever again. You tell him, Anthony: promise me you'll say that.'

He nodded and said, 'I will, and I will say it with absolute certainty. May I ask, what did you say to Joe? In the letter?'

'To say that I'm content, and to tell him to make sure you're safe,' she said.

'Thank you,' he said and went over to her, took her hand and squeezed it.

'Anthony, what on earth are you wearing?'

'My new baggies — do you like them?'

'I think they're, er, huge.'

'They're supposed to be. That's why they're called baggies.'

'Will you wear them tomorrow, for your father to see them?'

'Yes, that's why I bought them. I thought he'd approve,' Anthony said grinning.

'Good thinking,' Margaret said, and smiled too.

***

Gary unlocked the front door quietly and edged inside the hall. He listened — nothing. He went into the kitchen, expecting to see his mother. The room was empty. He ran upstairs and listened at his parents' bedroom door: silence. His and Kevin's room and Derek's room were also empty. He was relieved, but he was also worried. He couldn't remember the last time that he'd come home and found no one in the house.

He wandered back downstairs and filled the kettle. The kitchen was tidy and clean. He looked around for a note: nothing.

Gary sat at the table with his head in his hands, waiting for the kettle to boil. He felt flat and dejected. Recent events had dragged him down badly. He was enjoying being with the others, and was glad to be rid of Steve, Phil and Paul, whom he now recognised he'd despised for a long time. His hatred of his father had been a shocking realisation. He thought back to the encounter of yesterday and imagined with a surge of adrenalin the carnage that might have resulted if Anthony had shot him. He smiled grimly. He thought that, if pushed, Anthony would have shot him: he was that kind of nutter — the type that did what came into his head without thinking about the consequences.

The bell rang. He got up and opened the door.

'Hello, Gorgeous, is Kev in?' Tina said, smiling at him.

'No, I dunno where he is.'

Tina stood there waiting to be asked inside. Gary didn't move.

'Shall I come in then?' she asked.

'If you want,' he said standing aside.

Tina moved past him; he caught a strong whiff of her perfume as she walked through to the kitchen. He followed her.

'Good, the kettle's boiled. Shall I make the tea?' she asked.

'All right.'

Gary watched her. She was wearing her usual outfit — short skirt, white tights, platforms.

'It's hot in here,' she said, and taking off her leather jacket hung it on the back of her chair. She was wearing a tight white T-shirt. She saw Gary looking at her chest and said, smiling, 'What are you looking at, Gary?'

'Nothing.'

She made two mugs of tea and sat down opposite him. He was feeling uncomfortable in her presence. He always did. He thought she was the sexiest girl he'd ever met she oozed sex appeal.

She looked him in the eyes and asked, 'When will Kev be back, do you think?'

'I've no idea; I've just come back myself.'

'Oh, where've you been? With a nice girl?'

'No.'

'You're very quiet today, Gary. I've not upset you, have I?'

'No.'

'You still like me, don't you?' she asked him, looking deeply into his eyes.

Gary felt incredibly aroused. Tina seemed to sense what was going through his head. She leaned forward and took his hand. Her low-cut T-shirt revealed her cleavage. Gary stared. He swallowed hard.

Tina stroked his hand.

'You know I really like you, don't you, Gary?' Her voice was husky, inviting.

'Do you?'

She nodded and carried on stroking his hand.

Gary felt himself hardening; he shifted position. She smiled at him.

'Do you ever feel jealous of Kev? Do you sometimes wish it was you with me instead of him?'

Gary couldn't help himself nodding.

'Sometimes I wish it was you, Gary,' she breathed.

Gary stared at her breasts.

'They are great tits, aren't they?' she said with a giggle.

He nodded again.

They were silent for a moment then Gary felt Tina's foot move against his. He looked into her face; she was smiling.

'What do you want to do, Gary?' she asked.

Gary was silent.

'Let's go upstairs,' she said, her foot rubbing his calf.

'OK,' he croaked.

She got up and came around the table and took his hand and pulled him to his feet. She put her arms around his neck and pressed herself against him. He felt her breasts against his chest, and felt his cock touch her crotch.

'Oh, Gary, that feels so nice,' she whispered into his ear. 'Come on, let's go before someone comes, if you see what I mean,' she giggled.

Tina slipped off her heavy shoes and skipped up the narrow staircase. Gary followed, breathing hard. He wanted her. He followed her into his and Kev's room. As soon as she was inside, she closed the curtains, lifted her T-shirt over her head and turned around to face him. She stared at him as she unclipped her bra and wriggled out of it. She smiled as she stood in front of him, pushing her large breasts out.

She looked at the bulge in his trousers and whistled, 'Oh, Gary, let me have some of that.'

Gary stood still. He couldn't wait to get his cock out, but he was feeling hot shame too.

'What's wrong, Gary, don't you like me?' Tina said in a wheedling voice.

Gary stood motionless, silent.

'Don't you want to suck my tits? Would you like me to suck your knob instead? What do you want Gary?'

Gary was rooted to the spot. He wanted her so much but at the same time he was feeling a rush of sickening guilt.

Tina looked at Gary; she couldn't help taunting him, 'Kev doesn't wait for a second invitation. Maybe you're not as big as you think you are Gary; maybe you're just Kev's little brother after all?'

Tina moved towards him, she cupped her breasts and said, 'Do you want some of this?'

Her words, or maybe it was her graphic invitation, reminded him of the disgusting scene in the bus shelter with Katy. Gary felt a sudden wave of revulsion. Instead of lust he felt only loathing for this girl.

'Put your clothes on,' he said, and walked out.

As he went downstairs, he heard her contemptuous voice call after him, 'You're nothing, Gary Abbott, nothing. You're a worthless piece of shit.'

Gary went into the hall, picked his coat up and shrugged it on. He opened the door to find his mum and dad on the pavement outside.

'Hello, Gary, off out?' his mother said cheerily.

'Just for a walk.'

'OK, I'm making bangers and mash; it'll be ready in half an hour. Don't be late.'

'All right, Gary?' his dad said as he followed his wife into the house.

'Yes, why wouldn't I be?' Gary said.

His father put his hands up and said, 'OK, OK, sorry I asked.'

'Dad's been helping me with the shopping,' his mother said.

Abbott smile was sheepish. He said, 'Yeah, well, once in a blue moon; I don't want to overdo it, do I?'

'See you later, Mum,' Gary said and walked away.

***

Victoria had had a hard day. The events of the night before had left her feeling as if she'd gone ten rounds with Joe Bugner. Today had been full-on: meetings, staffing problems, a financial hole in the budget that had appeared out of the blue. All day, she'd been hoping to hear from Joe, so, when he'd rung, she'd been elated.

As Joe's battered black Zephyr came down her street, she couldn't stop herself smiling: it was partly his wry manner, partly his physicality, mostly it was the fact that he made her feel alive, properly alive, maybe for the first time in her life?

She got in, leaned across to kiss him; he kissed her hard in return.

'Where to, madam?'

'Take me there and back, and don't spare the horses.'

'Very good, hang on to your hat.'

They were quiet for a while, neither sure what to say, slightly awkward.

'How are you?' he asked finally.

'I'm well, thank you, and you?'

'Very well. All the better for seeing you; it's lovely to be with you again, it really is.'

She smiled at him. He took her hand and held it as he drove.

'It sounded as though you had a particular destination in mind,' she said.

'I do. We're off to see the wizard.'

'Oh? Sounds exciting.'

'Hmm, well, not exciting exactly.'

'Tell me more.'

'Well, it's more about me, I'm afraid. The point is that I want you to get to know about me, what I'm all about, and that means seeing me in all my different guises.'

'Am I going to discover your true identity at last?'

'That sort of assumes we only have one identity, doesn't it?'

'True. OK, so am I going to see a new or perhaps a true part of you?'

'You'll have to decide when we get there.'

'You know, Joe, you're as slippery as a bucket of eels. Why do you like to tease me all the time?'

'Hang on to that thought — there's a friend of ours.'

Victoria followed his gaze to see Gary sitting on a wall staring vacantly into space. Joe sounded the horn and, although Gary looked in their direction, he didn't recognise them.

'Hang on a minute, I'm just going to check on him,' Joe said turning into a side street.

'Wotcha, Gary,' he said as he walked slowly towards the dejected-looking figure.

Gary looked up but still seemed not to recognise Joe. Then his face cleared, and he smiled.

'Everything all right?' Joe asked.

'Yeah, I s'pose so,' Gary replied in a weary voice.

Joe sat down next to him.

'Anything I can do?' he asked.

'Nah, I'm OK.'

'You look a bit pissed off.'

'I'm all right, really.'

'Are you all right about the trip tomorrow?'

'Yeah, I'll be there.'

'Good, I think Anthony needs you there.'

'Really?'

'Of course, you're a hero in his eyes.'

'Me?'

'Definitely, he really looks up to you.'

'I don't know why: he's much cleverer than me.'

'It's because you're tough, Gary.'

'Believe me, he's tougher than me, tougher than anyone except maybe Susan,' Gary said.

'Well, maybe the thing is that you're all stronger when you're together?'

Gary nodded.

'How's the land lie at home?'

'Well, I don't know what you said yesterday but things are different today.'

'Better or worse?'

'Better, but it doesn't feel right, sort of unnatural.'

'Fingers crossed it becomes the norm?'

'I s'pose.'

'May I ask you a question, Gary?'

'Yeah?'

'Have you ever worn glasses?'

Gary reddened and looked down.

'Is it worth giving them a try?' Joe suggested.

'What, for everyone to call me Joe 90, or four-eyes?'

'I know; it's a hard one.'

'I'll see. I dunno.'

Joe got up. He put his hand on Gary's shoulder, 'See you tomorrow.'

Gary nodded and watched Joe walk back across the street.

'Is he all right?' Victoria asked.

'Not sure. I hope so. He's a really nice kid underneath all the bravado.'

'So, don't keep me in suspense. Where are we going?'

'We're going to see a friend of mine, someone very important to me.'

'Oh?'

'My mentor — my saviour really.'

'What, Stewart Simpson?'

'No. Do you remember I said that there had been two people who had changed my life? I want to introduce you to the other one. We're going to go on a trip down memory lane.'

Joe spoke as they drove.

'My first few weeks and months in prison were tough; they're supposed to be, I guess. I was lucky enough to be resilient, able to get on with others, even the shits and the bastards. But after a while it gets to you. I was beginning to buckle. But I was moved into a cell with this bloke. He was a wise man. He talked to me, listened to me, taught me how to see the world differently, how to relate to people in a way that gave me strength and resolve. He also taught me something special, something that has helped me greatly ever since.'

'I'm all ears.'

'He showed me something amazing, something so obvious that it's usually overlooked. He taught me to pay attention to people: what they do, what they say, how they are.'

Victoria turned to look at him. He looked back and smiled.

'I know, it sounds ridiculous, but I mean it. He made me realise that people communicate loads of things — about how they're feeling, what they're planning, what they're avoiding, what they hope will happen, what they're dreading happening — so much. By paying attention it's possible to understand someone in a very different way than most people ever realise. It's why you think I can read minds. Of course, I can't: all I can do is pay attention to what people are conveying.'

'But surely everyone can do that?'

'Of course. It's just that most people don't.'

'So, who is he?'

'A most unusual man. A special man.'

***

'You're going to have to tell me what you want, Frank. Saying "tidy it up" isn't enough,' Janice Gordon said.

'Well, pick someone off the telly and copy that; just make it look better than it is now,' Frank said.

'Don't get me wrong: I am very pleased you're doing something about it. You've let it get into a complete state. I don't think you've washed it in recent memory, have you? It smells awful, Frank.'

'Come on, Mum, you can do something with it.'

'No, I'm not going to. Dad always did the hair cutting and I'm not going to start now. Anyway, if I did, you'd complain that it isn't how you wanted it.'

'Yes, I know, but surely you can do something, anything?' Frank persisted.

'I know what I'll do.' Janice wheeled over to the kitchen and opened a drawer. She took out her purse and pulled out three, pound notes.

'Go off and have it done properly; make it look nice.'

'No, that's a waste of money,' Frank said, refusing the cash.

'Not to me. It will be a pleasure to see you looking half human.'

Frank thought for a minute. He didn't want to go to a proper hairdresser. He never had before. His father had always cut his hair.

'I'm sure you'd do a good job,' he encouraged.

'I'm sure I wouldn't. Come on, Frank, grit your teeth and make yourself look presentable,' Janice insisted.

Finally, Frank gave in. He took the notes she proffered and got up.

'Good luck. I expect I won't recognise you when you come back,' she said.

Frank walked past 'Blades' every day to and from school. He had seen kids from his class in there a few times. It had never occurred to him to go in, not until today. He walked slowly down the street. He was feeling nervous. He wasn't sure why. He didn't know what to ask for, how much it would be, or even if the result would make him look or feel different. He drew in a deep breath and quickened his pace. He reached the doorway and looked in. There were two barbers in action with one customer waiting. He pushed open the door and walked inside. The stench of cheap aftershave and a thousand cigarettes assaulted him. He sat down and waited for his turn.

'You having that lot off?' said the bald man waiting, nodding at Frank's hair.

'Yeah,' Frank muttered.

'That'll cost a bit, not like my one pound all-off.'

'Hmm.'

Frank was feeling self-conscious. He sat back and put his face in his hands. His fingers pressed against the silver ring. He took his hands away and looked at it. He smiled as he thought of Robbie. He imagined him sitting next to him now, whispering something funny.

'What do you think?' the barber nearest Frank said to his customer.

'Not bad,' said the bloke grudgingly, looking at himself in the mirror.

Frank looked at him. He had a huge head of permed hair. He made a note to ask what style it was, to ensure he didn't get that one.

'Here you go, son, take a look at that,' Frank's waiting companion tossed 'Forum' in front of Frank as he got up for his turn.

Frank looked at the cover of the crumpled magazine. He saw the smiling face of the pretty girl. He picked up the magazine and started to flick through the pages. Despite Robbie's claim that he had a great collection of girlie mags, he had rarely seen pornography. He found himself engrossed by the naked flesh and explicit articles. Despite himself, the public place, his own self-consciousness, he felt himself harden. He imagined himself with the girls in the photos and doing what was being described in the letters. He shifted uncomfortably and hoped that his state wasn't too obvious. He remembered the time he had sat next to Ailsa in the park, how her closeness had made him feel so aroused. The words and pictures blurred; Ailsa's image sharpened. He wanted to feel her arm against his again, the warmth and softness of her thigh. God, how he wanted her to look at him and smile. He thought he would do anything to hold her hand, kiss her lips, smell her scent. He also really wanted to feel her breasts, to part her thighs, to feel her hand on his erection.

Frank put the magazine back on the table, drew in a deep breath and willed himself to think of something else. What should he ask for when his turn came? He watched the hairdresser snip busily at Bald Man's head: no help there. He looked at the pictures on the wall. He recognised some footballers and pop singers: none of them looked in any way like him. The door opened, and a couple of youths swaggered in. They sat down next to Frank and lit up cigarettes. One of them picked up Frank's magazine.

'Cor, lovely.'

The other one looked across, 'Let's have a look. Hmmm, not bad.'

Frank felt dirty. He wanted to leave but didn't like to draw attention to himself.

'Did you hear those gun shots last night?' one of the newcomers said.

'Yeah, and I know what happened.'

'Yeah? Spill the beans then.'

'You know Tony Bishop?'

'Yeah?'

'Well, his mate was in a ruck with a couple of his mates, and they were having a ruck with some kid up Manor Way when another kid suddenly pulls out a gun and starts blazing away at them. According to Tony this kid was like a lunatic, firing this fucking gun at them.'

'Fuck me! What happened?'

'I dunno. I only heard all this from Tony's sister's boyfriend, but the kid with the gun and his friend, you know, the one in the fight, ran off and disappeared.'

'Was anyone shot?'

'No, but I think Tony's mate nearly was.'

'How can someone nearly be shot?'

'I don't fucking know; I'm just telling you what happened.'

'Who was the kid with the gun?'

'Some little shit, that's all that they said.'

'Well they must have seen something.'

'I don't know. The only thing I heard was that he looked like Beethoven or something.'

'What did Beethoven look like?'

'I think he had a load of poofy blond hair, you know, kind of flowing hair.'

'So, let me get this straight: the police are looking for a kid with a gun bearing a remarkable likeness to a dead composer?'

'All right, all right, smart-arse, I'm just telling the story.'

Frank screwed his eyes up tight. This was bad for Anthony.

'Your turn, son,' Bald Man said to Frank, as he paid.

Frank went to the barber's chair and sat down.

'Yes sir, what would you like?'

'Not sure,' mumbled Frank.

'You must have some idea.'

Frank felt his face reddening. He looked at the pictures on the wall.

'Like that,' he said, pointing at David Essex.

'Good choice. All the girls will fancy you, looking like him.'

Frank didn't want all the girls fancying him, just one. He shut his eyes and waited for the ordeal to be over.

'There you go. What do you think?' the barber said a few minutes later.

Frank opened his eyes. He saw his mouth fall open. He looked completely different — naked. He wanted to put a hat on straight away, to cover himself up. He looked closely at himself for the first time in ages. Was it really him?

'Fine,' he said.

He got up and paid. As he left the hairdresser's he heard the next customer say, 'Give me a David Essex, mate.'

***

'Hello?' Anthony said, answering the phone.

'It's Frank.'

'Hello, Frank, how are you?'

'I'm fine. You?'

'All fine with me. I'm all set for tomorrow. You are coming, aren't you?'

'Yes, I'll be there.'

'So, to what do I owe this unexpected pleasure?'

'I've just overheard a conversation about the gun.'

425

'What? Who? Tell me, Frank.'

'I was having my hair cut and a couple of blokes were talking about it.'

'What, strangers?'

'Yes, exactly. People are talking about it.'

'Were we recognised?'

'Well, the only thing I heard was that the kid with the gun looked like you.'

'In what way?'

'Apparently he looked like Beethoven.'

'In what way?'

'He had hair like you.'

'What does my hair look like?'

Frank was suddenly exasperated. 'Anthony, you've got fluffy blond hair that makes you look ridiculous: surely you know that?'

'Really?'

Anthony was silent. Then he said, 'You've got long greasy hair, Frank. You look like a tramp: hasn't anyone ever told you that?'

Frank laughed and said in triumph, 'Not anymore, Ludwig.'

'What have you done to it?'

'What you have to do: cut it off.'

'I like my hair,' Anthony said.

'Get rid of it, Anthony. If that's what people know you by then you have to get rid of it.'

'Do I really look ridiculous?'

'I'm sorry, Anthony: I hate to hurt your feelings, but it doesn't do you any favours.'

'OK, thanks, Frank. Leave it with me.'

'In the meantime, I'd wear a hat if I were you, and I don't mean something Beethoven would wear. Have you got a baseball cap or anything like that?'

'What do you think?'

'Well, stay in till tomorrow and we'll get you a hat once we're out of town.'

'Thanks, Frank. Sorry I was rude about your hair.'

'Me too, about your hair,' Frank said.

***

'What are you going to wear tomorrow?' Susan asked as they sat in Katy's bedroom.

Katy was attempting to master a new chord on her guitar.

'Whatever gangsters' molls wear when they visit prisons,' she answered.

'Silly idiot, we're not going into the prison.'

'I know, but I don't want to look out of place when we're waiting outside.'

'I'm going to wear jeans and a jumper,' Susan said.

'Me too. I thought I might wear this one: what do you think?'

Katy proceeded to pull a tight nylon top over her head. She wriggled into it and stood in front of her mirror pushing her chest out. She looked at herself critically front-on, then in profile.

'Do you think I look a bit too busty?' she asked.

'For what?'

'Well, I don't want the prisoners getting any ideas, do I?'

'Katy, you're not going to get anywhere near any prisoners. You'll probably have more trouble from prisoners' wives, turning up looking like that.'

'Like what?'

'Like a tart.'

'Oh, you're such a wet rag sometimes.'

'I wonder if Anthony is nervous.'

'Dunno. He's hard to work out, isn't he?'

They heard the doorbell ring. Susan got up and went to the top of the stairs to listen. She came back two minutes later with Anthony behind her.

'Talk of the devil: look what the cat dragged in,' Katy said as she saw him.

'Hallo, Katy,' he said staring at her breasts.

'We were just talking about you,' she said, pleased with the effect her figure-hugging top was having.

'Me?' Anthony said, surprised but pleased.

'Yes, we were wondering if you were nervous about tomorrow.'

'Totally petrified. In fact, putting it in Gary's terms, I'm absolutely bricking myself,' he answered.

'Still, you've got nothing to worry about, wearing your baggies,' Katy said, holding her hand over her mouth to stop herself laughing.

'I know. They're great, aren't they?' Anthony said proudly.

'Yes, Anthony, they are,' Susan said.

'Anyway, much as I'd like to chat about the latest fashions, I am here for a reason.'

They looked at him expectantly.

'Can either of you cut hair?'

'Oh no, you're not going to get rid of your lovely hair,' Susan said.

'Yes, I have to.'

'But, how about just trimming it a bit, making it a bit trendier?' Katy suggested.

'Nice idea, but Frank said I've got to get rid of it all.'

'Why?'

'Well, partly because apparently people might think I was involved with those gunshots last night, and partly because I look ridiculous.'

'Ah, well, maybe that makes sense, the first part I mean,' Susan said.

'And the second,' said Katy. She went on, 'I'm brilliant with a pair of scissors.'

'Well, I'm sure you are but I don't want anything too, um, trendy.'

'I'll get Mum's scissors and we can have a try,' Susan said.

When she returned, both girls started fiddling with Anthony's fine hair. He listened to them talk of layers, flicks, perms, various partings. He sat still and enjoyed the attention. He particularly liked their scent, their fingers in his hair, their breath close to his face. Every now and then he felt one of them press against him; he revelled in it.

'What exactly do you want to achieve?' Susan asked him.

'Well, I suppose I want to stop looking like someone who can be bullied all the time, and who looks different to how I look now.'

***

Gary quietly let himself back into the house. He paused in the hall and listened. He could hear voices from the kitchen. He wondered whether his dad was swigging lager, in which case it wouldn't be long before the easy-going man of half an hour ago would be the brute of last night. He also was more than a little concerned about what Tina might have said. He gritted his teeth and pushed open the door.

'Hello, love, you're just in time,' his mum said.

Gary looked around. Kev and Tina were sitting on one side of the table, his dad the other. They all looked up at him. Nothing was amiss. He breathed a sigh of relief and sat down next to his dad. He looked across the table at Tina, she was flicking through the paper, avoiding his eye. Kev was looking at him closely.

'What?' Gary said.

'Nothing,' Kev said.

'Guess what, son?' Brian Abbott asked.

'What?'

'I've given up the booze,' Abbott proclaimed.

'Really,' Gary said, without enthusiasm.

'I know — you're thinking that it'll be a one-day wonder. This time it's for real: I've got it cracked this time; you'll see. Yep, I've seen the error of my ways, at last.'

'One day at a time, dear,' Jenny Abbott said.

Gary saw Kev frowning at him.

'Great, well done, Dad,' Gary said, with a bit more conviction.

Jenny started serving the meal. As soon as their plates were put in front of them, Kevin, Gary and Tina started eating.

'Hang on a minute, you gannets, wait for Mum to sit down,' Abbott ordered.

'It's all right: best to eat it hot,' Jenny said from the sink.

'No, I'm not having that. You've made it; you've put all the effort in the least they can do is wait for you to sit down.'

Jenny dried her hands and sat down.

'You'll have us saying grace next,' tittered Tina.

Brian Abbott put his cutlery down and stared at her. Tina reddened and stopped giggling. They ate in silence.

'Lovely. Thanks, Jen,' Abbott said and patted his wife's arm.

She looked pleased but edgy.

'It's lovely, isn't it?' Abbott said to them.

They nodded.

'Well, say so then,' he told them.

'Lovely, Mum, very nice,' Kev said.

Abbott looked at Gary.

'Yeah, delicious,' Gary said, forcing himself to sound bright.

Abbott grunted.

They ate in silence.

Gary caught Tina staring at him. Rather than sexy, she just looked sulky. He wished he hadn't been tempted by her. He wasn't even sure now what had made him so excited.

'Who were those freaks last night?' Abbott said suddenly to Gary.

'Who?'

'Those people at the door last night, you know, your friends.'

Gary thought quickly. His father had been very drunk. He couldn't have taken on board much of what had happened, and he surely couldn't remember the faces at the door.

'Oh, just some friends of mine; we were having a laugh,' he said.

'Not at my expense I hope?'

'They seemed very nice to me,' Jenny said looking at Gary.

'Yes, they're nice,' Gary repeated.

'I'm sure they're "nice",' Abbott said, in an imitation of a genteel voice, 'but I don't want them here again, get it?'

'Yes,' Gary said. He did not want them at his house, ever again. He didn't want to be at his house either.

'Jam roly-poly for afters,' said Jenny.

'Cor, luverly,' Abbott said, clapping his hands together and beaming at her. The others nodded dutifully.

'Allow me,' Gary's dad said, and got up and collected empty plates.

'Thanks, love,' his wife said as she picked up her oven gloves. Opening the door, she lifted out the heavy earthenware dish and brought it over to the table.

'I hope there's custard?' Abbott said happily.

***

Victoria had lost track of where they were. She had quizzed him further on his past: about his comfortable early life, his two years in Germany on National Service, his work for the insurance company, and more about his time in prison.

'I'm doing better, aren't I?' he asked after a while.

'Yes, well done. You're improving. Thank you. One thing I don't know, well millions of things of course, but one in particular,' she said.

'Fire away.'

'What happened to your girlfriend?'

Joe paused, 'She didn't stick around.'

Victoria thought about asking more. She wanted to know everything about Joe but was beginning to feel as though she was prying. She was more comfortable with him now, less unsure. She would uncover as much as she needed to know, but slowly. Right now, she was just happy to be with him.

'Thanks, Joe, thanks for letting me in.'

He took her hand and squeezed it. She smiled; his touch felt really good.

She said, 'I saw your gang at school today, all in a huddle, very secretive.'

'Did they seem all right together?'

'Yes, very all right. I have never known a group of teenagers bond so quickly, especially when I think about their starting point.'

'I'm glad,' Joe said.

'What does Grace think of them?' Victoria asked.

'She's very fond of them — Frank in particular, I think.'

'I'm not surprised. He's like his mother: they're both one in a million. But I think that they're all unusual in their own way.'

'Maybe that's why they're getting on: they recognise something of themselves in each other?'

'Yes, maybe that's it.'

'Susan's joined; did you know that?'

'Yes, I saw her with them today. She was very funny. Those two girls are so alike — well, very different too of course.'

'Anthony is growing by the minute. You're probably used to teenagers changing in front of your eyes; I'm finding it hard to keep up with him. It's him and Gary that I find the most amazing: they're acting like brothers these days.'

They drove in companionable silence. Then Victoria asked, 'Will you tell me about him, please, the special man?'

'What do you want to know?'

'Well, what he was in prison for is what I'd really like to know, but you'll probably say that that was then and it's not relevant now.'

'You're right, as usual. But I know why you'd want to know so here it is: he was also in for murder.'

'Tell me more — all of it.'

'This is a very upsetting story, Victoria. I'm going to tell it, but it's hard to hear — and to tell. He was in the army during the war but came home to find that his world had been shattered: his wife was dead. She had gone to live with her parents when he'd signed up — he'd insisted on it. Then, unbelievably, their house was hit by a stray bomb, 20 miles north of London itself. His marital home had also been destroyed in the last year of the war. He decided to disappear. He found a little cottage and became a recluse. He lived off the land: he grew his own vegetables, reared hens and sheep, caught trout from a nearby river. He had a collection of dogs and cats for company. He had managed to find a way of being that was tolerable. He wanted nothing more from life. But something came along to ruin it. He started being bothered by local youths. Although his place was out of the way, it also became intriguing to a gang of teenagers with nothing better to do. They found it great fun to gather around his place at night, drinking and smoking, laughing and swearing — just being unruly shits, I imagine. They then started to call to him, to taunt him, and then openly antagonise him. He tried to ignore

432

them; he thought they'd get bored and go away. No — the opposite in fact: the more he stayed silent the more they tormented him.' Joe paused. He wiped one eye then the other, as he drove.

'Didn't he call the Police?' Victoria asked.

'I asked him that. He said he didn't want anything to do with the law, with society. He had given up on everything. I suppose he thought he could sort it out himself. Then it got out of control.'

'What happened?'

'Slowly, he started to lose it: he began to plan his revenge. He set traps for them, including digging holes for them to fall down; then wire across the path that brought them off their bikes. All this made matters worse, of course: it provoked them to even greater hostility.'

'This is making me feel very bad, Joe,' Victoria said.

'I know. It is a nightmarish thing. Do you want me to continue?'

She nodded.

'So, a battle of wills had broken out. For the kids it was fun, for him it was a living hell. He slowly descended into a trough; he began to lose track of what was right and wrong. He had no means of attack which was proportionate. He was powerless. Then, they sent him over the edge. They killed his cat. It was a horrible thing: they tied fireworks to its tail and set them off. It sent him over the edge. He went mad, Victoria. He shot them. He killed two of them and three were badly injured.'

The silence in the car was immense.

'He spent the next ten years in Broadmoor. His defence was that he was mad, and I guess he probably was. Then he was moved from Broadmoor in 1964 to my little abode, where I met him. I thank God that I met him: he was an exceptional man.'

The car was slowing down. Joe eased it into a narrow lane.

'Where are we?'

In the deep darkness, Victoria could see a large black shape.

'St Nicholas Parish Church.'

'Why?'

'We're going into the churchyard to see my hero.'

They got out of the car. Joe flicked on a torch, took Victoria's hand and led her along a metalled track. They branched off onto a grassy path.

433

'Here he is. Victoria: this is my dearest friend.'

***

'Oh, Frank, you do look good,' Janice said, as he walked into the living room.

'It's just a haircut, Mum,' he protested.

'I know, but to be honest you looked like a tramp an hour ago: now you look like a pop star.'

'David Essex?'

'Hmmm, maybe.'

Janice was looking at him; she was smiling.

'What?' he asked.

'Nothing — it's just that you look very nice, honestly you do.'

Frank smiled, bashful.

'We shall have to do something about your wardrobe too. We can't have you looking like a hobo with hair like that.'

'Well, actually, I was wondering about that,' he said.

'Have you got a girlfriend, Frank?' she asked gently.

'No, no, no, I just felt like, well, just sorting myself out a bit, you know.'

'Yes, I know.'

'I'm going out with the others tomorrow and I just wanted to look a bit smarter than usual, that's all.'

'What are you going to wear?'

'Well, I thought maybe my denim jacket, some clean jeans and the shirt you gave me for Christmas. What do you think?'

'Which shoes will you wear?'

'These,' Frank opened the bag he'd been holding and pulled out a pair of black suede wedges.

'Well, I think they look ridiculous, but I guess they're really trendy and if you like them then they'll be great,' she said.

'Thanks, Mum, I knew you'd like them' he said smiling, very, very, pleased to have such a wonderful mother.

Frank went into his room and opened his wardrobe. It smelled of musty, unwashed clothes. He pulled out the shirt he had in mind. It was crumpled and didn't smell great. He sniffed at the jacket he was wearing not good either. He grabbed all of his shirts, trousers and underwear and carried them into the kitchen.

'How do you work this thing?' he called to his mother.

She laughed, 'I knew you never used it.'

After a quick lesson, Frank shut the door on the majority of his clothes and turned on the machine.

'You'll need an iron too: any ideas?' Janice asked, smiling.

'None,' he admitted.

'It's in the cupboard next to the front door; the board is there too.'

'I'm sorry, Mum,' he said.

'What for?'

'For being such a slob.'

'Don't be silly. I'm sorry too.'

'What for?'

'For being so useless.'

Frank looked at her. He felt tears rush to his eyes.

'Stop that right now. You are the greatest woman in the world, by a mile.'

'And you're the greatest man,' she said.

***

'That's it,' Katy said, looking at Anthony.

Both girls stood back and admired their handiwork.

'Certainly different; not sure it's better though,' Susan said, considering him carefully.

'Can I see?' Anthony said.

He got up and stood in front of the mirror. He gaped. His pale, fine hair had disappeared. Instead he saw a hard-looking boy with very short, jet-black hair looking back at him. He smiled. The smile made him look even more peculiar. He smiled again, but this time with a sneer.

'It's fantastic! I actually look like a nasty piece of work. In fact, I look like a bad lot, as my father might say,' he said.

'You look like a skinhead to me,' Susan said.

'I'm still the same person, don't worry.'

'Really, that's a shame,' Katy said, imitating Susan's sad voice.

'Watch it, buster, unless you want a knuckle sandwich,' Anthony snarled at her.

Both girls started giggling.

'You're going to have to work on your hard man image a bit,' Katy said.

'How long does the dye last?' Anthony asked.

Katy looked at the bottle. 'It says, "apply regularly".'

'I'll ask Dad in a minute,' Susan said.

'My pater is going to have a fit when he sees me,' Anthony said, unable to hold back his laughter, 'what with my baggies, and now this. Thank you so much.'

He looked at Katy and Susan. He wanted to kiss them both, to hug them. He suddenly felt embarrassed and self-conscious.

'You silly boy. Just be yourself with him tomorrow, that's what's important,' Susan said.

'Thanks, anyway,' he said.

Katy cuffed his stubbly head.

'I'll do anything to help you two, anything,' he said.

'Well, we might take you up on that,' Katy said.

'It's late; time to go I think,' Anthony said, regret in his voice.

'I'll walk with you, if you like,' Susan said.

'That would be lovely. Bye, Katy, see you tomorrow. Thanks, so much for the new hairdo.'

Katy hugged him, 'Bye then, Dirty Harry.'

He felt his eyes sting with tears, happy tears. He followed Susan out.

'We're just off, Mum,' Susan called as she left the house.

They walked down the quiet street in silence. Susan glanced across at Anthony as they went under a streetlight. He looked so different, shockingly so. He looked back at her questioningly.

'I don't know what to think about you, you look so different,' she explained.

'I am different, and not just appearance.'

'Meaning?'

'Because life's so different suddenly, it's like I'm in a dream. I can't quite believe what's happened to me, Susan. Honestly, the last five years of my life have been non-stop misery, loneliness and at times I've thought "what's the point of going on?". Now, I've got some amazing friends, I'm not the pathetic little shit everyone thought I was, and life is looking good: it really is like a dream.'

'How did you keep going, though, when everything was so awful?'

'I have always thought that one day things would turn around for me. I couldn't see how, or why, or when; I just had this idea that life would sort itself out. It's funny, Susan, I've inherited some of my father's traits, of course I have he's very determined; he doesn't give up ever: fortunately for me I'm the same. Also, luckily, I'm not an evil bastard like him.'

Susan laughed and said, 'Now how do I know if that's true?'

'Hmmm, good question: you'll have to trust me on that one.'

'Well, I'll risk it for the time being,' she said, putting her arm through his.

They walked together in silence again. They stopped outside Anthony's home.

'Susan, I know it's rather forward of me, but may I kiss you goodnight?'

'Oh, Anthony, what century are you from?'

'Well what do you want me to say: "give me a feel of your tits"?'

Susan punched him, 'Right, that's it! You've blown it, matey.'

'So that's a no, then?'

She leaned towards him and kissed him quickly on the lips.

'You, silly boy,' she said and walked quickly away.

'Bye then,' he called as he watched her go.

'Bye then,' she called and waved.

***

Katy heard raised voices downstairs. She put her guitar down and went quietly onto the landing and heard her father say, 'How could we have been so stupid?'

'It's my fault. If I hadn't been so obsessed with having another daughter, giving Susan a twin, none of this would have happened,' Anna cried.

'That's ridiculous. Then we wouldn't have had Katy at all,' John said.

'Well, now we haven't got her anyway.'

'I can't even think why we didn't tell the truth from the beginning. It's not as if adopting a baby is something to be ashamed about.'

'We were playing happy families — trying to make it true.'

'What upsets me the most is the way she looks at us: she hates us right now,' John said.

Katy felt her face burn with a toxic mixture of emotion. She drew in a deep breath and went downstairs. She paused outside the kitchen then walked in.

Anna and John looked up sharply as she came into the room.

'We thought you were out,' Anna said, colouring, her hand over her mouth.

'I realised,' Katy said simply and sat down.

'Katy, it's not…' John began to say.

'I already heard you, Dad: don't bother saying it, whatever it was going to be,' Katy said.

They stared at the table, each one struggling to find the right thing to say, not even knowing what the right thing was.

'I know you did it for the best reasons. I know you love me, and I know that I love you too,' Katy said, without raising her eyes to them.

'Oh, Katy, it's so true,' Anna said with such force it shocked them all.

'I can't help myself feeling as though something has been taken away, as if I've lost something,' Katy went on.

John and Anna nodded miserably.

'I want to make you feel as bad as I do, to get revenge or something: isn't that awful?'

'No, it makes perfect sense to me,' John said.

Katy looked at him. He seemed very old; her mum did too. They were in their early fifties, but they suddenly seemed much older.

'How can I get this horrible feeling out of me? How can I get back to where I was before?' Katy implored.

John took his daughter's hand and said, 'We're trying to understand how you are feeling, Katy. We're all mixed up too. It's a funny thing in a way. We feel very, very badly towards your birth mother, for chucking a hand grenade into our lives. But we also feel as though we owe her a massive debt for giving us the greatest gift — our beautiful daughter and Susan's wonderful sister. Does that make sense?' John asked.

'Yes, it does. I do feel mixed up. I hate her for ruining everything, but I can't help wanting to see her, to find out about her: what she's like and why I'm like me.'

'So, maybe what we have to do is let her into our lives? That way we all take responsibility for what happens,' Anna said, and looked at first Katy and then John.

'Do you think so?' Katy asked, looking at them both, hoping for reassurance.

'Yes, I do think so,' Anna said.

'So, are you OK for me to meet her?'

'Yes, it's the right thing to do,' Anna said.

'What happens if I like her, or love her, or hate her, or can't make up my mind?' Katy said.

Anna reached across the table and gripped Katy's ears and said, 'No one knows, Katy, but whatever happens we're on your team and we'll back you up — forever.'

Katy stared at her mother's face for ages then said, 'Thanks, Mum, you can let go of my ears now.'

When Susan came back, she found the three of them sitting on the sofa in front of the television. Katy was in the middle, expounding on the costumes being worn by the dancers cavorting behind Cliff Richard.

'Room for a little one?' Susan asked.

'Yes, right here,' Katy said budging up so that Susan could squeeze in beside her.

As their daughters watched the television, Anna caught John's eye and puffed out her cheeks in relief.

***

'I'll do the washing up, Mum, you can leave that,' Gary said.

'What a good boy,' Brian Abbott said.

'We'll do it together. You go and watch the telly, dear,' Jenny said to her husband.

Brian said, 'If you're sure I can't help you?' and got up and went to give his wife a cuddle.

Gary shut his eyes and felt his stomach heave.

'Don't be long, Jen. Let's watch the telly together,' Brian Abbott said.

When he'd left the room Gary and his mother set about the dishes in silence. After a few minutes Gary asked, 'You all right, Mum?'

'Yes, I'm fine, love.'

'Sure?'

'Sure.'

'He's in a funny mood; it makes me feel a bit nervous.'

'I'm in a funny mood too. I'm not sure why.'

'What did that bloke say to you yesterday?' Gary asked.

'Mr Gregory?'

'Yeah, him.'

'Well, it was all about some kind of insurance policy; I'm not sure really. To be honest I didn't pay much attention. I think I was so tired I sort of blanked it all out.'

'He didn't say anything about Dad though, did he?'

'No, nothing to me. He did have a chat with him, though; I didn't hear it. Why?'

'Oh, no reason; it's nothing.'

'Gary?'

'Yeah?'

'Did that boy really have a gun last night?'

'No. It was a water pistol: he's a total jerk.'

'It looked real.'

'I took it off him and threw it away as soon as we all left,' Gary reassured her.

'Don't challenge Dad again, will you? It's not worth it,' she said, looking at him closely.

'Well, let's hope he's a new man,' Gary answered.

'Give him a chance, Gary. He's doing his best, you know.'

Gary put the dried dishes away and said nothing.

'I'm going on a trip tomorrow with my friends,' he said.

'Where?'

'Somewhere near Brighton, to see Anthony's father.'

'Which one's Anthony?'

'The one with the water pistol.'

'You won't spend too much time with him, will you? I think he might be a bad influence.'

Gary snorted with laughter. He made a note to tell Anthony his mother's concern.

'You'll be OK, won't you?' he asked.

'Yes, don't worry about me, Gary. I'm feeling great.'

Gary went to his bedroom. He reached under Kev's bed and pulled out a tattered magazine. He took out his new glasses and put them on. He flicked through the pages and marvelled at how much easier it was to see the pictures and read the text. He threw the mag back under the bed and picked up his sellotaped *Of Mice and Men*. He lay down and started reading from the beginning.

***

Victoria read the inscription on the gravestone:

'Captain Paul Smith,

1908 – 1974

A wonderful man'

Victoria put her arm through Joe's and waited for him to speak. Finally, he did.

'He was the kindest man imaginable. He cared deeply about others. Everything he taught me was positive and decent.'

'What *did* he teach you?'

'How to see inside people; what to say to give them strength; how to help them find solutions. He just made people feel better. It was as if he could touch someone and — Hey presto! — they'd be cured. I don't mean in a physical way: it was more like he could give people a mental boost. He helped me see how I might be able to do something similar. It's so awful that he couldn't help himself.'

'How did he die?'

'He became very ill: as well as being depressed, he developed some horrible neurological condition they never actually diagnosed. Towards the end, he could barely stand and was struggling to do anything for himself. He decided to take matters into his own hands.'

'Do you mind if I ask how?'

'No.' Joe paused and went on, 'I'm sorry, Victoria, I don't know how you'll feel about this, but I want to tell you the full story: in the end, my friend took a large overdose of anti-depressants with a bottle of whisky.'

'Where were you when you found out?'

'I was with him when he did it,' Joe said.

'Didn't you try and stop him?'

'No, he had decided to go. He was certain; absolutely sure it was what he wanted.'

Victoria closed her eyes. The trees swayed in the breeze; traffic hummed in the far distance. She felt the warmth and strength of the man next to her.

'What a poor man.'

'I tried for a long, long time to get him through it. Nothing helped him. He was determined to end things. In the end I started to think that the kindest thing I could do was to help rather than hinder him.'

Joe was silent. He drew in a deep breath and carried on, 'I told him that I would be with him and that I'd stay with him until it was over. I

442

owed him so much. I couldn't let him do it on his own. He didn't want me to be there, but I had to be.'

'Doesn't that make you an accessory to a crime?'

'Probably. That didn't seem very important, and it still doesn't. I owe him so much, Victoria. He was my sanity at a mad time. I owe everything meaningful to him. He gave me a future, and, in a way, I can't explain, he continues to do so. He was a healer. He made people feel better. He taught me everything.'

'What a terribly sad story. Do you wish you had saved him?'

'I do of course, but I also feel grateful that he allowed me to be with him at the end. That is a great privilege.'

'Yes, it is,' she said, thinking about finding her father dead, wishing that she'd been with him. 'Thanks for letting me meet him. I feel very honoured.'

'Thank you, Victoria. that means a lot to me.'

They stood close together.

'Let's go, I'm cold,' Joe said finally.

They walked back through the gloom of the graveyard.

'Do you want to go home, or have something to eat, or better still a drink?' he asked.

'Yes, let's find a pub.'

They drove back to town, thinking their own thoughts.

'You must wonder what you're going to find out next?' he said.

Victoria thought for a minute then said, 'Well, my first thought was "Oh no, not more death," and you being complicit too. Then I wondered what I might have done if it had been my friend. Maybe I would have done the same thing. In fact, it made me wonder what I'd have done when you killed that awful man that was conning your mother — maybe I'd have done the same thing. I suppose what I'm saying is "there but for the grace of God go I".'

Joe gripped her hand hard as he drove.

'Thank you,' he said.

They were coming back into the town now, driving past the brightly lit forecourt of the cinema, when Victoria said suddenly, 'Pull in, Joe. There's something going on over there.'

Joe braked quickly, and they looked towards the cinema entrance. They saw a crowd encircling some kind of fracas. Victoria got out and ran towards the throng. It was immediately clear what was going on — three young men were beating up an Asian youth. As Victoria pushed her way past the onlookers, one of them was viciously kicking the prone figure in the back.

She ran up to the attacker and, putting her arms around him, pulled him away saying, 'That's it, that's enough, no more.'

'Yeah, leave him alone, he's done nothing wrong,' said someone in the crowd.

'Yeah, you should be ashamed of yourselves,' said another.

The three assailants shambled off sniggering.

Victoria bent down to the young man's side and said, 'It's OK now. They've gone away: you're safe now. Are you hurt badly?'

He looked up at her and then around to see if it was safe. He shook his head and sat up.

'No, I'm all right, thank you.'

Joe put his hand on Victoria's shoulder. She was trembling.

'What were you all doing?' she shouted to the people looking on. 'Why didn't someone do something?'

No one answered. She looked back at the young man. 'Do you need an ambulance?'

'No, thank you. I'm fine now.'

She helped him to his feet. He gathered himself and limped slowly away.

'You Paki-lovers make me sick,' a beery voice said to her.

Victoria turned slowly to face the source of the comment. He was an overweight man, about her own age.

She said, 'I'm sorry about that, sir, I really am.'

'You're a fucking smart-arse bitch, aren't you?' he said, sneering at her.

Joe took Victoria's arm and led her away.

'You're a fucking smart-arse shit, too,' the man shouted at Joe.

Victoria and Joe walked back to the car. They got in and drove off.

'You're amazing,' he said to her.

'That man! Grrr — How primitive can you get?' she said.

'Nevertheless, you are amazing, Victoria: that's a fact.'

'I feel terrible now. I feel dirty, like I've been in a sewer; do you know what I mean?'

'Yes, I do,' Joe said.

'Let's go home; can we?'

'Yes, that's a good idea.'

When they arrived outside her house she said to Joe, 'Will you come in?'

'I'd like to, but only if you really want company.'

'I do — someone decent and respectable: you'll do.'

When they got inside Victoria led Joe into the kitchen. He said, 'Can I give you a great big hug?'

'At least that, but especially that. I'm tired Joe, can we go to bed soon?'

'Yes.'

They heard the sound of glass smashing outside. They ran to the front door and looked out. Three figures could be seen running down the quiet street. One of them yelled, 'Paki-lovers!'

The windshield of Joe's Zephyr was in a thousand pieces and the wing mirrors had been torn off. Joe looked down the road. He could dimly see three men waving at him.

He waved back and called, 'See you soon, lads.'

Victoria picked up the phone to call the police.

'I'm not sure it's worth the aggro of getting them involved,' Joe said.

'But we have to report the crime and, what's more, I can give a very good description of who is probably involved.'

'Probably?'

'OK, well it's only circumstantial, I accept; but surely we should take some kind of action?'

'I agree, but not the police.'

'We must, Joe. We can't just let it go.'

'OK, leave it with me. You go and have a hot bath. I'll sort out the police and get some fish and chips.'

After the call to the police, and fish and chips consumed, Joe said, 'Can I use your phone?'

'It's very late.'

'I've got to get a car for tomorrow's trip.'

'Don't forget we're using mine'

'That's very sweet of you but there'll be six of us and one of us is Frank: I can't see us squeezing into your little car.'

'I've got an idea. If the minibus isn't in use, I'll book it out and we can go in that. What do you think?'

Joe put out his arms. She smiled and let herself be hugged, then hoisted high.

'You're a living legend, Victoria Court.'

She laughed and said, 'Put me down! Right now. Now, I say!'

Joe start singing 'She's a walking miracle — Oo-oo!'

Victoria shrieked and hugged him tight.

***

When his alarm clock went off, Anthony woke up knowing that something big was due to happen, but for a split second he couldn't remember what. Then it all flooded back. He immediately felt a wave of excitement. The previous day's events rushed through his head; especially how wonderful it had been to kiss Susan last night.

He got up and looked in the mirror: it was true. He rubbed his head. It was so short it felt like sandpaper. He pulled a hard face to emphasise his toughness; he couldn't help laughing at how ridiculous he looked, but he did feel very different, and in a good way.

He went to the bathroom. He contemplated shaving but decided against it. He could not claim to have a beard, but a few whiskers were definitely showing, and he thought he ought to cultivate them, especially as he was going for the tough look.

He dressed carefully, paying particular attention to the look of his new baggies. He wished he'd thought of new shoes too; his sensible black brogues didn't really go with everything else but since the trousers were so huge it wasn't really possible to see his feet anyway.

'Anthony, what would you like for breakfast?' his mother called through the door.

He walked into the kitchen. She looked up and shrieked, 'What has happened to you? What have you done? You look awful, utterly awful.'

He couldn't help laughing.

'What do you think, Ma — suit me?'

'You confounded idiot: you look like some kind of petty criminal.'

'Really? That's fantastic.'

His grandmother peered at him, 'You look like a common little thug. Well done, Anthony. You would have made your father very proud.'

'You're not getting into the wrong company are you, Anthony?' his mother said, looking worried.

'Absolutely not. You've met them all: they're really nice, decent people.'

'Yes, but why do you want to look like an ugly brute?'

'Because I'm tired of looking like a victim.'

She looked at him and said, 'I'm sorry, what we did to you is inexcusable. I'm so sorry.'

'It's OK, Mother, everything's going well now. Plus, today is goodbye day to the real culprit, at last.'

'He'll have a fit when he sees you,' his granny cackled.

'That's the plan. I want him to understand that things are different now.'

'Who's going with you?'

'Well, Joe is driving us all: it's Gary, Frank, Katy and Susan.'

'You've got tremendous resilience — not something you got from me, that's for sure.'

'Don't say that, Margaret: buck your ideas up,' her mother said.

'That's right, Granny. Come on, Mother: you've kept us going despite everything. Plus, it was your determination that put him away, and got us away safely.'

'Took me twenty years too long.'

'We're fine now: that's what counts.'

She touched his head.

'You're a lovely boy, Anthony. It's just a shame you've got a head like a coconut.'

After breakfast he checked everything again. He had the letter, the wedding ring, some money. He looked at himself carefully: all was fine. He was ready.

'Bye then,' he called.

'Good luck. Don't let him get into your head; and come home safely.'

'Give him hell, my boy,' his granny cheered.

He went outside and took a deep breath. He was nervous but ready to go.

**

Frank got up and did some stretches. He could tell that he'd lost his conditioning, but he felt OK. He had a bath, shaved and put on his clean clothes and new shoes. They raised him another couple of inches. He brushed his new hair. He felt good.

'Wow, Frank, you look amazing,' his mother said.

'What would Robbie say now, do you think?' he asked.

'Hmmm, maybe: "You look like a primped-up lounge lizard with low moral fibre and unsavoury ulterior motives?"'

'Yes, or maybe: "If you want to pull a bird, you'll need a new personality, Frank, not a new costume?"'

'Yes, that's better. So, who is the lucky girl, Frank?'

Frank paused then said, 'Well, I thought I'd just see how Ailsa is, you know, just to see how she's doing?'

'Yes, I do know. That's very nice of you to think of her.'

Frank was fiddling around with stuff in his pockets. He looked embarrassed.

'She sent me a card; I never answered it. I thought maybe I could just call, just to say hello.'

'Robbie would be very pleased if you did.'

'Do you think so?'

'Definitely; I'm sure.'

'Good. Yes. I think you're right, Mum.'

'What time are you leaving?'

'In a few minutes. What time does the post come on a Saturday?'

'It's different every week, maybe soon.'

Janice looked at Frank. He was looking very edgy.

'Waiting for anything in particular?' she asked.

'Well, I wrote to Ailsa. I thought I might hear back from her today.'

'Ah, I see.'

'I'd better go; I'll see you tonight, Mum.'

'Good luck then — hope it goes well.'

He bent down and kissed her cheek. She got him in a tight headlock and kissed the top of his head.

'Mmmmm, nice after-shave.'

Frank went out onto the street. He looked up and down hoping to see the postman — no, no sign of him. He sighed and set off. He rubbed his thumb against the silver ring as he walked: it had become a habit already.

***

Katy was at the door when the post arrived. Her heart leapt when she saw the now-familiar handwriting.

'Is it from her?' Anna asked as she came into the hall.

'Yes,' Katy tried to hide her excitement.

'I hope it's OK for you, Katy, I really do.'

'Thanks, Mum. I'll just quickly read it and I'll be back.'

Katy ran upstairs and into her room. She shut the door behind her.

'Dear Katy

I read both your letters. I'm not surprised that you feel a bit mixed up. I do too.

Now that we are in contact, I would like us to meet, how do you feel about it? I understand that you and your family are going through an upheaval so maybe you're feeling that it might not be a good idea? Perhaps we should talk on the phone first? I don't know Katy; I want this to be right for both of us. Would you like to think about it?

In case you would like to talk here is my phone number 01 580 4468

I look forward to hearing from you

Yours

Jane x'

Katy sighed. The whole thing was getting her down. She wanted so much to return to life as it had been, simple every day. She also felt the adrenalin kick in, if she thought about dialling the number and hearing her mother's voice for the first time.

There was a quiet knock on the door.

'Come in.'

The door opened slowly, and she saw Anna's anxious face looking questioningly at her.

Katy held the letter out to her and rolled on to her bed with her face in her pillow. Anna read it.

'I'm so sorry you've been put through all this,' she said, stroking Katy's hair.

'It's all right, Mum, I'm getting used to it now.'

'Will you ring her?'

'Do you think I should?' Katy's voice was small.

'I don't know if I'd say you should: maybe it's more about weighing up the pros and cons.'

'I want to, but I'm scared too.'

'I know; I feel the same.'

'She seems quite nice in her letters.'

'Why don't you think about it today, or for as long as you want, then decide.'

'OK.'

'Can I come in?' Susan called.

'What is this, Piccadilly Circus?' Katy protested.

'Yeah, like you hate being the centre of attention,' Susan said.

'I'll let you two get on. See you later,' Anna said, leaving.

'Much later, Mum: we're off to Sussex today,' Susan said.

'Ah yes. Have a good trip — don't be too late back please.'

Anna left, and Susan looked enquiringly at Katy.

'The letter's there.'

Susan read it.

'Before you ask: yes, I'll ring her, but I'm not going to rush into it,' Katy said.

'You mean you'll wait for a minute or two?'

'No, I'll leave it a week or two more like,' Katy said.

Susan smiled indulgently and said nothing.

'Ready to face the convicts?' Katy asked, jumping up.

'Yes, come on. It's time we went, and don't talk about Anthony's father like that.'

'No, he's more of a shit than anything else as far as I can tell.'

'Well, that may be true, but we've got to support him, not make it worse.'

'Right, let's go, I'm ready for action,' Katy said, looking at herself in the mirror. She flicked back her hair, pulled down her jumper, turned one way then the next, and checked to see if her flares covered her boots — they did.

Susan pushed her out of the way and studied herself. She said, 'Do you think I look like a librarian?'

'Yes. Why you wear such sensible clothes I just don't know: you're more like Mum's twin sister than mine.'

'Thanks Katy: just the kind of compliment I needed.'

'Sorry, I didn't mean that; you'll always be my sister, you know that, don't you?'

'Of course, you idiot. I've been telling you that.'

***

Gary walked towards The Beeches. He had been desperate to get out of the house. His dad had been totally unpredictable: chatty and cheerful one minute, abrasive and challenging the next. His mum had been, as ever, totally indulgent of him and his moods.

'Where are you going, Gazza?' his dad had asked as Gary was about to leave.

'Nowhere.'

Abbott looked at his son closely.

'What's wrong with you, boy? Are you trying to wind me up or something?'

'No.'

'Well look here, old bean,' Abbott said in a parody of BBC English, 'clearly you are not going nowhere; therefore, you must be going somewhere: wherefore art thou going, old man?'

Gary couldn't help himself saying, 'Out.'

'Ah, that makes everything clear, crystal clear. The fact that you're not telling me where you are going makes it even more fascinating to me. Try again, Sonny Jim.'

'It doesn't matter, love. He's probably seeing a nice girl or something like that,' Jenny said.

'Ah, of course, Romeo it is. Wherefore art thou going Romeo. Off to shag a bird is it?'

'No,' Gary said as he shrugged on his parka.

Abbott stood in front of the door; arms crossed against his bulky chest.

'Off to do some shoplifting. Or, maybe you take drugs. No, I know, you're off to your poetry circle to discuss your latest creations with your intellectual buddies?'

'Something like that,' Gary muttered.

'Read me a poem before you go, old man: fill my head with your dazzling wit and wisdom, oh Wordsworth son of mine.'

'Oh, Brian, don't be so silly,' Jenny said, tugging at his arm.

Abbott's face went red and he turned to his wife. Gary could see where this was going and, for the sake of peace in the house, and specifically his mother's safety, he dragged from his memory the poem they'd last read at school.

'My name is Ozymandias, king of kings, look down on my works ye mighty and despair.'

Abbott grinned and said to his wife, 'The boy's a genius. I'm telling you, Jen: he's on his way to Oxford, or Cambridge, or prison — not sure which: prison probably.'

'Bye,' Gary said quickly and opened the door and sped out.

'We'll come and visit you in prison, son, don't worry,' Abbott called cheerfully after him and slammed the door shut.

He was a hundred yards away from the gates to The Beeches car park when he saw a nasty looking shit of a skinhead walking towards him. He looked down. The last thing he wanted now was any aggro, not with the poison of the last few minutes still in him.

'Wotcha, Abbott, you ugly tosser,' the figure said as they converged.

'You what?' Gary said unprepared for the venom in the youth's voice.

'It's me, Gary — Anthony.'

Gary stopped and stared at him. He even did a comedy eye rub to clear his vision.

'What's happened to you?' he said in a high-pitched voice.

'I know: it's brilliant isn't it? Katy and Susan did it, last night.'

Gary studied Anthony closely. The boy in front of him looked pretty hard.

'Fuck, I wouldn't want to meet you in a dark alley,' he said.

'That's the right answer,' Anthony said, smiling broadly.

'Are you ready to go?' Gary asked.

'Yes, I've got everything under control.'

They walked together into the car park. Joe was there, leaning against a lamp post. He waved at them.

'Is that you, Anthony?'

'Yes, my new guise, what do you think?'

'You look like a nasty piece of work to me, but I guess that's the idea?'

'Yes. And that too is the right answer.'

Katy and Susan were walking towards them. They were smiling at Anthony as they approached.

'Jesus, Anthony, you look like a total knob,' Katy said.

'It's such a shame: you look so awful!' Susan said.

'Here comes another stranger,' Joe said.

They all looked towards the gate to see Frank appear. They were silent as he approached them.

'What's up?' he asked.

'Frank, is it you?' Katy asked in wonder.

'Yes, who else is it going to be?'

'How about a younger, taller, better-looking David Essex?' she said.

'No, it's me.' He looked closely at Anthony. 'Never mind me, where's young Beethoven gone?'

'I took your advice, Frank. What do you think?' Anthony said.

'It's done the trick, definitely.'

Gary felt his face flush. He knew this was the right minute to do it: self-consciously, he reached into his inside pocket, brought out the hard, plastic case and opened it. He fumbled with the thick, black frames and put the glasses on. He looked defiantly around at the others and said, 'OK, I look like a wanker, you can call me Joe 90 all you like, but at least I can see you laughing at me now.'

They stared at him, dumbfounded. In an instant he'd gone from squinting, surly thug to studious young man.

'You look great, Gary, doesn't he?' Joe said and looked at the others for confirmation.

They nodded.

'Actually, I think you look much, much better, Gary. I thought you were really ugly but now you look rather handsome,' Susan said, weighing him up.

'No, you're still really ugly, you just don't look so stupid anymore,' Katy said sweetly.

'Nice one, Gary: takes some guts to wear glasses,' Frank said.

'Look at us: I look like a bully, Gary looks like the swot,' Anthony said, laughing. 'Talk about role reversal.'

'I do not look like a swot,' Gary said curtly.

'No, no, you're right: that's the wrong word,' Anthony agreed hastily. 'You look more like an intellectual.'

Gary grunted.

'Listen, we've got a problem,' Joe said.

They looked at him questioningly.

'Last night the windows in my car were smashed by some imbeciles, so we have no car to get us to our destination.'

'Oh no, what are we going to do?' Anthony said, crestfallen.

'Well, I've been in touch with some friends to borrow a car but the only one I can get is a four-seater. There is a solution available but only if you're all comfortable with it. They looked at him expectantly.

'We have a volunteer driver available, but you've got to be happy with the arrangement,' he said again.

They nodded, waiting.

'Victoria Court has offered to take us all in the school minibus,' he said at last.

There was a long silence.

Joe went on, 'She really wants to do it, I think. She seems determined to, but she knows it's up to you all.'

Katy said excitedly, 'Is she your girlfriend, Joe?'

Joe smiled, 'Well, since you ask so nicely, yes: she and I are stepping out together.'

'I knew it! I can always tell,' Katy squealed.

Joe turned to Anthony, 'It's your day, Anthony. How do you feel about it?'

'I'm fine. I like her. If everyone else is all right about it, then I am.'

Susan remembered the look she and Miss Court had shared as she'd taken revenge on Steve, Phil and Paul in the canteen.

'I think she's great, a good laugh. Plus, she's prepared to drive us,' she said.

'All right,' Gary said.

Frank was silently twisting his silver ring. He said, 'Yes, I'm fine; it will be more space for us all.'

'It's got a radio; we can listen to Capital,' Katy said.

'Come on then, let's go time waits for no man,' Joe said, and started striding towards the school.

As they walked up the drive, Joe manoeuvred himself next to Gary. He lightly tugged at his coat and drew him behind a few steps.

'Well done, Gary, you're a bloody marvel.'

Gary looked at Joe and couldn't help himself reddening with pleasure at the compliment.

Joe went on quietly, 'Will you watch out for Frank today? It's a big thing going in a car — or bus in this case — you know, after the accident.'

Gary nodded and said, 'Yeah, I will.'

They caught up with the others.

***

Victoria sat in the driver's seat of the minibus waiting. She was nervous. She really wanted to be with these people. Ever since the awful scene in the boys' lavatory she'd felt responsible for them all — before that even. She had to admit to herself that Joe's close involvement in their lives had left her a little shut out. Not that she resented his closeness to them, just that she wanted to be important to them too.

She and Joe had had a strange evening: the trip to see the grave, the horrible brutality of the assault outside the pictures, Joe's car getting smashed up, and then falling asleep in Joe's arms: safe and secure.

She looked in the rear-view mirror and saw the oddly assorted group walking towards her. She smiled in relief. She got out of the bus and waited for them to get close before she said anything. She saw Joe and Anthony were together: Anthony talking and Joe listening. She hadn't recognised Anthony for a moment, his appearance was so different she'd assumed it was someone else. Behind them came Frank and Gary, also in deep conversation. They too appeared radically altered; then Katy and Susan: she could hear Katy singing from fifty yards away.

'Hello, Miss Court,' Anthony said as he got close. 'Thank you very much indeed for the kind offer; we're all extremely grateful.'

'It's absolutely my pleasure, Anthony.'

'I'm glad you're here: you might want to see my mother's letter to Joe,' Anthony said, handing her the note.

'No, it's fine. I don't need to see it, but thanks anyway,' Victoria said, glancing at Joe who nodded.

'Well, I must say you all look rather different out of school.'

'So, do you, Miss,' Katy said. 'I like your jeans; where did you get them?'

'Oh, they're just old things, but thank you though. Now, because we're not at school and are, I guess, friends for the day, please will you all call me Victoria. Well, all except you, boy, you can call me Miss,' she said, looking at Joe.

'Yes, Miss,' he said.

'Who's sitting where?' Victoria asked.

'Well, we can swap around but, to start with, can I have a volunteer to sit next to Miss, please?' Joe asked.

Victoria looked quizzically at Joe. He'd obviously asked for a reason. When no one offered, Joe said gently, 'Frank, will you take the first shift?'

Frank looked uncertain. Joe glanced at Gary.

'Come on Frank; I'll sit at the front too,' he said.

'We'll sit at the back and cause trouble,' Joe said.

'Will you put the radio on, Vicky?' Katy said.

Victoria looked at Katy. She couldn't help herself laughing at Katy's immediate informality.

'Certainly, we'll listen to Radio 3.'

'Come off it! That's for boring old squares and losers,' Katy said.

'Like me you mean?' Victoria said.

'I prefer classical music,' said Anthony.

'There you are: I rest my case,' Katy said triumphant.

'I prefer classical too,' said Susan.

'Spare me, please. Come on, Victoria: just to get us on our way,' Katy pleaded.

Victoria put the bus into gear, turned on the radio and tuned into Capital and Kenny Everett. She concentrated on her driving but glanced back at Joe every now and then in the mirror, each time he saw her eyes, he winked. She smiled.

Part 6

Limiting Deceleration

Frank

Frank had woken up full of energy, excitement, but gut-wrenching nerves too. Without thinking, he put his fingers on the silver ring. Now, as before, his breathing slowed, muscles relaxed, stress subsided.

'How are you feeling about today?' his mother had asked him, looking into his face.

'It feels weird going back, seeing the old places, the old people. I'm not sure to be honest, Mum.'

Janice could guess how he felt. She couldn't bring herself to go back.

'You don't have to go, love: only if you want to.'

Frank nodded. He did want to go; he did want to be back home, his real home. He knew it would feel like a ghost town and everywhere he looked he would see ghosts. He was drawn back to see them though, to feel them there: they were waiting for him. But it was Ailsa he wanted to see most of all.

'You look great, Frank, you really do,' his mother had said as he was leaving the house.

His walk to join the others had felt strange. It was as if he were facing up to something stupendous, an event that was much, much greater than anything he'd ever experienced before. He wondered if it might be how he might have felt as he walked to the start line of the Olympic 100 metres final. He felt very conspicuous as he walked, as if everyone were watching him. It wasn't his new appearance that was making him feel wobbly, it was what lay ahead. Despite his conversation with Joe the day before, and the reassurance of the ring, the anxiety of getting into a car was making him feel twitchy.

As it turned out, it had been much more straightforward than he had imagined. The switch to the minibus had been a surprise and a helpful distraction. Gary had been funny, as had Victoria. All three of them had chatted about everyday things: favourite television programmes, bands, comedians, just chatting. He had enjoyed the trip down.

When he'd got off the minibus, he'd felt bad about leaving Anthony. He knew that his new friend was facing a tough challenge and he'd wanted to be there to support him. He'd given Anthony a rough hug, just as he would have done — had done — countless times to Robbie.

He walked to the bus stop and checked the timetable for the bus to Brighton: he had a few minutes. He went to the telephone box and rang his mother.

'It's me.'

'How's it going?'

'All right so far. I'm just at the Little Chef outside Lewes.'

'Going to get the good old 292?'

'Yep, assuming it comes of course.'

They were silent. Frank pictured his mother, clutching the phone hard, willing everything to be all right for him. He knew that she was feeling as much tension as he was, more maybe.

'I'm feeling pretty good actually, Mum; I'm looking forward to it, seeing the old places and people. Will you come with me next time?'

'We'll see. Maybe, if you look after me.'

'I will; of course, I will.'

***

As the bus went along all the familiar roads it was as if he were watching a film — not really there in person but observing himself. He got off outside Withdean Stadium, the home of so many of his races over the years. He walked around it, peered over the fence and had finally plucked up the courage to go to the entrance to see if it was open; it wasn't.

'Can I help you, son?' a voice called out.

An elderly man was trimming back bushes. It was Jim Stevenson, one of the blokes who maintained the place.

'No, I was just…' Frank trailed off. What *was* he doing exactly?

'Frank? Is that you?' he said.

'Hi, Jim.'

'How lovely. How are you doing, son?'

'Fine thanks, Jim, I'm fine.'

'You're looking good, Frank. Do you want to come in and wander about?'

'Can I?'

'Sure — come on. There's some building work going on; that's why it's all closed up.'

Jim opened the main gate and let Frank through.

'Give me a shout when you're done,' he called and shut the gate, leaving Frank in the stadium on his own.

Frank walked onto the cinder track and stood by the finishing line. He looked around: it was grey, damp in the air; it was quiet except for the road sounds outside. He walked around the track, trying to bring back the events of only a few months before the intense, vivid colours of summer, the excited buzz of the crowd, the electricity in the air. He reached the start line and looked down the track: there was nothing, no one. He waved, just in case. No one was there. He shut his eyes, fighting back tears. He looked up again: surely there would be a sign of some kind? Nothing. He sighed and walked slowly down the straight, trying to bring back some echoes of the past — just one, maybe: still, nothing. Jim saw him coming.

'How's your mum?' he asked.

'Oh, not bad. We're getting used to life.'

'She's made of steel; you are too,' Jim said.

'She is.'

'Are you running?'

'No, I can't. I've lost it, Jim.'

'I know. I'm sure it's hard. Keep looking though, won't you?'

Frank smiled and put out his hand. They shook.

Frank walked slowly along the main road towards Brighton, gradually getting closer to his street. He kept his head down; he wanted anonymity right now. In fact, he wished he was invisible.

 He saw the house and walked past it, not daring to look. He kept on going and saw his old school in the distance. He could hear the sound of a football match in progress and walked up the side of the main building to the fields at the back. There was a knot of people watching the match. In the middle of them was Mr Lewis, Frank's games master, shouting encouragement to his team. Frank stood a few yards back and watched the match. He recognised the players from his year, some of them friends, some of them fellow track and field team members.

The game was to-ing and fro-ing, most of the action taking place in the muddy middle third. No one was taking any notice of him and for a few minutes he enjoyed being on his own and just watching the match. The ball was blocked and deflected towards him. Instinctively he stopped it with his right foot and passed it back to the defender nearest to him. It was Kevin Moriarty.

Kevin looked at Frank in surprise then cried out, 'Frank, you bastard, what are you doing here?'

Frank smiled and looked away.

'It's Frank,' Kevin turned around and shouted to his teammates.

In seconds Frank was surrounded by his old school mates, some parents and Mr Lewis too. He tried to edge away but he was caught in a swarm of excited and friendly people. They were genuinely delighted to see him. The referee blew his whistle to regain some order. Slowly they all moved back to the pitch. Ruffled, Frank found his equilibrium and began to walk away.

'Don't go, Frank. Cheer on the lads,' Mr Lewis said.

Frank didn't want to stay, but his old teacher was lightly holding his arm, encouraging him to stand on the touchline.

'What's the score?' Frank asked.

'One-all; we've got twenty minutes left.'

Frank nodded and watched the game. He felt conspicuous but understood he had to play his part.

'You doing all right?' Mr Lewis asked, without taking his eyes from the match.

'Up and down.'

'It's great to see you; we all miss you.'

'Really?'

'Yeah, really.'

'Thank you,' Frank said. 'I miss all this.'

Frank made himself stay till the end. He clapped as they all filed off towards them. He had seen the goals go in, but he couldn't absorb the score. After a few minutes of banter with his friends, he slipped away. Once out of the main gates he speeded up and jogged back towards his street. As he slowed to a walk, he found himself touching the silver ring; it calmed him down.

He walked slowly towards his house, stopped opposite and looked.

Frank had had no preconceptions as to what he would find when he came home. Now that he was looking at the place of his past, his family's past, he wondered why it had been such a hurdle to overcome. Yes, it was his house. Yes, there was evidence of it being lived in — new curtains, a different car outside — that was about it. It was just a house. It didn't have any resonance for him. He looked at the upstairs windows. What did he think he would see? There was no glimpsed impression of Robbie, nor his dad: nothing familiar, touching or even upsetting. It was just a house. He stood staring at it. He conjured images from his past: the door opening and his parents striding out together with tennis racquets, his brother on his tricycle or, later, on his bike, his father up a ladder painting the window frames, or digging up the lawn to plant rhubarb or getting out of his car to go into the house. He could picture it all, but he couldn't bring the images to life.

'Hello?' a girl's voice said.

Frank jumped. He hadn't heard anyone approaching. He turned to his right, blushing.

'Hello,' the girl said again.

Frank saw a girl standing beside him. She was a teenager, nice looking, friendly, cheerful.

'Er, hello,' he said.

465

'You're looking at my house,' she explained.

'Oh, I'm sorry.'

'It's all right. I just wondered why, that's all.'

'Oh, nothing, I mean, no, I was just passing.'

'But you've been standing here for ages.'

Frank looked at his feet, embarrassed. He straightened and said, 'I'm sorry, I'm off now.'

She looked at him. He looked at her.

'Did it used to be your house?' she asked.

Frank nodded.

'Oh, that explains it.'

'Yeah, my mum and I moved a few months ago; we live north of London now.'

'Oh, I see.'

'Anyway, I'd better go,' Frank said edging away.

'Do you want to come in, you know, to see the place again?'

'No,' Frank said forcefully. 'I mean, no thanks, but thanks for asking; that's kind of you.'

'That's all right.'

Frank and the girl stood still, looking away from each other. Frank didn't want to be rude but didn't want to talk either. After an awkward silence he said, 'Do you like living here?'

'Yes, it's nice. It's much nicer than our last house. Did you like it here?'

'Yes, but things changed, and we had to move.'

Frank cursed himself. She was bound to ask, 'what things?'. He changed the subject.

'Do you live with your parents?'

'Yes, I've got two brothers too.'

Frank felt sure she was about to ask him if he had any brothers or sisters, he said, 'I'd better go now.'

'Really? Oh, OK.'

'Well, the thing is, um, I've got things to do, you know.'

'Yeah, I've got loads of things to do too.'

'My name's Frank, Frank Gordon.'

'Oh, my name's Alison Baker. Nice to meet you.' She put out her hand; Frank shook it.

He said, 'Sorry again, for staring at your house. I didn't mean anything by it. I suppose I just...'

'It's OK; it's your house too, isn't it?' she said.

'Not anymore, but thanks for saying it.'

'Bye then. It was nice to meet you,' she said.

'Bye then. Good luck.'

'With what?'

'I don't know. I just said it, you know, as a thing to say.'

'Yes, I know. Good luck to you, too.'

They paused another moment then Frank waved and walked away.

He walked quickly, keen to escape again. He got to the corner and looked back. Alison was still there. She waved. He waved. Blushing furiously, he started running hard down the street to the park. He didn't stop running till he got to the bench where he had talked with Ailsa last year. He sat down and stared out at the water. Life had seemed so easy, everything worked out well — in those days. He closed his eyes and thought about Ailsa. He remembered her scent, her closeness, the feel of her against him. He remembered his erection and how he'd had to pick up his bag to avoid embarrassment. He'd never really spoken to Robbie about Ailsa. He thought now that Robbie must have fancied her. Poor Robbie, he would never have the chance to go out with a girl, to have sex, to get married, to have children, to do anything. Frank put his head in his hands and cried for his little brother. He gave in to the tears this time. He couldn't help it.

The next thing he knew he was being licked by an eager tongue. He lifted his hands, and on the bench next to him was a very small dog, a terrier of some kind. It was nuzzling into him, wagging its little tail like mad.

'Come on, Hilda, leave the man alone,' called the dog's owner, a middle-aged man wearing wellies and an anorak.

'It's all right, I don't mind,' Frank called, stroking the wriggling creature.

'She's wet and muddy, and we're late,' the owner called.

Frank picked up Hilda and hugged her to his chest.

'Thank you, Hilda, thank you,' he whispered into her ear.

He put her on the ground, and she shot off busily sniffing, dashing here and there, getting on with her own affairs.

Frank rubbed his eyes and got up. He felt much better.

***

Frank rang the bell and waited. The door opened. 'You're very early,' said the man, looking dubiously at Frank.

Frank shook his head in confusion. The man went on, 'It doesn't start till two p.m.'

'What doesn't?' Frank asked.

'The party.'

'What party?'

'Ailsa's party.'

Frank understood at last.

'Oh, I didn't know there was a party. I just called by to say hello. It doesn't matter. I'll go — Sorry to have bothered you.'

'It's all right; I'm sorry about the confusion.'

Despondent, Frank turned away and heard the door close behind him. What a total failure he was: he'd come all this way and he was going without even seeing her. He felt stupid, red-faced with embarrassment, and utterly dejected.

He had gone a few yards when he heard the door open and Ailsa's voice, 'Frank?'

He turned around to see Ailsa at the door. She waved.

He waved and stood still, not knowing what to do. She came down her path and walked towards him. He watched her getting closer and closer. He felt like a rabbit caught in the headlights of an oncoming car.

'Frank,' she said and stopped.

'Hello. I'm sorry about this. I didn't know there was a party — is it your birthday party?'

'Yes, I'm fifteen today.'

'Oh, sorry. Happy Birthday to you.'

She smiled uncertainly. 'How come you're here?' she asked.

'Well, some friends of mine were going to Lewes and I thought it would be nice to see the old place, and... well, I thought it would be nice, well, I wanted to say hello to you too.'

'I got your letter.'

'Oh, good. I'm sorry it took me so long to write.'

'It's OK. I understand.'

'Do you?'

'I think so. You've had a terrible time.'

'Yeah, but no reason for not writing I'm sorry.'

'I was going to write back, but I got caught up with the party — you know how it is.'

'Of course; there's no hurry.'

'Do you want to come in?'

'Well, I don't want to get in the way.'

'I'd like you to.'

'Well, if you're sure.'

Frank followed Ailsa into her house. She was looking very pretty. He was glad he'd come.

'This is Frank, Dad,' Ailsa introduced them.

'I'm sorry, Frank; I didn't realise,' he said.

'It's all right. How were you to know who I was? I'm just a stranger on your doorstep,' Frank pointed out.

'I know, but you're Frank Gordon: you're famous.'

Frank shook his head and looked away.

'Do you want a drink, Frank? Something to eat?' Ailsa asked.

'Thank you, just a cup of tea; that would be lovely.'

Ailsa put the kettle on and steered Frank into the living room. They sat down, she looked at him.

'Nice haircut,' she said smiling.

'Do you think so?' Frank put his hands to his hair; it felt strange to him.

'Are you running?'

'No, I've given all that up.'

'What a shame! For good?'

Frank nodded.

'How's your mum?'

'She's doing OK. She uses a wheelchair these days and she's getting around pretty well.'

'That's good.'

Ailsa got up and made tea. She came back with some sandwiches on a plate.

'I bet you're hungry, aren't you?'

'Yes, thanks very much.'

Frank wolfed the sandwiches down.

'Do you like this dress?' she asked getting up and giving him a twirl.

Frank looked at her.

'You look beautiful,' he said.

'Thank you; you look great too.'

They sat in uncomfortable silence.

'Will you stay for the party? It's only a few friends, nothing exciting.'

'Well, I'm not sure. I'm not really a party sort of person.'

'I'd like you to.'

'Well, if you mean it, then, yes, that would be great, just for a few minutes maybe.'

'We're going to the pictures later too; will you come along?'

Before Frank could answer Ailsa went on, 'Frank, there is something you ought to know, though.'

'Yes?'

'Well, I know you won't think it important — I mean I know you're here because of Robbie, and, well you know, but the thing is…' Ailsa was struggling.

Frank knew what was coming. He helped her out, 'Your boyfriend is coming?'

Ailsa nodded.

'That's all right; it would be nice to meet him,' he said, with as cheerful a voice as he could muster.

'Really?'

'Of course, as long as he's a nice guy, that is, and I don't think you'd go out with a wan — er, with someone who wasn't nice.'

Ailsa looked miserably at Frank.

'Don't look so sad: it's your birthday,' he said.

'I know. It's just that you're so nice, Frank, I wish... well, anyway: he is nice, and I'd like you to meet him.'

'I can't stay for long. I've got to catch the bus back to Lewes at two thirty.'

'That's lovely. You'll know some of the others though, mostly from my year at school — and Robbie's too, of course.'

Ailsa looked out of the window. 'Here's some of them now. Oh, and some more. Are you ready?'

Frank stood up and stretched.

'Yeah,' he said, twisting his silver ring.

***

Frank stood awkwardly in the corner of the living room, unsure what to do with himself. He watched a group of teenagers come into the room. They were chatting and laughing and handing presents over to Ailsa. She said, 'This is my friend Frank, you know, Frank Gordon.'

The two girls and two boys stopped chattering and looked at Frank. He felt like a specimen in a museum. He smiled and said hello.

'Hi, Frank,' they said.

More people arrived; Frank was relieved. He felt less of a freak as numbers increased. He shifted from foot to foot and retreated even further into the corner. The room soon filled up. Ailsa didn't forget him. She kept close and made sure he was included in the cheery chatter. He couldn't bring himself to speak though; he felt tongue-tied and frozen to the spot. He also felt incredibly old and lumbering and totally out of place.

The doorbell rang again and more came in.

'Here's Patrick,' she said and went over to a good-looking boy, tall and well-dressed.

'Patrick, this is my friend Frank, the famous runner.'

Patrick looked up at Frank, impressed.

'Hello, Frank, it's very nice to meet you.'

'You too,' Frank said, feeling like a little boy now.

'Ailsa has told me about you, and your brother. I'm sorry about what happened.'

'Thanks,' Frank mumbled.

Patrick got caught up with some of the others and Frank was released. He watched Ailsa and Patrick together. They looked great. She looked over to him questioningly. He smiled; she smiled. He wondered if he could go now.

'Hello again.'

Frank looked round to see Alison smiling at him.

'Oh, hello, do you know Ailsa?'

'No, I just gate-crashed the party,' she said.

He smiled.

'Alison, this is my friend Frank Gordon. He used to live in your house,' Ailsa explained.

'I know I caught the peeping tom peering in through our windows earlier today,' Alison said.

Ailsa looked at Frank uncertainly.

'It's true. She caught me red-handed.'

'Are you coming out to the pictures with us later?' Alison asked.

'No — in fact, I've got to leave in a minute.'

'Oh, what a shame, after we've been through so much together,' she said.

'Will you come again, Frank?' Ailsa asked.

He looked at her. Patrick was back, standing next to her.

'Of course; soon I expect,' he said, knowing that he never would.

'Good, I hope I'll see you again,' Alison said, looking genuinely pleased.

'Er, I'd better go, Ailsa. Thanks for — well, thanks,' he said.

She led him out to the hall. He heard people saying goodbye as he followed her, his head down, embarrassed.

Ailsa shut the door of the living room and turned to him.

'Thank you so much for coming it means a lot to me.'

'It was awful, Mum, the way she just wanted someone to look after her,' he'd said feeling sad for her all over again.

'How was Ailsa?' Janice asked carefully.

'Fine, yeah, great. She seemed great.'

She left it at that. She didn't want to push him. It was obvious that the day hadn't gone quite as he'd hoped.

'Did you see the house?'

'Yeah.'

'What was it like?'

'The same, just the same. Well, more or less. I met a girl, she lives there.'

'What was she like?'

'Yeah, friendly, nice.'

'What's her name?'

'Alison Baker.'

'You know, you're a handsome young man, Frank. You'll discover that lots of girls will like you.'

'Hmmm.'

Janice looked at Frank. Her heart went out to him.

Anthony

Anthony was excited. He'd been rehearsing today's events in his mind over and over again. He knew exactly what he wanted to say, how to say it and how he'd respond when his father's tirade of abuse was inevitably released.

Coupled with the nervous anticipation of today, his head was also swimming with the overwhelming excitement of recent developments with Susan. He couldn't quite believe that he was close to having a girlfriend. He, Anthony Alexander, with a girlfriend! Not just a girlfriend, but Susan Walker. She was so kind, intelligent and decent. She was also very pretty. He wasn't sure what she saw in him, but he didn't want to analyse that too deeply: the fact that she liked him was enough.

Last night had been sleepless. The tension at the prospect of seeing his father had made his nerves jangle uncontrollably. Last evening's kiss with Susan had been wonderful but had added another layer of nervous energy. He felt himself becoming manic as the torrent of emotions piled in on him.

Susan was sitting next to him on the minibus. She was an inch away from him. Her presence filled his head — her scent, her breath, the touch of her clothes next to his; her voice: so calm, sensitive and thoughtful. He wanted to hold her hand, to draw strength and security from her touch. He didn't dare he thought he might start to cry if he did.

He'd been so happy to see them all turn up this morning. During the fitful night, he'd started to dread that recent events had been imaginary, and the horrors of his real life had returned. Standing with them all outside The Beeches had made him smile like a lunatic.

'Susan?'

'Yes?'

'This is all hard to believe for me. I've spent the last few years feeling lonely, being laughed at, getting beaten up: now look at me. It's weird don't you think?'

'It must be; it's good though, isn't it?'

'Very.'

'How are you feeling about the visit?'

'Terrified: I'm absolutely scared out of my wits. I know it's hard to believe when you've got parents like yours, people who treat you with love and respect and kindness. My father is bad. I don't know if he's evil; I'm not even sure what that means. He's just bad, that's all. Plus, going into a prison is making me feel scared too. But I'm also excited. There's something in me making me feel elated — I want to laugh out loud the whole time.'

'Something making you. What do you mean?'

'A sense of destiny or something, I don't know. It's like it's the end of an era, the end of a race or reaching the top of a mountain. The fact that, whatever it is, it is nearly here, and I can hardly bear the pressure.'

'Well, it's nearly done now. A bit longer and then you can relax.'

Anthony nodded. He wanted to hold her hand so badly. He suddenly felt empty: he'd run out of fuel before the day had even properly started. He felt his eyes close.

'Are you all right?' Susan said, looking at him, worried.

Anthony opened his eyes and smiled at her.

'Yes, thank you.'

He put out his hand; she took it and squeezed it tight.

***

Anthony was beginning to feel sick now. He'd been imagining the moment when he would see his father. He remembered how he'd felt when that critical, haughty stare descended on him: shame, fear and self-disgust. The memory made his stomach cramp and his face burn.

They'd stopped at a Little Chef for coffee and had dropped off Frank. Anthony had felt a wave of anxiety when they'd said goodbye. Frank made him feel stronger and more secure. Anthony had punched him on the shoulder and tried to say good luck or see you later or something, but he felt tears coming into his eyes and all he could say was, 'Bye.'

Frank had taken Anthony by the shoulders and stared into his face, looking hard at him, unblinking. He'd said quietly and with great force, 'Cool, calm, slow.'

Anthony had looked up at Frank and nodded his understanding.

When they got back onto the bus after the stop-off, Susan sat next to Katy. Anthony was momentarily panicked but felt relief flood through him when Joe sat down next to him.

'Want to talk about it?' Joe asked.

'Sort of. I'm not sure what to say though.'

'I thought it might be helpful to picture the scene a bit before we get there?'

'Yes, that's a good idea. The thing is, I've never been to a prison before. Have you?'

'Yes, I have. I've been to prison; I spent several years in prison.'

Anthony looked into Joe's eyes. Joe was calm, relaxed.

'Gosh, I'm sorry,' Anthony said, sorry that he'd asked.

'Thanks, Anthony.'

'Was it awful?'

'Yes.'

'What do I need to know?'

'It's a very strange environment. The physical nature of it might make you feel depressed; there is an oppressive state in and around a prison. It will look and feel big, heavy, dead. When you get near it and into it you will smell it. It smells of hopelessness. The smell will get into your hair, clothes and skin. You will feel desperate for clean, fresh air as soon as you get into the place. The warders will make you feel ashamed, small and dirty. The sound of it will shock you. There is a lot of hard noise: doors banging shut, railings being clanged, people shouting and swearing. You'll hear jeering and cheering. You will hear shouting and screaming. You will see men looking hopeless. People look and are unhealthy. People will look either hard and nasty or lost and miserable. You will see men shuffling and stooped. The smell of cigarettes will make you gag. The smell of unwashed people will make you gasp for clean air. Other visitors will shock you too. They will look hard, lost, angry, sad, desperate. No one will be cheerful or positive. Anthony, prison is a terrible place, do you understand that?'

Anthony swallowed. He hadn't really given any thought to what was coming his way. All his imaginings had been of his interaction with his father, not the place itself.

'It's all right, Joe, I'm fine,' he said, trying to breathe normally.

Joe nodded, 'Well done, I knew you were up for it. So, do you want to take me through what you picture happening?'

'I am going to tell him to leave Mother alone, to stop writing, to leave us to get on with our lives.'

'What do you think he will say?'

'I think he will sneer at me. He'll tell me how pathetic I am, how we have ruined him, that he gave us everything, that we threw it back in his face and that we will never manage our lives without him: that kind of thing.'

'And how do you think you'll respond?'

'I'm not going to respond. I'm going to stay silent until he finishes then just repeat myself, that's all. I know I can't persuade him. I can only be clear about what I want.'

'That's very wise, Anthony.'

'Anything else, do you think?'

'No, the only thing I can add is to expect it to be different to what you imagine. Something will happen that you hadn't thought of. If you can, try and be nimble, be ready for whatever happens.'

'Yes, I expect something out of the ordinary; there is no such thing as normal in this situation.'

'May I say one more thing?'

Anthony nodded and looked at Joe expectantly.

'You're in control of what is going to happen. Nothing can happen that you can't get away from: you're in control, Anthony, and you're free. He cannot control you; he cannot imprison you. You can get up and leave when you want. He cannot get up and leave. You have the power. He has none. You have some wonderful friends pulling for you. He has none. He can say anything he wants to you, but he can say nothing that changes the facts: you are a kind, caring, decent, loving, intelligent, brave and resourceful man. He is a convicted criminal in prison. Where does the power lie?'

'You're right I know. It's just that he has many years' experience of beating me.'

'But he hasn't beaten you. He has many years of trying to beat you, but you've still won. Who's on top now?'

'It's ingrained, I suppose.'

'I know what you mean. I have absolute confidence in you, Anthony. I think you're great, and so does everyone else here. We're here to back you up: you have your army behind you.'

'I know, and it feels amazing.'

'Well done. I'm telling you, Anthony: you're tough as tough can be. Before we get there, though, may I suggest something?'

'Sure.'

'Sometimes it's helpful to prepare one's sub-conscious mind for an event or experience. We think we're ready, but the reality is different to what we pictured. I was wondering if you'd let me prepare your sub-conscious; you know, get your mind ready for what might happen?'

'I don't know. Maybe. What do I need to do? What will you do?'

'Well, I was thinking of asking you to imagine what is going to happen and then suggesting a response to you. It will help you cope if you need that extra bit of steel. You don't need much, Anthony; you're already very resilient.'

'If you think it will help, let's have a go.'

'Well done, Anthony, you're brilliant.'

Joe was silent for a moment, then said,

'Close your eyes for a minute. I want you to imagine something for me. It's this: if you feel that things are getting difficult, that you're feeling stressed, wound up, angry, scared, panicky, excited — anything that makes you feel that you aren't in control — then you must imagine warning bells suddenly clanging, red lights appearing everywhere, klaxons, tyres squealing. Do you know what I mean, Anthony?'

Anthony nodded.

'No, you think you know what I mean but it's just in theory. Listen to me, Anthony, listen very closely. This is important, you must absorb this. I want you to feel the rising tide of fear, the rush of blood to your face; you're feeling sweaty; you're having to swallow. He is making you feel as though you're going to say or do something you'll regret. When you feel those sensations, Anthony, that is when the alarm bells are going to clang, the red lights are going to come up, everywhere you look you can see people running for cover. That is when you apply the brakes. Are you hearing me, Anthony? You must put the brakes on. Put the brakes on, brakes, Anthony, brakes.'

Anthony nodded again.

'Feel the panic, Anthony, feel the anger. Feel the fear. Feel the feeling of losing control. Feel that awful rush of sickness at how he is making you feel. Feel it, Anthony, let it wash over you — what are you going to do?'

Anthony said, 'Put the brakes on.'

Victoria saw Joe's raised hand in the rear-view mirror and stamped on the brakes. Anthony was flung forward in his seat as the minibus screeched to a halt. Joe grabbed his arm and held him. The sound of squealing brakes and skidding tyres filled his senses.

The minibus was still. Everything was silent. Anthony looked around the bus; they were all staring at him.

His heart was pounding, head reeling.

'Everyone OK?' Victoria called.

Joe looked at Anthony. Anthony smiled weakly and nodded. The engine started up again and they moved off.

'Sorry about that. It's all OK,' Joe said and let go of Anthony's arm, but not before he gave him a final squeeze of reassurance.

'Phew, that shocked me,' Anthony said.

'I'm sorry: will you forgive us?'

'Of course, as long as I can get my own back.'

Joe smiled, 'I'm sure you will, Anthony.'

***

The minibus drew to a halt. They looked at the imposing, castle-like building in awe.

'Jesus, it's straight out of *Porridge*,' Gary said.

Anthony swallowed; he felt his insides turn to jelly. Joe put his hand on his shoulder. 'You'll be OK. I know you: you're more than capable, Anthony. Are you ready?'

'Absolutely. Let's go,' Anthony said.

They all got out.

'Can I come in with you?' Susan asked, looking at Joe.

'We'll have to wait here; only relatives will be allowed in,' Joe said.

'Don't worry everyone. Everything's under control: I'm fine,' Anthony heard himself say.

'Good luck. We're all behind you — and with you,' Joe said, shaking Anthony's hand.

Victoria stepped forward, hugged him and said, 'You're very brave, Anthony, very brave indeed.'

'Yeah, I'd be bricking it if I were you,' Gary said and thwacked him across the back.

'I am,' Anthony laughed.

'Just as well you're wearing your baggies then,' Katy said and hugged him too.

'I'll walk with you to the gate,' Susan said, and taking his arm they walked away.

'Thanks for coming, Susan; it's so kind of you,' he said blinking back tears.

'Don't be silly. It's important, isn't it?'

'Yes.'

They neared the immense main gate. They looked up, daunted. Anthony shivered.

'I've got something for you,' Susan said.

Anthony looked at the small shell.

'It's just a seashell, from my collection. If you hold it up to your ear you will be able to hear the sea, and you will hear my voice too. It will say "Come back soon, come back safely".'

He held it to his ear and listened. He couldn't hear anything.

'Believe me, you'll hear it when you need it,' Susan said.

Anthony stared at the shell in his palm and took a deep breath, 'OK, time to go.' He reached for Susan and hugged her. She hugged him back.

'Come back soon, come back safely,' she said again.

They drew apart and he went up to the gate.

***

Anthony was jittery. He was breathing quickly, doing his best to stay calm and in control of himself. He sat on one side of a metal table waiting for his father to arrive.

He had had to empty his pockets and leave everything with the stern-faced warder who'd checked his identification. He had had to put his shell in with his few coins and keys. He'd briefly held the shell to his ear and thought that perhaps he could hear Susan's voice over the sound of the sea.

He looked on as prisoners came to sit opposite other visitors. He saw that some of them looked pleased to see their loved ones, others had blank faces. There was a general hubbub of conversation all around him. He felt self-conscious, ill at ease, regretting that he'd even thought of coming on this ridiculous exercise.

As Joe had predicted, the smell was overpowering. He couldn't identify one smell over another: it was a thick fog of cheap detergent, cigarettes, unwashed clothes and bodies, of hopelessness.

He saw a figure walking towards him. The man was shuffling; he had a slumped and dejected aspect, clearly someone who'd been here for ever and had long given up hope. Anthony saw him get closer and then recognised something about him. His heart started thumping in his chest. This broken old man was his father.

He sat down and stared at Anthony for several seconds then mumbled, 'Is that you?'

Anthony could only nod.

'You look very different.'

Anthony nodded again.

'I imagine I do too?'

'Yes,' Anthony croaked.

'I don't suppose you thought your dear old father could sink so low, did you?'

'No.'

They looked at each other, trying to reconcile the past with the present.

Anthony had been prepared for a battle with the perpetrator of fifteen years of neglect, abuse and contempt. He had not been ready to talk to a broken man, a poor pathetic wretch like this.

'I'm sorry, Anthony, I've let you down so badly.'

Anthony was silent.

'I've been such a bad father. I've spent every hour of every day regretting everything. Everything I've done to you. How you must hate me. I'd do anything to make it up to you, but I've left it too late.'

Anthony stared at him. Despite everything he couldn't bear to see his father like this.

'When I think about how hard and cruel, I was to you, I can't stand it. All the years you must have wanted someone kind and caring, someone to be proud of you, to give you what you wanted. Instead I criticised you, ignored you, put you down. Oh God, Anthony, how I hate myself.'

Anthony shifted in his chair. He couldn't look at him.

'Now you've grown up and I've lost you forever. Look at you: you are grown up. You've become a man without me even knowing it was happening.'

There was a long pause.

'Anthony, what I did — you know, the fraud thing — it was stupid I know. I got it into my head that if I could make more money, I could give you more. I realise that it was stupid; I don't know what I was thinking. I must have been mad: I was mad, I'm sure of it.'

Anthony looked closely. He saw a sad and broken man, full of remorse. He couldn't see his father: he was gone, no sign of him.

'Talk to me about you, Anthony, how are you? What's school like? I hope it's going well for you. Are you doing well? I guess it's really difficult to settle into a new place, with new people. Maybe it's hard to get used to everything since I... since I abandoned you.'

'It's going well, actually,' Anthony said.

'Well done, Anthony, really? Oh, I'm so glad, thank you, Lord, for helping my boy through all of this awful mess; a mess caused by me, by me alone.'

'I've got some friends. They're waiting for me outside.'

'So, they know about me then? I suppose it's not surprising. I have to accept my punishment and the public humiliation that goes with it.'

Anthony felt a twinge of pity. This was not what he had expected. He said at last, 'Have you got friends here?'

'No one really understands me, Anthony. I'm left alone. I think I'm a bit different to everyone else. It's a very lonely place. I get picked on, I'm not sure why.'

'Sounds like my school,' Anthony said quietly.

'I don't think so, Anthony, this is not like any school. Did you bring me anything?'

'No.'

'I'm not surprised. Why would you want to bring me anything, unless it was to get your own back on me, for what I've done to you.'

Richard Alexander put his head in his hands. Anthony could see his shoulders shaking as he cried. The man was so beaten it was impossible to feel anything other than pity. After a long silence, his father said, 'I must look pitiful to you — do I, Anthony?'

Richard Alexander looked up and locked eyes with his son. Anthony looked away.

'You do pity me; I can't bear it.'

He had aged ten years. He was pasty, dishevelled, dirty, a forlorn figure.

Anthony heard himself say, 'What would you like, if I came again?'

'You kind boy. I don't want anything. Just seeing you is a gift from God.'

Anthony swallowed. He shut his eyes. He wanted to get out: it was unbearable.

'Will you come again do you think?'

For the first time, he sounded hopeful.

Anthony said, 'Well, I'm not sure; it's not easy to get here.'

'No, of course not. I just thought — no, it's not reasonable to ask you to come again; I realise that.'

'Maybe I could. I don't know.'

'It's all right, Anthony. I understand. You don't want to come and visit someone like me, in a dirty, squalid place like this. I do understand you know.'

Anthony looked at his father's face. Gone was the haughty look, the contemptuous sneer. Instead he saw a look of abject defeat, someone craving love and kindness.

'What I'd do to make things up to you, Anthony, if only I could change history. If only I could turn back the clock, I would be the father you wanted: I know I would.'

'There is something you can do for me, Father.'

'Yes? Tell me, Anthony, tell me.'

Anthony hesitated. He didn't want to say it, but he had to: it was why he was here.

'Will you stop writing to Mother?'

He looked at his father's face. He saw it: a flash of the old persona — just for an instant, then it was gone again.

'The love between husband and wife is hard to understand, Anthony. Writing to your mother is what keeps me sane in this insane place. You can't want me to go mad, son, surely you don't want that.'

Anthony kept his eyes lowered and said, 'I'm sorry, Father. I thought that maybe it was hard for her to hear from you, even though I know how much you love her. I thought it might upset her.'

'I can't see how that can be true. I need to know that she still loves me and, most important of all, I need to tell her how much I love her. I know it's hard for you to understand.'

Anthony felt his heart begin to thump. This was it: this was what he'd been expecting. He took his courage in his hands and recited from his father's letter, *'I shall continue to write to you despite your protests. I shall continue to do my best to make your life as wretched as mine, be assured of it.'*

He looked at his father's face again. He shuddered. The wretched pathetic face had gone. In its place was the face he knew so well.

'So, my loving, dutiful little boy has been reading private letters, has he?'

Anthony stared at him in silence.

'Answer me, boy. Have you been prying? Of course, you have. You are the type that would: sneaky, dirty — a loathsome little cheat of a boy.'

Anthony could not tear his eyes away from his father: he had grown bigger; his face was hard and menacing, his eyes glittering and sharp — a hawk's eyes.

'Answer me, Anthony: have you been reading my letters to my wife?'

With a huge effort, Anthony said slowly and deliberately: 'No, just one, but I understand that there have been many.'

'God! That bitch. I suppose she's been lying to you, like she lied to me, to the police, to everyone.'

Anthony forced himself to speak, 'Not lying, just stating facts.'

There was blazing fury in the face now. There was some kind of evil power surging across the table that separated them. Anthony wanted to put his hands up to shield himself.

'No, I shall not stop writing to my wife. Who I write to has nothing whatsoever to do with you. I shall write to my wife, and when I am out of here, I shall come and talk to my wife, and I shall make it clear to her what a terrible mistake she has made.'

Anthony felt his heart hammering. The venom in that face was shocking. He clasped his hands together to stop himself shaking. He felt suddenly elated: this was it! This was what he'd come to do. It was working out exactly how he'd imagined it would. His excitement was making him get hysterical. He felt the hardness between his legs. It thrilled him.

'What are you laughing at, boy? Look at you. You look like you should be in here. You look like excrement on the pavement of a council estate. You are making me sick just looking at you.'

Anthony was laughing now. He undid his zip; he put his hand inside: it felt so good, so powerful.

'Stop writing to her, Father. It's over.'

'Oh, and how are you going to make me do that then, dear Anthony?' Richard Alexander said in a mocking voice.

'If you don't, I shall kill you.'

As he heard his father's bark of scornful laughter, Anthony was overwhelmed by a visceral wave of rage. He reached inside his trousers and grasped the butt of the gun. Instantly, he felt himself flung forward against the table, the clanging of alarm bells, red warning lights filling his head.

***

The hands gripping his shoulders were rough. He was dazed. Anthony shut his eyes tight and dragged his mind back into the present.

'Come on, son, time for you to go,' the hard voice of the warder was saying.

As he was half pulled to his feet, Anthony felt the heavy weight of the gun pulling at the elastic belt he was wearing inside his baggies. He bent double as if he had been punched in the stomach and quickly zipped up his flies.

In front of him, he saw his father being escorted away. As he walked off, the face that was turned to him was pure malevolence. Anthony stared back then, without thinking, he pointed two fingers at him, cocked the trigger and fired.

'What happened there? What did he do?' the warder said, as Anthony composed himself.

'Nothing. I just miss him so much; I can't stand it.'

The warder grunted and pushed Anthony back into the main entrance area. Once there, he collected his bits and pieces but, rather than leaving, he sagged onto a hard bench and reflected on the last few minutes. His overwhelming feeling was one of nausea. Being confronted by the poison that had spewed out of his father had made him feel physically sick. The need to destroy that mocking, evil face had been so great he had given no rational thought to the notion of shooting him: he had not been able to stop the instinctive drive to do it. It was only now that the purpose of Joe and Victoria's stunt was becoming clear. The alarm bells had not gone off, but he could have sworn that for an instant they were clanging everywhere. The force that had made him lurch forward had been so great, he had assumed it had been the warder throwing him against the table. He shook his head to clear it. He was holding Susan's shell. He put it to his ear.

He heard it quite clearly... 'Come back soon, come back safely.'

He closed his hand around it and at the same time saw his mother's wedding ring on his middle finger. He had forgotten to give it to his father. He realised that he'd messed up the whole exercise. Far from keeping his father away from them, he was sure that another letter was being written right now, one even worse than before. He had failed, totally failed. All he'd managed to do was enrage his father and make himself look ridiculous. Why did he say he'd kill him? That was just a childish reaction. Now that he thought about it more clearly, his whole venture had been based on a child's attempt to wreak revenge. He shook his head in frustration. With a heavy heart he heaved himself to his feet. He wanted to get out now. He needed to be surrounded by nice people: his people, the people he loved and who loved him.

He walked towards the exit, saw the gates up ahead and quickened his pace. He took his turn to get out into the free world. Once out, he breathed in fresh air in greedy lungfuls. He saw the minibus parked in the far corner and started running hard towards it. He couldn't get there quick enough. As he got closer, he saw them get out and walk towards him. He started crying. His heart was hurting, his lungs were straining for air. He fell into the huddled group: he had made it.

'Let's get out of here,' Joe said, 'let's get the fuck out of this dump.'

They got on the bus, all of them dragging Anthony inside. Victoria was behind the wheel, Gary and Katy next to her. Right behind were Joe, Susan and Anthony. The doors were slammed shut and Victoria gunned the engine: it stalled and cut out.

'Sorry,' she called and tried again. This time, with wheels squealing, they got away.

'What's wrong?' Susan said, looking anxiously at Anthony.

'Sorry, I was laughing at the getaway driver,' Anthony said, crying and laughing, and crying again.

'How did it go?' Katy asked.

'Terrible.'

'Why, what happened?'

'I messed it all up — I blew it basically.'

'No, I don't believe that,' Susan said.

'Did you tell him to sling his hook?' Gary asked.

'Yes, it didn't make any difference. He's evil; he really is.'

'Well in which case there was probably nothing you could do,' Joe pointed out.

'I know. I just feel that I let my mother down.'

'I don't suppose she thought you could change him: she knows him better than anyone after all,' Victoria called from the front.

'Yes, but I let myself down too.'

'How?' asked Katy.

Anthony paused then slowly undid his flies, reached inside and pulled out the gun.

'Oh no, you total idiot: you took a gun into prison. Anthony, you are insane,' Susan said horrified.

'I know,' he said sadly.

Anthony untied the gun from his belt and handed it to Joe.

'I'm guessing you didn't use it?' Joe asked, taking the gun.

'No, I came so close though. I was about to when your little trick stopped me.'

'Thank God for that.'

Victoria saw the gun in the mirror. 'Anthony, what on earth...!'

'Sorry, Miss Court,' Anthony was appalled by his own stupidity.

'We're taking that to the police right now,' Victoria said.

'Must we?' Joe asked.

'Of course: we have no option.'

'Why don't we just chuck it away somewhere?' Gary asked.

'I agree, no one need know; it'll just get really complicated otherwise,' Katy said.

'I agree. Let's make it simple for ourselves,' Joe said.

'Where on earth did you get it?' Victoria asked.

'I took it from my headmaster's office at my old school,' Anthony said.

'Anthony, you're lying,' Susan said.

'It's a long story. Let's get rid of it.'

'Hang on a minute: I saw you throw it away,' Gary said.

'No, I picked up a rock and threw that.'

'Don't tell me that was you firing the gun on Thursday night?' Victoria said incredulous.

'Um, well, Gary was in a bit of a mess. I had no choice,' Anthony said.

'Look, it's over now. Let's find somewhere to dispose of it,' Joe said with finality.

'He beat me,' Anthony said.

'What do you mean?' asked Susan.

'He made me lose control: despite all our preparations he got under my skin and I lost it.'

'Lost it? I think you saved it, Anthony. You're free: he's still there. You came out again. You're safe now, out of harm's way,' Joe said.

'That's right: you went in and faced him; now you're free of him,' Susan said.

'I wouldn't even have gone in,' said Gary.

'God, nor me,' Katy agreed.

They slowed down as the Little Chef appeared on the other side of the road.

'There he is,' Gary pointed.

They all clambered out as Frank walked towards them. Anthony ran up to him and hugged him.

'How did you get on?' Frank asked.

'Come on. I'll tell you all about it.'

They all got in again. This time Joe sat at the front with Victoria; the others clustered together at the back.

After ten minutes, Victoria spoke up.

'OK, everyone pay attention. I am not happy with it — but there is a lake over there. What are my instructions?'

'Let's get rid of it,' Anthony said.

Victoria indicated, and they turned off the main road onto a narrow lane. It twisted and turned through some woods until it came to an end a hundred yards from the expanse of water.

'What is this place?' asked Joe, looking around for signs.

'I think it must be a reservoir: that looks like a pumping station over there,' Victoria said, pointing to the far side.

'Have you got a carrier bag of some kind?' Joe asked.

Victoria reached into her bag, but Gary said, 'I have.'

Joe wrapped the gun in it and put it in his pocket.

'Right: we all get out, we all stroll along the bank, we all throw stones and rocks now and then. Then we talk and decide to have a long-distance throwing competition. Gary, Frank and Anthony, you all find a heavy stone and throw it as far as you can. Then I'll throw the bag. But we keep on throwing for a few more minutes. Everyone clear?'

They clambered out of the bus and walked along the bank, apparently just out for a stroll. One by one they started to throw stones out into the water. Joe nodded to Anthony to start the competition. Taking it in turns, they threw stones as far as possible.

Joe said, 'OK, find a nice big one now,' and got ready to take out the bag.

The three boys hunted for and picked up large rocks and were ready to hurl them when Anthony said, 'Wait, Joe, I've got something.'

He twisted his mother's wedding ring from his finger and handed it to Joe.

'Can you put that in the bag too?'

'Sure?'

'Yes.'

Joe nodded to Gary who ran up and threw his rock high and far into the water; then Frank, then Anthony, and finally Joe. The four objects sploshed heavily into the still water.

Anthony watched the spreading ripples. He pictured the bag sinking to the bottom of the lake. He pictured his mother's face, her downcast expression replaced by a hopeful smile. He thought of his father's face: nausea overwhelmed him; he fell to his knees and was sick. Wiping his mouth on his sleeve, he straightened up and took in a lungful of fresh air.

He turned to his friends and grinned. 'No need for these awful trousers anymore,' he said and, hopping from foot to foot, took off his baggies to reveal his school trousers underneath. He rolled up the discarded trousers and flung them with all his might into the water.

***

Anthony sat at the back of the minibus, next to the window, Susan beside him, the others all around. He had tried to be chatty and upbeat, clever and confident, but deep within he felt beaten and abused. He gradually became silent; everyone was.

'Are you all right?' Susan whispered to him.

He opened his eyes and looked into hers. He nodded and smiled. He felt her take his hand and he squeezed it tight.

'What a peculiar day,' he said.

She nodded.

He felt her move close against him, her thigh against his. It felt wonderful. He rested his hand on his leg and let his fingers graze against her thigh. She didn't move. He pressed his calf against hers. They sat like that in silence, close and intimate. After a long time, Anthony said, 'Thank you. You are such a lovely girl.'

'You're not bad yourself.'

'What do you see in me, Susan?'

Susan thought for a moment, 'You're clever, brave, funny, different to everyone else and, believe it or not, you're quite good looking.'

'Really?' Anthony asked, surprised.

'Really.'

'That's what I think about you, except that I think you're absolutely beautiful.'

She smiled, 'That's very sweet of you, thank you.'

'Will you come back to my place?' Anthony asked Susan.

'Just for a minute. I've got to talk to Katy. I think she rang her mother today.'

'Ah, of course. Well just for a minute would be great,' Anthony said, a bit disappointed.

Soon they pulled into the school car park.

'Who's coming to London tomorrow?' Victoria called to them.

'Why?'

'We're off to London. Katy has a project,' Victoria said.

Everyone turned to Katy.

'I'm going to meet my mum, my real mum,' she explained simply.

Susan looked at her for explanation.

'I'll tell you in a minute,' Katy said.

'Thank you so much for everything,' Anthony said to Victoria.

They all called their thanks to her.

'Listen, will you take my phone number, in case there is any change of plan?' she said.

They all jotted down her number and slowly walked away.

'She's so nice, isn't she?' Anthony said to the others.

'Yeah, she is. We had a great time when you were inside,' Gary said.

'She is nice. It's such a shame she's a headmistress. She could have been something much nicer,' Katy said.

'Like what?' Susan asked.

'I don't know something more enjoyable — for her, I mean.'

'I think she probably does enjoy doing her job,' Frank said.

'Funny thing to enjoy though, don't you think?' Katy said.

'Actually, I'd like to be a teacher,' said Susan.

'You would! You're always telling me that I'm wrong,' Katy pointed out.

'That's because you are always wrong,' Susan replied.

'I think you're all right, Katy,' Gary said, then blushed.

'Hmm, that's not much of a vote of confidence,' Katy said but looked pleased.

They reached Anthony's house. They said goodbye.

'Are you coming in for a minute?' Anthony asked Susan.

'Five minutes only,' she answered, then: 'See you in a split second, young lady,' she called to Katy. Katy waved two fingers and walked away.

'She's funny; you're both really funny,' Anthony said as he unlocked the front door.

'Is that you, dear?' Margaret Alexander called.

'Yes, Mother.'

Anthony and Susan walked into the sitting room. They sat down either side of Mrs Alexander. She looked tired and sad.

'How did it go?' she asked.

'It was fine, Mother, it was fine. He was the same. We didn't really talk much; we only had five minutes together. I told him to stop writing. He didn't say much. I don't know that he'll take any notice, but we tried.'

'Well done for trying. I knew you'd do your best.'

'He did, Mrs Alexander, he really did,' Susan said.

'Thank you.'

'Would you like a cup of tea?' he asked his mother.

'No, I'm fine, I'm fine.'

Anthony looked at his mother's face. He wanted to make everything all right for her, but he didn't know how. He had failed today, despite his efforts. He had failed miserably. He sighed.

'I'm just going to get a couple of books for Susan.'

They got up and went into his room. He felt suddenly shy and self-conscious alone with Susan in his bedroom. He sat awkwardly on his bed.

'May I sit down?' she asked.

'I am sorry. Of course: please sit down.'

He moved to the end of the bed; she sat down next to him, demure, her hands in her lap. He felt jittery. There was a ticking clock in his head. He only had a minute or two and the seconds were disappearing fast.

He said, 'I'm not very experienced with girls, you know.'

'I'm not with boys,' she answered.

Anthony realised something: he hadn't considered that Susan Walker, someone that he looked up to and admired so much, might be nervous too. He felt his confidence rise. He took her hand and held it gently.

'Thank you for being so fantastic,' he said.

She looked into his eyes.

'That's a very good starting point. Do continue.'

He reached towards her and ran his fingers through her hair.

'You've got beautiful hair. I'm so envious.'

'Your hair is nice too, as kitchen scourers go,' she said smiling.

'You have a lovely smile too.'

'So, have you.'

'Don't I look like a tosser?'

'No, you're handsome.'

'Why did everyone always say I was a wanker, a tosser, a shit, a bender, a bastard, a fucking this and a fucking that?'

'Because boys are idiots and they were probably jealous of you,' she said.

'Really?'

She nodded.

'Susan, I want to kiss you, but I don't know how to go about it: what's your advice?'

'Just do it,' she said.

Anthony moved nearer. His head swam. Then, leaning close, he let his lips find hers. He put his arm around her and pulled her towards him. He felt her hand on his shoulder and they kissed.

Anthony tried to get his head around what was happening. It felt so wonderful: to have a beautiful, intelligent girl willingly kiss him. He drew back slightly and looked at Susan: she was lovely.

'I know you have to go but, before you go, tell me honestly: do you really like me?'

'I do. I honestly do. Do you like me?'

'Oh, I do. I definitely and completely and absolutely do, Susan. You're a million dollars.' Anthony felt tears run down his face as he smiled.

***

That night, Anthony's dreams were full of mixed up images from the day. His father's face, twisted with derision and fury, kept appearing in the most incongruous of settings. He lurched from sleep to complete wakefulness when he realised that he was ardently kissing his father in the back of the minibus on the way home from the prison. He got up and went out. As he walked along the dark streets, he thought about how his life had changed over the last few months. He could hardly remember the years of misery he had endured at school and home. His life now was so different. He saw the Anthony Alexander of yesterday as a character in a book, someone he'd been observing rather than being. Everything had changed: he had friends; he had a girlfriend. He had grown taller; his voice had broken; he looked like a tough teenager not a skinny little posh boy. His father was gone — he couldn't come back and ruin things. He was sad about his mother though. He wondered what he could do to help her. His life had changed for the better, much, much better: surely it was time for things to improve for her too?

He thought about the day ahead. He couldn't wait to see Susan again, but he knew that today was Katy's day and she'd need Susan close to her at all times. He felt sad for Frank too. When they'd picked him up at the Little Chef, he'd seemed depressed. Something had happened — or maybe something hadn't happened. He had tried to get Frank to say how it had gone but he'd just said it was all right. Anthony knew that Frank wouldn't talk if he didn't want to. He made a mental note to spend time with Frank today, to give him as much encouragement as possible. He looked up to Frank; he wanted him to be a hero again.

Anthony loved his group of friends. He smiled as he thought of Gary, once his absolute nemesis. He remembered the trip to Fosters to buy his baggies. He thought about how Gary had stayed throughout the whole event, even though he must have been so embarrassed to be with him. He was close to Gary's house now. He crossed over and turned the corner, pausing outside number 45. It was quiet, dark, no sign of life. He thought back to the events of two nights ago. He shuddered. That had been terrible: he would have shot Gary's father, if it hadn't been for Gary's mother; he would definitely have shot him. He closed his eyes and thought about the difference a split second could make.

He speeded up and walked quickly home. He wanted to be on good form for the others today; he was determined to pull his weight, just as they had for him.

Katy

Katy's heart had been hammering when she'd made the call to her mother. She'd been rehearsing what she was going to say the whole of the journey to Lewes. When she'd got into the telephone box down the side road off the main shopping street, she'd gone blank. She put her hand on her chest and felt the thudding. She closed her eyes and counted to ten, trying to slow down her breathing. It worked. She got her 10p coins at the ready and rang the number.

'Hello?' said the stranger's voice.

Katy tried to think of something to say. She couldn't.

'Hello,' the voice said again, patient, quiet.

'It's Katy.'

'Oh, I wondered if it might be.'

'Yes.'

'Well, hello, Katy. I'm Jane.'

Katy wanted to hear the voice some more. It was a lovely voice, soft and husky.

'Hello,' Katy said, feeling like a little girl.

'You're brave — for ringing I mean,' the voice said.

'Are you really my mother?'

'Yes, I'm your mother.'

'Are you sure?'

'Yes. It's lovely talking to you, Katy; you sound so grown up.'

Katy fed another coin into the box.

'Would you like to meet one day?' Jane asked, tentative.

'Yes, but I'm a bit scared to.'

'Me too.'

They were silent for a long time.

Then Katy blurted out, 'How about tomorrow?'

There was a pause then, 'Ah, well, I'm a bit busy but, yes, that would be OK if it's in the morning.'

'It doesn't matter — another time,' Katy said, feeling embarrassed. Had she sounded too keen?

'No, tomorrow is fine. Can you get to central London?'

'Yes, I can get the tube there; it's easy.'

'OK. Do you mind meeting in a public place?'

Katy paused. She wasn't sure. She wasn't sure about anything. She said, 'That's fine.'

'All right, I shall see you at a café on Wardour Street — it's called the Black Flamingo — at midday: is that all right?'

'Yes.'

There was an awkward silence then Katy said, 'Jane?'

'Yes?'

'I want to meet you, but I won't stop loving my parents. You know that, don't you?'

'Yes, I understand, Katy; I do.'

'I want my sister to come too, is that OK?'

'Sure, whatever you want.'

The pips went again. Katy put in another 10p but didn't know what else to say.

'OK, bye, then,' she said and put the phone down, hearing the stranger saying goodbye at the other end.

Katy rested her head on the cool window of the phone box. She wanted to meet her mother, but she couldn't help wondering if she was sneaking behind her parents' backs. She picked up the phone.

'Hi, Mum, it's me.'

'Everything all right?' Anna said, in a worried voice.

'Yeah, everything's fine. Um, I just wanted to let you know that I've just spoken to Jane. We're meeting in London tomorrow.'

Katy heard her mother sigh, then she said, 'Thank you for telling us, Katy. Is Susan going with you?'

'She better had.'

***

Katy peered out of her bedroom window waiting for Susan to get back from Anthony's house. When she'd come in from the Lewes trip, she'd had a cup of tea with John and Anna. There was a tenseness about them. She had tried to lighten the mood, but it hadn't worked. She knew they were trying to be the loving, decent parents they had always been. She understood, though, that her going to meet Jane was a huge risk to everything they held dear. Although she was excited about the meeting tomorrow, right now she was just feeling guilty.

'Who's going with you tomorrow?' John had asked.

'We're all going Susan, Frank, Gary, Anthony, Miss Court and Joe,' Katy answered.

'I know it's probably not what you want, but I'd be happy to come along with you, you know, just for support,' he said.

'Thanks, Dad, we'll be all right.'

'What did you think of her?' he asked.

'I don't know; it's hard to tell. She seemed nice.'

'Do you think she understood what she's doing?' Anna asked.

'I think so. She was kind of quiet and gentle, I suppose. She seemed understanding.'

'Did she say anything about who your father is?' John asked.

'Look, you know how I feel. You're my father, Dad, and, Mum, you're my mum. The only thing is that there is someone else who is relevant, but she's not my mum. That's how I feel about it.'

Anna's and John's faces cleared a bit.

'Let's all have dinner together tonight, just us. What do you think?' Anna had said.

'That's exactly what I want,' Katy said.

Susan came up the stairs and flopped down on the bed. 'What a day,' she said.

'I know. Everything about it has been topsy-turvy. How is Anthony?' Katy asked, biding her time before broaching the big issue.

'I think he's all right. He's unusual, Katy. There's something different about him. He's got this strong mentality; I think that's it. What would get some people down makes him even stronger. You wouldn't think so to look at him, but he is a really strong person.'

'He's great, Suzy. I think you and he are great together, both tough as old boots. Poor Frank seemed down in the dumps though.'

'Yeah, I don't think his day went the way he wanted. He went into his shell again, didn't he?' Then, 'Come on, Katy, we can talk about Frank later. What's she like then?'

'Well, it's hard to say. She's got a husky voice. She's a Londoner. I thought she was nice, but it's hard to tell over the phone. Anyway, I was so nervous.'

'So, is she famous?' Susan asked.

'I don't know; she didn't say.'

'Ah, hmmm, so maybe she isn't World Famous then.'

'OK, you win I didn't think she would be famous really. I was just dreaming.'

'Was she friendly, though.'

'Very, she sounded nice, she really did.'

'Did you tell Mum and Dad you're seeing her?'

'Yeah. They were a bit cranky, but I think they're just glad that I told them.'

'It must be so hard for them,' Susan said.

Katy heard the tiniest wobble in her sister's voice. She sat next to her and said, 'And for you too?'

Susan sighed, nodding.

'But you're coming tomorrow though, aren't you? I can't do it without you.'

'Of course. I'm hardly going to let you out on your own, am I?'

504

'Come on, let's go downstairs. *Starsky and Hutch* is on soon,' Katy said jumping up.

***

Katy did not sleep well. She felt so many emotions, all at the same time, and all of them messy. She was very excited about meeting Jane but was incredibly nervous too. What if she just didn't like her? She wanted her birth mother to be beautiful, clever, talented, successful, generous, kind and dazzling. Katy knew that it was perfectly possible that she wasn't any of those things. She also had a strong premonition that whatever happened would mean a massive shift in her life, in her relationships with Susan, her parents and herself. She didn't know in what way; she just had a sense that her life was about to change forever.

What was troubling her the most, though, was trying to prepare herself for the meeting. She wanted to see Jane, but from a distance, so that she could get a sense of her mother before actually engaging with her. She didn't know what to say to her. She wanted to know about her father but didn't yet know her mother in any meaningful way. She wanted to look great, to make her mother feel proud of her. But she didn't want to look showy either: she wanted to appear casual, as if she didn't really care what her mother thought of her.

Until now she hadn't given any thought to her mother's everyday life. Did she have a husband? Any children? Did she, Katy, have any brothers and sisters — or maybe she had uncles and aunts and cousins?

Again, she put her hand on her heart and felt it pounding. She looked at the digital clock next to the bed: 05.23.

'Are you asleep?' she whispered.

'Not anymore.'

'I've been awake for hours.'

'I'm not surprised.'

'I'm a bag of nerves.'

'Me too.'

'I don't know if I can go through with it.'

'That's all right. You don't have to you know.'

505

'I'm going to, though. I'll be all right once we're off.'

'I know.'

'I like the drama of it — it's just the tension that's freaking me out.'

'You can't have one without the other.'

'I know.'

'You should talk to Joe. He's good at handling things. Anthony said he couldn't have gone through with yesterday without Joe being, well, being there.'

'I will. He'll help me; but you'll help me too, won't you?'

'Of course, you dimmo.'

'Do you know what scares me the most?' Katy asked, clutching Susan's arm.

'What?'

'That I might really love her, or, I might really hate her.

'I know. I thought that too. But you can't really love or hate someone after a first meeting. Think of tomorrow as just meeting someone at a bus stop, or in a shop.'

'Yeah, that makes sense. You're right; you're always right.'

'Except when I'm wrong.'

Katy shut her eyes. She thought of all the times Susan had got her out of trouble. She squeezed Susan's hand as tight as she could. Susan squeezed back.

***

Katy, Susan, Anna and John had all hugged each other at the door. As the girls walked down the garden path, Anna had called: 'Be safe.' Katy turned around and ran back to her mother and father and hugged them again.

When they'd met the others at the minibus, Katy had asked, 'Joe, can I sit next to you?'

'Funny, I was going to ask you that,' he said.

As they drove off, Katy thought about what to ask Joe. She wanted him to say something that would settle her nerves, help her prepare.

'It must be hard to take it all in, isn't it?' he said.

'Yes, it is; it's all so strange. Ever since I learned that I had a mother who wasn't my mother, it's all been hard to come to terms with — impossible really.'

'What do you know about her?'

'Not much. She's in her thirties. She said she'd had some tough times but that she's coming through them now. She didn't say anything about who my father was, only that he was an older man, he was married, and that he's a nice man.'

'And how are you feeling about meeting her?'

'Really, really mixed up. I've got so many feelings all hitting me at the same time.'

'I'm not surprised.'

'Joe?'

'Yes?'

'Will you do some of your magic on me, to make me feel in control? Well, at least not out of control?'

Joe smiled, 'Oh, Katy, I can't do magic. I wish I could.'

'Well, not magic — just say something wise then.'

'You're the wise one, Katy: you know all about what's important to you.'

Katy laughed. 'Me, wise? I wish.'

'Seriously, if you were talking to Katy now, I bet you would be very wise, very helpful, wouldn't you?'

'But I can't separate myself from myself, that's the trouble. I need Susan to be my sensible self, or you.'

'Well, I think you could do it too. Why don't you try?'

'How?'

'Well, I shall try and be you: you talk to me as if I'm you.'

'All right, you go first: what do you want to say?' Katy said.

'Well, the thing is, I'm going to meet my real mum. I'm excited, nervous, scared; I'm intrigued to know about her, but I'm worried about what she's like. Also, I'm still really upset that she's even got in touch: she's trampling all over my life and the people in my life that I love. I want to hug her, swear at her, cry, laugh, just say nothing, not stop talking

507

— everything. I honestly don't know what to do or say or how to be. What shall I do, Katy?' Joe said in a rush.

Katy looked into Joe's face. He had sounded like her. He had told her what was in her head. She shook her head.

'Katy, what should I do?' he said again.

'Well, what can you do?' she asked him.

'I don't know it's all too much.'

Katy thought for a minute.

'What makes you think you should be doing anything?' she asked.

'Well, I think I should be preparing myself for what is going to happen, but I don't know what is going to happen. I can only think of what might happen, and how I might be, might feel, what I might think, or say. I want to feel everything in the best way — be on top of things feel in control, enjoy the moment and, well, I think I want to experience it as if I'm a character in a book, with time to live it all in slow motion. Does that make sense?'

'Yes, it does, very much so,' Katy said.

Joe said, 'Is it possible though?'

'What: possible to deal with everything, understand everything, be aware of everything?' Katy asked.

'Exactly. I want to be able to be, well, in control of myself, and of what happens, but I know I'm going to be all over the place. Katy, help me. How am I going to cope with it?' Joe asked.

'I suppose you've just got to relax and let it happen,' Katy said.

'How, though, when I'm feeling so mixed up?'

Katy thought about this. She tried to think how someone else might manage, someone thoughtful and capable, someone she admired. Joe was watching her, waiting for her answer.

'What would you do, Joe?' she asked finally.

'I'm Katy: what would you do, Joe?' he said.

'I think I'd just accept that it's hard and relax. I can't do anything except be me, and just let happen whatever happens.'

'Ah, the Doris Day approach?'

'What?' Katy said, confused.

'Que sera, sera: whatever will be will be.'

'Oh, that old thing,' Katy said.

'But you think that's what I should do, though: just let it happen — have no expectations, no plans — just relax?' Joe asked.

'Yes, that's right.'

'Will you sing it to me?' Joe asked.

'Why?'

'It will help me remember,' Joe said.

'All right.'

Katy sang the chorus quietly, but Joe shook his head.

'So, everyone can hear,' he said.

Katy sat up and sang the old classic loudly.

Everyone had turned around to look at her, except Victoria who watched in the mirror. When Katy had finished, they all applauded, Joe clapping the loudest beside her.

'Will you be Joe again now?' Katy asked.

'Yes, although I enjoyed being you. You're a good person to be.'

'Do you think so?' Katy said, looking pleased.

'Of course, I wouldn't say it otherwise.' Joe went on, 'So, this is how I see it. You have your friends supporting you. You have your parents caring for you and loving you. You have a strategy for dealing with what is going to come up — just letting go and accepting whatever will be will be. You know we all have a very high regard for you. Tell me, how do you feel right now?'

'OK. Yeah, I feel OK.'

'So, we need a code word for you to remember, a word that when you think of it, or say it, or if someone else says it, you will feel how you feel now. What word do you want to have available?'

'What sort of word?'

'A word that means something to you, that sums up everything good — a word that reminds you that you're talented, intelligent, bright, kind and funny, strong and resilient; a word that reminds you that you feel in control.'

'Will Doris be a good word?'

'Tell me what Doris means to you, Katy.'

509

'It makes me feel warm and safe. It makes me feel that everything is all right.'

'OK, Doris it is.'

Joe took out a pen and tore off a piece of paper from a little notebook and wrote, 'Doris = safe, secure, fun, strong, talented, kind, bright and beautiful, in control, — whatever will be will be.'

He sketched something at the bottom of the page and handed it to her.

'Keep this safe; have it ready. Hold it tight whenever you need a reminder.'

Katy nodded and folded it carefully and put it in her jacket pocket.

'Thanks, Joe, I will.'

***

Victoria drove down Wardour Street. It was quiet.

'There it is,' she called out as they went past the café. She parked a few yards further down the street.

Katy drew in a deep breath and got up. They all got out and stood beside the minibus.

'OK?' Joe asked Katy.

'Yes, all fine: Doris and I are fine.'

'What do you want, Katy? Do you want to meet her alone? I'll come in if you want; we can all come in if you want,' Susan said, standing close to her.

'I'm all right. I think I want to do this on my own. Don't be far away though, will you?'

'Don't worry we'll all be nearby — just come out and we'll be there.'

'Good luck, Katy. You'll be fine, I know,' Victoria said, giving her a hug.

They all wished her well. Susan embraced her, trying not to cry.

'Whatever happens we're still sisters,' she said, pressing her face against Katy's.

'I know. Don't worry,' Katy said reassuring her, and herself.

Katy entered the Black Flamingo and went straight to the toilets. She sat on the toilet lid and counted to ten. She pulled out her folded-up paper and studied it for a minute, memorising the words. She saw that Joe had drawn a little guitar with notes flying out of it. She smiled and quietly hummed the tune. She examined herself in the mirror. She smiled, pouted, opened her mouth wide, closed it again. She took a brush out of her bag and buffed up her long dark hair. She carefully put on some dark lipstick. She liked what she saw. Breathing deeply one more time she went back into the café.

'Whadda you like, senorita?' the elderly waitress asked.

'A cup of tea, please,' Katy answered.

She sat at the very back of the café with a clear view of the door. She opened her piece of paper again and kept her concentration on it. She hummed the tune once more. She heard the door open and looked up. Two men walked in and sat down near her. One of them winked at her; she looked away.

Her tea arrived. She sipped it, nervous.

She looked at her watch: it was twelve o'clock. The door opened and in walked a middle-aged woman. She had greying hair, was wearing a shabby coat, old jeans and, to Katy's eyes, she looked a bit rough. She looked at Katy for a second then sat down near the door. Katy sighed with relief.

Five minutes went by and Katy was beginning to fret. She looked out of the window and saw the school minibus drive by. On the side window was a large white sheet of paper with DORIS written in big, black capitals. She smiled.

The door opened several times and people came in and went out. Every time she heard the rattle of the door handle, she felt her heart miss a beat.

Again, the door opened. This time a youngish woman came in. She was smartly dressed, glamorous. She had nicely brushed hair, was wearing make-up and looked confident. Katy caught her eye and smiled at her. The woman smiled back but didn't come over. Instead she sat down a couple of tables away. Katy sighed with disappointment. She looked at her watch again: it was ten past.

The two men got up to go. The one who had winked came over to her and said, 'On your own love?'

'No, I'm waiting for my mother,' Katy said in a clipped voice.

'Well, while you're waiting, we can get to know each other.'

'On your bike, mate,' she said.

'Charming! You don't mean that, do you?'

'Yes, she does,' the grey-haired woman said, and got up to join them. Katy looked into the woman's face and knew it was her.

'Bye, lads,' the woman said, and sat down opposite Katy.

'Pity, we could have had some fun together,' the bloke said and swaggered out.

Katy sat across from her mother and stared at her. She saw a stranger looking back, but someone incredibly familiar.

'I'm sorry about that. I lost my nerve,' Jane said.

Katy looked down at her piece of paper. She saw DORIS. She heard the tune in her head.

'That's all right. By the way, I'm Katy.'

She put out her hand, the older woman held it briefly. Katy noticed that her mother's was frail, careworn.

'It's lovely to meet you, Katy. I'm Jane.'

They looked at each other without blinking.

'You look lovely, Katy, you really do.'

'Thank you.'

'I know I don't look great; I'm sorry about that.'

Katy didn't know what to say. She opened her mouth, but Jane said, 'How did you get here?'

'I came up with my friends, in the school bus of all things.'

'Where are they now?'

'Outside somewhere.'

'What about your family, where are they?'

'My sister Susan, she's outside. My mum and dad are at home. They're shitting bricks, I think — oh, sorry, I didn't mean to be...'

Jane smiled.

'I'm sure they're nervous. I'm nervous. Are you?'

'Yes, but not too bad.'

They were silent again.

'So, let's find out about each other: is that all right?' Jane asked.

'Yes, that's what I want to do.'

'Me first then. My name is Jane Davidson. I am thirty-six years old. Both my parents were killed in the war. I grew up in a Barnardo's home. I can hardly remember anything from those days; I think I've blocked it out of my head. I remember it being grey and cold; I don't think I enjoyed anything, except singing. The only thing I ever wanted to do was sing, to be a singer. When I was a teenager, I decided I would go off and become world famous! Silly isn't it? I was terribly headstrong. I wanted everything immediately, especially fame and fortune. I thought I could be a celebrity, someone famous: a superstar. To be absolutely honest I was reckless; I'd do anything to get what I wanted. You probably think I was very foolish?'

Katy was silent; she was beginning to understand her missing half. Jane went on. 'I got a job as a cleaner at the film studios near where you live. I suppose I thought that if I was around the place someone would spot me, would see my talent. No one noticed me, and I became ill: I had depression. I got to be so ill that I had to go into a mental hospital. I was there for a year. When I came out, I was much better, but I didn't have anything. I lived in a hostel.'

Jane stopped and looked down. She had been talking in a small voice; it was hard to hear her. Katy looked away from her mother and saw the minibus drive past again, DORIS clearly visible.

She said, 'Do you want to go on?'

Jane nodded, 'A lovely, kind man helped me find a little flat. I moved in and started all over again. I got a job as an assistant to a photographer and things started to look up. Then, yes, you've guessed it, I became pregnant with you. I'm so sorry, Katy: I know you'll hate me for this, but I knew I couldn't cope. I was so, well, I was very weak, Katy. I could hardly look after myself. I knew I couldn't be a mother. I knew that if I kept you, I would ruin your life too. I can imagine that it's hard to understand but you were my priority and I made myself give you up for adoption. Can you forgive me?'

Katy studied her mother's face. She was looking imploringly at her. Her heart swelled with sympathy for this woman.

'Don't be sad. I think you were very brave.'

'Do you? Do you really? Oh God, if you can forgive me then that would make me so happy, Katy.'

Katy saw tears running down her face. She took in the woman's fragile appearance, her lined face, her pleading look.

'I forgive you. Thank you. Thank you for what you did for me,' she said with a catch in her voice.

Jane pulled out a handkerchief from her pocket and blew her nose.

'What happened next?' Katy asked.

'You were taken away and all I knew was that you would be adopted. I went back to work. I did get to be a singer, but I never became successful, although I loved it and still do. I have had all sorts of jobs — nothing wonderful, just ordinary work. I have had men in my life but no one special. I am really quite unspectacular in every way. The only amazing thing ever to happen to me was to have you; and now you're sitting here in front of me, and I feel as though I have won the Pools.'

Katy looked at her mother. She was a small, faded and unremarkable woman. She looked into her eyes and saw something burning there: she saw her own eyes, her desire, her ambition.

'What sort of things do you sing?' she asked.

'Oh, just ballads, jazz standards, hits from shows, that kind of thing. I just love to sing. I thought I'd be a film star one day, someone special. I soon realised that I didn't have any particular talent, nothing to set me apart from the rest.'

'Where did you sing?'

'Oh, you know, weddings, family parties, the occasional official function.'

'Where do you work now?'

'I work on the bar at a club near here.'

'What's it called?'

'The Phoenix.'

'Is it cool?' Katy asked.

'No, definitely not cool: honestly Katy, there is nothing special in my life. Anyway, I want to know about you: what are you like? What are you good at? What are your plans?'

Katy felt uncomfortable suddenly. She didn't want to talk to this stranger about herself: she felt on safer ground talking about her.

'Jane?' she asked.

'Yes?'

Just then the minibus drove by and she saw DORIS again. She smiled.

'What did you just see?'

'Oh, my friends keep driving past outside. They've got a sign up to remind me how I should be feeling,' Katy said, feeling a bit embarrassed.

'What does it say?'

'It's ridiculous, I know. It says DORIS after Doris Day.'

Jane raised her eyebrows in question.

'To remind me to be relaxed and just accept whatever happens — you know, que sera, sera: whatever will be will be.'

'Oh, that's so sweet.'

Katy nodded.

'Anyway, what were you going to ask?'

'I know it's going to be a difficult subject, but I want to know about my father. How do you feel about that?'

'I can't tell you who he is: I promised myself I never would.'

'OK, I understand that, but what can you tell me about him?' Katy pressed.

'Well, he was very kind to me. He helped me so much. I was incredibly lucky to have met him and I feel bad that things worked out the way they did.'

'You said he was married, in your first letter.'

'Yes. He was married, and I never wanted to break up his marriage, and never thought it was even likely. Things just got a bit complicated and before either of us knew what was happening, I was pregnant. I never expected him to leave his wife. In fact, I never wanted him to; I know he was very happy with her.'

'How did you know him? Was he in the films in some way?'

515

'No, he helped me get myself straight, after coming out of hospital. He looked after me; he was very, very kind.'

'Did you keep in touch with him, after I was born?'

'No, once the decision was taken for you to be adopted that was the end of things between us.'

'But do you resent him — just disappearing?'

'Absolutely not. He was lovely about everything; he could not have been more decent and kinder.'

Katy was quiet. She was trying to work out what she was feeling. She liked this woman. She wasn't the big personality she had been expecting — and hoping for: she was an ordinary person, just as she herself had said. But Katy wanted more. She wanted her father to be special, someone amazing.

'You're wondering something Katy, what is it?'

'Oh, this is going to sound so childish.'

'It's OK: just say it. I don't mind.'

'Well, the thing is, I'm sure I've got something extra, some talent. I thought that either you or my father — you know, birth father — would be stars, in show business. I don't mean anything against you. I hope it doesn't sound critical. I hope I don't sound like I'm disappointed.'

Jane smiled sadly. She nodded.

'Are you talented, Katy?'

'Well, people say I am. I think that perhaps I am. I don't know. I hope I am.'

'What are you good at then?'

'Well, I can sing quite well. I can dance, I can act. I, oh I don't know, maybe I'm just a jumped-up kid who wants to be famous.'

'I guess you're like me. I thought I would be a star one day. My father was famous: your grandfather. I wanted to be like him. He was a very successful singer. He sang with dance bands and orchestras; he was on the radio before the war. He made loads of records. I've got some of them at home.'

'What was his name?' Katy's eyes were shining.

'Sidney Davidson. You won't have heard of him: he's a voice from yesteryear.'

'Was he really famous?'

Jane laughed. 'Yes, he was. I never knew him but, yes, he was very successful. That's why I wanted to be like him, to follow in his footsteps.'

Katy felt a wave of pity for this woman. She had wanted success, stardom, to be famous, but things had worked against her.

'I'm sorry, Jane. You must think I'm very shallow.'

'No, you're just like me, Katy. We're the same: we want to be special. The difference is that you've got something that I haven't got, and never had.'

'What's that?'

'You've got a strong foundation. You've got a family.'

Katy nodded. She did have that, exactly that.

'Has Doris been around again?'

'Not yet; any minute I think.'

'Is your sister in the bus?'

'Yes, her name is Susan.'

'Is she nice?'

'She's amazing. She's very clever, pretty, strong, kind, generous; she'll do anything for me.'

'She sounds wonderful. You're so lucky to have a sister.'

'She is. I am.'

'And your parents?'

'They're great. They're just normal people, nothing special.'

'I know what you mean when you say that, but look at you and Susan: how do you think you got to be so amazing? What would you be like without them?'

Katy swallowed. She knew Jane was right.

'I didn't mean they weren't fantastic, just that they're not, I don't know, not talented. They're just normal people.'

Jane nodded.

'So, you've got no family at all? No other children? No brothers or sisters or cousins or anything?' Katy asked.

'I've got a brother. He's a comedian.'

'Not Jim Davidson?' Katy squealed.

'No, Eric.'

Katy laughed and said, 'OK, I get it. I've got to get a grip! By the way, Doris has just gone by again.'

'Good, I was getting worried about her.'

'Where do you live?' Katy asked.

'Camden.'

'Have you got a boyfriend? Anyone special?'

'No, I am on my own at the moment. How about you?'

'No, no one for me. I'm not bothered about boys really. I'm more interested in my career, whatever that means.'

'You're very beautiful, Katy,' Jane said looking at her directly.

'Thank you. You're lovely too,' Katy said.

'I'm old and done in; but thank you for saying such a nice thing.'

'I mean it — I really do,' Katy said.

Jane looked at her watch. She said, 'I need to go in a minute. I start work at one o'clock.'

'Can we meet again?' Katy asked.

'Yes, if you're sure.'

'I'm sure.'

***

Katy clambered into the minibus and sat down. They were all turned towards her expectantly.

'She's really nice,' she said.

Susan pulled her down on to the seat next to her. 'Was she? You're not just saying that?'

'Yes, she's lovely.'

Victoria started up the engine. 'Where to?' she asked.

'Can we have something to eat please? I'm absolutely starving,' Katy said.

'Where do you want to go?' Susan asked.

'It doesn't matter — anywhere will do.'

They found another café. Katy was full of her meeting with Jane, the others happy that it had gone so well.

'I knew I was related to a superstar,' Katy said.

518

'Sidney Davidson's not exactly Elvis, is he?' Gary said.

'Well, maybe he would have been if he'd lived. Victoria, you're old enough — do you remember Sidney Davidson?'

'Well, thanks very much. No, I don't. I've heard of him though.'

'Me too; I've heard him on the radio,' Joe said.

'See?' Katy said, sticking her fingers up at Gary.

'Let's go home soon. We need to talk to Mum and Dad,' Susan said, feeling the heavy weight of responsibility.

After their lunch Katy asked, 'Whilst we're here, can we find a club called the Phoenix?'

'We don't have to find it, it's there,' Anthony said, pointing.

'Really? Oh, yes. Come on,' Katy said, turning down the dark alleyway.

'Katy, I'm not sure it's the place for us,' Joe said.

'Why not?'

She retraced her steps and looked at the sign on the corner of the alley and read out loud, 'The Phoenix Club, Cocktails, Exotic Dancing and Adult Performance.'

Everyone was silent. They looked at Katy.

'She works behind the bar. Come on, I want to see.'

She walked purposefully down the alley towards the door of The Phoenix.

'Are you sure?' Susan asked, catching her up.

'She's lovely, Susan. I want to see her again. I want you to meet her, for her to meet you.'

They all followed her inside. They were met by a large man wearing a tuxedo.

'Are you members?' he asked, barring their way.

'No, we're just here to see a friend,' Katy explained.

'Well, you have to be a member to come in here.'

'How much is it to be a member?'

'One pound for a day, five for a month, twenty for the year.'

They stood in the foyer, uncertain. Katy could hear music in the distance and the sound of glasses clinking.

Katy looked at Joe. He shrugged. She looked at Susan. She shook her head. They heard the amplified voice of a compere, 'Ladies and gentlemen, she's back again, from Las Vegas. It's the wonderful, the sassy, the gooooooorrrrrgggggggeeeeeooooouuuuussssss Miss Mimi Mistral!'

'On your way, love, this isn't your kind of place,' the bouncer said.

'Don't talk to me like that, you ape,' Katy snapped, frustrated.

'Hang on, Katy, let me have a word,' Joe said.

Katy stepped back as Joe spoke quietly to the doorman who was shaking his head. Joe carried on talking and counted out some money.

'You're all over eighteen?' the bouncer said without interest.

'Definitely,' Joe said and led the way through into the bar.

As they went through the swing doors into the bar, they heard the singer launch into 'Love for sale'. They stood still, watching and listening to the singer. She had long chestnut hair, vivid make-up, a crimson velvet dress. She moved elegantly around the stage; she had a sensuous, deep, beautiful voice. They were captivated.

'Oh my God,' said Katy, and started to cry.

***

The dimly lit bar was almost empty. There were a couple of men sitting on their own at the bar. In front of the stage were small tables with two or three chairs around them, all facing the stage. No one was there. Jane and the pianist didn't seem to notice they carried on regardless.

Katy was spellbound. They all were. Jane had a stunning voice. Katy knew her exotic and glamorous appearance was a fiction, but it didn't matter she was a professional, a true performer. Katy felt that every song her mother sang was in some way directed to her, although she knew this couldn't be true as they were sitting in the bar area, well away from the stage. In any event, Jane was in another world, unaware of her seedy surroundings.

As they sat listening, they noticed that people were beginning to drift in, all of them men.

'She's wonderful, Katy, but this place is giving me the creeps,' Susan said.

Jane came to the end of 'Somewhere over the rainbow' and, bowing to the few single men now occupying the front tables, she walked off the stage.

The pseudo-American compere leered, 'That was the lovely, the beautiful and so, so sexy Mimi Mistral. Now, gentlemen, let's get this show on the road. Yes, she's back, she's London's top performer, especially with snakes, yes, that's right — snakes: it's Monterey Python.'

There were a few jeers as well as cheers and loud, bass music started to pump around the club. Seconds later, Monterey stepped on to the stage.

'OK, time to go,' said Susan and Victoria in unison.

'We can stay a bit longer, surely,' Anthony said looking longingly at the wiggling, wobbling figure on the stage.

'Yeah, we can stay a few minutes, can't we?' Gary said.

'We're off,' Victoria said and began to gather them all up.

Katy got up and attracted a few whistles.

'Aren't you staying, darling?' said a fat little man with wire-rimmed glasses.

'What, and watch you wank yourself; you mean?' Katy said. Then, remembering her headmistress, slapped her hand over her mouth and turned to Victoria.

'Well fuck off then, you little cock-tease,' said the fat man.

Frank stepped across and said, quiet menace in his voice, 'What did you say?'

He looked up at Frank and swallowed nervously. 'Nothing, son, nothing, it was a mistake.'

'Come on, you lot. Out. Now. You've had your bit of fun,' the bouncer said pushing them towards the door.

Frank stood still. He didn't like being pushed around. He looked the bouncer squarely in the face.

'Come on, Frank, let's go; let's get some fresh air,' Joe said. He put his hand on Frank's shoulder and steered him towards the steps out.

The bouncer said, 'Don't bring them back. That's it: no more.'

Joe nodded and followed Frank out.

They gathered on the pavement in the pale spring sunshine. Katy looked at the sign they'd seen earlier. There was a selection of photos, each one showing a sexy, scantily clad young woman. At the bottom was a picture of her mother holding a microphone, smiling brightly, looking fabulous. Katy stood in front of the sign, smiling back at her mother.

'Can we go home now?' Victoria asked.

'Yes, let's go. I'm exhausted,' Joe said.

They piled back into the minibus and set off.

'What was she like in the café, though? Not like that, surely?' Susan asked, as the minibus picked up speed.

'She's nothing like her. The difference is amazing. Jane's like a little bird, really: quiet and much older than I thought she'd be. Although she's much younger than Mum, she looks older.'

'What's happened to her, do you think?'

'She's had a hard life; things didn't work out for her.'

'And, did she mention who your father is, or was?'

'No. All she said was that he was very kind, that he helped her, that they didn't have any contact once I was adopted. But, Suzy, the point is that I was right: I have got it in my genes. You heard her. She's got talent too, hasn't she? You thought she was good, didn't you?'

Susan smiled, 'Yes, she was fantastic; she really was.'

'Did you think she was fantastic?' she said to the others.

They all nodded and looked impressed. Katy smiled delightedly.

'Thanks, everyone — thanks for today. It's been brilliant.'

Gary

Gary hadn't been sure what was expected when Joe had asked him to look after Frank. In fact, sitting next to Frank had made him feel nervous. What was he supposed to do if Frank went off on one? Still he wasn't going to let anyone down and as it turned out Frank had seemed very relaxed.

As they had driven along, Victoria Court had done all the talking. She had asked him about his article, what he'd thought of the Kipling poem; what he wanted to do when he left school; what he liked doing in his spare time. She was really nice, very friendly. She'd talked to Frank too, but not so much. Frank seemed happy just to sit in silence.

Most of the time, though, they had listened to Kenny Everett on the radio. That had been great: it was a helpful distraction from the tension he was feeling — he guessed they all were. Every now and then he'd glanced back at Anthony to see how he was. He looked edgy: chatty one minute, silent the next. One time he'd looked at him and he looked like he might be crying; then he saw Susan holding his hand. She was such a nice girl — kind and gentle; although he had to admit that he was a bit nervous of her.

Gary couldn't help himself glancing back towards Katy now and then too. She spent the whole time staring out of the window daydreaming. She joined in with the songs and laughed out loud at some of the stuff that Kenny Everett was saying but she didn't join in with any of the conversations on the bus. He couldn't help fancying Katy. Despite everything, especially that awful night in the bus shelter, he really liked her. He knew that she was way above him and wouldn't look at him twice, but he couldn't stop himself dreaming. He thought back to what had nearly happened with Tina yesterday. He couldn't deny the fact that she was sexy but compared to Katy she was just a scrubber.

The thing that occupied Gary's mind the most, though, was how amazing it was to be able to see so well. He hadn't realised how bad his sight was until he'd tried his glasses on the other day. Now everything seemed so clear. The detail he could see as they drove along was incredible. He was extremely self-conscious of his glasses, but no one had laughed at him and he was beginning to wonder if it might be possible to wear them all the time. Then he thought about what his dad and brothers would say, and Steve and the rest, and instinctively reached to take them off. As soon as he did, the world blurred over. He replaced them: it re-materialized.

'They take some getting used to, don't they?' Victoria said.

'Yeah, they're good; I just hate looking like a total prat,' he said.

'You don't,' Frank said.

'Well, a toe-rag then,' Gary said.

'Have you tried reading with them?' Victoria asked.

'Yeah, they help they make a big difference.'

'Well, maybe you'll get used to them and people will get used to you wearing them?'

'Don't hold your breath,' Gary said.

'See you later,' Gary had briefly said to Frank as he had left them at the Little Chef. Gary liked Frank a lot. There was something reassuring about him. He now felt a bit awkward sitting on his own with Victoria though. He didn't know what to say to her: she was the headmistress after all.

'I'm going into the town centre when Anthony is with his father; do you want to come?' she'd asked him.

'Ah — well — no. I'll probably stay and wait.'

When they'd reached the prison car park, Gary looked at the bleak scene in front of them. He peered around at Anthony. He looked pale and nervous.

As Anthony walked in through the gates, Gary said to Victoria, 'Um, can I go into town with you?'

'Of course. Katy is coming along too.'

'Oh, I didn't know.'

'Don't worry, I've got some business to do,' Katy said.

So, Joe and Susan sat in the visitors' waiting room, and Victoria, Katy and Gary drove off into Lewes. When they got there, Katy said, 'You can drop me off anywhere. I'll see you back here in thirty minutes. Is that all right?'

'Yes, we've got some business to do too, haven't we, Gary?' Victoria said.

'Have we?'

'Come on, let's go,' she said.

'Where are we going?' asked Gary trailing in her wake.

'Did you know I wore contact lenses?' she asked.

'No?'

'Well, I have done for a couple of years now; we could see if we could get some for you.'

'But, don't they hurt?'

'No. Anyway you get used to them really quickly.'

'I'm not sure.'

'Come on, keep up,' she called and walked quicker.

They stopped outside an opticians. Victoria looked inside. She turned to Gary, 'Want to give it a go?'

Gary peered inside. He looked at Victoria; she turned to face him.

'Can you tell I'm wearing them?' she asked.

He looked carefully: maybe her eyes were a bit shiny?

'It's hard to tell,' he admitted.

'That's it. Come on, let's see.'

They went in. The receptionist said, 'May I help you?'

'Yes, my son would like to try out contact lenses.'

'Well, I can make an appointment for you. When would you like to come in?'

'Well, it's a bit difficult. I'm away a lot of the time and I really want to be here with him; you understand, don't you?' Victoria smiled sweetly at the woman.

'I see. Well, if you could wait for a few minutes it might be possible to have a word with Mr Kelsey; he's our contact lens specialist. He has someone with him right now, but he might be able to squeeze you in.'

'Lovely. We'll wait.'

'Here you are, dear. Let's sit down over here,' she took Gary's arm and helped him gingerly onto a chair. 'He's very delicate, you see,' Victoria explained to the receptionist, who smiled kindly at Gary.

Gary scowled at the receptionist. He felt Victoria nudge him. He bowed his head, assuming the role of a delicate child.

Forty minutes later, they emerged from Mr Kelsey's consulting room. Gary's eyes felt weird to him, as though he had a brick tucked under each eyelid.

'These are just trial lenses: you'll need to get some made specially if you decide you want to wear them all the time,' the optician explained.

Victoria paid for them and they walked back to the minibus together. When they left, Gary winked at the receptionist, openly gawped at her chest and swaggered out of the shop.

'What do you think?' Victoria asked.

'I think I could get used to them; they're not great, but not terrible,' he acknowledged.

'I liked you in your glasses, but at least now you've got a choice,' she said.

Gary kept glancing at himself in shop windows. He looked OK, he thought.

'What have you done with your glasses?' Katy said as they arrived back at the bus.

'No more *Joe 90* for me,' Gary said smiling. 'I'm wearing contacts.'

Katy looked at him, 'Oh, well you look all right; for you.'

'Blimey, that's a compliment, coming from you,' he said.

'You're looking very cheerful, Katy. What's happened?' Victoria asked, noticing Katy's air of excitement.

'I'll tell you later. Let's get back to Anthony before he gets out,' she said.

The three of them sat in the front of the minibus as they sped back to the prison.

Gary had enjoyed himself. Being with Victoria had been a good laugh and she'd sorted out the contact lenses just like that! Now, sat next to Katy, he was feeling better in himself than he had for as long as he could remember. He wondered if he could ask her out. Knowing her, she'd probably just make a joke of it, but maybe it was worth a try? As they approached the prison, though, their moods dropped. They pulled up as far from the prison entrance as possible; Joe and Susan walked out to them.

'No glasses?' Joe asked.

'Contacts,' Gary explained.

'Nice one,' Joe said.

***

Gary saw Frank waiting in the car park of the Little Chef. He waved to him. They all poured out of the minibus to greet him. Anthony ran up and hugged him, Katy and Susan were next. Gary couldn't help himself pounding him on the back.

'You OK, mate?' he asked when they'd all calmed down.

'Yeah, everything's fine,' Frank said, he sounded a bit flat.

Frank looked at Gary, 'No glasses?'

'Contact lenses.'

'Pity, glasses suited you,' Frank said.

They set off, Victoria and Joe at the front, Anthony and Susan at the back, Katy on her own again. Gary sat next to Frank. He looked round at his new 'gang' and swallowed. He felt so happy that they were all back together; he didn't want to be apart again.

When Victoria had asked who was going to London the next day, Gary had felt a desperate need to be part of it all. He'd been the first to say yes, and he had looked around to make sure they were all joining in. He needn't have worried: everyone was up for it.

***

The day to London had been amazing. Gary had enjoyed every minute of it. He had tried to support Katy as much as possible, partly because he fancied her so much: he wanted to make a good impression. Also, though, he wanted everything to go well, for everyone. Now the day was over, and he felt deflated.

They were all suddenly quiet, reflective. Gary had lost his nerve about asking Katy out. He knew she was too excited about what had happened to think about him.

'See you then,' he said to the others as they reached his house.

They all clustered around him, none of them wanting to be the first to go. Gary looked at his house; his heart sank.

'Thanks, Gary, thanks for everything,' Katy said, stepping up to him and giving him a hug.

'I didn't do anything. I just, well, nothing,' he said, embarrassed but very pleased.

They all said goodbye and drifted away.

He walked up to his front door; as he approached, he heard Tina's voice behind him. He groaned inwardly.

'Hi Gary, is Kev in?'

'How do I know? I'm outside standing next to you,' he muttered.

'OK, no need to be horrible,' she said, hurt.

'I don't know where he is; I've just come back myself.'

He let her in to the house. She was wearing her usual tarty clothes. As they went into the hall she said quietly, 'I'm sorry about the other day: it was all my fault. I know that is what blokes want, and I thought you'd be pleased. Will you forgive me?'

With his contact lenses Gary was seeing Tina properly for the first time. Although she was, as usual, heavily made-up, her face was much younger and less confident than he'd realised. She was, he knew, the same age as him but he'd always seen her as more experienced: a woman of the world. He suddenly felt sorry for her.

'Doesn't matter. Anyway, I'm sorry — it was just as much my fault.'

Tina smiled, 'Thanks, Gary. Can we forget it ever happened?'

'Yeah. Of course.'

In fact, the images of two days ago were rushing back to him: he felt aroused all over again. They went into the kitchen. His dad was reading the paper; his mother was ironing.

'Look Jen: it's Beauty and the Beast,' Abbott said.

'Which one's which?' Tina laughed.

'You're both beautiful,' Jenny said.

'Is Kev in?' Tina asked.

'He's working late today — some kind of panic on, I think; isn't that right dear?'

'Fuck knows; that place is always in a mess. I didn't get any overtime, so I couldn't give a shit.'

'Oh, well, mind if I wait for him?' Tina asked.

'Lovely. You can keep me company,' Abbott answered.

'Cup of tea, dear? Gary do you want one?' Jenny asked.

Abbott said, grinning broadly, 'Hey, Gary, I met Jim Masters down the bookies. You never guess what.'

'What?' Gary asked without enthusiasm.

'Well, he'd had a few drinks down the Red Lion, nothing unusual there, drunken bastard, but then he was going past the pictures and there was this kid in the queue, a Paki, with a white girl. Anyway, Jim says to the Paki to get his hands-off decent girls and take his stink somewhere else. Well, the Paki only ignores him, can you believe it? So, Jim goes up and drags him out and starts giving him a kicking.'

'Oh, that's awful, Brian,' Jenny said.

'Yeah, well that's not the end of the story. First, the white bint starts screaming at Jim, then runs off to get the filth I s'pose. Then, guess what, your posh tart of a headmistress turns up and pulls Jim off the Paki. I think he'd kicked the shit out of him anyway.'

'Oh,' Gary said.

'There's more.' Brian Abbott was gleeful. 'Then Jim, Ray Kelly and Danny Warner follow her home and guess what? They smash up her bloke's car. They made a right old mess of it — smashed the windows, pulled the wing mirrors off. Fucking hell, I wish I'd been there.'

'Really,' Gary said.

'That'll show that posh madam what's what,' Abbott chuckled.

'Oh, Brian, that's terrible; don't talk like that. Now come on, let's all have a cuppa.'

'Let's have a proper drink. We must have some somewhere.'

'Oh, Brian, I thought you were on the wagon,' his wife said.

'Yeah, that was during the week. It's the weekend. Come on, let's just have a beer and relax.'

Gary looked at his mother. She was biting her lip, trying to find a way around this. She took off her apron and said, 'I tell you what, I'll nip down to the corner shop and buy us a bottle of Blue Nun: that's a nice drink.'

'Oooo, get you. Blue Nun is it? I like the blue bit but not the nun. You have that shit, Jen; get me a few lagers or something.'

'No, come on, Brian. Keep up the good work let's not slip back to the old ways. A nice glass of wine will be fine.'

'It's like living in a concentration camp here,' Abbott grumbled.

'Put the crumble in won't you, Brian, in ten minutes?' Jenny said to him as she left the room. 'I've put the oven on, so you don't need to worry about that.'

'Heil Hitler,' he called after her.

Gary turned to go upstairs.

'You'll have a drink with me, son? You won't let your poor old dad drink on his own, will you?'

'No thanks, I'm all right, Dad,' Gary said and went upstairs.

He lay down on his bed and turned the day over in his head. He heard the door close. He looked out of the window and saw his mother walking up the street, her head bowed. He lay back down and felt his spirits sag. His mum was so sweet and good-natured: why did she have to live the life of a slave, in fear all the time? He thought again about getting her into a refuge. He knew what she'd say: that she couldn't leave Dad, that he was getting better, that things had turned the corner and that Gary didn't know him like she did.

He thought about Curly's wife in *Of Mice and Men*. She had married a bully; she'd tried to find a way to escape. She had escaped from her prison by dying. Gary had a sudden premonition that his mum was going to end up the same way. He wiped hot tears from his face. She was so kind and gentle. She didn't deserve any of the shit she'd had to take over the years. He thought back to the shit he'd given her, and cringed. He rubbed his eyes and felt the unfamiliar pressure of his lenses. He had already forgotten them. He practised putting them in and taking them out; it was fiddly, but it was definitely getting a bit easier.

He got up and looked in the mirror. With his contacts in, he saw himself properly for the first time in years. He was surprised. He looked OK — not handsome, but not bad. He combed his hair; maybe he should get it cut like Frank's. No, he thought he was more like Woody from The Bay City Rollers. He smiled at himself: not bad. He didn't think Katy would ever fancy him, though; she was more likely to go for someone clever, maybe an actor, or a singer in a band. He thought about learning the guitar — that would make him more attractive. He would like to be more like Anthony: he was naturally clever, and he knew how to speak nicely, and what was the right thing to do and say. Gary felt dirty and stupid and rough. He felt trapped; he wanted to get out. How could he go, though? He couldn't leave his mum, not now.

He wondered if he could get his mum somewhere safe. He decided to talk to Joe: he would help. Joe knew how to get things done. The problem was his mum. She wouldn't leave her husband, no way. Why was she so loyal? He could not understand what kept her here. All she got was abuse; she was treated like a skivvy; she had nothing of her own. Gary could feel himself getting angry: the fury that had got him into so many fights over the years was overwhelming him again.

He heard music start downstairs. It was Elvis. His dad must have put on one of his crappy records. He could hear him doing his rotten Elvis impersonation and Tina's stupid giggling. He sat up and clenched his fists. He wanted to go down and kick the shit out of both of them. He put his hands to his ears and rocked from side to side, trying to block out their voices. He screwed up his face and fought to get his head straight. He stood up, started pacing, desperate to get himself under control.

The telephone rang; the music stopped. He heard his father's guttural voice briefly and the phone slam down. The music started again.

Gary wondered what Katy would be listening to now: something modern and cool. He was so ashamed of his house, his family and of himself. He felt like a piece of shit and he was sure the others must think he was thick and totally below them.

Elvis finished 'Jailhouse Rock'; the music faded away. In the space between songs he heard Tina. She wasn't giggling. She sounded different now, frightened; there was a pleading tone in her voice. Elvis started up again — it was 'Young and Beautiful' — but he could still hear her: she sounded seriously scared.

Gary listened hard. He could hear Tina pleading with his dad.

'No, I don't like that — stop it. Please stop it,' she was crying.

'Yes, you do. You've wanted this for ages. I've seen you looking at me, flashing your tits at me. Relax, sweetie, let me give you what you want.'

'No, please, Mr Abbott, no, no, please, no, no.'

Gary heard the side gate open and close. He leapt down the stairs and into the kitchen and stared. Tina had her back to the kitchen sink; her face was terror-stricken. Brian Abbott was thrusting himself against her, squeezing her breasts, and growling insanely. Tina looked into Gary's eyes and opened her mouth to cry for help, as Jenny came in through the back door. She stood and stared at the scene. Gary saw her face turn from shock to hatred. She dropped her bags, picked up the apple crumble from the worktop and, raising it high, brought it down on the back of her husband's head. A half second before it struck him, Brian Abbott turned towards her. The heavy dish smashed into his temple. He looked dazed, uncomprehending. For a second, he looked as though he was going to laugh. Then his eyes closed, and his legs gave way. Momentarily, he was supported by Tina, but she wriggled out from under his arm. He rolled away from her and collapsed on his back.

There was total stillness in the kitchen. Next door, Elvis sang 'I want to be free.'

They stared at the man on the floor. He was still. Jenny Abbott shook her head in confusion. She let the crumble dish fall to the floor; it landed with a dull *thunk*. Gary went into the front room and switched off the record player; the silence was shocking.

He went back into the kitchen and over to his mother. He put his arms around her.

'It's all right, Mum; it's all right. Please, Mum, it's OK now,' he soothed.

Tina stepped away from the unconscious form of Brian Abbott. She shuddered and crouched down in the corner of the kitchen crying.

Gary moved his mother to a chair and helped her into it. She seemed to be in a trance. He went over to Tina and bent down.

'You're OK now; come and sit down,' he said gently.

'I'm scared, Gary. What if he wakes up?'

'He's not going to wake up any time soon,' he said looking at his father's unconscious form.

He put out his hand to Tina. She took it and unsteadily got up. She burst into tears and flung her arms around him. Through her gut-wrenching sobs he heard her muffled voice say, 'Oh God, I'm sorry. I'm so sorry; it was me; it was me.'

Gary held her tight. He shushed her and said, 'It's all right now. It's over now: you're safe now.'

Tina held on to him even harder. He manoeuvred her into the front room and lowered her onto the sofa. He came back to his mother who was staring into space.

'Mum come into the front room. I'll make a nice cup of tea.'

Obediently, Jenny got up and followed him in. She sat down next to Tina, put her hands in her lap and bowed her head, just as she always did.

Bending down to Tina he said, 'Look after my mum. I'll be back in a minute.'

Tina looked at him blankly.

'Tina, listen to me.'

He saw her eyes focus on him properly.

'You're all right. We're fine. Look after my mum — keep her safe — just for a few minutes, OK?'

Tina nodded. She put her arm around Jenny Abbott and cradled her. 'Thank you,' Gary said.

He went back into the kitchen and looked at his father. He was still. His normally ruddy face was a waxy grey. The side of his head was all bloody flesh. It reminded Gary of the jam roly-poly they'd eaten last night. He bent down and put his hand on his father's throat. He couldn't feel a pulse, but his own heart was pounding so much he wasn't sure what he could feel. He looked around the kitchen. There was crumble everywhere. He stood still and considered what to do. As well as an ambulance coming, the police would certainly be involved. He tried to picture what the police would see when they entered the kitchen. He noticed for the first time that there was a bottle of whisky and a half full glass on the table. His dad had obviously had it hidden away somewhere. This was very helpful.

Gary decided what to do. He lifted the half empty dish of crumble and put it upside down on the floor beside his father. He picked up the iron from the ironing board and wrapped the flex around his father's foot.

He looked into the front room and saw Tina sitting next to his mum, holding her very gently. They were both covered in crumbs. He looked down at himself: he was too. He went back into the kitchen and considered his father's injury: how had it been caused? The sink protruded slightly from the worktops, could his father have struck his head on the corner as he fell? He stood back and gauged where his father lay in relation to the sink. He thought it was possible. To be sure, though, he picked up the tea towel on the table and wiped some blood from his father's head and dabbed it on the edge of the sink. He then used the towel to staunch the steady oozing from the wound.

He thought about the effect of the crumble being dropped when his father had had his terrible accident. How much would his mum, Tina and he be covered in crumbs if they hadn't been in the kitchen when the accident had happened? He couldn't judge. He thought it wise not to start brushing at the crumbs: that might make it worse. He backed away and into the front room again. He knelt down in front of his mum.

'Are you all right?' he asked her.

She was silent.

'OK, this is what happened — Mum, are you listening?'

Jenny looked up at him in bewilderment.

'We just found Dad in the kitchen. He was unconscious on the floor. We don't know what happened. When you came back from the shop, he was like that. We — me and Tina — had just found him like that too. That's it. That's all. I'm going to call for an ambulance now. Are you clear what happened?'

He looked closely at his mum. She didn't seem to be absorbing what he was saying. He looked at Tina. She nodded: she understood.

'Mum, you understand what has happened, don't you?' he said, gentle but firm.

There was a long delay then, 'I think so, love; to be honest, I've gone a bit blank,' she said at last.

'Mum, all we know is that he was on the floor, unconscious; we don't know what happened. You came in from shopping and he was on the floor. We didn't see anything either. Tina and me, we were in here listening to Elvis. We just heard a crash. None of us knows what happened.'

Jenny nodded, still vague, but her eyes were clearing.

Gary looked at her carefully. He couldn't see any blood on her. He looked at Tina — no blood. He nodded at them both.

'OK, I'm going to ring for an ambulance now.'

He went into the kitchen one more time. He looked down at his father for several seconds then said quietly, 'Bye, Dad.'

He backed into the hall, slipped off his shoes and leapt up to his room. He hunted feverishly for the bus ticket and a pen. He couldn't find the ticket. Where had he put it? He stood stock still and tried to calm down. He remembered: he'd been wearing his old baggies. Where were they now? He opened the wardrobe: there they were — clean and folded. He thrust his hand into the pockets, empty. He groaned. He gritted his teeth. He wasn't going to be beaten by anyone or anything. He recalled the scene: something about Joe's number had caught his attention — yes, the bus to Watford, the 306, it had been 4306.

***

535

'Hello?' Victoria said.

'It's Gary,' she heard him whisper.

'What's up, Gary?'

'Um, I'm sorry. Er, I've been trying to ring Joe — is he there?'

'Yes, what's up?'

'I need him here, quickly.'

'Tell me. Gary, what's up?'

'I can't tell you. I need Joe quickly, though.'

'OK, hang on.'

'Gary?' Joe said seconds later.

'Can you come here now, right now?' Gary whispered.

'At home?'

'Yeah.'

'Two minutes,' Joe said.

Gary went back into the front room. He sat down next to his mother. He positioned himself so he could look out of the window.

'What's happening?' Tina said, her voice trembling.

'I've rung for an ambulance and the Old Bill too.'

'Oh God,' she said crying.

'We're going to be all right, don't worry,' Gary said, sounding calm.

'I'm sure all this is my fault,' she whimpered.

His voice was quiet but brooked no argument, 'No, it's not. Be strong, Tina, for Mum's sake.'

Tina looked very scared. He held her gaze. She drew in a deep breath and let it out. She nodded.

They sat in silence. Then Gary said, 'Mum, when will Kev be home, do you think?'

She stared vacantly at the wall. Gary saw a car draw up outside, he could see Peter Gregory walking swiftly to the front gate.

'Hang on,' Gary said and ran to the door.

'Tell me,' Joe said.

Gary let him in and closed the door quickly behind them. He put his finger to his lips and opened the kitchen door. He stood back to let him see. Joe stood still and surveyed the scene. He looked at Gary with a raised eyebrow.

Gary whispered, 'I just need you to tell me what you think has happened here. But don't go in — footprints...'

Joe took in the body, the long trailing lead wrapped around Mr Abbott's foot, the upturned crumble dish.

'I think he got his foot caught in the lead, lost his balance and banged his head on the sink edge. Was he carrying that dish?'

'Yes. Does anything look out of place, anything not quite right?'

Joe looked again. He said, 'There is plenty of flex there. Something would have had to hold the flex around his foot to make him go over. How about you wrap it around the ironing board legs? It would have been because the flex got caught around both his foot and the legs that sent him over. You could shift the board so that it's all skew-whiff? Don't touch the metal, Gary — fingerprints?'

Gary nodded and fed the iron's flex in and around the legs of the board and pushed the board askew. He straightened up and stood back, beside Joe.

'Where's your mum?' Joe whispered.

Gary gestured to the front room. Joe looked carefully around the kitchen one more time.

'I think she needs to be with him when they arrive: you need to mix up all those foot prints, plus, I don't know what's happened here but if you want it to appear to have been an accident, she needs to be in here, very upset. She would be here, don't you think?'

Gary nodded his understanding.

Joe said, 'Do you need to worry about fingerprints on anything else?'

Gary studied the scene. 'Shit — yes, my dad's fingerprints need to be on the crumble dish. Shit! How can I do that?'

Joe said, 'You're not doing anything, Gary. Take your shoes off.'

Puzzled, Gary watched Joe taking off his own shoes. Then he understood. Joe put Gary's shoes on and did up the laces. He positioned himself awkwardly behind the unconscious man's head. He took a handkerchief from his pocket and unfolded it. Using the handkerchief like a tea towel, he picked up the crumble dish and rested it on Abbott's chest. He took Abbott's lifeless hands and pressed them against the dish. Then he let the hands fall back and replaced the dish on the floor. He paused, looking closely at the earthenware. He whispered, 'Gary, there's blood on the dish; does that matter?'

'Shit, yes. Can you wipe it off?'

Joe carefully wiped the dish with his handkerchief. He rested his fingers on Abbot's throat, struggled back to his feet and walked backwards to Gary. They swapped shoes.

'He's alive, Gary, just in case you were wondering.'

'Oh, yeah — erm, thanks.'

'I think you're OK, Gary,' said Joe. 'Time for the ambulance.'

Gary nodded again and sucked in his breath, 'OK, let's go.'

Joe said, 'You're going to be fine, Gary.'

Gary nodded, put out his hand. Joe took it.

***

Ten minutes later, two ambulance men hustled into the kitchen. They found Mrs Abbott kneeling beside her husband, quietly crying. They helped her to her feet.

'Come and sit in the other room. Let's get your husband sorted out,' one of them said gently.

'Come on, Jenny, come with me,' Tina said very tenderly and led her into the front room.

'You too, son; give us a little space.'

'How is he?' Gary asked.

'Leave us to it, son: go and wait in there,' they said, gesturing to the front room.

Next came two policemen. They stood at the door to the kitchen, watching the ambulance men at work, scribbling in their notebooks.

Then Brian Abbott was put on a stretcher and carried off. The siren's wailing disappeared into the distance.

After several minutes, the door into the room opened quietly and the police officers sat down in the two armchairs.

'Who would like to tell us what happened?' the older one said.

'How is he?' Gary asked.

'Not sure son. Pretty bad I think,' the older one said. He turned to Jenny and asked, 'So, you're Mrs Abbott?'

Jenny nodded.

'And you are?' he looked at Gary.

'I'm Gary. He's my dad,'

'And you?'

'Tina Castleton. I'm Kev's girlfriend. He's Gary's brother.'

'So where were you all when it happened?'

'We were in here, listening to records. Mum was out shopping,' Gary said.

'Well, I wasn't really listening; I don't like Elvis. I was just talking to Gary,' Tina said.

'OK, so what happened?'

'We heard this crash, and we rushed into the kitchen. Then Mum came back. We tried to get him to wake up and when we couldn't, I rang 999.'

'So, you weren't here, Mrs Abbott, when it happened?'

'No.'

'We're going to take a good look around the kitchen. Please stay here.'

'Can I go to the hospital soon? I want to be with Brian. Please can I go?'

'We'll take you down there. We just need a quick look around.'

They were left alone, the three of them huddling close together.

Gary was picturing the events of the last few minutes over and over again. He could see his father thrusting himself at Tina, his hands roughly squeezing her breasts, Tina's helpless terror, the look of savage fury on his mother's face as she had crashed the dish into the side of her husband's head.

Gary put his arm around his mother. He reached further and gently cradled the back of Tina's head. He felt her push her head back into his hand and heard her take in a long shuddering breath. He kept his hand there and let his arm rest gently on his mother's shoulders. The three of them held hands on Jenny's lap. They waited.

Then Gary heard his voice saying,

'Our Father, who's up in heaven

Hallo is his name

Your kingdom come; you will be done as he does in heaven.'

He paused; he couldn't remember any more. He heard Tina say,

'Give us daily bread — er — sorry, I've gone blank too. Isn't there something about trespassing?'

'Yeah, erm...' Gary said.

Then Jenny's voice cut in, strong and clear, 'Forgive us our trespasses, as we forgive those who trespass against us. And lead us not into temptation; but deliver us from evil.'

And Gary and Tina joined in:

'For thine is the kingdom, the power and the glory

'For ever and ever

'Amen.'

Victoria

'What do you want to do?' Joe asked, as they watched the five walk away from the school.

Victoria unlocked her car. She had been asking herself that very question for the last few days. What she really wanted was nothing. So much had happened over the last two days, few days, that having nothing to do seemed utterly appealing.

'Joe, has this been an incredible few days, or is this what your life is like all the time?'

'Well, it has been a bit hectic,' he agreed.

'A bit?'

'OK, more hectic than usual.'

'Here are the facts: a racial attack, criminal damage to your car, prisons, guns, disposing of evidence, strip clubs — and those are just the headlines.'

'Yes, quite a weekend.'

'So, in answer to your question, what I'd like to do is watch the television, have something to eat and drink and be safe, secure and without controversy or drama. Any chance?'

'Every chance. You don't regret any of it, though, do you?'

'Nothing from a personal point of view; but speaking professionally, I have to say that if a newspaper got to hear what the headmistress of the local comp got up to at the weekend, I would find it difficult to defend myself.'

Joe still looked at her and said, 'It's been fun though, hasn't it?'

'Yes, of course. It's been brilliant.'

He leaned over and kissed her. She felt his lips on hers and his hand on her breast.

'Get off me, you lech.'

'I'm sorry, I couldn't help myself,' he said looking contrite.

'Don't be too sorry; let's just find somewhere rather more private than the school car park.'

'Oh, all right. I'll control myself for the moment. Where do you have in mind, the Tesco car park?'

'You want to watch out, Joe Marshall, I might take you up on that,' she said, glancing around before reaching across to squeeze his balls.

'Get off, you lech,' he squealed.

They drove down Hillside Road, passing their fellow adventurers. Victoria hooted. They turned and waved happily.

'They're fantastic,' Joe said.

'They are — quite amazing, all of them.'

'What do you think will happen to them?' he asked.

'I don't know. I can't begin to guess. They've come so far in such a short space of time, I hope they stick together, though. Since they've got together, they're all so much stronger, and I think each of them can achieve so much.'

'What about you?' he asked.

'What about me?'

'Where are you going?'

'I'm going to get a takeaway, open a bottle of wine, drag you kicking and struggling into my bed and, I suppose, work hard and turn the school around: that kind of thing.'

'Nothing else?'

'Like what?'

'I don't know. You must have some ambitions, goals, targets?'

'Loads and loads; too many to even mention.'

'If I can help, I would love to. Can I help you in any way?'

'Maybe I'd rather help other people. How about you: what help do you need?'

'Ah, well, what I'd really want help with is getting my own back on the shitheads who smashed up my car.'

Victoria turned into her street and coasted to her house. Looking at Joe she said, 'I would love to get those shitheads, but only if it's legal and is commensurate with what a respectable headmistress should be doing.'

'Ah, pity. Well, let's think about that. Meanwhile I'm going to start kicking and struggling.'

***

Victoria looked down at Joe. In the dim light from the bedside lamp she could just see his face. He looked calm, focused, in control. She put her hands on his bare chest, feeling his muscles, his hard nipples. He closed his eyes with pleasure. She felt him move deep inside her, she let out a long involuntary groan. She felt his hands on her buttocks, squeezing and fondling them, lifting her up and down gently. The urge to move quicker was almost too much to resist but she kept herself in check, she just wanted to enjoy this feeling, without rushing anything. She put her hands on his shoulders and leaned down to kiss him. She felt his tongue on her lips; then it pressed inside her mouth, hard and insistent. She sucked on his tongue; it slipped away, then she found it again. His hands were in her hair, gently stroking, then pulling. All the while he moved inside her, probing, deeper, faster. She pulled her face away and looked into his eyes. They were dark, unreadable.

His hands gripped her bottom harder as she moved up and down, more and more quickly now, her breath shallow, faster. She gasped as she felt her orgasm rushing towards her. Arching her back, she let go. Victoria let the waves of pleasure shudder through her before falling forward onto him.

After a minute she extricated herself and rolled on to her side. She looked at Joe, the stranger. He was watching her closely. She looked away. She had become so close to this man. She loved being with him, but still knew so little about him. She was coming to terms with the fact that she would have to bide her time. She had only known him for a few days, after all; and what a few days. She thought back to the moment she'd first seen him at The Beeches: she had been drawn to him instantly. She thought about what had happened since — the awful scene in the boys' lavatories, the surprise arrival of Joe at school, the recruitment of her 'problem' students, their relationship building — first with Joe, then with each other — culminating in the extraordinary events of the weekend. Most of all, though, she was overwhelmed by the extent to which she had become what? Entranced, inflamed, obsessed by Joe? She had given up her mind, body and maybe even, she thought, her soul to him. Without him asking, or her meaning it to, it had just happened. She had seen how others were with him: they were the same as her. If she thought of Gary, Katy, Anthony and Frank before they had met Joe, and looked at them now, they were very different people. Her judgement had been that he would be a positive and safe influence on them. Was she right or wrong? Since Joe had turned up, her own judgement had become so unreliable, she couldn't even say what she was judging anything against. He had certainly been a positive influence, but were her vulnerable young people safe? What about her? Was she safe with this man?

She thought about Joe. He had killed a man, spent many years of his life in prison. He had associated with other people who had committed serious crimes. He had helped his friend commit suicide. There was no question that he was comfortable with the seamier side of life. He didn't appear to have a profession or any qualifications. He was nothing like the kind of man she thought she might want to be with, at least in superficial terms. What was she doing? She had to admit, though, she was utterly and completely alive, for the first time in her life. She felt wonderful.

'What do you think I'm thinking?' she said to him, knowing that he was paying attention; he always was.

'Er, what a fine mess I've got myself into?' he hazarded.

She nodded.

'Want to know what I'm thinking?' he asked.

She nodded again.

'How amazingly lucky I am to have found you. I can't quite believe it.'

'Truly?'

'Absolutely.'

'What are we going to do, Joe?'

'Stick together and work it all out bit by bit?' he suggested.

'You won't take me too far from the straight and narrow, will you?'

'Not too far; but you do like some excitement, don't you?'

'Yes, I do. You know I do,' she said smiling.

'Good. So do I.'

The phone rang. Victoria pulled on her dressing gown and went downstairs. She called up, 'It's Gary. He sounds upset.'

*****

Joe came out of Gary's house and got back into the car.

'What's going on?' Victoria asked.

'There's been an accident. Gary's father is unconscious.'

'Shouldn't we wait with him?'

'No, Gary's called an ambulance. He's OK; his mum is there too.'

'What did Gary want?'

'He thought I might be able to help but I couldn't; there's nothing more I can do.'

'Is it serious?'

'Hard to tell. He's out cold.'

Victoria felt uneasy. This was typical of Joe: untoward incidents, inadequate explanations.

She put the car into gear and asked, 'Where to?'

'Let's go and have something to eat. I just need to pick something up from The Beeches first.'

They went to the pub by the film studios. Joe led the way into the lounge bar and pulled out a chair for Victoria. They didn't talk much; both were exhausted. They ordered prawn cocktails, steak and chips and a bottle of claret. After they'd eaten and finished the wine, Victoria looked across the table at Joe. He looked back, attentive.

'Are you real?' she asked at last.

'Real?'

'You know.'

'Yes, I'm real. I do know what you mean, though: I'm a bit difficult to tie down, to sum up, to attach to anything.'

'That's it. You're a classic Will o' the Wisp. I'm used to things being straightforward. I like to know where I am.'

'Are you finding me difficult to be with? Is it making you want to get away before anything else happens?'

'Well, yes, and no. Don't get me wrong: I love being with you. My life has become exciting. It's great. And everything is sharp, in focus all of a sudden. But I feel like I'm on a roller-coaster.'

'It's the same for me, Victoria. You've changed everything for me. You know more about me than anyone has ever known, much more.'

'But I hardly know anything, well, except the headlines.'

'Exactly. So, you see what a desert I've been living in for so long.'

'Me too,' Victoria admitted.

'So, maybe we're rather well suited — don't you think?'

'In some ways, but not others.'

'How so?'

'Well, I have a professional role. I need to be taking steps to uphold standards, to be a role model. Since I've been spending time with you, I've made some really poor decisions. I've behaved in a way that only a few weeks ago I would have thought entirely inappropriate.'

'Well, it's just been a funny few weeks. I can't believe that we would carry on like this: life will just settle down.'

'Do you really think so? And anyway, if it did, wouldn't you get bored?'

'Almost certainly.'

'Hmmm, that's not encouraging.'

'Well, no one can predict the future.'

'Not even you?' she asked smiling.

'Ah, well, I predict a little bit of excitement coming our way. Quite when or where or who — that's not so clear to me. Do you mind me making a quick phone call, Victoria? I'll be back in a tick.'

'Don't be too long. I'd really like to go home soon.'

Joe lifted his jacket off the back of his chair and walked towards the payphone by the cigarette machine. He stroked Victoria's hair as he passed her. She closed her eyes and reflected on the last few weeks. Weeks? It was more like days. She wondered how the youngsters were feeling after all the ups and downs of the weekend. All being well, everything was dull and boring for them. Even better, they were just finishing their homework. It was, after all, only a matter of weeks before their GCEs and CSEs. It was incredible to her that she could get through a whole weekend without even thinking about school: the pressures of staffing levels, exams, the meeting she had tomorrow with the LEA at which she was expected to justify her serious budget deficit. It wasn't that she didn't care about those things, it was just that she was enjoying the rest of her life. She would have to start getting work-life balance back under control though. Time with Joe was thrilling, but it wasn't sustainable. She looked around to see where he was— no sign of him. It had been several minutes. Where was he? She put her jacket on and went up to the bar to pay. As she took her change, she said to the barman, 'Erm, you didn't see where my friend went did you?'

'Yeah, he left just now, with his friends I think.'

'What friends?'

'Some regulars. He met them in the public bar.'

'Oh, that's peculiar. Thank you.'

Victoria went to the door and peered out. She could dimly make out a group of people at the far end of the car park. She pushed opened the door and listened. She thought she could hear Joe's voice. Quietly she left the pub and wove her way between cars, keeping her head down as she went.

Joe said, 'Listen, lads, I know you want to give me a kicking but there's nothing to be gained by it. You smashed up my car, you got your own back on us for stopping you beating up that young kid outside the pictures. Why don't you leave it at that?'

'Yeah, but the point is, mate, we want to kick the fuck out of your ugly face; that's why we came out here.'

Joe said, 'By the way, you did a great job on my car. It's going to cost me a fortune getting the windows done, new mirrors, and I probably need a paint job too.'

'Ha, ha, we thought we'd give you a bit of air-conditioning.'

They laughed.

Victoria wasn't sure what to do. She stayed below the level of the cars and cursed Joe for getting her into yet another mess.

Joe said, 'You must be Jim Masters, Ray Kelly and Danny Warner?'

'You're a fucking smart-arse, aren't you?'

'Well, that's a matter of opinion. I'm sure you're right. All I ask is that you leave us alone now. You've made your point and I can't do anything about it.'

'You're right there: there's nothing you can do. There's plenty we can do. First up I'm going to kick your fucking head in,' the voice shocked Victoria.

'Come on, lads. This isn't going to get anyone anywhere. Let's shake on it and all go home.'

'Shake hands with you, you fuckin' wanker. You make me sick. Hold him, Ray, I'm going to have this shithead.'

Victoria found herself moving quickly to the knot of shadowy figures. She said, 'That's it, the game's over. We're all going home now.'

'Fuck me, if it isn't the Paki-loving bitch herself.'

Victoria's voice was cold, 'I'm not going to tell you again: please go now.'

'Are you going to make us?'

'Grow up. We're in a public place: all I have to do is call out and we'll be surrounded by people.'

'Yeah? Well let's see if you're right?'

To her horror, one of the men started walking towards her.

Joe said quickly, 'All right, if it's a fight you want, then let's get on with it.'

He took off his jacket, handed it to Victoria, then turned to face the three men. 'Before we start, may I ask you one question?' Without waiting for an answer, he said, 'There are three of you and one of me. Do you think you'd rather beat me up as a team or one by one? Actually, before you answer that one, if you don't mind, may I ask one other question?' Joe looked up and down the main street. 'OK, I was watching the television the other day; I think it was *Dixon of Dock Green*, or it could have been *Special Branch*, or maybe it was *Softly, Softly*. Anyway, the Police get called to a pub because there's a punch-up going on, disturbing the peace.'

Victoria was watching the three; they were exchanging glances, uncertain.

Joe was still talking, 'This is my question — are you ready? Are you? Are you ready, boys? I shall take your silence as a 'yes'. Ah, who's this I wonder? It looks like... yes — it's Dixon.'

Victoria saw the white police car slide into the car park.

'What the...? Fuck! The filth is here. Shit! Get the fuck out of here!' And the frenzied clattering of feet disappeared down Shenley Road.

Then Joe's arms were around her. She heard him say, 'Come on, let's get out of here.'

Part 7

Dipping for the Line

Anthony

Anthony was exhausted. The trip to see his father the day before had left him empty. The thrill of being with Susan had been both wonderful and overwhelming. Today's trip to Soho and the events that had taken place had finished him off. All he wanted to do was go home and be with his mother and grandmother. He needed time to process everything, to understand what was happening to him.

'Oh, no,' he said as they turned the corner into his street.

They looked and saw a police car outside his house. They stood still.

Anthony started talking quickly, 'Right, let's think. Nothing has happened today that would make the police come around. We got rid of the gun. Even if someone had seen us, no one could know who we were.'

Frank remembered the conversation in the hairdresser's two evenings before. He said, 'It's the other night, when you and Gary got caught up with those wankers, we met the other day.'

'OK, there's nothing for it. We just deny everything, agreed?' Anthony said, looking at them.

They nodded.

'I'll ring you later, once it's all settled down. Leave this to me.'

'Are you sure?' Frank said.

'Definitely, it will be easier to deal with if I'm alone.'

'I'll come in with you. I can give you an alibi,' Susan said.

'No, it's fine. I'll be all right.'

'Well, I'll come anyway,' she said with finality.

'Don't bother arguing, Anthony: she always gets her way,' Katy said.

'Good luck. Ring us, won't you,' Frank said.

Anthony nodded and, with Susan beside him, walked up to his front door.

'OK?' Anthony asked her as he opened the door.

'OK, I'm right here.'

Anthony pushed opened the door to the sitting room and stood still. His mother and his granny were sitting close to each other. They looked up. Opposite them was a large policeman and beside his mother was a policewoman.

'This is Anthony now,' he heard his granny say.

'Come in, son, come and sit down,' the policeman said, getting to his feet.

Anthony didn't move. He was trying to weigh up what was going on. He couldn't read it.

'Anthony, come and sit down,' he heard his granny say.

'What's going on?' he asked.

'Who is this?' the policeman asked looking at Susan.

'This is my friend, Susan Walker.'

'It might be a good idea for you to go home now, love,' the policeman said.

'No, I'll stay if you don't mind; is that all right, Anthony?'

He nodded and smiled at her in gratitude.

'Is that all right with you, Mrs Alexander?' the policeman asked.

Margaret inclined her head.

Anthony was thinking fast. He was rehearsing in his mind what he would say in answer to any questions about his whereabouts on Thursday. He knew that Susan would back up whatever he said.

'Sit down, Anthony. The police have something important to say. Do as you're told,' his granny instructed him, severe now.

He moved to the vacated chair and sat down. He looked at the policewoman, trying to look as if he had no idea of why they were here. He was aware of Susan standing behind him, her hands on the back of the chair.

The policewoman looked at him strangely. He couldn't read her face. She drew in a breath and said, 'Anthony, I'm very sorry to tell you this, but I'm afraid your father is dead. He died in prison today. I'm so sorry.'

Anthony stared at her. He looked at his mother; she nodded. He shook his head in stupefaction.

The policewoman went on, 'I'm very sorry; it must be such a shock.'

Anthony swallowed and nodded.

'How?' he asked finally.

'We're not able to give any details at this stage; I'm sorry.'

Anthony closed his eyes. He was still getting over the relief of not being arrested himself. He hadn't begun to absorb the fact that his father was dead.

'I know it's difficult, Anthony, but do you mind if we ask you one or two questions?'

Anthony shook his head.

'We understand that you visited him yesterday. That's right, isn't it?'

'Yes.'

'How did he seem to you? Was he in any way distracted? Did he seem different to normal? Can you think of anything unusual at all?'

Anthony thought for a minute. He wasn't sure how to answer. His mind was reeling. Had his father had a heart attack? Had he killed himself? Had someone killed him? He remembered his own last words to him. 'If you don't, I shall kill you.'

Finally, he said, 'No, he was more or less the same as normal, well, normal for someone in prison I suppose. I hadn't seen him for months.'

Anthony looked at his mother. She had her eyes closed, what was in her head? He looked at his granny, she looked back. Her expression was sad, her demeanour one of someone dealing with traumatic news but there was a glitter in her sharp eyes.

'What did you say to him, Anthony?' the policewoman continued.

'Not much, I didn't know what to say really.'

'Tell them about the letters, Anthony,' his mother said, looking at him for the first time.

'Oh, well, I asked him to stop writing the horrible letters that he's been sending.'

'What did he say?'

'He just laughed at me.'

The policeman cleared his throat now; he was leafing through a book.

'Anthony, your father was keeping a diary. This is yesterday's entry.'

He passed the diary to Anthony.

It read, 'The boy masquerading as my son came today. I do not believe that he carries my genes. He is nothing more than excrement. I am now convinced that Margaret must have been fucking some kind of Neanderthal or swapped my son with a low life in the hospital. When I looked at the wretched creature, I saw base stupidity and, worse still, I felt a sense of evil enter me. I must write to the authorities to warn them that there is a risk to public safety and decency loose and at large.'

Anthony stared at the policeman and his colleague. He looked at his mother and granny. He turned around to look into Susan's face. She was pale, but she looked back at him without blinking.

'I knew he didn't like me,' Anthony said at last.

'What else did you talk about with him?' the policewoman asked.

'Not much really. He spent most of the time telling me how sorry he was about everything.'

'Why the diary entry then, do you think?'

'I don't know.'

'Apparently you had some kind of turn. Did you faint or something?' the policeman asked.

Anthony felt his face flush.

'He said some awful things to me and about my mother. They made me flinch I suppose.'

'Your mother says you gave him her wedding ring. Is that right?'

Anthony's mouth went dry. Should he lie and, if so, what should he say?

'I'm sorry, Mother, I told you a lie. I was going to give it to him, but I was reeling from what he said. It went out of my head that I even had it. I threw it into a lake on the way home. I'm really sorry.'

Margaret Alexander looked at her son. He looked ashamed and scared. In fact, Anthony was feeling neither of those emotions. He was elated. This was a perfect alibi to explain all the throwing going on at the reservoir.

'It's all right, Anthony, you mustn't blame yourself,' his mother said.

'That's right. You've done nothing wrong, dear,' his granny was emphatic.

'One more question, Anthony. Who did you go to the prison with?'

'My friends.'

'Yes, could you tell us who please?'

Anthony paused before answering. This was not what he wanted.

'Gary Abbott, Frank Gordon, Katy Walker, she's Susan's sister, Susan. They're all friends from school. Victoria Court, she's our headmistress — she drove the school minibus — and Joe Marshall.'

'Who's Joe Marshall?'

Anthony thought for a minute. He realised he didn't really know who Joe was. He was, well, Joe.

'Oh, well he's a friend. He's, um, he's a really nice man,' Anthony tailed off.

He heard Susan say behind him, 'Joe has been organising a birthday party for an elderly lady at The Beeches and he asked us to help him. He's a lovely man.'

'That's right, he is,' Anthony said, nodding to emphasise the point.

'Can we have all their contact details please?' the policeman asked.

'Of course,' Anthony said, fishing his notebook from his pocket.

'Mrs Alexander, we're going to have to ask you to come with us, I'm afraid, to formally identify your husband's body,' the policewoman said gently.

Anthony watched his mother look up sharply, shaking her head.

'Come on, Margaret, I'll come with you,' her mother said.

Margaret Alexander shut her eyes and shuddered. After a long time, she unsteadily got to her feet.

'I'll come too,' Anthony said.

'No, I don't want you anywhere near that place or that man,' his mother said.

The policewoman said, still gentle, 'Anthony, I know that this news is a terrible shock for you: is there anyone you can stay with or someone who can be with you?'

'Oh. No — honestly, I'm all right. Thank you for asking. It's very kind of you.'

The two police officers looked at each other. The policewoman said, 'Shock is a funny thing, Anthony. I'm going to radio for a Liaison Officer to pop by; someone will be around in a few minutes.' She turned to Anthony's mother: 'Mrs Alexander, are you ready to come with us?'

***

As soon as they had gone Anthony put his face in his hands. He felt Susan touch his arm.

'What am I supposed to feel?' he said through his fingers.

'How do you feel?'

'Like a massive weight has been lifted from me. I can breathe for the first time in my life.'

'Then I guess that's what you ought to be feeling.'

'I don't feel sad, or guilty, or anything like that, isn't that terrible?' he said, looking at her for reassurance.

'No, not really. He has made your life a misery, and your mother's, and I suppose he was terribly unhappy too. Maybe that's why he's dead: because he was so unhappy, he decided to kill himself?'

'But that makes me feel bad for him, despite everything he's done.'

'I don't know, Anthony. It's all so unbelievable.'

Anthony nodded. It was incredible. He had been with his father only yesterday and now he was dead. He thought back over the conversation of a few minutes earlier.

'We must ring everyone and tell them. They need to know the police might get in touch,' he said and made for the hall.

He rang Katy first. She was totally over-excited. Anthony explained that the police might get in touch, but he wasn't sure she was taking it in. He heard her say, 'OK, Anthony, I've got it. Is Susan still there?'

'Yes.'

'Will you ask her to come home?'

Anthony said he would, although he really wanted Susan to stay with him.

'Tell her I'll go in a few minutes,' Susan said. When he put the phone down, she said, 'I'll wait until the police-person comes.'

He tried Gary next. Mr Abbott's harsh gravelly voice said, 'Yeah?'

'Is Gary available, please?'

'No, he's not, and anyway he wouldn't speak to a little ponce like you. Now get off the line.'

Anthony put the phone down.

'Phew, that man is an animal. He's as bad as my father. What is wrong with fathers.'

'Hang on a minute, my dad is lovely,' Susan said.

'I'm sorry. I'm sure he is.'

He couldn't reach Frank, Victoria or Joe.

'I'll keep trying, and you've got to go home,' Anthony said.

'In a minute,' she said and led him back to the sitting room.

They sat down next to each other on the sofa. Susan put her arm around his shoulders. Anthony started shivering. She gently drew his bristly head to her chest and cradled him.

'Anthony?' she said hesitantly.

He pushed himself away and looked at her, 'Yes?' equally uncertain.

'Um, well, I don't know if it's right or wrong, but...'

'Go on.'

'Well, er, I just wondered, would you like to undo my blouse?'

Very gently and carefully, and with great reverence, he started to undo the buttons of her blouse, his heart hammering, head spinning, his whole being rejoicing.

Katy

Katy felt the atmosphere as soon as she walked into her house. She called out, 'Where are you?'

There was a long silence then her father came into the hall from the kitchen. He looked stressed.

'Hi, Dad.'

'Hello, you're back.'

'Well spotted, Sherlock. Where's Mum?'

'I'm here,' she heard her mum's voice in the kitchen.

Katy went in and saw Anna sitting at the table. She looked white and even more anxious than John.

'What's up? It's like a morgue in here.'

'We've been wondering, you know, wondering how you were getting on,' Anna said.

'I know; I understand. It must have been very difficult for you,' Katy said, trying to see it from their position.

'OK, how did it go?' John asked at last.

'It was fine, well, actually it was wonderful. It started badly. She wasn't anything like I thought she'd be. She was sort of small and old, and vulnerable — fragile, I suppose. I thought she was nice, though, kind; gentle really. We had a good chat and we agreed to see each other again. Then, we went to where she works — a club up there. Guess what? She's a brilliant singer: really amazing. It's a horrible place but she's really good. I think you would have liked her. I really do.'

She looked at them both. They just stared back.

'What's wrong? Tell me what's wrong,' she said, feeling nervous now. She tried to guess what they were thinking and feeling. She said, 'Don't worry. We got on well, but it hasn't changed how I feel about you. You're my mum and dad; she's going to be more of a friend. It doesn't change anything; I knew it wouldn't.'

'Thank you, Katy, that's nice,' Anna said.

'Did she tell you who your father is?' John asked.

'No, she wouldn't say. She promised him, apparently. But, guess what? Her father is a famous singer: Sidney Davidson.'

They were quiet. She looked from one to the other, really worried now.

'What is it? Tell me.'

John cleared his throat and said, 'I'm your father, Katy.'

Katy smiled, 'Oh, no, I know that, Dad. You don't have to worry you'll always be my dad. Mum, you'll always be my mum. It's fine. Don't worry.'

'No, Katy, I'm your real father.'

Katy stared. 'What do you mean?'

'I'm your real father; it's me.'

Katy shook her head slowly. She looked at Anna. Her mother looked back at her, nodding in confirmation.

'I don't understand; I don't get it.'

John sat down next to her. Taking her hand, he said slowly, 'I met your mother, Jane, when she was discharged from hospital. She had been in a psychiatric hospital. She came to the council needing a place to live. Her case was assigned to me. I found her a flat and helped her move in and get set up. She was very vulnerable and needed a lot of support. I felt terribly responsible for her. I wanted her to do all right. I realised too late that I probably spent more time with her than I should have done. I wanted to make sure she was safe, comfortable, secure. She was and, as you say, is a very nice person, gentle and kind. I couldn't stand the thought of things going bad for her.'

John looked at Anna; she nodded for him to continue.

'I used to visit her after work, just to see that she was all right. I took her bits of furniture, crockery, utensils. I felt so responsible for her. I knew that she'd had a very bad start to life. I was beginning to like her a lot. I still loved Mum, of course. I never stopped loving her at any point in all of this. It was just that I cared for Jane too.'

John stopped and looked at Katy. She was staring back at him.

'Anyway, the thing was, that I knew I would have to say goodbye to her: it wasn't healthy. I told her that the next time I came around would be my last visit. She said she wanted to make a nice dinner, as a thank you for the help I'd given her. So, I went along, and took a bottle of wine with me. She had bought a bottle too. We got drunk and I made a terrible mistake. The thing is though, Katy, although I did something wrong, it has resulted in the most wonderful of things that can ever have happened: you came into our lives.'

'But I still don't understand. How was it that you were able to adopt me?' Katy said at last.

'Well, when Susan was born and her twin sister didn't survive, Mum and I were utterly distraught. We both decided that we would try and adopt a little girl: for Susan to have a sister after all, and for us to have two little girls. When Jane discovered that she was pregnant, she couldn't keep you. Don't feel badly towards her, Katy. She was only just recovering from being very ill; she didn't feel she could bring you up in the way she wanted to. So, she arranged for you to be adopted. I knew about it, of course, so I spoke to the adoption team and asked them if they had any babies that were about the same age as Susan. I wasn't very senior, but we were really lucky: Mum's Uncle Bill was the councillor with responsibility for adoption and fostering services. I told him that I knew of a young woman who had given her baby up for adoption and that, based on what I knew, the little girl would be perfect for us. Somehow, he brought pressure to bear on our behalf; but we still had to pass all the various tests before you could be given to us. Throughout it all, I was on a tightrope: I could never be sure that we would be able to adopt you. When we got the green light, it was the happiest day of my life.'

Katy turned to Anna, 'Did *you* know, Mum?'

Anna, white-faced, shook her head, 'No, Dad told me today.'

Katy's head was spinning. She put her hands to her temples. She opened her mouth to speak; then closed it again. She started shivering. She looked at her Dad. He was looking tense, waiting for her reaction. She turned to Anna. She saw the pain in her face and felt an overwhelming need to hold her and be held by her. She knelt on the floor and put her head in Anna's lap and burst into tears. She felt her mother's hands on her head, stroking her, calming her, as they always had. Anna and John heard Katy say through her muffled sobs, 'I'm so sorry, Mum, please forgive me. I'm sorry.'

'Don't be silly, Katy. You don't need to be sorry about anything,' Anna said.

'I do! I've caused all this: I've done this to you,' Katy cried.

John said sternly, 'No, it's me, Katy. I've done it. But I'm glad. I'm terribly, terribly sorry about how it has come about, but we have you and I'm glad.'

Katy looked up at her mother's face, 'And you, Mum, how do you feel?'

Anna looked at her little girl's pleading face.

'I'm glad too, you silly girl. I'm glad too, gladder than you can ever know.'

'Really?' Katy said, smiling through her tears.

'Really,' Anna said, smiling now.

Katy was silent again. Then she asked her father, 'Does Jane know that you adopted me?'

'No, she and I never had contact again. She just knew that you were taken into the care of the adoption service.'

'So how did she know where to find me, when she wrote to me?'

'She didn't. She wrote to the adoption team and asked them to send the letter on to us,' John explained.

'I've just realised something amazing. I can't believe it and yet I always knew it was true,' Katy said, exultant. 'We are sisters. We are sisters — I knew it.'

She got up and started to leap around the kitchen squealing, 'We are sisters — I knew it, I knew it!'

The telephone rang, she ran to answer it. It was Anthony. She told him to send Susan back immediately. She put the phone down and ran back to the kitchen. She paused at the door and collected herself. She was being selfish, as usual. She thought about what it all now meant. Her father was her dad, but her mother was only her adoptive mother; she knew that must be hard for her. She also knew that what her mother had heard today must have been a terrible shock. She composed herself and walked back into the kitchen.

'I'm sorry. I lost it for a minute.'

'It's all too much to take on board. We just need to take our time and get used to it,' John said looking at Anna.

'I'm finding it hard, Katy, hard to get my head around everything — it's very difficult. The thing is, I thought I knew all the facts, but I didn't. The only person who knew was Dad. There's been a big breakdown in what I thought was real and true.'

'Like it was for me when I found out I was adopted?' Katy asked, beginning to understand.

Anna nodded.

John's voice was quiet, 'Except that there's an additional thing, and that is that I was unfaithful to you.'

Anna nodded again.

'But why did you say anything, Dad? You kept it a secret this long: why did you say anything?' Katy asked.

'There were two things: I thought Jane might say something inadvertently, like, "your father was the housing officer at the council", something like that; or you might have said, "oh my dad's a housing officer, his name is John Walker", then it would all have come out. Also, and this is more important: I couldn't stand the secrecy and dishonesty of it all. I wanted it all out in the open. I realise that it's very painful for you, Anna, but it just seemed time to tell the truth, once and for all.'

Katy shook her head. She was still reeling. She got up and said, 'Would you mind if I went for a walk? I've got to clear my head for a few minutes. Don't worry, I'm not going to do anything stupid. I promise.'

***

Katy was in a whirl as she walked down the High Street. She was elated. She was also shocked. Her father had had an affair. No matter how much he said that it was just a mistake, he had been unfaithful to her mum. On the other hand, it had been with Jane, her new mother, who she liked; who was so gentle, like a little bird. Katy now felt really sorry for her mum, the woman who had loved her all her life and would do anything for her. She was struggling to work out whether it was good news, bad news, should she be happy or sad?

She wanted to be with Susan, really. Susan always knew what was sensible, what was right. She also wanted to tell Susan the news, the unbelievable truth. She had walked to Anthony's house, thinking that she would just tell her there and then, but she thought better of it. She needed some time to absorb it all.

As she walked, she remembered the last time she'd been confronted with such an incredible revelation. That time, she had been devastated, she'd fallen to pieces. This time, she was shell-shocked again — but maybe she'd developed a thicker skin; plus, this news was different.

She came to the side street leading to The Beeches. She turned right and walked into the car park. Entering reception, she asked if Grace was available for a visitor.

'You and everyone else,' the receptionist said, smiling. 'She's in the lounge.'

Katy walked down the corridor and into the lounge. She saw Frank was there, plus a pretty girl. They were laughing with Grace, who was looking severely at them.

'Hello, this looks like fun,' Katy said.

'Hi Katy, this is Chloe,' Frank said.

Katy looked at Chloe who looked back. They smiled thinly at each other.

'And how are you, Katy?' Grace said.

'Great, I've had some unbelievable news. You wouldn't believe it.'

Chloe cut in, 'I've come in with news too, Granny. I've just auditioned for a BBC show. It's called Grange Hill. I don't know whether I've got it yet, but I think I did really well, fingers crossed.'

'Well done, dear, very well done,' Grace said pleased, and proud. She went on, 'I know my eyes aren't what they used to be, but don't you two look similar? Don't you think, Frank?'

Frank looked at Katy and then Chloe. He couldn't see the resemblance, other than that they were both gorgeous.

'Hardly. I'm taller,' Chloe said.

'I've got much bigger eyes,' said Katy.

'You're both lovely, in your own ways,' Grace said.

'I'm a performer too,' Katy said.

'Really?' Chloe said unimpressed.

Katy ignored her and said to Grace, 'Do you know a singer called Sidney Davidson?'

'Of course, everyone knows him; he was a favourite of us old dears.'

'Brilliant! Was he amazing?'

'Terribly dashing — a lovely tenor voice.'

'What happened to him? Do you know?'

'I think he was killed in the war; just after maybe. Why do you ask?'

'He's my grandfather. I found out today.'

'Really? That explains why you've got such a lovely voice.'

Chloe was looking daggers at Katy. She said, 'My father is Stewart Simpson.'

'I know,' Katy said.

'You should audition for some television work too, Katy. You'd definitely get into something,' Frank said.

'I don't think so. I'm not as talented or as pretty as Chloe,' Katy said.

'I don't know. They often need plain girls for character parts,' Chloe said, smiling sweetly.

'I'm off now,' Frank said getting up.

'Wow, you're very tall, Frank,' Chloe said, looking up at him.

'He's an amazing athlete,' Katy said. 'He's going to win the Olympics.'

Frank blushed and looked at his feet.

'I think he will, if he wants it enough,' Grace said.

'Do you want it, Frank?' Chloe asked looking provocatively into his eyes.

'No, I'm nothing special,' he said, ignoring her innuendo.

'Well, just in case, can I have your phone number?' Chloe asked.

Katy was fuming. She didn't want this jumped-up girl getting mixed up with Frank. She sat in silence as Frank said his number.

'Bye, Grace, lovely to see you,' he said.

'I'm coming too, Frank. Wait for me,' Katy said.

She bent down and kissed Grace goodbye and said, 'I'll be around in a day or two. Can we talk about my grandfather?'

'Of course, dear.'

They left the room together. They heard Chloe call, 'I'll give you a call later, Frank.'

'You didn't like her, did you?'

'I did. She seemed really nice.'

'Really? Oh Frank, don't be fooled by the pretty girls.'

'You're pretty,' he pointed out.

'Do you think so?'

'You know you are; don't bother with the false modesty.'

'You know, Frank, you're very good looking. Did you know that? I'm not surprised Chloe fancied you.'

'She doesn't really. She was just trying to wind you up.'

'I'm not so sure. Let's see if she rings you, shall we?'

'What about you? Why haven't you got a boyfriend?'

'Because most boys are wankers and most men just want sex,' Katy said.

Frank laughed and said, 'That's the end of the chances of nearly everyone then. What kind of saint could get through your net?'

'Someone like you. Someone nice, thoughtful — not up his own arse.'

Frank was silent.

'Come on, I've got to go home. I must see Susan. Something amazing has happened and I've got to tell her. I'd tell you, but I have to tell her first.'

'Good or bad?'

'Mostly good, with a little bit of bad.'

'OK, so I'm pleased for you but a little bit sad.'

'Thanks, Frank, you're a nice bloke; you really are. Can I tell you my news later?'

'If I can find time away from Chloe,' Frank said smiling.

'Good luck with her mate — she's a man-eater.'

'Bye then,' Frank called, and they went their different ways.

***

When Katy got home a few minutes later, she found Susan sitting on the wall outside the house. She sat down next to her.

'Have you heard the news?' Katy asked.

'Yep.'

'I can't get my head around it, can you?'

'No, I can't. Plus, you'll never guess what: Anthony's father is dead.'

Katy stared at her, 'How?'

'They don't know — well, the police didn't say; maybe they know and couldn't say.'

'Jesus, what next?'

They sat in silence for a long time.

'How's Mum?' Katy asked.

'Like a zombie.'

'And Dad?'

'Like a zombie's husband.'

'And you?'

'I feel like I'm in a book or a film, something unreal.'

'Yeah, that's it: that's it exactly.'

'I'm very happy, though. Happier than I've ever been in my life,' Susan said.

'Me too. How's Anthony?' Katy asked.

'Lovely.'

'Are you two serious?'

'I think so. I know he's a total idiot and a prat and he's a bit embarrassing, but I do really like him,' Susan said, smiling as she said it.

'I really like Frank; did you know that?'

'I'm not surprised: he's gorgeous.'

'He is.'

'He keeps growing, have you noticed? I don't mean he's taller, just that he's sort of getting bigger.'

'I know. I suppose it's his confidence coming back.'

'I think our next job is to look after Mum and Dad,' Susan said.

'Definitely, come on: let's go in.'

'Katy?'

'Yeah?'

'Although you're my sister, properly my sister, you know it doesn't make any difference to me, nothing's changed?'

'I know. I just love the fact that we're twins after all,' Katy said, and yelled a massive 'Yeah!' She grabbed Susan and hugged her with all her might. They danced a jig of joy.

Katy drew away and said, 'Now, come on. I've got to go and ring Frank before that tarty scrubber gets her claws into him.'

Frank

When they'd all come back from London and gone their separate ways Frank had felt very alone all over again. The people and places of yesterday's futile trip were pushing back into his head. He didn't want to burden his mum with his misery; instead he meandered around town trying to burn off energy.

He didn't plan to visit Grace. He just found himself near the Beeches, so in he went. He saw the tiny, huddled figure sitting on her own at a table. He asked one of the carers if he could talk to her. The carer went over and said in a hearty, patronising voice, 'Grace, there's a handsome young man here to see you; you'd like to see him, wouldn't you?'

Grace looked at her and said, 'I don't know. Is he single?'

'You're a one, Grace. You'll get us all into trouble.'

'Who is it?' Grace asked.

'It's Frank,' he called over to her.

'Oh, Frank, lovely. Do come over. Will you get Frank a cup of tea, dear?'

Frank sat down beside Grace. She looked up at him.

'This is a nice surprise.'

'I just wanted to tell you something,' he said.

The tea arrived.

'Cor, Grace, you pull all the nice-looking men, don't you?'

Grace snapped, 'I've hardly pulled him, have I? Now get on and patronise some of the other inmates.'

Frank smiled as Grace winked at him.

'How's life then, Frank?'

'It's OK. I just wanted to let you know that I took your advice — you know, what you said about your medals. Well, I've got this ring and, every time I touch it, I think of my brother and it makes me feel better, more optimistic.'

Grace put her little bony hand on Frank's; she touched the silver ring.

'Was he like you?'

'Absolutely not. He was clever, funny, charming. I think he would have been on television or a politician or something.'

'I'm sure that he was very different to you, Frank, but you're special too, and I don't just mean your running. You are great. You will be something great one day.'

Just as he had done before, Frank felt very small sitting beside the tiny old lady.

'Thanks,' he said.

'What for?'

'Believing in me.'

'It's not me, Frank. You inspire people. We should thank you — do you understand? You're someone we can all look up to. You have a responsibility: whether you want it or not, you have it.'

Frank was beginning to understand.

The door to the lounge burst open and a very pretty girl came in.

'Hello, Granny, don't get up,' she said.

'Oh, that's the end of our little quiet time together,' Grace said.

'How are you, you old trout?' the girl asked.

Frank was about to stand up and defend Grace from this outrage when she said, 'I'm fine. How about you, you cheeky minx?'

'Who's this, your new minder?'

'Frank, this is my granddaughter, Chloe. Chloe, this is Frank. Frank is my friend.'

Chloe looked at Frank and smiled, 'You poor, dear boy, having to put up with this old baggage.'

Frank was tongue-tied. Chloe was dazzling. She oozed confidence as well. She looked very familiar.

'I know, you're thinking... "I know her",' Chloe said smiling.

'Yes — do I know you?'

'She's on some trashy television programme,' Grace muttered.

'Oh, of course: *Why Don't You?* Yeah, I know it. Chloe Simpson,' he said, recognising her now.

'That's it. Do you like it?'

'Not really,' he said.

Chloe's face fell, and she wiped away a pretend tear, 'Bastard.'

Frank laughed.

'Language, Chloe, really,' Grace said.

Just then Katy came in.

***

Frank had gone in to see Grace for some quiet reflection. He'd wanted her measured, wise words. All of a sudden, he was caught in the middle of a cat fight. He decided that it would be much safer to leave them to it.

A few minutes later, Chloe's and Katy's compliments were ringing in his ears. He had absorbed what Grace had said to him. Maybe she was right: he did have a responsibility, to Robbie and his dad, to his mum, to himself?

He left Katy at the corner and walked to the park. The grass under his feet was springy, welcoming him. Sitting on a bench on the far side, he stared off into the gathering gloom of the early evening. He found himself twisting Robbie's silver ring, feeling the now-familiar calmness fall over him like a cloak. He wondered whether he could bring the vivid images of Robbie and his dad back into his mind; he peered into the distance, but they wouldn't come. They wouldn't come yesterday at the stadium, or at their old house; not here — maybe never again. He felt tears prick his eyes. He knew they were dead, but he'd hoped they would at least come and visit him now and then.

572

Frank got up and started jogging around the perimeter of the park. He was shocked at how unfit he was; he'd never felt so flabby, heavy and sluggish. He kept going though, feeling the familiar sensation of muscles warming up, his breathing easing, his pace lengthening and now quickening. He let his mind go and waited to see where it would take him. Something was happening around him — he could feel it. Now it was visible. The grass was changing; it was lightening, from deep dark to vivid emerald green — everywhere he looked was colour. It was dazzling. He found himself looking towards the photographer again. He could feel, rather than see, his family around him. He put his arms out to touch his dad and Robbie. They were there. He was jubilant. They had come back to him; it wasn't a dream before; they were still here. He heard himself yelling in triumph. He knew for absolute certain they would always be with him. As he ran, he heard his dad calling him, urging him on, 'Come on, Frank! Come on, you can do it!' He ran hard for home. He wanted to tell his mum. She would understand.

Breathless, Frank opened the front door and shouted, 'Mum, I've seen them, they're back.' He slammed the front door and burst into the sitting room; his face flushed. Janice was sitting next to Ailsa. He looked from one to the other, bewildered. 'What's up?' he asked. 'What's going on?'

'We've been looking at photographs. Come and join us,' Janice said.

Frank just stood there, feeling stupid.

'Come on, Frank, you're making the place untidy,' Janice said.

Ailsa said, 'What is it, Frank? You look like you've seen a ghost.'

Frank sat down next to his mother. He tried to get his head around what was happening. Only minutes ago, he'd felt so close to his dad and Robbie it had been as though they had come back to him. Now here was Ailsa. She was right: he was surrounded by ghosts.

She said, 'It was lovely seeing you yesterday. I felt so bad about the whole thing. I couldn't bear it if I didn't see you again.'

'Oh,' Frank said.

Ailsa went on quickly, 'Plus, the thing is… We wanted to give you these. I was sure you'd want them — I hope we've done the right thing?'

Ailsa reached into a carrier bag and pulled out another one. She got up and handed it to Frank. He took it and looked inside. Seeing its contents, he closed the bag again and stared at Ailsa, his face a study of confusion.

Ailsa looked at Frank, 'We did do the right thing, didn't we, Frank?'

Frank pulled out one of the table tennis bats and looked at it. He saw Robbie's writing, in large, pink, felt-tip pen, 'Frank Gordon is a knob'. He closed his eyes and let the agony sweep over him as he relived, just for a moment, the hours of simple pleasure he and his little brother had had together. He felt his mother's hand on his arm, soothing, reassuring. He heaved a lungful of air into his chest, 'How… where… umm? You said we?'

Frank heard the bathroom door open. He looked up. Alison was there. 'Ah, here he is. Hello, Tom. Done any peeping recently?'

Frank could only stare at her.

She looked at the table tennis bat and said smiling, 'I found them in my wardrobe, right at the back. You were the only person who fitted the description.'

Frank's face cleared. 'Ah, I see.' He turned to Ailsa and smiled. 'Thank you, yes, you've done the right thing. Thank you.'

Gary

Gary went to the hospital with his mother in the police car. He stayed with her as they waited for news. After an hour or so a nurse took them to see his dad; a doctor was with him.

'How is he?' Jenny asked in a tiny voice.

The doctor said, his voice matter of fact, 'He's been badly injured, Mrs Abbott. It's hard at this stage to know how badly. Until he regains consciousness, we can't tell whether there has been any brain damage. All we can do is keep an eye on him and make sure he gets as much rest as possible. Right now, the best thing is for you to go home and come back in the morning.'

Jenny refused to leave.

Gary went home to get some things for his mum. Derek, Kevin and Tina were there. They were all puffing nervously on cigarettes.

'What's the latest?' Derek asked.

'Don't know; he's alive, that's about it,' Gary answered.

'What happened?' Kevin asked.

'I told them everything,' Tina said quickly.

Gary nodded.

'Is that it?' Derek pressed, 'He just fell over?'

'I don't know, Dell. All I know is that we heard this massive crash and when we got in, there he was, in a heap on the floor.'

'What were you two doing anyway?' Kevin asked Gary and Tina.

'I was waiting for you to come home. You didn't tell me you were going to work late,' Tina said.

'Yeah, but what were you doing?' Kevin insisted.

'Dad had put one of his Elvis records on and we were laughing about it,' Gary said.

Kevin looked at his younger brother and girlfriend suspiciously but said no more.

'The filth left a few minutes ago. They told us not to clean up the kitchen,' Derek said.

'Why not?' Gary asked.

'I dunno. I suppose they want to search it again. They said detectives would be coming next.'

Although Gary was just about keeping himself together, he guessed Tina's nerves were jangling. He would try to get a quiet word with her as soon as possible. She had to stay cool. He went upstairs, got a bag and went into his parents' bedroom. He hadn't been in here for ages. It made him feel sick to think about the abuse he knew his mum had suffered in here. He put some of his dad's clothes in the bag — trousers, a shirt, vest, pants, socks, a comb. He went into the bathroom and got a toothbrush and razor. He tried to think what his mum would want. He put her toothbrush in, a hairbrush, a flannel, an unopened bar of soap. He thought she would probably want some clean clothes but didn't like to look in her drawers. He went downstairs.

'Tina, will you help me get some clothes for Mum?' he asked.

'I'll come too,' Kevin said getting up with Tina.

Gary handed them the bag.

Kevin and Tina went upstairs. Derek asked, 'Was he pissed?'

'I don't think so, but there was a glass of whisky on the table'

'How's Mum?'

'Really scared, I think. She's not really saying anything,' Gary said, honestly.

'Poor Mum,' Derek said.

'Get off, Kev, leave me will you,' they heard Tina snap upstairs.

Gary felt anger flare in him. Derek looked over.

'I suppose you were getting off with her when it happened?' he said.

576

Gary reddened. 'Jeez, no, I wouldn't touch her with a bargepole,' he retorted.

'I would, tits like that; who wouldn't?' Derek said.

'When are the police coming back?' Gary asked.

'They didn't say.'

'I think I'll take the stuff down to Mum now.'

'How are you going to get there?'

'Bus.'

Derek grunted.

Kevin and Tina came back. She looked really pissed off.

Gary stood up and took the bag. 'See you later,' he said and went out.

Waiting for the bus, he had an overwhelming desire to talk to Joe. He crossed the road to the phone box and rang his number: no answer. He tried Victoria Court's — same result. He thought about ringing the others but decided against it. What would he say? What could they do?

Now, walking down the long corridors of the hospital, the smell of disinfectant filling his head, he readied himself.

'What's the latest?' he said to his mum as he sat down beside her.

'The same.'

He looked at the unconscious man. Gary had always known his dad as a large, loud and overbearing figure. He now looked small and old. He had some kind of plastic tube in his nose and was breathing in short shallow gasps.

'How are you?' he asked his mum.

'I'm OK.'

'Sure?'

'Yes, really, Gary, I'm doing OK. What's happening at home?'

'The police are going to come back: detectives,' he said.

'Oh.'

'It's all right. We know what happened,' Gary said.

She took his hand and squeezed it. They sat in silence for a long time. The hospital moved around them; they didn't see or hear it.

A girl came in and stood next to them.

'Hello,' they heard Tina say.

Gary looked up sharply. He hadn't recognised her. She had changed into jeans and trainers and was wearing a heavy coat. She had washed off all her make-up. Now Tina just looked like a frightened girl.

Gary stood up and went towards her then paused, uncertain.

'Hello,' he said at last.

'Hello, dear,' Jenny Abbott said.

'I just wondered — is he going to be all right?' Tina asked. She looked at Brian Abbott and then looked away.

'No news; he's not moved,' Gary said.

He went and got another chair and put it down next to his.

'Thank you,' Tina said and sat down next to Jenny. Gary sat beside them.

'Do you want a cuppa, Mum?' Gary asked, mostly to break the silence.

'Yes, please, that's a good idea,' she said.

'I'll help you carry them,' Tina said, getting up with Gary.

They walked back to the main entrance where the tea and coffee machines were.

'I'm going to have a fag,' he said and walked outside. Tina followed.

They stood huddled together in a dark corner of the car park. They lit their cigarettes. Tina started crying, 'Jeez, Gary. What's going to happen?'

'I dunno. We just have to stick to our story.'

'How's your mum?'

'I think she's OK; I can't tell.'

'I'm bricking myself,' she said.

'Me too.'

'It was horrible, Gary: he wouldn't listen. He just kept on making horrible comments; then he sat down next to me and put his hand on my leg. I tried to move away but he started getting angry. I said that your mum would be upset and all he did was laugh. I got up and tried to run out of the kitchen, but he caught me and pushed me up against the sink.'

Tina stopped. She was crying; her nose was running. She threw her cigarette away and crossed her arms over her head, to hide from the memory.

She went on through her sobs, 'He was all over me, forcing himself against me. He was so rough and horrible. I couldn't move.'

Gary chucked his fag away and moved closer to her. He didn't know what to do. He wanted to comfort her but wasn't sure how. He thought that he might scare her even more if he touched her. He felt utterly useless, pathetic.

'Will you hold me, Gary,' he heard her trembling voice.

He turned to face her and felt her move against him. He put his arms around her shuddering body. She rested her head on his chest, unable to stop crying.

Gary tightened his arms around her and said, 'Shush, it's all right now. It's all OK now — you're safe now, you're safe now.'

Slowly she calmed down. She pressed in against him.

'Don't let go, Gary; keep me safe.'

'I will, I will. I'll look after you,' he said, holding her tighter still.

***

Gary wondered how many more questions the police would ask. The uniformed coppers had been gentle with them back at home. These coppers were different. He knew from *The Sweeney* that plain-clothes detectives were a different breed to the normal plods. These had crafty, knowing faces. Jenny, Tina and he stuck to the story precisely. Gary had expected his mum to break down at any minute, or simply admit the truth. On the contrary, she was clear, straightforward and what impressed him most was that, despite everything that had happened and the fiction which they had constructed, his mum was playing the part of a frightened and desperate wife perfectly. He looked at her now. She was bent over, clutching the lifeless hand of her husband. He tried to imagine what was going through her mind. He knew what he was feeling: *Die, you bastard*.

'So, Gary, what were you doing before you came home today?' asked the copper with the Kevin Keegan perm.

'I was with my friends in London.'

'Who are your friends?'

Gary paused. He'd regretted saying that he'd been with them as soon as he'd said it. He didn't want any of them mixed up in this business. On the other hand, they could prove that he was where he said he was, although he wasn't sure why the filth would want to know.

'Some mates from school.'

'Names?'

'Anthony Alexander, Frank Gordon, Katy and Susan Walker.'

'Is that it?'

'Victoria Court — she's the headmistress of my school — and Joe Marshall.'

The detective with the white streak in his hair — like Dickie Davies off *World of Sport* — said, sharply, 'Joe Marshall?'

'Yeah. He's her bloke, and he's a friend of ours.'

Dickie wrote something in his notebook, then asked, 'And you, Tina, where have you been today?'

'Just at home, with my dad.'

'Mrs Abbott, how about you?'

'Just Brian and me, at home.'

'Mrs Abbott, I know this might seem a funny question but who does the ironing in your house?'

'Me. Why?'

'When did you last do the ironing?'

'Today. I was doing it before I went to the shop. I hadn't finished it: Brian wanted a drink and we didn't have anything in the house, so I popped out to the little shop by the garage; it's the only one that you can buy alcohol at on a Sunday.'

'How did you leave the iron and board, Mrs Abbott?'

'I left it up, but I turned the iron off. I remember that.'

Gary's heart was thumping: what were they getting at?

'Were the iron and the ironing board in the same place as usual?'

'Yes.'

'We noticed that the iron was plugged into an extension lead, that's right isn't it?'

Gary's heart missed a beat. He hadn't noticed. How had he missed that? How stupid, how fucking stupid!

'Yes, the lead of the iron didn't reach the socket.'

'But, Mrs Abbott, there is a socket right next to the board. It's right there isn't it.'

Gary froze. This was it: it was all over.

'Yes, but it didn't work today. I don't know why. It had fused or something. Brian said he'd look at it later. I got the extension lead out today.' Jenny spoke very calmly.

Gary closed his eyes. His mother's lie wasn't going to work. The police would check. They probably already had.

'I see. So, Mrs Abbott, you are telling us that the ironing board was in its usual position, that the socket next to it doesn't work and that today was the first time you used an extension lead. Is that right? That is what you are saying, isn't it?'

'Yes,' Jenny Abbott said.

Gary couldn't help himself: his head drooped, and he let out a long groan.

A nurse came in and picked up a clipboard from the end of Abbott's bed. She took a thermometer from her pocket and stuck it under the unconscious man's arm. She held her fob-watch, putting the fingers of her other hand to his wrist, concentrating on the rise and fall of his chest. Apparently satisfied with that, she withdrew the thermometer and waggled it to read the mercury.

She said, 'You're very warm, Brian; let's give you a bit of air.' She pulled down the bedcovers to his waist.

He was wearing a short-sleeved hospital gown, his arms and hands lying limply by his side. Out of the corner of his eye, Gary caught Kevin Keegan nod. Then, did Dickie tap his nose? Gary steeled himself for the next question: was it going to bring everything crashing down?

After filling in the clipboard, the nurse replaced it at the end of the bed and turned to the police officers, 'I hope you won't be staying too long; Mr Abbott needs peace and quiet.'

Dickie said, 'OK, sweetheart, keep your hair on; we're nearly done.' He got up, moved a few paces away and scribbled in his notebook.

Kevin Keegan said, 'How long were you out, going to the shop, Mrs Abbott?'

'About fifteen minutes, maybe twenty.'

'Were you two in the sitting room for all of that time?' he said to Tina and Gary.

They nodded.

'What were you doing?'

'Listening to Elvis,' Gary said again.

Dickie cut in, 'No, not what were you listening to? What were you doing?'

They were silent. Then Tina said, 'OK, it's a bit embarrassing but I was telling Gary that I'm going to split up with Kev; I was telling him all about what was happening.'

'Is that right, Gary?'

Gary nodded.

'And what is happening? What did Tina tell you?'

Gary swallowed. He thought back to the scene he'd overheard only hours before.

'Can I say, Tina?' he asked. She nodded.

'He wants more than Tina does — you know. I think that's it.'

'More what?'

'What do you think?'

'I don't know, son, that's why I'm asking.'

Gary was getting pissed off now. This copper was getting on his nerves.

'He wants to get his end away, what do you think?'

'Gary, please, that's enough of that language,' Jenny's voice was severe.

'Sorry, Mum,' he said.

'Say sorry to Tina, the poor girl,' his mum commanded.

'Sorry,' he mumbled to Tina.

'It's OK, Jenny. That's it anyway; that's what I was telling Gary,' Tina said.

Throughout the exchange, Brian Abbott's shallow breathing hadn't altered; he just lay there, oblivious.

'What's wrong with your eyes, Gary?' Kevin Keegan asked.

582

Gary had been rubbing his eyes. He'd forgotten that he was still wearing his lenses. He was suddenly aware of how bruised and uncomfortable his eyes felt.

'I'm wearing contact lenses for the first time. They're hurting, that's all. Plus, well, it's awful to see my dad like this,' Gary faltered; he couldn't help a tremble entering his voice.

'I know,' Keegan said. 'It's an awful thing. Now, Mrs Abbott, one more question.'

Gary gritted his teeth. When were the fuckers going to leave them alone?

'Yes?' Jenny said. She seemed to be coping better as each minute passed.

'Tell me about the crumble.'

'When I left, I told Brian to put it in the oven in ten minutes time.'

'Where was he sitting when you left?'

'At the table, facing the wall, the wall where the ironing board is.'

'I see. Now, Mrs Abbott, tell me very clearly. Where had you left the crumble?'

Jenny said, 'On the worktop, to the left of the ironing board.'

Gary shut his eyes and counted to ten.

At last, Dickie said, 'Will you all come down to the station in the morning? We'll need you to sign statements.'

They left them. Jenny, Gary and Tina waited several minutes before breathing properly.

'Mum, I'm so sorry,' Gary said.

'It's not your fault, love.'

'I mean the socket thing.'

'What about it?'

'They're going to check — they'll realise everything.'

'What do you mean?'

'Well, they'll see that you've lied about the lead.'

'No, love, the socket isn't working. It's true. I don't know why. You know the sockets in that kitchen? They're always going. That one went today.'

'Blimey, can you believe it?' Gary said, shaking his head. He got up, 'I'm going to make sure they've gone.'

He walked along the main corridor, through Reception and out into the carpark. He looked around. Shit! The Police car was still there. He spun back to retrace his steps, but it was too late. The doors of the car opened, and he heard Dickie call, 'Ah, 'allo, Gary, are you looking for us?'

'Err, naah. I just came out for a fag.'

Gary cursed under his breath as the two detectives walked towards him. As they came into the light spilling from the hospital entrance, Gary saw them glance at each other. Dickie nodded then said, all pally, 'Have you got a second, Gary?'

'Er, well, I need to get back to my Dad.'

'Yeah, we understand. The thing is, well, we were just wondering if you might be able to help us, Gary. You do want to help the Police, don't you?'

Gary definitely did not want to, but he made himself nod.

'The thing is, Gary, we know more than you realise. We might look like a couple of stupid bastards but we're not: we are bastards but we're not stupid. You understand, don't you, Gary?'

Gary had no idea what the fuck he was on about, but he knew he must keep himself together and do whatever needed doing: he nodded.

'The thing is, the little chat we're about to have is all about us doing a deal: you scratch our backs and we'll scratch yours — that make sense?'

Gary nodded again. He was ready; he wasn't sure what was going on, but there was something about the copper's manner that made him sure the next few seconds would decide their fate.

'So, I'm going to ask you some very simple questions. All you have to do is answer them honestly: all will become clear. Are you ready, Gary?'

Gary was ready, 'Yeah.'

'What kind of car does your dad drive?'

'What? Er, a Cortina, why?'

'What colour is your dad's Cortina?'

'Blue.'

'Light blue or dark blue?'

'Dark blue.'

'Do you know where your dad was on Wednesday 20th March, around 10.45pm?'

'No?'

'Are you sure?'

Gary's mind raced: what had happened then? He shook his head; nothing came to him. 'No — well… I'm not sure.'

Dickie was silent for a long time; he just stared at Gary. Finally, he said, 'How long has he had a tattoo on his arm, Gary?'

Gary gaped, what the fuck was going on? 'Er, I dunno; for as long as I can remember. I'm not sure, before that.'

'OK, Gary, let's cut to the chase. A man was savagely attacked on Theobald Street on 20th March. He was head-butted in the face, an unprovoked attack. He sustained some serious injuries; he's still not recovered. He can't recall much about what happened, but he does remember that his assailant drove a dark car, probably a Cortina, and he had some writing tattooed on his arm. Oh, yeah — and he remembers there were others in the car.'

Dickie stared at Gary; Gary stared back. Long, slow seconds ticked by. Finally, the copper said, 'So, Gary, you're a bright lad: are you up for scratching backs?'

Gary's brain was whirling. The shits had stumbled over his dad by accident! Maybe they were more interested in what had happened three weeks ago than in tonight's incident? Is that what Dickie was telling him? He decided: he was going to look after his mum – properly, this time.

'Yeah, I was there. My dad did do it.'

Dickie and Kevin Keegan smiled at each other. Dickie said, 'Well done, Gary. You've done the right thing telling us. Honesty is always the best policy, don't you think?'

Gary nodded emphatically, 'Definitely.'

Dickie said, 'See you tomorrow, at the station, 9am?'

'Yeah.'

Keegan was beaming, 'Give your dad our best wishes, won't you?'

The two coppers chuckled as they swaggered away. Gary heard Dickie say, 'What a result. I can't fucking believe it. This is medal time, fucking hell!'

Gary stood and watched them get back into the car and waited till it drove off. He walked slowly back to his dad's bedside.

Tina asked, her face anxious, 'Where've you been; I was getting worried?'

Gary sat down and put his head in his hands. 'You won't believe what just happened.'

'Oh no, not more. What now?'

He told them. Transfixed, in silence, they stared at the curlicued, black *Jailhouse Rock* vivid on the waxy skin of Abbott's beefy forearm.

Tina said at last, 'I'm glad we prayed. I know it's silly, but it made me feel better.'

'Me too. Maybe he's looking after us,' Gary said.

'Let's pray again,' Jenny suggested.

'I don't know any other prayers,' Gary said.

'What about "All Things Bright and Beautiful"?' Tina suggested.

'That's a hymn, dear, and I don't think it's very appropriate,' Jenny said.

'Oh, sorry.'.

'It doesn't have to be an actual prayer; we can just say, "Help us God",' Jenny said.

After a pause Gary said with great solemnity, 'OK, after three.'

'Help us God,' they said in unison.

'Er, amen?' Tina said.

'Oh, yeah, amen too,' Gary said.

'I didn't know you wore contact lenses,' Tina said.

'Yeah, well, I'm not sure about them now; my eyes are killing me.'

'Take them out then, silly,' she said.

Gary fiddled around for a while and managed to extricate them. He carefully replaced them in their little containers. After a couple of minutes, he reached into his pocket and pulled out his glasses case. He put on his black plastic glasses. He looked straight ahead, embarrassed.

'Let me see?' Tina said.

Shyly Gary turned towards her. She studied him.

'Very handsome. You look so clever. Don't you think, Jenny?'

Jenny Abbott smiled at her son, 'Oh yes, Gary's very clever all right.'

Victoria

Victoria watched the lights of the town flash by. She was dimly aware of the direction they were taking but didn't care. She was beyond caring. She was trying to get her thoughts and emotions under control. She was angry. She was cold with fury. She turned to Joe: 'What's wrong with you? Everywhere you go there's trouble. You're nothing but trouble. I get it — I understand what you did: you set up the whole thing as a trap for them. What I thought was a relaxing evening after an eventful few days was, in fact, your little game of revenge. I can't believe you did that. What's wrong with you? Are you a psychopath? Is that it? Are you? Did you spend the whole time in the pub waiting for them? All that time I thought we were having a heart to heart and you were planning how you were going to get even with the thugs who smashed up your car. I can't get my head around you, Joe. You're, well I don't know what you are.'

'I'm sorry, Victoria. It all got a bit more complicated than I'd expected'

Victoria fumed, 'Complicated! I was seconds away from getting beaten up. If the police hadn't turned up, you would definitely have been.'

'You're right. I'm so sorry. I didn't think...'

Victoria's furious voice was high-pitched, 'Think? You didn't think; you played your God figure. You thought it was all under your control; you thought "I, Joe Marshall, will make it so — and lo, it was so". You're not God, Joe. Just because you want something to happen in the way you want it doesn't make it happen that way. You think you know what's best for everyone; you think you can make everything right. You can't: you're just a man, a weak, self-centred, arrogant man.'

Joe had stopped the car. She didn't notice.

'May I have my jacket?' he asked gently.

She pushed it at him. Joe rearranged it and reached into the pocket. He took out the cassette recorder, stopped it, rewound and pressed play. They heard the exchanges outside the pub, him saying their names clearly. Then all the subsequent events.

'OK, so you've got your evidence. Now you can get them for criminal damage, threatening behaviour, assault, blah, blah, blah. But, Joe, we were having a quiet, romantic evening together. We didn't go out for a night of surveillance. I didn't go out in the hope of a punch-up in a pub car park. What's wrong with you?'

The car was moving again. Joe was quiet.

'Don't go quiet on me. Talk to me. Explain: please help me understand.'

Victoria now recognised where they were. It was the quiet lane leading up to the churchyard, where they'd come two nights ago. She wanted to punch and kick Joe. The awful conflict was tearing her apart. She loved him and hated him. Right now, though, she just hated him.

'I know I've done a terrible thing, Victoria. I got carried away. It's what I'm like, you're right. I have to take control of things, no matter what.'

'What, no matter if your girlfriend gets attacked by a group of drunken imbeciles? How could you have possibly imagined that that was going to be in any way taking control?'

'It didn't quite work out how I'd planned it. I was sure I would be back in the pub before you… well, quicker than it turned out.'

Victoria drew in a deep breath, 'But you thought everything else through. You obviously knew they were going to be there tonight: how did you know that?'

'Gary told me who they were, where they drink.'

'When did he tell you?'

'He gave me this, earlier.'

Victoria looked at the scrap of paper... 'Jim Masters Ray Kelly Danny Warner trashed your car; they drink at the Red Lion'.

'How did he know?'

'I don't know.'

Victoria thought for a minute then said, 'The tape recorder?'

'I picked it up from The Beeches.'

'The phone call?'

'I rang the police and told them there was a fracas at the pub.'

'Hang on a minute. Don't tell me you were looking through the window the whole time, waiting for them to arrive.'

'Well, not the whole time. I just noticed them; that's when I made the call.'

'Joe, you... you're just a manipulator, aren't you? Oh, I can see how clever you are. You asked me earlier if I would support you in getting your own back on them. I suppose you thought that that casual conversation gave you license to risk my safety. They could have had a knife, for God's sake!'

'I wouldn't have let anything happen to you, Victoria.'

'What if they'd just kicked my head in, like I want to kick yours right now?' Victoria was shrieking.

Joe just sat in his seat nodding.

'Don't just sit there nodding, you stupid fucking idiot,' she ranted at him.

Joe just sat in his seat, now shaking his head.

'Don't just shake your head. Are you trying to make things worse? What is wrong with you? When I think about it, I cringe. To think I put those damaged young people in your care: it makes me shudder. I've been taken in by you, but you let me, you let me think you could look after them. My God, what have I done?'

Joe took in a deep breath, 'I don't know, Victoria. I do this kind of thing. Until now I haven't had anyone to worry about; it's just been me. John taught me to take control of what happened to me, not to let the outside world control me. He helped me understand; he showed me how to take things into my own hands.'

590

'Hang on a minute — who's John?'

Joe put his head in his hands. 'I'm sorry, Victoria. I'm so sorry. I've messed everything up. I've let you down; I've let John down. I promised him and I've let him down.'

Victoria could feel herself becoming hysterical. What was he talking about now? 'Joe! Stop it! Who is John?'

Joe was silent for a long time then said, 'John is John Christmas.'

Victoria's fury drained away. 'What do you mean?' her voice was trembling.

'Can we go to the grave?'

Her head spinning, Victoria got out of the car and walked unsteadily after Joe along the path. They stopped in front of the gravestone again.

Joe took her hand in his. She snatched it away. He said, 'Captain Paul Smith was Captain John Christmas, an army doctor, a psychiatrist. He is your Uncle John, Victoria.'

'I don't understand. Is this one of your tricks, Joe? Please tell me it isn't a trick; I can't bear any more tricks.'

'It's true. I met him in prison. He was my inspiration, my saviour. When he came out of prison, he changed his name. He told me about you. He told me that you were a wonderful little girl; that he had always hoped to see you again, to keep his promise to see you. He knew that he never could — he could not face you knowing what he had done. He was broken by what had happened. But he never forgot you.'

'But I don't understand — is it just a coincidence that we met?' Victoria heard her voice: she sounded like that little girl again.

'No, it's all part of another one of my schemes, I'm afraid. Towards the end of his life, maybe just a few days before he killed himself, he asked me — made me promise in fact — that I would find you and make sure that you were all right. So, I did. I went to Ealing. I found out from your old neighbours that you were a teacher, that your father had died, that you had moved here to live with your mother. Then, because of my history, getting a job wasn't easy, so I asked Stewart if he could help me get a position at the Beeches. I needed a job: doing gardening and odd jobs suited me just fine. The coincidence was that your mother was a resident at the Beeches. When I first saw you, I'd had no idea that you'd turn up there. You probably realised that I was rather nonplussed the first time we met?'

Victoria was piecing together the parts of the jigsaw. She thought back to their first meeting. She remembered that he'd seemed to stare at her for a second too long. She'd dismissed the thought at the time, but now it made sense.

Joe put his hand in his pocket. 'May I?' he asked. Without waiting for an answer, he took Victoria's hand and placed a small object into it, closing her fingers around it. She uncurled them: for the briefest of moments, she was confused; then, like a light coming on in her head, she saw what he'd given her. It was a little wooden dog.

She held it tight. Her head was filled with the memory of John Christmas, his size, his smell, his warmth. She heard his voice reading stories to her. She remembered the feeling of love and peace that came from him, the overwhelming sense of safety that she'd had sitting next to him all those years ago. She couldn't help herself, she started to cry. She held the little wooden toy against her heart and cried for her long-lost friend. She thought about his life, his loss — his lost life — his pain and suffering. She couldn't bear it. She turned to Joe.

'That poor man, that poor, poor man,' she cried. 'That poor, poor man; that lovely, gentle man — why him? Why him?'

'I know. I don't know, it's not right. I wish I knew, but I don't.'

Victoria's mind came back to the present. She stepped back from Joe. She wiped her eyes with her fists then punched him in the stomach with all her strength.

She hissed, 'Tell you what, it's not easy being with you. You're driving me round the bend: you know that don't you?'

Joe was doubled over.

Victoria said, 'Can we go home now please, I'm desperate to be somewhere normal, no surprises.'

***

Victoria drove in silence. She tried to work out what to do next. Nothing was stable or secure in her life. Her mother had long gone into some other